The Winter Boy

by
Sally Wiener Grotta

Pixel Hall Press
Newfoundland, PA USA
www.PixelHallPress.com

The Winter Boy
by Sally Wiener Grotta

Published by Pixel Hall Press, Newfoundland, PA USA
www.PixelHallPress.com

Printed in the United States of America

Library of Congress Control Number: 2014913368

ISBN 978-0-9883871-3-3

Publisher's Cataloging-In-Publication Data
(Prepared by The Donohue Group, Inc.)

Grotta, Sally Wiener, 1959-
The winter boy / by Sally Wiener Grotta.

496 pages ; cm

Issued also as an ebook.
ISBN: 978-0-9883871-9-5 (ebook)
ISBN: 978-0-9883871-2-6 (hardbound)

1. Widows--Fiction. 2. Young men--Fiction. 3. Imaginary societies--Fiction. 4. Conspiracies--
Fiction. 5. Speculative fiction. 6. Science fiction. 7. Fantasy fiction. I. Title.

PS3607.R688 W56 2014
813/.6   2014913368

Daniel

Chapter 1

The Valley of the Alleshi stretches wide and green, surrounded by gentle mountains that cut the coldest of winds from the north and the wildest of hurricanes from the south. In the spring, summer and fall, the eight passes to The Valley flow constantly with pilgrims, traders, petitioners and emissaries — and, of course, Allemen, the leaders of the land, trained by the Alleshi. But in winter, heavy snow fills the high mountain passes. Only during those deep white months is The Valley isolated and inaccessible. It is a precious quiet season for the Alleshi.

As one such season approached, Rishana had just returned home from a strengthening class at the Communal Hall when she saw Dara through her mudroom window.

Dara was tall and lean, with flesh deeply etched by life. Her black hair was streaked with wide swathes of white. With precise, practiced grace, she walked up to the back door, raised her hand to knock, then noticed Rishana standing inside. So she opened the door and walked in.

"Dara, you're early!" Why was her mentor here, now, before she could bathe and prepare herself for their daily meeting?

"I'm not staying long." Dara followed Rishana into the spacious sun-filled kitchen and sat at the square oak table.

Obviously, Dara had something on her mind that she felt couldn't wait.

"Yes?" Rishana asked, as she sat down across from Dara. Her exercise suit was sweat-stained and itched. She raked the wet strands of her auburn hair that were escaping the tie-back ribbon, pushing them behind her ears. Then, realizing what she was doing, she draped her hands onto her lap, forcing her body to be still and receptive.

"It's time for you to choose your First Boy," Dara said with deliberate calm, her dark, age-yellowed eyes fixed on Rishana's. "I saw a worthy candidate this morning, the son of one of my Allemen. The boy could prove… interesting for you."

"My First Season isn't supposed to be until the spring," Rishana protested. "I'm not ready."

"Of course you are, or I wouldn't suggest it."

"What if I'm not, Dara? A boy's entire future depends on what I do, how well I'm prepared."

"You know you won't be alone. I'll guide you through your First Season."

"I don't understand." Rishana paused, trying to sort her thoughts. "Everyone has drilled into me how tightly structured my training schedule must be to fit everything I need to know into three years. Why would you now want to cut it short by four months... and so suddenly?" She studied her mentor, trying to read Dara's face and body the way she'd been taught. "Is there something special about this boy?"

"No, not at all, Rishana," Dara reassured her. "We're simply very pleased with how quickly you've learned. Waiting until the spring won't prepare you any better, but it would delay teaching you the finer points of being an Allesha, which you'll learn only by working with a boy in Season. Trust me; the timing is right."

The younger woman nodded, not so much in agreement as acceptance. Of course, she trusted Dara. Faith in the wisdom and power of the Alleshi was the foundation of her life, of their entire society.

"I don't have your experience or knowledge, Dara; I wouldn't know how to select a boy. Can't I simply accept this candidate, if you think he's the right one for me?"

Dara arched her back against the offensive suggestion. "*Absolutely not!* This is a decision only you can make. However, I can help you analyze what type of boy to choose for your First, which will define the kind of Allesha you wish to become."

"What do you mean?"

"Let me explain by telling you about this candidate." Dara focused on something only she could see in the empty air between them. "Unlike most Allemen sons, he's a rough one — arrogant, and a bit of a troublemaker. Still, he is bright and alert." Dara's voice was as disciplined as ever, enunciating each word clearly, forcefully. However, she paused between phrases more than usual, carefully considering each word before she said it. "He'll constantly try to provoke and test you, attempting to control rather than learn from you. But if you can reach him, as I believe you can, his strength of will, intelligence and good heart could be of great value for our people."

"Sounds like a strong candidate." Rishana wondered why her mentor seemed to be holding herself in tight check. Perhaps Dara was being careful not to unduly influence her in this important decision.

"Yes, but only a few Alleshi are willing or capable of taking on such a difficult boy. I was appointed your mentor because we believe you have within you that ability, and because problem boys have been my specialty. But you're under no obligation to follow in my ways. Should you select another kind of boy for your First, I will still work through the Season with you. It is your choice."

"How do I decide, Dara?"

"By meeting him, then evaluating your reaction. Does his coarse manner irritate you, or can you find humor and challenge in it? What do you see beyond the face he presents? Is it something intriguing that you'd enjoy unearthing, though the process would be difficult?

"Look into your heart," Dara continued. "Do you want to give a piece of it to this troublesome boy? Remember, once you are an Allesha to a boy, he becomes part of you, and that will change you. You must be honest about yourself — who you are, and what you want, both for the moment and for the course of your life. To choose a boy such as this one means that your first Alleshine Season — and Seasons to come — will be filled with conflict and stress. You will have to learn to be fierce, while instilling gentleness. It will wear you out before your time. There's no harder work, but also none more important."

"What if I choose another kind of boy for my First?" Rishana asked.

"Most boys aren't like this one. They're confused, mischievous, but willing to bend and eager to learn. Seasons with them start joyously and proceed toward harmony."

"Not much of a choice, is it?" Even as she said it, Rishana wondered why the words somehow didn't ring true. "Who wouldn't choose a life of joy and harmony over one of conflict and stress?"

"I for one, and possibly you." Dara sighed, a wistful smile softening her face. "Once you've moved past the conflict, once you've harnessed a problem boy's energy with discipline, the Alleman you create can become one of our most powerful and effective. Easy-to-train boys are fine for those times when you want to relax, but I couldn't have given all my Seasons and years to languid pleasure. I devoted my life to fire and stone, and with each of my problem boys, I became stronger, more alive." Dara's smile broadened, deepening the wrinkles around her mouth, and yet, for that brief moment, making her seem young once more. "And I couldn't be prouder of the Allemen they have become."

"I see. You've given me a lot to consider, Dara."

"I'll leave now, so you can meditate on your decision. After your bath, prepare a simple lunch, one that won't distract you from your thoughts. Then sit under one of your apple trees, among the fallen leaves. I'll be back in the late afternoon. Soon after, the Southwest Battai will come with the boy. Meeting him places no obligation on you, but will help you think things through."

Rishana was already deep in thought, weighing what Dara had said, and trying to decipher what hadn't been said, when Dara left as quietly as she could. On her way out, the older woman made sure that the outer front door of the house was closed, as a sign that Rishana wasn't accepting visitors.

Chapter 2

"*Evanya!*" Karinne greeted her friend warmly at her kitchen door. The two women always used the names of their youth when they were alone together, names from so long ago that no one else in The Valley remembered them.

One look at Evanya's shadowed face, and Karinne knew something momentous had happened. Silently, they secured the house and sequestered themselves inside the locked inner room, safe from any eavesdroppers. They spoke in hushed staccato tones, compressing every sound deep in their throats, though they knew no one could hear them.

"The boy has arrived," Evanya said.

Karinne's breath caught in her lungs. "So soon? We weren't expecting him until the spring."

"Mistral and Shria had no choice if we didn't want to chance losing him." Evanya shivered, though the room was warm. "He's determined to marry his girl; he had actually gone to their village council to announce their betrothal. If Mistral hadn't managed to get the girl's mother to block him…"

"But no woman speaks at the Birani council."

"She's a widow with no man to speak for her. So the council had to listen and honor her decision."

"Which was—"

"*An Alleman for my daughter or no man.*"

"I'm impressed. We should keep an eye on the mother, and see if she has the makings of an Allesha." Karinne struggled to rearrange her small, round body, trying to find a comfortable position. The inner room wasn't meant for women whose bones were no longer flexible, regardless of how well-padded they had become. "Perhaps it could be a good thing that he's arrived, that the waiting is over."

"Still, I'm concerned about the timing. I thought we'd have longer to train her. Four months could have made such a difference." Evanya paused. "There's so much she doesn't know, doesn't yet understand. And she's so young." She sighed deeply.

5

Chapter 3

In the nearly three years that she had been training in The Valley, Rishana had learned much about what it was to be an Allesha. She had studied how to control with the turn of a hand, to seduce with a glance, to disarm with a smile. Lessons with various Alleshine teachers had focused her eye to read the subtle signs in another's behavior, gestures and voice. Other Alleshi taught her self-defense and ways to avoid the need to defend.

She'd spent untold hours absorbed in The Valley's extensive library. Guided by Savah, Jared's Allesha, she had researched history, trade, treaties, and the cultures of the diverse peoples within and beyond the Peace borders, seeking hints about the long-ago hidden time before the Great Chaos.

Combining her new skills, observations and growing knowledge, she had practiced a range of responses to many different scenarios, altering her approach, posture and tone to achieve the most beneficial outcome.

All this time, Rishana's every waking moment had been consumed by the study and practice of the many disciplines required to become a successful Allesha. But now that Dara had set Rishana's mind in a new direction, she realized that her tight focus had distracted her from considering wider, more personal ramifications.

They had been training her to face this moment since she had come to The Valley with her Petition. Her teachers had been chosen carefully to set the path of her life. Their aim was now as clear as that of an arrow nocked into a bow by a master archer. Why hadn't anyone said anything to her, not even Savah?

Problem boys, problem life. Certainly, the challenges of such a future could be fascinating. But how dare they twist her training without asking her what it was she wanted — until now, at this late hour, when they felt confident of her answer. Confident, because they had already formed her into the Allesha they wanted her to be.

How like the Alleshi!

And now she was one of them.

"*No!*" she yelled into the empty house, startling herself with the sound, but feeling a certain satisfaction in the solid autonomy of her own voice. "Arrogant, manipulative, overbearing... I won't be like her!"

She shook her head to clear it.

"*Jinet, pull yourself together,*" she demanded of herself, using her name from her life before The Valley. "*Remember who you are and why you came here.*"

It had been five years ago this spring, but often it felt like yesterday. Jared's mutilated body carried home to her after that long winter wait. Bathing her husband for the last time and finding under the dried blood and encrusted dirt the gruesome geometric patterns carved into his flesh.

Mwertik Zalog runes.

Pushing the memory deep inside where she kept it locked away, Rishana straightened her back and closed her eyes. Then she took five deep, long breaths, releasing herself into each exhale. When she opened her eyes, she probed inward and found the knot of her anger. No, it would not be easily dislodged, but she didn't have to lose herself to it.

Rishana stomped into her bedroom, tore off her sweaty exercise clothes, and began the daily ritual of studying herself in the mirror.

The body she saw in her reflection was not the one of her youth. That had been the first difficulty for her when Savah had explained the importance of the wall-size mirror in every Allesha's bedroom. But her teachers had insisted she persevere; eventually, she had learned to evaluate her own body, wielding that knowledge in the way she carried herself.

All Alleshine skills began with this understanding of the physical self, a tool to be utilized, a power to be harnessed. But she had naïvely believed that the Alleshi would never use their skills on one another, on her. Now she felt like a fool. Yet, still she obeyed, by standing in front of the mirror, honoring the teachings of those who had not honored her.

All in all, it was an attractive womanly figure that Rishana saw in the mirror, one that had given life to two children and had reached the ripeness of maturity. Rishana's forty-three years had taken their toll, and her body had lost the taut, unstretched silkiness of her youth. The long, shapely legs might widen toward the curvy hips a bit more than she would like, but they were elegant and could be used to good effect. Her arms, too, had that same graceful length that made the motions and gestures she practiced in the mirror appealing. Though her breasts had become weighty rather than round, and her waist would never again be the hourglass indent it had once been, her body was tightening nicely, thanks to Michale's exercises. She was pleased that her shoulder-length auburn hair now shone with the highlights of her youth, thanks to the new henna rinse Hester had given her. And her skin was responding well to the lemon juice and olive oil treatments, helping to repair the years of sunburn and hard work. Not that anything would ever erase those freckles.

Rishana continued to stare into the mirror. If you can see a person's heart and destiny in her eyes, what did hers reveal about the Allesha she wanted to be? Had the Alleshi changed her so fully that she no longer had any choices that truly came from within her? Or was the woman who stared back at her still the freeborn, independent individual she had always considered herself to be?

Retreating into her steaming bath, Rishana gave herself fully to the sensual pleasure of it, and used it to clear her mind. As she dressed and prepared a lunch of fruit, cheese and bread, she turned her mind back to the question of her First Boy, and to the Alleshi. Later, she sat among the fallen leaves under the largest of her house-tall apple trees, nibbled at the meal, and considered her choices.

While her mind tugged her toward rebellion, she had shaped her day according to Dara's instructions — bath, meditation, lunch under the tree — and she recognized no contradiction in such behavior. Obedience to the Alleshi was deeply ingrained in her, as it was among all people and villages within the Peace borders. Starting in early childhood, all were taught to not give in to anger, but to follow whatever path the Alleshi decreed, until free will, unfettered by destructive emotions. could be restored.

A child of the Peace, she obeyed.

The resentment Rishana felt about being manipulated to choose a hard life, one devoted to problem boys, remained strong, but less emotional. She examined that anger, as she had studied her body in the mirror. And there, at the core of her being, where her ire had formed, she found her answers. She was calm and sure by the time Dara returned.

Chapter 4

Dara sat beside Rishana under the apple tree between Rishana's house and barn. A gentle breeze stirred the brown leaves on the ground, tossing them to the cloudless sky. Neither spoke. Nor did they look at each other. Instead, both leaned against the tree's rough, solid trunk, staring in different directions. Rishana took her time forming the words she wanted to say. They had to be simple, but effective.

"I was angry with you," Rishana said quietly.

"I know," Dara responded, just as calmly.

"You and the others have worked hard to form me as you needed me to be."

"Yes."

"Your chisel chipped at the stone of my being until you whittled me down to my essential self, as if I were a problem boy."

Dara turned toward her charge. "I knew you would understand."

But Rishana's sight remained focused outward and elsewhere. "Yes, I understand. But, I wonder, have you ever been wrong? What if, under that stone, you found a softness, a nature that required a gentler touch?"

"Under the stone is always a softness, Rishana. It is in such softness that true strength is revealed."

"So now I must choose. Do I wish to work with boys on whom I would use a similar chisel? Or do I want to use water on clay?"

"Yes."

"A boy to be chiseled is harder work," Rishana continued in the same cool apprising tone. "But the result is a stone-core strength, a man of unusual power."

"A man not unlike the woman you are."

Rishana was surprised to hear it, but still didn't turn toward Dara. Instead, she allowed her eyes to glaze over, hearing the meaning under the rhythm of their words, finding the truth that had been there all along.

Dara leaned back against the tree.

"The other kind of boy would shape under my hands with little resistance," Rishana continued, "and with a great deal of joy and pleasure. Yet you have known that I would choose stress and conflict."

"Because it is what will give you the greater joy and pleasure in the end."

"No, because you knew the kind of woman you had shaped."

"The kind of woman you've always been."

"You assume much."

"Yes."

"And now, I am the same as you."

"Yes."

"How will I know that I'm making the right choices for my boys?"

"You will know or you will come to those of us who know. It is in your blood, as well as in your training."

"So I will take this boy whom you have chosen."

"Only if you wish it. Your will has always been your own to command."

"A free will shaped by you."

"No. One unearthed by us, Rishana. It is your essential self that will be doing the choosing. We only helped you understand the shape of that self."

"Yet, before I make my choice, you already know what it will be."

"Yes."

"Because you know me even more intimately than I have known myself."

"Because I recognized you as my successor before anyone else. And I had been waiting long for you."

"Perhaps too long, Dara. Perhaps you have seen in me what you needed and wanted to see."

"No. I saw in you what you needed and wanted to be."

"I understand, but a part of me is still angry with you."

"Yes."

"What am I to do with that anger?"

"Accept it and use it. Without it, you would not have the free will we cherish and need. It is the inner conflict that will prepare you for the many conflicts ahead."

"So it is already decided."

"Yes."

"And it is my decision."

"Yes."

"Yes." Rishana looked up at the blue sky framed by the Sentinel Mountains. A solitary small white cloud drifted in the wind. It was a sharp, clean day, with summer a long-ago memory; winter wouldn't be held at bay much longer.

Chapter 5

Ryl cautiously pushed open the heavy oak door and peered outside. One of the serving girls was scurrying through the kitchen garden back toward the inn. Returning from an illicit rendezvous with a caravan lover, Ryl supposed. No need to fear her snitching on them. She'd have too much explaining of her own to do.

"It's clear. Let's go," he whispered to Sim, who hovered in the hallway.

Sim moved as though he never had to be wary of anything. Larger than Ryl in height and girth, with broad muscular shoulders, and much blacker than Ryl's swarthy coloring, Sim was, at nineteen, a year older. However, Ryl assumed the lead, running toward the trees surrounding the garden. It was the longer way around, but they'd be less likely to be seen and stopped.

Behind him, Sim stomped noisily and tripped over some roots. Didn't he know how to run in a wood? But Sim was okay. Not like most of the other Petitioners he'd met so far.

At first, Ryl hadn't known what to make of him. When Sim's family had joined the trade caravan that Ryl and his folks had traveled with for the last leg of their journey to The Valley, Sim had quickly become everyone's pal. Everyone but Ryl, that is.

No one ever had anything disparaging to say about Sim, which made Ryl look bad by comparison. Of course, Ryl's parents were used to having to explain away their son's behavior. But to Ryl's ears, Shria's sighs and Mistral's corrections had seemed more frequent after Sim had shown up.

Ryl had tried to egg Sim on, but nothing would rile him. Too damned easygoing, Ryl had decided. Regardless of how well-aimed the insult or well-contrived the difficulty that Ryl had cast at the other lad, it was like throwing feathers at a brook. No effect whatever.

Then one evening after supper, when everyone was relaxing around their campfires, soothing aching feet and backs, repairing gear and clothes, sharing stories, Ryl had wandered off. He preferred being alone to feeling so alone in the middle of everything.

Sim had followed, noisy as always. No way that boy could ever sneak up on anyone. As Ryl turned a corner around a wagon piled high with trunks of goods, he quickly pivoted. Sim almost ran into him.

"What the hell do you think you're doing?" Ryl demanded.

Sim shrugged. "We should talk, Ryl."

"What do we have to talk about?"

"I don't know. But we should get to know each other, don't you think? We're both going to be Allemen from the same Season if we're lucky."

Ryl figured his chances of being Blessed were as good as those of a fish learning to fly.

"You think I want to know you, huh? Okay. I heard your pa bragging what a good fighter you are." Ryl crouched with his fists in front of his face. "Show me what you're made of."

Sim shook his head. "I don't want to fight you, Ryl. I just want to talk."

"Talk with your fists. Maybe I'll hear you better."

"But Ryl, you don't have anything to prove to me. I'm sure I'm not as good as you."

"You've a lot to prove to me, though."

Ryl jabbed at Sim's stomach, but Sim blocked it. Then Ryl aimed for the chest with his right, and while Sim parried with his forearm, Ryl came in with a left undercut that connected solidly with Sim's face, felling him like a tree. Sim pushed himself up into a sitting position and wiped the blood gushing from his nostrils.

Ryl waited, knowing the yelling would start any moment.

Instead, Sim grinned at Ryl and asked, "How'd you do that?"

"You left yourself wide open."

"Could you show me?"

Ryl held out a hand to Sim to help him off the ground.

Soon after, they strolled back to the campfire, both bleeding and bruised, and laughing so hard that everyone turned toward the disheveled pair.

Mistral leapt up. "Skies! Ryl, what have you done now?"

Before Ryl could say anything or stalk away, Sim stepped between them. "Sir, I asked Ryl to help me improve my fighting skills. It's one of my weak points. He's really very good, you know." Then he turned to Ryl and winked. "Tomorrow night, I want you to show me that sneak attack again. Okay?"

Mistral sat down without another word. The boys' mothers bathed their wounds.

From then on, Ryl and Sim became close companions. Ryl didn't even blame Sim when he overheard Mistral say to Sim's father, "You've got a good boy there. He'll be a solid Alleman."

"If he's Blessed," Sim's father countered.

"Oh, he'll be Blessed. The Alleshi never let ones like him get away."

Ryl understood that it wasn't Sim's fault that Mistral liked him better than his own son. After all, Pa probably knew as well as Ryl what a fruitless journey this would be. Whatever powers the Alleshi possessed, Ryl was convinced that they'd be able to see right through him. Once that happened, no Allesha would be willing to select him. Ryl had long ago realized that not even Mistral would have picked him, if he'd had a choice in the matter.

Things got easier when they finally arrived at the Southwest Inn above The Valley, and the boys were housed in the Petitioners Wing, far from their parents' private rooms. What Mistral couldn't see, he couldn't complain about.

Not that the inn was that great. Ryl had to endure the Battai's endless questions during the interminable official interviews. But it didn't end there. The old busybody found Ryl wherever he was: in a corner by himself, wandering a garden, or even at supper with his parents.

Then there was the Healer examination — much more extensive and invasive than anything he had ever known. She probed and listened to his body so intimately that Ryl wondered once again at the propriety of a woman being a Healer. Among his people, only men took such roles. However, he tried to be charitable; she was so old and shriveled it was probably the only chance she had to touch a man.

The announcements began almost as soon as Ryl had settled into the Petitioners' wing. Arn, Jack and Mannockin were the first to be Blessed. Hanton, Yan, Daylor, and Staf were next. It didn't help when Sim reminded Ryl that those seven had arrived earlier and so had a head start. Each boy chosen represented one less Allesha available for the coming Season.

Ryl found himself eying the others, weighing his worth against each one. With little more than one hundred Alleshi planning to share the Winter Season, and scores of petitioning boys in each of the eight inns ringing The Valley, Ryl struggled to find reason to hope, to believe that any Allesha might actually want him.

What would happen if he were turned away, as most Petitioners were? Would Lilla go against her mother? Would he dare ask? Ryl couldn't bear the idea of putting Lilla through a council shunning. But what if it were the only way they could be together?

Hanging around the inn quickly got on Ryl's nerves. That's when he came up with the idea of stealing away to the tradegrounds. Anything would be better than sitting around doing nothing, listening to the other boys gossiping about the wondrous Alleshi and their damned Allemen, being cornered once more by the Battai, or running into Mistral.

Ryl had no problem convincing Sim to join him; all he had to do was mention Emmy. The daughter of Schul, the leader of their caravan, Emmy was a tease who had set her sights on Sim, but didn't give him any satisfaction. Then again, Sim hadn't pressed for it.

"She's not like that," Sim had insisted. "She's a nice girl who dreams of marrying an Alleman."

"She's not so nice, Sim. All you have to do is ask; you'll see."

Sim had refused to discuss it any further. But Ryl had noticed that Sim couldn't keep his eyes off Emmy during the entire trip, and he jumped at the chance of seeing her one more time.

Ryl and Sim cut through the woods, hoping to avoid people until they could lose themselves in the crowds at the tradegrounds. Not that they were doing anything expressly forbidden. No one had told them they had to stay put; just that they couldn't go below into The Valley unescorted. Besides, what harm could it do to spend some time among the caravans?

The day was balmy, with bright sunlight streaking through the trees. It was almost spring-like, except that newly fallen leaves crunched underfoot and the only green in the woods were old-growth pine and spruce. Sounds from the tradegrounds permeated the forest, an almost subliminal buzz which coalesced into a thumping, like faraway drums. The closer they got, the more clearly Ryl could discern competing strains of music and a cacophony of voices shouting out their wares.

As Ryl and Sim approached the edge of the woods, so many paths wove through the increasingly sparse trees, they no longer bothered trekking off trail. Sim spotted a young man in brown trousers and a black wool cloak walking on a parallel path. "Look, Ryl, an Autumn Boy."

"How can you tell?"

"From the way he carries himself. Don't you see it?"

"Looks no different from any of the other guys we've seen."

"No, Ryl, I'm sure."

Ryl was irritated at the fuss Sim was making, but mostly at the idea that it was over a boy who had received what he probably would never have — the mysteries and magic of an Alleshine Season.

"Hey, you!" Ryl called out as he cut through the trees to the other path. Catching up to the young man, Ryl grabbed his elbow and spun him around. *"Didn't you hear me calling you!?"*

About the same age as any of the Petitioners, the fellow was really pretty average, not very tall or broad, with muddy brown hair and a washed-out complexion. But something about him made Ryl feel small and clumsy.

"I didn't realize you were calling me," he said in a quiet, dignified voice. "How may I help you?"

"Well, my friend and I were having a disagreement, and I was wondering if you could help us resolve it."

"Yes, of course."

"He thinks you're an Autumn Boy. I said you're probably caravan trash. Which is it?"

"Ryl!" Sim had finally caught up, brushing dry leaves from his clothes; he'd stumbled yet again in his rush to stop Ryl. Composing himself, Sim said in that conciliatory tone that Ryl hated, "Please excuse us, sir. My friend meant no harm." Then he pulled on Ryl's arm. "Come on, let's go."

The Autumn Boy started to walk away.

Shrugging Sim off him, Ryl hissed, "Don't you apologize for me!" He stormed after the Autumn Boy, and shoving against his shoulder, demanded, "I still want to know what you think you are."

The young man looked Ryl up and down, studying him. "I don't believe you want to do this, but you can't figure out how to get out of it without being embarrassed. Let me help you. Yes, your friend is correct, I am just finishing my Season as a Blessed Boy. But you are also correct, I am Vetram, son of Vexam, the caravan leader. Now, I'm headed to the Southwest Battai's with a message from the Alleshi. I believe you were planning to enjoy yourselves at the tradegrounds. Let us continue on our way with no further unpleasantness."

"What is the problem here?"

Ryl hadn't heard the woman approach and nearly jumped at the sound of her commanding voice. One look at her and he knew he was in trouble. A tall, buxom old woman, with unruly grey hair that still had remnants of red, she needed no insignia or robe to declare who and what she was.

"No problem, Allesha," Vetram said. "My companions and I were simply having a… spirited discussion."

Her eyes glided over Ryl and Sim until Ryl felt there was nothing about them she didn't absorb and understand. "Tell me your names."

Sim bowed his head and turned his hands upward at waist level, in the appropriate traditional greeting accorded Alleshi. "I am honored, Allesha. I am Sim of the Emet."

The Allesha grazed his hands with hers, in perfunctory response to the ritual. "Welcome to our Valley, Sim of the Emet," she said, though she was looking at Ryl. "And you?"

"I'm Ryl of the Birani." Under the pressure of her unflinching gaze, Ryl belatedly bowed and opened his hands. "And I am honored, Allesha."

Filling his hands fully with hers, she responded "Welcome to our Valley, Ryl of the Birani." But she didn't move her hands away, staring almost transfixed into his eyes, reading his face. "Mistral's son," she added.

"Yes, Allesha."

With a nod, almost as though she were agreeing with something in her own mind, she pulled away. "You may proceed, but I suggest you avoid any further 'spirited discussions.'"

Ryl and Sim said, "Thank you, Allesha," almost in unison and took off for the tradegrounds as quickly as they could in a mannerly way.

Before they were out of earshot, Ryl heard the Allesha say to Vetram, "Tell Tedrac that his Allesha needs to see him again. Have him come to my home this afternoon."

Ryl's heart skipped a beat when he heard. *Tedrac! Skies! That was Tedrac's Allesha!* Tedrac, his pa's Triat. His mind raced, replaying the last few moments. Was there anything he could do to salvage the situation? All he could come up with was a jumble of memories with no future. Nothing left except the shouting. Why did everything always have to go so wrong for him? *To hell with them all,* he thought as he ran as fast as his legs would take him — faster, he hoped, than thought or broken dreams or Mistral's disappointment in him.

"Ryl, slow down!" Sim called after him. "You want me to break my neck on these rocks?"

But Ryl didn't stop until he looked up and realized he was in the middle of the tradegrounds. The first thing to hit him were the colors. More shades and hues than he had ever imagined. And the smells. Of strange and familiar foods, animals, incense, spices and people. A swarm of people bargaining, singing, dancing, arguing, laughing. Scattered throughout, individuals here and there silently scanned the crowds.

Sim caught up with Ryl, but was too out of breath to speak. Even when he was no longer gasping for air, he continued to stare with his mouth open, speechless.

Trade caravans were nothing new to either of them, to anyone living within the Peace borders. Whatever else went wrong with Ryl's life, the thrill he felt when one would arrive at his village had never diminished. It wasn't simply the amazing variety of goods, but also the travelers and the exotic stories they told. The biannual caravan arrivals at the Birani village were always filled with adventure and wonder.

But here, on the edge of The Valley of the Alleshi, was the Caravan Convergence. All year, except in deepest winter, caravans came to The Valley, bringing trade goods, tributes, duty gifts, messages and information from all corners of the world. So many that, although there were four tradegrounds in the foothills ringing The Valley, each with room for three or four caravans, none could stay longer than nine days. The frenetic pace of activity and excitement escalated even more during the three interim periods, when the newly formed Allemen from the previous Season, and Petitioners for the next, plus their families, filled the eight inns, tradegrounds and Valley pathways.

With such an abundance of choices before him, Ryl couldn't decide where to look or what to do. But Sim had no doubts, and for the first time since they had met, Sim took the lead, heading right for Schul's booths.

"*Sim!*" Emmy ran toward them through the crowds. "I thought I'd never see you again." Her grey eyes sparkled at the sight of Sim, whose grin was so wide that it almost split his black face in two.

"Hi, Emmy," Sim sputtered, happily abashed and unsure.

Neither seemed to be aware that Ryl was standing right there, next to them. "Hi, Emmy," Ryl said quietly.

"Oh… Hi, Ryl." Emmy's cheeks reddened when she glanced at him, though he doubted it was anything other than embarrassment. Not that it mattered. Compared to Lilla, no girl could hold his attention for more than a few moments of idle curiosity. Certainly not a caravan girl.

Still, Ryl had to admit her sudden blush was appealing. Emmy's long dark hair was threaded with bright, multi-colored ribbons, framing her small light-brown face. Somehow, the effect made her look fragile, though he had seen her successfully wrangle a stubborn mule with no help. Her dancing skirts and soft rainbow-colored blouse seemed to flow with all the colors of the Convergence, revealing curves that had been hidden under the shapeless rough-weave brown pants, quilted jacket and leather hiking boots she had worn during the trip.

Ryl stared, realizing Emmy wasn't as flat-chested as he had thought. Her breasts would be a good handful, if Sim ever got near them.

Sim and Emmy didn't notice when Ryl slipped away into the crowd. Nothing lonelier than being with people who are so involved in each other that you barely exist. It was a lesson Ryl had learned young. Looking back, he saw Emmy taking Sim by the hand and leading him away — hopefully, to someplace private. That poor fellow needed some relief.

Suddenly, a boy much smaller and younger than Ryl ran into him, almost knocking him down. The kid mumbled an apology that was heavy with a strange accent, then quickly disappeared into the crowds. Ryl understood how the kid felt; so much to see and do that he wanted to run about, too. Instead, he moved slowly, deliberately, as though this were an unknown forest, with strange creatures that required careful observation before he could begin the hunt.

Tendrils of smoke from an awning-covered booth wafted toward Ryl, laden with delicious aromas he couldn't name. Not really hungry, certainly not with the abundance of food at the Battai's, he was still drawn toward the grill that was sizzling with the fat of juicy oversized sausages. Next to it was a wood stove covered with fried breads and a bubbling pot of soup so thick he could probably eat it with a fork.

"Succulents and sausages!" the vendor called. "Come taste the best. Succulents and sausages!" Bent with age and missing several of her yellowed teeth, her small dark eyes danced like a young girl's. Her shapeless dress hung on her shriveled frame, but the fabric was as colorful as Emmy's. The old woman was smiling broadly, as if the world were hers to command and enjoy.

Ryl worked his way through the throng toward the booth. His mouth watering, he said, "I'll take a sausage."

"Certainly, young man." Damned if she didn't seem to sparkle at the sight of Ryl. Was the old hag flirting with him? "You've never tasted better," she said as she speared a large link and wrapped it in a flat of fried bread.

When Ryl bit into it, an explosion of hot spices and herbs filled his mouth, nearly burning the roof of his mouth, but it was so rich with flavors that he took another bite before fully swallowing the first.

"Go slow, young man. Enjoy what you have before you grab more."

His mouth was too full to respond, so he merely nodded and reached into his pocket for his purse.

"That's one and five," she said, holding out her hand for payment.

But Ryl's money was gone. Nearly choking on the food, he frantically searched his other pockets, though he always kept his purse in the one place. Skies! The boy who'd bumped into him! Pa had warned Ryl about pickpockets, but he hadn't really thought it could happen to him, that a stranger could reach into his clothes and take something without him feeling it.

The old woman's small eyes no longer twinkled, narrowing even more. She leaned further over the booth counter, shaking her open palm in his face. "One and five," she repeated, a hard edge to her voice that left no doubt that she was not one to be taken advantage of, not her, no sir, she had ways of dealing with people who tried to cheat her.

"I'm sorry, ma'am. My money…."

"*Ryl!*" Aidan's high-pitched voice cut through the crowd, and the slightly built boy was suddenly at his side. His improbably pale skin looked even more sallow in the bright autumn sun, especially against his close-cut black hair and dark slanted eyes.

Among the Petitioners Ryl had met at the Battai's, Aidan was particularly annoying, with his whining voice, fake friendliness and pompous book-learned smarts that had little to do with real life. Besides, Aidan was a gutless wimp. Ryl had even seen him weeping in a corner of the inn last night. Ryl couldn't imagine Aidan in an Alleshine inner room; he probably didn't even know what to do with a woman.

Ryl's instinct was to ignore Aidan, but at the moment he had other worries. "Give me some money," he demanded.

Aidan looked at the half-eaten sausage in Ryl's hand and at the woman with her outstretched hand, and *tsk-tsked* in a disapproving manner that he must have copied from an old granddad. "You shouldn't take what you can't pay for."

"Don't be a prig, Aidan. Give me one and five. I'll pay you back when we get to the Battai's."

Aidan shrugged, took some coins from his purse and, rather than give them to Ryl, put them into the vendor's hand.

"Thank you, young sir," she said to Aidan. "And would you like to try my succulents and sausages?"

"No thank you, ma'am," Aidan replied with a slight bow that made her sparkle once more.

Damn! Now Ryl was beholden to the wimp. No longer really enjoying the sausage, he quickly chomped on the rest of it, wiped his hands on his trousers, then turned away.

"Hey, Ryl." Aidan caught up with him. "The Battai's looking for you."

"And you took it on yourself to find me. How helpful of you."

"Ryl, do you want to hear what the Battai wants or not?"

"I know what he wants. He's got more questions for me."

"No. He has an interview set up for you. In The Valley. With an Allesha."

"What?" Could it be that he still had a chance?

"You're to meet an Allesha in her home this afternoon, if you're not too late already."

"But—"

"Don't worry. It isn't that bad. I had my interview this morning. She was nice. We had an interesting conversation."

"Conversation? Don't you know anything Aidan? An Allesha isn't for conversation. But I guess you can't be expected to know much about that."

Aidan looked at Ryl in a strange way, almost as though the wimp pitied *him*. "You're wasting time, Ryl. If you miss this meeting, you probably won't get another."

Not wanting to follow any advice Aidan could give him, but anxious not to botch this one opportunity, Ryl rushed off to the Battai's without a backward glance. As soon as he reached a clear path, he broke out into a full run, not stopping until he was at the door to the Battai's study on the first floor of the inn.

Chapter 6

In the late afternoon, the Southwest Battai brought the boy Ryl to the house of the new Allesha. They walked side by side, a study in contrasts: the lithe young man with the easy stride of a woodsman, and the short, plump man with a thin fringe of once-black hair, who had never been graceful, even as a child.

But it was the Battai who exuded comfort and confidence, while Ryl hid his nervousness with bluster. This particular path from the Southwest Inn down to The Valley was the Battai's personal domain, the defining geography of his position, his reason and right. Only seven other men — the Battai of the other inns overlooking The Valley — could claim similar privilege, authority and responsibility among the Alleshi.

Though most of the trees were bare, stands of evergreens alternately obscured and revealed The Valley below. About three hundred houses dotted the land, connected by gently winding paths and neatly landscaped green space, a meandering stream, a few tributary creeks and a small lake. Each Alleshine home was large enough for two people, set apart on its own patch of land with a barn, workshop or shed in the back. All were approached through a gate set in a wood fence or stone wall.

One, two or three-storied. Made of timber, stone or stucco. Rectangular and compact, or spread out in wings. Some even had curved walls. The Battai knew from experience that the variety of the houses reflected the wide range of personalities and backgrounds among the Blessed Sisters. It was the Battai's responsibility to try to understand each Allesha, and bring suitable Petitioners to her attention.

How many years had it been, the Battai tried to remember, since he had last taken a candidate for First Boy? Certainly, at least ten. So long that he had almost forgotten the raw excitement of preparing for such a meeting.

New Alleshi shouldn't be so rare. Then fewer boys would be turned away, as he had once been. He hated to fail a boy, to bring the news that a petition had been refused. No length of time could make the task easier, weighted as it was with his own boyhood disappointment.

The memory was as vivid as if it were yesterday. His parents had saved for most of his young life and had borrowed the balance to pay for the trip to The Valley and his petition. Yet, a gale on the sea had delayed them, and they had arrived at The Valley too late. All the Alleshi who would work that Season had already chosen their boys.

It was a matter of numbers, more than anything, for few boys who came to the inn weren't worthy. Just the act of making the trip to The Valley showed their desire to learn. But there were less than three hundred Alleshi in all, each choosing her Season, either to Bless a boy or to remain alone. Some worked only one Season in three, or less. And others were permanently retired from the cycle of Seasons. It was inevitable that most boys would be disappointed.

The Battai often wondered what had happened to the other unBlessed boys he had met as a Petitioner some forty years ago, when he had been turned away from The Valley. He'd heard that, in some villages, they never attained full manhood rights, while in others, it made little or no difference. So diverse were the many villages united under the Alleshi that even a Battai had difficulty keeping their various traditions clear.

In his maritime village, not becoming an Alleman meant he could never be a captain-owner of a seafaring fleet, though his uncle had chosen him as heir. Instead, a distant cousin had inherited the fleet, and the wealth and power it imparted. Too proud to bend his head to his cousin or any other, he hadn't gone to sea. But the seamen had so little regard for the beached that no landlocked position had been denied him. He had become a merchant-trader, the most successful in his village, which helped him get the attention and win the respect of both Allemen and Alleshi. Eventually, through hard work and concerted diplomacy, he had fulfilled his dream of returning to The Valley of the Alleshi, if only to live always outside, never fully accepted, but honored, needed and powerful.

The Battai knew that Ryl's life would be different if his petition were rejected by the Alleshi. The boy's people — the Birani — had been fierce warriors before joining the Alleshine Peace, not so long ago. Some of their leaders still doubted the value of Alleshine training. So Ryl would probably experience little or no stigma should he not be Blessed. Yet, the Battai's instincts, hewn over years of service to the Alleshi, told him that this boy would not be going home with his parents, that he would be accepted by the new Allesha.

Was he jealous of the boy and what he would have that had been denied the Battai as a youth? That was a demon that he had wrestled with and conquered years before. But, yes, the disappointment still lingered, a hard kernel in his heart that he kept walled away, so it seldom surfaced and wouldn't affect his work. He reminded himself that he could never have become Battai, if he had been Blessed by an Allesha. That was one position refused to Allemen. And, while some women from his village would have considered it less than appealing to marry a landlubber, his wife appreciated the wealth and comfort the Battai could afford his family.

Yes, he had to admit to himself, with a satisfied sigh, life did have a way of balancing out.

The Battai studied the new Allesha as she poured blackberry cider for all of them — except the boy, whom the Battai served. Sitting beside her was the boy's father's Allesha, who was said to be the young one's mentor. He knew what to expect from the old one. As stern as she was, he had dealt with her for many years, so he no longer feared her — well, maybe only a little.

As the Battai nibbled at the fresh fruit and pungent cheese that wasn't really to his taste (though he dared not show anything but relish for the young Allesha's offering), he looked closer, trying not to stare. She was tall and lean with soft curves. Her breasts were generous without being large, and her hips just wide enough for comfort. She was in her early or middle forties. Younger than The Valley's other Alleshi by at least eight or ten years. He saw signs of her people, the Attani, in her long limbs, thick auburn hair and graceful manner. The way the wind whipped those open lands sculpted the populace. Their strength came from bending, like laurel trees, but never breaking — and never moving from where they planted their feet. On important matters, she'd prove to be stubborn, an immovable force.

The new Allesha smiled at the Battai, and it seemed to light up her whole being, emerging from deep inside her. "Why have you asked for this audience, Battai?" she asked, using the ancient ritual question.

With a nod, the Battai put his plate on the table and crossed his small pudgy hands comfortably on the ledge the round bulge of his stomach formed with his chest. "I bring this boy and his Petition to your attention. I would be honored if you would consider it."

"Tell me of him."

"He's rash, to be sure, but bright and quick. Though much pressure was brought to bear on him by his parents and the girl he says he loves, I do believe he is here for himself, with free will and the desire to learn. I'm told that he's an adept hunter with keen tracking skills that equal the best, but he seems to have little knowledge of or respect for farming or the other gentler skills. In war games, he is said to have won most honors, and has been trained to the fullest ability of his village's warriors — though, he has not yet been bloodied. He should be an apt pupil in the arts of defense."

"Hey, old man. Don't talk about me like I'm not here."

The Battai turned to the boy, with no attempt to disguise his fury. "*Silence!* Don't shame me or yourself again with your insolence."

The boy glared, first at the Battai, then the old woman and, finally, at the new Allesha. But the Battai noticed how the younger one held the boy's gaze and seemed to transform his anger into burning embarrassment, so that the words of contempt he would have spoken were caught in his throat.

The young Allesha turned to the Battai. "Please continue."

"As you can see, he lacks discipline. He's a difficult boy."

"Is he fully matured, physically?"

"Yes, and certified as hale and whole by both his village's Healer and mine."

"But, Battai, you haven't yet told me why I should consider taking this boy."

"This boy holds great promise, for himself and his people, the Birani, but only if he is brought to full manhood. However, he won't reach true maturity without help, help that he has refused from his parents and all others. In my opinion, only an Allesha will be able to reach him, and among the Alleshi, only a handful, such as his own father's Allesha, who has summoned us here." The Battai nodded respectfully to the older woman, but she ignored him, as was proper. This was the younger one's interview to conduct and control.

The Battai continued, "I am told that you are trained to be such an Allesha. If that is so, here is a fitting First Boy for you."

"I assume he has had a full share of adolescent flirtations."

The boy huffed a bit, crossing his arms tightly across his chest, but held his tongue.

"Yes," the Battai said. "I understand that he was a rutting annoyance for a while, though he never forced himself, being popular among the girls of his region. But he has been settled now for well over a year, having chosen one girl, who apparently also wants him. Their betrothal feast is set for next summer, if, and only if, he becomes an Alleman."

The Allesha stared openly at the boy. Turning back to the Battai, she asked, "What have you told him about what it is to be a First Boy?"

The Battai was unprepared for the question. Did this new one mean to challenge how he handled his duties? Reflexively, he touched his gold badge of office pinned over his left breast. "I've explained the triple blessing you could offer. I've told him that to be Blessed by an Allesha is the finest thing that can happen to a young man. Even the son of the poorest, least respected family in the land, should he be an Alleman, can aspire to be a leader, honored by all, with his pick of the best women, most fertile land, fleetest ship, or whatever it is that's prestigious among his people.

"To be a First Boy," the Battai continued, "is to have an even deeper bond with his Allesha, one that will enrich his life and hers. First Boys are rare and valued above all other men.

"And to be a Winter Boy is to share the one Season in which the Allesha can devote all her time to him, with none of the daily distractions that descend on us during our spring and autumn Seasons, when The Valley is open to the world. Thus, a Winter Boy is the most rewarded and enriched by his Allesha."

"Does he understand the responsibilities of an Alleshine agreement? Does he have the maturity to honor it for the rest of my life?" the young Allesha asked the Battai.

"Yes, everything has been arranged. Please, Allesha, be assured, I have seen to every detail."

The young Allesha studied the boy while the Battai spoke. A boy of the Birani, a son of one of Dara's own? Could it be that Dara had actually brought Mistral's son to her? Why hadn't she said as much?

Attractive and fully grown, the boy could be mistaken for a man. And, yes, there was something of Mistral's dark wildness in him. His deep-set eyes met hers without flinching. Other than the crooked nose that looked as though it had been broken more than once, his swarthy face was made of straight lines, from his high cheekbones to his fine-chiseled jaw. No more than average height, he had the type of lean body that would look tall if he didn't slouch in that chair. His lower legs shook nervously, apparently unconsciously, readying themselves to dart. Underneath his bluster, she saw that he was eager to be accepted, willing to be responsible, praying to whatever or whomever he held sacred that she would Bless him.

Yes, she decided, and it was her free will that had brought her to it. But why would Dara bring Mistral's son to her with no warning? The young Allesha rose from her seat to signal the end of the interview.

"Battai, thank you. You have discharged your duties admirably. I will give you my answer tomorrow."

The Battai bowed first to the new Allesha and then, with deeper solemnity, to the older one. The boy mimicked the man's gesture, but with less grace, his movement made awkward by a muddle of fear, anger, resentment and hope.

Chapter 7

"Well?" Karinne asked.

"It is done," Evanya said. "Rishana will Bless the boy."

"Good. And Rishana?"

"I've done my best, but there is still so much she hasn't been taught."

"Anything you can't control, Evanya?"

"Of course. You know Rishana. Has anyone ever really controlled her?"

"No, but she is a reasonable woman. Logical and capable. Strong and good hearted. No amount of training could give us all that she is. We'll have to trust in her native abilities as we continue her training. We agreed from the beginning that she'd be a good match for the boy."

"Yes, but…"

"But what, Evanya?"

"Karinne, you won't believe what she suggested: a hunt on their first day. Just when we need to be close to her, guiding her through the delicate initial engagements."

"A hunt? She is full of surprises, isn't she?"

"You sound proud of her."

"Yes," said Karinne. "Yes, I am. What a wonderfully inventive idea. A hunt, indeed. Have you ever heard of an Allesha doing such a thing? And on her first day with her First Boy."

"But it's dangerous."

"Rishana's a skilled hunter. She knows our mountains and its herds as well as any."

"Not the hunt itself, Karinne. Them going away… on her first day. What if something happens? How could we control any problems that might arise? Perhaps a more experienced Allesha might experiment…"

"Don't you see, Evanya, how brilliant a plan it is? Keep a boy like this at home, and he'll always think of his Allesha as nothing but a woman like other women. Take him into the woods, which he considers his domain…. Think about it. You say he's a master tracker; well, Rishana is certainly anyone's equal in archery or riflery. For a boy from a village in which women aren't even considered fit for the hunt, it will shake him as no conventional first lesson could. Yes, Evanya, we chose wisely when we decided on Rishana."

"I still wish we'd had more time."

Chapter 8

Rishana busied herself throughout the day and into the evening, cleaning her house thoroughly, sweeping out anything from her rooms — and her mind — that wouldn't suit the boy.

Tonight, her First Season would begin.

It was still early when she finished, with hours left to fill. She felt too restless to read, write in her journal, or meditate. Besides, what she really wanted more than anything was to talk once more with Savah, Jared's Allesha.

The years had shrunk her world, taking away, one by one, those whom she could depend upon to love and protect her, whatever happened. First, all four of her grandparents in quick succession, though Grand-mamma lasted longest, followed some years later by her father and soon after, her mother. But those had been natural deaths, after good long lives. Then Jared, ripped from her too soon, with such sudden, senseless violence.

The one mainstay left from her previous life was Savah — and her children, Eli and Svana. But Eli and Svana were grown and off on their own. They were still an integral part of her being, as much as the breath in her lungs which sustained her but could not be contained. However, she had long ago recognized that it was right and proper, if bittersweet, that her children were forging lives that she could share only peripherally.

Savah was the one person remaining of those she had always de-pended upon for help, support, sustaining love.

Now, somehow, Rishana had become the elder, a guide and guard-ian to the young. Not simply as a mother, or even as a village leader, but as an Allesha to a strange, troubled boy.

Time had passed so quickly; she didn't remember getting older — certainly not wiser, like Savah or Grandmamma. Who was she to guide anyone?

Was it really so long ago when she had joined with Jared as his young bride, then known as Jinet? Her heart still brimmed with memories of their first flush of love. The joy of standing by Jared's side, when their union was affirmed at the village council fire, had been marred only by her trembling fear. For she knew that the marriage would not be sanctified until she made the requisite nuptial visit to honor the Allesha who had molded her Alleman husband. But when she had met Jared's Allesha, she had discovered a sweet grandmotherly woman whose presence exuded confidence and comfort. What's more, she had even been given the privilege of learning Jared's private name for his Allesha — Savah.

The bond between the two women had been forged with friendship, trust and love. Since Jared's murder, it had grown even deeper. through shared sorrow, need, and closer proximity. When the young widow had chosen to join the Alleshi, Savah had encouraged and sponsored her, becoming her closest advisor and supporter. At her initiation, it was Savah who had given Jinet her Alleshine name — Rishanna.

How unsettling that Jinet/Rishana hadn't planned her day more efficiently so she could have spent time with Savah. Just a few minutes of comfort, reassurance and Savah's intriguing questions would have helped. Instead, the young Allesha felt so terribly alone, on the threshold of an unknowable future, without Savah's sure hand at the small of her back.

Earlier that morning, Savah had stopped on her way to the library, to organize the small collection of books that she had selected and sent over for the boy's room. But Rishana had been in the middle of a planning discussion with Dara, and Savah had come and gone before Rishana could shake herself free.

Now it was too late. Savah was certainly already on her way to the Battai's to prepare for the Signing.

Rishana sat in the front window seat and looked outside. The half-moon was beginning to rise over the mountains, casting long shadows into the dark night, beckoning to her. She decided that a brisk walk in the cool evening air was just what she needed.

The walk quickly became an all-out run, as Rishana threw her pent-up energy and nervousness into pushing her legs and arms faster, harder. What a relief it was to abandon herself to pure physical release. It made her feel younger and stronger, reminding her what it was like to be in control of her own body and life.

She swerved a few times to avoid various Alleshi, Allemen and others walking on the paths. However, they were so busy with their own Season transition concerns, they barely gave her a backward glance. That is, except one woman.

Rishana didn't notice Kiv cutting through some shrubs from another path until the older Allesha was standing only a few paces ahead, directly in her way. Rishana had to stop abruptly in her tracks to avoid colliding with Kiv.

Tall and angular, with sharp features softened by her ready smile, Kiv greeted the young Allesha in a friendly, lighthearted tone. "Hello, Rishana, where are you headed?"

Rishana quickly composed herself, not wanting to show how unsettled she was by Kiv's sudden appearance. "I'm just getting some exercise."

"May I walk with you?"

Rishana's answer, "Of course," had as much to do with curiosity as courtesy. She had never spent much time with Kiv, certainly not alone. But she'd noticed how well liked Kiv was among their sisters, many of whom sought her out for her companionship and lively mind. In Council, Rishana had been impressed with Kiv's intelligence, but also noted the brittleness of her objections and counter arguments, especially with anything Dara had to say. Dara secretly called her The Knife, but did that have more to do with Dara than with Kiv?

Rishana initially reined in her usual quick pace in deference, but found that Kiv walked with greater energy than she had expected. Looking more closely, the young woman realized that Kiv wasn't as old as she had thought. Perhaps only ten or twelve years her senior. Then why was she already retired from the giving of Seasons?

As they walked, Kiv's small dark eyes slowly swept the landscape, noting all nearby activity, human or otherwise. Rishana had the impression that Kiv didn't want them to be overheard.

"Are you ready for tonight?" Kiv asked.

"As ready as I can be."

"Your First Boy is the son of Dara's Mistral, isn't he?" Kiv asked.

"Yes."

"They are a wild people. If he ever gets to be too much for you—"

Cutting Kiv short, Rishana reminded her, "Mistral *is* an Alleman."

"Yes, and your husband's Triat. I know. But Dara never really gained full control of him. His son will be even more difficult, especially for a new Allesha."

Was Kiv testing her, or did she not realize how easily her words could be taken as an insult? "Kiv, I don't wish to be disrespectful, but I would rather not discuss my Winter Boy."

"Please, Rishana, don't misunderstand me. I have full faith in your ability to shape this boy into a strong, capable Alleman. I just hope you'll remember that I'm here if you ever want to talk. It wasn't so long ago for me that I can't remember how confusing a First Season can be."

If she scrubbed her perceptions clean of Dara's disapproval of the woman, what would Rishana really see when she looked at Kiv? A brilliant mind, certainly, but also someone who cared deeply about the Peace and might be offering her hand in friendship.

"These are difficult times to become an Allesha," Kiv said.

"I would say they are difficult times for everyone."

"How true." Kiv nodded in agreement. "With the Mwertik hammering at everything we value, and our Council buckling under."

Rishana felt her stomach twist at the mention of the Mwertik, not really wanting to talk about them, wishing she could stop thinking about them.

"Tell me, Rishana, it's been only a few years since the Mwertik murdered Jared. Does the memory of it still keep you awake at night with questions of why it happened, and how it is that our beautiful Peace has failed so completely?"

"Failed isn't the word I'd use."

"No? We've become tame lambs grazing comfortably on the bounty we've accumulated around us, twitching nervously when the wolves strike, but doing nothing about it. Is it any wonder that the Mwertik's attacks reach deeper inside our borders with every passing year? Perhaps it's time to reshape our methods, to recognize that we must do something more than talk and trade when faced with enemies who understand nothing but violence."

Rishana shook her head, not so much in disagreement, but because she wasn't sure how to respond.

Kiv patted her arm. "All I ask is that you think about it."

As they parted, Rishana accepted Kiv's embrace, but the older Allesha's touch chilled rather than warmed her. Was it because "The Knife" was naturally cold, as Dara claimed, or because her cuts were so incisive?

Chapter 9

After leaving Kiv, Rishana continued her run, but it did little to dispel the disquiet she now felt. It wasn't just Kiv's comments, nor the mention of the Mwertik and Jared, that upset her. But she couldn't put her finger on exactly what the problem was.

As she approached her house, Rishana discerned a large, rotund figure of a man stopping at her gate. He looked at her closed front door, started to turn away, but then pulled something out of his pocket, wrote on it, and placed it under her gatepost message lantern.

She hurried to reach him before he could leave. "Tedrac?" she called out. "Is that you?"

"Hello, Jin—" he stopped in mid word. "Hello, Allesha. I was passing by and thought I might… But you must be busy. Don't let me disturb you. It was good to see you again." He turned to go.

"Wait, Tedrac. Please, won't you come in and visit with me for a while? It's been so long since I've seen you." She hesitated only slightly before adding, "Tedrac, please, I need to speak with you."

Bowing his head, he held his hands open in ritual greeting. "I am honored you will see me without prior arrangements, Allesha."

Tedrac, of all people, bowing his head to her!

Rishana acknowledged the gesture, and filled his hands with hers. "Tedrac, I welcome you to my home, which will always be open to you."

"No, not always, Allesha," he answered as he followed her inside.

She didn't argue the point, understanding that he wasn't so much disagreeing with her, as helping her move from the habits of their long-time relationship to the new forms. After all, she was no longer the wife of his Triat, but an Allesha on the threshold of her First Season, when her door would be closed to all outsiders.

In the kitchen, she gestured toward the table. "Please sit, Tedrac. I have blackberry cider and cheese. Or would you prefer tea and cookies?"

He eased his girth into the small bentwood chair. "Your cookies? Definitely. But please don't go to any bother."

"No bother," she said as she turned up the gas fire under her kettle. Once, many years ago, Tedrac had been walking-stick thin, but he enjoyed cookies and other sweets too much. No, that wasn't the whole of it.

She remembered meeting Tedrac just before her wedding. He and Mistral had come to stand behind Jared as he declared himself to her at the village council fire. Only when she felt the watchful eyes of his Triats as she responded with her vow did she fully understand that in marrying Jared, she was also accepting the other two men into her life — so close are the ties within an Allemen Triad.

How different those three were from one another. Tedrac had always been the quiet one, preferring to bury himself in books rather than expend any physical energy, slowing down and retreating even more after Lorel died giving birth to their only child, a stillborn son. Mistral was the exact opposite, filled with a restlessness that would not be contained, though his step was nearly silent, and his words few. Jared had been the balance between them, the one who was comfortable within himself, wherever he was and with anyone he met.

Yes, Tedrac had been an important part of her marriage and her life. And, now, here he was: Tedrac, the renowned scholar who seldom left his library and rarely traveled from his village, which was at least a month's trek from The Valley. Why had he sought her out, tonight of all nights?

She reached for a green-enameled tin canister from a top shelf. "If I remember correctly, you have a fondness for mint tea."

"I'm honored that you remember."

Turning from the counter, she met his gaze. "Please, Tedrac, don't do that. We've known each other too long to fall into ritual. Is it so very different from the old days, sitting here in my kitchen?"

"In one word, yes. You are now an Allesha."

"Yes, I know, and Jared is no longer here beside us, connecting us." She sat in the other chair, across the kitchen table from him. "But must everything between us be erased and forgotten, now that I am an Allesha? Did the Mwertik destroy that, too?"

"Of course not. If anything, Jared's death made Mistral's and my connection to you stronger than ever, because Jared is no longer there between us."

"Did you know that Mistral's son is to be my First Boy?"

Tedrac leaned back into his seat, crossing his arms over his chest. "I heard that you would listen to his petition."

"But when I agreed to hear it, I didn't know who he was."

"Would it have made a difference if you had known?"

It was the same thing she had been asking herself since the meeting. One of many questions, none of which she had been able to answer to her full satisfaction. "Mistral's Allesha thought it might. She claims that's why she didn't tell me... because she wanted me to judge the boy for himself."

"And you're discomforted by it." It was a statement, not a question. "You know you don't have to accept him as your First Boy. It is your choice."

"Is it, Tedrac? Is it really?"

"In the final analysis, yes. But no decision, at least none this important, can be made in a vacuum. Still, I do ask you to consider carefully. What you do today will change things for you, for your entire life."

She had seen Tedrac like this before, the consummate scholar and strategist, analyzing situations. If he followed his usual manner, he would soon be offering different viewpoints, working his way into the core of an issue, not directly but in spirals of ideas, knowledge, answers and new questions. Did he already know where he was headed tonight? Was this why he had come? "You sound like Eli."

"Oh?" Tedrac uncrossed his arms, which somehow changed his focus from portioning to gathering information. "I didn't know your son was here."

"No, not now. That was when I first came to The Valley."

"So he wasn't talking about Mistral's son?"

"No, of course not. Neither of us could have known back then that the boy would be my first Petitioner. Eli was warning me about other things, about how being an Allesha would change things for me."

"I see." He nodded his satisfaction and leaned back once more.

"Tedrac, why are you here? Was there something you wanted?"

"To pay my respects, Allesha."

"Please, Tedrac. Am I no more than a title to you?"

"Of course, you are. But you are also more than my Triat's wife, and far beyond the young woman I once knew as Jinet. What name could I use to encompass all that you have become?"

"Please call me Rishana. It is the name the Alleshi have given me."

"Then I am doubly honored, to be given your true name."

"Do you really believe that, Tedrac? That it is my true name?"

"Perhaps the question should be: do you believe it?"

"I don't know anymore. Tonight, I will shed even that, becoming a blank slate for a boy I did not truly choose for myself."

"Then don't accept him. Turn him away."

"You would have your Triat's son remain unBlessed?"

"I would prefer to not see my Triat's wife compelled."

"Does one preclude the other?"

"I'm not the one who can say, Rishana."

"I will not send him away."

"Then it's decided already. But you must remember, it is your decision, and no one else's."

"Why is that important to you, Tedrac?"

"Because I would not have my Triat's wife compelled."

"Is that all? Is there no other reason you've come?"

"I wanted to offer my friendship, Rishana. My help, any time you might need it. My support, whenever you want it. Beyond being my Triat's widow, or an Allesha, or even the Allesha to my other Triat's boy. For yourself." Tedrac leaned forward onto the table, his chair squeaking as he shifted his weight to reach toward her. "Rishana, Eli was right. Things are going to change for you, in ways you can't possibly foresee. If I can assist in any manner, I will."

She placed one hand over his. "Then I am the one who is honored, Tedrac."

The kettle whistled, and she got up to prepare the tea, using dried mint leaves and bits of lemon peel, the way he liked it. When she sat down again to serve the cookies and tea, the moment had been broken. But she couldn't shake a feeling that something more than what had been said had passed between them. And that something important, perhaps vital, had been left unsaid.

Chapter 10

Everything changed when Ryl heard from the Battai that he was to be Blessed. He could even put up with Mistral's constant instructions as he dressed and prepared himself. However, all that noise and nonsense Pa spouted about what it would be like when they would be Allemen together had begun to grate on his nerves, especially when he realized that Mistral still hadn't accepted the fact that Ryl and Lilla were promised to each other. Not that Mistral could do anything about it. No one would ever separate them again, once Ryl was an Alleman and master of his own life.

Shria was fluttering and smiling as she came into the Petitioner's Wing to walk with them to the Battai's study, "It's near time. Are my two men ready?" She fingered the fringes of Ryl's traditional leather tunic to untangle them, straightened the front where the lacing was pulling a bit, and stood back to admire her handiwork, her dark eyes shining.

"Ma," Ryl began to protest, but refrained. Instead, he spread out his arms and pivoted around once. "Well, what do you think?"

"Oh, Ryl…" Shria choked back tears of pride. "I can't believe this day has come so quickly."

Mistral stepped forward, pulling Shria to his side. Though Mistral wasn't tall, especially when compared to the men they had seen in the inner villages on their way here, Shria was diminutive and fit neatly under his arm.

"Look, Mistral," she said. "What a fine young man we bring to the Alleshi! Wasn't it only yesterday when you carried him to the council for his Naming?" With her free hand, she pulled her son toward her, so she could have an arm around each of them. "We'll miss you terribly, Ryl, but I'm so very proud of you," she said.

She held them both, but when Ryl's hand accidentally brushed against Mistral's, where their arms were wrapped around her back, he quickly stepped away.

"Come on; let's go," Ryl said as he strode down the hallway, not looking back to see his parents following.

The Battai's spacious office had been transformed into something mysterious yet wondrous by the simple act of turning down the gas lights and filling various nooks with candles. Shadows flickered on the wall-lining bookshelves and the green ceiling-to-floor curtains that covered the large windows.

During his three long interviews with the Battai, Ryl had stared out those windows, at the trail leading down to The Valley, convinced that he would never walk that path. The view was blocked now, but in his mind's eye, the path stretched open before him. He couldn't shake the feeling that it had to be a mistake. Yet he knew that the Alleshi didn't make mistakes. Still, why did they want him, when everyone else treated him as though he were nothing but trouble?

The Battai stood as they entered. Somehow, the man seemed taller, as though his ceremonial brown wool jacket with its Alleshine green edging, collar and cuffs gave him added stature. His gold badge of office gleamed on his left breast. Instead of sitting behind his massive oak desk, he gestured to Ryl, Mistral and Shria to sit with him at the large round walnut table, to await the other signers.

The Healer arrived first, having been in the inn since the early afternoon, when she gave the boy his final examination. Old and gaunt, she had more grey than black in her hair. Her ceremonial robe of deep blue, trimmed in the blood-red symbols of her craft, made her appear more substantial than she was.

The five of them had barely been seated at the round table again when they quickly stood for another woman who entered. Her yellow robe marked her as a Storyteller, though Ryl had never seen her before. She had a thick mane of pure white hair, but her dark face was so vibrantly youthful that he couldn't decide if she were older than a granny or younger than his mother.

The Battai then left the room by a side door. When he returned, he announced, "Please greet the Allesha."

Everybody immediately stood in respect.

A short, plump woman in her late seventies or early eighties glided gracefully through the door. She wore the traditional green robe; its hem dragged along the floor. Obviously, the robe was old but well cared for, and from a time when the Allesha was younger and taller.

While she embraced the Healer and the Storyteller, the boy pulled the Battai aside and whispered, "This isn't my Allesha, is it? I'm supposed to get that new one. Right? A younger one."

The Allesha heard the boy's question. "You're correct, boy," she said. "Your Allesha awaits you below in The Valley. I am here only to see that her Agreement is signed correctly."

"Sorry. I didn't know. I thought..." Ryl stumbled over his words, worried that this Allesha could break the Agreement before it could be made.

She nodded. "It's understandable."

After the Allesha accepted Ryl's, Mistral's and Shria's ritual greetings, she sat at the table and gestured to Ryl to sit beside her. The others arranged themselves in appropriate order around the circle.

"Tell me, boy, what do you understand about the Agreement you and your parents will be signing here today?" The Allesha spoke directly to him, as though he were the only person in the room.

"Well, I'm promising to become a Defender of the Peace, an Alleman."

"What does that mean to you?"

"I guess it means that I'll have to fight anyone who tries to break the Peace. But I'd do that anyway. You don't have to make me promise."

"Yes, I am certain you would fight for our Peace. But, sometimes, the most difficult battle is learning when *not* fighting will win it for you." She touched his hand and smiled. "Shall we read the Agreement together?"

They bent over the wide, round handwriting on the soft vellum while the Storyteller read another copy aloud.

Blessed is the Boy, son of Mistral, Alleman, Chancellor of the Birani; son of Shria, daughter of the Healer of the Reen; and grandson of the Headman of the Birani. The new Allesha blesses this Boy and welcomes him to her home, the House of the Apple Trees, to share her First Season. And Mistral's Allesha welcomes this Boy and his Allesha into her care.

The Boy acknowledges the new Allesha as head of the household and agrees to be bound to the Allesha's words and deeds, as she wills, for the four months of their Winter Season.

The Boy honors Mistral's Allesha and agrees to be bound to her words and deeds, as she wills, for the four months of the coming Winter Season.

The Boy and his family also agree to provision the two Alleshi, according to their needs and desires, for as long as they live.

The Boy vows that, for all the days of his life, he shall be a Defender of the Peace, and accepts all the responsibilities, obligations and allegiances that entails.

This Agreement is binding upon the Boy, his parents, his future wife or wives and any children he may have, down to the generations that spring from the Boy. Also, in accordance with the traditions of the Birani, the village of the Birani assume their Chancellor's obligation as their own.

"What do you think of it?" the Allesha asked the boy when the Storyteller had finished reading.

"It's awfully one-sided," the boy replied. "I promise to give her anything she wants, forever, and to accept whatever you Alleshi require of me as a Defender of the Peace. All she does is promise to give me a place to live for the next four months."

"This is true," said the Allesha. "Has anybody given you reason to believe it would be anything other than this?"

"Well... yeah... sure." Looking at the gentle old woman, Ryl felt twisted about and uncertain. "I mean, she's supposed to teach me stuff. How to do things, like be a leader, solve disputes, initiate me into the mysteries of... damn it... I don't know what you're trying to get me to say."

"I want you to say what you think, so I can gauge your understanding and commitment to this Agreement. So tell me, how can I judge whether you will honor it? "

"I thought that's what you're supposed to know, how to read and mold the future. Isn't that what Alleshi do?"

"We do many things. Right now, I'm asking you a question."

"Well, I've never broken a promise. Ask my pa. He doesn't like me much, but he'll say that about me."

"Son—"

The Allesha glanced at Mistral and, with a slight shake of her left hand, silenced his protest.

"Why do you honor your promises?" she asked the boy.

"Because..." Ryl hesitated; his sense of honor had always been rooted in deeds, not words. "Promises are oaths on your name. You can't let your name become nothing, mean nothing. It's not manly. It's not right."

"I see. And, if at some time in the future, you are convinced that the promise was forced on you or would lead to inequity, are you still obliged to honor it?"

"I think so. Yeah." Ryl was silent for a moment, then admitted, "I don't know."

"Good," said the Allesha "Not knowing is a good beginning."

"But you're supposed to judge whether I'll keep this Agreement, and I just said I don't know. How can that be good?"

"I'll let you think about that for a while. If, after you have been with your Allesha for a month or so, you still don't understand, then ask her to bring you to visit me, and we'll talk about this again. Now tell me of the girl you hope will be your wife."

"Lilla." Saying her name made Ryl feel warmer, more alive, even if Mistral winced at the sound of it. Ryl couldn't understand what Mistral had against Lilla.

"Did Lilla share in your decision to come to our Valley?" the Allesha asked.

"Did she ever! Her ma wouldn't have me anywhere near her, unless I came. Unless the Alleshi accepted and Blessed me."

"Did that made you angry?"

"Yeah, it made me angry! Lilla and I love each other, belong together, and that old hag got the idea into her head that no one except an Alleman would have her daughter."

"And Lilla agreed?"

"Yeah, Lilla agreed. Her ma can turn anything around so Lilla will agree. She's a shrewd one, she is. Could even turn Lilla against me."

"So, it's thanks to the mother, whom you call an 'old hag,' that we have the pleasure of your company?"

"Well...."

"Would you be here, if it weren't for her?"

"No..."

"Are you sorry that you have come?"

The boy saw the trap too late. *Damn, this old Allesha isn't as sweet as she looks.* "No, of course not. I'm excited as anyone could be about being Blessed."

"I'm glad to hear it," said the Allesha.

"You believe me, don't you?"

"Shouldn't I?"

"Well, yeah. My word is good. It's just that… oh, I don't know. It seems that you wanted to trip me up or something."

"No, I simply wanted you to speak your thoughts, so I could know the person we are welcoming into our community. I think I now know you a bit better."

"And I'm still to be Blessed?"

"Of course. Your Allesha has already chosen you."

"So you had no say in whether I'd be accepted?"

"None whatever."

"Then why did you put me through all that?" Ryl demanded. "You'll have nothing to do with me. You're not my Allesha. You're not anything to me."

The Allesha's posture and expression remained unchanged, but Ryl felt the room chill with her disapproval. "Hey, wait, are you angry at me now?"

"Shouldn't I be? You've told me I'm nothing to you."

He frantically sought some way back to the way things were before he had screwed up yet again. But what did that matter? What did anything matter, other than getting this Agreement signed and getting down to The Valley? After a moment of silence, the boy turned to the Allesha and said, "I'm sorry, ma'am. I didn't mean to insult you."

With a warm smile, the Allesha patted his arm. "I accept your apology." Then she nodded to the Battai, who spread out the three copies of the Agreement and placed ink sponges around the table and an ink bowl in the middle.

The Battai turned to the boy. "Before we begin the Signing, I must ask if you have any more questions for any of us?"

"No," Ryl answered.

"Fine. Let us begin," the Battai said.

Each person around the table rose in turn, took out a personal seal, pressed it on an ink sponge and applied it to the three copies of the Agreement. First the Healer, certifying that both the Allesha and the boy were healthy. Next, the Storyteller, who confirmed that she had studied both the Allesha's and the boy's bloodlines, and that they were free from familial or bond constraints. Then Mistral, giving his village's pledge to the two Alleshi.

But when Shria rose, Ryl was stunned. No woman of the Birani had her own seal, bound as she was by that of her father or of her husband. "Ma?" he blurted out, before he caught himself.

"You forget, son, I am of the Reen. I came to the Birani out of love for your father, but I still carry my past with me, which is as much a part of you and your future as anything that came to you from your father."

"But…" Ryl began to protest.

The Allesha asked, "You do know that each village has its own traditions, don't you?"

"But…"

"The women of the Reen are equals with the men," explained the Storyteller.

"I know."

"So, should they not also sign a contract, as men do?" asked the Allesha.

"Yeah, but my ma never did before."

Shria turned to her son. "No other contract has ever been so important to me, not since my marriage vows were witnessed." She moved slowly, deliberately inking her seal each time before firmly pressing it onto the three copies of the Agreement.

The Battai now spoke to the boy again. "It is time for you to sign your Alleshine Agreement."

Ryl stood, because it seemed the right thing to do.

The Battai asked, "Do you sanction this Agreement and all that it says or implies?"

"Yes."

The Healer asked, "Do you do this of your own free will, with no force or coercion?"

"Yes."

The Storyteller asked, "Do you understand that accepting this Agreement may change your life in ways you neither expected nor sought?"

"Yes."

The Allesha asked, "Do you promise to uphold the Alleshi, to honor us and obey our will, and to be a true and formidable Defender of our Peace, for as long as you live?"

"Yes."

"*Done!*" exclaimed the Battai, who now reached for the boy's right hand and pushed it into the bowl of red ink.

"Hey!" Ryl protested.

"Your right hand is the seal of a Blessed Boy," said the Battai. "Now, press it onto each copy of the Agreement." The boy obeyed, and when he had sealed the third copy, the Battai clapped the boy on his back, while handing him a damp cloth to wipe his hand. "Well done."

The Allesha rose and spoke to the boy. "Blessings on you, boy. We accept you into our community and honor you as one of our own." She pressed her seal onto the Agreements, binding the Alleshi to the boy.

The Battai poured seven glasses of wine from a decanter and raised his. "I propose a toast to the boy and his Allesha."

"To the boy and his Allesha," all rejoined.

"To my Allesha," Ryl added, in awe and wonder, but still not trusting that any of this could truly be happening to him.

Chapter 11

The forest smelled of the crisp end of autumn. The moon hadn't yet crested over the mountaintops, and the sky that showed through the leafless trees was filled with stars. Along the easy, generations-worn trail that wound down the mountain to The Valley, the boy and the old man walked side by side in silence, lost as they were in their thoughts. The Battai carried a lantern to light the way.

A sad sweetness seeped into the Battai's heart, of hope for the lad mingled with his own sense of time irretrievably lost. It was always such for the Battai, this final duty, taking a boy to his Allesha.

At a clearing near the end of the woods, the boy turned to the Battai, "You usually have so much to say. Why are you quiet now?"

"I was waiting to see if you have any last questions for me."

The Battai purposely slowed his pace to give the boy time to think. They continued walking, listening to the crunch of leaves underfoot.

"What questions should I ask?" The boy stared at the glimpses of The Valley lights through the dark wood, rather than looking directly at the Battai. His tone was uncharacteristically tentative. "I mean, are there any other things I should know that will help me?"

"What kind of help do you mean?"

"What happens when I get there?" The boy jabbed his hand in the direction of The Valley. "She's pretty old. Probably as old as my ma. I've never had a woman that old. Do I treat her like a teacher or a lover or what?"

"Treat her as you would any woman or man, with respect and good will." As the Battai spoke, he unconsciously shook his head, knowing this boy still had much to learn about respect and good will. But he quickly disciplined his actions and tone, reminding himself to keep his voice non-judgmental and his manner impassive. "She will be many things to you. Head of the house. Lover. Teacher. Friend. And what she will be will change often. After all, as I've explained to you, that's what the title Allesha literally means — Every Woman. So it is that an Allesha must be many women, to give what—"

"*No!*" The boy interrupted. "None of your philosophy, Battai. I need something I can use, now, tonight. Do I embrace her in greeting or open my hands in the traditional way or wait for her to approach me? What's this nonsense about naming her?"

"I've no doubt your village Storyteller has already taught you about the significance of naming."

"Yeah." The boy shrugged, then in a whining singsong voice that the Battai assumed was supposed to mimic a Storyteller, he recited the lesson. "Relationships define us. Important bonds and pacts change us. And the names we share within the privacy of those relationships represent this, sealing us to the 'other.'"

"So it will be with your Allesha."

"But so many names... how many can you have? One for every relationship? That'd be dozens of names. Maybe more. It's unnatural."

"Nothing is more natural. The Alleshi have simply taken what we already do, what our people have always done, and imbued it with layers of meaning we might not have otherwise recognized." The Battai paused, realizing that the boy wasn't ready to understand the nuances and import of name giving. Instead, he decided to take another tack. "You've already experienced this. What is your Father's name?"

"Mistral. Mistral of the Birani. You know that."

"Yes, but you don't call him Mistral of the Birani, except when you speak of him to strangers. If you were talking to others about a man related to you, you might say, 'my father.' In conversation with him, I've heard you call him 'Pa,' though I'm sure your name for him has changed as you've grown and your relationship has changed. You probably even have a name you use when you're angry with him. But none of your names for your father are those used by his wife or his Allesha."

"Sure, but how do I do it — name her?" The boy shook his head. "Skies! That's not important right now. Tell me about tonight and tomorrow morning. Will there be some initiation or ritual or something? What do I do or say to please her and get me into that inner room?"

"There's no second guessing any Allesha. All I can suggest is what I said before. Eventually, you will learn how to act, because that's one of the important things an Allesha teaches her boy."

Gradually, the forest gave way to cultivated greenery, the winding dirt path became a groomed gravel walkway, and the hills flattened to The Valley — so slowly that the Battai wondered if the boy noticed. Then again, this boy seemed to notice little that didn't directly and immediately affect him.

"But what about tonight, old man, what about the sex?"

"There'll be no sex for you tonight."

The boy stopped abruptly and pulled on the Battai's shoulder to swing him around, so the two of them were face to face. "What do you mean? Why not?"

"You'll have no intimacy until you are intimate."

"Now you're talking nonsense, old man."

"Until you understand how far from nonsense I'm speaking, you'll not learn any of what your Allesha has to give." The Battai started walking again.

"Well, that's what you're supposed to be doing, helping me understand." The boy followed the Battai, catching up to him easily. "Right, old man? That's part of what my pa paid you for. So explain. I want you to be able to tell her I understand, so we don't waste any time getting to that inner room."

"I won't be telling your Allesha anything. It will be up to you. She'll watch you, and, being an Allesha, she'll know when you're ready. Just try to remember this: attempting to control an Allesha will be a losing battle. Play her neither for a fool, nor for a weak opponent. She's shrewder and more powerful than anyone you have ever met." The Battai gestured to the slate-roofed cedar-shingled one-story house in front of them. "This is where I leave you. I wish you well, boy."

No lights shone through the front windows, which surprised the Battai. Wondering what the new Allesha had planned for this boy, he was certain of one thing: it would be an interesting match.

The boy seemed to want to say something, but nothing came out of his mouth. The Battai clapped him lightly on the back, pushing him forward through the gate. Knowing his role was finished, the Battai extinguished his lantern and quickly disappeared into the darkness.

The boy turned once more and, not seeing the Battai, whispered to the shadows, "Goodbye, old man… and thank you."

He walked through the open front outer door of his Allesha's home and called out "Hello?" in a thin, uncertain voice. Then he rapped tentatively on the inner door.

The Battai stood there for some time, watching the house from a distance, knowing he would see nothing, for he could go this far and no farther. Eventually, he made his way home through the cool night air, alone.

Chapter 12

When there was no answer to his knock, Ryl poked his head inside, and called out tentatively, "Hello?"

No answer. *Could it be she's hard of hearing?*

He left his coat, pack, satchel, bow and quiver in the vestibule between the inner and outer doors and cautiously stepped into the darkened greeting room. "Hello? Ouch! Damn." He rubbed his shin where it had jammed into some low-lying piece of furniture. "Anyone here?"

"I'm in the kitchen. Come on in."

He hated the relief he felt at the sound of her voice, the soft femininity that offered solace from the fears he didn't want to acknowledge. Behind him was the empty night and others' expectations of him. His unknowable future lay ahead, behind the black silhouette of a dark door framed by the light of the room beyond.

The kitchen was so brightly lit by gas globes that he had to blink to accustom his eyes after the deep dark of the evening. The Allesha stood at a stone counter with her back to him. Wearing a food-stained wraparound apron over a simple belted green dress. she showed a bit more leg than he was used to seeing in a mature woman. But then, those were legs worthy of showing.

"Please excuse my back," she said without turning toward him. "If I don't spoon the jam when it's at this temperature, the whole thing will be ruined. I hope you like bealberries. The harvest was good this year, so we have quite a bit preserved for the winter. Ah, there, that's the last of them."

She turned, looked at him quite seriously, then erupted into one of the most dazzling smiles he'd ever felt. "Welcome to my home... I should say *our* home, because that's what it will be for the next few months." She wiped her hands on the apron before placing them on his shoulders. They were about the same height so that she looked directly into his eyes. Then she quickly brushed her lips on each of his cheeks.

It was over before he had time to react. In fact, she had him sitting at the square oak table, though he wasn't sure how he had gotten there. She hadn't pushed him or anything. It was just those light, almost weightless kisses, and then he found himself seated across the table from her.

"Are you hungry? I don't suppose you had your supper."

"No, ma'am."

Looking across the table at her, he knew she was only an arm's reach away — but not *his* arm. His entire being was enshrouded in an itchy wool cocoon. It was a familiar discomfort, enclosing him, rooting him to the chair, as though he weren't quite in this room but apart from it and her.

"No to which, the hunger or the supper?" she asked.

"No, I haven't had supper, so I guess I'll be getting hungry soon, ma'am."

"Good." The word propelled her out of her chair. "The day was so filled with preparation, I didn't find the time to eat, either. I'll have a meal together for us shortly. Don't bother to help this time. Just sit there and talk to me."

"Yes, ma'am."

He felt as if he were a watcher at a Storyteller's tableau, but what he was watching was his own life. For almost as many years as he could remember, he had struggled, lashing out in anger even when he didn't want to, but had to, to break free of the deadening. Only with Lilla had it been effortless to step into the flow of his life, making it fully and truly his own. With Lilla, and when hunting, and sometimes when he was alone with his mother in her kitchen.

The Allesha set the table with homespun mats and napkins, pewter forks and bone-handled steel knives suitable for a headman's hunt banquet. He picked up the knife in front of him and felt the finely-honed edge with his thumb. *Superb. No old wife's knife this.* He bounced it in his hand, appreciative of the heft and balance. When he saw she was watching him, he quickly put the knife back on the table, in the exact same place and position.

She pulled a large covered clay pot from the oven. "It's roast chicken. Which do you prefer: white meat or dark?"

"If we could use some of those hot bealberries as a sauce, I'll take white meat. Otherwise, a leg and thigh would be good."

"White meat it is." She placed a blue and white pottery plate brimming with carrots, small white potatoes, chicken and hot berry sauce in front of him, and a similarly generous one at her place. In the middle of the table was a rattan basket filled with fresh baked hard-crusted bread and a tub of sweet butter. An earthen jug beside the basket held cool spring water.

"Please start eating; don't let it get cold." She whipped off the apron, sat down, picked up her knife and fork, then looked at him and put them back down on the table. "Or do your people practice some thanksgiving ritual before meals?"

He shrugged, and heard his voice echo in his own skull. "Some do. I don't, except when my parents insist. Usually, I just set aside bits of food for the spirits that live beyond our gate. Still, maybe this meal is different because it's our first together." Though he'd never tried it, letting a woman think she'd inspired a man to prayer had to be an effective way to impress and seduce.

"Yes, it is a special night, but hollow prayers can turn around and become a curse."

"Why'd you say that?" *Damn, is she reading my mind?*

"Please let us start this out right, with honesty." She reached with her right hand to touch the fingertips of his left. "You don't strike me as one who would bow his head in prayer. I can't imagine you bowing your head for anything or anyone. You face all that comes to you straight on, looking it in the eye, in confrontation or friendship or both, but always directly. If I'm mistaken, please tell me. Is praying at the table something you would do without being asked, because the words sprang of their own spirit from your inner self?"

"Not usually." *If she already knew the answer, why did the woman ask the question?* "Skies! You're right. Mouthing words is useless. It's only what a person does that counts."

"Well said and very true. Should you ever be moved to pray, to give thanks, I would be honored to share that with you. For now, shall we put some of our food on this saucer for the spirits, so we may take it outside after our meal?"

"Okay."

He chose and cut a small tender portion from each food on his plate and put it in the saucer; she followed suit with offerings neither less nor more than his.

But it felt *wrong*, this ordinary dinner, in a kitchen that was nicer than any he'd ever seen, but still just a kitchen. And, yet, sitting across the table, eating a meal she had prepared for him, was an Allesha. *His* Allesha, if he were to believe everything that had transpired.

He took a bite of chicken dunked in the berry sauce. "This food is good. I was hungrier than I thought. Thanks, ma'am."

"'Ma'am' sounds terribly formal, don't you think? I'm assuming you know that one of the first responsibilities of a Blessed Boy is to name his Allesha."

"They told me that. But… well, I'm not sure I know how to do that, ma'am."

"You will." While she buttered a piece of bread, she asked, "How was your day? I understand you took off for the forest in the early morning."

He hadn't slept the night before and had gone wandering before dawn when he couldn't stand it anymore. All the waiting to hear the Alleshi's decision. And those damned empty reassurances from everyone, when he knew and they knew that no Allesha worthy of the title would give him a second glance.

But here he was, and he still couldn't understand how it could have happened. Would she realize her mistake? Could she still send him away? Or was she playing some game? Was he there only to be laughed at when they told him the truth: that he really wasn't a suitable candidate? *So sorry, but get the hell out of here.*

He shifted in his seat and poked at his food.

"Our mountains are beautiful. I don't fault you for wanting to lose yourself in them," she continued. "But today wasn't your last opportunity to be in our forest. I hope we'll have many walks together in the woods, even when they're bare and covered with snow." She paused to savor a small bite of the chicken. "Actually, I was thinking… how would you like a hunt tomorrow? I was in my coldhouse today, checking our winter provisions, and there's still space for some meat. Would you join me in a hunt?"

"So that's why you chose me." The words erupted before he could swallow them. But once spoken, he allowed them to carry him, crashing clumsily through the cocoon's barrier into his life. "I knew there had to be a catch. You needed a hunter to supply your table. Guess I'll be doing that for the rest of my life."

"Are you trying to be insulting, or are you really that insecure?" She stared at him, as though he were standing naked.

"Skies! I didn't mean to…"

"No! Don't apologize yet. Listen first, and learn. Even if I never Blessed a boy, I'll always have whatever I need, for both comfort and sustenance. So, why do you think you had to sign the Agreement today?" The Allesha's eyes were full of fire, her body suddenly rigid. "It is a symbol of the bond between us; I am your Allesha and you are my First Boy, my Winter Boy. We are responsible to and for each other, until my spirit leaves my body."

She closed her eyes and took two deep breaths. In the sudden stillness, he sat rigidly, uncertain what he could say or should do, but knowing something was necessary.

When she opened her eyes, she asked, "Now, do you have something to say to me?"

"Yeah, I'm... uh... sorry." He grimaced. "Sometimes, my mouth rushes ahead faster than my mind."

She smiled at him and squeezed his hand firmly before starting to clear the table. That smile again, it was like sunshine breaking over a rain-soaked field, where only dark clouds had hovered seconds before. He welcomed the warmth of her smile, wanting it to go on forever. But she turned her back too soon, taking their plates to the sink.

"So, did you bring your bow, or do you need to borrow one?"

She put the leftover food in covered earthen dishes and placed them in the large varnished wood icebox, moving about the kitchen so quickly he had difficulty guessing where she would go, what she would do next.

"Yeah, I brought my bow. But don't you have any rifles?" he asked hopefully.

"Of course we do. However, where's the adventure or fair play in gunning down wild game? We use rifles for defense or when food is the only purpose of the hunt. But when I want to lose myself in our beautiful mountains, a bow is quieter, more sporting. Don't you agree?"

"Sure. I just didn't want you to think I don't know how to handle a gun. My village has had them for a few generations, ever since we came into the Peace." He didn't bother mentioning that only a handful of Birani had their own rifles, and that the only time he'd shot a gun was when he had sneaked away to the woods with his father's old smoothbore. Skies! He'd never seen Pa so angry.

"Yes, of course. So, we're agreed. We'll take our bows."

She picked up the rest of the cutlery and plates from the table, put them into the sink and quickly wiped down the table and counters. "The Allesha who brought us together wishes to come to our house tonight, to welcome you to The Valley." She handed him two wooden matches. "Please light the candle in the gatepost lantern to signal her. While you're out there, please set out our offerings to the spirits."

When he returned, she showed him to his room, to unpack and settle in, while she continued to clean the kitchen. "If you're finished before me, you can come and help. But tonight isn't for chores. We'll work that out later."

The yellow-painted bedroom was large, with big multi-paned

windows on the outer wall that must let in lots of sunshine during the day. As the Chancellor's son, Ryl was accustomed to comfort, but no one he knew — not even his grandfather with his headman's privileges — had a room as spacious and richly appointed as this.

The red maple furniture was substantial but simple, with straight, clean lines. Definitely a man's room, though with touches of femininity in the bed's patchwork quilt, the needlework cushions of the armchair, the forest-green linen curtains and the delicately painted bone knobs of the tall chest of drawers. Volumes of various sizes filled a low two-shelf bookcase. Gas lamps were placed on either side of the bed, next to the armchair, on the bureau — more and brighter lights than he'd ever seen in any bedroom. *These people must spend time in their bedrooms,* he thought, *doing things into the night that require lots of illumination.* He hoped that included activities other than reading. On one wall, two doors led to a small closet and a bathroom.

A number of the boys he had met in the Petitioners' Wing had been confounded by the advanced conveniences of the Battai's inn baffling. Not Ryl. His village had been converted from candle and oil to gas when Ryl was a child, so he knew how to use the keys on the pipes to turn gas lamp flames up or down. Similarly, he was already familiar with indoor bathrooms having flushing toilets and knew how to use those facilities, too. After all, his father had been the first in their village to build one, though some of their neighbors had warned against malodorous fumes and dirty water fouling the health of the home.

But the boy's pride and sense of superiority in his father's modern ways dissolved when he saw the spacious bathroom attached to this bedroom. Until then, he hadn't understood the measure of the Alleshi's great wealth. Both the large porcelain bathtub and the sink had two knobs; when he tested them, one produced icy cold water like at home, while the other pulsed with streams of steaming hot, like the shower at the Battai's. So much better than heating the water from the kitchen pump in his mother's iron caldron and then lugging it in that damned wooden bucket. What's more, even the air was warm, with the heat emanating from a tight rectangular coil of pipes under the small window. Even here, two wall shelves were filled with books, and several gas lamps filled all corners with light. They obviously expected him to spend some time in this bathroom, at least long enough to read.

Peculiar people, these Alleshi. Though looking about, he had to admit it would be pleasant to just sit in a bathtub like this, with hot water pouring over him. Did every bedroom in The Valley have a bathroom like this? How much more extravagant his Allesha's must be, if this were what was given a visitor they considered a mere boy.

The fourth door in his bedroom was locked. Did she sleep beyond, or was it the portal to that inner room the Battai had promised he would share with his Allesha? How could he get her to unlock it? When?

Damn these women with their rituals and ways, talking and taking their time, driving a man crazy with wondering and wanting.

He was almost finished unpacking when he heard a light knock at the door. "Our mentor is here. Please come greet her," his Allesha said through the closed hallway door.

The two women were seated on the sofa. One of them must have just said something hilarious, because they were shaking with laughter. They stopped abruptly when they saw him.

"Hey, don't stop on my account. I like a good joke as much as any man," he said.

His Allesha turned to him. "It was nothing. Just silliness between two friends that would take too many words to explain, and then it wouldn't be funny anymore."

Bet they were laughing at me. We'll see who laughs last.

His pa's Allesha got up to greet him. Ryl opened his hands to her in the traditional greeting given an Allesha, expecting her to fill them with hers, as she always had. Instead she put her two hands on his shoulders, pulling him toward her and brushed her lips on his two cheeks. The same gesture as the younger one's, but how different it felt. Her lips were dry, not soft. Her smell was sweet, rather than fresh and breezy.

"Blessings on you, boy, and welcome to our Valley. May your Season with your Allesha be joyous and fruitful."

"Uh, thanks."

"Come, sit with us." She patted the armchair next to the sofa.

The younger woman lifted a white porcelain kettle from its candle stand. "May I pour you some tea?"

"Okay… thanks," he said.

"It's natural for you to feel a bit strange tonight. Don't let it bother you," the older Allesha said. "We have some things to discuss, which may help you feel more comfortable. It's always easier when you know the boundaries and what's expected. First, however, do you have any questions for me?"

"Yeah, everyone says I have to name her. How do I do that?"

"Ah, the giving of names. Actually, you'll have two names to give, one for me, as well." She paused to sip her tea, then continued. "To name a thing or person properly is to seek to understand and, yes, in some part to possess its essence. But the essence of a thing is so changeable, that the naming of it says as much about the namer as it does about the thing being named."

Her words seemed double-edged, as though she had a secret obvious to everyone but him. "How can an essence — the core of a thing — be changeable? That doesn't make any sense."

She held up a small cake. "Name the essence of this."

"Food."

"True. But to a baker, it might be flour, sugar and water. A Healer might see it as a dual essence: a pleasant sweetness in moderation, but danger in excess." She took a bite, leaving half. "Now, it could be seen as proof of someone having been here, taking nurturance, leaving only half satisfied or so sated as to need nothing more." She put the cake down and wiped her fingers on her linen napkin. All the time, she watched him, as though he were a rabbit about to spring her carefully laid snare.

"So it is in the naming of people. The names you choose for us should have layers of meaning," the older Allesha continued. "We will change over the next few months because of our relationship with you. Your perceptions of us will evolve, too. Whatever names you give us should fit us today and next week and next year."

"That's stupid. You've already got names; I'll just use those."

"What names we have, we have received in relationships which have nothing to do with you or why you have come here. Those that you give us will define a whole new role for us — and for you. It will mark the true beginning of your Season with us."

"What if I can't find the right names?"

"Then the lessons you want and need the most will remain out of your reach."

"That's not fair!" The boy saw the know-all look the older Allesha gave the younger one. How he hated the way people did that, judging him before he even had a chance to prove them wrong. "So, if I don't come up with names you approve of by some complicated rules I can't hope to understand, you'll refuse to teach me."

His pa's Allesha shot him a warning glance, so like the looks his father sometimes gave him just before the yelling began — or worse, the silence. *But Fire and Stones! If she already knows what I'm thinking, all this tiptoeing around is pointless.* "No sex, then, is that what you're saying? So why did I go through all that crap?" He threw his napkin at the table, frustrated by its floating, lofting, soundless fall. Too bad he hadn't held onto his teacup. That would have made a satisfying crash.

"Calm down, boy. We will refuse you nothing you need," the older Allesha said.

"But you just said…"

"To reach a level of intimacy with your Allesha and with me, in which we can be effective, you must give something of yourself. Without names, we are nothing to you, only symbols, two of the many Alleshi. Your naming of us will make us flesh-and-blood women."

She clasped the young Allesha's hand. "It's time for me to go. Thank you for the tea." Then she turned to the boy. "You will walk me home. I want you to know where to find me."

The younger woman embraced them both at the door. She said to the boy, "We'll leave before dawn tomorrow. Please be sure to close the outer door before you go to sleep. Good night."

Now that the moon had risen, the night was bright. With the instinct of a woodsman to blend in, the boy extinguished the lantern he carried, and the woman followed his example. They walked for a few moments in silence. When she spoke, her voice scythed through the cool, soft air, commanding his full attention.

"You will be coming to my home often," she said. "Mostly, it will be at prearranged times, although you'll be welcome in my house any time the outer door is open. But do not wander from this path and do not enter any other building without permission. There are rules to be abided here and never broken."

Rules. When weren't there rules? "Like what?"

"I've already told you the one: Never go into any building other than my home and that of your Allesha. Do not walk off on your own, away from your Allesha's home, without her permission, and do not deviate from the path you are to take. Do not speak to any other boy in The Valley, until the end of your Season. You may see them about, though almost always with their Alleshi, since you are the only First Boy this winter. Speak only to those Alleshi who address you first. Don't—"

"Whoa! How do you expect me to keep track of all these rules of yours?"

"Simply use common sense, courtesy and respect for privacy whenever you don't know the right thing to do, and you should have no problems. Ask your Allesha or me if you're uncertain how to behave."

They stopped in front of a two-story wood and stucco house, surrounded by a stone wall. It was taller and took up less land than his Allesha's, with large evergreen bushes close to the building. The one thing the property had in common with the others he had seen in The Valley was the sense of solid construction and the feeling that the house and garden fit each other.

"This is my home. My outer door is closed because I've been away for the evening. Remember, come when you wish, when that door is open, or set a candle in your Allesha's signal lantern, if you want me to come to you. I'm giving this Season to you, as much as your Allesha is. The two of us will work hard to make it a good Season for you. But how good it will be, will be up to you."

"Yeah, I've heard that."

"Someday you will understand it. Goodnight, boy. Go directly home to your Allesha. I'll see you when you return from your hunt." She embraced him with her dry mouth on his cheeks and her long bony hands on his shoulders. Then she turned to enter her home.

Strange woman, he thought, as he retraced his steps along the path to his Allesha. *But at least a man can know where he stands with her.*

Chapter 13

By the time dawn had brushed first light onto The Valley floor, the boy and his Allesha had already hiked up the mountain, far from the paths to the inns and tradegrounds, traveling toward the wilderness above the ungroomed forest between the Northwest and West Inns. They stopped for a cold breakfast at a clearing. As they ate fruit and chicken, he studied her. How different she seemed from the woman who had greeted him the evening before.

Her auburn hair, which shone with the very colors of the dawn, was woven into long plaits that fell over her shoulders. Somehow, it made her seem young, even vulnerable, yet strong and self-sufficient. The way she had sprinted up the trail, sure-footed and long-legged, in her doeskin pants and boots, she seemed the image of a young woodsman, born to the forest. Now, her soft, beautifully tanned jacket fell open as she ate, and he saw the swelling rhythm of her breath in the tight knit of her tan jersey. How round her breasts were. Not bad at all, his luck in getting a new Allesha, rather than an old one.

"What about Mari? It's a good name, don't you think?" the boy suggested.

"Why?"

"Well, it's pretty, like you."

"But was I pretty yesterday? Will I be tomorrow? What do you think? Does it fit?"

He had no answer that wouldn't get him in trouble.

"You'll find it."

They cleaned the site and continued their trek uphill. The way was neither clear nor rough, but pleasantly wild. Tall bare trees scratched a blue sky, with the promise of a crisp, bright day. Light breezes blew the brown leaves in gentle whirls. They walked without talking, as is the way of hunters, climbing steadily upward. By noon, they saw their first fresh signs of long-tail eladar. A small herd had passed that way very recently, headed west. However, the Allesha set her feet toward the north.

"Hey, you're going the wrong way," he corrected her.

"That's not the herd we want. It's already been winnowed."

It wasn't natural, letting a woman lead a hunt, but he wasn't concerned. When she messed up, he'd take over. They'd not go back empty-handed with him doing the tracking.

They saw no more signs of eladar for the rest of the day — at least none fresh enough to merit following. Before the late afternoon sunset, each of them brought down a some partridges for their dinner. Watching her take aim and strike her prey had been quite a sight. Her arrows flew true at first shot, and her bow arm was strong.

"Who taught you to hunt?" he asked as they made camp.

"My father and mother."

"Your father *and* your mother?"

"Yes. You sound surprised."

"Women don't usually hunt. They're not built for it."

"Oh, really?" She stood apart and mimed a huntress stalking her prey. "We're lighter, tend to be more graceful, quieter when we walk." With an almost silent leap, she was by his side again, helping to snap kindling for the fire. "Did you know, in some villages, only women hunt, and men are expected to do the heavier work?"

"If you say so, but it's still not right. Yeah, I like it when Lilla comes with me into the woods. But I do the hunting."

"What does she do?"

"Keeps me company for the trek. Then stays and makes the camp, while I get the game. It's nice to come back to her in a clearing that she's made our own."

The fire built and lit, she popped up again, tousling his hair in a quick, playful swipe. "Well, no one could ever expect me to stay behind when there's fun to be had." She spread some leaves and fronds for cushioning under her blankets. "Nor do I expect anyone living under my roof to stand apart when there are chores to be done." She pointed to an area on the other side of the fire. "That looks like a nice spot for your bedding."

He pounded the dry earth with a log, using more energy than necessary for stamping out ground lumps. *Damn*, he reflected, *she not only expects me to help make camp, but she still isn't sleeping with me.*

"What about Jan. I like that name, don't you?" he asked. "It's solid and strong, like you, and pretty, too. What do you think?"

"I think you're not sure."

By the time their blankets were spread and leather flasks filled from the nearby stream, the fire had collapsed into glowing embers, where she buried their potatoes. When he saw that she intended to dress only her two birds, he plucked and prepared his, in angry silence.

✻

The young Allesha relished the quiet of her beloved wild woods. Every year, usually after the last harvest, she and Jared would take off together like this, leaving the children with family or friends. Making love by night, hunting by day, giving themselves fully to the wilderness surrounding them.

But in the years before his death, his missions had taken him away from her more and more, and they hadn't managed to find the time. She wished she had recognized the last hunt with Jared for what it was, something that would never be repeated, an ending too precious to have been treated like any other outing together.

How different everything was now. She was unable to give herself freely to the forest, because her First Boy needed her to adhere to a role, to be whatever and whomever necessary to help him grow and become an Alleman. When the Mwertik had butchered Jared, they'd killed more than an Alleman. They'd killed the woman she had been with Jared.

The sounds of late autumn on this mountain were more subtle than those heard in summer. A rustling breeze, a night bird's wings slipping through the air, small scampering paws. She gazed at the shimmer of red and gold hovering over the burning logs. When she spoke, it was softly, unwilling to disturb the peace. "On a night like this, the world seems to stand still. Nothing exists outside the light of our fire. I wonder if this is what it was like when the earth was born. Did it spread out from a campfire, stirred by some god playing with the embers?"

The boy seemed just as captivated by the mystery of the night. Staring into the fire, he spoke freely. "Our Storyteller spins a tale of life lost in a great ocean, thrown there in the beginning by Promin, because it wouldn't be still. But even in the deep of the sea, it bubbled with noise, until the ocean threw it out onto land. There, on the sand, it struggled to breathe the dry air, reviving only when the waves washed over it. But the waves withdrew, taking only the fish and coral back, for the beauty of their colors. All others were left, orphaned, to die or grow."

He paused to pull his cooked birds off the spit. Taking the scorching potato that she poked out of the fire with a stick, he gingerly bounced it from hand to hand, until it was cool enough to hold and eat.

She prodded him to continue. "To die or to grow…"

It took him a moment and a few bites of food to find the thread again. "Umm… and so life pushed its way up from the beach toward the forest and mountains. The weaker and the more foolish took root in the low lands. Only man made it to the summit of the tallest mountain. When he looked down, he knew that Promin had made him the strongest and most intelligent, to hold his place on high, above the rest of creation."

"But do you think it was Promin's purpose to give man the struggle so that he might prevail? Or was it an accident that sprang from one god's irritability?" she asked.

"It's just a story." He shrugged. "It's the fire. It makes men silent or talkative. I don't usually ramble on with Storytellers' nonsense."

"I enjoy such tales," she said. "Especially how a story changes with each telling, revealing something of the person who shares the tale. Don't scowl; it's nothing to guard against. You've given me a lovely gift."

"If that's so, show me something of yourself. Or are you scared to give me some of the advantage you now say you have over me?"

"I didn't speak of any advantage."

"No, but that's what you meant. I exposed myself to you, and got nothing out of it in return."

"Here, let me give you something of myself. I care nothing for such *advantages* as you see it. Let's see…" She paused to think and eat. "Yes, I remember another creation tale you might enjoy." She tore off the last bit of meat from the bird's bones, chewed it daintily while she composed herself, wiped her hands on a few leaves and then settled into a comfortable storytelling pose.

"It is said, in the beginning, everything was One, alone and complete. Nothing existed beyond the One. But even the One must obey Nature. The first law of Nature is that nothing may live that doesn't grow, and growth comes only from sharing. But the One had no one other, so the One began to shrink and die. That was when the One realized that the only way to survive was to break apart into the Many and the Multitude. And the One became the stars and the sun, the moon and the earth, the trees of the forest and the flowers on the plains, the animals of the land and the birds of the sky, Man and Woman. Ever since then, the One in all of us has been trying to find itself in the Others. That is why we are drawn to one another, to share, to unite, to be the One once again."

"Did you make that up?" he asked.

"No, it was told to me by my mother."

"It sounds like a woman's tale."

"Really? She told me her grandfather had given it to her."

"I didn't mean that as an insult. Women's tales can be good, too."

"Thank you."

"Why do I feel that you didn't take that right?" he asked.

"I suppose because you don't consider a 'woman's tale' to be the equal of a man's."

"Did I say that?"

"Don't worry so. We've had a pleasant evening; we've given something to each other that neither had before. Tomorrow, we'll find our eladar. Let's say goodnight and sleep the deep of the forest." She embraced him, with that now familiar two cheek brush of her lips, then wrapped herself up in her blankets before he could think of a retort.

Listening to the fire popping and the breeze rustling through the woods, he looked at the back of her long, curved body across the campsite from his own bedroll. *Steel would be a good name for her,* was his last thought before he gave himself to a dreamless sleep.

Chapter 14

The boy and his Allesha came across fresh signs of eladar by mid-morning. Following the tracks and droppings, they soon found themselves on the edge of a grassy plateau. A buck with a massive crown of antlers stood apart from his herd, regally poised on a mound of earth where he could keep watch, alert to every sound, any danger. Grazing nearby were his does, surrounded by their playful young. A lone older doe watched the young from the other side of the plateau; her soft gaze seemed almost sad.

The Allesha used hunting hand signals different from any the boy had ever seen, but it was clear how far off the mark her plan was. So much for women as able hunters.

Ignoring her gestures that they should separate and circle toward the right, he crouched to take aim at the buck. He pulled two arrows out of his quiver. One he stuck in the ground before him, to have at the ready. The other he nocked into the bowstring, and pulled it to his cheek, where the arrow's feathers, the string and his right hand pressed under his right eye, lining up to the buck's beating chest. *Steady, feel the wind. Adjust for it. Take a deep breath in rhythm with the stag. Now!*

Just as he released the string, a shove at his shoulder sent his arrow into the ground. "Damn you, woman!" he hissed. But she didn't really hear him, having broken into a long-legged chase for the eladar that had started at the "twang" of his bow and his whispered curse.

Running with a springing cat-like gait, she pulled two arrows from her quiver, and shot them, one after the other, into the throat of the older doe, puncturing the arteries for a bleeding kill. Still, she did not stop. Keeping pace with the herd, she called over her shoulder. "Boy! Get that fawn, the one with the limp."

A yearling had fallen behind the herd, because something was wrong with its leg. With the power of his arm on his longer, heavier bow, he felled the animal from where he stood. One arrow into the heart made a quick kill. The boy sauntered toward the fallen fawn with exaggerated ease, knowing that the woman was wearing herself out pursuing a running kill. The fawn's legs continued to jerk, but five quick knife slashes to the neck and legs brought her to her end. *So bled and so young, this meat will be tasty,* he thought with pride. *Not like that old doe, with its years of stringy muscle.* When the fawn's blood had spent itself into the earth, he swung the carcass up onto his shoulders and went in search of the woman, following a clear trail of blood and freshly trampled earth.

He found her kneeling on the ground beside a small stream, her forehead resting on the warm, lifeless doe. His anger had boiled away into the hunt and the search, and in the wake of his admiration for her prowess. Yet, he struggled to find it again, so he might vent it onto the woman who had dared jostle his nocked arrow and ruin his kill.

At the sound of his approach, she raised her head, saw him and smiled. And he realized that no anger could survive the onslaught of his Allesha's dazzling smile. It was in that moment that he knew her name.

"Tayar," he said softly.

"What?" she asked, obviously confused by the unfamiliar greeting.

"Tayar… your name."

"What does it mean?"

"It has no meaning, really. It's the sound of the eagle calling his mate to the hunt."

"Tayar. It's a good name." She patted the doe's body, and then rose to greet the boy. He braced himself to receive her hands on his shoulders and lips on his cheeks. Instead, she wrapped her arms around his neck, pressed the full length of her body against him, and quickly but firmly touched her lips to his. By the time he had raised his arms to encircle her waist, she had already slipped away and was on the move again.

"Woman, why—?"

"Call me Tayar, I like the sound of it." She was testing the strength of several nearby fallen tree branches.

"Tayar, why—?"

"But you do know it is your private name for me." Now she was pulling down some vines. When she discovered how brittle they were, she discarded them and took a length of coiled rope from her pack. "Don't use it within earshot of others… except our mentor, of course."

"Okay, but do you always have to be in such a rush? You're like a jackrabbit that twitches even in his sleep."

"When there's work to be done, I like to get it done. Right now, we need to gut these eladar, while we still have light. I'd like to sleep in my bed tonight."

What the hell, he thought, *why not say it?* "So would I."

"Really?"

"Yeah, well, you have your name. It's time already."

"Not quite time. Let's get to our gutting while we talk." She sliced through the belly of the doe with several swift strokes of her knife.

"That's women's work," he said with affected disgust.

She looked up from her bloody work and wiped her hands on the earth. "This is only our second day together, so I will forgive many things. You'll learn in time. But don't ever try to turn me into a servant. It's insulting — to both of us. Women's work, indeed! This morning we were hunters together. Now we must be butchers. In everything that we do, today or any day, you will do at least as much as I, giving your all. Otherwise, I'll never want to give my all to you. We were equals in the hunt. Now—"

"Equals! You knocked my arrow from its string, when I had that beautiful stag in my eye."

"What is a hunt to you?" she asked.

"Don't go changing the subject on me."

"I'm not. Please, tell me, what is a hunt?"

"It's a search for food and skins," he said. "And a chance to prove yourself against the wild."

"What do you have to prove? You already know you're an able hunter, a skilled tracker. Or, are you so uncertain of your abilities that you need to verify them every time you encounter nature?"

"Hey, stop turning everything around."

"You know what the hunt is to me? It's my chance to participate *with* nature, not conquer it," she explained. "In the forest, we return to our original home."

"Well, sure. I know that. Hell…"

"Then you understand why I couldn't stand by and let you kill that stag."

"No, I don't. It was a magnificent animal. Those antlers, damn, I've not seen too many racks like that."

"True, he's beautiful, but he's also necessary to the herd's survival. Kill the lead buck this close to first snow, and the does probably wouldn't find another until spring. They'd have no stag to protect them from predators or lead them to feeding grounds as the cold destroys the grasses. Winter will be hard enough. I'll not be party to making it even more difficult for them to survive."

"And that neck kill. Damn, that was good shooting, but you can't say you weren't just showing off, trying to impress me. A real hunter who wants to be sure of the kill goes for the easy shot, not the tricky one."

"But did you see that doe? She deserved an honorable death, not to be struck down with an arrow in her heart, suffocating on her own blood. Pierce the neck and the eladar will run out her life with dignity and less pain. At the same time, she'll bleed herself, giving us her dying gift of sweeter meat."

"I never saw it that way before," he admitted, having run out of arguments. "But it's still a tricky shot."

"Thank you. Now let's get to work. If we finish early, maybe we can take down more birds. Those partridges last night were rather tasty. I wouldn't mind having a small supply for the winter."

With no further protest, he took out his knife and expertly split the fawn's belly in a single cut, slicing through the skin and meat without puncturing the organs.

The boy felt her eyes on him as a hot buzz that started on his earlobes and ended in an excruciating erection. Great Mother, what a woman his Allesha was! If only he could figure out how to get the upper hand with her, so he could get into that inner room.

They finished the gutting in silence. When it came to binding two long branches into a travois for carrying the eladar, they worked well together. It seemed easier for both of them when they didn't talk. Then each took one limb of the travois and began dragging it down the mountain, back to the Allesha's home. When they sighted a flight of pheasant, she purposely didn't pick up her bow, leaving the birds to him.

When she went to retrieve the fallen birds, she called, "Good shooting!" and she saw his shoulders square with pride again. How little it took to prick this boy's ego — or inflate it. *When the inner man is solid, strong unto himself, without having to diminish others,* she thought, *then I'll have made an Alleman.* She tied the birds to the eladar, picked up her side of the sledge, and fell back into step with the boy.

Chapter 15

"*Tayar*." Dara let the sound of the name roll around on her tongue. "It suits you."

The two Alleshi were in Rishana's barn the morning after the hunt. Rishana had just finished caring for her two goats, Danide and Draville, and her half-dozen chickens. She sat on a bale of hay, while Dara perched on a nearby stool.

"I didn't expect him to find a good name for me so quickly. Do you think it was an accident, or could he be that insightful?"

"He's a special boy. The tough ones often are. But this boy… you're going to find some surprising depths in him."

"But, Dara, he's already pressing for sex."

"Of course he is."

"I'm not ready." Before Dara could respond, Rishana quickly added, "I mean, he's not ready."

"I know."

"I didn't want you to think that I would deny him."

"Rishana, don't you understand how much I trust your instincts? The boy hasn't yet given anything of himself to you. Until he does, he has no right to your body."

Rishana pulled a stalk of hay from the bale under her and proceeded to bend and break it into tiny shards. "He's learned to desire me. I'm no longer just an old woman to him. I'm Tayar, a huntress deserving of respect and the focus of his sexual ardor." Realizing what she was doing, she brushed the pieces from her lap and focused on Dara. "Haven't you taught me that we must find the crucial moment, the time of peak energy, when the boy is ready to begin his ascent to manhood? If I miss the signs of that moment, the key to his future may be lost to me."

"Rishana, you have as bright and active a mind as I have ever known, but only when you calm your thoughts and refuse to be troubled by them. Listen to the wisdom of your own heart. Trust yourself to recognize the moment when it comes." Dara slowly rose from her stool.

"Promise me one thing, Dara. If I fail to recognize the moment, you'll help me see it before it's too late."

The two of them proceeded outside, walking toward the house.

"Of course. But it won't happen." Dara smiled at Rishana. "Now, let's take care of more mundane issues. We must set up a schedule for his lessons with me. But he isn't to see them as anything but spontaneous — at least in the beginning. Otherwise, his need to rebel, to assert his individuality, would get in the way."

"How about morning, well after breakfast, so he can do some of his chores? Would that work?"

"Initially, yes. But we must be flexible and fit our schedule to the rhythm of your Season with him." As they reached Rishana's back door, Dara asked, "Shall we start now?"

Rishana nodded as she opened the door for her mentor. Before she followed Dara into the mudroom, she glanced behind her. Only then did she realize that she hadn't seen the bright, blue sky or noticed the clear, brisk breeze. Savor the details, Savah had often told her, but don't lose sight of the wide, far-reaching landscape. *Yes, Savah,* she responded silently to the part of her husband's Allesha who would always live in her soul.

Chapter 16

Tayar and her Winter Boy spent a busy afternoon in her barn, tanning the eladar skins and dressing the meat and birds from their hunt. They worked well together, but the Allesha knew it couldn't last; the boy's nature wouldn't allow him to calmly go forward. Nor would he learn without conflict. Rather than push him and risk rebellion at this early stage, she organized their chores so that everything would flow smoothly and easily.

Singing helped carry the afternoon through what might have otherwise been tedious and contentious. That the songs hadn't been part of her plan made it all the more pleasant for the Allesha. Humming as she worked was a life-long habit that had grown out of her father's love of music and his insistence that a tune made all work go more smoothly.

For a while, her low humming was the only sound the woman and boy shared. That, and the chopping, grunting rhythm of their butchering. One tune caught the boy's ear as a song he remembered, so he gave voice to her humming.

Hail fellows, game ye met,
Take the hunt away, away.
Eladar we chase to the mount,
Take the hunt away.

They weren't the words the Allesha knew, so she hummed along, enjoying the accompaniment of his mellow baritone that went off-key only on the upstroke.

Meadows left below the mount,
Take the hunt away, away.
Far above the clouds we hunt,
Take the hunt away.

Their cleavers thumped the song's rhythm, shaking the sturdy table with every other beat.

Death may come, but still we follow,
Take the hunt away, away.
Hunters gone, but game ye met,
Take the hunt away.

She stopped chopping just long enough to. "Well sung! Thank you." Then she resumed work. "Your words are different from the ones I know. Strange how a song can travel from village to village so intact and yet so changed."

"What's yours like?" he asked.

"It's a love song." She remembered the first time she had heard it as a youngster, and how embarrassed she had been that her mother could say such things. "Well, maybe more a humorous seduction song."

"Seduction, huh?" he grinned. "How does it go?"

As she continued cutting the carcass, she lifted her voice to the song, delighted to hear once again hints of her mother's warm tones echoing back to her. It was a sweetness of memory that lived within her, as much a part of her as her laugh, which often sounded like her daughter Svana to her own ears.

Jamie let me sleep by thee,
Nay, not today, today.
Jamie don't say no to me,
Nay, not today.

Jamie see my milky breasts,
Nay, not today, today.
Wide my hips and silk my lips,
Nay, not today.

Jamie how my pearl does ache,
Nay, not today, today.
But your spear fails me dear.
Nay, not today.

The boy smirked lasciviously at his Allesha. "Don't worry, my spear won't ever fail you."

A small smile played on her mouth, but she didn't meet his eyes. When they resumed their work, their blades no longer echoed in unison.

"Tell me about your village," she asked.

"You're changing the subject."

"Yes, but I really do want to know about your home, so I may know you better."

He opened his mouth, no doubt ready with a sharp or sarcastic retort, but stopped himself, shrugged and said, "I don't know what to tell you. It's a village, like any other."

"However, our villages are like our songs... the same tune, but different words and ideas."

"I guess so. Until the trip here to The Valley, I knew only the villages near ours; most of them were kind of like mine. But coming here was a pretty long trek from my home — almost six weeks. On the way, I saw some strange places and people."

"Such as?"

"There was a lake village, where the houses were built on really tall stilts. They said that was because of the annual floods. But when we were there, it was a long walk to the shore from the village — about ten times the distance to the old woman's house from yours — or maybe further. Can you imagine that much rain that it could swell a lake that wide?"

"Tell me of the people of this village."

"They call themselves the Fetreens, and they laugh a lot, even when there's no joke. At least, they didn't let me in on the joke. Maybe they were laughing at me, because all the guys were so much bigger than me, but they giggled like little kids. Undignified and silly, if you ask me, even if Pa and Ma seemed to like them. And the boy we brought with us finally smiled for the first time with the Fetreens. So I guess laughter can be good, even if it was too constant."

"What boy?" she asked.

"No one knows who he is. Pa said he was found near our border, after a Mwertik raid."

"What was he like? Did he tell you what happened?" She modulated her voice, to maintain the same conversational tone as before. But her heart throbbed in her ears. A survivor from a Mwertik raid? She'd never heard of any person or animal left alive once they attacked. Even children and infants. That was what made the elusive Mwertik so terrifying, their single-minded destruction, as though they wanted to wipe the earth clean of anyone and anything within the Peace borders. "Did your father learn anything new about the Mwertik from him?"

"The kid didn't talk, not to anyone. Ma said we had to gentle him, because he was frightened beyond any fright we could ever imagine." The boy leaned on his cleaver and stared into the distance. "He'd seen his whole village killed, and everything around him burned to cinders." With a shiver, he resumed his butchering. "You know what I think? I think someone must've hid him and told him to stay quiet. That's what probably saved his life. But that person never came back for him, and he thinks that if he makes any sound, he'll be killed, too."

The Allesha paused in her work, to look at her Winter Boy. "Is he quite young?"

"He's little. If he were from my village, I'd guess he'd be no more than six. Compared to the Fetreens, who are large people, he looked four or five."

"And he didn't talk at all?"

"Didn't make any sounds, except in his sleep, when he whimpered and moaned. Made it tough for me to sleep, I can tell you. But Ma insisted he stay close to me, which irked me. He never even looked at me, not directly, not when I looked at him."

The boy laid his clever on the table and turned toward Tayar. "Then one night, when he woke me up with his nightmare crying, like he always did, I reached out to turn him. Sometimes, pushing him into another position would stop his moans. Well, it wasn't really a push. All he had to do was feel my touch, and he'd flinch away. But this time, instead, he grabbed my hand with both of his tiny fists and curled his body around it. I don't know why, but that felt... oh, I don't know. You see, he was still asleep, so it was something that he did from deep inside, where the real boy was hiding from everything that he'd seen. He reached for me, needed me. That felt good."

'To win the trust of one so terrorized, that's quite an accomplishment."

"I don't know. Guess so. Anyway, after that night, I didn't really mind him staying close. I liked making him feel safe. I just wish he would've said even one word to me. He was like a trapped animal that didn't know the cage was open. But when the Fetreens laughed, he sometimes smiled, not with his lips, but in his eyes. It was a good place to leave him, if we had to leave him anywhere."

The Allesha heard the wistful loneliness in the boy's tone. "If you want, you'll probably see him again."

"Yeah. I'd like that. I'd like to walk into the Fetreen village and see the children playing and laughing and him with them, jabbering and making all kinds of noise." With a sigh, he picked up his cleaver and hacked at the eladar's hip joint.

The Allesha latched onto the glimmer of hope her First Boy's story offered. Perhaps the surviving child might yet tell them of the Mwertik. Would the Alleshi and Allemen finally uncover who the Mwertik were, where their home base was, perhaps even why they were so hell-bent on destroying everything associated with the Peace?

Turning her mind to the task at hand, she said, "So, you have seen how different things can be away from home. Maybe you now understand why I asked you to tell me of your village."

"Guess so, but it's really ordinary. No houses on stilts or anything."

"To you, it may be ordinary because you've known it all your life. To me, it may be exotic."

"Where do you come from?" he asked.

"My people are the Attani, from the Great Plains, where some ranches stretch as far as the eye can see, and the outer village homes belong to large farms that surround the entire community."

"Hey, I've heard stories about your people."

His fawn was much smaller than her doe, which meant he was finished sooner. He could have offered to help her, but apparently didn't think of it. Of course, she could have asked for his help, if she had wanted to use the moment for a lesson. Instead, she suggested he prepare the pheasants for storage. They continued to talk as they worked.

"Please tell me about your village," she asked once more. "If I visited, what would be the first thing I'd notice?"

"Well, I guess it'd be the trees. Our Storyteller says that when Arof, the first headman, led his people to the forest, they cleared a wide section right in the middle of the woods. I mean, they just chopped everything down, leveled it to the ground, as though the trees didn't matter."

"So, your ancestors didn't come from woodspeople, originally."

"No, that's why they didn't know any better."

The boy didn't see the small smirk that played across the Allesha's lips.

"Arof — that's my pa's direct ancestor — he and his people cleared the land and built their houses of the wood, at first. But bit by bit, all the walls were replaced by stone, as our people learned the truth about the forest, that it's alive. Yeah, I know; they weren't dumb. They knew the trees were alive, but they didn't really know about the forest, not at first. When they did, they finally understood they mustn't pull out or chop down any new tree."

"Do you mean that any tree that begins is allowed to grow wherever it might take root?" she asked.

"If it's outside. You can't have a tree growing in your kitchen or pushing through the stone hearth, can you? So homes don't have trees inside, but our spirit house does. It was built around a tree. The Storyteller says that it was the only tree that wasn't cut down by Arof and his people.

Not that they didn't raise their axes to it, but no man could finish his swing. Something inside them or inside the tree stopped them. Some say that was the beginning of our belief in wood sprites."

"What do you think?"

"I don't know. You should see that tree. I mean, I know the woods and still that one tree always catches my eye and pulls at my stomach whenever I look at it. Its branches spread out over all the old homes, and six tall men with their arms stretched could barely encircle the trunk. But it's more than just size. There's something about how old it must be, all that it's seen of man and nature. To bring it down would be sacrilege. Does that mean wood sprites live in it? I don't know. But if I were a wood sprite, I could think of no better place for my home."

"Your spirit house must be large indeed to hold such a tree. Please tell me more about it. What are the meetings like?"

"Well, I don't know if that would be right. Women aren't allowed in there, and we're not supposed to speak to women about the matters of men."

"Indeed? Then I would find your village exotic in more than one way. I've never seen a tree growing in the middle of a building. Certainly not one such as you describe. But even more unusual is that women should be excluded from the business and the spirit of the village."

"Yeah." His voice was tinged with a touch of sarcasm that she chose to ignore. "You Alleshi seem to think that women are equal to men in every way."

"You don't?"

"In a valley of women, it's only natural that women should be in charge. You don't have men to take care of things. But women and men were made for different purposes. That's why we're shaped different. Hell, I can't bear children or feed them from my body. Women can't carry the heavy loads I can."

"Those are physical differences. What does that have to do with leading a village or caring for its spiritual well-being?" she asked.

"We're the stronger sex, so we should be in charge."

"So, you feel that muscular strength, rather than intelligence, experience and nurturance, is the measure of a good leader."

"Look, I don't want to argue with you. You'll just get angry at me again."

"I'm not angry," Tayar retorted. "But I am indeed curious about how you think." With a wider than necessary swing of her blade, she broke the last joint. "Finished! Let's get this meat into the coldhouse. But first, pick a piece to give to our mentor as a gift."

She was pleased to see that he chose the best cut of his young, tender eladar. *This boy has his faults, but he is generous,* she thought. *We'll be able to use that instinct to his advantage.*

Chapter 17

After hanging the butchered game in the coldhouse, Tayar and her Winter Boy checked the eladar skins in their wooden frames, to be sure the stretches were even and secure. Then they returned to the house. The sun had set long before.

The Allesha kicked her bloodied boots off in the mudroom behind the kitchen. "I'm filthy. I must take a bath before we prepare dinner."

"May I join you?"

"In my bath?"

He nodded, his face beaming with hope.

She touched his face, letting her hand linger gently on his cheek. "Not tonight, but in time. I promise."

He put his hand where hers had been. Somehow, the skin that had felt hers, however briefly, was more alive, and that feeling remained with him through his bath. But when she greeted him in the kitchen with a light kiss, he realized that the tingle had faded on his cheek, only to be rekindled on his lips. Was this the magic of the Alleshi, to have lightning in their touch? *Great Mother, let us reach that inner room tonight!*

The boy was so absorbed with such thoughts he didn't notice how involved he became in preparing their meal. Responding to his Allesha's requests, his hands chopped vegetables, his legs carried him to the icebox and pantry for sausage, bread and butter, and his mouth tasted the offered spoonful of sauce without being able to judge the seasoning. His body obeyed, cut off from his mind and any objections he might vent about doing women's work.

He was acutely aware of his Allesha's every movement. She was clothed in a strange one-piece garment that wrapped about her body in flowing drapes. When he brushed against her in a manner that he hoped was nonchalant and seemingly accidental, he could feel the warmth of her skin as though no cloth separated them. If he looked closely, he could swear he saw the hint of her dark nipples sliding under the cloth as she moved. How he ached to absorb the whole length of her against his body. But just as he decided to act, she turned to look directly at him.

"Done!" she said. "Let's eat."

Uncertain what to do or say next, he followed her lead again, obediently sitting across from her at the table.

"It was a good day's work," she commented.

He nodded and ate, watching her as she spoke.

"The winter snow is expected early this year; we have much to do to ready this place for it."

He wasn't prepared to speak, focused as he was on other things.

"Tomorrow, after our morning chores, you'll take that cut of eladar to our mentor. Remember, you must name her soon."

That caught his attention. "Fine. Another name." His voice hid none of his anger for a beautiful spell broken. But he looked into her face and found himself unable to hold onto his frustration. *Damn, she actually shines. How come I didn't see that before? And I was wrong; she isn't that old at all. Could be Lilla's elder sister.*

Again, he heard little of what she said, lost as he was in the fantasy of possessing this incredible woman. He was unconscious of chewing or swallowing, and heard her words only as background music as pleasant as birdsong. Suddenly, all was silent, and he realized that she had just asked him a question. "Huh?"

"That's okay. We'll go over that later."

They both realized that he hadn't heard a word she had said. While he was worried that he had botched it again, she accepted the situation as part of the Fascination Stage in their relationship. *He's obsessed with my body right now,* she mused. *No, that's not quite correct. The obsession is with his own body and its needs. When he connects my mind to my body, he'll begin to be more concerned with my needs than his own.*

Savah had defined and described the stages of an Alleshine relationship early in Rishana's training. At the time, Rishana had thought the discussion too cold and precise, and had been uncomfortable with the idea that the human soul could be so thoroughly mapped, so completely predictable. But here before her was the Fascination Stage, clearly and classically embodied in her Winter Boy. A chill shot up her spine, though the kitchen was warm. She decided to visit Savah tomorrow while the boy was with Dara.

They washed the dishes together, although each was lost in thought. When everything was put away, they went into the greeting room. She turned to the boy and said, "I usually like to read in the evening, but I'd rather spend the time with you tonight. Would you be willing to read to me or tell me a story?"

"I'm no Storyteller," he said dismissively.

"Oh, I disagree. You've told me some wonderful stories."

"I don't know. Maybe. But I don't feel right just launching into a story on the say so."

"Would you feel more comfortable reading to me?"

"Sure, why not? What should I read?"

"You could select something that appeals to you from the books in your bedroom."

She sat on a cushion on the hearth ledge, stoked the fire and stayed there, enjoying the heat on her back. He went into his room and returned with a book so quickly that she was certain he must have grabbed the first one his hand touched, without really looking at it.

Settling into the sofa, he asked, "Tayar, please let your hair loose, so I can see the firelight through it."

She removed the pins that bound her hair and shook it out around her shoulders.

"It's beautiful. Thank you." His voice was soft and gentle in a way it hadn't been before, and her own delight in it caught her by surprise. He threw a cushion on his lap, ostensibly to hold the book, though she couldn't fail to see the sudden bulge he was trying to conceal.

He opened the book and began to read.

The days of my travels are more than I can number, though I can count the days of a year and the years of a cycle. Still, the beginning, when I first put one foot in front of the other, with my back to my ravaged village, is lost in the shadows of early life. So ask me not when I began and from where I came. I'll say only "it was back then, back there, some-where before today." Let that suffice, and question me no more.

Nor do my steps since then matter, though they be as many as the stars in a cloudless, moonless sky. One step after another after another and another I have walked. What I have set forth to tell you is of the stops between those unnumbered steps, when I have lingered here or there. The sights I have seen and the people I have met. Oh, there we have much to talk of, for our land is wide, with more in it than any village-bound folk could ever dream.

So I shall start my tales of the stops, the times not walking, when I met others, some like me, but most so very different. Where shall I start? It matters not, since each has been a separate event, isolated, just as the villages are isolated, seemingly untouched by others, except when they war ~ though, in many ways, they are connected by more than my steps.

When he paused, she said, "I believe this may be an old book, written before our Alleshine Peace or by someone who still remains on the outside," she speculated. "What is the title?"

He looked on the cover. "*The Traveler's Tales*. Why do you think it's old, Tayar?"

"Because our villages are no longer isolated, and war is a thing of the past for those within our borders."

"Hey, then maybe this is a story of the Before Times."

"Yes, very possibly from the period of the Great Chaos that preceded our Peace."

"Wow!" He glanced briefly at the book. "You know, I always wondered what came before the Great Chaos. Our Storyteller hints about an incredibly powerful culture that disappeared or perished, but that's all he says about it."

"We know very little about the world before the Great Chaos, beyond fables about a mighty civilization that had stolen the secret of creation from the gods."

"But did it ever really exist?"

"Something inspired the fables. Perhaps it was a society whose knowledge was so powerful that the people who came afterwards believed them almost godlike. However, the Great Chaos destroyed everything except a precious few remnants and ruins of that era. So all we can do is guess at the truth." She shrugged. "Please continue reading."

"Okay, that was the first page. Now, it looks like a new chapter or a story. Anyway, it has a title: *The Ungiving*."

On a bright yellow and blue summer day, sometime back in the years, I met a man at a lake. His net jumped with fish, but he pulled not, staring off into the depths of his inner despair. I sat beside him, not wishing to disturb his black reflections, since some people relish such darkness and do not welcome interruptions. But I sat so that he would see me out of the corner of his eye, should his eye be searching for other than his own inner self.

Such was his desire to see beyond that he turned toward me, nodded and spoke. "Hello, Stranger. Or, should I greet you Sister?"

"Hey, the Traveler is a woman!" The boy quickly browsed over the previous paragraphs to see whether there had been any hints about the sex of the narrator that he had missed. "Skies, why didn't she say so from the beginning? I've been picturing a man all this time."

"Maybe she said nothing of her gender, because it is who she is and nothing unusual in her own mind."

He nodded, then resumed his reading, his voice mellow and pleasantly modulated.

"Hello, Stranger. Or should I greet you Sister? I do not recognize you as of this region, but I have been alone some time. Perhaps you have lived among my old village, and I knew it not."

"No, kind sir. I am a stranger here, having just come from the east plains. Nor have I seen any village for some days."

The man sighed so deeply that I thought all breath had left his body. "My village is a day's distance in the direction you seem to have been going, before you stopped here, if you had continued in a straight line from the east plains to here to there. That is, the village was there two summers ago, when they cast me out from their sight. Since that day, I have had the company of no man, woman or child, heard no human voice other than my own. Though I have seen visions. Are you another? Can I touch you, or would my hand grasp only air and reeds?"

"I'm real enough to be hungry for that fish you have netted, if you will share with me. Here, touch me."

But he did not reach out to touch, fearing, I believed, to find me a phantom. When I extended my hand to him, he flinched, and I withdrew, not wishing to shatter his illusion with my solidity. He turned from me to stare inward again, neither pulling in his net nor offering me any of his fish, though I had told him of my hunger.

I left that sad man by the lake, starving for something he would never gather unto himself, though both the fish and I were within a moment's grasp. I walked in the direction he had indicated, to find his village a day later.

It was one of those fine summer evenings when the sun seems to hang in the sky forever and light reaches into even the most elusive shadows. And the village was as friendly as I've ever known. People flowed out to greet me, from their homes and their chores, while children played underfoot.

The bathhouse fire was stoked, so that I might bathe and steam and bathe again. As I scraped the dust of my travels from my skin, my clothes were removed and replaced with splendid garments of soft skins. The shoes seemed made for me. I was told later that they had measured my boots against those of the entire village, until they found the right ones.

Though that time was long ago, I have kept the clothes they gave me, in the bottom of my pack, where most travelers keep food and ointments. But those are things for which the need comes and goes, while these beautiful clothes filled an eternal need, to be connected with good, generous people, to remember that I was once at one with them, though *for only a short moment of an overly long life.*

They served a welcome feast that thrilled my senses with succulent tastes, joyful music and good conversation. All this they gave me simply because I had walked into their village. They asked nothing of me. Who I was, where I came from. Nothing. So I volunteered what I could, wanting to return their generosity with whatever I had to give. I thought it was little, but they seemed to enjoy my stories, as I hope you do, too.

As the evening's bonfire burned down to gentle embers, they gave me their names, in a gesture of open fellowship for a stranger that I have rarely seen matched by any people. I told them the name that the last village had given me, which I have long since forgotten. I offered to have them use that one or give me another, for which honor they thanked me and gave me one of their cherished names, which I have also forgotten.

Such are the memories of one who has seen much and had so many names that details are unimportant. Indeed, should you and I become soul mates, I still would not be able to share with you my true name, as much as I would wish. So, ask it not of me. Instead, name me as you would have me, and I'll live up to it as best I can.

As generous as they were, I did not wish to ask more of them, but my curiosity would not be still. I turned to the headman, at whose right hand I had been seated, and asked of the vanquished man of the lake.

The headman's smile faded, so that I was sorry that the words had fallen from my lips. But they were there, out between us, and, being the man he was, he gathered them to his heart and told me the tragedy that haunted his people.

"Yes, it is a difficult story to tell," the headman began, then hesitated. "How do I help you understand how a village that would welcome a stranger as you have been would turn out one of their own in such a cruel manner? For cruel it is to exile a man whom you have known since he was a seed in his mother's womb. But even then, there was something wrong forming in him. You could see it in the way his mother carried her burden, becoming more and more sallow and drained, not round and healthy as our women are in their bearing months."

"At first, we thought it was because she was a recent widow. We were wrong. It was the unborn child. He took so much of the mother that she weakened daily, until there was little left of her to face the trials of birth. When our Healer presented the infant to our council it was as an orphan whose very existence had killed his own mother.

"Yet, childbirth deaths are not unknown and should never be blamed on aught but the ways of the Great Mother. Look at our children. Can you tell by their faces or bodies or by the caresses they receive, which *child belongs to which parents or who are the two orphans among them? No, of course not.*

"Like these children playing or sleeping among us now, he wanted for nothing. But whatever we gave him, he demanded more. Fine, we said to one another, he has greater needs than most. So we gave even more to him, thinking that if we could satisfy his emptiness, fill him to brimming, he wouldn't grasp so. We showered the boy with all the village could gather, all our hearts had to offer. Yet nothing ignited in him but selfishness and dissatisfaction.

"Still, we accepted him and would have kept him close to us for the rest of his life, if only he had allowed us. But that, too, is a gift ~ allowing others to love you. No, he'd have nothing of it. Though he lived among us through the years of his youth into his manhood, he kept himself separate. Any gifts from us were thrown back in our faces, but he took whatever he wanted from our homes, our harvests, our storehouses.

"Then one day, an innocent child, who was too young to understand why this one man was treated differently, offered him a crock of juice. You see, she had never before pressed fruit into juice, and was proudly sharing it with everyone she could find. Well, when she offered the crock to this miserable man, he threw it back at her ~ right at her ~ cracking her skull.

"I don't think he meant to hurt her, but it was done nonetheless. The girl lingered in pain for days. Before we gave her body to the earth, we banished the man, that his presence shouldn't give sacrilege to her memory.

"We could have forgiven much," the headman said. "The selfishness, the denial of our gifts, even the child's death. But he was so adamant in his ungiving that he couldn't even proffer an apology. If only he had said one thing ~ 'I'm sorry' ~ we could have begun to heal. As it is, none of us can ever relinquish the pain of losing these two ~ the man and the child. It lives on within us, in every breath and heartbeat of our lives, for the want of one gift.

"We warned him never to come near our village again. We won't have him come close enough to steal from us, so we leave him food, goods and tools out beyond our fields. But we know he is there, a day's walk from us."

I remained with those good people through two full moons. Among them, I was as one of their daughters, blood and flesh of their ancestors. So thoroughly did I become at one with them that their sorrow seeped into me and became mine. Thus, I gave more and more of myself, aching to salve the wound inflicted by the man of the lake. At the hoe and at the loom, in the hunt and in the spirit house, what I had, what I was, I gave to them.

With the Healer and the Storyteller, I shared knowledge from the many villages I had visited. To the council, I advised of the wars and temporary peaces I had witnessed. Each child became my own. Each man, my brother. Each woman, my sister. I gave until you would think that nothing would remain of me, yet I left them carrying within me so much more than I could ever be.

Why did I leave these wonderful people? How could I tear myself from them? You would do well to ask it of me, for I have asked myself those same questions over the years of hardship and loneliness since then. But, you see, it's my feet. They needed their steps, one after another after another after another. And where my feet pull, my body must follow. But not my heart, my soul. Those I left in the trust of that generous village. Taking with me the same parts of each of them.

My feet carried me back the way I had come, though it was not my wont to retrace paths already taken. I had to see that man at the lake once more. He was sitting on a rock outcrop, next to a nest of eggs, but did not touch the eggs, staring instead into that deep despair he seemed to prefer above all else.

He spied me as I approached. "I know you. Begone, I'll not have that vision again!"

I continued toward him. "I'm no vision." And I used his true name, since I knew the names of all of the village, which had now become my village.

At the sound of his name, his face twisted with terror. He held his arms out, pushing away what could not be real. But still I moved forward.

"I have a gift for you," I said. And again, I used his name which I have forgotten since, as I have forgotten much, but I'll never forget the mournful moan that escaped his lips, unbidden.

"Noooo!!"

Then I embraced him.

He did not push me away, though that is what I had expected. Instead, his arms hung limply by his side, like the useless things they were.

I turned my back on that man and continued my travels, one step after another after another after another.

In quiet times, I often wonder why I did it ~ embrace him ~ a man so fearful of being touched that he had murdered a child. Did I offer it in the spirit of the village that had adopted me, as an attempt to shatter his emptiness and fill it with love? Did I believe that I could achieve what none of his people had, because I was infused by their generosity of spirit? Or was it that I was less changed by them than I had thought, so that I was able to demand of him what they would never consider?

Vengeance!

The boy reluctantly closed the book. Only then did he look at his Allesha. Though her face was in shadow, a single tear on her cheek caught the light of the fire.

"You know, that was a strange story." Perplexed, the boy shook his head. "An embrace for killing a kid. Not my idea of justice."

"No, it wouldn't be."

"I guess you see that as my failing."

Tayar sighed. "No, not at all. It's simply that it was right for those people."

"Do you think they're real, or just a tale?"

Tayar tilted her head, as she considered the question. "Could such innocent people survive our world, even now, when the Alleshine Peace has taken hold?"

The boy wondered why her sadness seemed to turn inward.

"Yet it does appear that the story is from a time before the Peace. How could such a village hold off the bands of brigands or marauding warriors of the Great Chaos?" she reflected. "I don't know. I'd like to think they could exist. Or at least that they live, here" — she pressed her hand to her breast — "in our hearts. Perhaps they're meant to represent the better part of us."

"I'm not sure about 'better.' How can it be good, when a village headman doesn't know how to guide his people through difficult times or deal properly with a murderer in their midst?"

Tayar got up from the hearth and walked over to the boy, touching his cheek again with that fiery static of flesh to flesh. "Thank you for your generous gift of that tale. I'll look forward to discussing it further with you. But right now, it's late and time for me to go to bed."

The boy stood, hoping for an invitation to join her.

She saw the question in his eyes. "No, dear, not tonight, but soon."

She brushed her lips gently against his. But when she turned to go, he wrapped his arms about her, pressing his full body against hers, so that she could feel his heart beating in her breast, his erection pressing through their clothes. He opened her lips with his tongue, and she responded, pressing her hips against him for such a fleeting moment that he could almost believe he had imagined it. But she pulled away, walked slowly to her bedroom and closed the door without looking back.

Chapter 18

At breakfast, the magic of the previous evening was gone. All the boy knew was he had slept alone, despite everything he had hoped and tried. Tayar said nothing of importance, so he ignored most of her prattle.

"Of course, I always take care of the barn animals before breakfast." She looked at him, as though she expected him to say something. He didn't. "Perhaps we could take turns with that responsibility."

With a grunt, the boy dropped his fork onto his plate and leaned back in his chair. She wasn't sleeping with him, but he was supposed to feed her chickens!

She ignored his sneer and continued. "I've been told that we can expect our first snowfall early this year. But we still have the windows to seal, the barn and house roofs to check, and—"

"Humph, no wonder you wanted a Winter Boy — for lugging, not loving," he grumbled under his breath, but not so low that the Allesha didn't hear it.

Her eyes blazed for a moment. Then she sighed in exasperation. "Did you hear nothing of what I said the other evening?" she asked. "I'm complete without you. That you might share in my life is for *your* sake. But it is up to you. Are you a guest to be catered to or a member of this household?"

"You mean I have a choice?" he asked.

"Of course. You always have a choice. But be cautious how you decide. Reverberations of what you choose will range far beyond what is in front of your face."

"Damn it! Why must everything be a lesson to you?"

"You came to me to learn. But, no, that isn't the only reason. Everything in life is a lesson, a chance to learn. Those of us who take advantage of such opportunities are enriched by them. Those who do not become rigid, set in their ways, old before their time — and boring." Her cheeks and ears flushed to nearly the color of her freckles. "I wouldn't wish such a fate on an enemy, certainly not on a boy in my care."

He was taken aback by her sharp tone and curt words.

"While we're on the subject of lessons, here's an important one for you. Your curse words have no effect on me. If you want impact, use language that has strength and originality, words that reflect who you are and what you want to say. Not the feeble echoes of boys, who in trying to sound like they are more than they are, reveal themselves as much less."

"Look, I don't know what I did to nettle you, but I'm sor—"

"You accused me of using you as a servant." She stood up abruptly. "I'm going to clean my room. I suggest you do the same."

Of course, the Allesha didn't expect the boy to clean his room. What he did behind his door, she didn't really care. And that worried her. Why had she reacted so fiercely? Not only was it unacceptable for an Allesha to lose control and show unintentional anger in front of her boy in Season, but it was unlike her.

The answer came to her while she scrubbed her bathtub with more energy than necessary: she was as eager as he to move forward. After the hunt, and then last night, she had believed they'd advance quickly past the barriers she had been told to expect.

No, fool! She flung the scrub cloth into her hamper. This boy can't allow himself to be that easy. She'd have to fight for him against his very nature.

When she came out of her room, she found the boy not in the house, but in the front yard, throwing stones at tree trunks. She sent him to Dara, with the venison rump he had chosen for their mentor. Once he was out of sight, the young Allesha closed her outer door and set off to find Savah.

Chapter 19

The boy hesitated at the inner door of the older Allesha's home. It didn't seem right to barge in, even though they had told him that an open outer door was a sign welcoming visitors. He walked around to the back, and found her taking off her boots in the mudroom behind her kitchen.

She waved. "Come in." When she saw what he carried, she said, "Oh, my, put that over there."

"No, I'll take it to your coldhouse."

"In a moment, dear." Stowing her boots on the floor rack, she walked toward him in her stocking feet. "For now, set it down so I may greet you properly and thank you for this handsome gift."

After he swung the haunch off his shoulder, careful to not let it drop onto the counter, she placed both hands on his shoulder, kissed each of his cheeks, and, to his surprise, brushed her lips quickly and gently across his.

He lifted the meat up again, but onto his opposite shoulder, realizing how heavily it had pressed on his muscles during his walk to the elder Allesha's home. Then he took it out to hang in the coldhouse.

When he returned, the Allesha was at the kitchen table, which was set for tea.

"Please sit," she said, gesturing to the chair opposite hers. "Now tell me, how does it go with your Allesha?" She sat opposite him. "What did you do last night?"

"I read to her, that's all."

She held up a plate, and he took a cookie. "Sounds pleasant."

"I guess it was nice enough, just not what I hoped it would be." He bit into the cookie, chewing it thoughtfully, though he barely tasted it.

"No, not yet."

"Why the hell not? Oh… she says I'm not supposed to curse. But damn it, she makes me feel like cursing."

Sipping her tea, she studied him over the rim of her cup. "Yes, I can see that. What did you read?"

"A story from some book by a woman, called *The Traveler's Tales*. It was pretty good, and reading to her made me feel that we were somehow closer. But then she pushed me away."

"I see."

"You're not much help, are you?"

"I can't make the world turn faster for you, just because you're in a hurry." She paused to put down her cup. "So, what questions do you have for me that I might be able to answer?"

"She told me it's time to pick a name for you, too."

"There's no hurry. You'll find it when you're ready."

"Did she tell you the name I gave her?"

"Tayar," the Allesha said. "It's a good, insightful name. You did well."

"But what about me? Am I to answer to 'boy' with you women for the rest of the winter?"

"That will be up to your Allesha, not me. But I can tell you that our boys earn their names."

"Well, she hasn't given me a chance to *earn* it yet. Damn! When's she going to let me in that inner room?"

"Patience, boy. This time will pass too soon. Enjoy it while you live it. Give your Allesha the courtesy and pleasure of being with her in the now, so that she may take you forward to your future. And, yes, into the delights of the inner room, too."

"Le'a."

"What?"

"It's a mountain on the far side of our forest. It watches over everything we do. The children of our village are taught that, if they ever get lost, they should climb to the top of a tree and look for Le'a. She'll show them the direction toward home, just by being where she always has been and always will be." He looked at her expectantly, but when she didn't respond immediately, he realized the old woman didn't get what he was saying. "It's your name."

"Le'a. I like it. Thank you."

Chapter 20

Rishana found the one the Alleshi called Peren in the yard outside her timber-and-daub barn, chopping firewood.

"Jinet!" the old woman called out, as she carefully lay down her axe and ambled over to her.

"Hello, Savah."

The sound of the old, familiar names comforted the young woman. It was the same — always would be the same — coming home to Jared's Allesha, whom he had named Savah when he had been a boy in Season. Nothing would ever change how rooted this one woman could make her feel. Alone with Savah, she could still be Jinet, the woman she had been before becoming the Allesha Rishana, or her First Boy's Tayar.

She bent down to Savah, fitting her tall lean figure easily and comfortably into the small, round softness of her dearest living friend.

Savah broke the embrace to place her hands on Jinet's shoulders and read her face. Then Savah walked to the block and picked up the axe. "Sit there while I do my chopping, and tell me what is bothering you."

"I'll do it," Jinet protested. "You should be the one resting."

"Thank you, dear, but no. Hester keeps telling me that, since retiring from the giving of Seasons, I need to find other ways to get my old heart pumping. Now you can tell her that I'm listening to her. Won't she be surprised?" She hefted the axe and began to build a slow rhythm of placing and splitting logs.

Recognizing that she never could change Savah's mind, Jinet sat down on the hard ground in the shadow of the stone wall that ringed the yard. She had to admit that Savah was building up a ruddy sweat that was probably doing her as much good as any exercise class at the Communal Hall.

"So, Savah, what library project are you working on now? I know you must have something. You always do."

Savah paused and leaned on the axe handle. "We're examining a large cache of books and scrolls we've recently acquired from far beyond our Peace borders. Some even have hints about the fabled civilization from before the Great Chaos. Wouldn't it be wonderful if we could finally discover who they were, what they knew? So much was destroyed during the wars of the Chaos. And, yet, if that civilization hadn't collapsed into centuries of horror and cruelty, we wouldn't be here, as we are today. The Alleshine Peace would have had no reason to exist." Savah stared into the space between them, lost for the moment in her beloved library. Then she resumed her chopping, fitting her words into the grunting syncopation of her efforts. "However, you didn't come to hear about that. Tell me."

Now that the time had come to speak about what had happened, the young Allesha hesitated putting it into words and acknowledging her shortcomings. But it was that very fear that made her push forward. "Savah, I lost my temper." She said it in a rush of words, hoping to outpace her shame. "I was emotionally reactive."

"Did you really think that would never happen? None of us is perfect."

"But this was with my Winter Boy, my First Boy." Jinet frowned. "Savah, my training was too short."

As Savah leaned over to put another log on the chopping block, she looked over at Jinet. A brief glance, but Jinet thought she sensed a shadow in it. Or perhaps the young Allesha was seeing what she herself felt.

Savah shook her head, then resumed the rhythm of swinging, chopping, removing the split wood and placing another piece. "I've reassured you repeatedly; you shouldn't need to hear it again. You are fully ready, have been for some time."

"Savah, please," Jinet pleaded.

Savah rested the head of the axe on the ground. "You're talking about more than this one incident, then?"

"I guess I am."

"It sounds like everything is going as planned with your First Boy. Perhaps the Conflict Stage came sooner than you had expected, but that often happens with problem boys. I wouldn't be surprised if some of your anger might have been because you were disappointed that it came so early. Or had you hoped to avoid it completely?"

"Fascination Stage… Conflict Stage…" Jinet bit her lower lip. "Why should any boy's Season follow such a rigid pattern? It's as though some mathematician had formulated it for us, and we were just going through the motions, surrendering our lives to her rule."

"I see." Savah put down her axe and sat next to Jinet.

"Do you? I had to believe that if anyone understood, you would." Jinet leaned against the stone wall and, with a sigh of relief, realized how tightly she had been holding back a fermenting jumble of doubt. "So many different boys come to us, from widely diverse cultures. How can you predict how all of them will behave, using a single set of rules? Deep inside me, I feel that there's something very wrong in this. It frightens me, Savah. Are the Alleshi… How do they know how to anticipate a boy's…? Savah, what are we, really?"

"Just a society of widows from the far and near reaches of our land who have banded together to try to keep war and chaos at bay."

"Yes, but to have such special knowledge and unerring insights?"

"Unerring? Never. The uninitiated may find comfort and surety in believing it of us… but no." Savah placed her hand on Jinet's knee. "Still, knowledge is a wonderful and strange thing. I've devoted the remaining years of my life to unearthing new knowledge for the pleasure it gives me and for the value it may offer our people. Of course, the Alleshi have always accumulated it for a grander, less personal purpose — to preserve it, use it — though some might say to control it. So you are right to fear knowledge. Its power is seductive."

Savah's easy acceptance that Alleshine power could be corrupted added fuel to Jinet's anxiety. Before she had come to The Valley, Jinet had believed with all her heart in the authority, wisdom and rectitude of the Alleshi. Now that she was one of them, she couldn't help have misgivings — about herself, and about the Alleshi for having accepted her.

"Jinet, every boy is unique. That we have given you the insights to see into a boy's heart and to help you prepare to attend to his needs and education doesn't negate his individuality. We Alleshi are very privileged to benefit from the best that our world has to offer. We have been given you. And you have been given this boy to teach and to love. Cherish the gift, the gifts, that have been showered upon you, because you are Jinet and Rishana and whomever else your boys will need you to be. Because you are Allesha."

"I'll try, Savah." Even as she said it, Jinet wondered how she could ever be all that Savah apparently believed her to be — fully and unequivocally Alleshine. "Sometimes, I feel a dark shadow forming just beyond the corner of my eye. I don't really know its shape or origin, but I fear it will overtake me. A hard seed of uncertainty that… Oh, I don't know what I'm trying to say."

"Yes, dear." Savah patted the young woman's hand. "The First Season can be most difficult, and you never were one to accept anything you hadn't struggled to understand. If you have doubts, look to them to guide you. I've never seen you fail when you listened to your own heart. In certain matters, I trust that even more than the combined wisdom of long-dead Alleshi."

Chapter 21

After seeing Ayne, Karinne knew she had to talk with her old friend Evanya.

Many years ago, when they had been young women known as Karinne and Evanya, whatever crises had beset them, nothing had seemed insurmountable. Now those names remained only as an ingrained habit that both clung to in the privacy of their friendship, something they could share that was aloof and apart from anything or anyone else in The Valley. They used the names most often as reminders that some conversations, certain subjects must remain private, hidden from the world. Neither found reassurance in the sounds of their old names, as they once had when life had been far less complicated.

Karinne didn't waste time on preliminary pleasantries when she found Evanya alone in her workshop. "If you don't tell Rishana soon, I will," Karinne insisted. "She needs to be prepared."

Evanya wiped the clay from her hands and flung the towel toward the sink. She didn't bother to mask her annoyance. "We agreed that it would be my decision."

"But Rishana senses that something is wrong. She's turning it inward, doubting herself, thinking that it has to do with her inexperience."

"Well, she's right... in part." Evanya sighed. "Karinne, don't you remember your First? When everything was still new, fresh, innocent. Of course she's uncertain, but her instincts are solid."

"It's those instincts that worry me. Do you really want her to guess the truth on her own? If it comes from you — or if necessary, from me — we'll have more control over the situation."

"Soon, Karinne, I promise. But let her remain innocent for a little while longer."

Chapter 22

When the boy returned, he found his Allesha in her kitchen. He strode across the room in three quick steps. Then, in a surprising gesture that might have been taken as mockery if he hadn't done it just right, he placed his hands on her shoulders, and pressed his lips on both of her cheeks, then firmly, but briefly on her lips.

"Sorry I'm late," he said. "The old woman needed some help with her chores. Didn't think you'd mind."

She held herself in check so she wouldn't show her wonder in his changed behavior. "I'm glad you were able to help her. Lunch is ready. Please set the table after you've washed up. I'll reheat the soup."

They discussed their afternoon chores while they ate, treading lightly, not wanting to pry or push in any manner that would upset the fragile equilibrium. But the Allesha knew how unfertile a placid balance can be. *Maybe that's one of the reasons this boy is always testing and unaccepting. His need to challenge for the sake of challenge is what marks him as a creature of power. It's up to me to spark and provoke him, to mold and make a leader out of the problem child.*

The boy broke through her reverie. "You didn't ask me about my visit with the old woman."

"If you have something to share with me, I trust you will."

"Well, yeah, I gave her a name, like you said to. Le'a."

"Why?"

"Does there have to be a why for a name? Can't it just be pretty?"

"Le'a. It has a good sound to it, but would you give our mentor a meaningless name?"

"Sure, why not?" He crossed his arms and grinned.

"Because I know how pleased I was when you explained why you had chosen Tayar for me. Because I don't think you do anything for no reason at all. And because I believe you're baiting me, the way a fisherman plays a trout, skipping some morsel over the surface of a stream. Do you think I'm so easily teased and hooked?"

"Hey, wait. You're twisting things." His sigh was more a huff of exasperation than acceptance. "Okay, look, the name does have a meaning.

But I didn't keep it back for any bad reason. Can't teasing be good or fun?"

"Teasing for fun is delightful. For power or control, it's offensive."

"Control? I don't understand."

"You will."

"Who's trying to control now?" He tossed his napkin onto his empty plate, got up from the table and started toward the back door. "I give up. Thanks for the meal. I guess I'll go out and get to work on the barn roof."

"Whoa, boy! We have dishes to do first. Then we'll both go up on the roof."

Without a word, he noisily stacked the plates and utensils from the table and carried them to the sink to wash in an over-full basin of soapy water. He was rough with the china and glasses, but his Allesha said nothing. *Let him simmer a while,* she decided. *We have time.*

He continued in angry silence for much of the afternoon. After cleaning the kitchen, they fetched the ladder and climbed onto the barn roof to inspect it. Several shingles were loose and a few needed to be replaced. Without a word, they set to work.

The Allesha felt that the boy wanted to come out from behind the emotional wall he had thrown up, but didn't know how to do it without appearing a fool. She considered helping him out of his discomfort, but realized that he'd have to learn to do it himself sometime. Might as well begin today.

Before they realized it, the sun was low in the sky, and they were almost done, with only one shingle left to replace, on the top edge of the sharply angled roof.

That's when it happened. Perhaps it was the lateness of the hour, or the tension between them, or her lack of focus on the task at hand. She slipped. Her fingers clawed and scraped at shingles as she plummeted.

"*Tayar!*" he cried out, diving downward, desperately catching her by her right arm when the rest of her body flew into the air below the eave. One hand over the other, he strained to pull her up to safety. Checking for injuries, he kept repeating her name, in varying intonations of anguish, relief and guilt. "Tayar. Tayar."

Ignoring her protests, he led her down the ladder, preceding her by one rung and bracing her body with his. Once on the ground, he picked her up, carried her into the house and gently placed her on the greeting room sofa. He ran into the kitchen for a damp cloth and bathed various scrapes and cuts on her hands, arms and face.

Satisfied that Tayar was truly safe, he tucked a quilt around her and lit the fire in the hearth. "Stay here; I'll clean up outside and take care of the animals," he said.

She was touched by his tender care, but needed to put the embarrassing incident behind her. As soon as the boy left, she went into her room, locked the door, removed her clothes and studied her body in the mirror. No real damage. A hot bath relieved most of the aches, various ointments salved the rest.

The boy was already preparing their supper when she entered the kitchen. At the sight of her, he rushed over to pull a chair out from the table. "Please sit. You should rest."

"I'm fine. Really."

"I know, but please…" The sight of her plummeting down the roof, almost out of his reach, was seared into his mind. He bustled about the kitchen, knowing he was being irrational, that it had been no fault of his that Tayar had fallen. Sure, he had wanted to punish her, but with silence, not with… he couldn't even allow the word into his thoughts, so horrified by what could have happened.

"What are you preparing?" she asked from her seat.

"I'm chopping up some apples I found in your coldhouse. They'll go into the frying pan with onions and bacon. It's a hunter's sauce for the roast you made."

"Sounds delicious. I have salad vegetables in the icebox that would make a good complement." She started to get up, but he shooed her down.

"I'll get it." He looked at her sheepishly. "But you'll have to tell me what to do. Salads aren't common around a campfire, and that's the only place I've cooked."

"Let's do it together. It's more fun that way."

He started to protest.

"If you wish, I won't get up from this chair. Come, bring the vegetables, the cutting board, that large wooden bowl, a small mixing bowl from that cabinet, and two knives."

He did as she said.

"Sit here, next to me." She patted the closest chair. "We'll cut the vegetables into pieces. Not too small. About bite sized. No, the spinach is best torn, like this." She showed him. "I don't know why; it just is. Everything that's leafy is torn. The rest are cut…. That's very good. Now bring me my oil, lemon juice, vinegar and… oh, please, may I get up for the spices? You'll never find them."

He nodded, trying to hide his surrender with a smile and a feigned interest in the secrets of salad making.

Tayar took a pinch of this and that, sniffing at each spice before sprinkling it into the mixing bowl. She was concentrating so hard on the salad, and then on concocting the dressing, he didn't think she noticed he wasn't really listening. Not that he didn't hear the words, but they didn't penetrate, until she started talking about the Before Times.

"It's hard to imagine," she continued, "but the variety and volume of these spices once represented great wealth."

"Yeah?" He looked more closely at the jars of spices, curious how they could be so important. It was the kind of detail that made stories about the Great Chaos of the Before Times so intriguing, compared to his own boring life.

"As the Alleshine Peace grew," she explained, "we gathered the seeds of spices from all our villages and dispersed them to the others. Nowadays, the only people who still covet and conquer for the sake of spice are those beyond our borders. How much easier it would be for them to just join us, but they haven't figured that out, yet." She looked at the boy, with hope and curiosity. "Maybe, you'll be among the Allemen who will help some of them — the outsiders — understand."

She stirred the dressing with a last flourish and tasted it again. "Yes. Done." She dipped a piece of spinach into the mixture and offered it to the boy. "What do you think?"

The boy continued to be solicitous over dinner, tender without being coddling, generous without being selfless.

If I had realized what the effect would be, the Allesha thought, *maybe I would have fallen sooner. Should I suggest life- or limb-threatening accidents as a tactic for working with problem boys? Or would it cut too severely into the population of our Valley?* She reined in her black humor when she started imagining bodies of Alleshi piling up under roof eaves, because their boys weren't quick enough to save them.

After eating and cleaning up from the meal, they adjourned to the greeting room.

"I'm glad you enjoyed reading last night," she said. "I think it would be nice if we alternate who reads each night, a gift we can give each other at the end of a day."

"Okay."

"What shall I read? Should I continue with *The Traveler's Tales*?"

"Sure."

Tayar picked up the book and began leafing through it to where he had finished the night before when he interrupted her. "Hey, wait. No. I mean, we've a few months to finish that book. I think I'd prefer to hear something else that you like."

She smiled. "That's a nice thought. I'll get a book from my room."

He stoked the fire, added a log and then settled comfortably into an armchair, with one of his legs thrown over the side. When Tayar returned, she sat in a corner of the sofa and built the cushions around her.

"You seem to be interested in the Before Times. This is a tale of a boy who was probably two or three years younger than you. It's called *Death to the Enemy*."

She cleared her throat, squirmed around in the cushions to make a burrow for herself, then began.

The old men usually met in council beyond the ears of any of us. But that one time they called in all young men who had reached the age of recognition. None of us had ever entered the council hall ~ not within our memory, though the naming ceremony of all male newborns was held there.

Our mothers cried and pulled at our shirts when the announcement was made. Such is the way of women, we knew, to cry at whatever goes past them ~ especially their sons, when they have long ago left the breast to enter the realm of men. But it was our fathers' instructions that caught our attention, made us think and gave us reason for excitement.

Our fathers lined us up two abreast by size, with the tallest leading the way. We heard the beginning of the chant as a low rumble, coming from behind the stone walls of the council hall ~ a deep, rhythmic throb that buzzed in the pit of our stomachs and climbed up our spines.

I was neither tall nor small, so I watched the first half of our double line of boys bend over two at a time, to enter the low crawlway into the council hall. As I got closer to the entrance, the chant became louder and more insistent. Two boys in front of me had just entered, when one word became barely distinguishable.

"Death... Death... Death..."

The buzz reached up from my spine, pulling my head down toward the ground, toward the crawlway. Such is how all men enter the council hall ~ on their hands and knees ~ in respect, in danger, not knowing if a club hovered, waiting to strike, or if a friend would greet with a hand and honored seat.

The crawlway was narrow and dark. I was guided by my companion's body on the one side, the wall on the other, and the chant pulling us forward, slowly, inexorably, becoming clear, one word at a time.

"Death... Death... Death to... Death to... Death to the...Death to the..."

The slight glow of a campfire and the smell of so many men and boys gathered in the one round room told us we had arrived, as the reverberating full chant washed over us.

"Death to the enemy! Death to the enemy! Death to the enemy!"

The pounding rhythm entered my body like a lover, taking claim, possessing it, reshaping and remaking me. I became the thunder. I became a man. I shouted the chant, throwing it to the boys who continued to pour into the hall as bent-over supplicants, straightening their backs against the words I flung at them.

"Death to the enemy! Death to the enemy! Death to the enemy!"

When all the boys had entered the hall, we stood in a proud, unified semi-circle before the old men of the council and continued the chant.

"Death to the enemy! Death to the enemy!"

Jabbing our right fists at the air above our heads with each "Death."

"Death to the enemy! Death to the enemy!"

Stomping our feet on the ground, with each jab of our fists, imagining trampling our enemy underfoot.

"Death to the enemy! Death to the enemy!"

So it would be. So it must be, before such a mighty force as we who had become the thunder, we who would wield the lightning.

"Death to the enemy!"

The old men watched us with such looks on their pale, furrowed faces, that you could imagine their withered members once more swelled for the sight of us and their remembered manhood. The oldest stood, the one we all called Grandfather, though none of us had any of his blood or sinew. (I think it was a title of respect, for he had outlived everyone who had truly known him.) He raised his small, claw-like hands over his head to call us to silence. Such was his position and our regard for him that, even in our fervor, we quit our chant long enough to hear his speech (though the words, "Death to the enemy! Death to the enemy!" continued to throb and echo in our heads and our bones).

"Men of our village." It was the first time anyone other than our friends had called us men. "Men of our village, our people call on you today, in need, in danger. How do you answer?"

As one voice we shouted, "Death to the enemy!"

"The women and children of your village will be slaughtered. Your mothers and sweethearts raped and butchered. Your fathers and grand-

fathers burned alive. How do you answer?"

"Death to the enemy!"

"Will you protect them?"

"Yes!"

"Will you place your bodies between them and the enemy?"

"Yes!"

"Will you drive the enemy out of our land and into hell?"

"Yes!"

"And should death find you, will you be there to block its path?"

"Yes!"

"Yes?" he asked.

"Death!" we answered. "Death to the enemy! Death to the enemy! Death to the enemy!"

He plunged his right hand into a pot of blood, slapped it onto each of our faces and smeared it onto our chests, while we continued to chant, "Death to the enemy! Death to the enemy! Death to the enemy!"

That night, my friends and I slept beyond the village gate. Already bloodied (though only in ceremony), we lay as warriors, outside the community, protecting it, separate from it, as was fitting. The next morning, we began our march in the direction the old men had pointed.

As we traveled, we played at war, practicing our spear throws and sword thrusts, rallying our pride and courage, teasing each other and bragging of our victories to come. For six days, we ventured forward, calling out our chant to speed our pace and steel our hearts, onward through familiar land into a strange, unknown valley.

That's where we met them ~ the enemy ~ a band of bloodied boys, standing, as though waiting for us, on the plains outside their village gate. The two groups stared at each other, in wonder. Then someone started the chant. I still don't know where the first call came from ~ their group or ours.

"Death to the enemy! Death to the enemy!"

Roaring our battlecry, we rushed forward, spear and sword poised, so that it wasn't necessary to strike. Just keep running, until metal bit through flesh.

I heard the cries and screams. I know I did, because they come to me still in waking nightmares and winter sweats. But they were muffled, unreal sounds, of birds screeching or devils wailing, not my friends, not my enemies, not boys like me, falling on my blade, slashing at my muscles till flaps of my flesh swung about like leaves on an autumn tree. I don't know when I fell, but it probably saved my life.

In the night, I awoke to the sounds of animals scurrying and picking over the piles of bodies. I feared opening my eyes and discovering either that I could not see (death, am I the enemy?) or what I would see. Eventually, I managed enough courage to look out through half lids.

What I had taken for the sounds of animals were two women who had stolen out of their village, in the hope of finding their sons alive. I lay quietly, until they left, sobbing. After some time, I heard one of them release a widow's wail, like a wolf's howl, baying at the moon, at the untimely night, at man's life that marches so willingly toward death.

I could have told her that, young or old, all come to death at some time, but that was before I had searched the dead myself, had seen the ugly truth of what we had wrought.

I found none alive in that field of blood and mud. All had killed even as their own lives were taken, falling one on top of the other, hacking and slashing pieces off their fellows as they fell, so that body parts were flung here and there. I could not know which arms or heads belonged to my friends, and which were my enemies, so alike they were in death. I found one complete body that seemed familiar, until I realized it was merely someone who looked like my own reflection. No friend of mine resembled me more in life or death. I still wonder what his name was. But that night and his face and the strewn body parts of two bands of warriors belong to a horrific memory I have worked hard to block from my mind's eye. Someday, I might succeed.

Now I am an old man. I sit on the council, and everyone calls me Grandfather, because I have outlived all who ever truly knew me. Tomorrow, I will send the young men who have reached the age of recognition to war.

"Death to the enemy!"

After a few heartbeats of silence, the Allesha closed the book.

"Do you think it's a true story?" the boy asked.

"Truth is in it, if you look closely and don't turn from what you see."

"But did that boy really exist?"

"I think so, in many places, at many times," she said. "I only wish our Peace could have come sooner for him and his friends."

"Yeah, I see what you mean."

"Do you? I hope so. It's important you do."

He was still thinking about the story, lost in deep contemplation, when she kissed his head and went to bed.

"Don't stay up too late. We've a lot to do tomorrow," she called to him from her bedroom door.

"Huh? Oh, yeah. Goodnight."

Chapter 23

For another week, their days followed the same pattern. Before breakfast, they took turns traipsing out to the barn to care for the animals. After breakfast, they retired to their private chambers, to give each some time apart. Then he would go to Le'a, or she would come to them. They finished preparing the property for winter and did other small chores in the afternoons. In the evenings, they read to each other.

Through it all, the boy was learning and growing. Not that he had developed patience. He often floundered between frustrated irritability and great tenderness. Obviously, he wasn't sleeping well, probably obsessing about the inner room and the promises it held, so close, behind the locked door, between their two bedrooms.

Unlike the boy, the Allesha was enjoying the sensuality of their encounters. As was appropriate for this stage, she worked at heightening it, with casual brushes of body against body, and seemingly involuntary sighs. But she wouldn't let it go further. She couldn't. As much as she, too, was looking forward to taking him into the inner room, he wasn't ready, and neither was she. But soon — she could feel it — the time was approaching when they would begin his full training, using the physical to reach the essential.

Near the end of that week, Tayar decided to accompany the boy to Le'a's, and then proceed to the storehouse. She had extra bealberry preserves, goat's milk and eggs to leave, and she wanted to get some honey.

The air was sharp and crisp. Though the sky was a clear blue, thick piles of grey clouds were looming over the western mountains, dusting the peaks with the first white of the year.

They kissed goodbye in the vestibule between Le'a's inner and outer doors. What started as a ritual embrace evolved into something much more. He wrapped his arms about her, pulling her body deep into his. She could feel his erection pressing against her, despite their layers of clothes. All the while, their mouths and tongues searched hungrily. It was a brief moment, but it left them both dizzy and breathless.

Only when the boy closed the greeting room door behind him did the young Allesha allow herself to collapse against the wall, while waves of pleasure and pain shot through her body. *How right you were Dara,* she mused. *This boy has more than a few surprises for me.*

So absorbed was she by the rippling tide of sensations that swept over her body that she barely saw the first few snowflakes falling in her path and on her clothes as she walked to the enormous storehouse. Nor did she notice Kiv rushing to catch up with her, until the older Allesha greeted her from behind.

"Hello, Rishana."

"Hello, Kiv."

Kiv fell into pace with Rishana. "I was wondering if you had thought about what we discussed the other day… about the Mwertik."

"Yes, but I'm not sure I know what it is you're suggesting we should do about them."

"I'm simply not willing to sit by and watch our Peace fail. Just because old paths have worked for us in the past doesn't mean they will carry us forward into the future. All the talk in the world isn't going to stop the Mwertik. And they obviously have no interest in trade. If we don't want to lose the Peace, it may be time to take action."

"Would you meet violence with violence, Kiv? Is that what you're insinuating? What would then separate us from the Mwertik?"

"We Alleshi have always prided ourselves in fitting the solution to the problem, yet we limit ourselves in the kinds of solutions we're willing to use." Kiv paused. "What if the only answer to the Mwertik is to stop them in their tracks, before they can kill again, before they destroy everything the Peace has achieved?"

Rishana couldn't ignore the ring of truth in what Kiv had to say.

"I see I've upset you, Rishana; that wasn't my intention. All I ask is that you use your own mind, rather than accept what others are telling you about how to think. Consider looking beyond the limitations we've imposed on ourselves. Somehow, we have to find an answer to the Mwertik, before it's too late. We'll talk about this again, after you've had time to think it over."

Chapter 24

The wonders of the storehouse never failed to captivate Rishana. So large, no single gaze could take in all that it held of produce and provisions, tools and materiel. It was a maze of tree-tall shelves and vats dug deep. Sunlight streamed in from the high windows, filling the cavernous open space in the center, shining on the many pools. Along the walls and in darkened rooms, sealed barrels and casks were piled high, protected from the light.

Over the centuries, as the Peace spread, more and more goods came in as duty gifts, tribute and trade, and were redistributed carefully to maintain balance and harmony. Farming communities, such as Rishana's Attani, supplied fresh and preserved foods. Seafarers brought goods and fish from under and across the oceans. While some villages provided raw materials from their mines, others worked the ingots and stones into highly prized finished products. The armory was filled with all levels of armaments, according to the sophistication of their sources, from knives, spears and arrows up to the newest rapid-fire guns that were carefully locked away as soon as they arrived, in the hope that they would never be used.

Before the young woman had come to The Valley, she hadn't thought to question the wealth and variety of the Peace, because her village was one of the old ones, so set in Alleshine ways and close to The Valley that she had never known want. Then, as an Alleshine initiate, Rishana had been assigned to assist Caith, the storehouse caretaker, in inventorying that first autumn's stores and gifts.

Rishana had taken her duties seriously, believing that the older woman needed her help. But Rishana had quickly learned how energetic and capable Caith was. Few in The Valley could keep up with that spry little woman. And few knew as much about the many villages of the Peace. Savah and other scholars had the library, but Caith's knowledge was rooted in the earth.

Early in her training, Rishana had heard the whispered rumors about the permanently sealed rooms, buried in a subterranean labyrinth, which were said to hold dangerous treasures from the Before Times.

Never one to put any store in hearsay, one evening she had asked Caith if the gossip were based on any reality. The caretaker had became suddenly somber and had refused to respond.

Neither of them ever again brought up the subject.

After her encounter with Kiv, Rishana welcomed the solidity of the storehouse, the embodiment of all that was right with the Peace. Rishana's footsteps echoed through the empty aisles where she was used to hearing dozens, if not scores of others calling, laughing, negotiating and whispering. For most of the year, the storehouse was a hive of activity with frequent deliveries and disbursements. But in winter, only Alleshi wandered in and out.

Rishana headed directly for a dark corner, where she lit a gas lamp. She took a jar measure of clover honey from a barrel near the wine rooms. Then she left her bealberries in the preserves section, put her milk and eggs in the dairy coldroom, and browsed among the spice sacks for inspiration. When she heard splashing and singing coming from the center of the building, she quickly lowered the lamp's flame and headed toward the central ponds.

Rishana found Caith sitting on the edge of the oyster pond, seeding the smaller oysters with grains of sand.

Caith waved. "Rishana, hello!"

Happy and relieved to see that mischievous old Allesha, Rishana rushed over to greet her, though a proper embrace was nearly impossible, with Caith's feet splashing in the pond and her hands covered with sand.

Other Alleshi had confided in Rishana that Caith never seemed to change, for she had been old before most of their sisters had come to The Valley. Her charcoal-colored parchment-thin skin had so many wrinkles it seemed impossible there could be room for any more, no matter how much longer she lived. Bones jutted out where flesh should have been. Nevertheless, she flitted about like a busy mosquito. Even in those rare times when her body was at rest, her hands were always reaching and fixing. It was hard to believe that tiny figure could burn enough fuel to maintain her constant pace, especially in one so old and in such a cool building, scantily dressed in her usual undyed wool shift. Yet, there she sat, happily kicking her bare feet in the icy water of the oyster pond.

"So tell me, how goes it with your First Boy?" Caith asked with a crinkling grin. "Are you here for your oysters?"

"No, not yet." Rishana laughed, as she sat on the floor, beside Caith. "It's much too early, as you well know. I came to bring you milk and eggs, and get some honey."

Caith wiped her hands on a cloth and cupped her tiny, calloused fingers around Rishana's chin, turning the younger one's face in this direction and that, with a strong, probing touch. Her age-yellowed eyes searched for the signs. "Mmm… Yes… Soon." She let go of Rishana and returned to her work. "I know the batch of oysters I'll give you. Sweet tasting, some with small pearls, others large. Yes, soon."

Rishana didn't question that Caith could read her face and see in it what she herself didn't fully know. Much like a farmer knowing that a crop was ready by the sweet smell of the morning breeze.

"But there's something else," Caith said. "Tell me. What's happened?"

Rishana could have taken the question to refer to any of a number of things, but she knew Caith well enough to understand what she was asking. "I ran into Kiv on the way here."

"Oh?" Caith placed the oyster she was seeding back into the pond and didn't pick up another. "What did she say to upset you?"

Rishana shrugged, not fully comfortable in examining what it was about Kiv that had made her feel off balance. "Mostly, she was giving voice to unsettling ideas I've had in my darker moments."

Caith's eyes locked on Rishana's as forcibly as the gnarled fingers that had left indents in her face. "Such as?"

"Kiv questions the manner in which we respond to the Mwertik. She says we're in a dangerous rut and need to consider new ways of thinking about them. She seems to be advocating becoming more aggressive." Rishana shivered. "What's most unnerving is that her ideas make sense."

Caith nodded, releasing Rishana's gaze with a sigh that could have been one of disappointment or satisfaction. Perhaps it was a mixture of both. She reached into the water for another oyster, pried it open slightly and inserted a grain of sand.

"Kiv has one of the brightest minds in The Valley, and when she brings her intelligence to bear on important matters, her arguments can be quite compelling."

"So, you agree with her?"

"I agree that the Mwertik are a terrifying force that require new kinds of thinking. But have you noticed that Kiv's ideas aren't new?" Caith continued seeding oysters, placing the completed ones in the water to her left, taking new ones from her right.

"Still, she's right. The Mwertik must be stopped."

"Yes."

"How?"

"Give yourself time to consider it. This winter may offer insights of a kind you never expected."

"Caith, do you think Jared was killed because the Peace — the way we keep the Peace — has failed?"

"I don't know enough about the circumstances of Jared's death. Neither do you."

Yet again, her mind reeled at the image of Jared carried home to her from the Red Mountains, with those grisly runes carved into his flesh. "He left to hunt a white antelope for Eli's betrothal feast. I couldn't persuade him to not go. After all his Alleman missions, to be ambushed and killed on a needless hunt. I'll never understand how… why…."

"I know, child. It's never easy to understand when we lose someone to violence."

"Irrational violence, that's what Kiv called it."

"So it is."

"She said that's our mistake, trying to meet irrational violence with rational talk. According to her, that turns us into sheep grazing happily while our people are slaughtered."

"Then we must find an answer that counters the irrationality while remaining rational."

"So, you don't agree with Kiv?"

"When you've outlived as many crises as I have, you learn to sit back and consider all implications before rushing headlong into rash action."

"What if we don't have the luxury of time, Caith?"

"Time is all any of us have. Over the next few months and for the rest of your years, you will hear plans and possibilities from every corner of our Valley. Each will try to win you over with her strength and wisdom."

"But these ideas of Kiv's… I am drawn to them, as much as I cringe at the thought. The idea of destroying the butchers who murdered Jared, who threaten our very existence."

"Yes, retribution is a heady temptation, but one that has no end once the spiral of violence begins. Would you so easily relinquish all that the Alleshi have fought for and forged over the centuries?"

"No, of course, not." Rishana decided that she was probably letting the combination of Kiv's cleverly seductive arguments and the unresolved tensions of her Season unnerve her.

"So, Rishana, tell me of your boy. It's Mistral's son, isn't it?"

"Yes."

Caith shook her head slowly, almost sadly. "Have you ever wondered why a woman would mate outwards, into a village so new to the Peace?"

"His father *is* an Alleman."

"But there's just so much we can teach. A man belongs first to his people, then to us. He'll not stray far from what he learned at his mother's breast and his father's knee."

"Caith, how can you say that? You have given your life to the Alleshine Peace. Do you no longer believe in what we do here?"

"I, more than anyone here in The Valley, have seen the changes we've wrought. But it's a slow process. No one man can make the full transition for his people. It takes time... son following father, grandfather and father's grandfather. Your boy's people are highly skilled at what they know. Hunting and tracking. But they're so new to the Peace, and still have a great deal to learn about the wider world. No, your boy's mother made an unusual choice, to leave the more fully civilized Reen for the Birani. Interesting tensions in that family have formed your boy. It's important to keep that in mind as you work with him; it'll help you through the ordeal ahead."

"I will," Rishana promised.

"Oh, don't be so serious all the time, child." Grinning mischievously, Caith got up, wiped her hands and feet, and slipped on her sandals. "I know what I'll do. I'll keep sending surprises for your boy, things he's never seen. Have to keep them guessing, you know."

Caith circled slowly, as though she could see through the walls and gaze on all that filled the multitude of shelves, pools and rooms. Then she stopped and pointed to a nearby pond. "Did you notice the beautiful sea bass the Hauks sent us? I'd wager your boy has never had anything of its like, landbound as his people are. I'll prepare one and leave it in your coldhouse tomorrow."

Rishana hugged the tiny woman, "It's perfect. Thank you."

She waved off the young Allesha's exuberant appreciation. "That's why I'm here. Caretaker is what I am, all I am. But I haven't forgotten what it's like, though generations have passed through this Valley since my last Season."

For a moment, the old woman seemed lost in memories that brought an even wider smile to her face. "Now, on with you. I've work to do." Caith reached up to take hold of Rishana's chin with her bony fingers again and searched the young Allesha's face once more. "Yes, and you've got work ahead of you, too."

After their farewell embrace, Caith started to walk away but stopped and looked back. "Remember, Rishana, I'm here, will always be here, if anything about your Season or The Valley upsets you.

Outside, the first snow of the season was falling thickly. The paths were already covered, with drifts forming where the wind blew them. The air tasted of childhood joy when Rishana lifted her head to the sky and stuck out her tongue to capture individual flakes. Looking back behind her, she saw her own footprints in the snow, where none had been before, and was sorry she couldn't fly or glide — anything to not mar the flawless perfection of her First Season's first snow. She bent down for a handful of snow and, throwing it into the air, ran through it. She didn't stop until she reached Dara's house.

Chapter 25

Out of breath, but rosy cheeked and exhilarated, Rishana/Tayar shouted through Dara/Le'a's front inner doorway, "Le'a! Boy! Come! Hurry!"

The boy burst into the greeting room from the kitchen, with Le'a behind him. "What's wrong?" he asked.

"Nothing's wrong. Look outside. Isn't it beautiful? How can you stand to stay inside? It's snowing!"

Le'a parted the curtain to look out. "So I see." Turning back to the young Allesha and her Winter Boy, she added, "But I'll enjoy the beauty from here, where I can stay warm and dry."

"Oh, Le'a, don't pretend you don't love it," Tayar teased.

"Go ahead, both of you." Le'a said to the boy, "If your Allesha wants to play in the snow, there's no avoiding it."

Tayar grabbed the boy's left hand, before his right arm was in his cloak. Jerked off balance, he stumbled out the door while trying to finish putting on his cloak and wave goodbye to Le'a, all at the same time.

"Hey, give a fella a chance, will you?" He pulled his hand out of hers. "I'll be with you in a minute, but how can I button up with you pulling at me?"

"Oh, don't be such an old stiff. A little snow never hurt anyone." Giggling, Tayar stuffed a snowball down the front of his shirt and ran, before he could react.

"Hey!" He sprinted after her, unsuccessfully dodging the soft, loosely packed snowballs that she threw. One landed squarely on his cheek, stinging his flesh with the cold, then quickly melting. He gathered snowy ammunition of his own to pelt her back. The wind carried her laughter and his, as though it were part of the flakes that flew in their faces, covered the land and coated their clothes.

He had seen her run once before, in that beautiful leaping stride that had made her seem more part of the eladar herd than any hunter he had ever known. As graceful as she was, she was also fast. He was confident that he was faster, but she did have a head start. *Skies, what a woman!* He didn't catch up until he had her cornered just inside her own gate.

Seeing him so close, she squealed like a child and tried to avoid his grasp by moving this way and that, in spurts of speed and feints. He lunged at her, wrapping his arms around her hips, and flung her into a snow drift, where he held her down with his own body, while stuffing snow down her sweater. "Let's see how you like it," he growled.

Her protests were swallowed by her giggles. But that didn't stop her from filling her hands with snow and smooshing it onto his bare head. They were both laughing so hard they could hardly breathe.

Suddenly, everything changed when one of his snow-filled hands pushed once more into her sweater and lightly grazed her bare bosom. He could feel her shiver below him, as much from the touch of his hand as from the cold against her breast. Her hands still held snow on his head, but, now, she pulled him forward, their bodies crushing his hand on her breast. It was the first time she had kissed him as a woman kisses a man, without being drawn into it by him and his impatience. He felt nothing but her body, the heat of her lips and tongue, her wet breath on his face, her taut nipple under his fingers. The snow and chill wind didn't exist. The world did not extend any further than this moment, these few feet of earth and flesh.

Tayar's lips traced a trail of soft, gentle kisses, from his mouth to his ear, where her hot breath carried the whispered words "Come, meet me in the inner room." She rolled out from under him and walked to the house.

In his daze, he sat in the snow drift, watching her. She turned to look at him before entering the house. When she disappeared from sight, he jumped up to follow her.

Chapter 26

The boy went directly into his room and quickly peeled off his snow-sodden clothes, leaving them wherever they fell. Nude, he started toward the door to the inner room, but stopped. *What if I'm not supposed to be naked when I enter? Skies! They never told me the rules for the inner room.*

He picked up his clothes, but they were encrusted with melting snow. So he hung them on the backs of various pieces of furniture, wiped down his body with a thick, large towel, and put on fresh underpants, trousers and shirt. *Bare feet would probably be okay. Wouldn't they?* He rubbed his chin, trying to decide, and realized he needed to shave. In his rush, he nicked his face several times, which meant he had to waste even more time stanching the blood. *Damn, what if she changes her mind while she's waiting for me? But there's nothing sexy about a bloody face. Should have left the stubble where it was.*

He checked himself in a mirror, raked his hair into place with his fingers, blew a breath into his hand to make sure there was no bad odor, then turned the brass doorknob, which was no longer locked against him. His heart thudded in his throat. He opened the inner room door and stared into a black emptiness, illuminated only here and there by dots of flickering candles. Water splashed ahead and to his right.

When his eyes grew slightly more accustomed to the dark, he saw her sitting in a small pool. Her face, shoulders and the upper swell of her breasts caught the candlelight, which seemed to glow from within her. As much as he tried to focus his gaze, the swirling dark water obscured the rest of her body.

Only when he heard her call to him softly, "Come, please close the door and join me," did he realize that he'd been gawking, stock still in the doorway. Pulling the door closed behind him, he stepped forward, and his foot sank into a deep, soft weave that covered the floor. A moist warmth enveloped him, gentler than that of a steamhut. He moved slowly, as in a dream.

The room was strangely shaped, with no corners or edges,

almost like a bowl, with the pool at the bottom. Everything was smooth and curved, covered with thick carpet, including the walls. Not even the floor was flat, reaching upward, not in a straight line, but like foothills, raised here and there in gentle undulations. The walls were a continuous curve of the floor. Surrounding the small oval pool was the only hard surface, an area of mottled stone that was cool to his bare feet.

The woman raised her arm out of the water toward him, offering him her hand. In so doing, one breast rose out of the water, though the nipple was still tantalizingly just below the surface, almost, but not quite, visible.

"Come, the water is warm and delicious." Her voice was a soft lilt, beckoning.

He started to step into the pool, but was stopped by her small gentle laugh.

"In your clothes is fine. But I think you'd be more comfortable without them."

Suddenly, he felt shy, uncertain how to undress in front of this woman. Tayar tactfully turned away, gliding to the other side of the small pool, where she poured fragrant oil from an amber vial into the water. He quickly stripped off his clothes and stepped into the warm water, to sit on a submerged ledge that followed the curved contours of the edge. Only then did she turn around again.

They perched on opposite sides, so close that if he straightened his leg outward, his toes would touch hers. But it felt to him as though an ocean separated them, held as he was by the awe of the moment, the fear of finding it to be only a dream.

Tayar reached behind her for two bottles and poured oil and soap into her palm. Then she rubbed her hands together and, with her eyes closed, slowly lathered her neck, shoulders and arms.

He watched her every movement, entranced, drawn to her through the warm swirling waist-high water, until he stood a breath away from her. He raised his hands to touch hers, riding the movement of her fingers and palms on her soapy, slippery flesh. When she reached for him, he massaged the lather into her shoulders, working his way downward to her breasts, fingering the tight, tall nipples, transfixed by the contours and textures filling his hands.

He quivered at her touch on his waist, chest, hips. When her hand grazed his stiff shaft, the shivers turned to unrelenting convulsions. His hands squeezed her breast, in rhythm with an inner pulse that, for that brief moment, became his total and involuntary focus.

It was over so quickly that he had reason to hope she hadn't noticed. After all, everything below his waist was under the dark water, and her eyes were still closed. He decided to proceed as if nothing had happened. *My stick's never failed me before,* he reasoned. *In a few minutes, it'll be as tall as ever.*

He continued to fondle her breasts, unlike any he'd ever touched. Small, but full, more oval than round, so soft and yielding in the cup of his hand. Her fingertips played the full length of his body, slowly climbing in gentle, feathery circles, raising bumps of pleasure wherever she touched.

Could this sensuous, submissive woman be the same controlling, obstructive Allesha who had frustrated him so*? Hell, who cares? She's mine now,* he thought to himself as he lifted her into his arms, stepped onto the ledge and out of the pond. Slipping slightly on the wet stone floor, he carried her across to the nearest cushioned platform and laid her down, with only a bit of a bump to her head.

Her body under his was a warm, inviting softness; her mouth, neck and breasts tasted windswept, musky, like an approaching autumn storm. With one hand, he gently pried her legs apart and entered her. Each time their wet bodies collided, he felt a fiery spark of lightning shoot from his groin up the full length of his spine. But he resisted giving into the ecstatic sensations that pricked every nerve in his body. *No, wait!* he told himself. *Wait for her. Wait, wait, not yet!* Even when he felt her shiver of pleasure, he held back, with a stringently rigid focus. It was her sigh, so throaty and dark, that broke his control, in sharp, penetrating tremors that squeezed everything he was into the narrow, piercing *now, now, now!*

Finally and fully spent, he collapsed on her, showering her with kisses, because women like such attention, though he would have preferred to turn over and fall asleep. He rolled onto his side and pulled her into his arms, against his chest. *There,* he thought, *now she knows how good she's got it for the next few months.*

They lay there for some time, in silence. It was the quiet that he couldn't take. Women like to talk afterwards, especially when the sex has been good. *Damn her. Do I have to do everything myself?* Teetering between languid comfort and a growing uncertainty, he finally broke the silence with a single word. "Well?"

"Very nice."

"Nice?" He bolted upright, to sit several feet away from her, with his back against one of the upward curves that formed the sides of the plateau. "Don't do that. I know what I felt. You enjoyed it."

She leaned back against her elbows. "Yes, you gave me pleasure."

"And it was great, right?"

"It was so nice that I was inspired. I now know your name — Dov."

"Dov? Does it have a meaning?"

"Of course it does. That's what names are for. In fact, it has many meanings. In one region, it's the spirit of the brown bear, playful and powerful, dangerous and protective. Elsewhere, it's a messenger bird that flies high and wide. I've heard that it's also used to describe the act of prayer, of hope. And it's a word of action, meaning to delve deeply, to dig into the earth or into people, to reach for the essence of a moment, a movement or a place."

"All that in one name?

"You deserve no less."

"Yeah? That's pretty good, *Tayar*." He lay down and pulled her once more into his chest. "Thank you."

Satisfied and depleted, he closed his eyes in anticipation of the deep sleep that always came after sex. How wonderful it felt to hold her. Her breasts pressed against his ribs, the nipples neither relaxed nor fully rigid. Her breath on his chest hairs was like a gentle summer breeze that barely stirs the tall grass. Her skin was cool to his touch, which surprised him, because he had built up such a sweat. Something about it bothered him. The more he tried to focus on what it was, the itchier his mind became, unsettled and unfocused. Fragments of ideas flitted like a swarm of gnats, biting him over and over again, but moving too fast for him to grab hold of them. Exasperated, he pulled himself out from under her cuddling embrace, to sit up once more. The Allesha sat opposite him, watching, but saying nothing.

He said the first thing that came to his lips. "This is all wrong."

"In what way, Dov?"

"I don't know. It just is." He shifted uneasily, searching the room, for the thoughts that eluded him. "It seems that... I mean, I feel strange, jittery, like before sex, not after. Not in my body. That's satisfied. But deep in my stomach or my mind." He swallowed his words into himself, needing to hold himself back from saying too much.

"Please tell me. What's bothering you?"

"It's like when you're hunting alone in the forest, and you've made your first kill. It could be a fine beast, plenty of meat, good skin.

You should be satisfied. But your instincts tell you that the mother of all beasts is just around the bend or over the hill. You want to rest, enjoy the kill, but something inside you won't let you." He balled his right hand into a fist and pummeled the ground. "Damn it! I know it's nonsense, but I can't shake the feeling. Stupid, huh? I mean, this is the inner room. I'm here. And, Great Mother, you're one hell of a woman."

"I think I know what you mean," Tayar responded. "Ever since you came to our Valley, you've believed that gaining entrance to this room would be the climax, the culmination of a great life experience. To some extent, you're disappointed that the sex has been, well, ordinary. Not unlike your previous encounters with women."

"Look, I wasn't saying…"

"Don't worry, Dov, I'm not insulted, because you're correct. It was somewhat ordinary."

"Hold on there. Don't you go turning this thing around on me," he protested.

"Oh no, Dov. Believe me, I'm not. You must understand that today is only a beginning, not a climax. So it's good that you're not yet satisfied. It proves how perceptive you are and that you are, indeed, an excellent candidate for Alleman."

"Well, that's okay, then. As long as you don't go blaming me for ordinary sex. Now come here and let me remind you how unordinary it is."

Tayar obeyed, realizing that he needed reassurance. He wrapped his arms around her, kissing and caressing her, with all the callow skill of his young life, as they slid together into a prone position. Then, balancing his weight on his arms and knees, he entered her, deliberately, almost excruciatingly slowly.

It might have been exquisite, if she hadn't known that he was motivated more by pride than tenderness. She turned from such thoughts, burying them to be attended to at some appropriate later time. For now, she gathered all her energy from her mind and heart, her memories and hopes, and focused it onto her pearl, and his erection inside her. Her determination drowned out everything but the slow, gentle stroke that, only then, began to ignite into a tense tightening of flesh. Once again, the boy seized on her slight frisson of pleasure as a signal that he had proven himself, and his methodical gentleness was suddenly supplanted by the hammering, reasonless imperative of his orgasm.

Tayar swallowed her frustration, cautious to remain more

Allesha than woman. On an imaginary slate behind her eyes, she jotted memory aids, to ease her frustration and turn it to purpose. *He'll learn, though he doesn't yet realize how much he does not know. He'll learn, because he must, because he can. And none of it is for my sake, though there may be pleasure to be had.* She focused on the throbbing, unrequited waves, willing them away, down to her thighs and legs, to dissipate before they reached her knees. *No, not for my sake, but for him, for the man he will become, and for his wife, his people, our Peace.*

Calmed by the rhetoric and mnemonic ritual she turned outward, to rest her thoughts where they belonged, on her Winter Boy. She listened to the deep breathing that wasn't quite a snore, setting her pulse to his inhales and exhales. Soon, she fell asleep.

Chapter 27

Dov awoke in tar-black darkness, to the sublime discovery that his hand cupped a warm, pliable, willing breast. Memories of where he was, of the events of yesterday, of making love to an Allesha, his Allesha, washed over him.

The inner room!

His palm rode the rise and fall of her sleep, buoyed by her beating breast. Was his hand too heavy, pressing her flesh? She didn't seem aware of it. In fact, she continued to sleep, her breaths steady and deep. He eased some of the weight of his hand, lifting it slightly, slowly. Amazingly, her nipple seemed to be drawn upward, stretching tall to maintain contact with his hand. He gently grazed the nipple, barely touching it, gliding his palm over it, feeling it become hard, delighting in her unconscious responsiveness. She was so vulnerable, yet all trusting, all his. If he knew where the candles were, he would light one, to see her face. Did she smile in her sleep? In the dark of the inner room, so much deeper than even a starless night, only his imagination could answer that question. His imagination and his hands.

Wanting to hold her closer, to feel the full length of her body against his, but hesitant to pull her inward for fear of waking her, he carefully encircled her head with his other arm. She turned to snuggle to him, apparently still asleep. He caressed her, devouring the feel of her body under his fingertips, filling his arms, pressing against his groin and chest, entangled in his legs. Her thighs parted when his fingers reached for her nether lips, and her mouth answered his when he kissed her.

Uncertain whether she slept or woke, wondering whether it mattered, he listened to her heavy breathing. Her body was ready; it wanted him. But should he be doing these things to a sleeping woman? To a sleeping Allesha? He hesitated only briefly. Then her tongue darted to play on his lips, as she reached out to pull his body closer, opening her legs to give him entry.

She moved under him, not a woman asleep, but one fully and ravenously aware. Their gasps of pleasure broke the silence, building to his quick, explosive orgasm.

Once more they lay quietly, wrapped in each other's arms. She was the first to break away, quickly standing and speaking in a voice too lively for any morning, but especially too much in control for one such as this.

"Sweet day, Dov. Thank you for a very nice awakening." Her voice traveled away from him in the darkness. How could she move around the many obstacles of the dark inner room, with no candles or lamps? "I'm going to bathe and dress. I'll meet you in the kitchen for breakfast." Dazzling sunlight flew into the inner room when she opened the door to her bedroom, which she left slightly ajar, illuminating the way to his own room.

Dov washed and dressed quickly, curious to discover what the new day would bring. Now that he had finally entered the inner room, everything would have different. But how?

Pausing at the kitchen door, he took a steadying breath and struck an attitude. How well he knew the importance of a first meeting on a morning after. Head tall, shoulders wide and chest out, he strode into the kitchen with pride and confidence, ready to be appreciated.

The room was empty.

Damn that woman! Couldn't she do what I expect, just once?

He stood in the middle of the kitchen, uncertain what to do. Should he go back to his room and wait?

Hell, I could stay there all morning until she comes looking for me, worried, sorry to be without me.

But his stomach rumbled with hunger.

The icebox was brimming with more food than an entire family could need and a wider variety than any region of villages could fathom. He gnawed on a chicken leg and downed several gulps from a red clay milk jug. When he heard the thud of a greeting room door, muffled by the walls, he tossed the chicken leg into the icebox, and slammed it shut. He wiped his mouth with the back of his hand, and his hands on his trousers.

When Tayar entered, he was sitting at the table, trying hard to not show anything but his well-rehearsed pose of powerful manhood. He turned to gaze at her, paused, then honored her with his ever-so-effective, quiet-but-earnest smile that he knew accentuated the dimple on his chin.

"Good morning, Dov."

She sparkled, not just her eyes, but her entire body. To look at her was to feel alive. He didn't even mind that she seemed unaffected by his practiced bearing, though he'd known women to melt when he'd favored them with such a look.

In midstride, Tayar leaned down to kiss him, so lightly that he almost didn't feel it. "I'm starved. What shall we have?" she asked, motioning for him to follow her. Peering into the icebox, she moved containers aside to see what was behind. She piled food into his arms, then filled her own. She gestured for him to put everything on the counter, then handed him a knife. "Please chop the fruit into bite-sized pieces."

Dov obeyed without thinking.

While she measured and mixed flour, eggs, and milk, with bits of this and drops of that, she chattered, almost like a young girl. Could it be like a girl in love? She did seem to have blossomed since yesterday morning. Her luscious auburn hair flowed, cascading from a thin pink ribbon tied in a small bow at the crown of her head. Her cheeks were flushed. With pleasure? Delight? Sex? Even her movements were lighter, her voice more spritely.

Could I have done this to her?

Suddenly, Dov realized that her voice had stopped. He searched his mind for her last words, but could only remember the upward lilt.

That's it. She's asked me a question.

How could he admit that he hadn't been listening to her, that her lovely voice was like background music to him? She'd be angry for certain and that would spoil everything.

"Fried fruit cakes," she said. "They're like breakfast flatcakes, but filled with fresh or preserved fruit. Oh, names are so different among our villages, but the ideas and food are often quite similar. Are you sure you've never had them?"

"Oh, yeah." He sighed with relief. "But we call them berrybakes and have them only for special occasions."

"What more special occasion could there be than this morning?"

"Well, yeah... I mean, of course!" Damn! Why was it that ever since she had walked into the kitchen, he'd felt breathless, awkward? But moments before that, there'd been no doubt in his mind or body, only the residual tingle of her flesh against his, the sure knowledge of his prowess. He chopped the fruit more ferociously, angry with himself, but unable to be angry with her. Not when she looked so beautiful and vibrant, transformed by his touch into this glowing, happy creature.

He dropped the knife on the counter, wrapped his left arm around her shoulders and started to reach for her chin with his other hand, to show her with a kiss just how special the occasion was.

"Careful!" She protested, as her bowl wobbled on the counter and almost spilled.

He jerked away from her, picked up the knife and resumed his chopping.

"Dov, please. You surprised me, that's all, and I didn't want to drop the bowl. Oh, don't turn from me. I like surprises, at least one as pleasant as that. Please give me another kiss."

Not her words, but the sound of them, the throaty melody of a mischievous giggle, pulled his heart to her, lightening it, lifting from it burdens he didn't even know he carried except for the sense of relief at their absence.

Her kiss tasted of laughter: fresh, playful and generous.

He stirred the fruit into the batter while she greased a hot griddle. The fragrance of sausages sizzling and berrybakes frying was too tempting to resist. She dangled a half-cooked fruit cake into his mouth, then bit off a juicy portion before it disappeared completely. Their lips met and lingered.

"Mmm, that's great!" he said.

"What? The fried cake or my lips?"

"Your lips, of course."

Tayar slapped at his chest. "You rogue. Do you think so little of my cooking?"

"Hey, wait; what would you have done if I said that it was the berrybakes?"

"I would have reprimanded you for thinking of anything but my lips, of course."

"So whatever I could've said would've been wrong. There's no way I could win."

"But, Dov, think about it. There's no way you could lose." With a flourish, she flipped the fruit cakes onto dishes. They sat down to breakfast, remembering to put aside choice pieces for their offering, then hungrily devoured the rest.

"You're not an easy woman to predict," he said.

"Good."

Dov waited for her to continue, but all she did was sip some juice. "That's what I'm saying. What does 'Good' mean?"

Taking another bite of berrycake, Tayar closed her eyes, focusing on the flavors. She swallowed and opened her eyes. "That I liked what you were saying."

Why couldn't she just speak clearly?

"Actually, it was more than your words," she said. "How do I explain?" Tayar put down her fork. "You were telling me that I'm full of surprises. I can interpret that in many ways, all of which are pleasing to me. That I engage your mind, make you think and question, am challenging. Great! So it should be whenever you deal with another. That you are feeling confused, off balance? Well, we did just have sex. I'd be disappointed if it were otherwise, if you were thoroughly clear-headed." She paused, then added, "Though, now that I think of it, sex can sometimes be a great whetting stone for the mind, but we're not at that stage yet."

"Okay, okay." He waved his fork in a reflexive gesture of dismissal, uncomfortable with having the morning turn yet again to lessons. Then he used the fork to spear a sausage and put it, whole, into his mouth.

"So, Dov, what are you are thinking? About the weather, our plans for today, the inner room, the fruit cakes?"

Unable to answer with his mouth stuffed, he quickly swallowed.

"Please take your time. I wouldn't want that sausage to get lodged in your throat."

Dov was amazed at how the sound of her voice, the vibration of humor and sex that filled the spaces between the words, seemed to change their meaning. In that breath of a moment, what he would have taken as a criticism or insult from anyone else, baiting him to take offence and crouch within himself, readying an attack… Well, somehow, Tayar made it feel more like an intimate touch, like when a woman bends her knees to make it easier to enter her. He didn't understand how she did that. It made him feel confused, unfocused.

They ate in silence for a few bites. Then, in a less challenging, more everyday tone that had just a twinkle of mischief, she asked, "Have you looked outside this morning, Dov? It's beautiful, all blue and white, with silver glints."

He turned toward the sunshine streaming through the window above the sink. "Yeah, nice day. The snow's piled high, though."

"Yes, exactly," she said.

"Okay, I get it, we've got some shoveling to do." *Why couldn't she just come out and say it, directly, without trying to sound like a Storyteller? She's got some work for me to do. I knew that was part of the bargain.*

"Yes, that, too. In fact, I think we should first go to dig out Le'a."

"Sure. I guess she's too old to take care of it herself."

"Oh, don't underestimate our Le'a. I just thought it would be pleasant to surprise her. Wouldn't it be fun traipsing through the high snow to get to her house? First snow always brings out the child in me."

"Well, I know I love playing in the snow with you." He used a deeper, modulated tone, hoping it was suggestive, seductive. But it seemed to have no effect on her.

"Great! Then that's settled. We'll go right after washing the breakfast dishes and tending to the animals. We can do our other chores when we get back."

He didn't know what else to do or say, so he concentrated on his plate, attacking the remainder of his meal. He was surprised when she didn't fill the quiet with more questions or lessons or plans.

Tayar got up and began clearing the table. When he didn't move to help, she glanced at him briefly. It was enough of a cue to lift him from his seat and into their after meal routine.

After the dishes were washed, Dov reached up to put away the last pan onto a top shelf when Tayar kissed his cheek. "Dov, dear, I'm going to feed the goats and chickens, and then change into proper clothes for shoveling snow. I'll meet you outside in about a half hour."

She was gone from the room before he could think of a response.

Chapter 28

Dov paced outside the house, kicking snow out of his way.

What started as a playful nothing, a release of excess energy, grew with each kick into a focus of frustration, a building fury that the soft flakes denied. A hard wet snow would have been more to his liking, resisting with a weight that clumped and thumped and echoed his anger, which seemed to surge from nowhere, go nowhere.

How could the morning have gone so wrong, especially after last night? Damn that woman! She doesn't know how to relax, to bend with the flow. Where's the soft yielding of a woman won?

She's just too old, he decided, *too set in her ways. It takes a young woman, like Lilla.*

How wondrous the first time with Lilla had been, in that pile of autumn leaves. Her sighs and surrender of will to his, the change from skittish virgin to full-blossomed, pliant woman, for the touch of his hands, his lips, his stick. The two had become one. But that went wrong, too. Lilla had sent him away, to this valley of sex witches.

No. He refused to believe it was Lilla. *It was her damn mother!*

So, for the sake of one old woman, he had to wait out here in the snow for another old woman.

Not that it was all bad, he had to admit. *Last night was...* He couldn't think of words to describe the delights of the inner room. *And I got to her. I know I did.*

Of course! That's the problem. I got to an Allesha. She lost control, and it was only our first night. Poor old thing. How embarrassed she must be. I'll have to be more gentle with her until she learns to be comfortable with the idea of being mastered so easily.

Continuing to pace the furrow of snow that he had plowed with his boots, the boy had found one reassuring thought among the jumble. He surveyed his surroundings for the first time, seeing the wintry transformation of The Valley. Dotting the white landscape were other boys and their Alleshi. They were too far away for him to see much more than their silhouettes.

Was that boy down the lane Sim? The height, bulk and carriage seemed right, but it was hard to tell. Ryl hoped Sim had been Blessed. He deserved it, like none of the other boys, certainly more than that wimp Aidan.

Ryl couldn't imagine Aidan in the inner room; probably wouldn't even know what to do. *His Allesha has her work cut out for her, unlike mine. Mine can just lie back and enjoy herself. I bet mine is wondering who blessed who, right now.*

He heard the door close behind him. Turning, he caught Tayar by the waist and lifted up into the air.

"Dov!" she squealed in mid-giggle as she hung there against the blue sky above his head.

He silenced her with a kiss as he pulled her into his arms, letting her feet touch the solid ground. Satisfied with the impact he'd made, he began to withdraw, but she pressed deeper into his body, while gently teasing his lower lip with her tongue. He felt dizzy, breathless and, once again, uncertain.

She's old, but what skill! Maybe, she does have a few things to teach me.

She spoke first, with a much calmer voice than he had expected or hoped to hear. "Phew, Dov, you certainly know how to greet a woman! Come, let's get our shovels from the barn. There's work to be done and fun to be had."

Could there be any more vivid picture of pleasure than my Allesha in the snow? he wondered as he sprinted after her.

On the walk to Le'a's, they played and chatted and stamped a path through the snow. She knew the problems were just below the surface, ready to erupt. But for the moment, Dov had turned his mind to life beyond his own skin, giving her the freedom to enjoy the brisk, clean day.

She lowered her shovel to the walk some distance from Le'a's, clearing the common path along the way. The boy followed her example. While she plowed and threw off the top half of the snow, he followed behind, scooping up the bottom layer.

Soon, Tayar began humming, as she usually did when she worked. Recognizing the tune, Dov added his voice to hers with a counter-rhythm that lifted the song in pace and tone. Her hum and his "ta, ta, ta's" blended in the cold air as puffs of energy that raised their spirits. When they reached Le'a's gate, they stood face to face, leaning on their stilled shovels as she hummed and he ta-ta'd a full cycle of the melody.

"Hurrah!" Le'a called from the doorway, clapping her gloved hands while slogging toward them, slowed by the snow and her heavy boots. "Thank you for the serenade. What a joyous greeting on such a beautiful day!"

"Hello, Le'a," they called back.

The two embraced the one, each in turn.

"I was just coming out to clear my walks."

"We're going to do them for you," the boy said. "So you can go inside, stay warm."

"What! And miss the fun? I'll have the pleasure of your company, and the work will be finished that much sooner. Here," Le'a said to the boy, "give me your shovel and get another from the barn."

When he was out of earshot, she grinned. "Well?" she asked.

"How did you know?"

"Because it was time. And I knew you knew it, by the way you had called us out to see the snow yesterday."

"Yes, it was time. And you were right about him. He does have some surprises in his manners and ways. But he knows almost nothing about a woman's body and little more about his own. And he's so tiring. Always testing, posing, prodding."

"That's why he's here, and why we gave him to you."

"I understand that now. But you'll have to forgive me if I continue to have uncertainties."

"There's nothing to forgive. You will be a formidable Allesha."

"Formidable? I don't like the sound of that."

"Shush, he's returning."

The boy found the two women shoveling side by side, with big smiles plastered on their faces. He had no doubt what they had been talking about.

She's told the old woman about last night and how good I am.

The three shoveled close to one another for a while, but in the pattern of paths, they separated: Tayar to the left, Le'a and the boy to the right.

"I enjoyed your singing." Le'a said to the boy. "Was it a song you know from the Birani, or did your Allesha teach it to you?"

"I know the tune, but I bet it doesn't have the same words as hers." He grinned mischievously. "It's a games song we use to taunt and trip up the other guy."

"In my region, our young people participate in very different kinds of games. We play in teams to strengthen our bond, and for the fun of it."

"Le'a, I guess I should have asked before, but I never thought about it. Who are your people?"

"My village is one of a confederation that rings the lakes about a thrity-day walk southeast from here. We're called the Terrali; those of my village are the Serterrali."

"What's a confederation?"

"During the Great Chaos, when war ruled our lands, and there were no Alleshi in this Valley or anywhere, some villages banded together for mutual protection." Le'a spoke between exertions, after she had tossed the snow on her shovel toward the side of the path, before bending to dig up some more. In the silences between, she sometimes grunted, but otherwise didn't show any of the strain he expected in one so old.

"When the wars ended, the union was already forged," she continued. "Now we are one people, living in five different villages, sharing what we have with one another."

"How is it ruled? If there are all these villages acting like one, who's the headman?"

"We have no headmen, only councils. Councils within our villages and a council of the confederation. The men and women of our councils debate and discuss any problems or concerns — often quite vociferously and, yes, sometimes with contention. However, when more than half agree to the form and substance of a plan, it's affirmed by all."

Dov shook his head in wonder at such inefficient and leaderless leadership. "You can be darn certain nobody argues with my grandpa, once he's made a declaration."

"Yes, that has long been the way of the Birani. Yet, when your father becomes headman, perhaps it will change."

"You don't know my pa—" He suddenly stopped, his tongue tripping over the realization that this woman had been to his father as Tayar was to him.

"Knowing your father as I do, I'm certain he'll welcome the day when his people will question the headman's authority and share in some of the decisions. Maybe you'll be the first to do so."

"That's right! I'll be an Alleman, too. He'll have to listen to me."

"He has always listened to you." She turned to touch his hand. "Your father loves you."

"Love is one thing. Listening is another."

"Yes, that's true. I'm glad you understand. It's important to listen carefully."

The path they had been shoveling now diverged into two. Le'a took the left fork, but when he followed her, she turned to him. "No, I think it will go more quickly if we separate."

"But the heavy parts…"

"If you hadn't come, I would have shoveled all of it. I can handle this one small length by myself. Up ahead, it converges with the one Tayar is clearing, and she'll help me for a while. Okay?"

"Sure, it's your back. Just don't break it."

"Thank you for your concern."

On their way back from Le'a's, Dov was surprised at how much of the common paths had been shoveled in a few hours. Even some of the walks surrounding his Allesha's home had been cleared in their absence. They lowered their shovels to clear the rest of her property. Working side by side, they talked.

"I guess you and Le'a aren't the only ones who enjoy working in the snow," he commented.

"It's the way of our Valley to take and give pleasure."

"Yeah, but I wasn't talking about *that*."

"About pleasure? Oh — you thought I was referring to sex." Tayar thought for a moment, then tossed a handful of snow into the air. "Snow falling onto a path can be beautiful and great fun. But it's also a responsibility, a weight to move out of the way. Does that diminish the essential joy of being out on a crisp winter day?"

He hated being cornered with questions that had no answers — at least none that made sense to him. "Is this still about the snow, about how everyone got out and shoveled, not only their own paths, but the common ones and others? You seem to be saying more than your words."

Tayar hugged him, then continued shoveling.

"What was that for?" He couldn't shake the feeling that she was trying to push him to do or say something.

"I do enjoy your mind sometimes. I know it is just the beginning, but you will be a true Alleman, listening to what a person really means, and not just his or her words."

He wanted to enjoy the moment, to accept what, on the surface, could be taken as a compliment. But he felt that damn cocoon descending again, separating him from her, from everything around him. "Le'a was talking about listening, too. Is this a continuation of some lesson she told you to give me?"

She stopped shoveling and faced him. "Dov, please don't do that."

He saw the warning in her eyes, and readied for her attack. "Do what?" he demanded.

"No, Le'a did not instruct me to discuss this with you. We — you and I — were simply talking while we worked, and I was enjoying being with you. But then you had to put a stop to it by challenging my purpose. Please learn to accept my friendship for what it is."

"Yeah, something that I'll be paying for the rest of my life," he mumbled.

She threw her shovel into a snowdrift and stormed toward her house, yelling into the wind so that he had to strain to hear her words. "I don't want to be with you right now. If you're smart, you'll stay out here until you understand what you've just ruined."

Glowering at her back, he attacked the snow with his shovel, tossing it this way and that into a mess of drifts.

Damn these women! Damn 'em! Damn 'em!

She watched him from her kitchen window. It was important that he try to understand what had happened, to learn from the experience. Of course, she knew he'd remain reactive for weeks. But such flashes of conflict, controlled carefully, would give seed to new ideas for him to consider and, eventually, become.

She could read his anger and confusion from the way he ravaged the snow. When it turned to stubborn resolve, she knew it was safe to leave him out there alone while she took care of the house and barn. She couldn't depend on his help with the chores today. There would be too much relationship work to do, which would, in its own natural way, end in the inner room. She began cleaning, starting in the kitchen, moving into her bedroom, and finishing in the inner room. Perhaps she applied more power to her mop and cloths than was necessary, but it felt good, a release of pent-up sexual tension not quite satisfied by a boy who had a lot to learn.

When the Dov/Ryl finished the walks around his Allesha's house and barn, his simmering anger still had not dissipated. So he moved over to common grounds. Le'a had warned him not to stray, but they couldn't object to his doing some extra work. Besides, he was tired of having those women control his every minute.

Turning a corner, he saw a boy who was also alone, bending his back to a shovel, in front of a house just across the way. He watched the other fellow for a few moments. When he stood up to straighten his back,

Ryl could distinguish the details of the dark face surrounded by tight black curls. It *was* Sim.

Ryl dropped his shovel, packed a snowball and threw it while running toward the other boy.

Sim jumped at the impact of the snow, but when he saw who had sent it flying, he grinned.

"Sim!" Ryl called out.

"Ryl," he answered through a hearty laugh. But after a short banter of punches and snowballs, Sim became quite serious. "Hey, we aren't supposed to be out here together. I'm pretty sure it's against code."

"Who the hell cares?"

"I do."

"Sim, you always were a wimp."

"Ryl, I know you don't mean that. My Allesha is teaching me about—"

"Yeah, how about those lessons? Not bad, are they? How long did it take you to get into that inner room of hers?"

Sim studied his friend.

"Hey, what are you staring at? Oh, I get it, she's still holding out on you, isn't she?"

"Ryl, it's good to see you, but I think I should go back to my Allesha now." Sim picked up his shovel and started to walk away. "I'll look forward to seeing you at the end of our Season."

"Hey, wait. Look, Sim, these paths need shoveling. That's why you're out here, right?"

Sim hesitated. "Yes."

"Me, too. So, if they need shoveling, and if it would cut our work in half, we might as well do it together, right?" Ryl wasn't sure why, but he definitely didn't want Sim to walk away just yet. "They couldn't mean that we're supposed to shirk our duties, just because we happen to see each other. Could they?"

"It doesn't sound logical, but—"

"Good." Ryl rushed to pick up his shovel and bent his back to the snow, before Sim could disagree. Sim, too, resumed shoveling, not noticing that Ryl was plowing a rather narrow swathe, to close the gap between them more quickly. When they were within speaking distance, Ryl asked, "So, how goes your Season?"

"Fine."

"You're in her inner room, aren't you?"

"I don't think we—"

"Well, maybe you need some pointers. First, you've got to pick a really good name for her."

Sim stopped shoveling. "Look, Ryl, you can't keep talking about our Alleshi and our Season. It's private, sacred."

"What the hell are you yapping about? I was just trying to help you."

"Ryl, I don't need your help just now, not about this. Maybe later, when we're both Allemen. But not now. I've worked too hard to get here to mess up on a lark." He turned to go, but glanced back to say, "Ryl, it really has been good to see you. I wish you well in your Season." Then he walked away.

"Hey, wait, Sim. Look, I didn't mean that about you always being a wimp. You were the only one at the inn that I could talk to. So you see, I'm trying to apologize. Can't you turn around and look at me?"

Sim stopped and looked back.

"They confound a man, these Alleshi, worse than any woman I've ever known."

"That's because they're not any woman; they're Every Woman."

"I didn't expect to hear that blather from you."

"Ryl, I'm not part of your Season. I'm not supposed to tell you anything, but I can say that the Every Woman is very real, not just something we've been told."

"Yeah. Well, goodbye, Sim. It was good to see you."

"Goodbye, Ryl. I hope you're happier when I see you next."

Happier? What did he mean by that? Of course I'm happy. I've punctured one of the sacred Every Women.

Ryl watched Sim walk toward a barn with a corral. Sim climbed over the fence to join his Allesha as she tended several ponies. The two of them embraced like true lovers, clasping with their full bodies. Somehow, it was also the way true friends greet, in delight and well-being. How he could see all that in one motion, he wasn't sure. But he did know that it was something he'd never experienced.

He swung his shovel onto his shoulder and proceeded back to his Allesha's house, where he could only hope to be welcomed as Sim was. But then, Ryl had never heard of anyone who didn't like Sim.

That's it. Sim's Allesha actually likes her Winter Boy. Does mine?

Chapter 29

Just before dinnertime, Tayar and Dov met in the kitchen, entering from opposite sides at nearly the same moment. She walked in from the mudroom; he came through the greeting room. Unsure of what to say, how to behave, the boy was torn between a pose of anger and his need to smooth the way back to the inner room.

Tayar greeted him formally, but warmly, with her hands on his shoulders, her lips to his cheeks, lingering longer than customary on each side, to breathe welcome to his ears. "Good evening, Dov."

She seemed different somehow — different from the morning, and definitely from last night. No less desirable, but less festive, more like a woman in her own kitchen than a girl at a hunt celebration. She was quiet and soft, wearing a calf-length, amber-colored dress that flowed and clung, hinting at the shape below the gossamer. Her hair fell free, curls reaching to her breast. Was this the same woman who chased eladar with the long gait of a wild animal, or the woman who teased and played with the impish skill of the best lover he'd ever had? The same woman who flared into burning anger at a single misspoken phrase? Every time he began to believe he knew what to expect on greeting her, she changed.

They prepared their meal together — he cautious, tentative — she quiet and thoughtful. Even her voice was lower, calmer, parceling out words without rhythm or tone. Tayar asked him no questions, only flat-toned requests to chop this or pour that. The boy obeyed, not knowing what else to do.

When they sat at their meal, she reached out both hands to touch his and said, "Let us be gentle tonight and speak only kind words." Then she sealed the request with a smile.

There was nothing for him to do but nod and be silent. However, conversation with his Allesha at meals had become so natural that he yearned to find gentle, kind words — whatever that meant — to fill the empty air between them.

Eventually, Tayar eased an opening through the silence. "I enjoyed working in the snow today. I hope you did, too," she said. "I looked out the window and saw all you accomplished. Thank you."

"You're welcome."

"How far did you go? Certainly further than I could see from my bedroom. Though I did glimpse another boy working in the same area."

Damn, she saw us. Gentle and kind... does that mean honest, too? But if she already knows, then honesty is the only possibility for fixing it.

"Yeah, well, I ran into Sim, a fellow I met on the caravan coming here. We didn't go looking for each other. It's just that we were shoveling the same paths. Sim was really worried that we shouldn't be working together. But I told him we needed to get the job done. Damn, am I in trouble again? If I am, then it's stupid. I didn't do anything wrong... really."

"Well, Dov, it isn't considered proper for two boys to meet and talk during their Season... at least not until the Service Days. And you did stray into paths where you don't belong. However, as you described it, the circumstances do seem unusual and not likely to be repeated. Am I correct in believing that it won't be repeated?"

"If that's what you want, sure. But what are Service Days?"

"Near the end of our winter together, you will spend time with other Blessed Boys and Allemen, learning more about our Peace and what must be done to keep it. It's a transition period that will lead directly to your apprenticeship and the forming of your Triad. But it won't be only talk. You'll help with whatever needs to be done to prepare The Valley for spring."

"Work, you mean."

"Yes, but fun, too."

"You seem to think that all work is fun."

"It can be, especially if you're working side by side with someone you like."

The way she looked at him just then, he realized she was talking about him, about liking him. Somehow it changed everything, though he didn't fully understand how.

The opportunity was too good to let slip away. "I like you, too, Tayar," he said, deepening his voice and focusing all the sexual energy he could into his eyes, then letting them flow over her body.

She appeared not to notice. "Thank you, Dov. That's nice to know. Now, let's talk about other things, to sweeten our meal." She took a bite of chicken. "Tell me of winter in your village."

"Judging by today, our winters are milder. Sure, we have snow that has to be cleared, to make it easier for women, children and the old to move around. But in the forest, we let our footprints make the paths."

"What do your people do with their winter days and evenings?"

"Folks spend more time around the home hearths visiting and talking, telling stories and practicing skills. Ma and the women do lots of weaving and sewing and stuff. They expect us — the kids — to give longer hours to reading books and doing lessons. The men do more governing business, so Pa is usually pretty busy during the long evenings. When he's there, that is. In the deepest winter, if he's made it home, he's stuck with us and can't go off on his Alleman missions. But it's a safer time, too, because no one comes from outside. Even the Mwertik Zalogs seem to burrow." He pictured the crowds of people that always pressed around him during the cold months. "Somehow, I get into more trouble in the winter."

"Oh?"

"I don't know why it happens. Anytime things go wrong, they come looking for me… especially Pa." He shrugged. "I can feel them watching me, cornering me, and before I realize it, I've screwed up again." He stared at his plate, pushing the remnants of food with his fork. Almost under his breath, he added, "Like this afternoon."

Tayar realized it was probably as close to an apology as he was capable of giving right now. She accepted it without acknowledging it, knowing she wouldn't accomplish anything by bringing things to a head tonight.

When she got up and started clearing the table, he stood and pulled her into his arms. They remained locked together for the length of a deep kiss, during which she carefully held plates in the air behind his head. She briefly considered letting one drop to the floor, to give the boy an even greater sense of potency, but decided against it. They were pretty dishes she'd be sorry to see smashed.

When he released her, she breathed a "thank you, sweet Dov," into his lips, but didn't move from the spot where he had anchored her. Instead, she hung there, motionless, apparently transfixed by his kiss. But if he didn't take the plates from her soon, she'd have to break the effectiveness of the moment to put them down.

Lifting the dishes out of her hands, he said in a soft, gentle tone, "Come, Tayar, let's finish in here. The sooner the dishes are done, the sooner we can return to the inner room."

"Yes, Dov," she answered demurely.

They cleaned the kitchen together, with quiet sighs and the "accidental" pressing of thighs. When the last dish had been dried and the food put away, he placed his hands on her shoulders, turned her to face him and kissed her, and then lifted her into his arms. He carried her from the kitchen, through the greeting room and his bedroom, into the inner room.

It wasn't a smooth or uneventful jaunt. More than once, her arm or head or foot banged into a door jam or brushed a wall, though she suppressed any reaction. A boy this untutored would not react well to laughter, she realized. So she kept her natural sense of humor in check.

In the inner room, he lowered her onto one of the platforms — thankfully, one well covered with cushions. He fell on top of her, pressing his lips to hers, his tongue into her mouth, his hands working to spread the material of her dress, so that he could cup her left breast.

Imagining herself as a girl with her first love helped transport her into an intoxicated state of desire. The throaty ache in her voice wasn't entirely contrived when she whispered to the boy, "Please help me take off our clothes." She refrained from adding that she didn't want him tearing her dress.

With awkward fumbling, they removed each other's clothes. He climbed on top of her again, touched her nether lips with his fingertips to feel their moistness, gently pried her knees apart, then entered her with a probing, anxious impatience unlike anything she could remember since her adolescent sexual experiments. She expected him to erupt immediately and prepared herself to protect him from embarrassment. However, even now, he worked to hold back his own orgasm, knowing that hers must come first. So she entered a deeper meditation, focusing on him pressing into her, accidentally rubbing her pearl, parting her nether lips with each thrust. Even though he didn't have much skill, she could appreciate the sexual power in this boy, power to be enjoyed as well as trained. The beginning of her initial orgasm ignited his. When it was over, he rolled off her and pulled her head into the pit of his arm, cradling her body with his.

She breathed quickly, in rhythm with the sharp, almost painful convulsions of unappeased sex that washed down her legs and up over her stomach. Willfully, she slowed her breathing, reaching for the strength she knew was buried deep in her lungs. Soon, the aching waves faded, replaced by a heightened resolve to teach this boy how to read a woman and a body's desires.

It will be just a few more days, she reminded herself. *Only a few more days of passive acceptance, until this boy is ready to learn. Then the real fun will begin.*

Chapter 30

Several days passed almost entirely in the inner room. If their mealtimes were erratic, the boy and his Allesha certainly didn't starve, eating when their stomachs' demands were more insistent than those of his young libido. Dishes were washed when no clean dishes were left. Little else required immediate cleaning, since they spent most of their time wearing little or no clothing, not disrupting their bedrooms, visiting their bathrooms on need, but not long enough to create more than a barely noticeable mess.

Soon the lessons would begin in earnest. But for these few days, Dov needed to establish himself within the domain of the inner room, to weld a bond with his Allesha that wouldn't break at the first pressure.

Tayar waited patiently. Not that she didn't have pleasure — small ones in learning his ways and patterns; more momentous ones in realizing that she did, indeed, have the skill to be the Allesha she'd been trained to be. Occasionally, the sex was enjoyable, just as the tickle of a feather on the bottom of your foot can be pleasurable. But far from fully satisfying.

In the early afternoon of the sixth day since they had first entered the inner room, Dov and Tayar emerged into a deep blue day. Surprisingly, even the boy acknowledged that the shimmering brightness outside was more enticing — for the moment — than the inner room. Besides, it was time to anoint themselves with creams, to soothe away the rawness that almost constant sex had rubbed.

Tayar saw that the candle in the gatepost lantern was lit. After dressing quickly and grabbing a woolen shawl from its vestibule hook, she went out to retrieve the note that Le'a/Dara had anchored under the lantern. Yes, she nodded to herself as she read, their mentor was correct. It was time to move on to the next stage. She called out to the boy, who was still dressing in his room, "Dov, Le'a is here, in the barn. I'm going out to help her. Come join us when you're ready."

Tayar/Rishana ran to the barn, as much for the pleasure of the open air after days of being enclosed in the darkness of the inner room, as for her excitement at seeing Dara and the prospect of having an adult conversation. She called, "Le'a!" before she reached the barn, and was rewarded by the sight of the older woman in the doorway, waving in greeting. Rishana threw herself into an embrace with Dara that would have unearthed any other woman less rooted in strength and weight.

"Rishana, you knock the breath from my lungs!"

"Sorry, Dara. I'm just so glad to see you."

"Yes, dear, I know. Shall we go inside where the boy won't see or overhear us talking about it?"

They sat together in the hay pile, near the back of the barn, asking after each other's health and well-being, waiting for Rishana to catch her breath and her thoughts.

"Dara, it's all such a jumble. The boy, the inner room, the childishness that erupts into surprising insights. I feel so frustrated, so in need of release. I want to just run at full gait until I'm so tired that I can't think or feel."

"You know the problem, of course. He didn't leave you alone at all these past few days, did he?"

"But how can I get away from him during this stage?"

"You can't, or I should say, you couldn't. Now we move on. You'll be relieved to know that was the worst part of working with a problem boy. Oh, you'll have days of confrontation and days of fire, but nothing is more difficult than holding yourself totally passive, to prepare him for what's to come." Dara reached over to massage the younger woman's neck and shoulders. "Yes, the tension is severe, but the worst is over."

At the sound of the barn door opening, the women moved farther apart. Dara/Le'a called to the boy, "We're over here, Dov, in the back."

He collapsed into the hay next to his Allesha, so their bodies touched casually, as lovers' bodies do, even in public. "Hi, Le'a. She been telling you about it?"

"Well, actually, we've been talking about other business that was important for your Allesha to know."

"Like what?" Leaning back on his elbows, Dov stretched to his full length and chewed on a piece of straw. Even in this position, his leg sought the warm of his Allesha's thigh.

"Dov, you know that some matters are strictly Alleshine. Let's not belabor a fruitless question. Tell me, how have you been?"

"I'm great, as though she didn't tell you."

"Good. Well, as you can see, the chickens and goats are fine for today. I expect that the two of you can tend to them from now on."

"The animals!" The boy turned to his Allesha. "Tayar, how could we have forgotten about them?" He seemed genuinely concerned.

Both Tayar and Le'a started to respond, but the younger woman allowed her mentor to reassure the boy. "Dov, I've been here every day, as Tayar knew I would be. Do you think she could neglect any creature that needs her care, regardless of how involved she is with you?"

"No," he brushed his hand along Tayar's arm. "She couldn't hurt anyone or anything. Can you believe it, I once thought her a hard woman? I didn't know her then, didn't understand what was under the surface."

"You do now?" Le'a asked.

"Yeah, of course. I mean, look at her. She's beautiful and soft."

"I wouldn't use the word soft to describe our Tayar."

"Hey!" Tayar playfully threw a handful of hay at Dov and Le'a; pieces fell into their hair and on their clothes. "It isn't courteous to talk about me as though I'm not here."

"Then Tayar, my dear, why don't you leave us alone, so Dov and I may talk freely. I'm sure you have matters that could keep you busy for, let us say, the rest of the afternoon. And please, take the eggs and milk from over there. I have more than enough from the past few days."

"Yes, Le'a." The young Allesha tried to not display her joy at being released from her responsibilities for a short while. Instead, she walked at a steady pace, picking up the basket of eggs and jug of goat's milk in midstride, without looking back. She put the eggs and milk into the kitchen icebox and then retired to her bedroom.

She stood in the center of her room, quietly pensive. *First, a pleasure meditation, then some vigorous exercises, and finally a centering meditation. The remainder of the afternoon should be just enough, if I time it correctly.*

"Come," Le'a said to the boy, "Walk me home. I've missed you."

As much as the boy didn't want to leave his Allesha and their inner room, he knew it would be a losing endeavor to disagree with Le'a. She wanted to talk to him, and talk she would. "I've missed you, too."

They brushed the straw from their own clothes and hair; Dov pulled an errant piece from behind Le'a's right ear. Standing face to face, he saw in her eyes the truth of what he had just said. "I really did miss you, but I didn't know it at the time. It doesn't make sense, does it?"

"Yes, Dov, it does. And thank you."

When they left the barn, a wind blew a blush to their cheeks. It was a clean chill that tingled their skin rather than cut to the bones. Le'a stood still, drawing the cool air deep into her lungs. It lasted longer than the boy thought natural, but then nothing seemed natural in the way she stood with her eyes closed and her body slightly swaying with the breeze.

"Delicious," she sighed before opening her eyes again. "Dov, try it. Take a slow, deep breath and hold it."

He began to protest, but the way she said, "Oh, go ahead and try it. It feels wonderful," seemed to be as much of a challenge as it was a promise. He decided to follow her lead and see where it took him.

"Good. Yes, but don't gulp the air. Sip it instead, to taste its subtle nectar. Now do you see it?"

"See what?" His eyes flew open, and he looked for whatever it was that he was supposed to see.

"Everyone sees something different, but it's always a welcome experience. Try it again."

He repeated the exercise, though a bit quicker than before. "There, are you happy?"

"I will be, when you are."

The two of them set off for Le'a's house. Even more snow had been piled up on either side since Dov and Tayar had shoveled the path.

"You don't get it, do you? I am happy, very happy. Everything's great, now that I'm in her inner room." He didn't mean to raise his voice, but skies! Who was she to tell him what he thought, how he felt?

"It's one of the things we hope to teach you... the ability to experience a newer, heightened level of happiness whenever life presents the opportunity."

"Every time you women talk, you tell a man something different. First, it's that leadership stuff and the Peace. Then... well, always... it's the sex. I remember one of you talking about teaching me to understand what isn't there, or something. And, oh, yeah, relationships too. Now you say it's to learn how to be happy."

"Please continue. I'm not certain I know what you are asking."

"It's just that you keep changing the *why* of me being here. Or is it that you don't want to tell me the whole of it? So you give out dribs and drabs of promises that you know I'd want, to keep me... to keep all the boys here, and all the villages within the Peace... in your control?

"That's quite an accusation."

"What? No, I didn't mean it that way, not as an accusation or insult. It's just that... Oh, I don't know. The rules seem to keep changing."

"As they always will, if you live your life well. That, too, we will help you learn."

The boy shook his head in frustration.

"Dov, do you know the difference between the reactive and the thoughtful?

"Is this another lesson?"

"No, it's the same one. But your response is an example of the reactive. Dov, think of it this way… You know the woods and its wildlife. All fine creatures, but they're reactive. Animals can't think out their responses. They seldom explore new, possibly more productive behavior, unless it's in reaction to stimuli. Only Man can be thoughtful."

"Look, it isn't that I'm not trying to understand, but I don't know what you're talking about."

"You will."

"You know, I might have missed you, Le'a, but I didn't miss you always saying, 'you will.'"

"You will. Miss it, I mean."

The anger that lived at the root of Dov's tongue started to boil forward. But the old Allesha smiled so broadly that he found himself laughing with her instead, because it felt better than arguing. Their laughter carried them through the rest of their walk, all the way to her front gate.

Le'a was truly enjoying the boy, not merely for who he was and had to become, but for himself. While it wasn't a surprise — not after the years of Seasons she had given to problem boys — with this particular boy, it was a bit distracting and could become perilous, if she weren't careful. But as long as she was aware of the dangers of such affection, she felt she could allow herself to take pleasure in small moments, while maintaining control over larger issues.

"Come inside, Dov. Let's have some tea and visit."

While she prepared the tea, the boy found the cookies where they always were and put a plateful on the table. When the water was hot, they sat, and she poured. Then she concentrated on enjoying her tea and cookie, giving the boy the space to take initiative. The quiet lasted for several sips of tea and half a cookie.

"Le'a… that stuff about reactive and thoughtful responses… I didn't understand what you were getting at, but you seemed to think it's important. Why? What's so important about it?"

"It's what keeps our Peace."

"How?"

"Our peoples are a varied group, with different needs and interests. When regions responded to each other reactively, we had wars. Generations of killing, conquest and subjugation which resulted in victims' anger and victors' pride, which led to even more war."

"You're talking about the Before Times."

"Yes."

"Please go on. I like stories about the Before Times."

"Many boys do. They're filled with adventure and uncertainty… things that the young find exciting."

"Are you saying something's wrong with liking the stories?"

"Not at all. They help us remember how destructive the Great Chaos was for all those centuries, before our Peace took root. Only by remembering can we hope to avoid the pitfalls of hate that outsiders try to use to destroy us. Even as we combat their hate, even if we must war with them, we must remember. Otherwise, though we may win battles, we will irrevocably lose our Peace."

"So how does all this relate to the other thing? The reactive stuff?" Dov reached for another cookie.

"When village leaders learned to be thoughtful rather than reactive, our Peace began to take root, as a reality that we could depend on to last and grow. It became necessary to teach more and more villages the way to Peace, to widen our borders and counter threats from beyond. And yes, to extend the blessings of the Peace as far as possible, not only for our future, but for theirs, too."

"So, being reactive… it's about war?"

"Only partially." Le'a sipped the last of her tea. "We can continue this conversation another time; I have another matter to discuss with you. Dov, do you remember what the word Allesha means?"

"Sure. Every Woman."

"Exactly, an Allesha is an Every Woman, because each Allesha must be every woman."

"That doesn't make sense."

"It will."

Le'a rose from the table, put her cup and plate into the sink, then turned to the boy who stood to hand her the rest of their dishes. After a ritual embrace, she said, "Now, it's time for you to return to your Allesha, your Every Woman. Remember to treat her well at all times, whichever woman she is." Then, having dismissed the boy, she proceeded with the washing.

Dov started to leave, but at the kitchen doorway looked back and said, "You know, Le'a, you are an interesting woman, but sometimes you're illogical. I guess that's just part of having a woman's mind. Still, I like being with you. And don't worry, Tayar is safe with me."

Le'a's hands were in the sink, so her back was to him when she said, "I'm pleased to hear that. Goodbye, Dov. I will look forward to seeing you again tomorrow."

"I'll try, but if she has me in the inner room all day again, I might not be able to make it. Bye."

She resisted the urge to go to a front window to watch him walk through the new falling snow on his way back to his Allesha's home. The early darkness of the winter afternoon would soon swallow him anyway.

Instead, she continued to wash and dry her dishes, then clean her kitchen, finding what activity she could in the mundane, knowing none of it would drown out the inevitable, or her part in it. What would happen, had to happen. No regrets for the innocence that would soon be shattered could change any of it.

So it must be. But I will miss the child once he becomes the Alleman we need.

Chapter 31

Tayar's front door was closed.

They had warned Dov never to enter an Allesha's house when the outer doors were shut. But they couldn't possibly mean that he should stay out here in the cold, night-black late afternoon, waiting for her to remember to open the door for him. Still, what if he ignored the closed door and walked right in, as was his privilege to do in his Allesha's house, at least for the next few months? Would that be one of the offenses Le'a had cautioned him about? Would simply going through a closed front door slam shut the door to the inner room?

Dov walked around the house, looking into windows, though most had drapes and plants obscuring anything but a corner here, a slit of corridor there. What little he could see showed no sign of Tayar. Even the open views into the mudroom and the kitchen didn't help; she was in neither.

Steeling himself to stomp through the closed outer door that should never have been closed to him, he was almost more sorry than surprised to find it was now open.

In the vestibule, he considered leaving his dirty boots on. She deserved mud on her floors. *But*, he realized, *I'd be the one who'd have to clean it. Besides, better to keep her happy.*

Stocking-footed, he entered the greeting room, started toward the kitchen, remembered that it was empty, turned toward his room, but knew she wouldn't be there. So he stood in the middle of the greeting room and called out. "Tayar! Hello!"

She came from her bedroom, flushed with happiness at the sound of his voice, or so it seemed to him. "Dov, welcome home!" She walked into his arms, with that full-body embrace of hers that pressed all the life her flesh held, giving it fully to him. Her lips, too, gave all, filling his mouth with the taste and delight of her.

Tayar took his hand, pulling him through the kitchen door, and continued to hold it as they sat down at the table. "How was your visit with Le'a?"

"Okay, I guess, but I missed you."

"That's sweet."

"Did you miss me?"

"Naturally. I felt the silence of the house. When you're here, you fill it completely. Even when we're in separate rooms, I feel your presence."

"Is that the same as missing me?" he asked.

"What do you think?"

Dov didn't have an answer ready on his tongue. *Of course she missed me. See how she fondles my hand. But why didn't she just say it? Could it be that she was happy to be without me?*

Tayar watched Dov's face as she might her kitchen window, where she would witness the changing of the weather from sunshine to thunderheads. His eyes were beginning to cloud over again. Not wanting to invoke his anger, she directed the conversation elsewhere. "The past few days we've ignored our duties; we can't let that continue. Today is nearly gone. But tomorrow, I'd like to be sure that we care for the chickens and goats, and do our other chores, as we had before. I'd also like to go back to having real meals and not just snacks. Tonight, let's prepare a proper supper."

"Then back into the inner room, right?"

"I do miss our reading… curling up with a warm fire in the hearth, and a story to be shared. Please, would you give me that gift, that we return to reading to each other in the evening?"

"And then back into the inner room?"

"Yes, after we read, we'll return to the inner room." Tayar smiled a quiet seduction to reassure the boy that sex was still his for the taking, though paced according to a reestablished schedule of days and hours. "Now let's get supper. I'm famished." She got up and went to the icebox.

"I've never known a woman who loved food as much as you do," he said as he followed her.

"Thank you."

"Was that a compliment? I mean, most women don't like to be thought of as having big appetites."

"Oh, I don't know about that. It's another part of my passion for life. Be careful, my dear Dov, of women or men who can't take joy in food. If they haven't learned that one fundamental pleasure, I don't trust them to have or understand other important passions and generosities."

"Is everything a lesson to you?"

"No. Well, perhaps so, now that you mention it. Life is a lesson to be learned and lived, isn't it? I don't know if I would enjoy life so much if there weren't the possibility of new knowledge or understanding in every next moment."

When they began to eat, the Allesha slipped off her right slipper and reached under his trouser leg with her bare toes. Dov reacted clumsily to this new kind of touch. Within the time it took him to look up from his plate, he dropped his fork with a clatter, bumped his glass and caught it before it spilled. A protest started to form on his lips, but she countered with a sparkle of girlish mischief. It opened something within, a quiet thing that lit him up from inside. For that moment, which lasted only a few heartbeats, she saw the signs of the boy's center beginning to shift, ever so slowly, away from the self to the other. Just as quickly, it was gone.

"Tayar." He used a deep chest voice, suffused with sexual overtones.

"Yes, Dov." *Why does he have to always be so serious about it? He must learn to play, to tease, to laugh at himself.*

He reached for her hand and tried to pull her out of her chair. "I'm not that hungry. Are you?"

She remained rooted in her seat, with her toes playing with his leg. "What do you think? Of course I'm hungry. And so are you. We've hardly started our meal, and it's scrumptious." She filled a fork with meat and sauce and held it out to him. "Here, taste this."

"I'd rather taste you."

"But the one doesn't preclude the other. In fact, learning to relish flavors and textures will heighten sexual pleasure. Here." She held the fork out to him again. But when he reached for it, she pulled it away. "Close your eyes, and try to sense by smell when the fork is near. Now breathe in deeply, through your mouth, as though you're sipping the air."

He opened his eyes. "Hey, that's what Le'a said!"

"Yes, she enjoys this, too. Now close your eyes and sip the fragrancies of the meat and sauce. Taste the air. Separate out the different spices, the many flavors in the one approaching bite. When you sense that the fork is near, open your mouth, so that I may place the food on your tongue."

He did as she instructed.

"But don't chew it; roll it about," Tayar directed. "Each part of your tongue can experience different flavors. Now bite once, to release more flavor. Ah, yes, you feel it, don't you?"

He wasn't sure what he was supposed to feel other than the quiet of the moment, the close warmth of her voice, but he bent his head to a single slight nod, his eyes still closed.

"Now, chew your food slowly, feeling it flow to all areas of your mouth."

The layered flavors separated and exploded. Dov sighed, "Wow!"

"When you're ready, swallow."

Dov felt calm, yet excited. But not the excitement of heartbeats and quick breaths. More like the elation of a mountaintop sunrise. Tayar placed another forkful into his mouth, this time of salad, with its intermingling of different textures and tastes.

When he opened his eyes again, he saw his Allesha watching him. It felt different than her other looks, though he didn't understand how or why. "What?" he asked.

She caressed his fingers with the lightest stroke. "Don't look for explanations right now, Dov. Let's just enjoy our meal together, like this."

Leaving her hand still on his, she closed her eyes and placed a small portion of meat and sauce on her own tongue, rolling it, tasting it fully, experiencing the heightening of all senses that radiated from her mouth. She then opened her eyes.

He watched her, this achingly beautiful woman who seemed to be waiting so patiently that he felt she could wait forever, connected to him by their fingertips, the air they breathed, the food they savored, all becoming an essence of something else. "Tayar, is this it, the thing that the Alleshi do, that make them worshipped?"

"Not worshipped. We are — I am — merely a vessel of knowledge and experience from which you may drink deeply, to learn, to grow, to discover the delights of our world together, as you discovered the true taste of meat and salad just now."

Dov shook his head. "I'm not sure that's right, Tayar. I mean, it's more than what you say, isn't it?"

"Yes, much more, but then our winter has only begun."

Chapter 32

After awakening the boy's senses during their supper, the Allesha anticipated difficulty in persuading him to delay entering the inner room. But it was time to move onto the next stage. "What will you read to me tonight?" she asked as she settled into a corner of the sofa.

"It's your turn." He threw himself into the armchair, with a brusque energy that might have made less sturdy furniture creak.

"Is it, really? I didn't remember. But then I've had some rather nice distractions since our last reading."

His position shifted slightly, to a less rigid posture.

"Dov, does it really matter whose turn it is? I have a yearning to hear your voice." And, she knew, she needed to give him some place to keep his hands, so that his mind might be the focus, to explore without the distractions of touch. "I want to close my eyes and see the world your words form for me."

"Like the food? You do that with sounds, too?"

"Oh yes, with sounds, smells, touch, anything you can sense. Especially a loved one's voice."

"A loved one's voice, huh? Well, sure, if you put it that way…" Dov stood to fetch *The Traveler's Tales* from a side table, then sat down on the other end of the sofa. Stretching his legs toward his Allesha, he opened the book to the page where they had put a slip of leather to mark where he had stopped previously.

Tayar folded her long body into the back cushions, rested her head on her arm and closed her eyes, ready to receive his story.

"This story is called *The Empty Land*," he said.

The Village at the End of the World knew not how to welcome strangers, for few came to them and none with good reason. Even in a world repeatedly ravaged by war, in which places of peace were scarce, no one chose to seek refuge in a far-off village that cared so little for life they could not find the passion to war ~ or to love.

Yet, there I journeyed, seeking an end. For this was in the early years of my travels, and my feet were faltering, weighed down as they were by how little I carried. No mate, no children, no kin, no hearth, all gone, all dead.

No inn nor open door offered hospice. Only young children would look at me as I passed, though they were quickly taken in hand and pulled away by the back-turned adults. Where my feet ceased, there I lay, tired and in pain, on stony earth that appeared unfenced, unclaimed.

Almost as soon as I put my head down, I felt the toe of a boot poking my side "Hey, you! Get up, get out of my field. You can't sleep here."

I raised my head to look at the cracked, parched soil. If field this ever were, it could no longer be. "What do you grow here?" I asked the sun-baked man who stood over me, still pushing with his toe.

"That's my concern, not yours. Get out of here."

"I have traveled far to be here, and I'm tired. I saw no place in the village where a room or bed might be had. Where can I sleep?"

"That's your concern, not mine. Get out of here."

Seeking a reprieve from the prodding boot that bruised the same rib over and over, I stood and saw that I was a head taller than the man. And as little food as I'd had for longer than I cared to remember, his skin was so thin over his jutting bones that I felt well fed in comparison.

His hands flew at my face, pushing his words at me, like small birds of prey circling their quarry. "Get out of here. Go back where you came from. We'll have no strangers in our midst."

"Well, I'll not stay where I am unwanted." I swung my pack onto my back and continued walking in the direction I had been headed before my feet had stopped.

"Hey, where do you think you're going? There's nothing out there."

"Nothing sounds good to me," I mumbled, knowing he would not expend the effort to stop me, except for the diversion of my discomfort.

"You crazy? Didn't you hear what I said? Why d'you think this place is called the End of the World? Only death is beyond that hill. It's the Empty Land."

The Empty Land. The name echoed the void inside me. So I kept walking.

Soon after I left the Village at the End of the World, the parched, packed soil became sand ~ dry, coarse, unresisting grains that slipped out from under my steps. That brown skeleton of a man was right about the emptiness. No green of plant or spark of life, no water or succulents, no scurrying animals or clouds in the sky. Only the grey sand that undulated in small, amorphous hillocks.

It was in that emptiness that I finally found peace, enough peace to *be ready to lie down and die, if only my feet would allow me to stop and rest. Sleep gradually descended upon me as I walked, so that I would fall in mid-step, only to be awakened again at dawn, when my legs had already begun pulling me forward.*

I knew not how long I had walked, except that I had licked the last drop of water from my flask some time before, and my body thirsted for what would not be. I was weary of life and knew death was near, and I welcomed it. That's when I heard her, though the sound of her singing seemed a thing of dreams or of my approaching end. So I ignored it. But when I saw her, sitting cross-legged on the next hilltop, my feet changed their direction to reach her.

She did not acknowledge my approach, didn't even turn to look at me when I sat a few hands breadth from her, though I felt the warmth of her body bend to me. She continued to sing, unlike any song I had ever heard. More a vibration that I felt deep in my chest, its pace changing too often to have shape. I wondered if it were a lack of rhythm or too many rhythms that defined it. And how could that deep, throbbing sound be coming from such a frail old woman?

When she finished her song, if song it was, she smiled and bowed to the empty space in front of her. Then she turned, smiled and bowed to me in the same reverent manner.

The silence that now hung in the air seemed somehow sacred, so I dared not break it. Instead, I sat and waited for her to speak. She did, but only some hours later, as the sun dipped to the far hill. During the interval between her strange song and her greeting, she stayed as still as the air, with her head bent toward the sand, watching something in the emptiness that I could not see, and smiling with such serenity that I ached to see what held her eyes.

"Welcome, Sister," she finally said, at the end of day's light. She stood, walked a few steps, and stopped to look back at me. "Welcome."

By her look and her greeting, I understood that she was inviting me to follow her. Some time later, she stopped in a hollow between two hills and sat cross-legged once more. She nodded to me to sit beside her. When I was settled, she raised her hands toward a grey, dry twig that stood in the sand before her and began to sing again.

Hearing the song from the beginning, as I now did, I could sense its elusive pattern, one that fit the undulating hills and shifting sands, ever changing, deep and vast. I closed my eyes as the throbbing of her song pulsed through my veins. When I felt her move beside me, I opened my eyes to see her digging at the bottom of the twig. I bent to help, though I did not know her purpose. Some lengths below the surface, the twig ended in a big round root. The woman shaved that root with a small knife and held the shavings in her hand.

"Lean back and open your mouth," she said, and I obeyed. To my surprise, when she tightened her hand into a fist, a sweet liquid ran into my mouth. She repeated the process ~ shaving the root and squeezing its sweet nectar over my mouth ~ until my thirst was satisfied. Somehow, the sharp edge of my hunger, also, was slaked. Then she drank her fill. She snapped tiny tendrils from the round root on which we chewed while she replanted the twig.

The moon was more full than new; I could see the woman's face clearly. Deep lines shaped her face, written with years of smiling that crinkled eyes, cheeks, chin and nose. Age had twisted the joints of her body, but not her back. She moved with grace, despite ~ or was it in harmony with? ~ her knotty joints. Her gnarled hands rested quietly in the bend of her crossed legs, drawing my mind to thoughts of productive toil, calluses earned, gentle touches, love given and received. Yet I felt no incongruity in finding her here in the middle of nowhere, apparently living in the Empty Land, beyond the End of the World.

The woman looked at me with the same serene smile that had glowed from her that afternoon, when she had spent hours watching the sand. Did she see in my face the questions that were forming? "Call me Alleen," she said.

The young Allesha opened her eyes in surprise at hearing the name, but resumed her pose before the boy noticed and could be pulled from the story.

"Alleen, I would give you a name to call me, but I have lost my names, back there in the world of villages, the world of war."
"I will call you Roen, for the song that called you here."
"It was a song unlike anything I've ever heard."
"Yes, it exists only here."
"Here in the Empty Land, or here in you?" I asked.
"You use the blind people's name for this place, and yet, did you not see how rich this land is?"
"I've seen sand and clear sky."
"And?"
"Nothing else, other than you and the water root you showed me."
I looked about the moonlit emptiness and wondered what she expected me to see.
"Then sleep, my child. We have a busy day beyond this night."

When I awoke the next morning, Alleen was gone. I followed her footsteps, which had not yet been filled in by the shifting sands, to find her sitting on a hilltop, as she had been the day before. Her head leaned to one side as though she were listening to something I could not hear. Then she nodded to the space in front of her and altered her gaze to an area of sand just downslope from her knees.

I sat beside her, copying her posture as closely as I could, and stared in the same direction. I saw nothing.

I did not believe her mad. Therefore, I reasoned, she must see something I could not or did not. I continued to imitate her pose and manner, looking where she looked, even controlling my breathing to match her rhythm. My lungs protested at first, unaccustomed to thoughtful breath, preferring independence rather than concurrence with any other living being. But there was peace in her rhythms, as there is in gliding along in a dance with a lover who follows a breeze-blown flute. Soon, I realized that her rhythms were the most natural, easiest breaths, filling my lungs as they needed air, expelling when it was time. I was no longer imitating, for to imitate is to impose something unnatural, belonging to another's way, onto your own.

We sat thus long enough for the sun to move halfway to its midday height. Yet the only thing I had seen was the play of light along the vast emptiness, as the sun searched out and, sometimes, stepped over the hills. But, there, just below us, I saw a movement that was not the play of light, though I had thought it so. It was the movement of sand, like a stream or rivulet, flowing from below our feet to join other currents crisscrossing the vast landscape. I watched in wonder the multitude of branching, converging, diverging currents of sand. I saw whirling rapids and peaceful pools, cataracts and sprays, tiny trickles and wide gorges ~ all of sand. Not grey sand, as I had originally thought, but so many colors that they could not be seen together without the eyes trying to blur them into something pale and easier to digest.

As the day before, I heard the vibration in my chest before my ears registered the song. It was the sound of the rivers of sand, flowing through the land, converging, diverging, whirling and pooling. And it was a song that had come out of my lungs, as I inhaled and exhaled, as I breathed the air of those eddies of sand, and felt myself become not a stone in the currents, but another rivulet carried over the land.

The many rhythms of the land reverberated in my chest and, as I recognized the counterbalance coming from my companion, the clarity of the song's form filled my heart with joy. Then another sound flew to my ears, so alien that I had forgotten its sweetness, for I had not heard my own laughter for far too long ~ not since before that burning day I last saw my birth village, when it had become an unrecognizable pile of rubble, a single large funeral pyre.

The tears came in the whirling eddies of my laughter, and Alleen held me. Her song changed subtly, no longer calling forth the land, but calling my sorrow out of the deep, dark hole where I had buried it. At first, she matched the rhythm of her song to my sobs, but that too changed, carrying me along with it, to something more like our sand-river rhythms. Soon, she had me turned outward, though still cradled against her. She pointed to the foot of our hill. "Look." Awe was in her voice. "Do you see who our song called forth?"

Drawn toward us in the currents of sand was a slash of black. But it was black in the same way that the sand was grey. A black that held gold and amber and other shimmering colors. When I saw that it was a large viper, I flinched, but Alleen held me still.

"Calm, child. He has come only for our song today. Tomorrow, he may be hungry, as we may be. But today, let us welcome him in the spirit of our beckoning."

Still holding my hand, she sat facing the snake as it approached. The vibrations of her song shaped a new rhythm, one that moved in slipping curves. The snake raised his head, so that he towered over her, and she bowed to him with reverence as she continued to sing his rhythms to him. He did not move to strike or to leave, but coiled back down in repose, listening, watching.

Her song changed yet again, adding some small, hopping rhythms to those of the snake and of the sand and of my laughter and tears. In the corner of my eye, I saw a tiny brown movement to my left, but could not turn to look, fearful of disturbing the snake. It was gone as quickly as it had come, then back again, on the right. Up again, its head popped out of the sand, between Alleen and me, hidden from the snake by our knees. It was a little mewmit, a cousin to those minor barnyard nuisances children so often befriend. It crawled out of its hole and stood upon its hind legs, cocked its small round mottled head to listen to her song, then curled up in the shadow of my thigh.

Every time Alleen added another rhythm to her song, another life was summoned and revealed itself. The song held them, all enemies to one another, in repose and wary peace, as at a watering hole. Creatures that crawled and dug, flew and hopped, slithered and pounced ~ each held by its own rhythm, as I was, cradled and soothed, cajoled and sustained.

One by one, Alleen released the creatures by slowing each individual rhythm until it faded and its creature withdrew. Eventually, only the *tiny mewmit remained, asleep against my thigh. Alleen took the mewmit in her cupped hands, blew a gentle breeze across its fur to awaken it, and remarkably, spit some of her own precious moisture into her palm just before the mewmit's nose, so it might drink. She lowered her hands to the sand, near the hole, and the mewmit scampered into it.*

When all had gone, Alleen bowed to the land and then to me. "I'm hungry, aren't you?" she said as she stood.

I realized that, yes, I was not only hungry, but drained. Her parting song had buoyed me so high that, when it ended, gravity and heat, hunger and thirst could no longer be held at bay. But more than that, the energy of all those rhythms, all those creatures, where life should not, could not be, had been a shock. So much life where I had sought only death. I was as weak as a newborn. Alleen helped me stand and supported my weight as we walked across a flat area to the bottom of another hill, where even in the midday sun we found some shade.

From a fold in her robe, she pulled out what looked like an old piece of dried leather. She cut it and handed me half. Grinding it with my teeth, I felt like a pre-tool primitive softening a hide. Tiny morsels broke off and mixed with what little saliva I had into a pungent sweetness not unlike dried fruit. However, my jaw was aching before my hunger was satisfied, and the effort seemed greater than the value of what little nourishment might be had from it. But Alleen appeared so content, so patient, relishing the flavors that she fought out of the toughness, that I chose again to imitate her, hoping to discover whatever it was she was feeling.

An hour, perhaps more, we chewed, swallowing what small flakes our teeth were able to separate from the whole. I soon understood that the answer was not to fight its resistance, but to work it with patience. My breathing slowed, making me realize how rushed, how tense it had been. And I felt the peace of the land, of Alleen, enter me, claim me, calm me and revive me.

In all that time, we hadn't spoken. At first, I was too drained. Then, too busy with chewing. But when no reason for silence was left, I did not know how to break it.

"Questions are always a good place to start," she said, as though she knew my thoughts. "But if your questions haven't found their form yet, perhaps you would like to start with your story."

"My story is drier than this land."

"And probably just as lively."

Her smile caught my heart as I realized how true her words were ~ about the land and about my life. They drew my thoughts together into a question, the first of many. If I were to point to any one moment when my life turned from the path where it had been pushed to a path of my own choosing, it would be the moment of that first question. "Yes, lively, where yesterday I saw only emptiness. How is it that you see, can call forth, what no one else knows to exist?"

"I look and listen."

Alleen said nothing else. Instead, she dug at the base of a tiny dry twig that I hadn't noticed. I guessed that it was probably another water-root plant.

I leaned over to help her dig. "How is it that you see and hear so much?"

"Take a deep breath. What do you smell?"

I shook my head, because I smelled nothing out of the ordinary.

"Now, go over there." She pointed to an area away from our shade. "Does it smell the same?"

I walked where she indicated. "I don't know. The taste of the air seems the same, but, well… it doesn't seem possible." I returned to the shade, where she continued to dig, and inhaled deeply "Could it be that the air is somehow weightier here than there?"

"Yes! That's the water we'll find here. I'm pleased you understand so quickly. You're ripe to learn."

My delight in her approval ignited something in me. I knew then that I wanted to learn, needed to learn all she had to teach.

"Yes, ripe and healthy. I called well yesterday when I called you to me. Soon I will be able to rest."

We had reached the root and she was crushing moisture into my upturned mouth before I could ask the questions that stirred in me. So she continued with her previous thought.

"This moisture isn't hidden by the sand if you can smell it out, if you know what twig marks its resting place. So it is with all life in this desert. I have learned to temper my senses ~ to see, smell, hear the small steps, feel the diverse vibrations of life ~ to awaken the wide spectrum of colors. It's all there, for anyone to discover."

Alleen reburied the root after we had both relieved our thirst. Then she beckoned for me to follow. At the top of yet another hill, we sat, and she gestured at the landscape that stretched to the horizon. "What do you see?" she asked.

"Sand and sky."

"And…?"

I struggled to find something, anything to describe to her. "Hills so small they look as though they were poured through a giant's hand."

"Go on."

"Well, I can see that the sand ripples like a lake. Even so, there is no breeze, but the air isn't still either. I can feel the slight pressure of it against my face"

"Yes! A good beginning, but there is so much more." She searched my face as she had the landscape, studying me. "Yes, you are ripe to learn, and I shall teach you."

At no point had she asked me whether I wanted to learn her secrets, her ways. Hers was a declaration of fact, of fate. For she knew and under-stood me, as she knew and understood the snake and mewmit. I obeyed her completely, placing myself, my new future into her care and guidance ~ though I had not known until that day that I had any future. My lessons began with the ease of breathing, with no preliminaries, no explanations, no pause between declaration and instruction.

"Sit here with me, as we were earlier. Today, let us silently seek out what our eyes may find. Or perhaps I have forgotten the measure of time for beginnings. Let us say that we will give the days yet to come to learn-ing to see. Now close your eyes to look inside yourself, to calm your heart."

I did as she instructed, and rested in the quiet for several breaths.

"Now, slowly, open your eyes and focus, look for the details, the life and beauty that surround you. See each grain of sand as separate from all else."

I kept the silence that she had commanded during our daylight vig-ils and tried to focus on individual grains of sand. But how can you see only one grain of sand, when so many uncounted grains fill your vision?

"Patience, child," she would tell me in the evenings. "This first les-son is the most difficult, but you make it more so. Don't struggle. Your eyes will find what your soul needs."

"But a single grain of sand, separate from all others?"

"Trust me, if you can't trust yourself. I know it is already there inside you to see the fullness of life."

I did trust her, almost unquestioningly, as a drowning man will not question a thrown rope. If I did not see, it must be in how I sought to see. So I changed my manner of focus. I did not look at the substance of the sand, but at the light and shadows that played upon it. Eventually, I saw light and shadow as the definition of sight, delineating shapes to my eye. I used the minute lines of shadow and saw them as boundaries of space between substance. So intent on this exercise was I that I did not realize until the end of that day that I was, indeed, seeing individual grains of sand. But more than that, I saw a minuscule hole ~ a small enlargement of shadow ~ where a tiny creature lived. I watched that hole until I saw a long spindly leg reach out and catch an even tinier insect for its supper. Then I returned to the wonder of shadow and light, of individual grains of sand, of the ecstasy of true sight.

That evening, I didn't need to tell Alleen of my discovery, my transformation. "You are ready to move on to the next lesson," she said. "Tomorrow, you will close your eyes and listen."

Listening was more difficult, because it was so restful. With my eyes looking only onto the red curtain of my lids, I often lost myself in a half-consciousness, akin to that warm, comforting haze that comes just before sleep.

After days of struggle, I no longer fought the haze and found, to my surprise, that I did not sleep. Instead, I rode the air that gently pressed on my inner ear, feeling it change timbre ever so slightly from time to time. When I tilted or turned my head, I could feel the shape of the sounds where the air curved over hills and rode over flat land unheeded. And there, in the far distance, I knew that a storm was forming, but I felt no fear of it, because I realized we would have ample warning from our ears and eyes, should it veer toward us.

So it was with my lessons of smell and taste, which were the same sensation. I learned to taste the air with both my mouth and my nose. It was wondrous beyond wonder. But when I sensed all the life around me on my skin, when each hair on my body reached out for it, like tendrils seeking their own kind, then and only then did all my senses coalesce so I was no longer able to separate them ~ just as I could no longer separate the snake from the mewmit from the currents of sand that formed the land, nor you from me. We are all of the same substance, the same life. Though there are many differences between us, those are merely the shadows that delineate our boundaries. Our light is the same.

How long I stayed with Alleen, I cannot measure; time did not exist for us. Each day was a new adventure, new knowledge to discover, new places and creatures to encounter and explore. But one evening, after another hope-fulfilling day, Alleen made me cry from deep within my soul.

"I have taught you almost everything I know. There is only one more lesson for you, and it will be the most difficult. Therefore, I will teach it quickly, so you cannot delay in understanding."

She took my hands in hers. They were now so similar, dry and cracked. By our hands and our spirits, you would see us as sisters, though once we had seemed so different.

"Roen, my sweet child, death is the nature of life."

I knew the truth of her words, and my face tasted moisture even in that dry place.

"When I join the land, you must leave."

"No, I can't leave our creatures."

"These animals are not our creatures," she said. "Though through them we have learned much, we belong to humankind. Would you have our knowledge die here in the desert, where no other human heart beats? Why do you think I called you to me? I am too old to return to our peoples, but you must. Take what we have learned here to the blind ones. Teach them of life, so that they can no longer commit the sacrilege of cruelty and war. Your task will be difficult, and you will not succeed in your lifetime. But if you choose your students well, what I have taught you will live on and branch out. In the time of generations, what we have learned here may yet have meaning beyond our own lives. Promise you will do this."

My heart burst, knowing that her words had ever been true. We spent the evening together as though it were an anyday, seeking water and food, sharing our stories, our hearts. Soon I was calmed, and she was reassured. We slept in a hollow, near a water-root twig. Before sleep claimed me, I reached out my hand, and she held it.

The next morning, I felt Alleen's hand on mine, but it no longer held me. I pressed my ear to her heart, though I knew it would be silent. As I lifted my head from her body, pain welled up from my womb and careened through me, reverberating against my skull. I felt the land flinch at the unnatural sound of my scream, and the creatures came. Not one by one, as had been their custom when Alleen and I would call rhythm by rhythm, but all in one swoop, converging on the small hollow. They came not to listen, but to mourn, each adding his own rhythmic sorrow to mine, lifting it, so that it rested not on my heart alone, but on theirs, too. The burden was not lightened, but in their act of sharing, it was less cold. Somehow, the creatures took a portion of my pain into themselves ~ of Alleen's death, for she belonged to them as much as to me ~ but also of the emptiness inside me that originally had brought me to them.

The creatures and I continued our songs as I buried Alleen where she lay, in the hollow where we had slept our last night together. Then they swarmed over the mound, in farewell. When they had gone, I lay my head on the sand where she now slept. I could not bring myself to leave her, so I stayed there through the day, crying at times for my own pain, laughing at times for the joyous memories, aching to reach and touch her, to sing with her, to share the day and night and days and nights with her.

But she was no longer there. In time, not even her body would remain, so scant are water and meat in the desert. And I knew Alleen would not have refused that one last gift to the creatures that had shared so much with us.

So it was that my feet honored her last behest. One step after another, I moved across the desert, my feet once again carrying me where they wished, as the days passed unwilled, unwanted.

While I was still in the desert, I continued to sing to the land and to the creatures. But my songs took on new rhythms when I once again saw the Village at the End of the World.

Dov gently closed the book and rested his hand on its cover. His fingertips caressed the embossed leather, though his mind was elsewhere, still adrift in the desert.

Gradually, he returned to the now. First, to his hand on the book, then to the sofa, where his legs stretched toward the woman who curled into herself. When she opened her eyes, it seemed to be a gift for him, bound up somehow with the Traveler and her stories. A gift that pierced his protective shell as a mewmit cracks open a walnut, or a miner strikes a stone in search of a gem.

Something broke inside him, in the pit of his stomach. New feelings erupted, too intense and strange. So he swallowed them, without thought, as he might swat at a fly that annoyed and distracted him.

The Allesha saw these changes and more, in the seconds they played on his face. *Yes, sweet boy,* she thought in the silence of her mind, *it's all there inside of you, just as Alleen taught Roen, taught all of us. There is no empty land, no empty man. Life, Dov, you can try to swallow it, to hide from it, but I'll dig it out of you, one way or another.*

She leaned forward to drape her body over his legs, bringing her mouth to his ear. "Meet me in the inner room, Dov," she whispered.

Chapter 33

On entering the darkness of the inner room, the boy lit a single gas lamp, which threw small dim islands of light here and there among the shadows. Just enough illumination for him to make his way to the pond to await his Allesha.

Playing with the currents as they danced over his body, he directed the pressured streams of hot water to bubble against his shoulder blades, his stomach, between his toes, around his genitals. But when his heel pressed against one of the openings, water shot up into the air, drenching his face, hair and the surrounding floor. A small amount even went up his nose, with a shock of stinging discomfort that reminded him that it had been far too long since he'd entered, and she still hadn't appeared.

Damn that woman! Why can't she be where I expect her to be? Why does she keep changing the rules?

The water was no longer pleasurable for the simple reason it was where she probably expected to find him. He climbed out, dried himself off and threw the towel over the puddle that had formed on the stone floor. But he didn't know what to do next. Should he leave, return to his own bedroom and let her come looking for him? She deserved that, but what if she didn't follow him? That would mean no sex tonight. Still, he couldn't just stay there at the pond like a hungry puppy begging at a closed kitchen door.

As a hunter, he'd often hide in a thicket, to await the game that was certain to come his way.

If I must wait, let it be as a hunter, as a man.

He searched the room for a place of power, where the advantage would be his. In the few spots where the dim light of the doorside lamp fell, he could discern dark hints of the soft shapeless platforms. He knew them to be like a field of boulders reaching up to the wall, so that he could never decide where the wall started and the floor ended. So like a woman's body, a woman's mind, it was eerie.

The single lamp threw more shadow than light, but they were shadows of different densities, softly blending into the light. Like the desert in that story.

Part of him felt that the woman was trying to push him toward something again, and that part of him resisted. But on a deeper level, he was curious.

Hell, why not try it? No one's here to see me make a fool of myself.

He climbed to a high platform and sat cross-legged with his back against a curve in the wall. If she came into the room, he would see her before she could see him. He tried to plumb the shadows and light, as Alleen and Roen had in the story, to discover details that had eluded him before. It wasn't that different from reading a dark forest for animal signs, except without the variety of textures and shapes that made a forest. Here, everything seemed so much alike in its softness and moist warmth.

But not so alike, maybe. Over there, near the pool, the stone floor glowed, reflecting, almost magnifying the dim light from the one lamp. Where the carpet met the stone, the essence of the light changed as the cloth almost absorbed it, forming the only hard edge in the room. Not so much a physical hardness as a sharp transition of material and light.

His eyes flowed over the platforms and humps, the light and shadow. His vision seemed to be changed by what he beheld, pulled this way and that, following the contours onward and upward. But there, about halfway down and to his left, among the deepest shadows, the undulations changed dramatically, into smaller curves and a different kind of shadow that held an internal glow, just beyond his ability to perceive it. He stared deeply into that area, but could see no more than nuances that nagged and worried him.

As he climbed down toward that shadowy area, his concern grew into a burning temper, which he didn't recognize as embarrassment. "How long have you been hiding there?" he demanded.

"Wonderful, Dov, you found me." Tayar ignored his question and his anger. "Which sense did you use?" Stretching, she reached up to him.

Standing over her, he chose to hold onto his fury, banking it against an even deeper fire that burned at the silhouette of the deliciously naked woman. He winced when she laughed. But it was that deep-throated laugh of hers. A laugh he couldn't possibly mistake as anything but her delight in being found.

"Was it a game, then?" he asked, trying to find a path out of his anger and pride.

"As much as life is a game, my dear."

She held her hand out to him again, and this time he took it, pulling her up to her feet and pressing her body against his, flesh to flesh, mouth to mouth. Then she glided back down toward the platform, still holding him, crushing only one finger under their bodies. After a few minor adjustments, they lay together, their mouths pressing, their hands exploring. But she broke away and rolled onto her side.

"Tell me, which sense did you use to find me?"

Dov didn't know how to answer her. That, in turn, made him feel trapped and out-maneuvered. He held himself in tight check, not wanting to lash out, not here in the inner room, where everything had been so wonderful until tonight, until she had lain in wait for him, watching him, cornering him.

"I knew you'd find me, but I wasn't sure if you would use sight, sound or smell," she said.

"Sight." He said the one word as an automatic response to her list, not sure where to go with it.

"What did you see?"

On edge, he found it difficult to believe it could be as simple as she seemed to be implying. "Well, these humps and platforms, they're all different, but their shadows have similar shapes. No, not shapes, but types of shapes." He glanced around, trying to find an anchor for his thoughts, some way to keep his anger from coming to a boil and ruining his chance with her tonight. "Do you see that hump there?"

She sighted along his outstretched arm. "Yes."

"Well, it's larger than the one just above and to the right of it. Their shapes are different, but they're more alike than different."

"Yes, I think I see what you mean. Their angle of curve is similar, as are their proportions."

"Yeah, that's it. And the way the light from the lamp falls on them makes shadows that are nearly identical. Well, all the shadows in this room are like that. Not identical, but more similar than different. Only, here, where you were hiding, the shadows were more different than similar."

"Excellent." She kissed him lightly on his mouth again. "You did very well, indeed."

He liked her praise, but not the idea that she might have been judging him. "Why did you do that?"

"What? Kiss you?"

"No, hide and wait and watch me."

"For the same reason you did."

He stared at her. So close and luscious and naked. But each time she spoke, it felt as if she were slipping farther and farther away.

"Dov, why did you decide to sit up there and search the light and shadows of this room?"

He shrugged his shoulders.

"Wasn't it because you wanted to try what the Traveler had written about?"

"I suppose."

"Me too."

"So it wasn't some sort of test?"

"Test?" she laughed. "No, it wasn't a test, but it was a challenge… to both of us. Did you enjoy it?"

"I didn't think of it that way. I was curious. I never saw things like that before, though I use something like it when I'm tracking. But this was harder, because everything looks so much the same in here. I guess, now that I think about it, it was, well, maybe not fun so much as strange and new." He shrugged, trying to shake off that damned familiar itchy cocoon that hovered, ready to descend on him and ruin everything. "But we're in the inner room now. Let's get back to why we're here." He tried to pull her to him, but she resisted, not quite withdrawing, but not yielding either.

"Dov, this is why we're here. Sensuality is about using our senses, all our senses, to heighten pleasure. You used sight to find me. Why not try smell?"

"You're clean. Clean people don't smell."

"That isn't true, Dov. Clean people have many odors, all belonging to their bodies and the way they live, what they eat and drink. When we wash, we remove the dirt and odors that don't belong to us and reveal those fragrances that are essentially ours." She lay down on her back. "Come, Dov, lie beside me. But, no, don't use your hands. Close your eyes and use your nose to explore me, the many parts of me."

"I don't understand."

The Allesha knew if she insisted, the lesson would be drowned out by his adamance and anger. So she quickly altered her plans. "Here, let me show you. Lie back and close your eyes."

Dov obeyed, with a slight huff of annoyance that she supposed was meant to demonstrate that he was doing this only because she insisted.

Tayar stretched out against his side and leaned over. The nipple of her right breast lightly brushed against his chest as she nuzzled his neck, closed her eyes and inhaled slowly, deeply. His fragrance was fresh, subtle, like an herb garden at dusk; yet, it was also bright, giving her a feeling of being enveloped by irrepressible life. When she moved her nose around the edge of his ear, it touched, not his skin, but the tiny hairs that reached up from his skin. He turned his head to press closer, raising his arms to pull her into his body.

"No, Dov," she giggled, pushing his arms down. "You need to lie there and be passive right now. Don't move."

Her nose continued around his chin, across his shoulders and down one arm, resting here and there at pulse points, where his scent was more pungent — like the fresh-cut peat she used to love to play with as a child.

She continued exploring the aromas and textures of his body, down his arm, snuggling her face fully into his palm, but moving before his hand could close around her. Upward again, along the crease between his arm and torso, her nose traveled, just barely touching. Her mouth followed her nose, absorbing the spice of his flesh.

"Hey, this is supposed to be about smelling me. You're nibbling. Isn't that against the rules?"

"What rules?" Tayar raised her head slightly, so he could see the sparkle in her eyes. "Be still and enjoy."

With her nose, lips and mouth, she caressed and inhaled the whole of him, down to his feet. Experiencing him as she would the sweet smells of a wheat harvest or the edgy tingling of the air just before a thunderstorm. Then, upward once more, stopping only briefly at his groin, to enjoy that mushroomy musk, neither ignoring nor acknowledging his quick gasp of pleasure, pain, uncertainty. If the boy were more advanced, she would linger there. But he wasn't ready for that lesson, not yet.

Her hands now trailed her mouth and nose, sensing him fully through touch, taste, smell, no longer able to distinguish individual perceptions. All of it had become one delicious sensation, taking Dov into her as she never had before. Up and up along the side of his torso, where pleasure bumps prickled all over his skin, along his arm and hand, nibbling at his thumb briefly, then across his chest, her tongue circling his stiff nipples, up to the warm moist hollow of his neck. Pressing her full body onto his, to feel him through the pores of her skin, kissing his ears and eyes and nose and lips, with her mouth fully on his and her tongue probing, her teeth lightly nipping at his lips.

Suddenly, she pulled away from him. "Like that," she said.

The rush of the room's air onto his flesh where her nose and mouth and body had been was a shock of loss. One moment, every follicle on his body was alive and tingling, so that he wondered whether he'd ever be able to breathe fully again without audibly gasping. The next, she was gone.

"That's what I meant when I suggested you explore the smells of my body," she explained in a voice too matter-of-fact and far away for him to hear her words.

"Uh huh." He reached for her.

"No, Dov, not yet. It's your turn."

"Later," he said with a heavy, sexually charged voice. "Right now, I want you. And none of your tricks."

He rolled over onto her, with his legs pressing hers apart, holding his weight off her on his hands that held her wrists against the floor. He slid into her with an ease that astonished him. He was even more surprised by her sudden, violent shudder, when his full shaft first pressed deep into her. Her crescendo of pleasure grew with such speed and intensity that, somewhere in the back of his mind, he vaguely wondered at her heightened response. His stick felt like an extension of his spine as he pushed into her, again and again, shooting bolts of lightning, blinding him, deafening him.

He felt dizzy, almost unconscious. Yet, at the same time, his mind had never been clearer. He saw, smelled, sensed her with every nerve in his body, her wrists against the palms of his hands, her legs pressing against his, her sweat trickling, then pouring, mingling with his sweat, his body. It was a flashing, grinding, blaring awareness that focused all its energy into her, squeezing, pulling, throbbing, until his explosion of pleasure/pain pleasure/pain pleasure/pleasure merged with hers in a fiery joyous agony.

He lay on top of her, both numb and sensitized, adrift and unable to move. Suddenly, he felt her tighten herself around his shaft, squeezing it with inner muscles where no woman should be that strong.

"Hey!" His eyes flew open, focusing in shock onto hers only inches away, seeing in them that she had controlled those muscles. Each time she did it, violent surges racked his body. The last wave of pleasure/pain threw him free of her body, onto his back and into a deep, dark, warm sleep.

The Allesha watched the sleeping boy for a few moments, a gentle smile forming on her lips. As quiet as a cat in the wild, she climbed down from the heights of the room. She knew that for an hour or two she would be free of his needs and demands. She would certainly have enough time to retreat to her bathroom, to bathe the sweat from her body, before he would tumble out of that deep sleep. She might even have enough leisure to take her pleasure to the next higher level before returning to his side, so he would find her there in the morning.

But the day will come, she fully understood for the first time, not in her head but in that inner part of her that was the Every Woman. *Yes, someday, the boy will transport me, too, into that deep exhaustion that comes with complete sexual satisfaction.* Then he would be ready to leave her, to be her first Alleman, her first untouchable. Dara was correct, again. *Power is in this boy— power and joy — and what fun it will be to unleash it. Fun and sorrow.*

Chapter 34

After completing their morning chores, the young Allesha sent the boy to their mentor.

Le'a's outer door was open, but Dov couldn't find her anywhere in the house or barn. He went into the greeting room to sit on the sofa and wait. After all, she had told him that he was welcome in her home, as long as the outer door was open.

His eyes wandered over the room, as his fingers fidgeted with the fringe on a pillow. It was sort of similar to Tayar's greeting room, but different, too — as different as the two women were from each other, as different as the one's fruit and cheese and the other's baked sweets.

Not one to be still for long, Dov got up and paced, touching this little lamp, that funny piece of pottery, picking up and leafing through a book without seeing the words on the page. In his restlessness, his mind sought something to consider, as his hands sought something to touch, his feet a place to go. That was when Dov remembered last night, how Tayar had hidden and let him make a fool of himself.

Now, he was waiting again. This wide-open room, with its flimsy curtains and squared walls, had no dark or hidden corners. But he couldn't forget his embarrassment when he had discovered Tayar, lying in wait, watching him. Somehow, that awkward discomfort from last night spilled into the sunny greeting room. His impatience became a smoldering irritation that burst into a full blown anger, propelling him out the door and onto a public path he had never walked before.

Dov didn't pay much attention to where he was walking, focused so inwardly that nothing else existed or mattered. Of course, he knew he shouldn't be wandering off where he didn't belong.

"Don't try to test the limits of our rules," Le'a had warned him more than once. "The Alleshi are unpredictable, and you can never know when we will anger and if we will forgive."

But skies! A man has his limits, and these women had pushed him too far, testing him, watching him, trying to make and unmake him, so he didn't even know what he thought anymore.

After some time, Dov started to notice his surroundings. Nothing looked familiar; nor could he remember how he had gotten there. In fact, it was the first time since he had been a child that he would have to acknowledge he was lost — not that he would admit it to anyone, as embarrassing as that would be for him and his reputation as one of the Birani's more skilled trackers.

All Dov knew was that his anger had carried him away from where he belonged into an unknown area of The Valley.

Great Mother! Now what have I done?

He had to find his way back to Tayar or to Le'a, before anyone saw him. He crouched behind a large bushy evergreen, while he tried to glean his bearings.

Judging by the mountains, he was near the center of The Valley. In front of him was a building larger than any he had ever seen. It had curves where other buildings had corners; a raised courtyard seemed to have taken a bite out of a side. Something about it reminded him of the inner room. Maybe it was the strange curves or the lack of symmetry or the essential womanliness of it.

He was so fascinated by the sight of the strange building that he didn't hear a woman approach him from behind.

"Boy! How dare you spy on us!"

Startled, he jumped to his feet so suddenly he almost lost his balance.

This Allesha was older than Tayar, though younger than Le'a. Her stern face might once have been pretty, but it was ravaged by time, filled with sharp angles that seemed hewn by her frown. Though thin, almost gaunt, nothing about her was insubstantial. Her stone face cut to his heart, reminding him again of Le'a's warnings. *Could this be one of those unpardonable crimes?*

"I demand an answer," she hissed. "Who are you that you sneak into our Valley and hide here? Do you spy for the Mwertik?"

"No! I belong here." He straightened his back against the insult, but still felt off balance, as though his own feet wouldn't support him and this woman were a storm that could blow him down.

"Not here." One bony finger pointed to the large building. "No man or boy belongs here, not now."

"I guess I made a wrong turn. But I do belong here in The Valley. It's my Season."

"What is your name?"

"I don't know how to answer you, ma'am. I'm not supposed to use her name for me, not to you… I mean, not to anyone else, right? But my before name was Ryl… Ryl of the Birani."

"Ah, yes. Mistral's son. It would be you."

"Is this a crime, to be here, to see this place?" He looked beyond the evergreens at the building. "What is it, anyway?"

"Something no boy sees until the end of his Season."

"Does that mean this is my end?" Dov tried to quiet his stomach, steady his heart; however, his words still quivered

"That is a question I cannot answer. Your fate is in the hands of your Allesha."

"But that's great! Tay— I mean my Allesha — wouldn't send me away. Not now."

"Don't be so certain of yourself, boy." she said in a raspy whisper so deep that it reverberated in his gut rather than against his ears. Then, with a piercing look, she silently commanded the boy to follow her.

Though he kept pace with her, she didn't look at him. The boy's imagination carried him to the heights and depths of his emotions. *Tayar the huntress would understand. Tayar the woman, would want him by her side. Tayar the Allesha, whose true name he would never know, would discard him like an old unwanted boot. But she couldn't. Not now. Could she?*

Soon his surroundings began to look familiar; she was taking him back to Tayar.

Dov knew he had to say something to the woman, but what? "Ma'am… uh… what should I call you?"

Without slowing, she turned to glare at him, drying the words in his throat. "Allesha." She turned away again, her sharp face pointing like an arrow toward their destination.

"Allesha, I'm sorry."

"Yes. Of that I have no doubt."

"Can you help me?"

"I'm not your Allesha."

"But you're the one who found me. I mean, you don't really have to tell her. Do you?"

"No, I don't." She bit off her words, as though saying anything to him was distasteful. "*You* will tell her what you did, and she will decide."

"Will she do it… send me away? Has any boy ever been sent away by his Allesha?"

"That isn't the question you should be asking."

"What question should I be asking?"

"I cannot tell you."

"I know, you are not my Allesha."

"That is correct." The woman stopped and pointed him forward.

Down the plowed path was his Allesha's home. "Go and tell her I await her."

Dov started for the house, but saw, to his dismay, that the front door was shut. "I can't. The outer door is closed."

"This is your Allesha's home, in the middle of your Season. You may enter her house whenever you wish, until she withdraws that privilege. Go; I will wait for her to open the outer door to me."

As reluctant as he was to confront Tayar, the boy was anxious to get away from the sharp old Allesha. He darted into the house, shutting the outer door behind him.

"Tayar!" he called as he went into the kitchen.

"Tayar!" He entered the inner room by way of his bedroom.

"Tayar!" He stood at the door to her room, but doubted that the old one outside meant for him to go in there.

He ran to the barn, but it, too, was empty, except for those stupid chickens and goats. Back in the house, he stood in the greeting room that seemed as cold as that old woman outside. *"Tayar! Tayar!"* he called over and over again.

He went outside and told the strange Allesha, "She's not here."

"We'll go to your mentor and wait there."

"She's not home either."

"How do you know?"

Did she think he was lying?! "Well, she wasn't before."

"Let's go look."

"Sure, let's go look." This time, he took the lead, angry at this interfering old woman, at this Valley with its rules, at his Allesha for not being home, for being part of The Valley that never really wanted him anyway.

Well, I had a few weeks. That's more than the guys back home. And do I have some stories to tell! It might not be so bad after all, getting out from under these women's rules.

But what about Lilla? Would she still stand with her mother against me?

And Pa? He'd never forgive me, but that's nothing new.

And what would become of Tayar and Dov?

Chapter 35

The Alleshine Library was unlike any other building in The Valley. Carved into the western mountain, it had burrowed further inward with each generation to accommodate the centuries of knowledge the Alleshi had accumulated. It was so extensive that no one knew where the original caves were. Even those scholars who had given their lives to searching the twisting tunnels and deep caverns never found the legendary ancient knowledge that was supposedly buried somewhere in the heart of the mountain.

In the unadorned entrance hall, five Alleshi bent over scrolls, papers and books strewn about on desks and tables. The closest looked up when the young Allesha entered. Tayar/Rishana mouthed one word, "Peren?" using the sisters' name for her husband's Allesha, her dear old friend, Savah. The scholar nodded toward the door to the far left, then buried her face back in her work before she could see Rishana's mimed thank you.

Beyond the indicated door was a long corridor that led deep into the mountainside. The first room on the right was filled with wooden crates. From their markings and Elnor's obvious excitement as she unpacked them, Rishana gathered it must be the new shipment from beyond the Peace borders that Peren had mentioned with such fervor the other day.

A rugged individualist originally from the Merton Mountains, Elnor didn't fit Rishana's image of a scholar. Too much energy flowed from her compact frame, even when she sat contemplating a thorny passage in a book. Yet Elnor was fascinated by the process of unearthing lost knowledge, and devoted all her off Seasons to assisting Peren. If Elnor were here, Peren probably wouldn't be far off.

Elnor reached into one of the crates and pulled out a small volume. Holding it gingerly with gloved hands, she opened the ancient book slowly and cautiously, and, while perusing the brittle yellowing pages, walked quickly to the next room. That was where Rishana found Peren/Savah. Elnor quickly withdrew back to the crates and whatever other hidden treasures they might hold.

"Jinet," Savah said with no preliminary greeting.

Falling back on the names of their old, long-established

relationship, returning to who they had always been for each other, regardless of how life around them had changed, was part of the comfort of being with Savah.

Today, Savah was so engrossed by the small volume in her hand that she might not have even noticed what name she had pulled out of her memory. "Look what Elnor just brought me! This book may predate the Great Chaos." She donned linen gloves to protect the ancient paper from the oils on her hands, before leafing through it. "The language… it's so intricate… I recognize some word roots, but… I must get Elnor to work translating it. Do you realize what wealth we have here?" She gestured to the shelves of books she had already catalogued. "And so many more in the crates in the other room. We must bring this region into the Peace. Learn what they know. Save what they have, but have forgotten."

"Savah."

The sound of Jinet's voice, full of concern, pulled the old Allesha's attention away from her beloved books. "But that isn't why you're here, is it? Let us go where we can be quiet and undisturbed."

Only a few tiers deeper inside the mountain, they settled into a small study that Savah had made her own. It had an icebox, a rack of clothes, even a sofa that had obviously been slept on more often than sat upon.

"Savah, don't tell me you've moved into this place."

"Well, not exactly moved in, but the days do speed by, and I have been known to forget to sleep or eat sometimes."

"You mustn't strain yourself."

"Yes, well, Hester has already taken me to task. But there are so many books that we have yet to understand, and I have so little time left."

This wasn't what she had come to discuss, wasn't something she wanted to consider, not when so few remained among those who had framed her life, anchoring and supporting her. "Savah, please…"

"Don't worry, dear, I don't plan on dying any time in the near future." Savah shrugged away what could neither be foretold nor forestalled. "Anyway, Hester made me promise to sleep at least six hours every day, and I told her I would if I could stay here as much as I wish. So, this is my home away from home. Cozy, isn't it? I rather like sleeping under the mountain, surrounded by all this knowledge."

"But Savah, what of sunshine, of sharing the company of your sisters?"

"Oh, I don't stay here every night. But when I work late, this comfortable sofa is far more inviting than the winter air." Savah's sigh seemed to deflate her, revealing a bone-deep fatigue. "Now, what is your question?"

"Actually, it's about a book, *The Traveler's Tales*. My Winter Boy found it in his room among those you brought."

"Very good!" Savah nodded. "When I organized the books in his room, I put that one on the bedside table, so he would grab it first."

"Tell me about the author, Savah. Is she of the tribe of Wanderers?"

"Well, she comes from the same source." Savah's back became straighter, her eyes crinkled, and she seemed to tap into a reserve of inner energy now that the subject had returned to books and history. "The Great Chaos destroyed an entire civilization. People became wanderers, with no homes of their own. When the Alleshi brought Peace to our land, the tribe of Wanderers remained nomadic, preferring their new ways to their old ones. Why do you ask?"

"Alleen. The First One. Didn't she end her life in this Valley?"

"Yes, but why?… Oh, I see, you've read *The Empty Land*."

"Yes, and, in it, she dies in the desert."

"Are you sure of that?"

"Savah, please. Tell me, don't educate me. Not now. I don't have the time today."

"Did you notice that *The Empty Land* is the first story in that book in which the Traveler mentions names — not only hers, but that of her teacher?"

"Yes."

"Because of all the names she had been given and had taken over the years of her travels, those two were rooted so deeply in her heart that nothing could burn them out of her. In the end, when she finally found her home—"

"Her home? Our Valley?" Jinet followed Savah's train of thought to its only logical conclusion. "She took the name of the one person she could not lose inside herself?"

"Yes, my dear."

"And the Traveler is our First One?" Jinet nodded. "That explains quite a bit."

"Doesn't it, though? Then you noticed the other thing about that book that is so important — the pattern of the stories. She does keep tempo, doesn't she?" Savah smiled, waiting for her companion to see what was so apparent to her scholarly mind.

"In what way do you mean? The rhythm of her language is musical."

"True, but what of the order of the stories, their pattern? They are familiar, aren't they? Think, Jinet. It's a pattern that concerned you on our last visit."

"The stages? The stages of growth in a boy in Season!" Jinet's breath caught in her throat.

"Calm, my dear, there's nothing here to upset you. Nothing to make you feel—"

"Controlled?"

"Really?"

"How is it possible that the very book my First Boy chooses to read to me is one that predicts what he will do and need over the next couple of months? A book that was written hundreds of years ago, when The Valley was new and empty, and only one Allesha — Alleen — existed. It's not right. He's a special boy."

"Of course he is."

"But you're saying he is like every other boy the Alleshi have ever taught, and that this book would work into all their lessons."

"Because it is a very special book, written by a wise woman who knew that no boy is like another, no woman like another, and yet we are all the same at the core. Though we may react differently to the same lessons, a good story will reach everyone, teaching what is needed."

"If it's such an important book, why did you never suggest I read it to prepare myself?"

"Ah, because I wouldn't have wanted to deny you the pleasure of discovering it with your First Boy."

"Savah, are you disappointed in me?"

"Never! Why would you ask such a question?"

"Because I do ask questions. I can't blindly accept all that we are, the power we have, and the assumptions that have been made for us and by us."

"Why do you think I love my books so much? Because they make me question presumed 'truths.' Please continue questioning. Then you will not only be Dara's successor, but maybe a little bit of me, too, will live on in you."

"Oh, Savah." She reached over to hug her friend and mentor. "Thank you."

"And thank you, dear Jinet." Savah returned the embrace, then shooed Jinet to sit down again. "Now, tell me, have you talked to your boy about the Mwertik yet?"

The young woman was flustered by the unexpected change of subject. "No, Savah, we've just begun."

"It's never too soon for some things, dear. We have difficult times ahead. You won't want your boy to be unprepared."

"Savah, have you heard something I should know?"

Savah hesitated only briefly. "Nothing new. But if he has the kind of power within him that his father does, then you'll need to be even more diligent in forming and directing it."

"I don't understand. I'm following the stages."

"The stages are a path, not the destination. Think about your boy, the kind of Alleman he must become and the world he will be facing. He needs to learn about the Mwertik." Savah paused. "At least, the little we know. If you are uncertain how to proceed, discuss it with Dara."

Thoughts of Dara and the Mwertik carried the young Allesha to another question, one she hadn't planned on asking. "Savah, what is it between Dara and Kiv?"

"Why do you ask?"

"I ran into her the other day."

"Kiv?" Savah walked over to the icebox, poured two glasses of juice and handed one to Jinet. "Tell me," she said.

"Actually, I don't think it was as accidental as she wanted me to believe." Jinet put the glass down untouched. "Savah, what do you think of Kiv's ideas?"

"Which ones? She has so many."

"About the Mwertik. About how we should respond to the threat they pose against the very fabric of our Peace."

"Don't get caught up with Kiv, not now during your first Season, when you can't afford distractions." Savah sighed as she sat down, plumped a cushion behind her back, then settled into it. "Kiv and I were once quite close. Did you know that I was her mentor for her First Season? She came to us young, though not as young as you. And not as a widow, but after her husband had broken the marriage. You should have seen her. Brilliant, dynamic, passionate about the Peace, caring so deeply about helping strengthen it through her boys."

"What happened between her and Dara?"

"The rift developed gradually. They had such different ways of working with their boys. Did she say anything about yours?"

"She offered to help me with him. Suggested he might be too much for me to handle. I don't know if I should have been insulted or pleased with the offer of friendship."

"Neither. Kiv is not part of your Season and shouldn't have any-thing to do with you — or your Winter Boy."

"Why?"

"Please, Jinet, you have trusted me all your adult life. Trust me on this. Engaging in Kiv's debates and arguments might be an interesting exercise for you, but not when you're in Season."

"What about trusting me? There's something you're not telling me. Is it about Kiv and Dara?"

"Jinet, I have buried myself here in this mountain to seek the answers we need. I'm only at the beginning. Please allow me a bit more time to decipher what I have found before I share it."

"I don't have the luxury of time, Savah. Kiv is asking pertinent questions; Dara is the mentor of my current Season. I need to understand."

"Yes, Jinet — Rishana — you must understand. And you will. But you've only this one short Season for your Winter Boy. When it is over, you can concern yourself with other matters. For now, focus only on the boy." The older woman stood and patted the young Allesha's arm. "Now, I have books to study, and you have a boy in Season."

Chapter 36

Le'a/Dara had known from the beginning that Ayne would have to meet and evaluate the boy. But now that the time had come, she caught herself fidgeting, twisting the napkin on her lap. After all these years, why did Ayne still have the ability to instill fear and uncertainty in Dara? Or was it that Dara had learned to care too deeply for this boy and his Allesha, and she worried that Ayne would sense it and rightly rebuke her?

Not that Ayne displayed anything other than calm courtesy, sitting at Dara's kitchen table, sharing a pot of tea. But this was the woman who could bring the most unruly Council of Alleshi and Allemen to order simply by standing quietly and looking around a room. She was seldom outvoted or overridden in Council or private conversation.

The boy was late, but such changes in schedule often occurred in the early Season. It gave the two women time to talk.

"Kiv is definitely up to something," Ayne said.

"Kiv is always up to something." At least with Ayne, Dara didn't have to conceal her distaste about anything to do with Kiv.

"No, Dara, this is more than her usual complaining and agitating."

Dara's tea remained unconsumed, something to keep her hands busy rather than to be ingested. "What have you heard?"

"That's the problem. I haven't heard anything." Ayne paused to nibble on a cookie. "I fear we shouldn't have allowed her to be so thoroughly trounced and humiliated in Council last summer."

"But her proposals were ridiculous."

"No, not ridiculous, but dangerous and highly seductive. However, the way it was handled silenced her too thoroughly, so we have no way of knowing what she is now thinking or planning. I believe she may be privately sounding out some of our sisters, trying to gather them to her side."

"Who?"

"I don't know anything definite. It's a feeling I get when I come upon her talking with another."

"We must find out—" Dara was startled by the sound of voices in her greeting room. Dov had finally arrived, but the woman with him wasn't Rishana. "Kiv!? What's she doing here? And with the boy!"

Ayne ducked into the mudroom and grabbed Dara's coat from a hook. "Keep her in the greeting room," she whispered. "I'll take the back path."

Dara nodded while she quickly put their cups and plates into the icebox. Before opening the door to the greeting room, she took a single deep breath to compose herself and push her fear down into her stomach, where Kiv couldn't see it.

Dara greeted Kiv in ritual embrace, as was appropriate in the presence of an outsider. "Welcome, Sister. Would you care to freshen up in my room? I'm sure the boy would excuse us."

"Thank you, Sister, but the boy has something to say to you first."

The two women looked at the boy, who squared his shoulders and attempted to appear unconcerned. However, as both Alleshi continued to stare at him, his pose slipped, and he erupted into words to fill the tense silence.

"I really messed up this time." He spoke directly to his mentor, trying to avoid Kiv's glare. "Well, you weren't here, so I went for a walk, and I guess I ended up somewhere I wasn't supposed to be. She," he nodded toward Kiv, without looking at her, "found me and I'm afraid I might have broken one of those rules you told me about. I know I wasn't supposed to walk off on my own, but she said that my Allesha could decide to send me away because of it." He shook his head. "Damn, I'm sorry, but why weren't you here?"

"Was that an apology?" Kiv asked, in a cutting manner that made her opinion clear.

Before he could reply, Dara answered, "Yes, it is an apology of sorts — the best apology he is capable of giving at present."

Kiv narrowed her eyes at Dara, but wasn't about to contradict another Allesha in front of the boy.

"Thank you for bringing his trespass to my attention." Sure that Ayne had disappeared onto the paths beyond the barn by now, Dara took Kiv's elbow and gently guided her through the vestibule to the outer door, "I will tell his Allesha of it."

"He must be properly disciplined," Kiv insisted. "Coddling boys will not help us when the Mwertik come."

Dara glanced back through the vestibule's inner door at the boy who paced the far end of the greeting room. She spoke softly, so he wouldn't hear them. "I don't see the Mwertik at our mountain passes, but if they ever do come, let's hope our strength is rooted within each individual and in the deep bonds that we forge here with our Allemen. Otherwise, what use is discipline?" She formed her face into a smile she did not feel. "Thank you, Kiv, for bringing the boy back to me." Dara closed the outer door as quickly as she could without it appearing that she was shutting the door on one of her own sisters.

As soon as she returned to the greeting room, the boy rushed to her, hugging her tightly. "Oh, thank you, dear, sweet, wonderful Le'a."

She gave Dov a stern look and pushed him away. "Tayar has an important decision to make."

"I thought you... I mean when you sent that mean old woman away..."

"No, Dov, I may be your mentor, but Tayar is your Allesha. Let us go to her, now."

"She isn't home. That's why that woman—"

"Call her Allesha. It is her title, which she has earned."

"Well, that Allesha brought me here because Tayar wasn't home."

"Then we will leave a note for her, and return here to await her signal."

"Le'a, will Tayar send me away?"

"That is not my decision."

"I know; you're not my Allesha. She..." he pointed to the door to indicate the woman who had just left, "said the same. But Le'a, you know Tayar, and you know the rules."

"However, I still don't quite know what happened, do I?"

"Yeah, it's like I told you."

"If that's true, then we have nothing to discuss until Tayar makes her decision. But if something else happened, something that made you leave here, even though I had left the outer door open for you when I went out on a quick errand. If there were some reason you willfully fled the safety of my home to brave the uncertainty of The Valley, to break rules you don't understand fully but knew were in place, then we would still have something to talk about before returning you to Tayar for her judgment."

"Well..." He hesitated.

"Shall we sit while you explain?"

They sat in the greeting room, the place of formal meetings, while the boy told the Allesha what had happened. Not everything, and certainly with details missing or skewed, but enough that she knew the taste of his fear, the shape of his confusion.

Chapter 37

When the young Allesha returned home from the library, she found a note from Le'a/Dara under her gatepost lantern.

"Kiv came to my house with your Winter Boy. She found him near the Communal Hall. He awaits your judgment. If you wish to have us come to you, please light your signal candle. Otherwise, we'll wait here for you. D."

Kiv! What was she doing with Dov? Why was he near the Communal Hall? And why now, just when Savah warned me to keep Kiv away from my Winter Boy?

Whatever happened, Dara expected her to make a judgment over him. Better that it should be here, in her home, where she felt centered. Rishana lit the candle, then went into her bedroom.

Looking through the clothes in her closet, she considered the persona she should don. Stern, almost but not quite unapproachable, would be good for this scene. Surprise the boy with an Allesha he doesn't yet know.

When Dov and Le'a arrived, the young Allesha was seated in a tall, straight-backed chair in the greeting room. She did not rise when they entered. Nor did she speak, smile, nod or otherwise acknowledge them. Still, the boy felt her eyes on him. Le'a took another straight-backed chair, so he sat, too, pulling a small cushioned stool from the wall to join them.

Where had those two chairs come from? he wondered. *All of Tayar's greeting room furniture is deeply upholstered.*

The silence roared in his ears. He looked at Tayar, but was that indeed she? This stern woman had almost as many sharp angles as the Allesha who had found him. The black dress she wore sheathed her body from her neck to her wrists, down to her ankles. Her hair was pulled into a tight bun at her neck, with not one wisp escaping. She sat bolt upright, neither allowing nor ignoring his questioning search of her body and face.

Le'a gestured to the boy, indicating it was time for him to speak.

"They say you will judge me," he said.

Tayar inclined her head, not so much nodding as recognizing that he spoke.

"Then judge and be done with it! You never really wanted me here anyway, so here's a good excuse for you to be rid of me."

"I've yet to be told what it is I am to judge." Her voice was low, each word fully formed before the next was uttered.

"Whether I'm going to be thrown out of here today."

"Really?"

"Yeah, that old Allesha who found me said this could be the end of my Season, because I saw that building that I wasn't supposed to see until the end."

"I see."

"Do you?"

"I see that you were somewhere you weren't supposed to be. How did that happen?"

He looked to Le'a, but she was nearly as blank as Tayar.

These women aren't going to make it easy. I should just get up and walk out of this house and away from this Valley. But what if there's still hope?

He leaned back, resigned that his only chance would be to tell the truth. "I went to Le'a's, but she wasn't home. The outer door was open, so I went in, like you told me I should, but she wasn't there. I got edgy just sitting there, not knowing what was going on. I guess it was another test that I failed, because I couldn't just sit there like that, doing nothing, waiting, so I walked out."

The boy paused briefly and glanced at the black-sheathed Allesha. He thought he saw a flicker of Tayar in her eyes, but it was quickly replaced by an aloof stare. Taking a deep breath to steel himself against the emptiness, he threw his words at her like a battering ram.

"I started walking, and I didn't watch where I was going. Stupid, huh? And when I realized that I didn't know my way back here, I got… well, okay, you want the full truth, I got scared. I remembered what Le'a had said about not breaking any rules, because I could never know when you'd get so angry that you'd never listen to me again. But you are listening, aren't you? Well, that's something. Then that other one found me, near that strange building. Damn it, what do you want me to say?"

"I believe I now understand what happened," the younger Allesha said in a flat, monotone. "Tell me, how do you think I can judge you?"

"Isn't that your job?"

"Yes. But I must gauge not only what happened, but whether it has damaged your Season."

He knew he should have a smart response, something that, once said, would fix everything. "I don't know what to say, except, I'm sorry. But I don't understand any of this. Does everything have to change just because I went for a walk?"

"Was that all it was, a walk? When you put it in those terms, it does seem silly, doesn't it?"

Was that the beginning of a softening in her eyes, a crinkle of life? "Yeah, it does," he said.

"But it wasn't only a walk, was it? You were angry."

"Sure, I was angry. Wouldn't you have been?"

"No."

"Well, no, I guess you wouldn't have been. But then, you're the one in control here, aren't you? You've no reason to get angry; you hold all the arrows in your quiver. I have nothing."

"Nothing? You had an Allesha and a mentor, two women who were devoted to you and your needs. All we asked was patience and respect. What we received was anger and disrespect."

"No! Tayar, please don't believe that. I may think all kinds of things about you, about this Valley, but, damn it, it has nothing to do with disrespect. I know I'm not what you expected or wanted, but don't think I don't respect you."

"You're unconcerned with how your actions will affect others, and consider only your own comfort and satisfaction."

"Hey, wait."

"No, you wait, boy. You need to think over what I have said. If you can learn from this experience, then there may be hope for your Season."

"But—"

"Did you not hear me? I suggest that you say nothing. Go into your room. Or, better yet, go sit in the inner room, and consider all that transpired today. We'll discuss your situation again in an hour."

The two Alleshi stayed as they were for several moments after the boy had slammed his bedroom door behind him. Tayar/Rishana heard the door to the inner room thud also, though the thick walls usually muted any such sounds. Only then did the pose fall from her body and face.

Le'a/Dara relaxed, too. "You handled that quite well, dear."

"Dara, it's too much. Making such a fuss over what is essentially nothing. We both know how good it is to walk off excess energy. That poor boy is a foaming sea of emotions. Emotions that I have purposely unleashed. Now I have to punish him for reacting to all that he has experienced?"

"Yes."

"Is that all you have to say?"

"You need nothing more from me. You already know what I would say."

"Do I, Dara? Tell me, what happened with Kiv?"

Dara's mouth contorted as though she had just tasted soured milk. "That woman tried to terrorize the boy. She threatened him and then insisted that he be punished immediately."

"Is my Season damaged?"

Dara stared into the space between them, biting her lower lip pensively. "I don't think she really learned anything about him." Her voice was low, hesitant.

Rishana was taken aback by Dara's cryptic response. "What?"

Dara shook her head, as though to clear it, then focused on Rishana. "I mean, Kiv didn't have enough time with the boy to develop the leverage to unbalance him. But she did instill a heightened fear of the Alleshi in him, of our unpredictable ways."

"Then perhaps meeting Kiv will prove useful for him."

"*Never!*"

"Dara, don't you think you're overreacting, allowing your differences with Kiv to cloud your perspective?"

"You don't really know her, Rishana. All through her service, Kiv took only soft, easy boys, molding them against their own natures to make them hard, like her. How relieved I was when she decided to retire early. But now she spends most of her time in Council calling for a hardening of Alleshine ways, to prepare for an all-out war against the Mwertik." Dara, who was usually so steady and self-possessed, was becoming increasingly agitated. "How can she be so blind to our history? It's people like her who created the Great Chaos of the Before Times, destroying all semblance of civilization."

"Still," Rishana countered. "She has a point about the Mwertik. All they understand is violence. Our ways are based on establishing communications and trade, as a remedy to war. But you can't initiate trade with those who have no interest in listening, with those who seem to want nothing more than to destroy everything in their path. She's right; we have been like sheep to the slaughter."

"Would you want us to become like the Mwertik, then?" Dara asked, attempting to sound rhetorical, but unable to mask her bitter sarcasm. "Destroy everything our Peace stands for, in order to save the Peace?"

"Of course not."

"No. I've seen you with your Winter Boy. You are no more like Kiv than a lioness is like a shark." She paused to take a single deep breath. "Rishana, if you ever feel seduced by Kiv's violent ways, think about Dov, and how different he would be if he were trained by someone like Kiv."

"Yes, I have considered it."

"Oh? And what have you decided?"

"That I prefer Jared and Mistral over Kiv Allemen like Gerard or Tevan. Still, if Jared had been more fierce, like a Kiv Alleman, would he be alive today?"

"Would he have been the Jared you loved and believed in, if he had been trained by Kiv?"

"No."

Dara leaned back into the hardwood chair. "I'm glad you understand."

"No, Dara, I don't understand, not fully. Too much is going on under the surface, beyond my grasp. I wonder if it has been purposely hidden from me."

"Rishana, we will deal with your uncertainties later. Right now, your Winter Boy awaits your judgment, which you will have to shape before he decides he's had enough of stewing alone in the inner room."

Rishana knew Dara was deliberately deflecting her questions, but she also realized that Dov was her more immediate concern. The rest could wait. "My judgment! It's ridiculous to even think I would banish him."

"Of course it is. But he's predisposed to think in terms of extreme consequences for even the smallest of indiscretions, a trait that Kiv heightened with her threats."

"So I have to soften the fear without weakening the lesson." Rishana paused in thought, then added, "And I need to get him back on path somehow."

"Oh, he is very much on path. If he hadn't rebelled about this time, I would have wondered what we were doing wrong. His kind need to rebel… to feel some control over situations that confuse them. They can't allow anything to be easy for them, or for the people around them. But you knew that, didn't you?"

"Yes, of course, Dara. But I'm still stuck here, in this dark persona." Rishana brushed the cloth of her severe, long dress. "What do I do now? I can't be completely changed when he comes out of the inner room in an hour."

"Correct. But what if he doesn't come out? What if you go in to him first?"

"Fully clothed in the inner room? As I am, now?"

"Definitely."

"To tell him of my judgment."

"To first let him tell you—"

The young Allesha nodded. "Yes, that fits."

Chapter 38

Stomping into the inner room, Dov threw all his anger at the door, slamming it behind him. But it gave him no satisfaction. True, it made a nice loud *thwack* when it crashed into its frame. Then, slowly, almost languidly, it glided on its hinges, gradually widening the beam of light that fell from his bedroom into the dark inner room.

Everything in the room was too soft, too anchored. He wanted something to throw, to hear the crash of destruction, the force of his power.

"Damn her!" He punched a wall, but the woven covering was so thick that he hardly felt it.

"Damn her!" He ran the perimeter, jumping from platform to platform, throwing himself against the opposite wall.

"Damnher... damnher... damnher!" He leaped down to the stone floor surrounding the pond, wondering what Tayar would do if she found him there hours from now, having misstepped and fallen onto the hard surface. But he landed safely on his feet.

Wearied and bored, Dov sat on the edge of a nearby platform, lit a candle and carefully surveyed the room to make sure he wasn't being watched again.

He didn't know what to do with himself. Tayar had told him to think. If he could quiet his mind, he would refuse to think, simply to avoid doing what she had commanded. Instead, his thoughts catapulted through the events of the day, of last night, of his entire stay here in this Valley, in this house, in this very room, where she had smelled him last night. *Skies, that felt great!* Everything she did here in this room felt incredible.

Well, not everything. Not the way she had lain in wait, watching him from the dark, spying on him, so he could be made a fool.

He knew what it was about. *It's how they keep us guessing, keep their control over us, with stupid rules that they never state clearly, so you can't help but break them.*

But that didn't make sense. Not Tayar, so gentle and generous, soft and yielding.

Tayar had sent him here to the inner room for a reason. Of that he was certain. Was it anything more than to put him aside so she could talk with Le'a and not be bothered with him?

"Go and think," she'd said. Think about what? A walk that broke some stupid, vague rule?

Damn her. Damn the lot of them. Well, no, not everybody. Not Le'a. And not the Tayar who had played with him there in the pond and tickled him over there on that platform and awakened with him there, and there, and there.

But what about the woman who wasn't really Tayar, that formidable, unknowable black-sheathed woman who'd sat so rigidly in that damned straight-backed chair, and was probably preparing at that very moment to send him away?

The boy wandered the landscape of his confusion and anger. Back and forth his thoughts boomeranged, never landing anywhere.

After some time, the door to the Allesha's bedroom opened. The light streaming behind and around her was almost blinding, so that he was unable to see the details of her shadowed face or body. But it was obvious that she still wore that long black dress.

The dark silhouette of his Allesha glided forward only as far as the platform nearest her door, where she sat. One half of her face caught the candlelight, and he realized that she was looking at him, waiting for him to speak. He said the first words that came to his mouth. "I should have smelled you."

"Oh? Why?" she asked.

"Because you wanted me to."

"Oh. I see."

"You sound disappointed."

"No, not disappointed." She spoke slowly, her tone softer than before. "It's only that I thought you were about to say something else."

"Something you wanted me to say?"

"Something I thought you would be ready to say."

"Is that why you sent me here to the inner room?"

"I suggested you might want to come to the inner room, because it's a good place to think. Don't you agree?"

"I don't know what you mean."

"No, I suppose you wouldn't." She looked toward him, though he no longer felt as though she was looking at him, but at something that was far away.

"Don't you know that I hate that?" His skin itched with anger and irritation, a buzz of frustration that made him want to run again. "When you say things like that, it makes me feel I'm not the person you were hoping to find."

"I am sorry to upset you that way."

"That sounds like a real apology."

"Of course, it is. I'm sorry if I made you feel uncomfortable, if I gave you any reason to think that I was hoping to find anyone other than you."

"Does that mean you want me here?" he asked, not sure he wanted to hear the answer.

"Ah, I see. You need reassurance."

"I just want to know where I stand. Do I pack up and leave, or do I stay?"

"What did you think about for the past hour?"

"I don't know if you really want to hear that."

"Why not?"

"Because I was angry."

"What made you angry?"

"What do you think? You made me angry." His voice strained with the effort of not yelling.

"Tell me." Did her back seem to be a little less straight? She almost appeared to be settling in, waiting to hear him read another story. When he didn't say anything further, she closed her eyes.

Eventually, he filled the quiet with his words. "I know I shouldn't have stormed away like that. Not from Le'a, especially after you both told me to stay away from strange paths. But, damn it, I can't just sit and do nothing. And I can't prattle on to a stone statue with her eyes closed." His hands balled into tight fists. "Damn it! Look at me!"

She opened her eyes.

"Tell me one thing. Can I still call you Tayar?"

"Of course, that's the name you gave me," she said, then retreated into herself once more, looking at nothing, certainly not him.

He considered matching her silence with silence. But didn't she just say that she was still his Tayar? It wouldn't be a good strategy to put up a block right now.

If she wants to hear me speak, I'll talk until she can't stand it anymore, until she calls me Dov once more.

"So, I was angry. I know I've got a bad temper; it just erupts sometimes. Maybe too often. I guess you could help me with that, couldn't you? I'd like that… to learn how to control it, so it doesn't keep getting in my way."

She closed her eyes again.

"I guess that isn't what you wanted to hear." He paused, searching for another path. "You said something that really got me going. All that stuff about me being disrespectful. About me doing it even if I didn't intend it. If I did something that made you think I don't respect you, then I'm sorry."

He thought he saw her head incline a bit.

"And do you really believe I'm that selfish, that I think only about myself? I mean, how could I love Lilla so much if I didn't think about her? And Ma? And yeah, you, too."

Was that the beginning of a smile? No, it must be just the play of the candlelight.

"I wonder though, what love really is," he said. "I know what it feels like to love Lilla… like I can't breathe. And you make my mind and my body feel things I never knew existed. But what about you? Damn! Is that what you meant?"

She opened her eyes and leaned toward him. "Yes?"

He was startled to hear her voice again, so soft a whisper that he could almost believe he had imagined it.

"I mean, about smelling you. It's always been about what I'm feeling, hasn't it?"

"Tell me."

"When I went for that walk, I was angry. All I could think about was how I felt. I didn't think about you or Le'a. And last night, when you wanted me to smell you, all I could think about was how good I would feel if I were inside you. They're connected somehow, aren't they?"

"Are they?"

"Please don't do that. Not now. I need to know…."

"You need."

"Okay, it doesn't really matter what I need, does it? But wouldn't it help us get back to where we were if you helped me understand?"

"Yes, it would, Dov."

"You called me Dov."

"That's the name I gave you."

"Does that mean we can go back?"

"Oh, no, we'll never go backwards. We've climbed a difficult hill, with mountains ahead."

He stared at her, not sure what to do or say.

"Come up here; sit beside me," She patted the carpet next to her. "We have so much to discuss, and this separation makes it more difficult."

He stood, but didn't move toward her.

"Dov, I believe you still have something to say."

He knew he needed to find the right words — now — before he lost this one chance, perhaps his last, to fix everything. But the more he tried to unravel the jumble of thoughts, the foggier everything became. The distance to Tayar, who sat just a few steps away, stretched until he wondered if he'd ever bridge it again.

He sighed deeply. That's when he remembered what Le'a had taught him about clearing his mind. He closed his eyes and took a slow deep breath. Focusing on the air slipping through his mouth, down his throat, easing into his heart, he took another breath, and another.

When he opened his eyes again, he looked at Tayar, and saw her fully, the woman who waited for him patiently because she knew he had it in him to bridge the distance that had always existed between them. She patted the platform again, and he climbed up to sit near her, though not even their thighs grazed.

"Tayar, I'm really very sorry that I thought about my anger before I thought about you. I didn't mean to hurt anyone or show disrespect. But I did. I would like to learn how to not do that."

"So you shall." She leaned toward him and brushed her lips across his cheek.

"Tayar, may I ask you a question? What do I do now? I mean, I've apologized, and I think you've accepted my apology."

"Yes."

"Well, we are in the inner room. So, would you… I mean, may I? Skies! Why don't you take off that damn dress? I'd really like to smell you right now. When I thought you were going to send me away, I was very sorry I hadn't done that. Not just because you had asked me, but because I couldn't remember what you smelled like. And because of how you made me feel when you did it to me. Wouldn't you like me to make you feel that way?"

"I look forward to it, Dov. But not now. This afternoon's turmoil has taken a great deal out of both of us. We need some quiet time together, before we can fully enjoy each other's bodies. Dov, don't look so dejected. Pleasure is outside this room, too, in our daily lives together."

"Uh huh."

She stood to leave. "I'll meet you in the kitchen."

"After dinner, we'll come back here, right?"

"After dinner, I would like to read to you."

"And after reading?"

"Yes, Dov, after reading."

"I will smell you."

"If you wish."

"No, Tayar, if you wish."

Chapter 39

Tayar was relieved when she was able to shed the ugly black dress. However, she knew that she mustn't diminish the effect of her earlier severity by now appearing soft and yielding. She chose a no-nonsense costume for the evening — grey wool trousers with a white high-neck sweater — and gathered her hair at the nape of her neck with a silver clasp.

The boy was subdued throughout their meal, but with mischievous undercurrents that his Allesha found appealing. More than that, Tayar was relieved she hadn't broken his spirit. He had found his way through the day's confusion, coming out at the other end still whole. She was astonished at her sense of pride in him.

I wonder what surprises he's cooking up behind that mysterious smile.

As they washed the dishes, he brushed his body against hers more than was his norm.

Good. He's learning the art of tension. A bit awkward, but it's a beginning.

Dov's smile grew wider and more open as they moved into the greeting room. "What will you read to me, tonight, Tayar?" He asked as he settled into one corner of the sofa and gestured to her to sit in the other.

As she sat down onto the sofa, she picked up two thin books from a side table and handed one to him. "Dov, you know that before our stories were written down, people kept the tales in their hearts and minds. Imagine now that two men are speaking at the village fire. The booklet you hold contains the words of one man." She held up the companion book in her hand. "This has those of the other. Shall we read them to each other?"

"No, that's not the way it's supposed to be. You're reading to me tonight. Come, settle back and put up your feet."

"Dov, this is very special, but for it to work, it requires the two of us."

"But…"

"Please, Dov, this is part of what we were discussing earlier. Think beyond yourself."

"I was. I am. Damn!" Exasperated, but resigned, he huffed. "Okay, what do I do?"

"Thank you. I'll read a line, then you read a line. We'll go back and forth like that."

"Who starts?"

"I will."

The battle is over, and we have won,
she read.

> *The battle is over, and we have lost,*
> he responded.

But victory tastes foul in my mouth,
as I call out the names of the dead
to our village fire.

> *No family is untouched.*
> *Many hearths will never again burn warm.*

All my sons, both my daughters,
butchered by those animals.

> *My wife collapsed to her death bed*
> *when she heard our line was no more,*
> *butchered by those animals.*

As in our fathers' time.

> *As in our fathers' fathers' time.*

They came to the walls of our village,
bloodying our fields,
destroying our generations.

> *They cut down our trees,*
> *burned our homes,*
> *destroying our generations.*

Until we pushed them back
to their own walls.

> *Until they burst into our village,*
> *trampling even into our spirit house.*

We saw the truth of them,

> *We stood face to face,*

And knew them to be animals.

> *And knew them to be animals.*

We saw how they cage their women
away from the world.

> *We saw how they force their women*

                                        into the world.

So little do they respect
their wives and sisters

                        That they send them to do battle
                        beside their sons and brothers.

And their gods are so fierce
they hide their faces when they pray, in fear.

                        They insult even the gods,
                        trying to look them in the face.

No respect for their own.

                        No respect for their gods.

When two peoples are
so different from each other,

                        When a people is so uncivilized,
Can there be anything other than war
                        Generation after destroyed generation?

The battle is over. So much have we lost.
                        The battle is over. All we were is gone.
No crops to be harvested,
we steal from the gods' storehouse.
Hunger-driven sacrilege.

                        What few children remain
                        beg morsels of the enemy.
                        I gag on their bounty.

Is this what it is to be victorious?

                        Why was I spared for this shame?
To see my people ruined.

                        To witness my people's end.
I cannot fathom the gods' purpose in all this.
                        I cannot allow them to occupy my village,
                                        my home.

And yet I live,
can that not be my hope?

                                        And yet I live,
                                        to plan our revenge.

To see my son's wife
delivered of her burden.
A son it shall be.

                        I shall destroy the destroyers.
                        For that alone,

> I will tomorrow's heartbeats.

I shall hold him at the village fire,
and call his name,
standing for his father.

> *My plan must be sure, strong.*

His life must be rich, good.

> *For that I will live.*

For that I shall live.

> *Their end.*

His future.

> *Their atrocities will be repaid tenfold;*
> *such animals require slaughter.*

I must find new paths to end this cycle,
to give my grandson a new peace.

> *When an enemy is so uncivilized,*

Can we not find any way other than war?

> *Generation after destroyed generation.*

The battle is over, let it be for all time.

> *The battle is over, I await my moment.*

I shall go to their spirit house
and speak my heart.

> *He comes, their leader,*
> *to gloat and demand.*

Be my enemy no more,
son after father.
Let us join to rebuild.

> *Come, my enemy,*
> *be no more.*
> *Die on my knife.*

My grandson calls from the womb.
I can do no less.

> *My children cry from their graves.*
> *They must be avenged.*

I must now be braver than before battle,
standing before them,
stripped of all weapons.

> *I must now gird my heart, as before battle.*
> *There he stands,*
> *an animal awaiting slaughter.*

Though my men surround us,

189

what I ask they, too, fear.

> *"Peace," he says. Ha!*
> *So the victor masks his unsheathed whip.*

Must we kill,
as in our fathers' time?

> *He comes with lies,*
> *as in our fathers' fathers' time.*

Our generations have died,
hate filling their short lives.

> *My children are gone,*
> *and yet you, old man, live.*

I say "No more!"

> *I give you my knife!*
> *I say "No more!"*

"You have killed me. Why?"

> *"You would destroy us."*

"No, I said peace."

> *"On victor's terms."*

Too late, I see.
When two peoples are so different.

> *When a people is so uncivilized,*

There can be nothing but war,

> *Generation after destroyed generation.*

Tayar's eyes were hooded with sorrow. "So many wasted lives, all that hate, the lost, destroyed hopes and dreams." Her words were a sigh.

"You're acting like you're mourning people you knew. It's only a story," Dov said with a dismissive shrug, "from way back in the past."

"Does that make the people any less real?"

"No, but it happened so long ago that even if it had ended differently, they wouldn't be any less dead."

"How people die shapes our world." Tayar paused, wondering how she could teach a boy to care, when strangers may always be just that — unknown, perhaps unknowable.

She touched the book on her lap. "These two men died long ago, but they live today, because of us, because of our connection to them, through these words. As we read, they became as real to me as any people alive today. Their villages became my village. I'm saddened, because two of my people, two villages of my world, lived generation after generation in hate and fear, not knowing how to end the cycle of war."

"I guess I don't take it as personally as you do."

"I hope someday you will, because that's an essential part of what it is to be an Alleman. When you care deeply about other people, even those long dead, you'll be driven by something more potent than any pledge or promise. And you'll not rest until you can make this life better for the living — and for future generations."

"If you say so. Now, come give me your feet."

"What?" she asked, surprised at the turn of subject.

"Put your feet up here on my lap."

She saw that it was important to him, so she complied. He removed her slippers and socks, and bent toward her feet. Unfortunately, he was sitting in such a way that his face overshot them.

Was that what all those hints were about throughout the evening? Does he want to smell me, now, rather than wait for the inner room?

Bend as he would, this way and that, he couldn't get his nose close to her toes, without contorting into an awkward position. Seeing his frustration, she stretched sensually, to try to be more accessible. It didn't help.

"Dov, you know what I would enjoy?"

"What?"

"I really love having my feet rubbed."

No doubt, he was trying to enact some fantasy he had concocted, and didn't quite know how to extract himself without feeling foolish. When Dov straightened his back, she knew he had resolved the moment and was ready to proceed.

He cupped his hands around one foot and began rubbing it. "Like this?" he asked.

"Mmm, yes. Your hands are deliciously warm. I'd like to show you how wonderful it feels. Please give me your feet, too."

"But I wanted to do this for you."

"So you shall, but wouldn't it be more fun to do it to each other, at the same time? I'd enjoy it."

Reluctantly, he said, "Okay."

Tayar repositioned his left leg between her legs and after removing his slipper and sock, settled his foot between her breasts. Then she did nothing, waiting for him to take the lead. When he resumed massaging, she initially mimicked his movements. Little by little, she built on the motions, altering them only slightly, so he didn't quite recognize the lesson for what it was. Soon, his fingers discovered the curves they were meant to follow, the nooks where a circle motion fit, the open stretches that pulled his palms inward and along a tendon.

Tayar rode the rhythms of their hands and their breaths, gauging when it would be safe to go forward with the planned lesson without diminishing the one he was already learning.

"Dov, you didn't tell me what you thought of *The Battle Is Over*." She pushed his left foot away, repositioning her legs around his right leg and removing the slipper and sock from the foot resting on her chest, so each had a new foot to massage.

Tayar watched his face while Dov considered his response. So it was that her fingers unconsciously played with the ridges on his sole before she actually noticed them. When she did look to see what it was that had pulled her hands into an unfamiliar pattern, she saw prominent scars that appeared to be a purposeful design. "Dov, what is this?" She stroked the jagged lines and lopsided circle of the scar.

"I burned myself when I was a kid. Pa says I stepped on some fire-hot medallion when I was just learning to walk. I don't remember doing it, so I must have been really young."

"How dreadful. Did it inhibit your ability to walk as a child?"

"I don't know much about it. Whatever happened then, I can outrun anyone I know now, so it doesn't matter."

Determined not to be distracted from what she had planned for this evening, the Allesha waited the few moments it took for them to return to their mutual massage, then asked once more, "Dov, tell me what you thought about *The Battle is Over*."

"Well, it's sort of like the story you read to me before, *Death to the Enemy*," he said. "You know, the one about the kid who went to war and then grew up and sent other kids to war. I guess it's the cycle thing, each generation going to war, killing off the boys and piling up anger. The way the stories tell it, it sounds really stupid."

"Yes. That's true. But the cycle of hate is hard to break. How would you do it? If you had walked into that spirit house, just before the one man stabbed the other, what would you have done to try to prevent the murder?"

"I don't know. I mean, wouldn't it be too late at that point, with the knife already unsheathed?"

"True."

"So how do Alleman do it? How do they break the cycle?"

"In the past, whenever we've encountered villages that would rather fight than seek common ground, we have stood away for a time and watched, trying to find what the people wanted or needed most. Quietly, we seed small influences. The right teaching tales introduced into a community can create powerful tensions for change. As they become more amenable to our presence, our Alleman may help the villages develop a trade that's too profitable to take a chance on war destroying it.

"Arranging marriages between prominent families in each village has been known to help. Or we teach each village a new skill that the other needs, so they must barter for each other's help. In one case I know of, the Council of Allemen relocated a village to more fertile land that contained a rich copper mine, to get them away from their enemy. But that was an extreme situation that created other problems we're still trying to resolve. Hate doesn't disappear overnight, not even after a couple of generations. But, eventually, peace supplants war, simply because it's better — and more profitable."

"Don't those villages take offense at our interfering? I know I wouldn't want a bunch of outsiders telling me how to run things, or secretly trying to change me, or — *skies!* — moving my village just to suit some far-reaching plan of a bunch of old women and their cohorts."

"True. If the path we choose is offensive, does it matter that the goal is worthy? Peace that extinguishes a people's pride or disregards their history is tenuous and certain to fail. Yet how can we not try, when so much is at stake?" She remembered what Savah had told her, and she pushed ahead into her personal hell. "Then there are the Mwertik Zalogs." Despite her best effort, the words came out as a hoarse whisper, revealing her deep-seated pain.

"Tell me." Dov's voice was gentle and kind. His hands continued to give, though Tayar had stopped massaging his foot.

"You're too young to remember a time before the Mwertik raids, when the Great Alliance was indeed whole and inviolate, when all living within the Peace knew true security. Then they came. From where, we don't know. We don't even know their name or village."

"But they're the Mwertik Zalogs."

"All 'Mwertik Zalogs' means is 'murdering raiders,' in the language of the first border village they attacked." She looked at him, measuring time by lives. "We initially heard of them about eighteen years ago, around the time you were born. Even then, it was something that happened elsewhere, a concern beyond our influence. But year after year, the raids came closer and more frequent — always unrelentingly brutal. They take no hostages, ask for nothing, just murder everyone in sight. They burn the fields, poison the wells, slaughter the animals, raze the villages. We've never seen anything like it, not since the Great Chaos. Total and mindless destruction, with no apparent reason or purpose."

"Yeah, my pa told me."

"What did he tell you of them?"

"That no one can predict where and when they'll attack. That's why

Pa insisted that we wait for caravans for every portion of our trip here, even though I know he goes off on his Alleman solo ventures."

"Yes, he does, because he must. I wish it weren't so." Tayar sat up, so that her foot slipped from his hands. "Dov…"

"Hey!" He reached for the foot, but was stopped by something in her eyes.

"How would you deal with the Mwertik?" she asked.

"Like they deserve. Let them come near my village or my family or you, and they'll see how quick an arrow can fly or a rifle shoot."

"But then you'd be no different from them, would you?"

"Yeah, I would. I'd be protecting my people. They're just murderers."

"But do we know that, Dov?"

"It's the one thing we know about them; they're murderous animals."

"Like the men in *The Battle Is Over*? Dov, what if one of the men in that tale were a Mwertik?"

"Which one?" He paused to consider his own question. "Bet it would be the one who killed the other in his own spirit house."

"Would that alter the way you interpret the story? Earlier, we were ready to understand both men and how they could hate each other. Now, if we cast one as a Mwertik, why does that change our empathy? Does the need to break the cycle of hate change when it's our hate?"

"I don't know what you want me to say."

"Don't say anything, if no words form in your heart. But promise me you will think about it."

"Why is it so important to you?" he asked.

"Because I do hate the Mwertik. Yet if we are to survive as a people, if we are to find a path back to the Great Peace before it is ruined, we must learn how to turn even them."

"Turn them or destroy them."

"No! Destroying them would destroy us as well."

"But," Dov said, "if they war against us, we must fight — and fight to win. With the Mwertik, that means crushing them completely."

"How can we be so sure? I hate them with all my being, but I hate even more what that feeling does to me. I don't know what they are, other than vile, skulking murderers. But I need to find out. How have we failed so thoroughly that they should seek out and butcher our people, destroying everyone and everything in their path? What is it about who we are and what we do that should spawn such malice? We know nothing about the Mwertik. How can we know whether we can or can't turn them, until we try?"

"So, if it's war, you still wouldn't fight?"

"Dov, I would fight to my last breath for our Peace. But I'd rather live for it, even though that's often the harder choice. If I am to believe in all that has shaped who I am, I will have to learn to respect the lives of even my deepest enemies."

"I don't know if I could do that... respect the Mwertik." Dov visibly shuddered at the thought.

Tayar doubted she could either. A part of her wanted to revel in the pain of Jared's savage murder, holding it close to keep the memory vivid. "Let's try to forget about the Mwertik for the moment, Dov. Imagine you are already an Alleman, and you have been sent out beyond our borders to try to bring peace to those two villages in this story." She touched the book from her lap. "What would you do?"

"I don't know enough about them. So, I guess, I'd have to find out what I can."

"Yes. That is one of the primary reasons your father and some of our other Allemen are sent out beyond our borders, to learn what they can of the ways and wants of other people."

"Has Pa brought any new villages into the Alliance?"

"Oh yes, he specializes in First Meets. Hasn't he shared any of his experiences with you? They're quite stirring."

"No, Pa doesn't share anything with me, except a home and Ma."

"Yes, I see. Well, someday, you must ask him about his work. He's quite good at it, and I believe that you have inherited much of his talent."

"There's nothing of him in me," Dov said angrily.

Tayar chose not to dilute the lesson by trying to tackle that deeper pain. Instead, she stood, leaned down to kiss him, and whispered, "Meet me in the inner room."

Chapter 40

Dara/Le'a was in her bedroom preparing for the boy's daily visit when she heard him call from the front door. Dov was early, and from the breathless joy in his voice, she wondered if he'd jogged all the way. When she entered the greeting room, he lifted her off her feet and twirled around.

"Well, someone is in a good mood," she said from on high.

Dov set her back on her feet, and brushed his greeting kisses on her cheeks and lips. "Oh, Le'a! Have you ever seen a more wonderful day?"

She recognized the signs. Rishana/Tayar had obviously used yesterday's crisis to move forward into the Awakening Stage. Judging from the boy's excitement, last night's inner room session must have been lively. "Come into the kitchen, if you can calm down long enough to sit with me."

"For you, anything." He held the kitchen door for her, in a playfully exaggerated display of courtesy.

While Le'a put on the tea kettle, Dov piled a plate with jaut0bakedcookies. Then they sat together, he beaming, she watching and waiting. She waited some time. He seemed content simply sitting there, grinning and daydreaming. The whistling kettle propelled him from his seat, to prepare and pour their tea. Yes, an endearing stage, indeed. If only she could relax and enjoy it.

Dov sipped the tea, ate two cookies with appropriate expressions of appreciation for her baking, and still wasn't forthcoming with conversation. So, Le'a decided to start it. "Tell me, what did you read last night?"

"Oh, it was a strange story called *The Battle Is Over*."

"An interesting choice. What did you think of it?"

He reached for another cookie and nibbled it thoughtfully. "It was easy to see why my person... I mean the person whose words I was reading...was so angry. Everything that mattered to him had been destroyed by the other guy's people. So, he killed him. But, if I'd been reading the other guy's words, I think I would have seen it from that side, and not understood why I — that is, he — was killed. Do you know what

I mean?"

"Do you see how that can relate to what we discussed about reactive and thoughtful behavior?"

"They're completely reactive, aren't they?"

"Are they, Dov? What about the man who wanted to break the cycle?"

"Yeah, but he didn't succeed. I don't think he could ever succeed, because… oh, I get it. It was one way, wasn't it? He was being thoughtful, but it was so new for all of them that he was the only one, and everyone else was being reactive, so it didn't work."

"Unfortunately, you're correct. That's why life was so savage during the Great Chaos. Only when we were able to break the cycles of hate and violence could we begin to establish the Alleshine Peace."

"Are there cycles the Alleshi failed to break?"

"Oh yes, we have failed many times, but we have always persevered. Generations pass. Time can change even the most obstinate enemies, just as a small stream can wear down even the highest mountain."

"But that won't work with the Mwertik, Le'a. It's one thing for Tayar to believe it will. She's so gentle and kind; she thinks listening carefully and giving whatever is needed can solve anything. But if we went to the Mwertik like that we'd just be going into their spirit house to be slain." He shook his head slowly.

"Our Tayar is a creature of great hope and faith." Le'a stared out the window, remembering when she, too, believed that their Peace was inevitable and inviolate, rather than the fragile weave she now knew it to be. "The Mwertik appear to war not for hate or survival, but because that is what they want. They have no concern for anybody, not even their own, apparently taking joy in killing. But somehow, we have to get them to listen to us."

"When we beat them at their own game, they'll have to listen."

"Like the men in *The Battle Is Over*." She sighed, letting the boy see her disappointment in his response. "Then the cycle of hate will continue to escalate."

Dov's dark eyes flashed at the slight rebuke. "Well, what would you do?" he demanded.

"Somehow, we must forge a way to persuade the Mwertik to sit down and listen to us willingly. Until then, we must watch carefully, listen closely, try to learn what it is that they need and want from us."

Dov crossed his arms over his chest and glared at her. "Well, while you're looking for answers, I've got to worry about keeping Ma and Lilla safe, and yeah, you and Tayar, too. I still think the one answer would be to fight the Mwertik on their own terms."

"Then you would be like them, just as reactive, entering into their cycles of violence."

"So, what would you have me do? Nothing? Should I just sit here inside your Peace borders and wait, like a pig in the pen rooting about happily, not knowing that all his life he's been marked for slaughter?"

"But you are not a pig, nor any kind of animal. You are human, learning to be an Alleman, learning the thoughtful path."

"Well, I don't think the Mwertik see it like that."

"Then we'll have to find a way to show them, won't we?"

Chapter 41

Tayar/Rishana tried to lose herself in her cleaning, but her mind was elsewhere, struggling to decipher the various conflicting conversations she'd had with Kiv and Dara. When she realized that she had polished the same table three times, She collapsed into her bedroom armchair. She opened her journal, hoping that writing down her thoughts would help her sort what she knew to be fact from what she could only assume or extrapolate.

If Kiv is as malevolent as Dara would have me believe, then how could Kiv be an Allesha? Or are my own lifelong beliefs about the Alleshi flawed?

If Kiv isn't the vile woman Dara would have me think, if she is exactly as she appears — simply a woman struggling to find answers to help save our Peace — what does that say about Dara?

If I can't trust Dara's judgment and integrity…

Rishana couldn't finish that sentence, unable and unwilling to imagine how rootless her First Season could become, if Dara weren't who and what Rishana needed her to be.

Rishana was so distraught that she didn't notice the design her fingertip unconsciously drew in the fresh furniture oil on the chair-side tabletop. Over and over, it traced a circle and jagged lines, almost as though her finger had a will and memory of its own.

As her finger doodled, her mind wandered, not so much in circles as in escalating spirals. Kiv and Dara were each pulling at her, insisting on her loyalty, demanding that she have faith in them and the way they trained and guided not only her, but also their boys and Allemen, their allies and enemies.

Enemies! She suddenly realized, *Dara doesn't just adamantly disagree with Kiv and distrust her. Dara hates and fears Kiv!*

But that's not possible, not between two Alleshi.

Shaking her head in denial, she saw the designs her fingertip had drawn absentmindedly in the oil on the sidetable. She stared at the various circles and lines that were the shape of the scar on Dov's foot.

Without her eye to guide them, the designs were distorted. One was smaller than the actual scar and shaped slightly differently, as it must have been when it was first burned onto an infant's sole, before it was transformed by his growth.

When she saw that one shape, her heart contracted into itself, a painful clutching weight in her chest. For what she saw was identical to the runes that had been carved into Jared's flesh by his murderers.

The boy didn't seem to notice anything out of the ordinary about their afternoon and evening together. Even in the inner room, the young Allesha managed to suppress her inner turmoil, maintaining the outward appearance of full involvement. But she slept fitfully that night.

The next morning, she applied extra makeup to hide the dark circles under her eyes. As soon as it was feasible, she sent Dov off to Le'a, and rushed to the library to find Savah.

Rishana/Jinet walked briskly through the library's winding corridors and practically collided with Savah outside her study. Savah took one look at her and knew immediately that something was amiss.

"Jinet, what's wrong?" Savah asked, as she guided her into the small room.

"Savah, tell me about this symbol." she brandished a small piece of paper.

"What is it?" Savah asked, as she took the paper and glanced at the design Jinet had drawn.

"How could you forget?"

Savah looked from the symbol to Jinet and back again; she appeared to be weighing the paper against the young Allesha's face, reading both. "Jared?"

"Yes. The horrid mutilations." The room seemed smaller and darker than Jinet remembered, or was it that she was so focused on the drawing that she couldn't see anything else?

"Why now? What has happened that has so unnerved you, my dear?"

"My Winter Boy has a scar on his foot that matches that." Jinet pointed to the drawing. "Or almost matches it. His foot has grown since he was burned as a child, by some medallion, he said. It's distended and distorted by the years. So I didn't recognize it at first."

"A medallion?"

"Well, he doesn't remember what happened. Mistral told him that he stepped on a red-hot medallion when he was only a baby, just learning to walk."

"Yes." Savah nodded. "That's a likely explanation."

"Savah, are you going to tell me what that is?"

"But I thought you knew, Jinet. It's a Mwertik symbol. As far as the Council was concerned, the mutilations were the final proof that the Mwertik had killed Jared."

"Yes, I know that." Jinet's voice rose in undisciplined irritation, and she didn't care. "But why would it be burned into my Winter Boy's foot?!"

"Perhaps…" Savah paused. "His father is one of our Mwertik specialists. It's not unlikely that he could have found one of their medallions. Isn't that a possible explanation?"

Jinet sat down with a thump. "I didn't recognize the scar at first. How could I have not seen it for what it was?"

"Is that was this is about, dear? Do you fear that you are forgetting?"

"No! I will never forget."

"Of course not, dear. But it frightened you, the possibility. Didn't it?"

"I don't think so, Savah. But I don't know. It's just that," she pointed to the paper, "coming on top of Kiv's concerns."

"Kiv," Savah stared at the paper in her hand. "Sometimes, I think that busybody retired just to give herself more time to stick her sharp nose into everybody's business."

"That's almost exactly what Dara said."

"Oh? Yes, I suppose she would."

"That's one of my problems, Savah. Dara hates Kiv." Jinet stared at the small, gentle woman who had taught her more about love than anyone other than Jared himself. "Savah, do you agree with Dara about that, too?"

"Hate is a very strong word, dear. I fear how far Kiv may be willing to take her call to violence against the Mwertik." Savah paused. "I wonder what she would do if some of our own stood in her way. Yes, I suppose when it comes to Kiv, Dara and I tend to agree, but hate—" She shook her head, though Jinet wasn't sure if it were in denial or in response to something else.

Jinet trembled with fear and, she had to admit, anger, too. "Don't you see that's wrong?"

"Of course it is, dear."

"No, I don't just mean Kiv. If the Alleshi can't mitigate their own disagreements"

"Yes, I see what you mean."

"But, Savah, you were just talking like Dara."

"Would you rather I speak as Kiv would?"

"Of course not. But does it have to be either/or? Aren't we the Alleshi, the Peacekeepers?"

"Does that make us any less human?" Savah asked. "Any less fallible?"

"No, but it should make us that much more accountable for our own actions and responses."

"Do you see how Kiv has already affected you, made you question your most fundamental truths? You must not listen to her."

"It isn't only Kiv."

"No, you're correct. The more the Mwertik raid and kill, the more people Kiv may persuade to her way of thinking."

"That isn't what I meant, Savah. Kiv is an Allesha, no less than you or Dara or any of us."

"Jinet, dear, there are things you don't yet understand."

"I wonder… the more I learn, will I understand even less?"

Chapter 42

Evanya found the unsigned note from Karinne under her gatepost lantern. "We must talk. Come to the library immediately."

Heading for the library, Evanya set a steady, heightened pace that would not seem untoward to anyone who watched her. Her mind raced, imagining scenarios of danger, despair, destruction, one after another. Only after a few moments did she realize that in each she was picturing Karinne, not as the old retired Allesha she was now, with her thick, round body and tightly coifed grey hair, but as the young woman Karinne had been when they had met, decades ago, as Allemen brides.

How simple their lives had been when their greatest concerns had been little more than being good Allemen wives, maintaining their homesteads, caring for their children, helping their neighbors. Perhaps that was why the two of them still clung to the names of their youth — Evanya and Karinne — in the privacy of their friendship, in a vain attempt to invoke a time of innocence and faith.

Inside the library, Evanya found Karinne in her private study. "She's seen the brand," Karinne said without preliminary greeting.

Evanya nodded. "As we knew she would."

"But we didn't prepare her for it."

"How could we without telling her the entire story?"

"Evanya, we don't dare wait any longer. His Season must be turned."

"Not until I know how much damage Kiv has done," Evanya insisted. "If Kiv has succeeded in seeding enough doubt that we can't predict how Rishana will react, then we'll need the remainder of the Awakening Stage to solidify her bond with her boy."

Karinne's frown creased her face even more deeply. She gestured for Evanya to sit. "The brand isn't our only problem. Rishana is beginning to doubt you, and maybe even me."

"Tell me."

"You allowed her to see your hate and fear."

"My what? I don't hate anyone."

"Even Kiv?"

"Ah, yes."

"It can become a wedge, separating her from us."

"Never, Karinne. Whatever else she feels or thinks, she would never turn from you."

"Evanya, how can we be sure of that? Yes, she will always love me, because it's ingrained in her as part of her love for her dead husband. But should she ever realize that I've deceived her by withholding the truth, what is it that she would be turning from, other than a phantom of lost faith?"

"You've always been true to yourself. How could she not see that?"

"I didn't tell her the truth about the brand; she'll remember that. She came to me with questions, important ones that cut to her heart, and I diverted the conversation." Karinne's voice trailed off. "Once she realizes that I'm more than her Savah and much less, too, she won't be easy to control."

"She never has been. If she were, she wouldn't have been the right instrument for us."

"True," Karinne said, a glint of pride softening her voice only briefly before it turned to ice. "I knew when we started the sacrifice it would require: to be willing to gamble losing the full faith of one of my own. Now, it's beginning to happen, and I fear everything may unravel at the smallest pinprick."

Evanya was silent for a few moments, weighing what Karinne had said. "How do I regain her trust?"

"She'll be watching for signs of dissembling now." Karinne paused, then said, even more adamantly, "Only honesty will win her trust now, Evanya. That includes the truth of your complicity in all this. And mine. The sooner, the better, if we want her to not only understand, but accept."

"I need a bit more time, Karinne. Time to find the right way."

"You're trying to avoid what must be. I've never seen you like this. If one of your problem boys had behaved in such a manner—"

"Yes, I know. I know. As soon as I'm sure the bond between them is strong enough to withstand whatever might come…" Evanya sighed. "It's been so pleasant these past few weeks, watching them, remembering the wonder and joy. I miss those days, Karinne. How alive we once were. How innocent."

"Our innocence died years ago, by our own hands. You can't allow yourself to become soft now, Evanya, not after everything we have done to get to this juncture. The boy is here, and Rishana is the Allesha we shaped for him. If we weaken when we are so close, it will all have been for nothing. How many deaths would then be piled on our heads?"

"I'm not saying I won't do what must be done. Just that I wish—"

"As we all wish. But only action will save us, not dreams."

Evanya nodded. "Soon, Karinne. Soon."

"What will you do if she asks you directly?"

"I'll deal with that when it happens."

"No, Evanya! You must be prepared. Should she ask you directly — and I am convinced that she will, and soon — you *must* tell her the truth."

"And if she doesn't ask?"

"Then we will know that the damage is greater than we thought."

"Soon, I promise. But it must be gradual, so we don't overwhelm her or damage her Season."

"This is one promise you must not break."

Evanya stood suddenly. "Karinne, how could you? You know I never willingly—"

Karinne didn't move, nor did she adjust her position in any way. She just glared at Evanya, allowing her eyes to cut through to the core, where memories welled up between them. "Your will is your own and ever has been," she said in a steely quiet voice.

Evanya felt the weight of years and guilt descend, and she stood not quite as tall. "Karinne. I will do my best."

"Your best is better than that of anyone I've ever known, dear."

But Evanya knew that more than Karinne or even Rishana was depending on her. If she failed, how would they ever salvage the Peace?

Chapter 43

Dara/Le'a allowed herself the guilty pleasure of watching her two charges as they blossomed during the Awakening Stage. She observed Rishana carefully, almost convincing herself that the young woman's Season remained untainted. Was it so wrong to squirrel away this bit of joy against what was to come?

Rishana had her own style for teaching the sense-awakening lessons. And the boy responded to them with intoxication, like a blind man whose eyes were suddenly opened to colors and light. Of course, his habit of lashing out whenever he felt uncertain or threatened was so ingrained that he was still reactive and often rebellious. He was.however, trying hard to learn and master his temper.

A few days into the Awakening Stage, Dara knew she could delay the inevitable no longer. At the end of Dov's visit with her, she decided to walk back with the boy. Rishana/Tayar had a right to learn the truth.

The sky was heavy with winter clouds and the promise of more snow. Le'a and Dov were approaching Tayar's house when the young Allesha strolled toward them, her arms filled with wicker boxes and mesh bags from the storehouse.

"Hello! Here." Tayar thrust most of the packages at Dov.

He grunted, but said nothing; he was too busy juggling the various strange shapes that didn't fit into a neat pile in his arms.

When everything was balanced, Tayar stroked Dov's hair. She knew the effect to be one of unconscious familiarity, which is why she had started with such gestures. Now it was as natural and heart-born as she would have it appear. She hoped that Le'a didn't notice how stiffly she held herself as she leaned in to embrace her mentor.

Once inside, the young Allesha asked Dov to put the food away and prepare the vegetables for dinner. The two women went into her bedroom and closed the door.

Dara sat in the upholstered armchair while Rishana perched on the edge of her bed. Rishana finally broke the tense silence. "Dara, are you just going to sit there and not say anything?"

"Ask whatever you will, and I'll do my best to answer."

"You hate Kiv," Rishana said. "And you fear her, too."

"Yes," Dara said, but she didn't lower her gaze in shame. "Have you listened to Kiv? Do you understand what she's trying to do to us?"

"Does that give you the liberty to turn from all that we are, all we must do and teach?"

"It's Kiv who has turned. She doesn't believe our ways can hold our Peace in the face of the Mwertik." Dara's hands tightened into fists. Seeing what she was doing, she deliberately opened them, and slowly smoothed the black wool of her trousers with her flat palms.

"But to hate one of our sisters."

"I apologize to you; I have allowed my fears to gain a foothold and turn bitter; it may have affected your Season."

"I don't want or need your apology."

"What is it you do need?" Dara asked.

"Do you know that's the first time any Allesha has ever asked me that? You always do or tell, never ask."

"Perhaps you can teach us to ask more often. So now I'm asking you, Rishana, what do you want?"

"The truth."

"The truth is a large and complex thing."

"Let's start with just one portion of it. Why do you hate Kiv? Why do you fear her?"

"That she will change everything I have ever loved and believed in. Change it so fully that I will no longer recognize my own world, my own people."

"Is she that powerful, then?"

"No, not personally. But she has a powerful ally — our great terror of the Mwertik. When people are so frightened by the unknown, they will listen to even a madwoman."

"Kiv isn't a madwoman. She's an Allesha who is trying to find solutions, as we have all been taught to do."

"But her solutions are unacceptable."

"Nothing seems acceptable. It's either war or our old ways." Rishana saw a glint in Dara's eyes. "Or do you have some other plan?"

"What if we could find someone the Mwertik would listen to?"

"Have you?"

207

"Not yet, but we're working on it."

"An intermediary?"

"Of sorts."

"Who?"

"Whom do you think?"

Possibilities whirled in Rishana's mind. But a part of her had no doubt once the question was asked. Who else could it be that she would know? "Dov?" she asked reluctantly.

"Yes. Dov."

"But why? How?" Rishana paused, suddenly seeing the answer as clearly as the drawing on the paper she had taken to Savah. "The scar on his foot!" She shot up onto her feet.

"Yes, the brand," Dara said, measuring out the words. "The Mwertik mark their own."

Rishana pictured Jared, mutilated just as her Winter Boy had been, and was certain Dara couldn't possibly mean what she was saying. "We know they mark their victims."

"Yes, but in a different way; they carve into their victim's flesh with their knives."

Rishana felt numb, as though her skin had suddenly become a dead shell. "What are you implying? That Dov is Mwertik? *Fire and Stones! How is that possible?*"

"Mistral…" Dara hesitated, choosing her words, "…found him as an infant."

Rishana whirled to stand over Dara. "Found him? Are you saying he isn't Mistral's and Shria's son?"

"Not by blood."

"But how?" Tayar pictured her Winter Boy, so raw and open, so ready to love and learn. "Damn! He doesn't know, does he?"

Dara shook her head. "It's a complicated story, which I promise to tell you some day, but we haven't the time right now."

"Another promise, Dara? Why should I believe you?"

"Because you now know enough that you will seek the truth, with or without my help. I'd rather it be with." Dara pulled her shoulders back, making Rishana realize how hunched over the older woman had been. "Rishana, your boy will be looking for you soon. When we have the time, we'll sit together, and I'll answer all your questions as completely as I can."

Rishana nodded once, in acceptance of the promise she no longer needed or trusted, knowing she wouldn't rest until it was fulfilled. "Tell me one thing: do you have a valid reason to believe that the Mwertik will listen to him?"

"We think so. Everything will depend on his training. On you."

Rishana wanted to shout, to explode with anger, but she was trapped. The only way out for her, for Dov, was to do exactly what Dara expected of her. "Yes, I see that now." She paced about the room, back and forth, measuring the limits of her life, so completely delineated by all that had been decided for her and for him.

"Will you accept my apology?" Dara asked tentatively.

Rishana glared at Dara over her shoulder, then quickly turned away. "No," she said. "No, I can't. But I won't cheat the boy of his Season. Especially now."

"And you'll work with me to shape it?"

"Do I have any choice?"

"Not unless you want to turn to Kiv's ways."

"Damn it, Dara!"

"Yes, I know."

"Do you? Do you understand how betrayed I feel right now? You were my mentor. I thought you were my friend."

"I am and always will be."

"But you lied to me, manipulated me."

"I didn't lie so much as not tell you the truth."

Rishana felt as if she were seeing Dara for the first time, and she didn't like what she saw. "And you hate, Dara."

"Don't you?"

Rishana was thrown by the question, because she did feel hate welling up in her heart. "No, I won't become as you are. I won't hate — not Kiv or you — or anyone."

"And the Mwertik?"

The Mwertik. It always came back to them, and to the memory of Jared's beautiful flesh slashed by Mwertik knives; the same pattern seared into the sole of a child's foot. "I haven't won that battle yet," Rishana admitted.

"But you can win it. Work with me to mold the boy into what he could be, what he must be."

Rishana stared at Dara, and her perception shifted once more, forcing her to see through her own illusions. Dara was nothing more than a woman struggling and sometimes failing. And that was the greatest betrayal of all — that the older Allesha was not the embodiment of wisdom and experience that Rishana had once believed her to be.

"Yes, I will work with you because Dov will need all we can give him if he is to survive your machinations." Rishana closed her eyes and took two cleansing breaths. However, when she looked at Dara again, she didn't feel any calmer. "I must go out to Dov," she said. "He's certainly finished his chores."

As Rishana reached for the doorknob, Dara said, "Kiv must not find out about the boy."

Rishana turned to Dara. "Why not? If she knew you have an alternative, perhaps she'd stop pushing for war."

"We can't know what she might do about him… or *to* him." Dara hesitated, then said in a whisper, "Some wonder about the timing of Jared's murder and how it might have fit into Kiv's plans."

"This is too much! Don't you dare use my memories of Jared to try to control me!"

"I'm not saying I know anything of the kind; only that we have very good reason to be wary of her. Please, Rishana, help me keep the boy's secret."

"For Dov's sake, not yours."

"Of course. I understand. But—"

"No! Don't ask anything more of me right now. I've had enough of your intrigues for one day."

Dara nodded and said no more.

Chapter 44

Evanya found Karinne in her library sanctuary, still lying on her makeshift bed, though fully awake. Books were spread everywhere, tucked around her legs, stacked on tables and piled on the floor. Obviously, Karinne had spent another sleepless night trying to drown her worries in her studies.

"Rishana knows," Evanya said without preamble or greeting.

Karinne put down the ancient hide-bound book she had been reading. "How much?"

"That the boy is Mwertik." Evanya sat in a nearby chair.

"And the rest?"

"Only that we plan to use him as a bridge to the Mwertik."

"You told her?"

Evanya shook her head. "I helped her recognize the brand." She sighed. "How could any people be so barbaric, branding an infant as you would cattle? No wonder Mistral reacted as he did."

"Your Mistral always was a hothead."

"True, but can you imagine any Alleman, any civilized person, sitting still while a baby is being tortured? Not even your precious Jared."

Karinne ignored the taunt. "I'm not sure that I believe it was torture, any more than a tribal tattoo is. We must learn more about them before we can judge their ways." Karinne waved her hand between them, as though to dismiss the direction of their conversation. "So, will Rishana continue?"

"Yes, but not for us or herself, only for the boy's sake."

"I knew she would," Karinne said with pride. "What of the boy? Does he know?"

Evanya shook her head. "No, not yet."

"You must help her prepare him."

"But I've lost an important measure of control."

"No one has control over Rishana when it comes to what she considers right and wrong, any more than you could have controlled Mistral when he saw an innocent baby being hurt."

"She is going to be difficult, even secretive," Evanya said.

"Does she know of my involvement, or the others?"

"No, Karinne, all her anger is directed at me."

"Good. We can use that."

"You're as fearful as I was, Karinne."

"More so. Not just for myself, but for Rishana."

"And when she finds out the full story?"

Karinne sighed. "By then, I hope she will understand."

Chapter 45

That night, before supper, the young Allesha retreated to her room to be alone and prepare herself for the evening ahead.

She had held herself tightly all day, forcing her mind to concentrate only on the boy, struggling with every fiber of discipline to contain her fury. Only now could she allow herself to think back on the morning's conversation with Dara, the days and weeks spent with Dov, the months of her training, the years of her devotion — seeking hints, truths, answers to questions she feared asking, even in the privacy of her own mind. Wherever her thoughts carried her, they returned, over and over, to visions of the drawing she had made of the scar on Dov's foot, the runes gouged into Jared's flesh. One branded for life; the other for death.

Mwertik. The very name of evil. Murderers in deed and in essence.

Yet, if the boy is Mwertik... A Mwertik, in my inner room. Touching me as intimately as Jared ever did. Not just my body, but reaching deep into the heart of me. If giving myself as an Allesha means that my boys will become a part of me, change me, will I, too, have some Mwertik within me?

"Jared, forgive me; I didn't know," she cried in a strained whisper, knowing Dov couldn't hear her through the thick walls, but not wanting to break the silence too loudly, not when there could never again be a response.

Damn Dara! If only she had told me earlier, at the beginning.

If only I had never learned the truth.

A Mwertik, in my inner room. A boy I can't desert; an enemy I cannot abide.

"Jared, did you know?" she cried aloud.

Dov was Mistral's boy. How could Jared have not known? Mistral and Jared and Tedrac. Yes, Mistral would have told his Triats. Was that what Tedrac was hinting at when he sought her out, just before her Season began? Of course it was.

"That doesn't mean you knew the rest, does it, Jared? About Dara and Kiv and the divisions within the Alleshi and how everything we were taught to believe has been distorted?

"Jared, what do I do if he is Mwertik?"

He is my Winter Boy, one who could become a potent Alleman, if I do my job right. Do I dare give him that power and ability? Do I want to continue to devote myself, all I am, to this Mwertik?

I hate the Mwertik. As much as I abhor hate.

I hate the Mwertik because they taught me what hate is.

How is my hate any different from Kiv's — or Dara's?

Kiv and Dara. Enemies, not only of the Mwertik, but of each other. Allesha against Allesha, conspiring to outwit each other, to control me.

What was Council doing during all this? Are they blind? Of course not; they're Alleshi.

No, that's my mistake. There is no "they," no unified whole working together to guide our people.

Factions, then? Arraigned behind Kiv or Dara, choosing for or against aggression or manipulation.

She rose from her desk chair to pace the room, using physical activity to try to her focus her mind. But her back-and-forth movement did nothing to help her untangle the winding paths of her thoughts.

And Savah? What does Savah think of all this? Certainly, she agrees with Dara about Kiv. She said as much. That doesn't mean Savah was party to Dara's plotting. Does it? Savah, whom I'd trust with my life and all I love?

She refused to allow herself to turn from the obvious. *Of course Savah knew.*

Savah and Dara, then. And who else?

In her mind, she roamed The Valley, picturing each lane and house, trying to sort the Alleshi by loyalties. Then she came to her own gate.

Where do I stand? With Dara or with Kiv? Or completely alone?

If I can no longer trust Dara, can I still believe what she has said about Kiv? I understand Kiv, her vehement loathing of the Mwertik, of all that conspires to destroy who and what we are and have. But is she capable of murder? Am I? If I stood face to face with those who killed Jared, what would I do?

"Jared, what happened up on that mountain? You left me for a stupid hunt, to find a white antelope. You returned on a slab of wood, a frozen corpse."

Was it the Mwertik? Can I trust Dara's insinuations about Kiv and Jared? Or was that no more than a clumsy parry to keep me away from Kiv? What does it say about me that I'm willing to consider that an Allesha, one of my sisters, might have been party to Jared's murder? What does it say about Dara that she would set my mind in that direction?

Is anything about The Valley as I had believed?

Feeling unbalanced, she collapsed into her armchair.

My First Boy is Mwertik.

I hate the Mwertik.

But I must not allow myself to hate the boy.

Not Dov.

If Dov is truly a Mwertik, if he is what he has been taught to hate and fear, I can't desert him now, regardless of how many lies and half-truths led me to this point. Not when he will need me and everything I can teach him, now more than ever. As I was taught. In ignorance. Because he is not yet ready to learn the truth. Because I do not yet know the full truth.

So, I go forward. For the boy's sake.

Even if he is a Mwertik.

Chapter 46

A few days later, Tayar walked with the boy to Le'a's, on her way to the storehouse and Caith.

To Dov, Tayar seemed distracted. While their conversation wasn't less lively than normal, underneath the banter and smiles, something seemed to pull at her. He didn't recognize his new awareness as anything unusual; he concentrated instead on trying to discern what she was thinking. When they parted at Le'a's gate, he started to ask Tayar what was bothering her, but realized that she wasn't ready to talk about it — whatever it was.

Dov found Le'a in her barn, sitting on a stool in a small room he had never entered before. Le'a was so involved in working a potter's wheel that she apparently didn't hear him enter. While her legs pumped up and down in an even rhythm, making the wheel turn, her hands and fingers worked the clay. When Le'a reached for more water to smooth the paths her fingers plied, she glanced at him, clearly aware of his presence.

Back home, he had never paid much attention to the potter's work. Making the jugs and jars that women use hadn't seemed a worthy task for a true man. But watching Le'a at her wheel, the boy felt something spark within himself. Though his eyes focused on her fingers and the clay, his mind pictured a particular glade two days' walk from his village. There, by a pooled part of the stream, he liked to sleep so he could witness the forest's rebirth, as it awakened to the dawn. Somehow, the way Le'a worked the clay reminded him of that.

She stopped pedaling the wheel and, as it gradually slowed to a halt, leaned back to look over her creation. "What do you think?" she asked.

"Nice."

"Nice? Is that the best you can say? If you like it, tell me why. If not, don't give me an empty compliment."

"Hey, what did I do to get you angry at me?"

"Nice is something you say when you don't want to make any commitment. It's a safe word. I hate safe words. They don't belong between friends. Give me cruel honesty over safety any time. Then I would know you care enough about me to give all you are to our friendship."

"Look, Le'a, I'm sorry I upset you. I didn't know what to say. I've never seen anything like that. Skies! It was a lump of wet clay, but you pulled and poked and coaxed, until it became that... I don't know what to call it."

"You can call it a vase, though I may end up making it into a pitcher."

"A pitcher? But I've never seen one like that."

"You still haven't told me what you think of the shape, the form."

"It curves like a woman. Not that it looks like a woman, but it makes me want to touch it, to see if it feels like a woman."

"Wonderful! Then I've accomplished what I wanted. Thank you." She pointed to the vase on the wheel. "Why don't you try it?"

"I'd ruin it."

"Don't be silly."

"No, I don't want to touch it. I mean, I do want to touch it, but not like that. It needs to be preserved, not changed."

Carefully, with knife and hand, Le'a removed the vase from the wheel, placed it on a nearby shelf, and draped a damp cloth over it. "In that case, after I fire it, I'll give it to you, to keep safe and touch whenever you wish." Opening a barrel, she took two fistfuls of clay, balled them together and slapped it on the wheel. "Now make something for me."

He looked at the clay, then at her. "I don't know how to work a wheel."

"You'd be amazed what you can do when you try."

Le'a's mind was obviously set, so Dov stepped closer to the wheel. "Okay. What do I do?"

Le'a punched the center of the clay down. "I'll pedal for you. Pull up that other stool and sit across from me. First, wet your hands in the bucket." Dov did as ordered. "Good. Now, take these sides..." she pointed to the edges her punch had created, "between your thumbs and fingers, with your thumbs on the inside. As I pedal, the wheel will turn, slowly at first, then faster, okay?"

"Yeah, but what do I do?"

"Lightly squeeze the clay between your fingers and thumbs."

Dov placed his hands as she had described. When the wheel started, he felt the clay move under his fingers. At the slightest touch, it climbed up into his hands as it thinned out between his fingers and thumbs. "Hey, wow."

"Don't glance away!" Le'a's warning was too late. The clay was already wobbling out of control.

"Damn!" He hit the lump and stomped away. "I told you I couldn't do it."

"Dov, come back here. Don't give up so easily."

"I don't know how to do it."

"You never will unless you try. Everyone makes a mess the first time. When you were learning how to shoot your bow and arrow, did you hit the target the first time?"

"But archery is something I needed to learn, to be a man. This is nothing."

"Nothing? To make a thing of beauty that's also useful? To learn how to do something you've never done before? No, I don't think you believe that. I think you're just afraid of failing."

"Look, I'm not afraid of anything."

"I don't believe that either, because I know you're not a fool. Only a fool has no fears. A brave person goes forward despite them."

"It's just a stupid lump of clay."

"That's all it is right now. But you can make it into something else, into anything you wish."

"You're not just talking about the clay, are you? Okay, what's the lesson today?"

She pulled the lump off the wheel, rolled it into a ball, wet it, then punched it down onto the wheel again. "I want you to make something for me from this clay."

"In other words, you're not going to tell me, are you?"

"Come here. Dov. Stand beside me, and let's do this together. Place your fingers over the back of my hand, your palms over my fingers and the tip of your thumbs over my thumbnails. Good. Now let your hands float rather than press on mine."

With his hands on hers, she moved them up and down, side to side, to give him a feel for following her motions. "Yes. I think we're ready to start. I wonder what we'll make."

"Don't you know?"

"Oh, I have ideas, but my hands and the clay tend to take over. First, let's wet our hands again." He kept his hands on hers even as she dunked them into the frigid water. "Remember, remain on my hands whatever I do."

"It feels strange. You'd think that it would be easy to let you take over, but I have to keep controlling from my shoulders, so I don't put any pressure on you. It's harder than it was when I was doing it myself."

"That's true. And there's a lot to think about in what you say." She began pedaling.

Forcing himself to keep his hands as light as a bird's feather, he rode her movements as she pressed outward with her thumbs, rolling the clay up with her fingers. A simple bowl quickly formed. "That's pretty neat," he said.

"Yes, but let's see what we can do with this." She started to put her full left hand inside the bowl. However, with his hand on hers, she had to first widen the mouth, so both could fit. That done, she placed one hand inside and the other outside, and pressed them together, creating a indent where the bowl had bulged. Working from the base to the mouth, she alternated between softening and exaggerating the curves.

The wheel slowed. With a sigh of pleasure, Le'a pulled her hands away from his, dunked them into the water and rubbed off the clay. "Yes, I do believe you have a feel for this."

"Can I try again?"

"Of course." She punched down the piece they had just created.

"Hey! Why'd you do that?"

"To give you a starting point."

"But we made that… you and me, together. And now it's gone."

"When I work at the wheel, I'm constantly destroying what I've created."

"But that's not like you."

"Dov, I'm an Allesha. I will always be changing. Whenever you think you know me, beware, because you'll never see the whole of me. Then again, isn't that so with any person?"

He stared at her, uncertain how to answer.

She pointed to the clay on the wheel. "Why don't you try it on your own this time? But shall I pedal for you?"

"Okay." Dov stepped forward, wary but intrigued. Hesitating only briefly, he formed the clay into a ball. After dunking it in the water, he put it dead center onto the wheel and punched it down, as he had seen her do. Le'a began to pedal once more.

Dov pressed his thumbs and fingers around the rim, trying to recreate the movements and sensations they had shared. Like a living creature, the clay played with him, flowing up and around his fingers that rode the ever-changing shape. When he tried to force the clay to his will, it started to wobble again. This time, however, he didn't stomp off in anger. Instead, he pulled his hands away, wet them again, and as she slowed the pedaling, he re-balled the clay and started over.

Dov rode the clay once more, following it as it formed itself into a tall vessel. Seeing the shape develop, he gently guided it to curve here and there. It was like walking on a fallen branch across a river. He could go forward, but only carefully, stopping his effort and allowing the clay to take over whenever it began to protest. Then he pressed his will again, until his next retreat. The clay eventually formed into a strangely shaped bowl with a wide neck. After a while, Dov released the clay and watched the wheel spin down until it was still. "That was nice," he sighed.

"Nice?" But this time her voice held a tease, not scorn.

"No, You're right. Not nice at all. Sort of scary. It felt like it was alive and claiming me. When I let it, I felt so peaceful. But I couldn't let it win, could I? Then it would be doing the potting, not me. I mean, I needed to put myself into the thing, not simply sit there and let it take over. But I couldn't force it, or it would fall apart again. So I had to coax it and watch it. Hey! That's what this is about, isn't it? Reading things, reading people. It's what Tayar's been teaching me, and you knew that, didn't you?"

"How does that relate to the clay?" she asked.

Dov stared at the bowl on the wheel. "Well, she says that touching is like a partnership. It's a gift, too. But a gift is valuable only if it's what the person receiving it wants. The clay was like that. I couldn't just make it move the way I wanted. Instead, I had to learn from it — learn how it wanted to move — then make small adjustments to influence it. But they couldn't be so far off from its natural way that it would break or bend. I've got it, haven't I?" His entire being felt suddenly alive with excitement and discovery.

"Excellent! I knew you'd figure it out on your own. Of course, there's more. But you've made a key connection. I'm very pleased."

Dov knew her words should have sounded encouraging. Instead, they made him feel that he had let both her and himself down. "What did I miss?"

"Is influence a gift?" Le'a asked. "You started out saying a gift must be something the receiver wants. But then you explained how the clay taught you to be more effectively influential. Are they related?"

He couldn't decipher what she was asking. "I don't know. You tell me."

"Actually, they are. Many of the same skills that you use to tailor your gifts can be used to influence those around you. When necessary, we must convince others that our gifts are indeed what they want and need. However, the power of influence can become addictive. That's a trap you must never allow to ensnare you."

"Isn't that what all this is about? Being an Alleman and everything? I mean, you're supposed to teach me how to change things, and that requires knowing how to get people to change."

"Yes, and to leave things unchanged when that's the best path. Then there are personal relationships, which are quite a different matter. You wouldn't want to always be in control with your family, your wife, your friends, would you?"

"Sure, why not?"

"Because, they would become less than your friends, and you'd be more than a companion, less of a man."

"Huh?"

"Come, let's clean up here. We'll go into the kitchen and talk over tea."

"Sure." No longer elated, feeling instead like he was hovering over a precipice, Dov didn't understand what had gone wrong. For a brief moment, he had glimpsed the shape of what they were trying to do to him, and it had felt so very right. Why did it now seem so unattainable? Why couldn't Le'a or any of them ever be satisfied with who he was?

Chapter 47

In the storehouse, Tayar/Rishana found Caith perched on the top rung of an impossibly tall ladder, her feet resting on a high shelf. Mumbling to herself, Caith read the labels of the goods stored there. She found one of the items she sought, tossed it into a mesh bag that hung on a hook on the ladder, and pushed off with her feet, so the ladder rode its rails to the next section.

All the times Rishana had seen Caith do that, she was still amazed at the old woman's nonchalance and energy. During her training, when she had been apprenticed to Caith, Rishana had worried about the seemingly frail old woman dangling so high. Though Rishana had attempted to take such risky responsibilities onto her much younger frame, she never did gain Caith's easy mobility in the upper stacks.

The young Allesha's heart still leapt into her mouth, watching the tiny caretaker deftly swing about like a flying mouse. Should Caith ever fall, no Healer would be able to mend her old brittle bones. Still, this was what Caith loved, who she was. If she had seen Rishana below her, the younger woman had no doubt the older one would take even more risks, to prove how capable she still was. So Rishana didn't announce her presence. Instead, she wandered through the shelves and storage rooms.

It hadn't been Rishana's intention to collect provisions, but the variety of what was available was so tempting that she soon had her own bulging mesh bag. When she rounded a corner, Caith was waiting for her, arms on her skinny hips, a wide grin adding even more wrinkles to her dark, parched skin. "So, you've come for your oysters."

"Yes, Caith."

"Your boy is progressing well." It wasn't a question.

"Yes," Rishana responded to her retreating back, as Caith led the way.

"Quickly, in fact. Some had told me not to expect you for a while, but I knew they were wrong. Your First Boy is special; he'll surprise all of them. He's an interesting one."

"That he is."

The old caretaker turned to face the young Allesha, and with her

222

rough, calloused hands, pulled Rishana's face down, to look into her eyes. "Yes, interesting." Then she trotted ahead once more.

Rishana had difficulty keeping up with tiny Caith, who turned unexpectedly through this aisle and that. Without warning, they ended up not at the oyster ponds, but in Caith's room. Rishana noticed new piles of books spilling out of the wall-covering cabinets and towering in corners. It made her realize that it had been a long time since she had last spent an evening with Caith in this cozy room, talking about everything that had ever entered their minds and lives.

"Come, sit." Caith cleared papers and books from the upholstered armchair for Rishana, then pulled the wooden desk chair closer for herself. She poured two glasses of wine from a crystal decanter and handed one to Rishana. "Taste this. I think the Friants surpassed themselves with this vintage."

Caith swirled the red wine in her glass, watching the light dance on the liquid. Then she closed her eyes, breathed in the rich, earthy fragrance, and sipped, playing the various pungent, sweetly acidic flavors over her tongue.

Rishana found she couldn't give herself to the wine as fully as she would have liked. Nevertheless, she drank in silence rather than disturb the wonder of the moment for Caith.

With a sigh of pleasure, Caith put her empty glass on the desk, and leaned toward Rishana. "So, how are you doing?"

"I'm fine."

"No, dear." She placed her hand on Rishana's knee. "Start again. How are you doing?"

"I don't know." Rishana paused, weighing how much to disclose. "He's fascinating to watch as he learns. I believe he'll be a fine Alleman, maybe even one of great power and influence."

"Of that I've no doubt. But does he give you pleasure in the inner room? Does he have any native skill?"

"Yes. There, too, he has learned."

"Good... Good." Caith leaned back. "Does he make you forget that you're an Allesha and he's your Winter Boy? Does he ever make you feel like a woman with a man?"

"No. I won't let that happen. Don't worry, Caith."

"No, not yet."

"Never!" Rishana shook with the insult that she could ever be so unAlleshine.

"Don't be so sure. Oh, yes, I know they tell you that it would break the trust, but I've never really followed any rules that *they* force...

Whoever *they* might be."

"Caith!" Rishana couldn't believe what she was hearing.

"The day he makes you forget is the day that you'll realize how deeply you love him. That's when you'll know how fine a job you have done as his Allesha. But you need to prepare for it now, Rishana. You have the potential to be one of the best I've ever known. Your boys will become powerful Allemen, because of the power and skill within you. That's why you will forget who you are in the end." Caith sighed. "I'm sorry; there will be much pain for you."

"Oh, now I understand. You're talking about the difficulty of End of Season separation. I think I'm prepared for that."

"No, that isn't what I'm referring to, but—" She paused to look deeply into her young companion's eyes. When she spoke again, it was with a lighter, happier voice. "Enough of this. There will be great pleasure, too. And, at the end of it all, we'll still have good wine like this. Do you want another glass?"

Rishana smiled. "No, thank you, Caith. I think I need to keep my head right now."

"Well then, let's go. I've put aside a very special selection of oysters for your First Season." She pulled her coat out of the closet. "I think I'll go with you to help prepare their new pond."

Rishana was speechless. Caith hardly ever left the storehouse anymore except to attend important Council meetings. "I'm honored."

"Bosh! Let's go. We've got work to do, and pleasure to prepare for." Caith was rushing ahead through the towering shelves once again, with Rishana following in her wake.

In Rishana's inner room, Caith helped her remove the oyster pond's stone cover, and showed her how to regulate the water temperature to assure that the mollusks stayed alive and healthy. Caith then sat back on her haunches and studied Rishana.

Rishana broke the silence of Caith's scrutiny. "I wish you were my First Season mentor." She hadn't meant to say it aloud, nor had she realized that was how she felt. But when the words poured out of her, she knew the truth of them.

Caith didn't respond, and Rishana didn't know what more to say, still unsure how much she could safely disclose. The only person she trusted more than Caith was Savah. Yet, she hadn't even spoken to Savah about Dov's true identity. "This Valley isn't what I thought it was, Caith. I never realized how fragmented the Alleshi are."

"Politics." Caith spat the word, as though she had bitten into a worm-rotten apple. "They couldn't let you have a normal First Season, could they?"

"Who?"

"Who do you think? Those old crones."

"Dara and Kiv?"

"Yes, them, too."

"Caith, they hate each other."

"Do they? Yes, I suppose it could have grown to that by now."

"Tell me, please."

"Rishana, you know I keep myself apart from the Council. Let them wrestle with day-to-day arguments. I prefer staying in my storehouse and watching the years unfold."

"You know more than anyone about what's happening in this Valley. Don't pretend you don't. I've seen you."

"Oh?" Caith raised an eyebrow. "Have you now?"

"Yes, I have. You might not take sides, but you know exactly which side faces where, don't you?"

Caith asked softly, "Tell me, child, what have they done to you?"

"I've never had any choice in anything. I've been nothing more than a pawn, pushed this way and that, to make me fit into their plans." In the soft warmth of her inner room, the words tasted bitter, cold, but as true and solid as the granite floor around the pool.

Caith crossed her legs, folded her hands on her lap and spoke in a quiet voice that made Rishana's sound even louder by comparison. "Rishana, how do you work with your First Boy? Do you tell him the shape of every stage of the Season from the beginning?"

"Caith, they're using me for their personal ends."

"To be an Allesha is to be of service, to be used."

"But not like this. When did it start? Was it from my first day of training. or earlier? Who decided I was to be Dara's heir, a specialist in problem boys? Who really chose this boy for me? And what about Kiv and Dara? How can hate be allowed in this Valley? Doesn't being an Allesha mean anything anymore? Did it ever?"

Caith reached out to catch Rishana's windmilling hands. Locking eyes with the young woman, she tried to infuse her own calm strength through pure will. "Hush, child. Don't let them tear you apart."

"But Caith—"

"You're no one's pawn, unless you allow it."

"You don't know—"

"I know more than most realize. Now, take a breath." Still holding the young woman's left hand, though more gently, Caith breathed with Rishana, guiding her by example to slow her rhythms. After several long, slow breaths, she nodded. "Let's break down your fears into small bites."

"Tell me about Kiv," Rishana said.

"She's allowed her terror of the Mwertik to take control."

"Is she dangerous?"

"I don't really know, but there's always some danger whenever we allow our fears to direct our actions. How far has fear taken Kiv? I hope not as far as Dara seems to think it has, but I can't know for certain."

"So you've seen it too? Dara and Kiv."

"Yes."

"I don't know what to think of them."

"Then don't. Not now. You need to put aside all such concerns and concentrate on your Season."

"But my First Boy—" Rishana stopped in mid-sentence. Not even with Caith would she dare expose Dov's fearsome truth. Not until she was sure she understood the perils that lay in wait for him… and for her.

"Yes?"

Rishana stood and held out her hand to help Caith up onto her feet. "You're right. He must be my focus right now. Thank you."

Caith's creased face formed an enigmatic half smile. "You're very welcome, my dear."

At the front door vestibule, Rishana helped Caith on with her coat, then started to put on her own. But Caith shooed her. "No, child, I won't have you walking all the way to the storehouse again. I will enjoy the solitude of my stroll, and you must meditate and prepare."

"Thank you. For everything."

They embraced as Alleshi do, in ritual respect and bonding, but also as two women wanting to give something of themselves to each other. Before turning to leave, Caith said, "Come see me again. Soon."

Chapter 48

Throughout the afternoon, Dov was fidgety and unpredictable. One moment, he'd be attentive and happy, the next, moody and irritable. Rishana/Tayar had been told to expect such confusion as the boy struggled between his newly heightened sensitivities and deep-rooted habits. The strain would be fueled, rather than soothed by the vivid sensuality of the Exhilaration Stage. Then, during the Conflagration Stage, something in him would ignite, churning his fears and uncertainties to the forefront. With a boy of such power, she had no doubt Conflagration would be intense and difficult to direct. But first, tonight, she would use the oysters to initiate Exhilaration.

After dinner, Tayar and Dov settled into the sofa, heads at either end, legs entwined, as had become their way. He picked up *The Traveler's Tales* from the end table and opened it. Tayar leaned back into the arm pillow and closed her eyes while he paged through the book to find his leather page marker.

"The next story's called *The Northern Border*," he said.

One year, I wintered in the sun-seared south, where the people were as dried out as the thin leached soil. So it was with little sorrow that I followed my feet to the north and west at the first hint of spring's shriveling hot winds. As I traveled, I kept pace with the season, watching spring touch the earth again and again, gradually changing from a flavor of death to that of life.

Finally, in a high mountain range, I found a deep, wide-open cave. A creek babbled nearby and trout dashed through the currents. As spring progressed, the bushes along the banks grew heavy with food for the picking. It was a safe place, bountiful and quiet. I could curl up into myself to heal the wounds that the south had flayed into my soul.

I was not alone. As Alleen had taught me, I called life to me each dawn. Then one morning, a new life responded, one I hadn't known existed there.

Tracks of dried tears streaked the child's dirty face. Her clothes were torn and filthy; her tiny hands were caked with mud and blood; her legs scratched and bruised. She crawled into my lap as I sang to the animals and the sun, looking up to me with hope, fear and hunger. I continued my song; it seemed to calm her. By the time all the animals had crept away, one by one, she was asleep, her hands wrapped around my belt to hold me there, perhaps to assure herself that I was real.

She did not awaken when I carried her to the stream, though she slept fitfully, with small fearful squeals and twitching muscles. I bathed her scratches and bruises, relieved to realize that most of the caked blood was not hers. She did not appear more than three or four years, but was so frail and thin that she might have been older. As I washed away the filth, I saw how fair she was, unlike the dark babies I had once carried in my womb, held to my breast and buried in the smoldering ruins of my village.

I realized the child was awake when I felt the sudden stillness of her body. I continued to wash her and applied unguent to her bruises as though it were normal to be responsible for a strange child. When I washed her face, our eyes met; hers were the blue of glacier ice. Her tiny hand reached up to brush my tears, and she whispered, "Mama." Hearing her small voice form that sound and give it to me bound me to her as no rope or chain ever could.

I called her Dawn, for the morning song which brought her to me. She fit into my life so easily that it was hard to believe it had not always been so. When we fished and swam and gathered our food, she stayed by my side, her eyes fixed on me as though she feared that, if she looked away, I would disappear. At night, we slept curled together, though she kicked and cried, unable to escape whatever demons stalked her dreams.

Our days were happy and quiet. Too quiet. She spoke no word, other than that first "Mama." I tried to coax her tongue with my own, but she'd only look at me, as though she didn't know the purpose of my utterances. I chose to not press her. In time, I thought, she will learn how very safe she is with me. In time, she will have so much to say that words will spill from her.

I knew how to be patient.

I was relearning how to love.

Finally, one day, she felt secure enough to venture out of my sight. We had been walking along the bank of our stream, gathering our noon-day meal, when a butterfly lighted on her hand, then flew away. Laughing, she chased it downstream, actually turning her back on me in her delight. I followed her, careful not to catch up, to let her have her private adventure.

So it was that she was around a bend when I heard her scream. It *was a sound out of nightmares. My legs pumped faster than ever in my life, but at first sight of what lay ahead, I stopped in midstride and crouched behind a clump of bushes.*

In the clearing, two sun-baked, fair-haired men fought with knives, while two others jeered in a guttural language not unlike some I had learned in my travels. All four men were enormous, with bodies made strong through breeding and training, far beyond the needs of peaceful folk.

"Get him, Kar!"

"Watch his left!"

"Kill him!"

Tucked under the arm of one of these goading spectators was Dawn. She kicked and struggled, but she was so small, dwarfed by the single arm as a rabbit is to a tree, that he didn't even shift as she flailed against him. My eyes darted over every speck of the clearing, seeking some way to wrest my child from these savages.

Kar's knife bit hard into the belly of his adversary, who struck out blindly, already dead, though his legs and arms didn't yet know it. With a final slash to the throat and a kick to the stomach, Kar finished off his opponent, who fell with a gurgle to the ground. Kar wiped the blood off his knife on the dead man's tunic, then turned to the one who held Dawn. "Shut that brat up, or I'll do it myself."

My heart careened into my throat when I saw him brandish his knife toward Dawn.

"Na, Kar. She's Murat for sure." The one who held Dawn nodded to the dead man, then held the child up in front of him, so Kar could see the resemblance. "She'd be a good hostage."

"Shit, they've none of mine, what do I care of hostages to trade? And she's too young for anything else. Hell, give her to me and we'll be done with it. I can't stand that bawling."

"Wait!" I ran out of my hiding place as he grabbed Dawn. "I can keep her quiet."

"Well, what is this?" Kar lumbered toward me, so casually threatening that I knew the taste of my own death.

"Mama!" Dawn screeched.

"Mama? You're no Murat." He rubbed the heel of his hand on my cheek. "What are you?" He turned to his companions and laughed. "Hey, look at this. It isn't dirt. It's her skin. She's the color of shit. That's what you are, a piece of talking shit."

"The child is frightened, but I can quiet her if you will let me hold her," I pleaded.

229

"Why the hell not, Kar?" said the third man. "We've got bounty here. More than we've found all trek. Let's take both and go home."

"Here." He thrust Dawn into my chest. "Now shut her up."

I stroked and kissed Dawn, while checking her over for wounds. "Pshaw, child. I'm here. I know. But you mustn't cry." Slowly, her sobs subdued, not because she was comforted, but because I think she understood that our lives depended on her silence.

I felt a jab in my back. "Move!"

I walked in front of the men, carrying Dawn. Whenever we came to a diverging path, a kick or shove would indicate which direction to go. I hummed to the child to calm us, as I would to my dawn creatures, but under my breath, my lips to her ear.

By their choice of campsite for the evening, I knew our captors were dull to all I could see and feel around us. They did not read the signs of snakes nearby, nor that water would be easier to find further on.

When they raped me that night, Dawn held my hand, which I stretched above my head, as far from what was happening as possible. She somehow knew that by being near she could diminish the violence, help me see that those three men weren't important. Her short life had included men like these, of that I had no doubt. No wonder she chose not to speak. But her hand in mine said more than words ever could.

The days and nights soon bled into one another, differentiated only by what I learned of each man and of their people. Kar was the leader because he was the strongest. He leaned on his physical strength as a cripple does a staff. His senses were uninitiated, his mind followed only straight and obvious thoughts.

Thim was the smallest of the three, but still larger than any man I had ever encountered. That first day, he had mentioned that his child was held hostage by the Murat. So I tried to talk to him, thinking that he might feel some common bond with me. I learned that it was a son of thirteen years and his eldest, before Kar told him to "shut up about that damn kid of yours."

In coloring, Dac was even fairer than the others, with nearly white hair, though his skin was burnt to a permanent ruddiness. He was the most brutal when he took his turn on me, making me realize that what he felt for me was less than hate, because I wasn't even human to him.

From their boastful banter, I learned of their people, the Mukane, and of the Murat, whom they said were Dawn's tribe. For as long as history, the Murat had been the Enemy, and that defined their whole existence. Kar ranted about his murdered brother and uncle, Thim of his raped daughter and captured son, and Dac of a diverted stream. The very word

Murat was a vile curse on their lips.

On our fifth afternoon of captivity, I saw signs of danger on the land. Small animals scurried, not from our tramping feet, but toward us, in their haste to flee from whatever was ahead. The smell of something large and bloodied changed the tenor of the breeze.

Dawn had been walking by my side. I gathered her up in my arms and whispered to her to hold tight. Dust bellowed over the rocks in our path, and I knew it was near, so I coughed, pulling my body to the right in the natural way of uncontrollable coughs. Before Kar could grab me, the wild boar charged in their midst, and I flattened our bodies against the other side of a large boulder.

Huge and wounded, the boar ran at them with madness in its eyes and death on its tusks. It gored Kar, ripping apart his groin before Thim and Dac could unsheathe their knives. Crouching low, the two men approached the boar from opposite sides. The boar pawed the ground, lowered its head and charged Dac, who was slightly closer than Thim. Before it reached Dac, Thim slashed its back. The boar turned toward Thim, and was slashed by Dac. When it turned again, though Thim's knife caught its hind, it would not be deflected before ramming into Dac, who had straightened up just in time, so that the tusks bit into his legs instead of his abdomen.

By now, the other sounds I had heard grew louder ~ calls and hoots and stomping feet ~ as a band of men cleared the knoll of rocks. Large blondes so similar to my captors that they might have been brothers, they carried spears as well as knives. The boar turned from Dac and ran toward the newcomers, only to be stopped by a wall of spears raining down on it.

"Ha! Got him, finally," one gloated as he pulled his spear from the boar and pointed it at Dac and Thim. Soon the two were surrounded by a circle of blades.

I tried to flatten myself and Dawn even further behind the boulder. If only we could avoid being seen.

Two men, dressed with more beading than the others, strolled over the crest. From the way the others' posture changed when they arrived, I realized they must be leaders of the group. That was when Dawn slipped from my grasp and ran forward, shouting with glee "Nonni!" As the smaller of these two leaders turned to her, crying, "Nasserit," I ran also. "Dawn!"

She was in his arms, hugging and kissing his face, when I reached them. However, four warriors blocked me, their bloody spears aimed at my chest. The man Dawn called Nonni and I stared at each other. Neither of us knew what to think of the other, but realized that we both loved the same child. He barked a command, and the spears were withdrawn. For the moment, I was to be spared.

The other leader had entered the circle that held Dac and Thim and the fallen Kar. He kicked Kar, who didn't move. Then he bent to look at Dac, who moaned and writhed on the ground. "Bisrit!" he called.

The man who held Dawn looked at him, then at the child. He was needed, but didn't know what to do with her. I held out my arms, and he placed her there. Then he stepped into the circle and bent to examine Dac's legs.

"How bad is he, Healer?" the other leader asked Bisrit.

"Do you wish him to live, Darrint?"

"I haven't yet decided. Would it be difficult?"

"No, not difficult. No main vessels are severed. The muscle and flesh can be sewn. If he were not Mukane... Do you have a purpose for him?"

"Sew him up for now. We can decide to kill him later."

"As you say." Bisrit called to another, who brought his satchel of Healer tools and medicines. Two men had to hold Dac down when Bisrit dug through the sinews of his legs to sew together skin and ligaments. As I looked on Dac's pain, I remembered his brutality, and felt no pity.

The band camped at that spot and had a feast of roasted wild boar. In the afterglow of their meal, the men discussed the fate of Thim and Dac. When Dac admitted that he was the son of the Mukane headman, they decided to spare them both as hostages.

Then the leader turned to me. "What of that?"

"What is it?" asked one man.

"A woman," said another.

"We've enough women who aren't burnt black."

That was when the Healer Bisrit stood and came to stand beside me. "My granddaughter has bonded with her. Whatever she may be, it is likely she saved Nasserit's life. I give her my protection and claim her for my hearth. Any who would refuse me that right risks the wrath of their Healer." He turned slowly to look into the eyes of every man gathered around the fire. None challenged him.

"Come," he commanded me, and I followed him to his night space, which was set apart from the others. I slept by his side, with Dawn curled between us, though I did not allow myself to sleep deeply.

Their village was not far from where we camped. In two days, we reached the stream that marked their northern border. The warriors splashed across it, hooting and laughing. Women and children poured out of the village to greet them. Men and elders followed, with wide welcoming smiles. Suddenly, I found myself in the midst of a throng of people whose appearance was so similar to one another that I doubted any outsiders had ever lived among them. Even the young women were large, strong and very pale, as though they stemmed from the same colorless but fierce forebearers as Kar, Thim and Dac.

The Healer had me walk between him and Dawn, our hands linked, so all would know my place. Still, everyone stared and pointed, as much at the color of my skin as in wonder at the return of the child who had been believed dead.

Soon, the crowds parted, making a path for an old, stooped woman, who leaned heavily on a staff and dragged her left leg behind her. When she saw Dawn, she fell to the ground. "Nasserit!" she called and lifted her arms to the child, who ran to her. Weeping and laughing at the same time, the old woman touched the child on her limbs and face, head and body, trusting only her hands to prove what her eyes beheld.

The Healer took me to them, and said, "Mother, this woman saved Nasserit's life."

She reached up to me, and I bowed to put myself within her grasp. Holding my hand, she said, "Child, whatever I have is yours, for you have returned to me all that is left of me and mine. Please tell me what name I shall call you, other than deliverer."

"Please, ma'am, do me the honor of naming me for all to hear, for I am reborn today, knowing that Nasserit is finally safe with her family."

She looked at me fully, seeing all that I asked. For should she name me, I would be one of hers, belonging to her village, and finally safe, as Dawn was. By now, the entire tribe surrounded us, watching in awe the reunion of the child and great-grandmother, and the stranger with brown skin who dared to ask such a boon before anyone knew her.

No sound was heard from the group, until the old woman spoke once more. "You are truly my child because you restored the last of my line to me. So, I name you Meysrit, for the fruit tree that nourishes us even in winter." She looked up to the Healer, who nodded, then took me by the hand once more. Dawn stayed with the great-grandmother.

That night, I slept in the Healer's hut, alone with him for the first time. But he did not touch me, nor did he lie near me. He seemed still youthful, though not young. I had no reason to doubt his virility. So I judged that either he found me repugnant or he honored me for Dawn's sake. Or maybe, his protection, which he had given me, extended even into his own hut.

As a member of the Healer's hearth, I assisted him in his duties. At first, I was given only menial tasks, such as washing the rag bandages or chopping herbs. But, as time passed, he saw that I, too, had some skill in the healing art. The Healer learned to trust my eyes for harvesting our medicines from the earth, once he had shown me the shape of the plants and leaves. And he would use my hands when more than two were needed to tend to the wounded or sick. Some initially resisted my touch, fearful that my darkness might be contagious. But the Healer either ignored or ridiculed their objections.

Soon, he assigned me the care of the hostages, though the Healer continued to check my work, making sure I followed his instructions in everything. The hostages were kept in a fenced pen like animals, though they were not treated as well as the animal stock that fed the village. But they were not to die, unless the headman decided otherwise. The Mukane held too many Murat prisoners, which made an exchange inevitable.

In the hostage pen, I saw Thim reunited with his son. He seemed torn between his joy of being with the boy once more and the shame of living as a prisoner among his enemies.

Dac's leg wounds were slowly healing, but the flesh was knitting together too tightly. So I worked the muscles with massage and exercise, which was painful to him. I do not doubt he saw my efforts as torture, my revenge for his brutality.

Why did I do it ~ try to help his legs heal properly ~ though it was not part of Bisrit's orders? Should the Healer have discovered it, I could have been punished. I'd seen other women, true Murat, punished for much less. To bear such risk for a man who had shown me only violence and cruelty was foolish indeed. Yet, I continued. I have no easy explanation for my actions.

One day, while I was in the pen with the hostages, the guards brought in a new prisoner, a boy of ten or eleven years. His wounds were so severe that blood poured out of him more quickly than I could apply cloths. When Bisrit came, he worked furiously to save the child, even though he was Mukane. That was the Healer's way, to see only the patient and his needs, while he worked on him.

As he ministered to the child, he barked at me for this tool, that herb or another bandage. We worked as we often did, reading each other so clearly that it was as though we were a single person with four hands. But regardless of how hard we tried, we could not stop the torrent of the boy's lifeblood. It was like trying to hold a river in your hands.

When we finally gave up, I leaned back on my heels and looked at the boy, so young and fair. Then I saw that all the hostages had gathered around us. One woman was straining against two of her fellows, who held her back. When the Healer and I left the pen to clean the blood from our hands and clothes, the woman broke free, ran to the dead boy and held him to her body, rocking him and crying out with piercing wails that echoed through the village.

That evening, we sat by the fire between the Healer's hut and that of his mother. Dawn played nearby, and her great-grandmother sat at her door, sewing. I was chopping herbs we had collected by the stream that afternoon, while the Healer sorted them. It was a clear, peaceful evening, with stars filling the sky. But I was not at peace. I turned to the Healer, as we worked together, "Please, sir, may I ask a question?"

He nodded.

"Please, tell me, why do you war with the Mukane?"

"They are our enemies."

"But why?"

He looked at Dawn, then at his mother, who pretended not to watch us as she sewed. "They massacred my sons and daughters, my brothers and father."

"But, sir, those horrors are the fruit of war, not the cause."

The great-grandmother put aside her sewing and stared at me.

The Healer did not mask his distaste for my words. "They're animals who understand only death and destruction.'

"Would you be surprised to hear that is exactly what they say of you?"

Scowling, he raised his voice, as though he were about to lift his hand to me. "Do you take their side, after all that we have done for you?"

I bowed my head in fearful respect. "No, never. But when I look at Nasserit, I see the woman she will be, the man who will take her to his hearth, the children they will create together, the grandchildren who will follow. And that is a joy in my heart. Then I realize it is only a dream that could easily be snuffed out. She nearly died once, though she's barely five years. Will she live to be six, seven, ten? What's to keep her alive when so many are killed? What then of her children and grandchildren who would never be born? What then of your village that will lose yet another generation? Must there always be war?"

"These are women's words."

From the other side of the hearth, the Healer's mother spoke so softly that we had to strain to hear what she said. "Women's words raised you, formed you, created this village from our willing wombs. Shall we remain quiet as the fruit of our lives are killed? Listen to Meysrit, my son. Even a woman's words can be born of wisdom."

"Mother, I am not a child to be advised by women!"

"That is true, my son. You are the Healer, the one responsible for the health of all. You battle Death himself for our sakes. Does not Death come most often because of this war? Yet the Healer does not know or seek its causes, does not fight to end its ravages." She sighed so deeply that even Dawn ceased playing to look at her great-grandmother. *"Son, you and Nasserit are the last of our family. That isn't how it's meant to be. This hearth should be busy with lovers' games and infants underfoot. So much dying, and what does the Healer do? He stanches the blood, but does not stop the knife from striking. Would you ignore the call to end all this death, because these words are women's words? Be not so proud, my son. Be great instead."* She picked up her sewing again, looking only briefly at me before concentrating fully on her work. But in that nodding glance, I saw that her eyes shone.

The Healer was not pleased to be lectured by a woman, even his mother, especially in the sight of another woman and his granddaughter. He stomped away from the hearth.

I finished chopping the herbs and stored them in the correct containers. Soon everything was put away. Dawn was back in her great-grandmother's hut, where they slept. I, too, retired. I didn't hear the Healer return until close to sunrise.

At the morning meal, he told me we needed a certain root, which could be found only in a remote mountaintop glade, a day's trek from the village. He instructed me to pack food and water for three days. After informing the headman where we were going, he waved to me to shoulder the pack and follow him. We walked in silence until the late afternoon.

His words, when they erupted, came with no warning. *"This war has always been, as far back as we can remember. There was no beginning; there will be no end."*

"Then there will be no life for Nasserit."

"That is the way of things. I cannot change it. I am but one man. I cannot stand alone between the two tribes."

"If you believed it could end the warring, would you do so? Would you stand between them?"

He did not speak again for quite a while. Then, as though no time had passed since I had asked the question, he answered it. *"Yes. I think I would. How could a Healer not? But I don't believe it would work. So I won't."* Under his breath, he added, *"Still, I must do something to end this death."*

Again, we walked in silence. Later, we spoke only about the camp we set on the bank of a gentle stream. The Healer chewed the evening meal so lost in thought that I could have fed him sand, and he would have given it the same attention as he did the tender chicken.

"They really are animals, you know," he said. "You've seen how they butcher our people, steal our food, take our women. They tortured and raped you, would have killed Nasserit. Yet you want me to make peace with these vipers."

"What of your men? When they battle, do they fight with less savagery? Are your hostages treated better than those that they hold?"

He did not respond, but curled up in his blanket on the other side of the fire.

As I drifted off to sleep, I heard my voice whisper aloud what churned in my mind, before I could stop it from passing my lips. "War makes animals of all men."

The climb to the mountaintop glade was gentle and easy. By midmorning, we arrived at our destination He found the first plant, dug it up and showed it to me, so we could both work the glade, seeking what we needed.

I was emboldened by our conversations of the day before, so I ventured to return to the subject without his prompting. "Sir, I do wonder why the Murat and Mukane fight."

"For their fathers and brothers, sisters and children, for all our people who were murdered by the enemy."

"Revenge."

"More than revenge. Honor. Anger. Hatred." He paused. "Yes, and revenge, too."

"When did it start?"

"No one knows. It has always been."

"Then why did it start?"

We sat on the ground, on either side of the glade, no longer pretending to hunt for roots.

"The Storyteller says that, many generations ago, the border stream flowed in a different bed, one closer to our village. But the gods saw that our people flourished and were fruitful, which made them glad. So Ansit, the father of the gods, blew on the stream and sent it swimming in another bed, further north, so we might have more land for our many children. But when the Mukane saw the stream had been diverted, and their southern plains cut by it, they grew angry, not understanding that it was the will of the gods that the Murat grow. They came in the middle of the night when all Murat were asleep, oblivious that their neighbors whom they had always treated fairly had become murderous. After that bloodbath, the Murat never again attained the numbers that had gladdened the gods." He paused. "I don't tell the tale as well as Hanit, but *that's the essence of it."*

"So, the cause of the war can't teach us how to end it. Even if we knew how to turn back the stream, I don't think it would change anything about the war."

"So, it will continue." Bisrit sighed the words.

"Sir, why do you now seek a way to end the war?"

"Because I am the Healer." He paused. "My mother's words cut deeply. Your words, too. I've attended too many deaths that I could do nothing to combat. Then Nasserit was gone, dead like her mother and father. Or so I believed. But you returned her to me, and with her, you returned my hope, which I had thought killed long ago." He slapped his chest with his open hand. "It's a cancer, this hope. It eats into you, destroying what you always knew to be the truth, leaving you with a gaping hole that demands to be filled. I would fill it with peace, but then, I've become a foolish old man who dreams that hope might be turned to peace."

"No, Bisrit, neither foolish nor old, but newly young. Hope belongs to the young. It's Nasserit's gift to us."

"But it's impossible. The stream cannot be forced into its old bed, and the dead will never again live. War is in the food we eat and the air we breathe. It has changed our people. Now they don't even wish for peace, but enjoy battle. I know and understand, because I was the same myself, until you came."

I felt myself stand and walk toward Bisrit, drawn by his words and his need. We sat side by side, with my hand in his, in silence. But it was a soft, comforting silence, enfolding us rather than separating us. When he spoke, his voice was no longer gruff or commanding, but tender. "So, what are we to do, Meysrit?"

I looked at him, uncertain whether he was speaking of the war or of this new warmth we shared. But he answered my unasked question with another. "How do we stop this war and make peace for Nasserit?"

"We must find out what the Murat and the Mukane want more than they want the continued war," I replied.

"And what would that be?"

"I don't know, Bisrit. Perhaps we can find it together."

That night, he did not sleep on the other side of the fire, but in my blanket. His touch was gentle, and we enjoyed each other's bodies fully. The next day, when we set off on our return journey, we knew our course, if not where it would lead.

So Bisrit and I began to seek a path to peace. In the hostage pen, I talked with the Mukane. Each one I asked, "What do you want more than anything else?" Their answer, always, was "freedom." But when I asked, "Do you want it more than fighting? Would you promise never to fight the Murat again, if you were given your freedom?" their answers ranged from jeers to angry insults.

Bisrit fared no better among the men of the council and the villagers who came to him for healing. "The only thing that will stop these Murat in their killing," he said as we lay together in our hut, "is when all Mukane are dead."

We decided to approach the question from another direction. "What would it be like if there were no more war?" I asked the Mukane and he asked the Murat.

At first, their answers were blank stares, as though it were a thing so alien that their minds could not form around it. But, one at a time, over the days, weeks and months, I could see their faces change. My Mukane hostages would gaze into the sky, seeing the shape of peace, and their shoulders no longer bowed. The women stopped dreading childbirth for its futility. The children laughed more, even though they were enclosed in that brutal pen. And the men told tales of life as it had never been. Of what a life it could be if there were peace.

The cancer of hope, as Bisrit had called it, was beginning to grow.

Then, one evening, Bisrit told me that the headman Darrint had called him into his hut to ask about this nonsense that had been spreading through the village. They talked of peace, of what could be, if only war did not exist. The headman dismissed the Healer for an old fool, but Bisrit persevered. When he left the headman's hut, he hadn't been thrown out. Instead, he said, he left a seed of the cancer in Darrint's uneasy heart.

"But now what?" he asked when we were alone in our own hut.

We sat side by side, thigh touching thigh, our faces turned to the fire. "I think Dac could be the key, though he is the most stubborn of the Mukane hostages. Still, he is their headman's son, the only one left."

I felt the muscles of Bisrit's leg tighten and throb, though he remained outwardly calm. "How can you bring yourself to work with such a man, when you still cry out at night for what he did to you?"

I tried not to see the memories of those horrific times in my mind ~ the repeated rapes, the terror ~ though they were ever near. I turned to look at Bisrit. He took my right hand in both of his, gently, firmly.

"If I can't conquer my own hate, Bisrit, how can I hope to help make a better world for Nasserit?"

"And for her sake, you will forgive him?"

"No, never forgive. But we must move forward, and Dac could be the key."

"How would you proceed?"

"There's a bond between Thim and Dac, and Thim can be reached through his son. You know, Bisrit, I believe Thim loves his son Wen as much as we love Nasserit."

I saw a protest for such a comparison begin to form in his eyes. But then he thought a moment and nodded.

The next day, in the hostage pen, I spoke with Thim's son. "Wen, I need your help with Dac. His legs are mending, but we need to get them to heal in the right way, so he won't be a cripple."

The boy looked at his father, who nodded to him. "How can I help?" Wen asked.

"Now that he's stronger, he resists my treatments. But you're Mukane, and his companion's son. He'd likely trust you enough to allow you to do what is necessary. I'd like to teach you how to massage and exercise his legs."

"Would you teach him more than this work on Dac's legs?" Thim asked. "It would be good for Wen to learn the healing craft. Maybe it would keep his mind off the pen's fence and keep his spirit from getting old too soon."

I nodded to Thim, then said, "So, Wen, you have your father's permission. What do you say?"

"Okay."

"You don't sound too enthusiastic."

"Well, ma'am, it'd be something to do."

"Fine then, come with me."

When Dac saw me approach, he started his daily rant. "Stay away from me, woman!" He spotted Thim and Wen behind me. "She's a witch. They send her in here to torture us. We don't have to let her near us." He pushed himself up from his pallet to call out to all the prisoners. "Rise up! We can fight them. This fence isn't so strong that it can hold Mukane!" But he fell back into a recline, still weak from his injuries.

While I stretched his legs out to remove his bandages, I talked to Wen, ignoring Dac's curses. "As you can see, Wen, the wounds are healing, but the muscles and flesh are knitting in a way that could make Dac a permanent cripple."

"Get your hands off me, bitch!"

"We need to teach these legs to walk again."

"Hey, shit woman, I told you to get off me."

"Not just to walk, but to be strong again."

He started to kick at me.

"Look, Wen, at the muscle here. Do you see that it is too tight for

Dac to be able to put much strength behind his kick? He's as weak as a baby.When we're done with him, his legs should be able to do real damage."

"I'll show you how weak I am, whore!"

He lifted himself onto his elbows, but Thim pushed him back down. "Dac, don't be a fool. Can't you tell she's trying to help you?"

"You're the fool, Thim. You hear her words and forget everything. Why should she help me?"

Fed up with his bellyaching, I addressed him directly. "If I were a sane person, I would have asked the Murat to leave you up in the mountains to die. Right now, I'm all that stands between you and a life on your belly. So shut up, before I remember too clearly how you cared for your prisoner."

Dac started to spit out another curt reply when Wen placed a hand on his shoulder. "Uncle, I know you're not scared of her, 'cause you're not scared of anything or anybody. We'll wait and watch and see if she can do what she says. If not, no pen fence will be able to protect her. Heh?"

Dac slapped Wen on the back. "Thim, you've got a good boy here, a real Mukane man."

I'll never know how much of Wen's stance that day was real and how much was his way of getting Dac to cooperate. But from then on, Dac became, if not amenable, at least less hostile. Wen learned quickly and well. Any time Dac yelled at the boy or refused to push further, Wen would force, prod, argue, even belittle the man, until all the exercises had been tackled with vigor. If I had tried to force his legs in like manner, I would have been deemed cruel. But it was what Dac needed to strengthen his legs. So I merely observed as the boy worked the man, occasionally making suggestions to Wen for adjustments to the movements.

While I watched, I would talk with Wen about my travels, the people I had met and, mostly, what his life could be, if only this war would end. Dac pretended not to listen, and, when he did acknowledge my presence, he derided my words. I could only hope that somewhere under his blustering he heard me.

When the boy wasn't working with Dac's legs, I had him do the same for other wounded men and women. He was too harsh for new injuries, but just the right challenge for those on the mend. With Wen's help, the injured Mukane healed much more quickly. Dac eventually walked with his old swagger, even learned how to run again, though a bit lopsided. All the while, the cancer of hope grew where only anger and revenge once had flourished.

I felt the first hint of new life in my body, in the middle of night, near the end of winter. Uncertain whether it was merely another form of hope or truly a new child, I decided not to mention it to Bisrit.

Then I felt him stir beside me and I knew he was awake. I placed my hand on his back, so he would know I, too, did not sleep, should the thoughts that had awakened him be ones he wished to share.

"You know, Meysrit, it's a fool's dream. What good will it do if we convince the entire village and all the hostages? In the Mukane village, I have no doubt the hearth talk is of war, not peace."

"Yes, Bisrit. But we knew it would be that way. Didn't we?"

"I don't know what I knew. I never believed we'd get as far as we have, so how could I have foreseen this?"

"We need to persuade the headman to release some of the hostages. At least Dac, Thim and Wen."

"That he will never do, not without an exchange," he said.

"We can't wait for an exchange. We must spread the dream to their village before the war season resumes."

"And Dac? If he is released, will he speak for us at the Mukane council, to his father?"

"I'm not sure, Bisrit, but I think so."

"We'll need to be certain. Until we are, I cannot ask Darrint to consider releasing him."

"I don't know if I can ever be sure."

"You must."

When the spring muds began to dry up, I knew we were running out of time. The war season was upon us. I sought Wen and invited him to walk with me outside the pen, as I had a few times before. It was the only way we could talk without being overheard. As we walked, I realized that I was looking up to see into his eyes. How tall he had grown over the winter, and broad in the shoulders. It was good to see that he now carried himself with pride; I could only hope that it was, in part, because my friendship was more powerful than a hostage pen.

"Wen, I am pleased with your work. You have done well."

"Thank you, ma'am."

"Please, I have told you to call me Meysrit."

"Yes, of course, Meysrit."

"Wen, you know my dream for you, for your people and the Murat."

"Yes. Peace." He stared up into the trees that rustled with a coming spring storm. "But it is only that... a dream. War is the way of our peoples. They don't know how not to fight."

"Wen, if you could create peace, would it be something you would want? Is it something that you want more than you want to kill Murat, even though they have held you hostage and killed so many Mukane?"

He stared at me, and I felt that he was measuring the substance of my words. "Meysrit, I'm tired of the fighting and killing. It's all I've ever known. I'll never forget my family and friends who were butchered, but if I could do something to stop the murders, without becoming less of a man, then, yes, I want peace."

"What of the other hostages? What do they think of my dream? Would they prefer peace over war, if they could have it?"

"I think many would. The women argue for it most, but you'd expect that, wouldn't you? I've heard men talk as men will of what can never be. Peace. It's a wonderful word. But how can you stop fighting without laying bare your neck to the Murat's knives, giving the Murat victory?"

"Still, Wen, if they could find a way toward peace without giving the Murat victory, would they prefer peace over war, even though it would mean wiping the sand of the past's marks, ignoring their hearts' call for vengeance?"

"If such a way could be found, what man wouldn't want it?"

"Including your father?"

"Yes, especially my father."

"And Dac?"

"Dac's a hard one to read. But, yes, I think even Dac, as long as it wouldn't offend his pride."

We returned to the pen and found Thim and Dac playing noughts. Wen and I sat beside them, watching their game. Dac was obviously already beaten ~ outmaneuvered and cornered. Still, the two of them played on. Eventually, Thim made a mistake that gave Dac an opening. I had seen it happen before. Once Thim knew he had won, he would give the game to Dac.

I turned to Wen, as though I were continuing our private conversation. I tried to make it appear that I didn't care that Dac and Thim would hear our words. "Wen, how does a Mukane hold a promise?"

"With honor, of course," Wen answered.

Dac looked at Thim, but neither said anything.

"And if honoring a promise meant being ridiculed among your own people?"

"You don't make the vow, unless you know you will honor it."

"What if honoring it meant death?"

"Then you better be sure that such a promise is worthy of your

death."

"How could a stranger know she could trust a Mukane's word?"

Dac concentrated on the game, but his angry grunt seemed to be for me.

Wen searched my face before answering. "A Mukane wouldn't make a promise to a stranger; what hold could a stranger have on him that it could be demanded? Only a friend is worthy of a promise, and a friend would know the value of Mukane honor or be no friend of mine."

With their faces still buried in their game, both Dac and Thim nodded.

"Yes, Wen, a friend would know the weight of your honor, as I do. So let me ask you one more question. If you were set free today with no exchange, no battle, but simply allowed to walk out of this pen with enough provisions to find your way home safely, would you promise to speak of peace to your people? Would you try to explain our dream to them of what life could be, if only the Mukane and Murat didn't war?"

"Did the Murat ask you to ask this of me?"

"No, Wen."

"So, it is just another of your dreams."

"I believe it could be made to happen, because I believe everyone is tired of the killing. It's a waste, not only for all who die too young, but for the living who know no other way. So, Wen, if I could persuade the Murat to release you, would you try with all that you are to convince your people that peace is better than war?"

"Yes, Meysrit, I would. But my promise would be to you, and not to the old men of this village."

As though he had always been part of our conversation, I turned to Thim. "And, you, Thim, would you make such a promise to me, if I could persuade the Murat to release you?"

"Yes, Meysrit. Not only because of any vow I would make to you, but because of one I made to myself."

"And you, Dac?"

Dac continued to stare at the pieces of the game, working out his next move. He moved his nought. "Ha! You thought I was beaten didn't you? You'll never win, Thim, because you don't persevere. You'll be beaten in seven moves."

"Dac?" I had imagined all kinds of responses from him, but certainly not to be ignored.

He looked at me for the first time since I had sat down. "If you get me my freedom, I will fight for your peace."

I didn't know what to say. Had it been too easy? Could I trust him?

Did he understand all I was asking of him? But, when I looked at him, I saw the smile spreading across his face. And I believed him, despite all the lingering disgust I felt for what he had done to me. This man was a fighter, and he had vowed to fight for my dream.

He held out his hand, and I hesitated only a moment before I clasped it. "Thank you, Dac; I am honored to have your promise."

Bisrit argued with the headman for days. Eventually, what convinced him to let the three men leave was that he risked little by doing it.

Bisrit and I joined many other Murat who walked to the stream with Dac, Thim and Wen, to honor their promise, and our dream of peace. It was like a festival procession, filled with laughter and chatter, singing of hope.

Before stepping into the water to cross into Mukane land, Wen turned to me, put his hands on my shoulders and said, "You have our promise, Meysrit, and our thanks. We will teach our people that peace must come."

Thim embraced me and whispered in my ear, "You are an amazing woman. I would take you with me, but I haven't the right, for all that I did to you when I didn't understand. When we win your peace, I will return and ask for you." Then he kissed my hands and said for all to hear, "Meysrit, I vow to you that we will make our people listen."

Dac stepped toward me, with a grin so large that I did not recognize him. Then he reached for his knife in his belt, which had been restored to him, took my hand in his, and, before any Murat could jump to my defense, cut the meat of my thumb and sucked my blood into his throat. He had no words for me, just the blood vow. The three turned their backs and crossed the stream toward their home.

That night in our hut, to celebrate, I told Bisrit of the child I carried. He simply nodded. "Don't you have anything to say?" I asked.

"Meysrit, you are my heart and mind. Did you think I would not notice?"

"But you said nothing."

"Neither did you."

"Are you pleased?"

He pulled me into his body and whispered to my flesh, "More than I could ever say."

That night, we held each other in our sleep, as we had many nights. It was an uncommon joy made common by daily practice. Finally, I realized, I could allow my feet to rest.

Five days later, the Mukane attacked.

No more or less bloody than other battles, this one was, nonethe-

less, more destructive for being focused on the Murat home village. Bisrit was slain, trying to keep two Mukane from dragging me out of our hut. Dawn came running and screaming toward us at the same moment, and was struck down by a killing blow. When the Mukane men were done with me, I bled my unborn child into the earth, then lay in the bushes, waiting to die.

The great-grandmother found me where I lay, willing myself into oblivion. When the Mukane were taking our women away with them, she hid me. Days later, when I returned to my body, the first sight to fill my eyes was her. She was so changed I didn't know her. But, soon, my mind filled with her and our memories together, and I recognized my own unfathomable loss in her horror-stained face. She tried to show me their graves, to tell me what she had done for them and who still remained to rebuild the village. But I could not hear those words. As soon as I could walk without falling, I asked for her forgiveness.

"Why, Meysrit? For living, when they died? Then I must ask you to forgive me."

"No, Mother, for being a coward. For causing this horror with my foolish dreams."

"The dream is not foolish. Those who continue to fight when they no longer remember why, they are the fools. Give it time, my daughter. When those who fight have killed each other off, the dream will remain and guide the living."

"Perhaps, but I can no longer believe in it. The dream is dead with all that I loved. I cannot stay here. Would you come with me? Nothing remains to hold you here."

"My feet hold me here, just as yours must flee. But you knew that the first time you saw me, did you not? My left foot drags behind me, pulling me into the grave beside all whom I have birthed and buried. Yet I live. I wish I could learn the secret of dying, to shake this earth from me. You are the last of my family, Meysrit. I would have you free of all this. But I would want you to stay by me until I die."

I hated myself for leaving her, not helping her live out her life. But I burned inside with rage for the murder of Bisrit and Nasserit and all the others, for my shame in having spread the cancer of hope. I would go into the wilderness and die. I would walk until my feet finally stopped, and there I would wait, alone, because I didn't deserve to share my death with anyone. How could I, when I had proved myself so unworthy of sharing life?

I left the great-grandmother there, beside the graves of all we had loved. Out of habit, I took my pack, knife and walking boots. But I emptied the pack of the food and water she had put in it, as soon as I knew she could no longer see me, regardless of how long and hard she watched.

For the second time in my life, I turned my back on the ashes of my home village. My babies and my man were dead. Where my feet would take me did not matter. One foot in front of another and another, they carried me. The days and nights melded into a single grey, walking nightmare.

Some time later ~ how much later I cannot say, though my great thirst did mark days passing ~ I glanced back from where I had come. And I saw, on the horizon, two figures running toward me. Fine, I thought, death comes in pairs. I will sit here and await them. As they approached, I recognized the strange lopsided gait of one whose legs would never really be the same, no matter how hard I had tried. At that, too, I had failed, as I had failed with everything that really mattered. What a dolt I had been to think that such a man could ever be turned! I closed my eyes and waited for Dac to come and end my suffering. I could ask no less of my enemy than death.

I felt them approach. They were out of breath from their run. I prepared for the blow, but it did not come. Instead, they sat by my side and waited.

Eventually, I opened my eyes. To my right was Wen. His breath was still ragged, but it wasn't exhaustion that I saw. His face was weary ~ if I could believe my eyes ~ with shame. And Dac, who sat to my left, actually appeared concerned. He held out a water flask. When I didn't take it, he pressed it against my lips, pouring the water into me while gently holding the back of my head. Despite my resolve to die, my throat hungrily gulped the liquid. But he would not let me have my fill.

"Slowly, Meysrit. Let your stomach remember the feeling of water," Dac said. He wet a cloth with the water and began to bathe my face. I shrank from his touch. Wasn't it supposed to hold a knife?

Then I heard Wen's voice. "Meysrit, are you okay?" I saw the boy, who was a boy no longer. "We were so worried about you when we heard... Damn it, Meysrit, we couldn't stop them. We tried. You've got to believe me, we tried, but they were already setting out. They'd been preparing for war all winter. They couldn't... wouldn't... hear us. Please Meysrit, do you understand? Dac, do you think she understands?"

Dac allowed me to drink some more water, but he held the flask. "Yes, Meysrit understands. That's what she does best, isn't it Meysrit?"

"Dac? Where's your knife?" I asked.

"Here it is, Meysrit. Do you need it for something?" He held out his blade, with the handle pointed toward me. When I didn't react, he

placed it on the ground between us.

I couldn't fathom what game he was playing this time. But Wen, dear Wen, and Thim. Thim had promised to return for me.

"Where's Thim?" I asked Wen.

"He's dead," Dac answered, because Wen couldn't.

"Why? Did the Murat kill him during the raid on our village?"

Wen's face distorted and he cried out, "Meysrit, don't you understand? We tried to stop them. Pa stood in their path and they went right through him. His own people... my people... they killed him!"

"Thim?" Another death to my tally.

"Yes, Meysrit, Thim is dead. But it was a proud death, a good death," Dac said. "He did you honor to the end."

"Meysrit, you do understand, don't you? Pa kept his oath, and we will, too. You have to understand."

I slept and awoke to find that they weren't a hallucination. After they fed me, I was able to listen more clearly to what they said.

"Please, Meysrit, please say you forgive us for failing you."

"I failed you, Wen. I should have realized."

"No, Meysrit!" Dac interrupted. "You were right. It was our timing that was wrong. That's all I wanted you to know. We will win this peace of yours, even if it takes our lifetime."

"Dac, Wen, I release you from your promise to me. Don't waste your lives."

"Didn't you understand anything Wen told you about a Mukane vow?" I could hear the old sneer in Dac's voice, but it seemed somehow more muted, the way he used to talk to Thim when they argued over noughts. "You don't have the power to release us. It will be done, as we promised."

They stayed with me until I regained my strength. When one went to hunt for our food, the other remained by my side. They talked to me about the dream, until I could see its shape again, though it was new and reformed, made fully their own.

When I was whole once more, they didn't try to persuade me to return with them. I think they understood I could not go back there, where my future had been obliterated. They filled my pack with food and water and walked with me for two days, to the east, until they were certain I was on a safe path. Then they said goodbye to me.

Wen held me and whispered into my ear, "My pa loved you, and he wanted to return to you. But he was proud to die, knowing the dream would live. I'll make your peace, Meysrit, and my children will remember your name."

    Dac looked at me, grinned, pulled me roughly into his arms and pressed his lips hard against mine. Then he shoved me away from him, pushing the palm of his hand against my back to start me on my path. I did not look around to see them leave.

    So my feet began their journey again, one step in front of the other. My heart was heavy with the pain of my burnt village. But somewhere, deep inside, I could feel the tiny seed of hope that Wen and Dac had planted there.

    Hope is indeed a cancer.

Chapter 49

The Allesha heard her Winter Boy's voice catch as he read the last lines of *The Northern Border*. Tayar counted a few breaths, to give him time to compose himself before opening her eyes.

"Why do all these stories have to be about failures?" he demanded.

"What?" Tayar hadn't expected him to take that tack and was unprepared for the question.

Dov's eyes were streaked with red; his face clouded with angry confusion. "You say I'm supposed to learn how to make peace among people, but all the stories we read are about how impossible that is."

"Not impossible."

"No? Have we read a single story that shows how peace can be made when people war?"

"Yes. The one you just read."

Dov glared at Tayar. "Her man and children were killed. Her village destroyed."

"And her enemy swore to fight for her peace, though it would take him a lifetime."

"Even she didn't believe it would work."

"Didn't she say she took away with her a seed of hope, and that hope is a cancer? In the years that followed, the Traveler devoted her life to finding ways to create peace, refining her approaches. Eventually, she did win."

Dov picked up the book to thumb through the pages again. "Where did it say that?"

"Well, it didn't say it — not in that story — but that is what happened."

"So, did she ever go back? Did Wen and Dac win the Peace?"

"I don't know," Tayar admitted.

"What do you mean you don't know?! You said—"

"What I know relates to the larger issues. The Traveler moved about our land sowing the seeds of hope. Over the years, they germinated until, eventually, they became what we have today — peace wherever the Alleshi and their Allemen are honored."

"That's no good. It's like talking about a feast at the next full moon, when I'm asking how to hunt for tonight's dinner."

"Still, the story does give us hints. What did the Traveler do that changed the way the Murat and Mukane thought? More to the point, how would you have handled it differently?"

"No!" Bolting upright to sit against the sofa's arm, Dov pulled his legs away from Tayar.

Stunned, the Allesha drew herself up into her corner.

"I don't want to do this! No questions and answers and more questions tonight. This story deserves…"

"Yes?" It wasn't so much Dov's reaction to the tale that worried her as his combative tone.

"I don't know. But it's more than a lesson for you to drill into me. It's Dawn and her great-grandmother and the Healer and Wen. I guess they're all dead and maybe it doesn't matter whether they died of old age or war, but… it does matter. So don't play that game with me tonight."

"I didn't know you considered it a game. I thought we were exploring ideas together."

"Sure! And your goat Danide exists only as a pet."

"What?" He was veering in too many directions for Tayar to work out exactly where things went wrong.

"You use her. You get your milk and cheese from her. When she's no longer useful, I guess you'll eat her."

"How does that relate to our evening conversations?" Tayar asked. "Do you think I'm using you?"

"How the hell do I know? You don't tell me anything. You just ask impossible questions and push me this way and that. Skies! They're as far from normal conversations as Danide is from a pet."

"Dov, what's happening right now is very much like what happened between the Mukane and Murat."

"I don't—"

"No, you don't. Still, I can hope that you would."

"That I would what?" he demanded through clenched teeth.

"Tell me, why did the Mukane and Murat continue to war?"

He crossed his arms over his chest. "They always had."

"Exactly! It was a snake biting its own tail."

"What the hell is that supposed to mean?"

"That's an old saying. When the snake feels the bite, it reacts by biting its tail more, which makes it even more painful, so he'll bite even harder, and so on. It continues round and round, until it dies. If the snake could learn not to bite in reaction, it could break the cycle and live. But the snake doesn't even recognize that he's the source of his own problems. Instead, it reacts instinctively, in anger and pain."

"Yeah, so what?"

"Why are you angry at me, Dov?"

"You think you know all the answers. Why don't you tell me why I'm angry."

"Because you were upset by the story, and all that emotion got in the way of your thinking clearly. Once it started churning, you didn't know how to stop it. Like a snake biting its tail."

"Fire and stones, woman! Why can't I just be angry at you? At always being pushed and pulled, being told what to think and feel, what to do, how to do it. You never stop, you never let me be."

Tayar felt a hard knot twisting in her chest, recognizing the signs. *This shouldn't be happening now. Not Conflagration. Not yet.*

"I'm a good lover, a good man. I don't need to be treated like this, like a kid who doesn't know how to think, what to do with his hands, how to be himself. I'm the headman's grandson! I'll probably be headman. I've got a good woman waiting for me. Who the hell are you to tell me what to do, what to think?!"

"Dov—" *How do you stop a snake from biting its tail? Distract it by inflicting new pain or giving it something even more interesting to bite. Are my only choices to hurt or be hurt?*

"So you have an inner room and all kinds of sex craft. Well, it isn't enough anymore to make up for making me feel like this."

But if we're in Conflagration, I have no choice but to go forward with it.

"Don't you dare." Her voice was low, simmering with ferocity. "You're angry. So what? What are you going to do about it? Destroy yourself? Fine. I'm going to bed."

When Tayar turned to walk away, something in Dov cracked. He caught her by her arm and spun her around, so they were face to face. "Where do you think you're going?"

"Away from you." She tried to turn, but he clasped her upper arms tightly. She didn't bother struggling.

"You talk of truths, woman. Well, here's one for you. I see you for what you are. I see your lies and your games, and I've stopped playing them."

"Only a child talks of games."

"A child, heh?" Dov tightened his hold once more, lifting Tayar off her feet, so that she was like a rag doll, dangling in the air. Yet her face was rigidly unmoved, her eyes fixed on his.

Releasing her, he pushed her away in disgust. She almost lost her balance — but only almost. Calmly, even gracefully, after the first faltering steps, she brushed away the wrinkles in her sleeves where he'd grabbed her and settled into the nearest armchair. She even reached for a book and opened it, as though it were over for her, and all she wanted to do was read.

He snatched the book from her and flung it across the room. When he reached down to grab her, she kicked out with both legs, propelling him backwards into the opposite chair.

Tayar leaned forward. Though her face remained an impassive mask, her entire body pulsed with danger. "Boy, you have no idea how close to disaster you are."

"Sure, because I won't be controlled by you."

"Because you won't control yourself." She leaned back into the chair, as though it were of no consequence to her. "Well, you'll learn, or you'll be ruined. It's up to you."

"Damn it!" Dov's blood throbbed in his temples; he couldn't fix his thoughts. "What the hell do you want of me, woman?! I'm tired of all this."

"Then end it. Of course, to do that, you'd need to understand the beginning, wouldn't you? But you'd rather hurt and be hurt."

"What the hell are you ranting about now?"

"The rage and fear that's rooted at the beginning of all this."

He started to protest, "It was just a story." Then he realized that wasn't really how he felt. "No, it was more than a story. It was people who lived and died and never won. But to you, it was nothing more than a teaching tale; the people didn't matter."

"No, that wasn't the beginning. It was simply a spark from the tinderbox."

"The people never really matter to you Alleshi and your Allemen, do they? You talk of big issues, about trade and treaties and the fruits of Peace. You move whole villages to suit your plans. You send men off wherever you need them, never noticing what your whims do to the individuals in those villages, to the families of those men. To their sons — to my mother."

Tayar just sat there, watching him.

"Sure, you dress it up with smooth words and pleasant touches, seducing an entire world with your tricks. No wonder you work so hard to twist boys like me to do your bidding. If enough of us become men who know enough to resist you, you'd have real problems, wouldn't you? You'd have entire communities that haven't succumbed to your witchery.

Then where would all your power be? You'd be just a bunch of old dried up women nobody wants or needs. I'd pity you, if I weren't so disgusted. So you can drop the mask. The game is over, and you've lost."

Tayar reached back to rearrange the pillow behind her.

"You don't believe it yet, do you? But you will. Yeah, you made a man out of me, but not the one you expected." He thumped his chest. "This is a man you'll never control."

She leaned back into the pillow and crossed her legs.

"Damn it, woman, don't you have anything to say?"

"Until you reach your truth, anything I say will be meaningless to you. When you reach it, my words won't be necessary."

"Didn't you hear me? I've reached my truth, and it's nothing like yours."

"No."

"No? You don't believe me or you don't agree with me?"

"No, I have nothing to say."

"Skies!" Dov slammed his fist onto the table beside him, cracking a leg. "Who the hell do you think you are?"

Tayar glanced at the table. "That's too bad. I liked that piece. I wonder if we'll be able to repair it."

"To hell with the table." He smashed it, splintering the cracked leg and kicking the pieces away. "What about me? You care more about your damn table than about me."

"No, I don't think we'll ever repair it now." She leaned forward in her chair. "What about you?"

"I told you, I won't play your questions games anymore."

"But it wasn't my question. It was yours, as the answer must be. When you know what it is you want—"

"No!" The tortured screech erupted from deep within him. The force of it propelled Dov from his seat, to pace the room, each step pounding his anguish. "You don't know when to stop, to leave a man alone. How am I supposed to think with all the questions and probing and pushing and wheedling?"

When he reached a wall, he punched it, tumbling books from a shelf. Driven by his anger, he ricocheted off the opposite wall and back. "You just keep pushing and pushing, so a man can't breathe or think." The next punch felled a picture, smashing its glass. He stomped on it, then grabbed another larger picture, and flung it with all his might, for the sheer satisfaction of its destruction. He didn't see her quickly covering her face with both arms. The heavy frame and shattering glass missed her, crashing against the table in front of her. Punching or pulling down another picture and another, he smashed all within his reach. He grabbed a small stone sculpture from a table, feeling the gratifying heft of it in his hand as he prepared to hurl it.

"Dov! Stop!" she screamed.

Fire and stones! he suddenly realized, *I was aiming! But not at Tayar?!*

He stared at the heavy stone piece in his hand, almost surprised to find it there.

I couldn't, I wouldn't... would I?

Uncurling his fingers, he watched it drop to the floor, heard the thud of its deadly weight. He glanced at the woman, her face contorted with horror, and he looked away.

"Why does everything I touch turn rotten?" Dov barely realized that he spoke his thoughts aloud. He swatted at his face, where it felt as though an insect buzzed, surprised to find his cheeks wet. Wiping the tears with both hands, he continued to pace, but his feet no longer stomped. His closed fists hung like dead weights at his side.

Reaching a wall once more, his legs seemed to lose their will to hold him; he slid slowly to the floor. When his hands fell into his lap, he stared at them, bloodied and useless. He picked a small splinter of glass out of his thumb, then pressed his hand against his trousers to stanch the blood.

The Allesha's deep sigh broke through to the depths of his thoughts, awakening him to his surroundings. Looking at her, he felt as though a sharp knife that had been lodged in his stomach had been wrenched out, leaving a gaping, rusting hole in his gut. He searched her face the way he had studied his hands. "I believed in you. That you were—" He paused.

"That I was what?"

"No, don't do that anymore. I'll find the words, the answers, without your prodding."

"Yes, Dov."

He heard her without understanding. But in the silence that followed, one word did get through to him. "You called me 'Dov.' But it's not really my name. It's the name you gave me, and I chose to accept it, because you were my Allesha. You were the emblem of all I had been taught to believe in. But you're not. You're only a woman. There's no magic in you just because you have the title Allesha."

"That's true."

"What? You admit it so easily, now that I confront you?"

"I have always acknowledged it."

"Then why all the poses, the demands, this Season?"

"The Alleshi have no magic, just as Allemen do not."

"Yeah. Allemen." He slowly shook his head. "I wanted to be an Alleman."

"You don't now?"

"Why should I? I'd just be trying to be like him. What is he that I should want that? He can't help anyone."

"It hurts to stop believing, doesn't it? When you can believe that someone has all the answers, life is quite pleasant. Safe. But now you're angry at me and your father, because—"

"Keep my father out of this!"

"You mean you never did believe in him?"

"Never!"

"Then, please, explain it to me."

"It's like that story. The way the Traveler tried to spread that cancer of hope. It sounded like she might really win the peace. I wanted her to win it. But she failed. Because she had no answers. No one does. Pa goes off on his missions. He says he fights for the Peace. But what does he really know of peace? If he wins, it's as much a mistake as if he loses. Because he has no magic, no power. Like you. You wouldn't know what to do, would you? If you were sent out to a village like that one in the story, you'd just guess, and maybe you'd guess right. But that's all. No one has the answers. It's all a lie."

"Dov, which do you think is the greater achievement? For a sorcerer to create peace using some secret magic formula that sets him apart? Or for an ordinary man to struggle to learn and grow, to reach with all his being, that he might someday be wise enough to help two warring villages work toward peace?"

"You're doing it again. You spout such fine words, but they mean nothing."

"Dov, you're correct. There is no magic. All I can promise you is a great deal of hard work."

"I don't understand. You're acting like you still want me to be an Alleman. Haven't you heard anything I've said?"

Tayar didn't respond immediately. Instead, she looked at him; he had the feeling she was swallowing the words she really wanted to say. "Dov, we've been through a lot tonight. We're both exhausted. I hope you will want to continue your work here, so you may become an Alleman. But it is up to you. It has always been up to you. Tomorrow or whenever you reach your decision, you must let me know how you wish us to proceed."

Dov stood, but held his arms at his side, willing himself to not reach for her. "You're leaving." He was too worn out to let his anger boil once more, but it continued to hover as a buzz in his head, a rough rawness in his throat.

"No, Dov, I'm going to sleep, because it's nearly dawn and I'm tired, and because we can accomplish no more tonight. I suggest you clean those wounds on your hands. Use the sap from a leaf of the k'mri succulent that's in my kitchen window. It will speed the healing. Good night, Dov."

Chapter 50

Even after a series of deep relaxation exercises and a bath, Tayar/Rishana was still too distraught to sleep. She replayed each moment in and out of sequence, recoiling against the pain and violence, the unfettered wildness of the boy. Was it truly just the next stage in his development as a problem boy?

Or was it in his nature as a Mwertik?

One image kept intruding on her thoughts, unbidden and unwelcomed. Jared, alone and cold in the Red Mountains, set upon by Mwertik with knives and spears — raging, rampant Mwertik, not unlike her Winter Boy.

It wasn't that she hadn't been warned to expect his explosive response to all the changes they were forcing on him. Why else would the stage be called Conflagration? Until the boy had plumbed the full extent of his frustration and fear, faced his own anger and seen it for what it was, he would be blocked by it.

But it happened too soon and was so shockingly violent. Or was it? Did other Blessed Boys destroy pictures and tables when Conflagration ignited in their Seasons? She couldn't imagine her son Eli or Jared getting blood on their Alleshi's walls — and certainly not Tedrac. Mistral, maybe. But not like this.

Would Dov have hurled that heavy stone figurine at her head if she hadn't stopped him? Had she pushed him too hard, releasing poison into their Season that damaged it irretrievably?

She had nothing to compare it to, nothing to assuage her horror — or her fear of his Mwertik blood.

So it returned, again and again — the picture her mind had built of Jared's murder, twisted now into an ugly parody of her own Winter Boy seizing her, hurting her, almost bashing her with that stone sculpture.

Throwing on clothes without any attention to what they were or what pose they represented, the Allesha wandered out of her bedroom, relieved that he wasn't anywhere to be seen. The greeting room was a shambles, but picking up the pieces just made her doubt burn stronger.

Standing in the middle of the room with a shard of broken glass hanging limply in her hand, she heard a silent cry echo in her heart. *Somebody, help me!*

At that moment, she knew how much she needed Dara. Despite all the lies and treachery, Dara was the one person who had possibly been where she was right now, who understood problem boys and maybe even the Mwertik.

She lit the candle on her gatepost, knowing that Dara usually awakened before dawn, and hoping her mentor would be watching for her signal. Then the young Allesha went into her kitchen and heated some cranberry cider, to give herself something to do while she waited. She was seated at the kitchen table with her hands wrapped around a steaming mug when she heard the soft tapping at her mudroom window.

It wasn't Dara.

"Kiv?" she didn't hide her surprise or disappointment.

Framed by her black hooded cloak, the older woman's face reflected the room's light, softening the sharp angles of the long nose and pointed chin that had inspired Dara's derogatory nickname for her — "Knife."

"Good morning, Rishana. I saw your candle and wondered if I could help."

"But Dara—" Caught off guard, Rishana struggled to find the right words or pose.

"Oh, she's not home right now. I believe she's at the library."

"But how could you know? "

"Your candle."

"No. I mean know that Dara isn't—"

"I saw her. So, how may I help?"

Was Kiv watching Dara? Had she been watching Rishana — and Dov?

"Kiv." Rishana felt the shape of the name roll around on her tongue. Was she truly a threat, as Dara would have her believe? Or did Kiv offer fresh views worth considering, even possible solutions? Whichever it was, Rishana needed to know the truth.

After surreptitiously glancing toward the greeting room to make certain that the door was closed and no evidence of last night's violence could be seen, Rishana said, "Please come in."

Rishana poured a mug of hot cider for Kiv, and they sat opposite each other at the table.

Kiv studied Rishana. A probing look of tender concern, reading the signs in the young woman's face as they had been trained.

"I've been worried about you, Rishana. But I'd never interfere with

Dara's mentorship."

"Kiv, what is it between you and Dara? Why are you always at loggerheads?"

Kiv wrapped her long, thin hands around the hot mug, closed her eyes and breathed in the pungent steam. "We disagree about essentials." She said it without opening her eyes, though her knuckles whitened.

"Tell me, please," Rishana asked.

With the steam still wafting about her face, Kiv stared at Rishana once more. "Surely that isn't why you lit your signal candle."

"Perhaps in some ways, it was." Rishana paused, gathered her resolve and pushed ahead. "I want to know."

Kiv put down the mug, withdrew her hands onto her lap and squared her shoulders. "Our Peace is collapsing, and the Alleshi do nothing but carry on as always, seducing boys and mouthing platitudes."

Rishana struggled not to protest. Instead, she concentrated on remaining silent, so that she might fully hear and understand what Kiv had to say.

"The Mwertik," Kiv continued, "have been testing us, raiding here and there, pushing deeper into our lands with each thrust. No doubt readying their forces for a flat-out attack. Yet we act as though they're nothing more than an annoyance to be dealt with in the same manner as other outside villages we eventually bring within our Peace."

Kiv sighed, letting Rishana see her deep-seated pain. "But the Mwertik are not like any other people we've encountered. They want nothing from us — not our prosperity, our goods or our land. Nothing other than our total destruction. That's why they salt our fields, poison our wells, destroy our mines and workshops, burn our villages, leave no one alive. They're vicious marauders who live to kill and destroy."

Kiv's words — the familiar litany of Mwertik atrocities — descended on Rishana, a dark echo of her deepest fears.

"Dara and Peren would have us use subtle, generational influences to bend the Mwertik to our ways. But we won't survive long enough. We must act *now!*" Kiv's right fist slammed onto the table surface. "Or surely we will be destroyed." Kiv picked up her mug, leaned back in the chair and slowly sipped the cider, allowing it to fill her mouth before swallowing the heat into herself. "Now you know what I think. Does that give you the answers you seek?"

Rishana shook her head, unable to accept or reject Kiv's vision of their world. "But war isn't our way. The reason for our entire existence is to prevent war, not pursue it."

"We have the armament and the skills, but not the will to fight for our very existence. Instead, we take the most powerful boys and turn them into spies and negotiators. Look at your own First Boy. He's unruly and undisciplined, but anyone with eyes can see the power in him. What a warrior he could become, to lead our forces against the Mwertik."

"But we do give our Allemen defense training."

"I'm not talking about defense." Kiv nearly gagged on the word. "Are we to sit here in our Valley until our world shrinks into itself, one destroyed village at a time? Until they come here, to our own mountain passes, to our hall, storehouse and library? Are we domesticated dogs who sleep at the hearth and dream of a bone we buried long ago? If we love our Peace and our people, we must be willing to fight for them, or we'll have nothing left to defend."

"How? We don't even know where to find them. No one has ever lived to tell us what they look like."

"I'm not sure." Kiv's small, black eyes bored into Rishana. "Jared and Mistral must have brought back some intelligence."

Rishana's mind reeled. Of course Mistral would know better than anyone. But Jared? Why hadn't she seen it before? Certainly, as close as Jared and Mistral had been as Triats— and Tedrac, too, their third. How wide did it spread? What other connections had she missed? If Jared, then what of Savah? Suddenly, her breath caught in her throat with a stranglehold she couldn't break.

Kiv reached across the table, grasped Rishana's hands in hers and shook them twice with a force that jarred the young Allesha's shoulders. "Rishana!" Her voice grated with its calm, caustic insistence. "Get ahold of yourself, girl!"

Rishana yanked her hands away, as if they had been immersed in scalding water.

"What on earth has got you so riled, child?"

Rishana felt beads of cold sweat on her upper lip. "I'm so very tired, Kiv, and when you mentioned Jared and the Mwertik…." She shook her head, hoping that Kiv would read her turmoil as a widow's grief and nothing else.

"Yes, of course." Kiv picked up her mug and sipped it.

"Kiv, are you sure about the Mwertik, that they are so different from the others we have turned, that we couldn't win them over with our usual methods?"

Kiv set the mug on the table and leaned forward on her arms. "Yes, I am certain. They are murderers who would destroy us. I would have us survive instead." Kiv stood. "I believe I hear your Winter Boy moving about. It wouldn't do for him to find me here."

Rishana had not heard anything coming from the other room, but being tired and worn out, she didn't disagree. She walked with Kiv to the back door. "Thank you for answering my signal candle," she said out of courtesy, though she wasn't sure she felt anything akin to gratitude. If anything, she felt more confused and conflicted than ever.

"We must talk again, Rishana. I believe there's much you don't know."

"Yes, but not now, not in the middle of my Season."

"We have so little time. Do you think the Mwertik are delayed by such niceties?"

"Perhaps not, Kiv, but one thing worries me about what you say. If we fight as they do, how would we be different from them?"

"Because we would fight to survive, to save the Peace for the many villages and people who depend on us. They fight to destroy the Peace. It's an important distinction, don't you think?"

"Yes, Kiv. That it is."

Kiv stroked Rishana's shoulder in a surprisingly warm and tender gesture. "You know, Rishana, your boy isn't the only one with power in him. But such power can be frightening when you don't know how to best use it or whom to trust. Remember, my dear, you can depend on me to tell you the truth. Untarnished and sometimes unappealing, but always the truth." Kiv drew her fur-lined hood around her head and walked away.

As she watched Kiv's retreating back, Rishana noticed the sun's red glow already crowning the eastern mountain. She closed the door on the chill morning, made her way back to her room and fell into her bed, still fully dressed.

Chapter 51

Dov tossed about on his bed, trying to reconstruct all that had happened. When he thought back on the gentle beginning of the evening, it seemed entirely unrelated to what had followed. So, too, did the violence that his mind refused to own. He knew that everything had changed, but how?

Eventually, he must have slept, because one moment all was dark outside his window and the next, early morning sunlight filled The Valley. Still dressed in the clothes from the night before, he walked into the greeting room and was forced to recognize the shambles he had made of everything. It was an easy matter to pick up books and put them back on the shelf. Not so the blood smears that stained the two walls where he had hammered his anger.

Remembering his mother's claim that vinegar in soapy water would clean anything, Dov tackled the blood stains, with varying degrees of success. He swept up the shards of glass and tried to put the pictures back together. Finally, when he could no longer avoid it, he examined the wrecked table.

What is it about me? Is there something evil inside me that wanted to smash this table just because she liked it?

Dov gathered the fragments of the table and set out for the barn. After only a few steps outside, the bitter cold cut through his cotton shirt. *What am I doing? It's winter!*

He returned to the house, put on his coat, gloves and boots, and took the table pieces to the barn. There he was greeted by the anxious bleats and cackles of the unfed animals.

"Shut up! Let a man think." he yelled at them, and immediately felt ashamed.

Danide butted him gently and nuzzled a gloved hand, looking for a scratch behind her ears. The boy bent down to pet the goat with the lively affection the animal had learned to expect from him. "Oh, Danide, what am I going to do?"

As though the goat understood the words, she walked to the bin where her food was kept, butted the lid, then looked at the boy.

"Okay, Danide, I'll feed you, but that isn't what I meant."

While the boy fed the animals, he continued to talk to Danide and her sister, Draville. The goats' eyes followed Dov, almost as though they were listening. "Well, girls, I guess I really did it this time, and I don't know how to fix it. Not just the table, but everything."

With the animals fed and quieted for the moment, Dov went to the workbench and tried to reassemble the broken table. Eventually, Danide and Draville wandered in to be near him.

As he fit the pieces into place, Dov saw that most of the fragments could be put back together, if he took care. However, the one leg was shattered. Dov searched the barn, but found no suitable replacement. Then he remembered seeing a pile of carpentry wood in Le'a's barn. He scratched the goats goodbye and left, with the pieces of the broken table leg in hand.

In Le'a's barn, he found some good-quality lumber, but none that matched the table. The closest was some nice, straight cherry wood. Le'a must know where to get the right one, he thought.

The outer door of Le'a's house was closed. So he sat on the back steps, staring at a piece of cherry wood and the broken leg.

When Le'a returned from the library, she found the boy crouched in deep thought on her back steps. "Dov! What are you doing out here in the cold? Come in quickly, before your backside freezes to the steps."

"Hi Le'a. This cherry's nice, but not quite right. I need a piece of fine-grain walnut, like this. Can you help me?"

"Of course. But come inside."

Le'a preceded him into the warm kitchen, coaxed his coat, gloves and boots off, then sat him at her table. But the boy wouldn't release his hold on the wood for longer than it took to remove his outer clothes. She turned up the fire under her kettle. Soon it was boiling.

"Be careful not to burn yourself," she said as she placed a steaming mug in front of Dov. "Sip it slowly. Have you eaten?"

"About the lumber — Le'a, can you help me?"

"Put those things down and hold the mug. You need to get some warmth in you."

"But it's important, Le'a."

"Even if it's important, it can wait a few minutes."

"No!" Dov stood up, jarring the table and almost spilling his tea. "I need your help, but if you can't…"

Le'a placed a gentling hand on his shoulder and guided him back to his chair. "Of course I'll help you, Dov. Now, sit down and sip your tea while I prepare our breakfast. After we eat, we'll see about the wood."

Dov sat down, but still held the fragments of wood in his hands. Le'a took them from him, meeting only initial resistance, and placed them at his feet.

"Now tell me what's happened?"

"I broke her table."

"I see." Le'a busied herself with preparing breakfast, to make it easier for the boy to talk. "Did you break anything else?"

"A couple of pictures, and I got some blood on her walls."

She spun around to look at him. "Blood! Whose?"

Dov held up his battered hands for her to see. "Mine." Then, realizing what she feared, he added, "You don't think I'd hurt her?" His voice quivered on the question.

"No, no, of course not." Still shaking, but determined to not show it, Le'a turned back to the counter and cracked eggs into a bowl.

"Well, I wouldn't. At least, I don't believe I would. But I don't know, something got into me. You don't think I'm... that I'm bad, do you?"

"No, never, Dov. I wouldn't be surprised if that's why you broke the table and hurt your own hands." She picked up the bowl and leaned against the counter. While whisking the eggs to a froth, she looked at the boy, reading his face, letting him read hers if he wished. "Something apparently upset you last night. You became angry. But you vented your anger onto the table and your own hands. You chose to not hurt your Allesha."

"You're wrong."

"Oh? Did you hurt her?"

"Yeah." He didn't meet her gaze and swallowed his words deep into his chest, so Le'a had to strain to hear him. "I did hold her too tight, and I guess I went a little crazy."

"Is she all right?"

"I think so. But that isn't what I meant about you being wrong. I don't know if she's still my Allesha."

"I see." Le'a turned back to the counter to chop some sausage and vegetables, and adjust the fire under her frying pan. "What happened?"

"I found out the truth. Well, I guess I always knew it, but then she admitted I was right, and that made me angrier."

The truth? Did Rishana tell him about his birth already? It's too soon. Le'a continued to busy herself with scrambling the eggs and turning the toasting bread.

"I guess I didn't want to be right," he continued. "Not about that. Now, everything is changed, and I don't know what I'm supposed to do. I mean, she said she thought I could still be an Alleman, but well, I don't know if she meant it, or if she was tired or scared and just wanted me to leave her alone. And if she did mean it, do I want it? I don't know. It's all lies, and it would make me part of the lies. But I'm tired of not being part of anything. It seems that it might still mean something, but I don't know what."

Holding her emotions tightly, Le'a kept her back turned to him to give herself time to regain her composure. "Dov, please set the table, breakfast will be ready shortly," she reminded him.

"Huh? Oh. Okay."

"Please, do go on. What is this truth that you found out?"

"About the Alleshi and their Allemen? That they aren't anything, really."

Recognizing the signs of Conflagration, Le'a stifled a sigh of relief. Nothing out of the ordinary. Not yet.

They met back at the table, where Dov was laying the plates, condiments and utensils. She doled out the eggs and bread, freshened their tea, and they sat down to eat. He tackled the food as only a hungry boy can.

"Tell, me, Dov, what do you mean by saying we're not anything?"

"Well, you know, not anything magical. Just ordinary people."

"Magic? Hmmph, this is no hearthside tale we're living. Of course there's no magic or sorcery. Only lots of hard work and responsibility."

"That's what she said."

"Of course. Please pass the preserves."

Dov handed her the jar of strawberry jam. "But everyone always talks about how special the Alleshi and Allemen are."

"Dov, others — those who are not Alleshi or Allemen — may attribute magical qualities to our successes because it's a simpler answer to their many questions and fears. We can't allow ourselves the luxury of simple answers." Le'a paused, took a forkful of eggs, but put it back down on her plate, and sighed. "The luxury or the danger."

"What danger?"

"Believing in magic would make us lazy and set us on a path to failure. We've too much we must accomplish: maintain the Peace, build trade, help our villages prosper, bring new villages under our influence, protect our borders. At the same time, we must continue to learn, amass new knowledge for our people, train the next generation. We've no time to waste on believing in magic. It's something reserved only for the innocent, the young, and the gullible."

Dov hid his uncertainty by concentrating on his eggs. She allowed the silence to continue for a few minutes, knowing he had more to digest than food. When he finally looked up from his plate, she gave him a half-smile that was both sad and peaceful. "Dov, do you understand what really happened last night? You're no longer innocent or young. You cannot drift in ignorance. Now, you must either take hold of your future or see the choice disappear from your grasp."

"You know, she said I can still be an Alleman. Even after all I said and did."

"Yes."

"And you, Le'a, do you believe I can still be an Alleman?"

"Always, but that isn't the important question. You need to decide whether you believe in yourself— and in us."

"I don't know. It wasn't just what I found out, but what I did, Le'a. I really messed up." Feeling suddenly too tired to even move, he yawned.

"Dov, did you sleep at all last night?"

He shrugged.

"Come." She guided him to his feet and out of the kitchen. "I think you need to lie down. While you nap, I'll see if I can find your lumber for you." Le'a led him upstairs to her second bedroom and opened the door. "Rest here. I'll be back soon."

He stretched out on the bed and was asleep before she left the house.

Bundled up against the cold, she carried the wood to the storehouse, certain she would find its match among the vast lumber stores there.

Chapter 52

When Dov awakened, he didn't recognize where he was. Then it all flooded back — last night's horrors and the morning's greyness, and being brought to this room by Le'a.

This was *his* room, he realized with a jolt. Dov looked around and saw the bookshelves, the bureau, and the four doors, so similar in idea, if not structure, to his own room in Tayar's house. And yes, one door led to the bathroom, another to a closet, the third to the stairwell hallway, and the fourth was locked.

Pa's inner room.

The room he had shared with Dara when he had been a Blessed Boy.

Unable to avoid picturing his pa with Dara, he tried to blur it with memories of his time with Tayar. The sex, the readings, the chores, and all the lessons — everything a lesson. In his mind's eye, he saw his father as a struggling innocent, brought to the Alleshi by his own father, who viewed them as magical.

But did Pa? Or did he know in his heart that they were as ordinary as anyone?

"Hello?"

Startled by Tayar's voice calling from below, he rushed downstairs, barefoot and disheveled. She stood in the greeting room, clearly surprised to see him there.

"She, uh, Le'a told me to sleep there." Dov pointed upward, to the second floor.

"You slept here?"

"Yeah, well, no, not last night. After breakfast."

"Oh."

"Yeah." How awkward he felt, as though Tayar had discovered him somewhere he shouldn't be.

"Is Le'a home?" she asked.

"I don't know. Le'a!" he called out.

"Le'a!" she echoed.

"I guess not," he said.

They stood on opposite sides of the greeting room, stiff and unmoving. Tayar seemed shrunken within herself, paler than usual.

"Are you hungry?" Dov asked, needing to say something. "I guess that's a silly question. You're always hungry. I had breakfast with Le'a, but I'd like something else to eat now."

"As well you might. It's far past lunchtime. And, yes, I'm hungry. Let's see what Le'a's pantry has to offer."

They went into the kitchen, made tea and took some brownies from the jars on the counter. When they could busy themselves no longer, they sat at the table.

At first, Dov looked everywhere but at Tayar, not wanting to meet her gaze. But he gradually realized she was fully focused on her mug of tea, the flavors of the sweets, on everything but him, as though she, too, didn't know what to say, how to act. Eventually, he broke the stillness. "I'm sorry about everything. I don't know how it happened, why I did it."

"You were angry."

"Yeah, but I didn't have to smash everything, scare you."

"Maybe you did." Tayar's voice sounded cool, distant, almost as though she wasn't fully there.

"That's the thing. I break things, hurt people. You said I have to decide whether I want to be an Alleman. And Le'a said that I have to decide if I believe in myself. But I don't. Believe in myself, that is. I think there's something evil inside me that destroys things. I'm tired of doing that. I've got to put an end to it. So I can't be an Alleman. Because I'd just end up hurting you again. I think I should leave. I know the passes are still snowed in, but I could stay at one of the inns, couldn't I? Not as a guest; I don't have any money. But I could work for the Battais, as one of The Valley's maintenance crews or maybe in the steam plant."

Tayar shook her head slowly. "Do you know how sad it makes me feel?"

"You don't understand. I'm trying to protect you. Le'a saw the blood on my hands." Dov held up his scabbed-over palms, then quickly retracted them, anchoring them under his arms. "You know what she thought?" Dov lowered his gaze, staring at the floor without seeing it. "There's something in me, Tayar. And it's bad, really bad."

"No…" Tayar held the word as though she were testing it, making sure it fit her mouth, her thoughts. Then she was silent for a few breaths before adding, "Just human, like the rest of us." But her voice was tight, almost strangled, and too quiet.

Dov knew then that he had broken something precious, and no amount of glue, nails or lumber would ever fix it.

At that moment, Le'a came into the kitchen. "Hello, Tayar. I'm glad you're here." Le'a thrust a piece of wood toward Dov. "Look at this. Isn't it beautiful? It's a near-perfect match to the grain of the leg, and just the right size and shape. And this" — she handed him a small glass jar filled with dark liquid — "is the stain for it. One of our Alleshi is a skilled carpenter, so I took the broken leg to her. She selected the wood, turned it on her lathe and mixed the stain to match. She recommends several applications, with intermittent fine sanding, and this beeswax to finish it." Le'a pulled another jar from a pocket and put it on the table. Then she prepared a mug of tea with water from the still-hot kettle.

"Le'a, Dov has decided to leave us." Tayar's voice was so devoid of emotion that it was almost deadened.

Le'a sat down, folded her hands on the table and looked at him. Dov felt too ashamed to meet her gaze.

"I see." Le'a didn't say anything else, which surprised Dov.

He glanced at her out of the corner of his eye, and then at Tayar, who studied her teacup. Was she avoiding looking at Le'a, too? Or only him?

After biting into a brownie, Le'a spoke again, slowly, insistently. "At the beginning of this Season, a boy came to us, signing his Agreement, but uncertain what was to come. If you were to continue, it will be a man — an Alleman — who will leave us, far more knowledgeable than most, but still only beginning to learn. Right now, you're caught in the middle of your Season, unfinished, neither the boy nor the man. Even if you wanted to, you can't go back to what you were. You've learned too much. Your only choice is to either go forward or leave." She paused long enough that he raised his eyes to her. Only then did she add, "You say you have decided to leave. But I wonder, have you considered where each path would carry you?"

"I haven't really thought about the future. I just want to stop the hurting that I do."

"So you must. But first, I would like you to describe what you think your life would be like as an Alleman if you stayed."

He felt trapped, wanting to get away from this table, from these women and their constant questions that prodded and poked and couldn't be answered.

"Dov, before you try to respond, do something else for me, please," Le'a asked.

"What?" Trapped, too, by the glimmer of hope Le'a's words seemed to offer.

"Close your eyes, and sip the air, the way you've learned."

A hope that somehow things might go back to the way they were, but better, even though he knew in his heart that would be impossible. Everything good had always been impossible, out of his reach, not meant for the likes of him. Everything but Lilla. But that door, too, was now slammed shut. Lilla's mother had made it clear — only an Alleman for her daughter.

"Please," Le'a said gently. "Focus on the air filling your lungs, slowly."

He did as she asked, not because he believed it would help, but because of that faint hope, and because he was stuck here with these women for now, and had no choice.

"That's right. Now release the air, through your lips, in a thin stream, slowly... slowly. Again."

His breath reached deeper into his lungs with each inhale and exhale, until his heart was quieter and his mind clearer.

"Yes, good," Le'a said. "Now tell us how the two paths appear to you, where they would lead you."

"If I leave here today, my life would be without you, both of you. I'd be sorry for that. As difficult as you can be, I'd miss you." He looked at Le'a, and then Tayar. Two women who would go on to live out their lives unconnected to him, as they had before he had come to this Valley. At one glance, they were old and young, strong and vulnerable, needing nothing from him, yet needful.

"I don't really see much else about such a life," he continued, "because I've never heard of anyone failing a Season. That's the worst of it. I would have failed, and I'd carry that shame with me my entire life. But if it meant that I'd be doing the right thing, then what's the difference if it made me look bad?"

"What if you stayed?" the younger Allesha asked.

He shook his head, but decided it wouldn't hurt to play their games one last time. "If I stayed, I suppose I'd become an Alleman. Lilla would be my wife. But then I'd have to leave her side whenever the Alleshi called for me. Our children would grow up not knowing when they could depend on their father to be with them."

"It doesn't sound like much of a choice." Le'a paused, then asked, "But tell me, what kind of Alleman would you be if you stayed? What would you want to achieve?"

The women watched him, not like hunters cornering a prey, but as though they were truly interested in what he had to say. No one had ever asked him what he wanted. No one other than Lilla. He and Lilla had talked a lot about the home they would make, the house they'd build, and how they'd raise their children. It was one of the things that had made him feel so complete when he was with her, knowing it would continue through the years of their life together. But this was more than dreams to share with your future wife. Dov considered the question carefully before answering.

"I don't think it's enough to bring peace to strangers," he said. "Sure, it's important, and I'd like to be part of that, but it's not enough. If I were an Alleman, I'd want to find ways to make life better for the people closer to home."

"Yes?" Tayar whispered.

"It seems to me that all these skills and wisdom that the Allemen are supposed to have should be used to help."

"Yes, that is a vital part of being an Alleman — protecting the people within our Peace borders," Le'a said.

"No, not just protecting them. Making them feel like they're part of it, rather than just people who fill villages within the Peace borders. They're kids and wives and husbands, with names and fears and hopes. They need to be part of all that the Allemen and Alleshi do. Sure, they're the reason for it, but they're not part of it, not really. Do you understand?"

Dov's eyes burned with his vision of a future he had never before imagined. "If I were an Alleman, I'd work to make that happen, even if it meant changing what it is to be an Alleman. I wouldn't want anyone to see me as anything more than I am. No magic. Just me. That way, anyone who met me would know that they could do as much good and learn as many skills as any Alleman."

"And what of the Mwertik?" Tayar asked softly, almost tentatively.

"I don't know. I mean, I'd have to teach our people how to fight them, but it wouldn't be enough to win that fight, would it?"

"Why?" Tayar asked.

"Because the Mwertik aren't what the Peace is about. It's the people who live within the Peace."

"A most worthy path. Do you see anything its equal in the other direction?" Le'a asked. "What would your life be if you left here today?"

"Lonely, but I could still try to help people and protect the Peace."

"How?"

"I don't know how, Le'a, but I could learn."

"Yes. I believe you would learn. Though why do it by yourself, when you can learn with us and your fellow Allemen? Is the lonely struggle so enticing to you?"

"No. But that isn't the point." Suddenly, the vision and the hope it had given him were gone. "I destroy things."

"Dov, do you agree that you are not the boy you were?" Le'a asked.

"I suppose so."

"In the same vein," Le'a added, "who you are today is merely the beginning of the person you can become."

Why did Dov get the feeling that Le'a was addressing Tayar, as much as she was talking to him?

Tayar stared at Dara, then reached across the table and lightly touched Dov's hand. "We can help you."

Dov looked from one woman to the other. Moments before, he'd firmly believed that leaving was the right and honorable course. Now he didn't know what was right or wrong. Dov placed his other hand over Tayar's, feeling the warmth of her flesh, the solidity of her offer. Embarrassed, he gave a slight chuckle that came out more ironic than mirthful. "I don't suppose you're offering to leave with me?"

"Dov, I don't believe we could allow you to take our Tayar away from us," Le'a bantered.

He took one hand away from Tayar, to reach out for the older woman, too. "Then I suppose I should stay."

Before Le'a would take his hand, she asked, quite solemnly, "Is this a decision to stay or the relinquishing of a decision to leave?"

"It's my decision to stay."

"Are you sure? Do you really understand what you are facing, what will be expected of you, how everything could change for you, perhaps in ways you never imagined?"

"It's my decision to change my life, Le'a, isn't it?"

"It must be."

"Then why can't you accept it? How many times must I repeat it until you believe it?"

"It isn't my beliefs that are in question," Le'a started to respond.

At the same time, Tayar said, "Every day."

"What?" he asked Tayar.

"You asked how many times you must reaffirm your commitment. Every day. Not to us, but to yourself," Tayar said. "Throughout your life, you will face choices. Some difficult, some painful. Each time you make the right choice, you'll be affirming your vows as an Alleman. Whenever you go against the good and right choice, you'll be returning to old destructive ways. Eventually, you will believe in yourself. Not because of who you once were, or even who you are, but who you want to be."

"You women won't let anything be easy."

"We fight for what is worthwhile, even when it's a hard-headed boy," Le'a answered.

Chapter 53

The yound Allesha didn't have a chance that afternoon to talk privately with Le'a/Dara about Dov's violent twisting of the natural order of the stages, so she still had no gauge to help her understand the boy's outburst. In fact, since last night, she hadn't conferred with any Allesha other than Kiv, who'd sliced up her innermost beliefs even more than Dov's hard hands on her.

Somehow, she had to sort out the truth. *Who is right? Kiv? Dara? No one?*

And what of Dov? Did being a Mwertik make him intrinsically evil? *Am I a fool to believe the human spirit is greater than the cycles of hate — even when it's my own hate — of the Mwertik?*

But she didn't have the luxury to mull over the questions bombarding her. She was an Allesha in Season. To stop now would mean deserting her Winter Boy. Whatever he might be, he was still her charge and responsibility — more than ever, now that she knew the truth.

But that didn't make it any easier for her to go forward into the Exhilaration Stage. So she lingered longer than usual in meditation before joining Dov in the inner room. She was determined to use whatever discipline she possessed to bury the terrors that haunted her. She almost convinced herself that she had succeeded.

Dov was sitting cross-legged on the floor, next to the small oyster pond. No longer uncomfortable with his own nakedness or hers, the boy seemed newly young and open, scorched clean by the previous night's violence. His scabbed hand splashed in the frigid water, but he didn't ask questions. He simply sat there, playing with water where only stone floor had been before, curious what it was and why it was there.

Tayar sat beside him, took an oyster from the cold pond and held it out to him. Dov turned it over several times, feeling the deep, rough ridges and sharp edges.

"It's an oyster," she said.

He bounced it in his right hand, then looked closely at the edge. "Sort of looks like a mussel. Not the shape, color or feel, but the way the two sides fit each other."

She walked over to the nearest wall and picked up a short, wide knife from a ledge alcove. Light and well-balanced, it was meant for one purpose only. Why did the feel of it in her hand turn her mind even now to how Mwertik had used much more brutal knives?

After sitting back down next to the boy, she took the oyster from him, held it in one hand, wedged the knife into the joint and flicked it open. It was done easily, belying the many hours and slip-knife cuts she'd endured learning this one skill. Another twist of the knife separated the meat from the opened shell.

"Here." She lifted the half shell to his lips and let the juicy morsel slide into his upturned mouth. "But don't chew. There's something hard in the middle that could chip a tooth. You'll want to spit it out."

She watched him, remembering her first taste of an oyster. Salty sweet. Pungent and fresh. On a clear moonless night, alone with Jared on a sandy beach — he had fed her oysters, told her stories and showed her what she was preparing to teach Dov.

Dov's jaws worked as he rolled and pressed and sucked on the juicy flesh, until he isolated the small, elusive pit, forced it from its meaty prison, and spit it into his palm.

She held up a candle. "It's a pearl."

The flickering light reflected along the pearl's opalescent surface, as he rolled it about on his hand. "Pretty thing."

"And considered a rare treasure." Tayar place her hand under his, closing his fingers around the pearl. "It's yours, as are all the pearls in these oysters." She gestured toward the small pool.

"Is this my reward for passing a test, for not leaving?"

"Dov, you do ask some provocative questions."

"That's no reason not to answer."

"Tests and rewards. I hadn't thought of it that way. The pearls are yours because I have chosen to give them to you. Because I know you will want to have them in the years to come."

"Because they're valuable?"

"Because they will be precious beyond value."

He started to protest, hesitated, then smiled. "I suppose you'll explain it to me when you're ready."

"No." She took the pearl from him and placed it in onw od the open half shells on the floor. Then, with her hand in his, she led him to their warm bathing pool, a few steps from the oyster pond. "Soon enough, the answers — and the mysteries — will be yours, just as the pearls are yours. Come." She stepped into the warm swirling waters. "Bathe me."

Dov stopped to fill his hands with oil and soap from amber and blue bottles they kept on the side of the pool. Then, with gentle, insistent caresses, he massaged a warm, lemon-scented lather into her flesh.

Tayar closed her eyes to ride the gentle tingling of her body wherever he touched. She nuzzled the curve of Dov's neck, burrowing into his warm musk, feeling his quickening pulse against her cheek. Buoyed by the water and his hands cupping her buttocks, she wrapped her legs around his waist, and he entered her with only a slight resistance. It was a still, quiet moment. At first, the only movement was her inner muscles, which she squeezed, increasing in speed and momentum, until her body began responding to him with tightening waves of pleasure. He pressed deeper, moving with her, quicker with each thrust, breaking the silence with wordless rhythmic gasps, until all was still once more.

In the dark warmth of the inner room, the only sounds were their breath and the soft lapping of the water against their bodies. Slowly, Tayar slipped off Dov and gently rinsed the soap, sweat and semen from their bodies. Then she led him back to the oyster pond.

"These oysters are here to help me teach you a wonderful lesson. Do you know about a woman's pearl, Dov?"

He looked at her quizzically.

Stretching her legs into a V in front of her, Tayar lifted a candle with one hand, while with the other, she spread her nether lips to expose her pearl. He watched in silence, then reached out to touch it gently with the tip of his forefinger, sending a shiver down her legs.

"I never heard it called a *pearl*, but I've seen it."

The Allesha quickly crossed her legs and put the candle down beside her, disciplining herself to focus on the lesson and not on the sudden astringent chill heat of her nether lips. "I've heard Healer scholars say that a woman's pearl has as many sensations packed into its tiny shape as a man's whole organ. I don't know if that's true, but it is very sensitive to pleasure — and to pain."

"Yeah, well, I *have* seen it before."

"As with any other part of the body, there are many ways to touch a woman's pearl." She was pleased that she was able to keep her tone even, unperturbed, still in control. "The problem is it's so very sensitive that I can't show you by using my own body, as we have before. At least, not initially. That's why we have these oysters."

Dov watched her in silence, absorbing her every word, gesture and move.

Tayar removed an oyster from the tank, opened it with her knife and put aside the empty top shell. With two fingers of her right hand, she gently moved the meat of the oyster within the shell. "See how moving the flesh causes the pearl to move, too? Here, try it."

Dov took the oyster from her and imitated her action. But his eyes kept drifting from the shellfish to her pubis. "Show me again."

She opened her legs and leaned back on her left elbow while, with her right hand, she parted her nether lips. Then, realizing what he wanted, she pulled her hand away and supported herself with both elbows.

Using the same touch she had shown him on the oyster, he rubbed her nether lips with two fingers, watching closely at how the movement manipulated her pearl, unaware of the fiery sparks his tentative caress ignited. His concentration was so profound that her deep sigh and slight shudder made him jolt.

Suddenly self-conscious, he sat more fully upright and stared at the oyster in his left hand. He massaged the oyster meat once more and mumbled, "It's not the same at all."

Taking a deep breath to calm her body, she closed her legs, leaned forward and smiled. "No, it isn't the same, but we can use it, to learn and experiment." She brushed his shoulder with a gentle kiss and pressed her body closer, waiting until she felt his muscles relax before continuing. "A woman's pearl is unpredictable."

"Yeah, well, it's part of a woman," he quipped.

Tayar bit back a retort and instead, gave Dov a half-smile of acknowledgment. Then she took the opened oyster he had in his hand, and demonstrated different patterns of touch. "The number-one rule is that a direct touch is usually too painful to endure — except when a pearl demands to be touched."

"So, how am I supposed to know?" He shook his head in frustration.

"By learning to read me. As you alter the rhythm, pressure and placement of your touch, my responses will vary; you can't even depend on what you think you've already learned. One moment, a certain touch will send chills up my spine. The next, it may be uncomfortable or even painful. And yet another time, I won't want to you stop doing that very same thing."

"Why don't you just tell me when you want something or don't want it? You've never been shy before."

"I'm not being shy now. I'm trying to teach you how to read me so you can understand what I want before I understand it myself."

"I'm not a mind reader."

"No, but if you learn to read people, some will think you are."

"You're not talking about sex anymore, are you?"

Tayar smiled.

"This is it, isn't it? What it is to be an Alleman."

"Part of it."

"Knowing a woman's pearl?"

"No. Pearls and oysters — and the inner room itself — aren't the goal. They're a road we travel together as you learn and refine your skills."

"But it's about the pearl, too, right?"

"No, it's about the woman, about learning to read me and anticipate my most intimate impulses, needs and desires."

"How?"

"Watch for subtle changes in my skin and eyes, my breathing and posture. Notice when my muscles contract, twitch or become suddenly flaccid." She gently traced his inner arm with her fingernails and gestured for him to look at his skin as it reacted to her touch. "Watch for pleasure bumps like those, or a flush of color, or the widening of my pupils. Be aware of a slight elevation of body temperature or a quickening of the pulse. Listen to the rhythm and depth of my breath."

"But even if I can see all that, what does it mean?"

"All I want you to do now is be aware of any changes in my body, face or voice. Just looking for them will help hone your senses." With a grin, she leaned closer to him. "Come here; I've had enough theory, haven't you? After all, this is the inner room."

She led him to a carpeted platform, where he lay down and reached for her to join him. Instead, Tayar sat beside him and leaned over to take his member in her mouth.

"Hey!" Dov bolted up and pulled away, to sit against the upcurve of the platform.

Tayar rolled back onto her haunches next to him. "What's the matter, Dov?" she asked, using gentle, yielding tones.

"That's... it's unnatural."

"Why, dear?" Her hand rested on his thigh, just inches from his groin.

"It just is. Only perverts..."

"Ah, I see." As natural counterpoint to her words, her hand moved slowly upward, over his smooth, muscular flesh. "But Dov, can anything we do together, here in our inner room, be perverted?"

"It isn't the way I want you."

Tayar languidly drew her hand along the boy's penis, then raked her fingers through the surrounding coarse hair. "Do you remember smelling me?"

"Of course. That was great."

"You didn't think it would be, though, did you?" She varied her touch slightly, using her nails on his inner thigh.

"No, but that isn't the same. I never heard of anyone using smell for sex."

"Do you like kissing me?" She played her lips along his neck until he could resist it no longer; he bent to fill his mouth with hers. Withdrawing from his lips, she stroked then kissed his shoulder and chest, punctuating her words with action, using her lips and hands. "I certainly enjoy kissing... smelling... tasting you." Her hands grazed his groin, while her mouth and tongue explored the textures and flavors of his abdomen and thighs. His sweat tasted acrid, both nervous and aroused. "And I will kiss you wherever I want, because it gives both of us pleasure."

She kissed the smooth tip of his phallus lightly, then more deeply and still deeper, until it gradually filled her mouth. Dov's protest was swallowed by a deep-throated groan. She felt his hands reach for her head and start to pull her off him. Instead, he stroked her head and back, down to her stomach and lower, reaching to caress her pubis, using his fingertips to manipulate her nether lips as she had shown him with the oyster. His hands were stiff and awkward, but he was so eager to please that her body responded, with a sharp, tense, almost painful contraction.

"I can't hold back!" he moaned.

"Then don't," she mumbled.

"No!" He rolled over onto her and entered her. The extended gusts of his orgasm lasted long enough to ignite her own. Then he fell away from her and immediately collapsed into a deep sleep.

While he slept, Tayar retreated to her bedroom for a pleasure meditation to relieve the ache in her nether lips, knowing that soon, she would no longer need to do it for herself.

Exhilaration jarred the rhythm of their days, so that the boy and his Allesha lost track of time. In the dark inner room, morning became the time they decided to have breakfast, whether or not the sun had recently risen. Night was another relative term that had nothing to do with a moon, stars or sleep. All was blurred by the acute sexual revelations of the stage.

Gradually, Tayar taught Dov to read her flesh, the tone of her sighs, her breath. She constantly changed her signals, becoming a different woman with each encounter, forcing him to see and learn her anew. Soon, he was experimenting more freely with his hands, lips and tongue, first using the oysters and pearls with her guiding him, then practicing on her body with her releasing all control so she might enjoy the pleasure he gave her. How difficult it was to then direct his attention away from focusing on her pearl and back to the entire woman.

One evening, when Dov had discovered how her pleasure could build from one release to the next, he suddenly became silent. It seemed to her that he was quivering on the brink of the next step, but was unwilling to acknowledge his doubts. Instead, he studied her even more closely, seeking answers in his newly acquired perceptions. Tayar allowed a single tear to trickle and a gasp to catch in her throat.

Gently licking the tear from her damp cheek, Dov asked, "Why are you crying, Tayar?"

"Tears aren't always a sign of sadness. I don't think it's a coincidence that we use the same word — touch — to describe both inner and outer experiences. You touch my skin, and it touches my heart."

"But you never cried before. Does that mean that you weren't touched before? That I didn't satisfy you?"

"You've always given me pleasure, Dov."

"But I wasn't a very good lover before, was I?"

"Is anyone ever as good when they start as they can become when they learn and grow?"

He paused, then shrugged his shoulders. "There's something I still don't understand. Why is sex the way you train Allemen? I mean, it's got to be more than how you get us to come here and listen to you."

"Yes, much more. Imagine you're an Alleman who's been sent into the midst of two warring tribes, seeking a path toward peace for them. Each side makes demands which change constantly, yet you need to find what will truly satisfy both. It takes patience, knowledge, flexibility and, above all, an instinct for understanding strangers that grows out of constantly focusing and refocusing your perceptions."

"You mean that the Peace is like a woman's body?"

"In many ways, it is. Both require the same skills — constant care, creativity and awareness — as does any relationship worth having."

"But isn't sex sort of an extreme way to teach it?"

"As you said, it got you here." Tayar paused and gave him a small, pensive smile. "But it's much more than that. What you learn in passion, you'll never unlearn. It becomes as much a part of you as the instinct to breathe or think."

"So, you expect me to use sex as an Alleman?"

"Actually, no. It's too powerful, weighted by a wide variety of taboos and social conventions. Using sex in diplomatic situations can become a barrier to achieving understanding."

"But the Alleshi use it."

"Only here in our Valley with very special boys, and only as a teaching aid."

"Then I think it's time for you to get back to work. Teaching, that is." He grinned, leaning over to lightly trace her right nipple with one finger, while he played his tongue and lips along her neck, sending chills down her spine.

The Exhilaration Stage lasted almost a week. One morning, while sitting in her bedroom, writing in her journal about the past couple of days, the young Allesha realized that the stage was aptly named. Not only for the boy, but for her, too. She felt heightened, energized. Just the memory of the evening Dov had decided to search for an oyster pearl that most closely resembled hers, while the two of them laughed uncontrollably, caused a shiver of pleasure. Yes, he was a good student, and was becoming a superb lover.

Just then, she glanced at the wall mirror, and what she saw shocked her. She closed her eyes, blocking out the woman in the mirror, not wanting to see the unfettered joy that seemed inappropriate for an Allesha in Season.

Not without Jared.

Not with a Mwertik.

She took slow, deep, calming breaths. When she opened her eyes again, she barely noticed that her smile had dimmed; instead, she was focused on the days and weeks ahead.

It's time to bring Dov's new sensitivities out of the inner room, to teach him how to use and control them. If he is to be prepared for all the duties and dangers of being an Alleman, and to survive whatever lies ahead, I must teach him to read people and situations, as well as he has learned to read me. And it must all be accomplished before his Service Days. How little time I have left!

Resolved to move forward, the Allesha rose from the chair, ready to take her Winter Boy to the next stage. But as she stood, tears suddenly erupted, streaming down her cheeks.

Everything's such a tangle! Kiv and Dara. Jared and Dov. And always the Mwertik, out there, hovering over everything I love. Murderers. Butchers. Must Dov be sacrificed as Jared was?

Stop this immediately! she chastised herself. *What use can I be to Dov if I can't control my own emotions? I can do this. I must do this.*

She gathered all her strength, burying her unreined emotions deep within, where they couldn't affect the boy's Season. Too soon, it would be over. Only then would she have the freedom to deal with her personal demons.

When her tears were spent, she washed her face and brushed her hair, determined to erase all signs of her private turmoil before leaving her bedroom.

As she crossed the greeting room, she heard the boy coming from his room. She turned to embrace him, but he held her at arm's length and looked deeply into her eyes. Yes, there were definitely drawbacks to having taught him to read her so well.

"What's wrong?" His voice was soft with concern.

"Dov, I must go out for a while." She barely controlled the tremor in her voice.

"Are you okay?"

She hugged him quickly, to break the hold of his eyes on hers. "Everything will be fine." She darted into the vestibule, put on her coat, grabbed her hat and gloves and left the house.

Dov went to the front window and watched as she ran through the snow. *She forgot to put on her boots,* he realized, and almost rushed after her to give them to her. But he stopped himself. *She doesn't want me to follow her.*

Chapter 54

Tayar/Rishana fled through the snow with no conscious destination. All she knew was that she had to remove herself from her Winter Boy before she tainted his Season with her inner turmoil. Only when she realized her blind escape had led to the library did she recognize that she no longer sought comfort or reassurance. She needed answers.

Rishana entered the library with the confidence of one familiar with its paths, so that none would have reason to offer to guide her — or ask questions. After all the time she had spent in the library with Savah, sometimes helping with her research, Rishana felt sure she'd have no difficulty finding her way. But she made a wrong turn and eventually found herself much deeper in the bowels of the mountain than she had ever been. The well-groomed, angular hallways with their regularly spaced gas sconces became increasingly darker rough-hewn narrow tunnels with fewer and often dim or extinguished lights. In some places, she had to duck to avoid hitting her head. She doubled back a few times, but became even more disoriented among the twisting, forking paths of the labyrinth.

Then, as she rounded yet another barely lit narrow bend, she peered down a pitch-black tunnel with no illumination at all. Tired and defeated, she leaned against the chill craggy wall and wondered if she would ever again see the light of day. If she never found her way back, would they even know where to look for her?

When Rishana had first heard the rumors of those legendary caverns of lost knowledge that were supposed to be locked away somewhere in this stone warren, she had scoffed. How could anything be truly lost here in The Valley? Now she was beginning to understand how deep and dark the secrets of the Alleshi could be.

Suddenly, a tiny flicker of light approached from out of the darkness, so unexpected and incongruous that she thought she imagined it. But as it drifted forward, she saw it for what it was — a candle — and the figure of the woman carrying it came into welcome focus.

"Elnor! Thank goodness." Rishana was so relieved that she didn't see the furtive glance that Elnor gave her as anything other than surprise.

The older Allesha walked into the dim light where Rishana had cowered, pinched the wick of the candle to extinguish its flame and pocketed it. "Rishana, what on earth are you doing down here?"

"I'm lost."

"Obviously." Elnor, who was usually so loquacious, said nothing else. She walked away, looking back only once to be sure that Rishana was following.

When they reached an area of the library that was familiar to Rishana, she thanked Elnor, who barely nodded before moving on. It wasn't long before the young Allesha located the room she sought.

On a high shelf deep in the room, Rishana/Jinet found Mistral's journals. She rolled a ladder over to them, sat on its upper step and browsed through the dozens of small leather-bound books. Soft and flexible in her hands, they conveyed a sense of the years and miles these journals had traveled to rest here under the mountain. She leafed through them, following the chronology of Mistral's service, but the ones she sought were missing. Mistral's journals stopped abruptly about eighteen years ago, leaving a large empty space on the shelf.

She knew that Jared had delivered his journals to The Valley every year of his adult life, as did every Alleman. After his death, their son, Eli, had brought Jared's last journal to the library, fulfilling his father's final obligation to the Alleshi. Jared's journals were in the same section as Mistral's, on a shelf about shoulder high. Once more, most of the shelf was empty, with Jared's last journal dated from eighteen years ago. Scanning the nearby shelves, she looked for Tedrac's journals, convinced by now that most of his would also be missing.

"You won't find it here." Savah's soft voice punctuated the silence as loudly as a rifle crack.

The young Allesha spun around to look at the small, round woman she had once believed was her dearest living friend.

"Come," Savah said from the doorway, before turning to leave.

They walked in silence, until they were in Savah's study. To Jinet's astonishment, Savah removed a set of keys from her bodice and locked the heavy oak door behind them.

Savah was the first to speak. "Your feet are soaked. What are you thinking of, going out in the snow wearing nothing but those house shoes? Where are your boots?"

Choosing to not hear Savah's concern, Jinet shook her head. "Savah, you lied to me."

"Never," Savah said emphatically. "Now take off those wet shoes before you catch a cold."

"Forget the damn shoes!" Jinet's heart pounded in her ears. "How can I ever trust you again?"

Savah recoiled as though struck. "Do all the years we've known each other mean nothing?"

"That's what I should be asking you."

"I never lied to you. I always told you the truth."

"What form of truth, Savah?"

"There is only one form of truth. I just couldn't tell you all of it. You weren't ready."

"I'm ready now."

"Are you, dear?" Savah sighed deeply.

"No more secrets, Savah!" Hearing her own shrill voice, Jinet took a deep breath and said more evenly, but no less vehemently, "You've no choice and neither do I. I know too much already, and yet I don't know anything."

Without another word, Savah pressed a seemingly solid plank on the wood-paneled wall behind her makeshift bed, and the plank's face slid sideways to reveal another lock. Savah opened that lock with a key from the same ring, and a section of the wall opened. Behind it was a small alcove. She stepped back, so Jinet could see that its four shelves were lined with journals. Jinet stood and took one at random.

Savah pointed to the upper shelf — "These are Mistral's." — Then to the second shelf — "These are Jared's." — And to the next-to-last shelf — "Tedrac's."

"The bottom shelf?" Jinet asked.

"Mine."

Jinet leafed through the journal in her hand. When she saw Jared's familiar scrawl — the writing of a man whose hand could never keep up with his thoughts — her throat burned with tears she refused to shed. She didn't notice Savah leaving the room until she heard the door close once more and the key turn. Savah had locked her in! But Jinet refused to be distracted, not even by the fact that she was now ostensibly Savah's prisoner. She pulled a chair closer to the alcove and began to read.

Savah returned later, after Jinet had skimmed through one of Jared's journals and half of one of Mistral's. Jinet looked up from the page she was reading.

"Do you understand now, my dear?" Savah asked.

"No."

Savah glanced at the open volume in Jinet's lap and picked up the one on the floor beside Jinet's chair. "No, I suppose not. These two won't make any sense unless you read the others that came before them."

"Then tell me."

Savah sat in the other chair and leaned back into its deep upholstery. "We didn't set out to have a Mwertik among us, but when it happened, we realized what an opportunity it could be to mend our world through him."

Jinet steeled herself to ask, "Jared knew?" though she dreaded the answer.

"Yes."

"In other words, he lied to me, too." It came out as a gasp, as though the air were suddenly too thin to fill her lungs.

"Jared would never have hurt you."

"That isn't what I asked."

"He couldn't always tell you everything. I swore him to secrecy."

"So your poison seeped even into my marriage."

"No, Jinet!"

"What would you call it when you make a man lie to his wife?"

"Necessity. But it never changed the way he felt about you, or how I feel."

"And here in The Valley, how have your lies — your necessities — distorted things?" Jinet felt her body tighten against the onslaught of ideas that shook her very being.

"Jinet, please. You don't understand."

"You're right I don't. You've brought hate into this Valley."

"No, the hate was here. Hate of the Mwertik, created by the Mwertik, perverting our Peace, making the Council question our most basic precepts and reason for being." The venom in Savah's tone was undeniable. "Kiv—"

"You hate her… one of your sisters!"

"I hate what she represents, what she is trying to do."

"Such as…?"

"I fear she has brought the Mwertik's own violence into our Valley and our ways."

Shocked at what Savah was implying, Jinet stood abruptly, letting the journal fall to the floor. "Savah, I pity you. You've become so warped by your own fears—" The young Allesha struggled to find the right words, but was lost in the torrent of her disbelief and anger. She stomped toward the door.

"Wait!" Savah took a satchel from under her bed and filled it with a dozen journals from the cabinet. "Here, take these with you. When you have finished those, please return to me. Then you can ask me any questions, and I'll give you honest and full answers, to the best of my ability — and more of their journals to read."

Jinet snatched the bag without a word and turned to leave.

"Jinet, please. Don't judge me and throw away everything you believe in before you have more knowledge."

"Knowledge, Savah? Is that all this is to you? We're not talking about another book you've rescued from oblivion. These are people's lives. Jared, a man you claim to have loved, and my Winter Boy. People who can be hurt while you sit here safely under your mountain weaving your stories. Yes, I will read and ask you questions, but I'll never return to you, not to what we once were."

Jinet chose to not see the hurt in Savah's eyes.

Chapter 55

Jinet/Rishana stood with her hand on her front gate latch, a thick snowfall drifting about her. She ached for the warm haven of her home, but dared not go inside. As cold and tired as she was, she still wasn't in control of her emotions. Until she was, she knew she must stay away from her Winter Boy.

She had to find shelter, and someone to talk to who wouldn't endanger her Winter Boy. But where? Who? In the past, she would have turned to Jared or Savah or, more recently, Dara. Whom could she trust here in this Valley that had proven so different from what she had believed it to be? Different and devious.

The snow had turned to pelting ice by the time Rishana reached the storehouse. Huge and filled to brimming with its accumulated weight of history, the storehouse was concrete proof of the far-reaching, generations-old Peace. Whatever storms raged outside, here she knew she was safe.

Rishana surveyed the nearby aisles to confirm that no one had seen her enter. Good. Now she needed to find a warm corner where she could be alone while she sorted out her thoughts. She retreated to a room on the far side of the storehouse, where she had once helped Caith inventory piles of thick lush furs, gifts from the Diaghts, who were seeking trade rights. After turning up one of the gas lamps, Rishana kicked off her drenched shoes and socks and wrapped herself in a large bear fur. Then she opened the satchel, arranged the journals chronologically on the floor beside her, and began to read. She had gone through about a third of the first from Mistral's pile of journals when Caith entered the room.

"I saw the light and wondered who was in here," Caith said with a smile as she walked through the door.

Caith paused in mid-step at the sight of Rishana hunched over with a heavy fur tented around her shoulders. Sweat trickled from the young woman's temples. When Caith leaned down to touch her face, it was ice cold. Rishana looked up from the book on her lap; her eyes were shining feverishly.

"I'll be right back," Caith said. She returned a short time later with a large hot mug, which she handed to Rishana. "Drink it slowly and breathe in the fumes."

When Rishana sipped the brew, she wrinkled her face in distaste and lowered the mug.

Caith wrapped her small, gnarled hands around Rishana's, which still held the mug, coaxing her to bring it back up to her face. "I know it's bitter. But we don't have the leisure to fight this thing gently. You've got a chill that could turn into something much worse. Then what would happen to your First Boy's Season?"

At the mention of Dov, Rishana spoke for the first time since Caith had entered. "My Winter Boy. I must…." But her words were slurred and indistinct. She forced herself to swallow more of the brew.

"Good, but sip it slowly and breathe the aroma in through your nose." Caith watched as Rishana obediently finished the drink. Then Caith tried to guide her out of the room. "I stoked the fire in my steam room. It should be ready by now."

Rishana wouldn't budge until she had gathered the journals into the satchel. Then, with one fist clutching the bear fur around her and the other wrapped around the satchel's straps, Rishana walked in silence beside Caith.

They disrobed in the small anteroom, where Caith retrieved three jars from a cabinet while Rishana concealed the satchel beneath the large fur. As they entered the steam room, the warmth enfolded them like a welcoming cloak. Caith took the chain of keys from around her neck — the ones she never let out of her sight — and put them in a hanging pouch far from the doorway. Then she poured oils and herbs from the jars and ladled water onto the heated rocks until aromatic steam filled the small room. They could barely see each other through the fog as they reclined on opposite wooden benches.

"I am very old," Caith said. "I remember people in their youth who were long dead by the time you were born. Sometimes, their faces are clearer in my mind than those I saw just yesterday." Caith paused, as she drifted through a cloud of memories. "With my First Boy, I was as young as you, maybe younger. They said I was the youngest Allesha ever, but how could they know? No one had marked my birth or counted my years. I thought myself so mature, especially after all I had survived to get here. Only when I was well into my First Season did I understand how much I still had to learn."

Rishana's whispered "yes" was little more than an exhale, a release of breath.

"My First Boy was a handful, questioning everything I tried to teach him." Caith rolled onto her side to gaze through the steam toward Rishana. "Actually, you remind me of him, especially at times like this. He'd take his lessons deep into himself, as though he had to chew them completely before he could reshape them into something fully his own. Only then would he discuss them with me.

"Of course, back then, things were simpler. All I had to contend with was a rambunctious boy and the confusion typical of any new Allesha with her First Boy. With the help of my mentor and our sisters, I became stronger, more assured and capable." Caith sat up and stared into the fog. She could almost see Rishana across from her, a shape that appeared to be sitting and leaning forward. "I never had reason to doubt the grace of any Allesha."

"You do now?" Rishana asked.

"My doubts aren't the issue, are they?"

"I need to know what you think."

Caith considered the various answers she could give, then said, "Our sisters are split into opposing forces, and you're caught in the middle."

"Why?"

"Fear does terrible things to people. And we've got a lot to fear right now. The Mwertik seem to want to destroy us. How do we fight what appears to be unreasonable hatred?"

"Seem? Appear?"

"We don't know anything about them for certain."

"Don't we, Caith? Doesn't anyone?"

Caith breathed in the steam, letting it fill her, seeking strength from it. "Yes, there are some who may know. Dara, maybe."

"And Kiv?" Rishana asked.

"No, Kiv is only guessing — I hope."

"So you agree with Dara that she's dangerous?"

"Her ideas definitely are. Some feel she is traveling a path that will change all of us." Caith paused, remembering Kiv as a young Allesha not so many years ago. "Kiv has always been passionate, though with a fiery temper. If her hate has taken hold of that side of her, then I don't know what she might do." She shook her head sadly.

"What of Peren?"

"She's your husband's Allesha," Caith said dismissively.

"She manipulated me, lied to me. I feel as if my whole world is coming apart."

"In many ways, it is."

"What do you know of my First Boy?" Rishana asked.

"You mean that he is probably Mwertik?"

The young woman gasped. "How did you know?"

"I didn't, but my guesses tend to be pretty good. Better than Kiv's, I hope."

"I love him, Caith." Rishana's voice now came from the left side of the room, though Caith wasn't sure when she had gotten off the bench.

"Of course, you do. He's your First Boy."

"But I hate the Mwertik. His people."

As Rishana paced closer, Caith could see her furrowed face before she gradually disappeared back into the steam.

"They killed your husband, want to destroy all you love. And you have just been through the Exhilaration Stage. You're raw, wide open, and you feel so close to your chosen boy."

"Yes, but that isn't why, Caith."

"No, it isn't. Still, even in a normal Season, Exhilaration wreaks havoc on a woman's equilibrium. And yours is not a normal Season."

"Dara and Peren want to use him."

"Because they hope he may be the key to saving us."

"But he's more than their pawn," Rishana said. "He has his own hopes and needs. He has a right to make his own choices."

"Then he will have to be told when he is ready."

"How do I tell a boy that the father he has struggled to love for so long is not his father? His mother not his mother? That he's a Mwertik Zalog, a member of the very people who would destroy our Peace? It will crush him."

"If so, then he isn't the hoped-for intermediary others would have us believe."

"That's cold, Caith."

"No, it's reality. But I don't believe he will be destroyed, because you won't allow it."

"I'll be the one doing it." Suddenly, Rishana was hovering over Caith, staring at her. "I still don't know where you stand."

"By your side, Rishana."

"Do you agree with Peren and Dara, or with Kiv?"

"With you — uncomfortable with the choices at hand, knowing we must proceed with one if we are to survive without destroying ourselves."

"While our world splinters and breaks."

Caith took Rishana's hands. "Our world is changing. You must decide for yourself whether you wish it to change by violence or subterfuge, or a combination of the two."

"And my Winter Boy? What of him?"

"Love him, protect him, prepare him. If you're smart, you'll also enjoy the short time you have left with him. It will go by so quickly, and then all you'll have will be memories."

"It hurts, Caith."

"I know, Rishana."

"I'm not just talking about him. I'm afraid of trusting Dara… that she hasn't been fully on my side. And Peren. I believed in her as completely as my own mother." Tears mixed with the trailing sweat on Rishana's cheek

"I know, child. It's painful to discover that the people we love aren't who we thought they were."

Rishana pulled her hands out of Caith's and sat back on the opposite bench. "Are you who I believe you to be?"

"No, of course not."

"Who am I to believe in, then?"

"Yourself, Rishana. The rest will come only after that."

"What of Peren and Dara?"

"You must give them a chance to earn your trust again."

"And Kiv?"

"I cannot say, because I don't know what she is proposing. Is her strategy a reasonable one? Does it have a hope of succeeding? I will talk with her when she comes for supplies."

"No! I forbid it!" Rishana suddenly stood towering over Caith.

"How else can we protect you and your Winter Boy?"

Rishana started to protest, considered her options and nodded. "Fine. But if you—"

"I promise, child. I would never do anything that would hurt you. I know it's hard for you to trust me right now. But we must find out."

"I need to be able to trust you. I have no one else."

"You have yourself and your boy." Caith reached up to grasp Rishana's hand. "Listen to your own heart. I've seldom seen one so strong and true."

Rishana squeezed Caith's hand, then released it and walked toward the door.

"And be careful, child."

"Of everyone," Rishana said before leaving the steam room.

Chapter 56

After Tayar bolted from the house, Dov tried to busy himself with chores, but didn't get much done. He was constantly drawn to look outside into the snowstorm, to scan the path for his Allesha.

When Tayar did reappear almost two hours later, her shoulders were hunched under the weight of a heavy satchel, and her eyes downcast. *What's made her feel so defeated?* he wondered. *Something's dreadfully wrong.*

Dov rushed to the door, but she turned away once more before he could call to her. When he saw her disappear into the heavy snowfall, he hesitated for only a moment, then quickly threw on his overclothes, grabbed her boots, and sprinted after her. But the deep snow was churned up by so many crossing footprints, he couldn't be sure which of the various intersecting paths she had taken. He called out, "Tayar!" The icy wind whipped his face, muting the sound of his voice, even to his own ears.

Fire and Stones! What could have been so upsetting that it would drive her out in a storm like this without her damn boots? Doesn't she even have enough sense to find shelter?

Realizing that he, too, needed shelter, but not wanting to return to the empty house where he'd be alone with his worries, Dov set his feet on the one Valley path that he knew as well as the way home through the dark Birani forest.

Dov found Le'a in her kitchen, spooning a batch of cookies onto baking sheets. After their greeting embrace, he watched Le'a as she lit the oven and bent to put the cookie sheets into it. He could discern no hint that she knew what had happened that morning that could have so unnerved Tayar.

Straightening up, she gestured to the table, but he remained standing. "I really didn't expect you today, Dov. Not in this storm. Is something wrong?"

"I don't know. Well, yes. I'm certain there is, but I don't know what. Was Tayar here earlier?'

"No. Why? What's happened?"

"It was strange. Suddenly she wasn't anything like herself. Then she ran off. Didn't even put on her boots."

"Dov, you know about the Every Woman."

"No, Le'a, this was her, the real woman, and she was…" Dov paused, picturing Tayar with her red, darting eyes and nervous mouth. "…scared. I'm sure that's what it was. She flew out of the house before I could see anything more. But it was something else, too. It was almost as though she had stepped off a cliff, where she'd expected solid earth. Does that make sense?"

"Yes, it does."

"You know something, don't you, Le'a?"

"I can't say, Dov. I wasn't there, and you haven't given me much information."

"I have so little."

"But much more than you would have had only a week ago. I'm proud of you, Dov. You've learned well."

"This isn't about damned lessons. Tayar is out there, without her boots, in this storm. I'm worried about her."

"I'm sure she's inside somewhere, warm and safe."

Dov bussed Le'a's cheek in farewell. "I've got to find her."

Le'a put her two hands on his shoulders. "Dov, go home. You mustn't be wandering about The Valley. Even if the weather were fine, you're not permitted."

"Surely, in a situation like this."

"No, Dov. I will let Tayar know you're worried, and she'll return home soon enough."

"But you said you don't know where she is."

"I can find her easily enough by notifying my nearest neighbors, who will send word to their neighbors and so forth, until the entire Valley is alerted. Tayar is undoubtedly visiting with another Allesha and will return soon."

Dov could tell that Le'a wasn't exactly lying to him, but her mouth was tight as though she were holding back something important. However, he understood that he'd learn nothing more by pressing her. "All right," he said. "But I have her boots with me. Will you make sure she gets them?"

"Of course," Le'a said without meeting his gaze.

"I'd really rather go with you. You're not a woodsman. You might need my help in this weather."

"It's my Valley, and you aren't allowed where I would look. Go home, Dov. It's where you belong." Le'a embraced him quickly, then patted him on the back, almost as though she were pushing him out the door.

Dov didn't know why he hung back, hiding behind a large evergreen tree, to watch Le'a's house. But when she came out, he saw that she didn't carry Tayar's boots. And she didn't stop at her nearest neighbors, but went much farther afield. He followed her until he realized she was headed toward an area he'd never been, at the far edge of The Valley. Whatever she was up to, he didn't dare go where he had been forbidden. Especially when he noticed another Allesha across the way, who appeared to be watching him. He waved goodbye to Le'a's back, as though they had been walking together and were only now going separate ways.

As he trekked back to his Allesha's home, he replayed the day in his mind, still finding no answers. But one way or another, he was determined to find out what was going on.

Dov spied Tayar from his bedroom window when she finally returned home in the late afternoon. Though she still carried that heavy satchel, her back was straighter than before. She wore boots, but not the ones he had given Le'a. He rushed through the greeting room, flinging open the door to the vestibule just as she was reaching up to hang her coat on a hook. "Tayar! Are you okay?"

"Hello, Dov." Her smile was bright, and her eyes crinkled, but for some reason, it didn't feel right to him. Almost as though her expression was artfully pasted over, like a mask.

Tayar brushed a lock of his hair off his brow, then embraced him with her full body pressing against his. But she stepped away too quickly, with no appearance of being touched by any of it. She bent to pick up the satchel.

"Here, let me carry that for you," he said as he reached for its leather strap.

She yanked it out of his grasp. "No, it's really not as heavy as it looks." Shouldering the bundle, she stepped past him into the greeting room. "What smells so good?"

"I made some soup. I had to do something. You were gone a long time."

"Why don't I drop this off in my room and meet you in the kitchen? I'm famished."

"You should be." Dov struggled to not sound irritable. "You've been gone all day."

"I'm sorry you were worried, but I'm home now." Tayar stroked his arm, then walked toward her bedroom.

How could she act as if nothing happened? What's she hiding? Shaking his head, Dov went into the kitchen to wait for Tayar, determined that she wouldn't sidestep him again.

Tayar took some slow, steadying breaths and adjusted her smile before walking into the kitchen. But she couldn't stop her heart from beating loudly in her chest.

Dov stood at the stove, ladling vegetable soup from the pot into a bowl. On the table was a small pile of overstuffed chicken sandwiches and a fruit salad. He certainly had been busy while she was gone. She strolled up to him, leaned against his back and wrapped her arms around his waist as he filled the second bowl with the steaming soup. Giving him a bear hug, she breathed in the fragrance of the boy and kissed the back of his neck. Then she settled at the table.

He brought the bowls over and sat down opposite her. After placing some bits of a sandwich into their offering saucer, she tasted the soup, allowing the heat to fill her, while playing the flavors and textures over her tongue. "Mmm, it's as good as it smells."

Tayar could feel his eyes on her, worried and aware of her every nuance. *Why did I have to teach him to read me so well? It's going to be difficult to redirect his attention tonight.*

"What's wrong, Tayar?" Dov asked, his voice soft with concern. "Why did you run out of the house like that?"

"I had some things I needed to take care of."

"At the western mountain?"

"What?"

"That's where Le'a was headed when she went looking for you. What's over there that I'm not allowed to see?"

"Nothing that you won't have access to once you're an Alleman. It's our library."

"So why is it off-limits to me now?"

"Every place in this Valley, other than our two houses, is forbidden to you right now. You're in Season, and there are rules."

Dov glared at her. She could almost see the old problem boy reasserting himself.

"Why were you so upset, Tayar?"

She considered denying it, but realized it was too late for that. "I learned something that surprised me. It's over now."

"Is it? Then why are you hiding?"

"I'm not aware of hiding anything."

"But you're not telling me anything, either."

"I don't have anything to tell you, just questions I'm trying to answer."

"About me? And why Le'a went running to the library?"

"Please, Dov. It's been an exhausting day. I need to relax, take a long bath and then enjoy a pleasant evening with you. Why don't you find something to read to me tonight while I rest?"

Tayar watched him struggle between his need for answers and concern for her well-being. Putting down her sandwich, she placed her hand on his. "Dov, I just need some quiet time on my own and then with you. Please."

He met her gaze. "Of course." Only then did he begin to eat.

Tayar finished the soup and sandwich, and got up to leave the room. Bending down to kiss him, she said, "Thank you, Dov, for being so caring. Coming home to you was wonderful."

He returned the kiss gently, with no demands or expectations.

Chapter 57

Caith was organizing the baked goods when Kiv came to the storehouse for supplies.

"Good afternoon, Caith," Kiv said cordially.

"Hello!" Caith responded in the same friendly manner. "You've come at the right time; Beatrice just left some of her nut pies. You must have one." Caith took two pies from the shelf. "In fact, I was about to enjoy a piece. Please join me."

In her room, Caith removed a pile of books from the old leather armchair to give her guest a place to sit. Then she settled into her desk chair and cut two generous portions of the pie. She gave Kiv the larger slice, and they ate their first bites in respectful silence for the craft of the baker.

"To what do I owe this honor, Caith?" Kiv gestured at the room, one she had seldom visited.

Caith put her plate on the desk and folded her hands on her lap. "I've wanted to talk to you for some time about your comments in Council. I want to understand your ideas, to learn how you've come to the conclusions you have."

Kiv pressed her fork into the last crumbs of pie, licked the fork, then put her plate down — all the while carefully studying Caith. "You've been talking to Peren." It wasn't a question.

"Actually, I haven't seen her all Season. She's buried herself in the library."

"Exactly. She hides away inside that mountain and thinks she knows what the real world is like."

"Tell me how you see it, please." Caith reclined back into her chair, affecting a listening pose.

"Our Allemen are being butchered. Our villages are endangered. Our Peace is at risk, falling apart because Peren and her intimates would rather close their eyes than act. We're attacked from without and deteriorating from within."

"Isn't that an exaggeration?"

"If anything, I'm understating things. The Mwertik are out to destroy us. If our survival requires that we destroy them first, then we must do it quickly, with whatever it takes. The longer we wait, the more powerful they become, and the weaker we will be."

"But if there were another way," Caith asked. "Perhaps, if one Mwertik could be turned. If we could find one of their tribe who hasn't yet been taught to hate us."

"You're talking about that foundling."

Caith's heart skipped a beat, but she kept a tight grip on her emotions. "Who?" she asked, showing only her curiosity.

"The boy Mistral and his cohorts found last summer after the Mwertik raid."

Caith didn't allow herself to sigh in relief. "Oh, him," she said. "I didn't think he was a Mwertik."

"I don't believe he is."

"If he were?"

"He would be dead."

"A child?"

"Don't be so shocked. It's nothing less than they do to our people. Age doesn't stop them; it won't stop me. And many more agree with me than don't. I've been out there, beyond our mountains, talked with our people. They want to know why we haven't acted."

"What do you tell them, Kiv?"

"That we will. Soon."

"But you can't speak for the Council."

"All it would take, Caith, is you distributing the weapons we've accumulated over the years. Open up the armory. Better yet, dig up the hidden vaults from the Before Times!"

"Kiv, you know better than to believe in legends. We have no such ancient technologies buried under this floor, or anywhere in our Valley."

"When I can prove what I believe, no one will stand in my way."

Caith desperately needed to defuse the moment. "Kiv, I've looked. All these years, I've searched." She shrugged. "Nothing."

"Then release the advanced rapid-fire guns you've got locked away," Kiv commanded.

"Too many of our villages haven't yet reached that level of proficiency and discipline."

"Only because we haven't given it to them. Don't they have a right to defend themselves?"

"And if I don't release the guns?"

"You're old, Caith. There's not much you can do about it."

"I'm not so old that I don't care what will happen after my death."

"Don't you want there to be a Valley after you're gone? Do you want this to be the last generation to live with the prosperity and safety of our Peace? That's what I would fight to preserve."

"But what if it could be preserved without violence?"

"The only response to unreasonable violence is to counter it with greater, more effective violence."

"Can you entertain the possibility there may be another answer?"

"The time will come when you'll all see how right I am." Kiv stood quickly, jolting the side table.

Caith reached out toward Kiv. "Please sit. We still have so much to discuss. I need to understand."

"I'm tired of all the talk." Kiv spun on her heels, reached back to grab the uncut pie, and left.

Caith fell into her chair, breathless and terrified.

Chapter 58

Ever since Peren/Savah had given Jared and Mistral's journals to Tayar/Rishana, she devoured them every spare moment. She read them when she retreated to her rooms after breakfast. She read when she used the toilet. After sex, when the boy collapsed into a deep, satisfied sleep, she returned to her bedroom and read. The more she read, the greater her compulsion to return to those pages, to hear Jared's voice in her mind's ear, to understand Mistral, to know the truth of her own life and that of her Winter Boy.

When Rishana heard the tapping on her bathroom window, she was in her bedroom lost in one of Jared's journals, taking advantage of the privacy the boy's visits to Le'a/Dara afforded her. She walked into the bathroom and looked out, but saw no one. The morning's snowfall had blanketed the yard once more, but now, the afternoon sun shone crystalline on the footprints that led from under her window to the barn. Wondering who had signaled her in such an unusual manner, she threw on her coat and boots and went outside.

"Caith!" Rishana was astounded to find the spry old caretaker in her barn, sitting on a bale of hay, pushing one of the goats away repeatedly.

"Hello, Rishana." Caith's wide smile wrinkled her dark crosshatched face even more. "How do I get rid of this pest?"

"She just wants her head scratched." Rishana sat down next to Caith and patted the ground. The goat responded by turning its attention to her. "What brought you here, Caith, in this weather?"

"Kiv was at the storehouse today."

"What happened? What did she say?"

"That's the thing, Rishana. Much of what she said sounds quite reasonable. It's *how* she says it that isn't."

"Please start at the beginning."

"I'm not sure where the beginning is. When did her hate become so poisonous?" Caith's eyes seemed to focus on something in the past.

"Dara claims Kiv was always like this," Rishana said. "Taking only easy boys and bending them to her will, instead of paring them down to their essential selves."

Caith shrugged. "Dara considers any Allesha who doesn't take on problem boys to be below her standards. Still, she is right that Kiv always needed to prevail over everyone else."

"You said her words were reasonable. In what way?"

"In that we do need to prepare ourselves to fight the Mwertik. It's not as simple as Kiv would have it. Still, if we have no alternative, what else can we do? And if we fight, dare we do less than be prepared to fight effectively and decisively?"

"What of my Winter Boy?"

"Yes, he may yet be the key. But he's only one person, and he'd be walking into a possible death trap to try to convince people who won't even recognize him as anything other than an interfering stranger, an unwanted interloper. Why would they listen to him?" Caith paused, then asked, "Have you read *The Northern Border*? It's one of Alleen's stories."

"My Winter Boy read it to me only a little while ago." Rishana cringed inwardly at the memory of how that one story had suddenly and unexpectedly brought on the Conflagration Stage.

"The Mukane could not be diverted from war, not even by the son of their headman."

"But the seed of hope that they planted…"

"Took generations to take hold. Too late for the child in the story and her entire family. Too late for so many who were killed." Caith shook her head sadly.

"So you no longer hope?"

"There's always hope. We have your Winter Boy. Still, we must be prepared should he fail."

"How?"

"By preparing for war while striving to avoid it."

"But once we start down that path, won't it be difficult to stop? Does training for war make it inevitable?"

"That, too, we must guard against. As I said, it's much more complex than Kiv would have. Perhaps even more than Peren, Dara and the others realize."

"So, you're saying Kiv could be dangerous, but she could be right."

"For your First Boy, the danger is very real, whether Kiv is right or wrong."

Rishana stood and brushed the hay from her clothes. "I can't say I'm pleased to hear this, but I'm grateful to you for coming and telling me. You've given me quite a bit to ponder."

Caith reached out her hand, and Rishana gently pulled her up onto her feet. "You're welcome, child. Of course, you now know what you must do."

"Yes. Prepare him the best I can. And protect him."

"Your protection won't reach as far as he must go." Caith embraced Rishana, then held her at arm's length, to study her face once more.

"What, Caith? What do you see?"

"You, my child. I was drinking in the sight of you." Caith's voice was even, as always, with a lilt, but something about it made Rishana shiver with fear.

"Caith, is Kiv a danger to you, now that you've talked with her? You know the old saying about awakening a wildcat when you could have walked quietly around her."

"Yes, Kiv is now awake to me. That's fine, as long as she isn't aware of your Winter Boy, and who, or what he is."

"But Kiv *has* met him."

Caith pulled at Rishana's sleeve, almost as though she were about to lose balance and grasped at the closest anchor. "Your Winter Boy? How? When?"

"He had a temper tantrum and wandered off where he shouldn't have been. She found him near the Communal Hall and escorted him back here."

"What did she say to him? Did he tell her anything important? Did she seem aware of anything out of the ordinary?"

"I didn't see her with him, Caith. But even if I had, how could I have judged when I knew nothing about any of this?".

"So, either Kiv has guessed that he might be Mwertik, and she isn't as hellbent she implied, or she isn't yet aware of the boy's role in Peren's plans."

"But the wildcat is awake to him, too. How much might Kiv deduce of the truth, now that she has met him? After all, Dara is my mentor and Peren my husband's Allesha. Would it be too much of a leap of logic for her to recognize that he's part of their plans?"

"I must divert her attention from him. Give her something else to chew on." Caith smiled mischievously. "She wants my guns, the rapid-fire ones we never let out, not even to our Allemen. Let's see how hard she'll fight to get them."

"Oh, Caith, please be careful."

"You know me, child. I'm always careful, as long as it doesn't interfere with my fun."

Caith embraced Rishana once more, then bundled up and left the barn. Following her outside, Rishana watched as the old caretaker defiantly left the well-groomed paths to trudge through thigh-high snow, flapping her arms to keep her balance, obviously enjoying herself. Rishana had no doubt that Caith was again performing for her sake. To reassure and, yes, tease — denying the power of age to impede her. How Rishana's heart ached for that tiny wonderful woman, the oldest Allesha and most youthful soul, dauntless, yet so fragile.

Chapter 59

The more the young Allesha read the journals, the more agitated she became. Not that it wasn't wonderful to read Jared's words and once again hear the sound of his voice in her mind. Reading his reactions and perceptions about the people they had known, remembering the shape of their days and the pattern of their life, made her feel as though she had returned home to him, to who they were together. But what an innocent she had been, thinking they'd shared everything, believing they'd been a team who never kept anything of importance from each other. Now she knew otherwise, and it hurt to recognize that a part of him had always been held back from her.

For that, she blamed Savah.

But Rishana/Tayar didn't have time to focus on recriminations. Two-thirds of the Season had passed, and Dov still didn't know the truth. Nor was he ready for it.

Certainly, Dov had grown and learned. He was no longer a child struggling to claim his portion of a room or a life. Wherever he walked, it was with the graceful strength of one who knows who he is and where he belongs, aware of his surroundings and curious about anything new.

She couldn't look at him without feeling the magnetic pull of his warmth, energy and intelligence — powers he was cultivating with her assistance. In their discussions, he often surprised her with insights that bridged perspectives that would have once been alien to him.

Yes, given the chance, he might yet become a remarkable Alleman. However, that chance would be his only if he developed the ability to navigate through the web of conflicts and conspiracies surrounding them.

The first step would be to help Dov confront some deep-seated demons, especially those related to his father. Now, more than ever, that rift must be healed, before he learned the truth of his heritage. Otherwise, it would color and corrupt everything that would follow.

After dinner, as they settled comfortably into opposite ends of the sofa, Dov seemed more subdued than usual. "Tayar, something's been bothering me. The Allesha who was at my Signing. Do you know which one?"

"Yes." Tayar remembered how pleased and honored she had been to have Savah oversee her first Signing. She now realized it wasn't a loving gesture at all. Savah had her own reasons for wanting to meet the boy.

"Well, I owe her an apology," Dov said. "You know what I was like before. So damned cocky and, well, scared. I said a few things to her I shouldn't have." He paused. "She told me when I was ready to apologize I should ask you to arrange for me to see her. I'm ready. Would you arrange it, please?"

Not wanting the boy to read her face, Tayar looked through the journal in her hand. "I could send a message to her tomorrow," she said without looking up. "But she's a very busy woman. It might be best to wait until the end of your Season."

"Please, Tayar, I'd rather not wait that long. I'm ashamed of the way I behaved."

"I'll see what I can do," she said noncommittally. Then, not wanting to discuss the matter further, she launched into the evening's lesson, "I've recently found an Alleman's journal that has some entries you'll find particularly interesting. I'll start with a meeting between two Allemen." She leafed through a few pages. "Actually, not the meeting, but the way it ended."

Dov removed Tayar's slippers and pulled her feet onto his lap so he could massage them while she read, occasionally pushing back her slacks to caress her legs.

Finding her place, she began to read.

We agreed that given the events of the past months, Mistral should return to the west...

"Pa?" Dov's attention was suddenly diverted from her feet to her face, astounded that she had uttered his father's name.

She nodded and continued.

... that Mistral should return to the west, and that I would forward his report to the Alleshi. But he seemed reluctant to leave our campsite, even though he had appeared restless and anxious during our meeting. So I stoked the fire and infused more tea. We sat and sipped in silence. Only after our mugs were empty did he relax enough to talk about what was bothering him.

"I'm tired, Jared," he said.

"Jared!" Dov exclaimed happily. "I know him. He's one of my pa's Triats. He's great!"

Tayar smiled.

Mistral's body was as straight and proud as ever, making me realize he was talking about an emotional or intellectual fatigue.

"I need to go home. Be with my family," he said.

I tried to comfort him, but what can a few minutes with an old friend do to ease a lifetime of difficulties? After her last failed pregnancy had almost killed Shria, something had broken in Mistral. Now, his family consists only of Shria and the boy. Mistral regrets not being with them, especially with the boy, during these important years.

I think of how much my children grow every time I am gone, changing without me. It's the natural order of things for children in their teen years to pull away from their parents. But by being away so often, we lose the opportunity to share that transition, to change with them and forge new bonds that might, if we're lucky, carry us into their adulthood.

How much more difficult this is for Mistral. The depth of the attachment he formed with the boy in infancy is so strong it's almost as though his heart is being ripped out of him. Yet Mistral is the one we send most often on extended missions. We need Mistral for his expertise in the Mwertik and their ways. But what is all of this doing to the boy, who lives too much without a father?

We must find a way to ease Mistral's burden. All I could do that evening was banter with him and give him companionship, something he must do without for much of his travels. We laughed together over my son's attempts to win his first girl, remembering our own follies. He talked with pride about how his boy was growing in stature and ability, excelling in his age group's races and contests, especially in archery and tracking. Mistral's smile changes when he talks about the boy. It's lighter, yet more deeply rooted.

"You should see him, Jared." he told me. "It's a marvel how much Ryl looks like me."

"Then he'll soon be winning a few young women himself."

When we parted, I promised to stop at his village to talk with Shria and see Ryl. I said I would try to spend some time with the boy, perhaps even take him on a hunt.

"Oh, and he did!" Dov said, his voice rising with his excitement.

"What do you remember of him?" Tayar asked.

"Jared was taller than any man I'd ever known, but he never seemed to look down at me. I didn't understand then how he did that."

"You do now?"

"I think it was his way of listening to me. When I spoke, he was completely with me, as though what I had to say was worthwhile."

Tayar pictured Jared with their own children, remembering how wonderful he was with them, always making sure they understood that they were the center of his world.

"How was the hunt?" she asked.

"Great! For two days, it was just the two of us. We took down a beautiful buck and a bunch of birds."

"What do you think about what he wrote? About how your father feels about you."

Dov shook his head. "You don't know what it's like. My pa doesn't—"

"Jared wouldn't lie about that."

"You know him. Jared, I mean." It was a statement, not a question. "You love him. I can tell by the way you say his name."

"My love isn't the point. I'm talking about your father's love for you."

"I don't blame you. Jared's quite a man. Ma thought so, too."

"Oh?" Tayar fought the spike of jealousy that threatened her composure, but not before the boy noticed it.

"No, Tayar, it wasn't like that. Not for Ma. You don't know what she's like, how she feels about Pa."

Once again, Tayar regretted having taught him to read her so well. She would have to learn how to better veil her thoughts around him if she ever wanted to regain any semblance of privacy.

"It was tough when Pa was gone, in a lot of ways. Some of the other men around the village tried with Ma, but not Jared. He came as Pa's friend, and mine, too. It was nice around the house when Jared visited." Dov stared off into his memories. "Wish he had been my father," he said softly, almost to himself.

"Would you like to hear what Jared wrote about that visit?" she asked.

"Yes, please."

Tayar turned a few pages, found the entry and read.

The boy, Ryl, is quick and lively. Mistral is right; he does remind me of Mistral, not just in his demeanor and appearance, but in his mischievous ways and frequent challenges to authority. If we can harness his innate power, he will be a worthy Alleman.

After I helped resolve some conflicts in the Council, I took Ryl on a hunt. As Mistral said, the boy has considerable skills in the woods and at the bow. He's already showing signs of becoming a master tracker. When he has the opportunity, I've no doubt he'll be quite a rifleman.

Unfortunately, Ryl carries a huge burden that affects everything he does and thinks. The boy is convinced that he's to blame for the death of the last child Shria carried.

"Hey, that's not true!"

"Let's hear what Jared wrote. Then you can refute it, if you wish."

Her most recent miscarriage came while Mistral was away on a mission, unable to return in time for the winter, although he had promised he would make it home before the snows. I'm not sure I fully understand the boy's convoluted logic, but he is unable to forgive himself for his inability to save the baby and protect the mother, just as he's unable to forgive Mistral for not being there when they needed him.

Dov fidgeted, but didn't say anything.

"I found it impossible to root it out of him in the short time we had together. But I fear it will cause him to distort his love for Mistral into anger. For what is that love if not a betrayal of the baby and mother?"

Tayar closed the journal and looked at Dov expectantly. But he didn't react or even glance at her. "What do you think about what Jared wrote?" she asked.

"Ma almost bled to death. I found her and ran for the Healer. But as soon as he saw how she was, he threw me out of the house." A shiver of tension shot through his body. "If my pa had been there, he could have helped, but not me. I was useless."

"Undoubtedly, Shria would have lost the child, whether Mistral had been with her or not." Tayar sat up, and moving closer to Dov, took his hand in hers. "Nothing you, or anybody, could have done would have kept death at bay. Not then, as a child. Not now, as an adult."

"She was only a tiny baby, my sister. Why did she have to die?" He quickly swallowed a sob. "And almost take my ma with her."

"There isn't always a reason. At least, not a reason we can fathom. But blaming others for our inability to change what may happen—"

"I know. It's stupid." Slipping his hand out of hers, Dov slumped into himself.

"So, what are you going to do about it?" she asked.

"What do you mean?"

"Can you forgive your father?"

"But you just said it wasn't his fault. If that's true, what should I be forgiving him for?"

"For letting you down. For not keeping his promise to be there when you and Shria needed him. For impregnating Shria with a child that almost killed her."

"Did you know my father before I came here?"

Tayar didn't hide her surprise at the turn of his thoughts. "Yes, I did."

"And you talked about me?"

"No, at least no more than polite inquiries about his family. But I still can know him through you, and now," she gestured at the closed journal, "through Jared."

"When I become an Alleman, one thing I look forward to is seeing Jared again." He said it lightly, filled with hope and plans for the future.

Tayar sighed, trying to release the knot in her throat. "Unfortunately, that's impossible." Burrowing the pain deep into her, determined that Dov shouldn't see it, she added, "He was killed."

"By the Mwertik? Was he the one?" Dov asked. "The one who was murdered a few years ago, when everything became so much stricter? The reason Pa wouldn't let us travel here alone, but insisted we join a caravan?"

His accurate mark almost jarred her tight control. Tayar nodded.

"I'm sorry. I really liked him."

Thankfully, Dov seemed to have run out of questions, at least for a short while, giving her time to regain her composure. When he spoke again, his thoughts took yet another unexpected twist.

"Jared said Pa was important. Do you think I'll ever make a difference the way Pa does? "

"You are your father's son. And he is justifiably proud of you, Dov."

"My father's son." He looked down at his hands and sighed. "Proud of me? I don't know. But... maybe... I think he does love me." He paused, as though he were listening to his own words echoing inside him. After a few breaths of silence, he raised his eyes to hers. "You know, it feels great to say it, but it's like someone else is speaking. Someone I never met, talking about a father I never really knew."

"In many ways, you don't know yourself or your father, not as you will. When this Season is over, you'll have opportunities to learn about each other, to become friends and Allemen together."

"The Every Woman," he said. "It isn't only about the Alleshi or even women, is it? It's about men, too. How we can change and grow and be different people to each other, if we allow it."

"Yes. In fact, some believe we can't ever know another person fully. But when we touch each other, we can sense a portion, a single aspect of the other."

Dov took her hand in his, turned it over and gently brushed his lips into the hollow of her palm. "Thank you, Tayar, for not giving up on me."

Chapter 60

After breakfast, Dov finished the dishes, swept the floor and went into his rooms. Falling easily into his morning routine, he gave little thought to what he was doing, consumed, instead, with thoughts about the passing of time.

Only a few weeks left.

In many ways, Dov felt his whole life was in this Valley. Everything before this Season and beyond the mountain passes was another world — something that had happened to someone he no longer was. Could he ever again be Ryl of the Birani, when all that was best about him was Tayar's Dov? Yet, once his Season ended, Dov would be nothing more than a secret name he would share with a woman he'd visit from time to time, but never again love.

No, that wasn't right. Dov knew he would always love Tayar. Somehow, he had to find a way to make it possible, to keep it alive and real. Not allow it to turn grey and indistinct the way his life before Tayar now seemed.

And what about Lilla?

How can a man love two women with his entire being? And two such different women? Or was it Ryl who loved Lilla, while Dov loved Tayar? Then who would he be when it was over? Who would stand by his side for the rest of his life?

Dov pictured Tayar once more, as she had been when he tried to talk to her about needing to apologize to that old Allesha. She'd been evasive, unwilling to share her full self. Not because she didn't love him or trust him, but because a part of her would always be separate from him.

She was his Allesha, his completely — for one Season. Not for a lifetime. At least, not as lovers.

He felt torn apart by that thought, inviting some of the greyness that hovered just beyond The Valley into his heart. An indistinct fog he quickly walled away, trying not to feel it. Not now, here in this home, where he had finally become more fully himself.

Dov found Tayar just outside the barn, pushing a wheelbarrow heaped with hay. Sprinting toward her, he called, "I'll handle that—!" In mid-sentence, he slipped in the mud, sliding several feet, his arms flapping and his center of gravity repeatedly shifting beneath him. Yet he remained upright, gliding to a stop just in front of the wheelbarrow.

"Well done!" Tayar exclaimed with a grin.

Dov looked at Tayar and saw the mud on her hands and knees. "Guess dignity and mud don't mix." He took the handles of the wheelbarrow from her and started pushing it. "By the way, where am I going with this thing?"

"Not everyone has your skill in navigating the slippery paths of this sudden melt." She pointed to her muddy knees. "I want to put down some hay before anybody else falls."

"Good idea." Dov hefted an armful of hay and spread it over the tracks of his slide.

As usual, they worked well together, falling into each other's rhythms, Dov threw the hay from the cart, while Tayar spread it on the ground. They moved the wheelbarrow forward as they covered the distance, returning to the barn periodically to refill it. In the manner of all their work, they mischievously threw hay into each other's hair, joked, sang and stole kisses.

The air still tasted of winter, crisp and clean. Along the edges of the muddy paths, the shoveled piles of snow sparkled in the blue-sky sunlight. However, Dov couldn't deny that the heavy clouds over the western mountains could as easily foreshadow a bitter afternoon rain as a nighttime snowfall. His Season with Tayar was winding down, nearing its end. His father would be returning soon to The Valley.

Dov stopped working and stared into the distance. "It's going to be strange, you know… being with Pa again… being whoever I'm supposed to be."

"You're not supposed to be anyone. Just yourself."

"Yes, but—" He shrugged and bent to pick up another load of hay.

Tayar placed her hand on his arm. "What were you trying to say just now, Dov?"

He scattered the hay onto the ground, straightened up and looked at her. "I was just thinking of what we talked about last night. I don't want things to be the way they were. With me and Pa, that is. But it's going to be tough. I've gotten so used to being angry. How do I start all over?"

"Yes, I see what you mean. It is difficult to reshape a long-established relationship."

"Hey, that's it, isn't it?! You and that other Allesha — the one you really don't want to go see with me. You're angry at her, aren't you? And you don't know how to be with her anymore. It's like me and Pa. That's why you don't want to send her a message from me. Because you'd have to go with me, be with her."

"Actually, I already sent the message. We should be receiving a response today or tomorrow."

"I'm glad. But that doesn't mean I'm wrong. You and that old Allesha… something happened between the two of you, and you're angry at her, like I was with Pa."

"Dov, there are things you don't know or understand."

"Sure, I realize that. You're an Allesha. But I'm right. When you're ready, you'll tell me so." With a decisive nod, he turned and gathered another armload of hay, resuming their task.

Chapter 61

Savah responded within a few hours, saying she would meet with the boy the following morning. Of course. What else did she expect? Savah had carefully planted the seed at the boy's Signing and undoubtedly had been expecting a message to arrive about now.

As much as the young Allesha tried to prepare herself, the turmoil in her heart would not quiet. She couldn't even decide which names to use in her mind for this meeting. Savah and Jinet, two women who had long ago learned to love each other, through their love of the same man? Peren and Rishana, two Alleshi dedicated to upholding and extending the Peace? Of course, neither was right; nothing she had once believed in was true. So why was it she always used the name Savah in her thoughts, and ached to be Jinet once more?

When the time came for the meeting, the young Allesha hesitated at the open outer door to the house that had once been a second home and safe haven. Now, she feared it as the lair of one who had betrayed her.

Dov squeezed her hand to lend her strength and support. She looked at him and couldn't help wondering whose meeting this really was. The boy seemed so confident, ready to take on whatever lay ahead.

After they removed their boots and coats in the vestibule, she knocked on the inner door and entered.

Savah rose from the sofa to greet them. "Welcome. What a delight to have you visit me!" As was seemly, she embraced the young Allesha first.

Jinet could almost close her eyes and feel the same enfolding warmth that small round figure had always instilled. Instead, her muscles stiffened, and she withdrew from the older woman as quickly as propriety allowed. She could not avoid, however, Savah's probing, pained look.

The older Allesha then turned to Dov. Striding forward, Dov opened his hands to her in the traditional gesture, but added a small self-aware nod to the ritual, not unlike that of a headman greeting an honored visitor. "I thank you, Allesha, for allowing us to visit."

After filling his hands with hers in welcome, she walked to the greeting room sofa and chairs, and gestured for Dov to sit. But to Jinet, she said, "Please bring in the tea and sweets."

It was a normal request, asked conversationally. How many times had Jinet taken care of such matters here in the home of her husband's Allesha? Still, she didn't want to leave Dov alone with Savah. Nor did she want to fall into the old relationship so easily. But she couldn't refuse without appearing unreasonable and upsetting her Winter Boy.

Why was Jinet not surprised when she entered the kitchen to find that the water in the kettle was cold, with no fire burning under it, and that no tea service had been prepared?

Dov watched Tayar as she disappeared through the kitchen door, unexpectedly leaving him alone with the old woman. He wondered if their exchange had been as natural and unplanned as he was supposed to think.

Turning his gaze to the older Allesha, he couldn't help but respond to her. What was it about her that made him feel so good inside? She wasn't beautiful. Nor did her smile light up her face like Tayar's. Small, round and grandmotherly, she exuded a deceptive softness.

"I never thanked you properly for your guidance at my Signing," he said.

She nodded her acknowledgment.

"However, that isn't why I'm here. I want to apologize for my harsh, thoughtless words."

"You had already offered your apology, and I had accepted it."

"That was before I really understood... or understand enough to realize how much I still have to learn and how much I never will."

"Tell me what you understand."

Dov paused, wondering exactly what she was asking him, uncertain what the undercurrents in her voice implied. "I used to say whatever words came out of my mouth. That got me into trouble more often than not. I'm sorry some of the words that poured out at my Signing were insulting. It isn't enough that I didn't mean them in that way. After we say our words, we have no control over them and how they may affect others. That's why I have to exercise greater control."

This time, her nod felt like a benediction. "Why did you feel it was important for you to come here today, in the middle of your Season?"

"Because it isn't the middle of my Season. It's coming to an end in just a few weeks, and I began it by insulting you. I wanted to make everything right. I know that simply saying 'I'm sorry' doesn't solve anything or make the hurt go away. I'll have to spend a lifetime making up for a lot of things. But I wanted to begin with you."

"I accept your apology as a very nice beginning, indeed." The old Allesha leaned back into the sofa cushions, but Dov knew enough not to take it as a sign that she was relaxing her focus.

"You seem to mean something more," he said. "I'm not sure what, but when you said 'beginning,' it sounded different to me." He shook his head. "I guess you still plan on giving me quite a bit to think about."

"Always." She smiled.

No, it wasn't Tayar's sunshine smile, but it relieved the tension and made him realize how safe and good it felt to be with her. "I'm glad. I've learned to appreciate the enigmas that the Alleshi are."

"Could you give me an example of the type of enigmas you feel we are?"

"Sure. Why is my Allesha so sad around you? Sad and angry."

"Why do you think?"

"I think it's because she loves you, and you did something that hurt her. But I look at you, and I can't imagine you doing anything to hurt someone else. Not on purpose."

"Just as you didn't insult me on purpose?"

Dov started to shake his head to deny the comparison, thought about it, then said, "Yes, just like me. I said things for my own reasons, but the result was that I hurt you."

"Sometimes, the only way we can grow is by working our way through pain to the other side, where the view is so different as to make the pain irrelevant."

The old Allesha stared at him, and Dov knew she was waiting for him to sense something beyond her words. But it eluded him. "I'll need to think about that one, too."

"Don't worry. When you need to understand, the understanding will be yours."

"That's the kind of high language that used to make me angry."

"And it doesn't anymore?"

"Angry? Not really. Just annoyed."

"Annoyed with what?" Tayar asked from the kitchen door.

Dov stood to take the heavy tea service tray from her. "Oh, those vague statements that you Alleshi spout when you don't want to answer a question, but still want to sound all-knowing."

"Is that what we do?" Savah asked.

"Sometimes," Tayar answered. While she poured the tea, she studied them. Savah had already won Dov over. But Dov was holding his own, Tayar realized proudly.

"Why do you do it?" Dov asked.

"Because language is more than a tool of communication," Savah said.

"There you go again," he said.

"Think about it. We use language not only to convey what we know, but also to examine new ideas, unearth new perspectives."

"And to avoid and twist truths," Tayar interjected, staring at Savah over the cup she held out to the older woman.

"Or to control how and when truth is revealed." Savah took the cup, sipped some tea, then placed it on the table in front of her, all the while holding Tayar's eyes, until the younger woman looked away.

"Control the way truth is revealed?" Dov shook his head. "That sounds deceitful."

"Yes, doesn't it?" Tayar nodded sadly as she gave Dov his cup.

He put it down untasted.

"Not when the truth abides," Savah said.

"But truth can't abide if people twist it," Dov insisted.

"Truth is as complex as words. How they are spoken is not always how they are heard. Isn't that what you were saying to me just now?" Savah said.

Dov nodded.

"Tell me, what kind of Alleman would you like to be?" Savah asked. "What would you like to do with your training? Mistral is one of our best First Meet experts. Is it something that would interest you?"

The young Allesha watched silently, wary but fascinated. Where was Savah going with this? How close to the truth did she dare take it?

"I don't know. He was away all the time," the boy responded.

"You know how dangerous things have become with the Mwertik. How important would it be for you to protect your family and village from them?"

"It's the most important thing," he said, with a depth of sincerity that pulled at Tayar's heart.

"Well, that's part of what Mistral has been doing all these years. Protecting you and Shria, the Birani, and the rest of our people," Savah said to the boy, but to Tayar it felt as though the older woman's words were meant primarily for her.

"I know that. But it still hurt as a kid," Dov paused. "You know, if I could do anything at all, I'd want to stop the hurting we do."

"I'm not sure I understand what you mean," Savah said.

"It's like at my Signing. I hurt you because I didn't think how anything felt to others. Only how it felt from inside me. Well, maybe everyone does that, seeing the world from a narrow viewpoint. Maybe, if we could understand the view from the other side, we'd be able to break the cycles. It'd be tough to fight someone you really know and understand, wouldn't it?"

"What about the Mwertik?" Savah asked.

"You're right. I guess sometimes understanding isn't enough. Sometimes, you have to fight to survive."

"But what if you could fight the Mwertik without violence?"

"That's not possible," he said.

"Have you ever fought with your mother?" Savah asked.

"Sure."

"Did you ever hit her?"

"No! Never." Dov huffed, offended at the idea.

"Exactly." Savah stood as a signal that the meeting was over.

Dov and Tayar walked in silence, each wrapped up in his and her own thoughts. It was another bitingly cold day, with the sun a pale yellow blur behind grey clouds. No doubt it would snow again tonight. Though winter was drawing to a close, spring still felt far way.

In the distance, other Alleshi were out with their Winter Boys, walking and talking, working and playing. They passed a gate where one couple was leaving the house. Dov didn't recognize the other boy. While no words of greeting were exchanged, the four of them nodded.

Dov was amazed at how natural it felt to be part of this Valley, hand in hand with Tayar, as so many other boys were right now, as so many Allemen and Alleshi had been through the generations. It rooted him, gave him a sense of belonging. But it also made him conscious of being just one among many. Would he ever be able to make a difference, do something that would make Tayar proud of him?

He replayed the meeting with the old Allesha in his mind. *What was she trying to get me to think or do? Why couldn't she just come out and say what was on her mind? Of course I would never hit Ma. Does she really think I could fight the Mwertik the same way? Skies! My ma loves me. The Mwertik hate everybody.*

And what is it between Tayar and the old woman? So much tension and hurt in their gestures and voices, so much left half said.

"Tayar, I'm sorry, but I like her," Dov finally said.

"Why are you sorry?"

"Because she hurt you. It's something about me, isn't it?"

Tayar stopped, looked at Dov, then resumed walking. "What did you think of her?"

"You're evading my question."

"Yes, but I do want to know your impressions."

"She's powerful, isn't she?"

"Very."

"But still soft."

"That's how she likes to think of herself."

"No, I think she really is soft. Somehow that's the source of her strength."

"An interesting observation, Dov."

"But her ideas about truth are another matter; I prefer your direct way. I always know where I stand with you."

"Don't ever forget. I am an Allesha," she cautioned.

Dov wondered why Tayar's warning sounded more like an admission she was making to herself.

Tayar lifted her face to the pale winter sun, seeking warmth that it couldn't give her.

Before seeing Savah, she had wondered whose meeting it would be. Now she knew. Savah had controlled it — and her — throughout the visit, scaring the lesson into her heart.

Yes, I am an Allesha. I withhold truth when it is to my advantage, when I feel it isn't time to speak it. I am to him as she was to me. If I am correct to be angry with her, how much more right will he have to be angry at me?

I am an Allesha, no longer innocent or blameless. I am fully involved, and whatever I do will have implications for our future, for good or ill. You, my dear Dov, are only my First Boy, my first attempt to do it right. One of many to come, if I continue.

But damn it all, you're my Dov, and I won't let them devour you.

"You know, Tayar, the day's still young. We could visit Le'a, instead of go right home," Dov said. "What do you think?"

"Why don't you go see her? I have things to do."

"Are you sure? Do you think you should be alone right now?"

"Of course I'm sure. She'll be delighted to see you."

He embraced her, and she felt her body flow into his, finding the warmth the sun had denied her. Then she watched him as he tramped off. So confident and alive. At least she could take comfort in knowing she had achieved that much for the boy. If only she could be sure that he would feel the same way tomorrow. She considered going to see Caith, but rejected the idea because she knew she had much to do to prepare herself for the evening.

    Dear sweet Dov, she thought, *I hope you will forgive me. That you'll be more generous with me than I could be with Savah.*

Chapter 62

Tayar/Rishana opened her outer door and sank onto the vestibule bench, relieved to be home. Before removing her boots, she closed her eyes and retreated into the comforting quiet. Some calming breaths helped her focus and relax, but didn't salve her anger or shame.

"Hello, Rishana."

Rishana's eyes flew open at the shock of hearing another person so close. Silently, Kiv had appeared in the open outer doorway.

"Kiv! You surprised me." She heard the vibrato of fear in her own words and tried to soften it with a belated smile.

"May I come in?"

"Of course." Rishana struggled to normalize her voice, to give the outward appearance of courteous welcome. When she leaned down to remove her boots, Kiv closed the outer door behind her, signaling passersby that Rishana wasn't accepting visitors. *How presumptuous!* But Rishana refrained from objecting and suppressed the vague sense of threat that bubbled in her stomach. Better to see the moment out, observe and learn.

"Will your boy be at Dara's long enough for us to have tea?" Kiv asked as they entered the greeting room.

Has Kiv been watching us? Is that how she knows Dov's whereabouts? Or is she pointedly giving me the benefit of the doubt that my Winter Boy is under control, unlike the time she found him near the Communal Hall?

"He shouldn't be back for about an hour."

"Good." Kiv led the way into Rishana's kitchen, sat down and waited for the young Allesha to put the kettle on the stove, set the table, and arrange cheese and crackers on a platter. At no time did Kiv pretend to offer assistance. Nor did she say anything more until Rishana sat opposite her and poured their tea.

"What would you say if I offered you an opportunity to avenge yourself on the men who killed your husband?" Kiv asked calmly, as though it were an ordinary, everyday kind of question.

Rishana almost choked on the cracker in her mouth. "I don't know

322

how to respond. I'm assuming you're being rhetorical."

"If I weren't, would you want to know, to help?"

Kiv's eyes drilled into Rishana so intensely that the young Allesha wondered what Kiv thought she could see. Was she that adept at reading the signs? Or that clumsy?

"What are you asking, Kiv? Do you want to know if I am willing to put my hand to a knife or a gun to kill another human being?"

Slowly, Kiv put down her mug, dabbed her lips with her napkin, then said, "You wouldn't necessarily need to handle the weapon yourself, if that would be distasteful to you."

"Kiv, I'm speechless. It's all so inconceivable."

"Beyond the shock, what's your reaction? Not what you want to say, but how you feel. Deep down in that part of you that still grieves for Jared, do you hate the men who butchered him?"

"Of course I do, though I wish I didn't," Rishana reluctantly admitted.

"Yet, that hate is one of the truest things about you." Kiv's voice had a lilt, as though the words gave her joy.

"I hope not. I wouldn't want to think the core of my being is rooted in hate."

"No, not rooted — forced by circumstances and the Mwertik to face hard realities."

"Yes," Rishana said softly, feeling the weight of her own defeat. Unable to resist Kiv's insistent, almost hypnotic gaze, she diverted herself by taking another cracker and a chunk of cheese. But she didn't eat. Instead, she nervously arranged and rearranged the cheese, trying to center it on the cracker.

"Think back, Rishana, to when you first heard of Jared's murder."

Realizing what she was doing, Rishana withdrew her hands into her lap and stared at them. "If I had been there with Jared, in the Red Mountains, I've no doubt I would have shot, knifed, clawed, done anything to beat them off him."

"Anything? Would you have killed them?"

"In the heat of that moment, what else could I have done?" Tayar's fists twisted white-knuckled into each other, but she would not cry. She refused to give her tears to Kiv.

"You've pictured the moment."

"Too many times."

"Wishing you had been there so you could have killed those men. Before they butchered Jared. Or, failing that, after he was dead."

"But I wasn't there."

"And had they been brought to you in chains, trailing behind Jared's corpse?"

"No." Rishana shook her head. "I don't think so." Just saying the words gave her the strength to straighten her back against Kiv's relentless assault.

"Does your fire chill so easily?"

"I'm human. If thrown into a situation in which someone I love is being attacked, I've no doubt I'd react violently."

Kiv studied Rishana in silence, then pushed her mug and plate away from her and stood. "Thank you, Rishana. I enjoyed our tea and discussion."

"So, will you be letting me know?" Rishana knew she had failed, that she had allowed Kiv to slip away from her.

"About what?"

"About your plans to kill the Mwertik who murdered my husband?"

"Come now, Rishana. You know we Alleshi like to discuss all kinds of possibilities, feel the measure of them, then talk them to death."

"I don't believe that's what you were doing."

"What else could it be? Do you think I have a Mwertik up my sleeve whom I was planning to deliver to you?"

"No, but I had the feeling you knew where you could find the men who killed Jared. That you were testing me to see if I'd want to participate in some violence against those monsters."

"How would that be possible?"

"I don't know, Kiv. You tell me."

"There's nothing to tell. I've learned what I wanted to know. Your hatred of the Mwertik doesn't run as deeply as I thought." She shook her head slowly. "It surprises me. If my man had been killed the way yours was, I would burn with dreams of revenge."

"Perhaps, if your man had been like Jared, you would want to honor him by living according to his beliefs."

"Ah, yes, the golden Jared. Rishana, you really should be more careful about the myths you choose to trust. The veneer on some is very thin, indeed."

Rishana bolted from her seat. "Don't ever use that tone about my husband again!" She was livid, shaking, but whether from anger or fear, she couldn't say.

"My apologies." Kiv took one more piece of cheese and popped it into her mouth. "I really must move on before your boy returns. Thank you for the tea, Rishana."

Chapter 63

"Dov, what I'll be reading tonight will be disturbing," Tayar said as she settled into her corner of the sofa. "Please allow me to read all the way through. Then we'll talk about it. Agreed?"

"Sure." Dov fell onto the sofa like a playful rag doll and reached for her feet, but she sat rigidly upright. "Aren't you going to lie down?" he asked.

"Not tonight." Her eyes were lowered, focused on finding her page in the journal.

"You're very upset, aren't you?"

Though his concern was sincere, Tayar couldn't allow herself to rely on it. So much could change before the evening was over, especially if the foundation she had helped him build wasn't as strong and resilient as she hoped.

Dov settled comfortably against the cushions. "Okay, so what will you be reading?"

"Some entries in an Alleman's journal, recording one of our first encounters with the Mwertik Zalogs. Actually, it was before they became known as Mwertik Zalogs, when we had no name for them."

She began to read before he could ask any further questions.

I rode into the Perlcain Mountains yesterday. The foothills rise so gradually from the western plains that I didn't note the change imme-diately. Then this morning, steep, boulder-strewn crags forced my sure-footed mount to pick his way carefully, slowing our progress.

It reminded me of my first mission to beyond our lands, when I real-ized that the borders of the Alleshine Peace are not lines drawn on the landscape by human hand to mark one step within, another without. Indistinct as this morning's haze, which hid the mountain peaks, the Alleshine borders are where chaos ends and civilization begins. All I know is that the last village I visited three days ago is part of the Peace, having joined a few years ago, but any people I might meet from here on will probably be outsiders.

I've been told signs of the nomads I seek abound in this area. The back side of the Perlcains is covered with dense fertile forest and dotted with trout-filled streams and lakes that empty into the great western ocean. If I were headman of a nomadic tribe, I'd certainly favor this area in the summer for its abundance of game and forage, though it would be too cold and bleak in winter. Perhaps, after all these trips to the border-lands, I may finally see them.

Tayar turned a few pages and resumed.

This afternoon, I saw the smoke of a single campfire downslope. Wary of strangers hearing my approach, I hobbled my horse in a pro-tected pocket canyon near ample grass and water. I followed the stream until it cascaded over a cliff into the lake of a lower canyon. Camped in a clearing by the side of the lake were three men far below me.

"Hey wait, I thought no one's ever seen the Mwertik. No one who's lived to tell about it," Dov interrupted.

Tayar raised her eyes from the journal and gave him a sharp disap-proving look.

"Sorry. I'll be quiet."

A narrow ledge wound down the steep forested slope, almost as though the water had carved it purposely many years ago into a gentle footpath. Following it, I found a small cave behind the waterfall. Neither the path nor the cave would be visible from below. Yet it afforded me an unimpeded view of the lake, the clearing, and the men. The ledge contin-ued downward, giving me access to many paths toward the clearing. I set up camp in the cave and established several lookouts.

Tayar quickly turned to the next section she had bookmarked, then continued reading.

I am almost certain these are the people I seek. Their clothes are adorned with the intertwining geometric shapes that were described to me. Not tall, they have a lean strength of the type that could overpower much larger men. Their dark coloring is similar to others in the region, even to my own people. But their carriage is much more tightly wound, with small, restrained movements that waste no energy. The roaring waterfall drowns out their voices, making it impossible to determine their language roots or try to understand their words.

My first day under the waterfall started cool, but the long midsum-

mer hours quickly turned muggy, with the air weighing heavily in my lungs. The constant roar of the cascade deadened my hearing. Gnats feasted on my flesh. I changed lookout positions frequently, trying to get away from them, but the biting nuisances would not be sated or avoided.

Throughout the day, new people arrived in the clearing; men appearing one, two or three at a time from all directions, while two large groups of women and children came only from the west. Men, women and children are all cut from the same cloth as the first three, with black, lustrous hair, chiseled features and caramel-colored skin.

Unlike the men's dun and brown tunics and leggings, the women dress in a multitude of colors, some of which may represent a hierarchy of position, for I noticed red and yellow in all their skirts and tunics, but only a handful wear blue accents. The oldest person in the camp is a shriveled, grey-haired woman to whom even the men pay respect.

Nearly everything they carry ~ clothing, tents and pots ~ is decorated with those strange geometric shapes made mostly of circles, spirals and jagged lines.

Tayar thought she heard Dov shift uncomfortably, but it could have been her imagination. Perhaps it was her fear that the description of the shapes would ignite some hint of recognition too early. Without pause, she continued reading.

The women have erected a sizable red tent on the far edge of the clearing, some distance from the much smaller tents put up by the men. Far busier than the men, the women cook, serve, wash and organize the camp, stopping periodically to go in and out of the red tent, which no man enters or even allows himself to be seen watching.

The last two men to arrive did so from opposite sides of the clearing, near the end of the long summer day. Both tattooed with a profusion of geometric designs, they wear only loincloths and armbands. But the way they carry themselves, with wide strides and heads high, screams more loudly than any amulet or device that these two are the leaders, probably the headman and shaman. Men swarmed from the camp to greet them with drums and chants. Soon, nearly all the men were dancing around the central bonfire, in rhythm to a coarse guttural rant.

Tayar skipped several pages of detailed description.

In the nether time between night and dawn, I was awakened by slow insistent rhythms that I felt rather than heard, like a faraway drum that thumped its message through the curtain of water. I crawled down the slope to crouch behind a large outcrop of boulders, closer than I had previously dared.

In the grey pre-dawn half-light, I saw a camp devoid of women. Men sat silent and nearly motionless at their morning fires, staring within, swaying to the reverberating rhythms. Only three or four children moved about, untended. The camp was eerily quiet, except for the low rumbling that grew in volume, so I could distinguish it as the syncopated moans of many women, in concert with one another, building ~ overpowering and unfathomable ~ erupting from the red tent.

The wordless chant swelled in tempo and timbre, sweeping through the camp. The men brandished knives and spears, and yet they retreated before it, as though it were a tidal wave pushing them to the far edge of the clearing. The children disappeared completely.

The thrumming rhythms raced through my body. I clutched my rifle and reassured myself it was loaded and ready, then made sure the straps of my backpack were tight and secure.

Suddenly, the deep resounding chant erupted into high, shrill ululations, piercing as ice water. I squeezed my rifle so hard that the ridges of the metal pressed into the flesh of my hands. Though the dawn air was cool, I wiped sweat from my brow before it could drip into my eyes.

Then the women burst from the red tent, dancing with wild abandon around the wizened grey-haired woman, who held aloft a newborn infant. I relaxed my tight grip on my rifle, realizing the exuberant chants were ones of womanly joy. Yet, the men were spurred on to greater anger, grimacing fiercely, calling out their own warriors' chants, which fought to drown out and overpower the women's jubilation.

Without warning, the men ran through the group of women, threatening with knives any who tried to resist them. Some of the younger women tried to block the way to the old woman and her charge, with the only weapons they had: their hands, nails, feet and bodies. But they were easily overwhelmed and roughly shoved aside. The men tore the infant from the elder's arms, and the women's song became shrieks of terror.

I can write this now, days after the event, and a part of me wonders at what transpired, how it was that I so easily broke code. But what else could I do? The men tossed the infant from hand to hand around the central bonfire. Closer and closer to the fire. I had heard these people were fearsome, but infanticide? I couldn't stand still and watch. I had to do something.

Rummaging through my backpack, I grabbed two flash-bangs. I scurried to the other side of the clearing, planted one near the rear of the red tent and another, with a longer fuse, further into the forest. After lighting both, I ran back to the side closer to the waterfall.

As fast as I had been, the infant was already in the shaman's arms. He held it high above a rush altar, then lay it down. The headman handed him a red hot brand from the fire. Grabbing the child's tiny foot in his bear-like claw, the shaman pressed the brand into the baby's sole, searing his flesh as though he were nothing but a herd animal.

That's when the first of my flash-bangs exploded with a blinding blast of white smoke, shattering the air with a percussive sound louder even than the men's bloodthirsty chants. Everyone hurried toward the red tent to see what had happened, leaving the infant alone on the altar, flailing his little arms and legs, wailing and screeching in pain.

I darted into the center of that camp, grabbed the child and ran for the forest, as the second flash-bang ignited, luring them farther away. As fast as my legs could carry me, I made for the path behind the waterfall. I had my pack on my back, but I was unbalanced, carrying both the rifle and the infant. As I passed the waterfall, I flung my rifle into the lake but didn't watch it fall, having to trust that the men who followed me would not see where I had discarded it, would not retrieve it, or, barring that, would have no ammunition for it, other than the round in the chamber.

I dared not look back to see if I were being chased. I had to assume they were at my heels. I had a screaming child in my arms, a steep slope to navigate, and a fierce tribe to outrun. Yet I had never felt so right in anything I had ever done. The child was scarred, but alive.

When I finally reached the hidden canyon where my horse awaited, I held the baby in one hand while I pulled my knife from my waist sheath with the other, and in midstride, cut the hobbling rope and jumped on his back, leaving the saddle and my other belongings behind me. I could control the horse with my legs, but I needed to free my hands. Quickly, I flipped my pack off my back, upended it to spill its contents, secured the child inside and slipped it over my arms so the pack rode on my chest.

Only then did I dare look over my shoulder to see the entire tribe pouring into the canyon, yelling and brandishing spears. Arrows flew at our backs, but Zeka galloped even faster than their arrows, saving our lives.

"Zeka?!" Jumping up from the sofa, Dov grabbed the journal from her hands, glanced at the page and recognized the handwriting. He threw the book down, breaking the spine. Kicking off his right slipper, he pulled his ankle over his knee to look at the strange geometric scar on the bottom of his foot. "You knew! That's why you kept touching this! How long have you known?"

"Dov, please sit down," Tayar said calmly.

The boy paced back and forth in silence, occasionally shaking his head in agitated denial.

When he finally looked at her, she touched the sofa cushion. "Dov, please."

He glared at the sofa, then at her, and threw himself down onto it. Only after a long silence did he talk, initially very softly, muted by the weight of memories.

"I loved Zeka. You'll never find another horse his like. One of my earliest memories is how Pa would put me up on Zeka's back, tell me to hold on tight, then walk us around. I thought I was higher than the sun on Zeka." He looked at Tayar. "It's true, isn't it?"

"Yes, I believe it is."

"Pa and Zeka saved my life." It was a toneless statement, more wrenching than the raging emotions she had expected.

"That's what he believed at the time." She kept her voice neutral, factual.

"What do you mean?"

"Your father had never seen the Mwertik before. None of our people had. He had no way of knowing. All he saw was an innocent baby being tortured, possibly sacrificed. It fit into our ideas of the strange nomadic tribe that had been raiding our borders."

"What are you trying to say?" He leaned forward, demanding yet fearful of the truth.

"Mistral found out much later that it was a ritual honor, probably reserved only for the first son of their hereditary headman."

"By roasting him — me — over a fire? Branding my foot like a beast's?" He slapped at his scarred foot in anger, as though he would cut it away if he could. "What if he doesn't survive the *honor*?"

"Perhaps it would be deemed a sign that he was too weak to lead the tribe, or that the gods did not approve of him."

"This is crazy! You're telling me I'm Mwertik!" The word curled like a curse off his tongue. "Pa stole me from my real parents."

"He thought he was saving your life."

"And when he found out the truth?"

"He didn't discover it until years later. You were already his son. His and Shria's. They couldn't give you up."

"Skies! Mwertik! Can you really believe it of me, that I'm one of them?"

"By blood, you're Mwertik, but that doesn't make you any less

Birani."

"How can a man be both? Especially those animals. They aren't anything like the Birani."

"Do you remember the story we read? *Death to the Enemy?*"

"This isn't a story; it's my life! Don't you understand? It's all over. I'm Mwertik. I shouldn't be here. I'm your enemy!"

"Never! You are and will always be my Dov."

"But what about Ryl?"

"Yes, what about Ryl? That's always been the central question, hasn't it?"

"Is this why Pa — Mistral — kept insisting I had to come here?"

"You're here because we believe you will make a great Alleman."

"But I'm Mwertik," he repeated yet again, spitting out the bitter taste that wouldn't be expelled. "How can you even want to be near me?"

"Because you are also Dov and Ryl and Birani and whatever — whomever — else you become. Because you are my First Boy, and will become my first Alleman."

"You're being sentimental and not thinking straight."

"No. I'm being realistic. It would have been much easier never to tell you, not to have had to put you through this."

"So, what am I supposed to do now?" He shook his head. "Hell, Mwertik! It sort of makes sense, though. In a twisted way."

"We can figure that out together. We still have a few weeks left in our Season."

"But it was based on a lie. I'm not one of you. I don't belong here."

"I hope you don't really believe that."

"I don't know what to believe."

"Then why don't we take a rest from all this?" Tayar rose, picked up the journal from the floor, gently tucked it under her arm, and walked toward her bedroom while saying, "I'll be waiting for you in the inner room, when you feel like joining me."

"What the hell do I do now?"

She turned to look at him. "Yes, it is difficult."

"No, not difficult — impossible!"

"I don't believe that, not for you. And I'm here. I'll always be here whenever you need me."

"Why? Because we have an Agreement, a contract?"

"No, because you're my Winter Boy."

"If you want, I'll release you from the Agreement."

"You don't have the power to do so, Dov. No one does."

"I bet that isn't true. They've just never had anything like this before."

"Don't you understand? It isn't about a contract; it never was. It's us. Tayar and Dov. We're a team. You're now part of me, for the rest of my life."

"But, hell's fires, I'm Mwertik!"

"Yes." She wanted to say so much more, but realized that her reassurances would sound hollow, meaningless to him. "I'll be in the inner room. I hope you'll join me."

Dov didn't answer; he didn't even seem to hear her.

Chapter 64

Tayar waited for Dov in the inner room pool longer than was comfortable. Waterlogged and dejected, she toweled herself dry, climbed up to a low platform, lit a candle and tried a calming meditation. She didn't expect it to work. The next thing she knew, she was struggling out of a deep, dark abyss of sleep. How long had Dov been sitting beside her, staring at her? Was it his presence that had awakened her? She closed her eyes and focused inward, clearing her mind for the ordeal ahead.

"Dov." Tayar toned her voice to be a soft invitation, to speak or touch or do whatever he needed.

But Dov didn't move, didn't even acknowledge that she had spoken. She touched his arm, a single gentle stroke. His eyes followed her hand down his arm, grabbing it when she reached his fingers, pushing it with his full weight against the carpet, covering her body with his.

She lay still and passive under him, accepting the press of flesh pushing her into the deep pile of the carpet. With rough caresses, his one free hand stroked her body between them, probing and demanding. Not cruel, just thoughtless, an attempt to drive thought away while reasserting that he did indeed belong here, in the inner room, with his Allesha. All this she understood and accepted, even when he entered her with no preliminaries, ramming his need deep into her.

Suddenly, he pulled out, moving as far away as he could on that platform. He clutched his legs into his torso and dropped his head onto his knees, making a tight knot of his body. Then he cried, though the only sign of it was a soundless heaving.

Moving quietly to sit only inches away from Dov, Tayar watched him. She ached to reach out, to smooth away the anguish throbbing beneath his skin, to assure him that everything would be fine, that his world hadn't suddenly collapsed, that the two of them could put his life back together. Instead, she disciplined herself, vowing to remain silent rather than offer false hope.

Eventually, his body stilled. He wiped his face against his knees and sat up. Seeing Tayar watching him, Dov straightened his back against the upcurve of the platform and returned her gaze with his old arrogance.

"Gawking at a Mwertik? Is it a new experience for you? What do you think you see?"

Breaking eye contact just as she would with a wild animal she didn't want to provoke, Tayar retreated to sit against the opposite wall.

"How long have you known?" He asked, but didn't give her a chance to answer. "Oh, of course. That day you disappeared. No wonder you were so frightened. A Mwertik for your First Boy! Does Le'a know?" He slapped his head. "Of course she knows. She's known from the beginning, hasn't she? *His* Allesha. He tells her everything." Dov's eyes glistened with new tears that he angrily wiped away with the back of his hand.

"Dov…" Tayar tried to gentle him with her voice and demeanor, but he would have nothing of it, swatting the air between them as though he were physically pushing her away.

"And the old woman today… I bet she knows too. That's what the both of you meant with your nonsense about different kinds of truth. Alleshine blather to make your lies palatable. Well, I don't swallow that, either. Truth is truth. Skies! Mwertik!"

No, Tayar realized, Dov had a right to rant. Even if she could soften the blow, it would be doing him a disservice. She leaned back, took a deep breath and tried to let it flow over her. But it was difficult not to cringe in the face of his fury, not to absorb his pain into herself. To wait until he was ready for her to help him.

"Who else knew? Jared?"

Hearing Jared's name used with such vehemence was a knife in her heart.

"That's why he was so nice to me, so attentive. He was keeping an eye on me." He expelled a lungful of air. "Damn. I thought Jared liked me just for me."

"He did, Dov."

If he heard Tayar's whisper, he ignored it.

"What about that nosey old biddy? The one who found me that time I got lost. That's why she hated me so much, wasn't it?"

"She knows nothing of it." Tayar enunciated each word, forcing him to hear what he must not forget. "We must keep it that way. She's dangerous." Tayar shuddered, picturing Kiv's sharp-featured face and chill resolve. "She hates the Mwertik."

"Who doesn't?" Something deflated within Dov when he said it, rounding his shoulders and slightly softening the ridges of taut muscles in his legs, arms and neck.

"Until we can answer that with assurance, we must keep all of this a secret."

"More lies?"

Tayar was relieved to hear the sharp edge of Dov's disapproval, not unlike her own. No, he would not be defeated. Not now, not ever. Even in the midst of this night's horror, he demanded, probed, refused to blindly accept. "No, not lies. Silence — for your protection," she said.

"Protection?" He rolled the word over his tongue, as though he were trying to digest it. "What is it you fear?"

"I can't really say."

"Damn it! After all this, you still won't be honest with me."

"Dov, you have to believe me. Your life depends on listening to me right now and doing as I say. You mustn't tell anyone. No one. Definitely not that woman."

"But she's an Allesha."

Tayar couldn't fail to recognize the many conflicting undertones coloring his use of the title. Nor could she blame him. "Yes."

"She'll know the minute she sees me again."

"You should know better than that by now. We have no magic, no ability to read minds. All we do is recognize and understand the signs in whatever is before us. But we're not infallible. There are ways to dissemble."

"But you haven't said why. What exactly is it you fear?"

"Something's happening. I can feel it brewing, boiling over, but I don't know what it is. All I know is you're in danger — very real danger. Just because I can't read the future doesn't negate that one horrible fact. Dov, please promise me you'll lock this secret up tightly within yourself until we can find out more."

"It isn't like I'd want to brag about it."

"I'm not talking about words alone. You must guard even your thoughts, so nothing becomes evident."

"But—"

"Dov, you must listen to me. We both know there are those who hate the Mwertik so deeply they would attack, even kill, without thought."

"Can you blame them? I don't."

"Even now?"

"Just because their blood runs in my veins," he slapped his forearm, "doesn't mean I suddenly no longer hate them. They disgust me. Animals!"

"Animals?" Tayar lingered on the word, lengthening it to give him time to make the connection.

"That's why you kept harping on that idea, isn't it? That only the unknown enemy can be seen as less than human." He mouthed the dictum, twisting it with his revulsion.

"Does it no longer make sense to you when it's now so personal?"

"It's always been personal."

"In what way?" she asked, pushing him to think it out.

"They're out to annihilate us. You can't say you don't hate them for that."

"Dov, I've had more reason than you can imagine to despise them."

"You mean you've met Mwertik? Before, I mean?"

"No, never." She paused, not wanting to tell him, knowing she had to. "They killed someone I loved. My husband. They butchered him with no provocation just because he was where they were, I suppose." Would there ever be a time when she would remember without dying a bit more inside?

"How can you stand to be here with me? A cursed Mwertik!" He choked on the name. "You didn't know, did you? When you chose me, I mean."

Taken aback by the abrupt swerve of his thoughts, Tayar didn't have a suitable response.

"No," he answered for her. "I know you didn't. They tricked you, too — Mistral and Le'a, or whatever her real name is — and that old woman today. They tricked both of us. That's why you were so uncomfortable about going with me to see her. Skies! I actually apologized to *her*." Dov's upper lip curled with dark irony. "Would you have even Blessed me if you had known?"

"I honestly can't say. But if I hadn't chosen you, it would have been a terrible loss never to have known you, never to have shared these months." Tayar shook her head slowly, feeling the sadness as deeply as if she were about to lose Dov, just as she had lost nearly everyone else.

"So the only reason I'm here is because of a bunch of lies."

Tayar fought to wrest control from his careening emotions. "You're here because you belong here."

"How can you say that?"

"Who is more suited to say it? I'm your Allesha."

"Only because they lied to you, too. Wait a minute!" Dov leaned forward and poked his forefinger in her direction. "It was Jared, wasn't it? The Alleman who was killed by the Mwertik? Your husband. I knew I'd heard you use the same tone before. That helpless anger with the pitch toward betrayal. It was when we were talking about Jared being dead and how I'd never see him again. When you read his journal to me."

Tayar didn't know how to answer, then realized that Dov had heard the truth in her voice. She lowered her head in a single nod.

"Hell, I don't understand how you can stand to have me touch you." Dov clutched his legs to his chest once more, but didn't burrow into them. Instead, he stared into the space in front of him, not really seeing her or the room. "What does it mean to be a Mwertik?" He seemed to be asking himself as much as he was asking her. "All I've ever believed is dead."

"Not the essentials."

"I'm Mwertik. Everything I've ever hated, that anyone I've ever cared about hates." He struck his chest with his fist. "*Mwertik*. It sickens me to think it."

"I understand, but—"

"Don't. Not now. I don't think I could take it right now. That Alleshine thing you do that contorts everything into a lesson, into making me think the way you want me to think."

Unable to deny that he was right about the Alleshi, about herself, Tayar didn't respond. She felt his eyes on her and knew he was studying her, seeking the signs he'd learned to read so well.

"Damn! You agree, don't you?"

She dared not be pulled by his questions into more dead ends. Of course, she agreed with him. But what value would there be for her to unburden herself when he needed her to be strong and sure, to be his Allesha? "Dov, you're asking so many questions at once. Don't you think it would be better if we followed one thought all the way through rather than scattering our energies?"

"Okay, tell me; why am I here? And don't go into your litany about me becoming a great Alleman."

"I chose to Bless you with this Season because I believed in you and your potential." Tayar raised her hand to forestall his protest. "But, yes, there is more to it. Dov, did you mean what you said about what you want to achieve as an Alleman?"

"You're evading me again."

"No, I'm going right to the heart of your question. You said you wanted to end the pain, to find a way to stop the cycle of anger and hatred. You're here because you, more than anyone else, may be able to do just that, by taking advantage of your rights and heritage as the son of the Mwertik headman."

"And you think they'll just let me walk in and take over? I won't even get near enough to speak to them before they kill me."

"Then we'll have to find a way for you to approach them safely."

Dov stood abruptly. "You're all lunatics! There's no way I'm going to just put my head on the chopping block." He towered over her, a shadowy figure with only parts of his face and body illuminated by the single candle

"I agree," she said softly.

"What?" Dov stared down at Tayar.

"I agree with you, Dov."

"Then what's all this about?" He sat down heavily on the edge of the platform. "What am I supposed to do?"

"I don't really know. Not yet. But we'll figure it out together."

"Together?"

"Dov, the only course we have is the one we're already on. But we can focus the rest of your Season to give you the training you need to protect yourself and find your own path."

Dov rubbed his face vigorously. "I've complicated everything for you, haven't I? It would have been better if I'd never come here. Better for both of us."

"But if we can find a way for you to help heal our Peace…"

"Yes, you're right. What does one life mean compared to that?"

"Everything." The single word encompassed so much, she couldn't find the energy to follow the many directions her thoughts tugged her. "One life means everything."

"You're being sentimental again."

"No, just hopeful."

"Even now?"

"Especially now, because you are here with me, in our inner room. It's a beginning."

"And an end," he said bitterly.

"Yes," Tayar sighed, feeling worn thin.

"There's no doubt, is there?" he asked, his voice low, almost inaudible.

"About you being Mwertik?" She shook her head. "None."

"You should have told me sooner, Tayar."

"Perhaps."

Exhausted, they eventually ran out of words and sat in the silence of their thoughts. Tayar didn't know which one of them fell asleep first, collapsing where they sat. But some time in the night, they ended up curled into each other. Whether it was because their bodies drifted together out of habit or because Dov had pulled her toward him, she wasn't sure.

Chapter 65

"I've decided I won't visit Le'a today," Dov said as they sat down at the breakfast table.

"What?" All morning, the boy had been saying and doing things that had caught Tayar off balance.

"I don't want to see her right now." After placing choice bits of his food onto their offering saucer, he poured apple juice into her glass, then his. "These eggs smell delicious." He placed a forkful onto his tongue, closed his eyes and savored the flavors.

It wasn't just Dov's words or actions. He still filled the room, but no longer rippled the very air with his energy. Instead, he now harnessed that energy, drawing it inward, as quiet as a sheathed knife.

"Le'a is an important part of your Season." She added her offering to his and began to eat, putting effort into making the meal and their discussion seem effortless.

"I don't trust her." Not a complaint or question. A simple, forceful statement of fact.

"You don't have to, but she has knowledge and skills you will need."

"How can I be sure she'll teach me true and not sabotage me?"

"Because she thinks you're her creation and will be her tool."

"Yes, that makes sense. But not today. I'll go tomorrow... maybe." He looked up from buttering his toast. "What are your plans for me?"

Tayar would not allow herself to pause before answering; he'd become too skilled at reading her fears and concerns. "To continue your training, but to add more survival skills. I don't think we can wait for your apprenticeship for you to learn how to protect yourself."

"You mean I'm still going to have an apprenticeship?"

"Of course." Sipping her juice, she studied him over the rim of the glass, giving her eyes a twinkle of familiarity to disarm her intensity.

Dov acknowledged her warm gaze with a half smile that came more from his mind than his heart. "But I'm Mwertik. What Alleman would be willing to take me?" He picked up his fork, then put it back down on his plate without using it. "Oh, of course! But is it within code to assign me to my own father, or the man everyone thinks is my father?"

Tayar was disconcerted by how quickly his mind grasped what she was just beginning to understand. "We don't know that's what they plan."

"He's the obvious choice. The only one who makes any sense. Bet they were planning to put me with Jared before he was killed. I would have liked that. But Mistral…"

Tayar clamped her mind against the might have beens — of growing old and comfortable with Jared, surrounded by their children and grandchildren, and welcoming apprentices such as Dov into her home.

"Maybe Tedrac. He is the third of their Triad. He's a respected scholar, and you'd do well to learn from him, especially about strategy and long-range planning." She pictured Tedrac, with his fine pale face, massive body and incisive mind. "But, no, he doesn't have the skills you'll need beyond our borders. Nor, as far as I know, does he have Mistral's expertise regarding the Mwertiks. The more I consider it, no other Alleman I know would be as suitable as Mistral for your apprenticeship. He has knowledge and skills you'll require, and a father's need to see you succeed. Besides, you'd be safe with him."

"Yes, he's already done his harm." Dov's words were bitter, but his demeanor remained calm and sure, as though Mistral were distantly removed from him.

"Dov, that's not worthy of you. Your father honestly believed he was saving your life."

"Yes." A flat acceptance of the facts.

"Give yourself time, Dov. The wounds are still fresh."

"But I won't really have that much time, will I? If they have their way, I'll be sent out from here in a few weeks and right into the thick of it, with him."

"Not right away. You'll have your apprenticeship. And if you work it well, it could give the two of you a chance to make your peace."

"It won't be pleasant."

"That will be up to you."

"That's the whole point, isn't it? That it's always been up to me. Not what I am or what others have done to bring me here, but what I will do about it."

"Yes, that's true. I'm glad you finally understand."

"Oh, I wouldn't say that. There's a lot I don't understand. But I don't intend to follow blindly anymore."

"You weren't exactly passive. "

"I was a kid punching at shadows without knowing why I always felt so angry." Even now, Dov's voice was smooth, though he didn't hide his chagrin.

"I wonder which of this Season's boys they trust enough to share your apprenticeship with you," she reflected.

"You mean Pa would have other apprentices?"

"I've never heard of a sole apprenticeship. All Allemen are formed into Triads; you know that."

"Then I just won't tell the other guys."

"You can't start such an important relationship with a lie. The young Allemen you train with will become your two best friends and closest allies for the rest of your life, your Triats. You'll need to be able to trust and depend on one another without reservation."

"Like Jared, Tedrac and Mistral. I wonder… how much did he tell them about me? How involved were they in his plans for me? How much farther does it go? Their Alleshi? And what of their Alleshi's other Allemen?"

"We must find out."

"Don't you know?"

"Until recently, I never realized how much I wasn't told."

For some time, neither of them had bothered with the pretense of eating. Dov now pushed his plate away and leaned on his forearms toward her. "It hurts, doesn't it?"

"Yes. But in a strange way, it makes what I had even more precious. Have you ever had a dream so wondrous you didn't want to wake up?" she asked.

"Sounds to me like you really don't want to learn the truth."

"What I want doesn't seem to matter anymore."

"So what do we do now?"

"Go forward. We have no other choice. But we'll need to broaden your lessons, to safeguard you against whatever hazards lie ahead."

"Like what?"

"How to take advantage of your new skills of perception so you can command effectively. We'll work on your voice and posture, the subtleties that will affect people around you."

"It doesn't sound like much in terms of protection."

"Oh, we'll cover physical defense, too. However, sometimes the simplest craft applied in a timely manner can help divert all but the most necessary violence. For instance, on first greeting, willfully controlling what you think about the other person will affect how they will react to you for a long time."

"But not everyone can read the signs."

"Not consciously, as we do. Still, everyone reacts to nuances, even when they don't understand why they feel a certain way about you."

"So, you control what you think."

"Not just control it, Dov. Create it, by forming specific sentences in your mind. Let me show you." Tayar leaned back into her chair, lowered her head while she composed herself, then looked up, met Dov's eyes directly and said, "Hello, Dov. Welcome to our Valley." She paused, recomposed her face and then asked, "What did you feel when I said that?"

"Happy, warm."

"That's because I was thinking, 'What a nice young man. I will enjoy knowing him.' I said it to myself as full sentences, clearly formed." Once more she withdrew into herself and when she looked up again, repeated the same phrase. "Hello, Dov. Welcome to our Valley."

"That time I felt threatened, like you were angry and wanted to tear me apart."

"I was saying in my mind 'Don't trust that boy. He's dangerous.'"

"So from the first moment you meet someone, you're trying to manipulate him."

"When necessary, yes. Given the dangers you face, I'd prefer you have some power over how people react to you rather than needing to resort to more extreme measures."

"And when it doesn't work?"

"Then you'll have to defend yourself in other ways. We'll prepare you for that, too."

"You mean *you* want to teach *me* how to fight?"

"No, you already know how to fight. I'm going to teach you how to win your fights."

"I usually win my fights."

"No doubt. But before coming here, your contests were with boys you knew, who had been taught to think and fight as you do. It's much more difficult when you don't know what to expect from your opponent."

"This is amazing. I thought the Alleshi were all about love and sex and understanding."

"So did I once. Now, I realize that power sometimes requires physical force and the willingness to use it."

"So, what makes us different from them? From the Mwertik?"

"I pray that we aren't very different from them, or that they aren't that different from us. Because then we can hope that this can end well."

"Then you agree with Le'a and Pa and that other Allesha? You want to use me just like they do."

"I plan to protect you, and teach you how to survive. The rest will be up to you, when you decide what you want. But if you choose to help save our Peace, you will end up putting yourself in the middle of a battlefield of wills and arms, and you'll need all the skills and help you can muster."

"Okay, let's get started." Dov stood, picking up the dishes to discard their uneaten breakfast into the scraps bin. "The goats are going to have a nice dinner," he said as he proceeded to wash up.

Chapter 66

After three days of neither seeing nor hearing from Tayar and Dov, Dara/Le'a decided she'd been patient enough. She found them in Tayar's barn. Sweaty and disheveled, the young Allesha and her boy were so intent on their grappling that they didn't notice her standing in the doorway.

Tayar lunged at Dov, throwing a powerful punch directly at his face. Grabbing her fist with his right hand, he turned his body to block her with his side and hip. Within the blink of an eye, she was behind him, flat on her face on a pile of hay. Dov leaned down to help pull his Allesha back up to her feet.

"Yes, but you're still expending too much energy." Tayar brushed hay from her clothes and reset the band holding her braid in place. "Let my momentum do the work for you."

"That leaves too much to chance. What if the other guy is stronger than me and resists?"

"If he's stronger, his blow will be that much more powerful and his fall surer, usually."

"It's that 'usually' I don't like."

"Adjust your actions according to your opponent's size and ability. You already know how to use force. What you need to learn is how to conserve your energy while impressing your opponent with your ease in defeating him."

"I'm not looking to impress him. Just beat him."

Tayar shook her head. "That's not always so. For some villages, the value of a man rests in his skill in hand-to-hand combat. Can you imagine how much more respect you'd win by deflecting a flying fist effortlessly? And if it's a fight for survival, you'll want to marshal your strength for the long battle."

"Okay, try me again."

Without pause, and taking him by surprise with her speed, Tayar threw herself at Dov. He pulled her fist past him, while blocking her body with his leg, his foot in front of her forward one, so that she fell to the ground. From her prone position, she smiled while reaching for his hand to pull her back up.

Just as Tayar reached her feet, Le'a applauded their performance, exclaiming, "Well done!"

Tayar spun around at the unexpected sound. "Le'a!" An unguarded edge of annoyance slipped into her voice.

At the same time, Dov stumbled back a step, stopped himself, and crossed his arms over his chest, planting his feet firmly where he stood. "How long have you been watching us?" He didn't exactly glare at the older Allesha, but the freeze in his tone was unmistakable.

"Only long enough to see that smooth move of yours, Dov." Le'a strolled toward them. "But you're leaving yourself open at the end. Let me show you. Tayar, if you will." Le'a motioned to the younger Allesha to come at her. "But slowly, please."

Tayar moved with exaggerated deliberateness, feigning an attack that allowed Le'a to easily catch Tayar's hand in hers. "This is the critical point, when Tayar trips against my foot. As soon as I am certain of her fall…" As Tayar mimed a fall, Le'a held onto her hand a little longer than necessary. "I use her momentum to pivot me around so I can check the surrounding area for other dangers." She turned as she spoke. "It's a quick circle that brings me to rest above her as soon as she is fully on the ground." Le'a gently rested her foot on Tayar's shoulder. "Now I'm in control. My fallen opponent can't get up, and no one can catch me by surprise."

Both Le'a and Dov reached to help Tayar up. Though Dov was a bit slower, being several paces away, Tayar clasped his hands and bounced onto her feet.

Le'a chose to not allow herself to be bothered by such a minor slight. "When you fight, it's too easy to focus only on the person closest to you. True, he may represent your most immediate danger, but not necessarily the greatest. Keep your eyes moving in a wide arc, but never lose sight of your direct opponent for longer than it takes to blink."

"Sure. It's how we run in the forest, sweeping our eyes to see roots or rocks in our path, animals and branches to the side."

"Exactly. Why don't you try it, Dov?"

He braced himself in front of Le'a.

"No, Dov. I don't have the flexibility or strength of our Tayar." Le'a sat down on a bale of hay. "I'll watch safely from here, where my old bones and joints can be comfortably immobile."

While Dov was distracted by Le'a, Tayar rushed at him. Her fist was only a breath from his jaw when he caught it and twisted it behind him, throwing his leg in front of her, pivoting, and coming to a stop just above her, his heel resting lightly on the flesh below her shoulder. But just as he was about to lift his foot, Tayar grabbed it in both hands, and shoved upward with all her might, felling him.

"Every maneuver has hazards." Tayar said, looking pointedly at Le'a.

Dov scooched over to sit next to his Allesha.

"Yes, learn to anticipate the unexpected." Le'a paused, waiting for Dov or Tayar to fill the silence. When they didn't, she continued, "I wonder if you realize how unusual it is to find an Allesha and her boy of the Season practicing defense. We usually leave such matters to the Alleman who will take you on as his apprentice."

"It's necessary." Tayar's eyes drilled into Le'a's, daring the older woman to challenge her authority as the boy's Allesha.

"But to take time away from other lessons, when he has so little left in his Season."

"Dov knows."

Le'a nodded.

"Don't you have anything to say to me?" Dov demanded.

"What would you have me say?"

"You could start by apologizing."

"Apologize? For training an Alleman with such a good heart he couldn't ignore an infant's cries of terror? For allowing Mistral and Shria to keep you as their son after the three of you had bonded so deeply that you would have remained a family even if we had separated you? For praying that you might somehow help us save our Peace?"

"No. For deceiving me. For letting me believe that after all this is over," he gestured with a sweep of his arm at the barn and The Valley beyond it, "I could return to a normal life."

"Dov…" Le'a' said softly.

"What right do you have? "

"Dov," Le'a implored.

"Sitting here so safely in this Valley, weaving your webs."

"Dov!" Le'a commanded his attention. "Dov, I do apologize. I wish none of this had happened. But we have to deal with whatever life brings us. Your life brought you here just when we need you."

"When you need me. When did you ever think about what I need? What I want?"

"What you want? Is that really all that matters?"

"Not the way you make it sound. But it should have counted for something. Besides, lying to me was a rotten way to start if you want me on your side."

"Dov, would you have come to The Valley, if you had known earlier?"

"Probably not."

"Then how could we have taken that chance? Are you sorry you are here, or that Tayar is your Allesha?"

"That's not the point."

"But it's precisely the point. Tell me, do you like the man you've become? Do you really think you would have been better off without our training, without Tayar's and my guidance?"

"You're twisting everything around again so I'll agree with you and think the way you want me to."

"No, I'm trying to help you understand."

"I don't believe you care a fig for my understanding. You just want me to accept whatever you say, so you can use me as your tool."

"If that is what you think, then you've made two major mistakes." Le'a countered. "The first was allowing me to see your antagonism and anger, forfeiting key information without getting any in exchange. The second was to confront me about it. Never back your enemy into a corner unless you have no other choice, and only after you have amassed all the ammunition you might need."

"Are you my enemy?" Dov asked.

"If I were, do you think I would answer that honestly?"

Dov stared at her without responding. Tayar rested her hand on his thigh, and he covered it with his palm. But he didn't break his concentration. Dov sat tall and watchful, studying Le'a's every move. Even so, his back was curved, and his limbs were draped comfortably. Everything about him displayed an intentional ease. Everything but his eyes.

Only then did Le'a realize his question hadn't been for the sake of answers, but to find out how she would respond. With a single decisive nod, she stood. "I'll expect to see you tomorrow afternoon. You can ask any questions you have then."

"You're leaving so readily?" Dov was still seated, though he had curled his legs under him, in an unconscious fight-or-flight posture.

"What would you have me do?"

"What you usually do. Argue, explain, try to shape my thoughts."

"Why waste my energy and your time on what would be fruitless for both of us?" Le'a offered him her hand. "Tomorrow, then."

After a moment's hesitation, he clasped it and stood. "Tomorrow." He didn't give or accept their usual embrace.

Tayar walked Le'a to the door, but the young Allesha said nothing as she accepted Le'a's brushed lips on her cheeks. Le'a clamped down on her disappointment, refusing to indulge in such a trivial emotion as sadness. Still, how painful it was to recognize the end of joy in this Season. New lines of allegiance had been drawn, leaving her out in the cold.

Chapter 67

For four days, grey skies glowered, erupting with daily cloudbursts that became snow at night. Muddy paths turned to treacherous ice soon after sunset, then remelted with the first daytime downpour. The mounds of shoveled snow and white field cover shrank into themselves, splattered and ugly.

Deeply chilled, Tayar ached for the long bright days of summer. Yet she dreaded the end of winter. Dov would be gone, out into a world that was much more treacherous than she had ever imagined. Struggling against time and her own visceral distaste for violence, Tayar spent nearly every waking moment researching, developing and working new lessons on defense, strategy and tactics. Whatever happened, she was determined Dov would be armed with every tool she had within her power to give him.

Dov returned to his daily visits to Le'a, though he no longer did it happily. Then again, these days Dov did nothing happily. Even in the inner room, he was solemn and deliberate, absorbing everything he saw, moving and speaking with care. Not that he wasn't tender and loving. With all the shared turmoil of the past days, the sex had become even more poignant. But Tayar missed his innocent wonder — and the laughter.

After a hearty lunch, Tayar and Dov slogged through the mud to the barn to practice yet another style of hand-to-hand combat. Their heads were down, trying to keep the rain out of their faces, so neither heard nor saw Le'a approach until she was standing in their path. Wet strings of hair were plastered to her face; her eyes were red and swollen. Grabbing Tayar by the arm, she spoke in staccato gasps. "Caith… She' s dead."

Tayar staggered. "Caith?"

Le'a nodded, tears and rain streaking her face.

Tayar pictured the impish caretaker. The title meant more than her responsibilities for the storehouse. Caith had watched over all of them.

How could she be gone? Then Tayar remembered their last conversation. "The guns!" she gasped, unaware that she had spoken out loud. The young Allesha ran toward the storehouse. Realizing Dov was following her, she yelled over her shoulder. "Stay here," without looking back to see if he obeyed.

Le'a/ Dara caught up with Tayar/Rishana only after the young Allesha slipped and fell in the mud. Though Rishana wasn't injured, she slowed down to avoid another fall.

"What do you mean *the guns*?" Dara asked.

Rishana shook her head, not wanting to put words to her fear. Not until she had reason.

Once inside the storehouse, Dara led her to the textiles section. There, Hester crouched over Caith, examining the frail old body through her tears. Michale, usually a paragon of fitness, hung on to Meika's neck like a limp dishrag. Meika stared at a smear of blood near her foot, her delicate face distorted with shock. Savah rested her hand on Hester's shoulder, while watching the Healer at work. But Caith was beyond healing.

Savah looked up at Rishana and shook her head slowly.

Rishana bent down, searching Caith's face, seeking even the tiniest flicker of her friend's spirit. But it was flaccid, empty, with no expression of life, nor of the last moments of what must have been a painful death.

When Rishana opened Caith's collar, she tried to not touch, to affirm the chill reality of dead flesh where so much warmth and laughter had been. But she needed the long chain of keys that Caith always wore around her neck. And she dared not delay.

Rishana started to reach with her other hand to lift Caith's lifeless head and slip the chain off, when it came free on its own.

"The clasp is broken!" she exclaimed, as she grabbed the keys and ran to the armory. Easily eliminating the rooms with the bows, arrows, spears, axes and other less sophisticated weaponry, she took only a moment to choose one door among the half dozen remaining.

"Rishana!" Dara's voice echoed through the storehouse.

"I'm over here. At the gun vaults."

Rishanna selected the key with the three identifying nicks, turned it in the latch and heard the familiar ratchet of the smooth tumblers. When she had been apprenticed to the storehouse caretaker, Caith had shown her the armory. Thousands of guns, ammunition, grenades and so much else. Some as old as the Peace. Others newly manufactured but given to the Alleshi for safekeeping. All carefully inventoried, oiled and locked away.

"If you do your job well," Caith had told her, "none of these will ever again see the light of day."

Rishana stepped into the room and turned up the gas lights, dreading what awaited her. All appeared normal. Slowly, she walked each aisle, her eyes sweeping over the rows upon rows of neatly stacked guns, thousands of weapons, ordered according to style and age, twenty to a rack.

"Rishana, where are you?" Michale called from the doorway.

"Back here." Rishana turned the corner to the last aisle, where the rifles with the new style magazines were kept. "They're gone!" she gasped. Taking a quick count of the empty racks, she instructed Michale, "Tell the others. Two hundred are gone." Feeling someone approach from behind her, she pointed at the bare wall. "I helped inventory the weapons that are supposed to be here." Bile burned her throat; she swallowed. "They were smart, leaving the other rifles closer to the door."

"Who? What are you saying?" Meika asked, but she must have understood. Why else did her voice quiver? Or was Rishana's own terror contagious?

"They didn't want us to know right away. Didn't realize I would guess." Rishana couldn't take her eyes from the empty racks.

"Know what?" Savah asked as she rounded the corner, out of breath.

"That some had been stolen."

"Stolen? By whom?" That was Hester's voice.

"Kiv."

Rough hands seized Rishana's shoulders and spun her around to face them. "What are you talking about?" Dara demanded.

"Caith told me that Kiv wanted the new rapid-fire guns. It irked Caith, and she had decided to… You know Caith. It was a game to her. Everything was always a game."

Suddenly, the horror — Caith's death, Kiv's treachery, her own silent complicity — descended on her. "They murdered her, Dara. And it's — oh, hell, it's my fault. I should have stopped her, stopped them. I should have known." Rishana had never felt so cold. Not even when Jared had been brought home on that wretched slab of wood. At least then, she had been innocent, could have done nothing to prevent it. But Caith. Dear-hearted, wonderful Caith. Every muscle in Rishana's body vibrated with guilt and sorrow. She couldn't stop shivering.

Rishana felt Hester's arm wrap around her waist, and she bent to the warmth of the older woman's soft body, allowing Hester to guide her out of the vault. She heard the click of the key locking the gun vault door behind them.

"Michale, you're the fastest. Go to Kiv's house." Savah said.

"She won't be there," Dara said.

"We need to be sure," Savah replied.

Rishana heard the retreating echo of Michale's footsteps.

"Meika, go to the Battais." Savah managed to not make it sound like the command it was. "We must know about anyone who has been through the passes. But make sure no one is told what has happened. Not yet."

Was Savah getting rid of those two for a reason? Or were they part of it all? What of Hester? That would make sense. The three Alleshi of Mistral and Jared's Triad: Dara, Peren and now Hester, Tedrac's Allesha.

How amazing it was to Rishana that her mind continued to absorb everything around her so clearly. Yet at the same time, she felt as if she were drifting through a dense haze, barely in control of her own feet, as Hester led her through the cold storehouse aisles to Caith's room.

Savah pulled Rishana's damp coat off her unresisting frame. But it wasn't Savah, her husband's beloved Allesha. No, it was Peren, who had once posed as Jared's Allesha, a woman Rishana didn't truly know.

Hester cleared books off the large armchair and gestured for Rishana to sit. After tucking a blanket around Rishana, Peren moved the desk chair to be next to her. Dara sat on the side of the bed, while Hester busied herself making tea.

"What were you and Caith up to?" Peren asked.

Rishana glanced at Hester. As ever, the Healer was a large, imposing presence, with her crown of thick grey hair pulled into a loose knot, still showing touches of the flame red that had once been her pride.

Peren read her hesitation. "Hester knows."

Hester was perched against Caith's desk, waiting for the water to boil. Always so calm and solid, Hester simply nodded.

"What do you know?" Rishana asked Hester.

"That your boy is Mwertik."

Shocked to hear it said so openly, Rishana scanned behind her for possible eavesdroppers. "Who else knows? Michale? Meika?"

"Michale knows nothing of it. Meika, some." Peren answered.

Meika, her son's Allesha. Did that mean he, too, was part of the conspiracy? "Eli?" she asked in a hoarse whisper.

"Only that there is a Mwertik boy whom we hope will help us," Peren said.

"But not that he's my First Boy?"

"Can't you just see him?" Peren asked. "Eli's so protective of you, especially since Jared's death. No, we didn't dare tell him everything."

The shrill whistle of the steam kettle pierced the air like a scream, startling Rishana into releasing the blanket. Only then did she realize she had balled her hands into tight fists. She wiped her moist palms on the blanket's soft weave and straightened it around her lap.

While Hester prepared the tea, her back was turned to the others. "What made you immediately assume it wasn't an accident?" she asked.

"An accident? What do you mean?"

"It appeared as though Caith had fallen during one of her high ladder antics. The contusion on her head and other injuries would be consistent with a fall." Hester handed Rishana a mug of mint tea.

"Then you don't think that Kiv…?" Here, in Caith's room, where everything had always been so reasonable and safe, the idea of murder was absurd, impossible.

"I don't know what to think now." Hester continued to pour tea for the other two and herself.

"Could Caith have fallen when she was surprised by them and realized what was happening?" Rishana asked.

"Possibly. I must admit my examination might have been clouded by my preconceptions of what I would find. I'll have to study the body more fully."

"I've always believed Kiv was capable of murder."

"Dara! Don't allow your personal feelings to color our investigation," Hester reprimanded.

"We must consider who's involved, Hester." Peren's soft voice belied her intensity. "Kiv has a violent nature. Perhaps this isn't the first time."

"We need to focus on here and now, and not what might have been in the past," Hester insisted.

"Even if the past may give us clues to what happened today?" Peren jabbed her forefinger in rhythm with her words.

"Let's examine one thing at a time, starting with what's in front of our eyes. Then we can work backwards." Hester turned to Rishana. "Tell us, what made you leap so quickly to murder?"

All three Alleshi watched Rishana, awaiting her answer, but she was unsure and embarrassed. After all, Kiv had said she wanted to kill Mwertik — not one of her own. "Caith was going to talk to Kiv. We needed to know the truth." Rishana swiveled toward Peren. "I didn't know who to believe."

Peren nodded sadly.

"And I had to find out what the dangers were for my Winter Boy."

"So, you enlisted Caith's help," Hester said.

"I asked her what she knew."

"What did she say?" Dara asked.

"That Kiv wanted the advanced rapid-fire guns to use against the Mwertik."

"Are we sure the guns disappeared only now?" Hester asked. "Couldn't they have been gone for a while?"

"Surely, Caith would have known." Peren paused. "Or would she? Two hundred, you said?"

"Caith kept them twenty to a rack. Ten racks are empty. And they were the deadliest. Anyone armed with just one can outshoot fifty riflemen, or more." Rishana remembered the jolting power of the gun she had tested; it fired bullets as fast as she could pull the trigger, shredding the wooden target in seconds.

"It'd be a massacre," Hester gasped. "We must determine who stole them, and when."

"Who has access, knows where and how the guns are stored, has the skill and experience to develop a workable plan and the ability to execute it without being caught?" Peren's voice was strained, and her face had turned sallow. "Kiv couldn't have done it alone. She needed people she could trust. Strong. Intelligent. Well trained. Steadfastly loyal to her."

"Allemen." Dara spoke so softly Rishana could almost hope it hadn't been said. "Kiv Allemen."

Rishana felt a knot of anger suddenly burst inside her. One by one, everything she had built her life on was falling apart. Had it ever been real, or just a gentle, comfortable mythology she hadn't dared examine too closely?

Michale burst into the room. "Kiv's gone!" Soaked through and gasping for breath, she collapsed onto the bed, next to Dara. "Not a sign of her."

"Are you sure?" Good, steady Hester, never accepting anything without solid proof. "At this moment, my home is empty, too."

"Kiv's house is a mess, as though she rushed about grabbing things to take. Even the icebox door is ajar. If she didn't ransack her own home, then we've another problem."

Hester gave Michale a mug of hot tea, watching her with a Healer's concern. As fit as Michale was, she was well over sixty, and the run from Kiv's house through the chill rain had obviously been a strain. Hester watched Michale slowly breathe in the warmth of the tea. Then, with a nod, the Healer leaned against the edge of the desk. "We have several questions we must answer." Hester counted them off on her fingers. "Who took the guns, and when?"

Peren started to protest, glanced at Michale, then leaned back into her chair.

Hester continued. "When and how did Caith die? Are the two events connected? Is Kiv anywhere in The Valley? Most importantly, can we stop whoever has the guns before they are used?"

"Hester, do you know when Caith died?" Rishana asked.

"I'll have to examine her more closely, but my initial assessment is that it could have been as early as yesterday evening."

"Damn!" Rishana jumped up from her chair, letting the blanket fall as she darted toward the door.

"Where are you going?" Dara called after her.

"It's time to find those answers before someone else dies."

Passing the many shelves, cabinets and ponds on the way back to the textiles section, Rishana realized how much she had depended on this storehouse to always be here — a rich, wondrous symbol of everything that was good about the Peace. And at the core, Caith's indomitable spirit. How could any of it ever be the same?

Caith lay where she had fallen — or was pushed. How small she was in death, now that no mischievous smile crinkled her round, dark face. Bolts of cloth were scattered about, as though they had tumbled at the same time. When the others caught up, Rishana asked, "Did you move her?"

"No, of course not," Hester replied, miffed at the affront to her professionalism.

"She fell like that?"

"Yes." Hester looked at Rishana and then at Caith. "But… oh my, I see."

"What?" Michale asked.

Rishana gestured toward Caith. "Look at her. How comfortable she is. She could be asleep in her bed. Where are the flailing arms and splayed legs of a fall? And why was her key chain broken, yet placed around her neck?"

No one answered. What could they say?

Rishana bent down and tenderly brushed an errant strand of hair away from Caith's face. Caith was fully, truly gone; this corpse was only a shell. Standing and turning her back on the body, Rishana started toward the rear of the storehouse.

"Now where are you going?" Michale asked.

"If you were planning to steal two hundred rifles in the middle of the night, which entrance would you use?"

"There's nothing there," Dara said. "We checked it as soon as Caith was found."

Rishana turned to face them. "Who found her?"

"I did." Michale choked on the memory. "Meika came in soon after me."

"Anyone else?" Rishana asked.

"No, no one." Michale suddenly realized, "No one knows what's happened! We have to call a Council."

Peren hooked her arm into Michale's. "You've a boy in Season, dear. We'll take care of calling the Council. But first, we must gather what information we can. Otherwise, the Council will have nothing to go on."

Dara moved to the other side of Michale. "No need to frighten everyone unless and until we know whether Rishana's correct or simply overcome with the emotion of events."

Michale pulled her arm free, and stepped away from the other Alleshi. "They have a right to know."

Hester took Michale's hands in hers in a gentle Healer's embrace. "So they shall, but it must be done properly." She paused, punctuating her words with a deep sigh. "I'm worried, Michale. Caith was beloved. We must be careful how our frailer sisters learn of her death." She shook her head slowly. "And the shock of learning it was possibly a murder."

"Yes, I understand," Michale said to Hester. "I just won't be party to anything—"

"None of us would want that, my dear," Peren responded. "All we're asking is that you wait until we know what we're dealing with. Then we'll call a Council."

"When?" Michale didn't look back toward Peren, but asked Hester.

"Give us until tonight. Then we'll organize a five-by-five rounder callout for Council to meet... shall we say tomorrow... late morning?" Hester turned to each of the others who nodded. "Then that's agreed. In the meantime, Michale, I'm sure you want to return to your boy. We'll get word to you as soon as we find out anything."

Rishana didn't wait to see Michale leave, but proceeded toward the back door. However, something caught her eye along the back wall — tiny, indistinct scrapes on the floor, at regular intervals — and she veered to follow them. Dara, Hester and Peren caught up with Rishana near the preserves aisle.

"What are you doing now?" Hester demanded. "The rear entrance is in the opposite direction."

"I've never seen those marks before, have you?" Rishana pointed at the floor.

The three older Alleshi shook their heads, though Rishana wasn't looking at them. Instead, she kept moving, following the strange scratches on the concrete floor. "They look like measurements, as though someone were trying to pace out a specific distance along this wall," Rishana said. "What would they be looking for? They knew where the guns were."

No one responded, though Rishana was sure they were all thinking about the same thing — the legends of the trove of ancient artifacts and weapons that were rumored to be buried under the stone floor.

Where the line of scrapes stopped, a track of scuff marks crossed their path. It appeared that something very heavy had been dragged along the floor. What was strange was that it came from the wall itself, as though whatever it was had been pulled from behind the wall.

Hester rapped her fist on the wall six times: twice several paces before the track, then beyond it, and finally just above it. She didn't need to say anything. They could hear how hollow that small section was. Intrigued, Peren and Dara studied the wall, running their hands along the cool stone, searching for a seam or release somewhere on its apparently solid face. Rishana and Hester followed the dark scuff marks into a storage aisle, where they found a large metal box behind barrels of cooking oil. An axe lay beside it.

About the size of a man's torso, the box was as seamless as the wall. Rishana saw no latch of any kind. Its silvery metal was of such a fine mill that the surface was glassine, with no visible imperfection — other than the jagged hole about twice the width of the axe head. Rishana peered inside, but couldn't see into the far corners. So she started to reach into the hole.

"Watch yourself!" Hester warned, pointing to blood on the sharp ragged edges of the hole. "Wait a moment." She retrieved a small burlap bag from a nearby shelf and wrapped it around Rishana's hand and wrist.

Rishana probed the box. Nothing. "Whatever they were looking for, they got it." She sat back on her haunches, shaking her head. "Is it possible? Could this be from the Before Times? From the civilization destroyed by the Great Chaos?"

When Dara and Peren rounded the corner, Peren said, "Well, that's something of a relief. At least we can now assume that their knowledge is almost as limited as ours." The other three stared at her, and she shrugged. "Don't you see? Somehow, they found the secret to opening that hollow wall. But they still had to use an axe to get at whatever was inside that box."

"Small consolation." Dara bent down to look inside the box. "Particularly when I think about Kiv getting her hands on—" Standing, she faced Peren. "Can we even begin to guess what she's unearthed here?"

"We still don't know for certain if Kiv is involved," Hester reminded them.

"Oh, she's involved. You can be sure of that," Dara said.

"We're fencing with shadows. We need facts." Rishana took off once more for the rear entrance, with Hester, Dara and Peren close behind.

Opening the oversized double doorway at the back of the storehouse, Rishana stopped and held her arms out to keep the others from walking any farther. She crouched down and stared at the ground. Two muddy paths cut through the melting snow. The left one led around to the front of the storehouse and the other headed outward, toward the mountains. "That's strange," she said.

Dara leaned down next to her and looked in the same direction. "What?"

"See the footprints and the roughness of older indents there?" Rishana pointed to the left.

Dara sighted along Rishana's arm. "Yes."

"Now look over here. What do you see?" Rishana gestured to the area in front of the door and to the right.

"Nothing."

"Exactly." Rishana stood and turned to the other Alleshi behind her. "What path anywhere in this Valley is that smooth in all this mud?" Pulling an overcoat, gloves and hat from the rack at the side of the door, Rishana came to a decision. "I'll be right back. Don't let anyone walk around out here."

Peren watched Rishana's every move. "Where are you going?"

"To get my Winter Boy."

"You want to bring him here?!" Hester asked, aghast at the idea that a boy in Season would even see the storehouse before the Service Days began.

"Rishana's right," Dara told her. "Mistral's one of our best trackers, and he's trained his son."

"But he's a boy in Season," Hester objected.

"In a few weeks, his Season will be over, and he'll be an Alleman," Dara said.

"But we can't wait weeks. We need him now," Peren acknowledged. "Go. Bring him quickly, but be careful what you tell him."

"Of course." Rishana didn't bother to hide her annoyance. No one had the right to tell her what to say to her Winter Boy.

Chapter 68

When Dov heard the front door close, he immediately put down his book and hurried out of his room. Tayar was flushed and out of breath. Her eyes were darting, and her lips pulled into a thin, tight line. Though she was usually so particular about tracking dirt into the house, she still had on her muddy boots and someone else's damp black coat.

"Tayar, are you all right? What's happened?"

"Come with me. Now." She pulled him out the door into the vestibule. "I'll tell you what I can on the way."

"The way where?"

"Please, just get your things and let's go. Now!"

He quickly stepped into his boots, closing only every other hook. Then he slipped on his coat, grabbed his hat and gloves, and followed Tayar outside. "Who's Caith?" he asked.

Tayar walked at a brisk pace. "My friend. An Allesha. The caretaker of our storehouse. She's dead." Her words came in spurts, punctuated with gasps for air.

Hearing a tremor in her voice, Dov said, "You're scared."

Tayar shook her head in a denial Dov didn't quite believe. Not that she was lying. More that she was struggling to keep her fears at bay by not admitting to them.

"I need you to read some tracks, Dov, before they're gone."

"You think she was killed."

"What?" Tayar grabbed his forearm. "Why would you assume that?"

"Well, a woman is dead, and you need me to track."

She shook her head and released his arm. "The tracks may not be related to her death."

"Then why?"

"Dov, please, no more questions right now. I'll try to answer after. Not now."

Though the rain had stopped for the moment, the air was heavy with a chill dampness that threatened another downpour. Dov followed Tayar along twisting paths he didn't know, until they arrived at the largest building he'd ever seen. It spanned as much land as some villages and was as tall as the tallest trees.

Stopping on a small knoll overlooking the building, she took two deep breaths before speaking. "This is our storehouse. Over there is the main entrance. Each side has one set of large receiving doors and a handful of entryways. The receiving doors farthest from us face the mountains. We tend to use them when we accept offerings and when we give supplies to those from beyond The Valley."

He couldn't believe he was actually at the fabled Alleshine storehouse. What's more, soon he'd be an Alleman, with access to all its wonders. "You want me to start at the far doors, don't you?"

"Please, no more questions; I don't want to influence what you see. All I can say is I believe someone was here within the past day, probably between sundown yesterday and this morning. Tell me what you can from the tracks."

"Well, the path we're on is a mess, but you know that already," he said.

"Dov, describe everything you see, even if you think it's obvious."

Taking off his glove, he crouched low, while peering down the path. He pushed his sleeve up and probed three small puddles. "The earth is rain soaked; the puddles are of varying depths. So I'm assuming a lot of people come and go along this way." He wiped his hand on his trouser leg and stood. "Two, maybe three people ran through here recently, probably within the last hour or two." He looked pointedly at her boots. "Including you."

They approached the building, walking along the left side of the path rather than on it, sometimes having to circle trees, bushes and rocks, often trudging through knee-deep piles of old shoveled snow. Dov stopped frequently to look closer at the mud and puddles. Every once in a while, he touched a track or probed pooled water. Tayar knew enough to stay behind him.

They circled toward the back of the storehouse, with pauses at the massive doors on the front and side of the building. At the rear receiving entrance, he saw what he supposed had bothered her. "That's unnatural," he said, pointing to the area beyond the door. "Doesn't anyone use that path?"

"Tell me what you see."

Dov crouched down beside the path and studied it. "It's too flat. The rainwater spreads too evenly. Was it groomed recently?"

"Is that what you think?"

"Either that or someone was trying to hide their tracks." Standing,

Dov stared at the building before him. The large double doors were enormous, but were dwarfed by the colossal wall. He scanned the area around him, then set off uphill, walking beside the smoothed-over path. In the manner of most trails in The Valley, it curved with the terrain, passing a handful of Alleshine homes at some distance. Dov saw a boy and his Allesha walking toward a barn, though he doubted they could see him through the trees. Not that they were looking at anything other than each other.

From time to time, Dov probed the ice-cold muddy water with his bare hand. At one curve, he stood, blowing on his hand to warm it. "Whatever they dragged to smooth the ground wasn't heavy enough. There are hoof prints under the water, recent ones, horses or mules, weighed down by heavy burdens. Heavier than whatever was dragged to erase their passage. I can feel the hoof prints under the puddles."

"Can you show me?" Tayar took off her glove.

Dov removed his second glove, so one hand could probe under the frigid water, while the other gently guided her. "Here. Do you feel that? It was formed at night, when the beast was so burdened it broke through the deeper ice." He moved their hands along the edge of the hoof print, then up to the higher smoothed earth that surrounded it. "They should have stood on it."

They straightened up, drying their hands on their pants and quickly putting on their gloves to warm their fingers.

"Stood on what?" she asked.

"The log. At least that's what I think it was. They dragged a log or two behind them, trying to erase obvious signs of their passage." Around a deeper bend, the path wound through a dense cluster of trees and low bushes that opened onto a small copse. Behind a bench were two muddy logs. "There!" Dov exclaimed, pointing. "If I hadn't been looking for them, I might have thought they had fallen naturally. But only at first glance." He turned toward Tayar. "That's what this is about: our first glance. They wanted to slow us down, give them time to get away before we saw through their subterfuge. I don't believe they expected to really fool us."

The glade was covered with recent hoof and boot prints. Because of the thick canopy of branches overhead, the ground wasn't as wet as the paths had been. Dov took long strides, careful to not step on any tracks, making his way to just behind the bench. He sat on the back of the bench, with his feet on the seat. Just as carefully, Tayar skirted the active area and climbed up to perch beside him.

Dov studied the ground in silence; he felt that his Allesha watched him with the same kind of scrutiny. Was this a test? Were other boys in The Valley going through similar field trials? Dov glanced at Tayar as naturally as he could, incorporating it into a visual sweep of their surroundings. How rigidly she sat, rubbing her hands repeatedly against her thighs. No, her fear was real, as was her urgent need to discover everything she could about the people and beasts who came this way last night. An Allesha had been killed, and Tayar needed his help.

"How many do you think?" she asked.

He stood and walked around the periphery, leaning down to look more closely at various prints. "Could be as many as thirteen. Mostly men, I believe. But three people took smaller, more hesitant steps, as though they were older or untrained. Women, probably." He pointed at the area in front of the bench. "Those three sat there to rest." Leaping over the path, to land neatly on a rock, he kneeled down. "But one left the group and headed downhill."

She stared where he pointed — toward the center of The Valley.

"And it looks like about nine beasts." He considered the size and stride of the hooves. "Large horses."

"What can you tell about the tracks that left the group?"

Dov followed the lone set of footprints away from the grove toward the houses on the lower slope. But they became lost among many in a frequently traveled path not far from the copse. He returned to Tayar, who knew enough to stay still rather than add her steps to the ones he had to read.

"Definitely a woman, or a small man." He climbed over the back of the bench and sat next to her. "She limps, leaning on her right foot more heavily than the left."

"How long ago were they here?" Tayar gestured toward the center of the glade.

"With all the rain, that's difficult to say. But given the hoof prints under the smoothed area back there, it had to be at night, late enough for the deeper ground to be frozen." He looked out beyond the grove. "The later the better, if they wanted to avoid running into people from those houses. They stopped here for longer than it took to discard those." He gestured toward the logs behind the bench. "Some of the men's prints are heavier near the animals. I think they rearranged whatever the horses were carrying... guns?" he guessed, looking at her for confirmation.

At first, she didn't answer, then reluctantly nodded.

"A large load of them from the tracks."

"Two hundred."

"Skies!"

"Dov, can you be more specific about when this happened?"

He paused, while trying to think out the timing. "I'd say about ten to fourteen hours ago."

Tayar started running back toward the storehouse, though she still kept off the path.

"What now?" Dov called.

"We'll need supplies. Come."

Chapter 69

Hester was at a storehouse side door filling her lungs with fresh air to rid herself of the taste of death when Meika returned. The younger woman had her four mountain ponies in tow, which she secured in the corral.

"Why in heaven's name did you bring those beasts?" Hester asked, as they walked to Caith's bedroom, where Peren and Dara had retreated. While Hester understood the need for such animals in The Valley, she had never gotten over her dislike of their messy, unsanitary ways. Why any Allesha would choose to keep such creatures rather than leave that duty to the Battais was a mystery to her.

"How did you plan to follow them… on foot?" Meika countered, though with more irony than irritation.

Hester had been so engrossed in examining Caith's body that she hadn't considered what they would do next. Of course, someone would have to go after the renegades and retrieve those rifles, one way or another.

On entering the room, Meika informed the others, "I've brought my ponies."

"Good." Dara stood and headed for the door. "Let's start packing."

Hester stared at Dara in amazement. "Do you really think you're the one to go after Kiv? Do you want to stop her or goad her even further?"

Peren started to rise from her chair, but collapsed back again, suddenly shriveled by the day's events. "Hester's right, Dara." Her voice was so low and indistinct it barely traveled to the doorway.

Hester walked toward Peren and looked into her face, while feeling her wrist pulse. But Peren shooed her away. "I know. I'll rest while you get ready."

"Me?"

"Who else is there?" Peren asked.

Hester wanted to protest, but Peren was right. No one else in their circle had even the slightest hope of talking Kiv into returning. Not that Hester felt Kiv would listen to her, either, but she had to try. Too many lives were at stake. Damn, she could already feel the ache in her back and hips from having to sit astride one of those nasty animals for untold hours.

Another downpour opened up as Dov and Tayar dashed into the storehouse. As far as Dov could see, rows and rows of enormous, roof-scraping shelves were filled with everything he could imagine, and then some. Stunned, he gawked like a child who had never seen a treeless sky, especially up at the top shelves that reached the impossibly high roof far above their heads.

Tayar nimbly scampered up and down ladders, filling his arms with food and packs and supplies. But when she piled a bottle onto the load he carried, he was suddenly unbalanced, forcing him to drop everything lest he careen into a pool.

"What do you think you're doing?" Dov didn't mask his annoyance as he bent to pick up the scattered goods.

"Leave it. I'll be right back."

Soon, Dov heard the clacking of metal wheels as Tayar pushed a large cart toward him. "Here, we can use this," she said, tossing stuff from the floor onto the cart.

"You can't be serious about following them. Do you have any idea what it's like in those mountains? All the rain down here is ice and snow up there. Bet it's a damn blizzard in some spots."

"I hope so. If not, we'll never catch them."

Dov picked up the last of the spilled supplies and dumped them onto the cart. "How do you expect us to be able to carry all we'll need for weather like that?"

"On my ponies," an Allesha answered from the other side of the pool. Straight, chestnut-colored hair framed the most delicate features he had ever seen, like a finely carved doll you'd be afraid to give a child. Though obviously an old woman, probably at least his grandfather's age, she moved with the grace and ease of one much younger. She was tiny, but had a sure, strong presence. Definitely a woman who was used to being deferred to.

"Perfect!" Tayar said as she continued to put more packages from the shelves onto the cart.

Dov grabbed Tayar's hands to stop her. "How many ponies do you have?" he asked the strange Allesha.

"Four," she answered as she walked toward them.

"And how many people are going?"

"We'll need you for your tracking skills. So your Allesha should come. Of course me, to handle my ponies. And another. A Healer Allesha."

Le'a and a large woman with an improbable mop of reddish-grey hair came around the corner. "That's me," said the big one. "But are we sure it's necessary? Tell us, boy, what did you learn from the tracks?"

Swallowing his pride, Dov ignored the belittling title. What else could this stranger, an Allesha, call him? But now that he looked at her, he realized she wasn't a stranger. He had seen her before, on the path from the Battai's to the caravan tradegrounds. Tedrac's Allesha. "I'd say about thirteen people left this building and headed toward the mountain. Three were old or women. "

"*Three* women?!" the small one gasped.

Dov nodded. "But one of the women returned to The Valley when they headed up the near mountain."

"She has a short stride and a limp that favors her left leg," Tayar added.

"A limp?" Le'a seemed genuinely puzzled and looked to Tedrac's Allesha to identify who it might be. But the Healer had turned inward and didn't respond.

"They had about nine horses, packing very heavy burdens." Dov paused only briefly. "The guns you're missing, I'd guess."

Jolted out of her reverie, the Healer stared at him, openly reading his posture and expression. "Are you sure the tracks returning to The Valley were made at the same time as the others?" When he nodded, she suddenly appeared smaller, sagging under the weight of her age and disappointments. "How long ago?"

"Ten to fourteen hours," Dov answered.

The other Alleshi turned to the Healer questioningly. "Yes," she sighed. "That's the probable timing."

With a chill, Dov realized they were talking about that woman's death, and the timing made them think it was murder.

"But it still doesn't mean—" the Healer protested.

Le'a glared at her. "What will it take to convince you?"

"Facts. That's what it will take. Unambiguous facts, not coincidences."

Le'a closed her eyes and took two deep breaths. When she spoke again, it was with less agitation but no less adamance. "Well, you're not going to get any closer to the truth standing here."

"On that, we are agreed," the Healer conceded, then turned to the small woman with the ponies. "But you have a boy in Season. We'll need someone else to tend the animals."

"You can't mean you plan to trek through these mountains in this weather." Dov gauged the Healer's weight and probable lack of fitness and became even more determined to stop these women. "Four people with four small ponies following others on horseback with a half-day head start and a load of guns! It's ridiculous."

"I'd match my sure-footed ponies against spindly-legged horses in these mountains any time," the diminutive Allesha said with pride.

"And when the snow reaches your ponies' bellies?" Dov couldn't believe how poorly they had thought this out. Damn, these were Alleshi; they should know better. "Even if you catch up to them, do you really think you'll be able to stop them? How will you be armed?"

"They wouldn't shoot *us*—" the Healer started to say, then stopped herself and shook her head.

Dov turned to Tayar. "Be sure to add several sacks of food and water for the animals to that cart. At least we'll have a Healer to treat frostbite and broken limbs if someone slips or the snow shifts."

"They made it through. I'm sure they expect to get out again, even loaded down as they are." Le'a said.

Dov studied Le'a and saw for the first time in months how old she was, as though something had defeated her so thoroughly she could no longer maintain her pose of strength. "If they make it out, it'll be because they had time to plan. They probably have stashes of supplies and spare horses along the way, and other men waiting for them in camps that are already set up. I've no doubt at least one of them is a master mountaineer, trained for winters." He looked from woman to woman. "Are any of you expert at surviving that kind of terrain in a blizzard?"

They stared blankly in response.

"I'm definitely not. But I know enough not to go into something I can't handle."

"We've no choice," Le'a still insisted, though with less confidence. "We can't let them get away."

Dov walked over to her and gently put his hands on her shoulders. "They already have."

"He's right," Tayar said. "We'd just be killing ourselves, with little hope of success." With the same determination that had driven her to accumulate the supplies on the cart, she started to put them back on the shelves.

"But what do we do now?" the small Allesha asked.

"Get word to our Allemen," Le'a said.

The small one nodded. "I've already told the Northwest Battai to inform the others to let us know immediately when the first Allemen springtime runners arrive."

"In the meantime, we must prepare." With a deep sigh, the Healer began ordering their priorities, counting them off on her fingers. "First, I'll finish my examination of our sister's body; we must determine how she died before we convene the Council." She turned to Tayar, who was still dutifully reshelving the cart full of supplies. "Leave that for now. You've a boy in Season; it's best that the two of you return to your responsibilities."

Tayar stared at the jar in her hands as though she were surprised to see it there. "But who will do it now?"

The Healer gently took the jar from Tayar. "We'll re-shelve this stuff. Who will take over as caretaker is another matter the Council will need to decide."

Tayar nodded, but in such a manner that Dov felt she was already thinking of something else. She absentmindedly gestured to Dov that it was time for them to leave.

As Dov followed Tayar, he could hear the Healer continue, "Confirming who's involved is crucial, though that will require more than one day to unravel. In the meantime, Peren should search the library. Somewhere buried in that mountain are answers. What, in heaven's name, did they unearth, how did they find it, and what's the key to opening that damn wall? But, I'm concerned about the stress on Peren's heart. We must make sure Elnor assists her in looking for the lost archives. Elnor's so used to crawling about the library for Peren, she won't ask inconvenient questions…" Her voice soon faded as Dov and Tayar walked toward the nearest door, putting more and more of the incredible volume of goods between them and the other Alleshi.

Chapter 70

Tayar was silent for their entire walk home; she didn't even appear to notice that Dov was beside her. After removing her boots and outer clothes in the vestibule, she was about to disappear into her bedroom when Dov touched her shoulder. "We need to talk," he said.

She turned and nodded. But when she collapsed into a corner of the sofa, she sat staring at the space in front of her and said nothing.

"Tayar, please! Talk to me. I don't know what to think about all this."

How pale she was, as though even her blood had retreated inward. Yet her eyes were red, almost feverish. "Yes, it is difficult."

"What is?"

"Caith." The name sent a shiver through her body.

"The dead woman?"

Tayar pulled her knees tightly to her chest. "Yes."

"Was she murdered?"

"I don't know. Possibly. Probably."

"Why?"

"Maybe because of me."

Dov hated that she was being so vague, walled up behind that intractable will of hers. "You? You mean you and me?"

"I don't know. But maybe."

"Because I'm Mwertik?"

"No, I don't think that's part of it. If it were… Oh hell!" Tayar turned toward him, locking her eyes onto his face in horror.

"We'd be dead, too. That's what you're thinking, isn't it?"

She considered it for a few moments. "No, that's not the right direction. It's about Caith and another… not you."

"Who?"

"Yes, that's the problem," she said.

"But you have someone in mind."

"The Allesha who found you that time you went wandering."

"Her?" Dov would never forget that woman's sharp face and cold, searing eyes. "You think she killed Caith?"

"No! It's not possible."

"Over the guns that were stolen?"

"That's how it appears. We just don't know enough."

"What do they plan to do with the guns?"

"Kill Mwertik." Tayar said it flatly, refusing to allow even a tinge of emotion to escape.

Dov considered the implications. Killing Mwertik had always seemed like a good idea before. Kill them before they get us. *But who is us?* he wondered. *Who am I?*

"And it's an Allesha behind all this?" he asked. "How is that possible?"

"We mustn't accuse her without the facts."

"But if it's true…?"

"If it's true, then your life just became even more complicated — and much more dangerous." Suddenly, the dam broke within Tayar, and tears poured down her cheeks unchecked. "Oh, Dov, I'm so sorry. So terribly sorry."

All it took was a slight nudge on her shoulder for Tayar to fall into his chest, sobbing. He wrapped his arms around her and gently stroked her hair. She burrowed her face into the curve of his neck, her body twitching with convulsive sobs. Eventually, her weeping subsided to softer, less explosive tears, though they continued to flow soundlessly, insistently, even as sleep overtook her.

Dov held her, stroking her hair, needing to find some way to give her comfort. Her body became less rigid, but he didn't know if it were in response to him or to the deadening of sleep. After a while, Tayar slid off Dov and crawled into the crook of the sofa's arm. He covered her with a blanket, and she snuggled deeper, pulling the protective cover closer.

Though the room was warm, Dov felt chilled. He knew only one thing for certain: it all depended on him now. He could rely on nothing other than his wits and abilities. Somehow, he had to protect Tayar while finding out the truth about these Alleshi — and about himself.

Chapter 71

Pursued by jagged arrows, circles and spirals, Jinet ran through a black landscape with no ground or horizon. The geometric shapes herded her, blocking her in every direction but one. When she tried to backtrack to reach Jared, who became Caith, then Dov, the spinning, pummeling shapes formed an impenetrable flesh-searing barrier between her and everyone she had ever loved, cutting and burning them until nothing remained but the black emptiness and the flaying shapes. Her children cried out to her in pain, but she couldn't see them, couldn't fathom which way to run to find them. If she could sit down and rest for a moment, she'd be able to think more clearly, understand what the shapes were trying to tell her. But she knew if she stopped, they'd devour her.

Suddenly, her feet, then her legs were mired in something she couldn't see; the shapes were gaining on her. The more she kicked and struggled, the deeper she sank — to her hips, waist, chest. Just as the vanguard of the shapes was about to fall on her, she reached down, grabbing handfuls of the ropey mass that entangled her. The familiar texture of the blanket pulled her out of the nightmare, but so gradually that she wasn't certain when the Mwertik emblems dispersed and the horrors of reality descended.

The greeting room was dark, with no light except the thin line of warmth framing the closed kitchen door. Still groggy, Tayar drifted forward, opened the door and was momentarily blinded by the brightness of the kitchen.

"You're awake just in time," Dov said from across the room. "I've warmed yesterday's soup, and it's ready."

She closed her eyes to adjust to the light, then opened them, seeking to make contact with her Winter Boy. "I owe you an apology, Dov."

"Sit and eat. We can talk over our food."

"I'm not hungry."

"That's not possible. You're always hungry."

"Please, Dov, I need to talk with you."

"Then talk, but you need to eat, too. It'll do you good." He reached into the icebox and pulled out the cold cooked chicken. "Do you realize how late it is? It's long past supper time."

Tayar sat at the table, watching her Winter Boy move with such sure, calm energy about her kitchen — setting the table, slicing bread and chicken, putting out the butter and cider, and ladling the soup into two bowls. How comforting it was to be cared for by a boy who once considered such work beneath his inflated dignity. But Dov was no longer a boy, as he had demonstrated to her and the others in the storehouse. He was a man. Her first Alleman — perhaps her last.

After taking his seat, Dov put pieces of bread soaked in broth in their offering saucer, filled his spoon with soup and lifted it to his lips, all the while staring at her. When he saw she wasn't going to eat, he put down his spoon.

"Please accept my apology, Dov. My behavior was unacceptable."

"Sure." He shrugged in dismissal. "But I'm not sure I know which behavior you're referring to."

"Collapsing like that, losing my control."

"Oh, that. You were just being human."

Dov started eating, but his pose was imperfect, artificial. What had he expected her to say? "Did you think I was apologizing for something else?"

"There's a lot, don't you think?" Dov put down his spoon and pushed the half-full bowl away. "First of all, you were really planning to go after them. Not just you, but other Alleshi, too. It was stupid."

"As you wisely pointed out."

"But I shouldn't have had to." He leaned forward, his forearms crossed on the table. "You're Alleshi."

Alleshi. The word used to evoke such calm and confidence, but her blind faith in the Alleshi was as dead as Jared. Somehow, she had to rebuild her life, relying only on solid knowledge hewn out of this mess by her questions and doubts. For Dov's sake and for her children, whose nightmare cries still echoed in her mind, she couldn't stop now. "What bothers you the most about our reaction, Dov?"

He stared at her, evidently surprised she had to ask him. "That it was just that: reactive. Explain to me how four Alleshi could have been so far off the mark? Going against all your own teachings?"

"I can't speak for the others. I was probably in shock."

"But isn't that what this is about? This Season? This Valley? Not falling into that trap. None of you even paused to think. You plowed ahead. It would have been a disaster."

Tayar was uncertain how to respond. Would they have gone ahead, up into a mountain blizzard? Or would common sense have intervened?

What are the true limits of the Alleshi? Did they diminish when they acted alone or in small groups? "Dov, I was proud of the way you handled things earlier."

"You're changing the subject."

"Not really. Just trying to look at it from another direction."

"Now, you're turning this into a lesson on strategy and tactics. It's more than that."

"Yes, on both counts. It is, by its nature, a lesson. And much more."

Dov studied her in silence, at first seriously. Gradually, his mouth parted into a small smile. "You're confused, too, aren't you?"

Tayar's first instinct was to deny it. But she'd taught him too well; he'd see through any dissembling she might attempt, especially now, when she was feeling so off kilter. Besides, perhaps the time for deception was at an end. The problem was balancing her need for honesty with his right to a full, rich, productive Alleshine Season. Did one preclude the other? "Tell me, what would you have us learn from today?"

Dov didn't answer right away. When he spoke, he weighed each word before he said it. "I think what disturbs me most is that we've covered this before. But when confronted with something real, it fell apart." He shook his head. "Is it all lies, then? The lessons and everything?"

"No, Dov, I honestly don't believe the lessons are false. It's because of all you've learned that, when you spoke today, four Alleshi listened."

"Alleshi," he said the word so softly as to be almost mouthing it, feeling the shape of the sound and tasting the bitter flavor of his disappointment. "So, what will the Alleshi do now?"

"They'll have a Council tomorrow. But you heard them as well as I did."

"Yes, but what will they do?"

"I'm not sure. As far as I know, nothing like this has ever happened. Somehow, they must come up with a way to stop the thieves."

"If they don't stop them, would it be so horrible? Don't look so shocked, Tayar. Forget for a few moments about my birth. Are we so sure it would be wrong to go after the Mwertik with overwhelming force?"

"It's not the Alleshine way. It goes against everything we've ever fought for and believed in… the very foundation of our Peace. To be the aggressor… it's wrong."

"Why?"

"Have you learned so little?"

"No, I'm simply trying to look at this from another direction, as you like to say. The Mwertik aren't the kind to stand still and listen. How do you expect to get their attention long enough to be able to perform your

Alleshine magic on them?"

"Magic? It's not—"

"I know." Dov voice rose in irritation, which he abruptly curtailed. "How can you influence a people who will kill you on sight?" He didn't wait for her answer. "Maybe the Mwertik prefer killing as a way of life. Or their hate is so overpowering that they'll never be anything other than what they are."

"That's terrible! I can't believe any people could be so... so...."

"Whether you believe it or not doesn't change reality, if that's the way it is," Dov asserted. "Then again, there's another possibility. What if they're the kind of people who won't respect you until you can prove you can fight as well as they? They kill us because they can, because they think we won't fight back. But if we kill a few of them, maybe we'll win their respect, be recognized as worthy opponents."

Tayar shook her head, not in denial, but in surrender.

"Don't you see?" Dov continued. "The people who stole those guns might have been wrong in how they did what they did, but maybe they could see no other way to stop the Mwertik. And they might be right."

"You've been thinking about this."

"How could I not?"

"What conclusions have you reached?"

"Conclusions? It's all guesses and questions and throwing stones at clouds. I know so little." He studied her face as though he were seeing it fully for the first time. "Tell me about the Alleshi."

"What do you want to hear?"

"How can I say what I don't know? Today, in the storehouse, I saw undercurrents and conflicts I'd never imagined. There's much more to the Alleshi than I had considered. Tell me about it."

"I don't know where to start."

"How about starting with the sharp one, the Allesha you think stole the guns? Whether or not she did, the fact that you and the others think she's capable of it — and maybe even of murdering another Allesha — that's what I want to try to understand first."

"I don't fully understand it myself."

"Tell me what you know of her."

"She has a powerful intelligence, a quick wit, and is devoted to our Peace." Tayar paused. "But that sounds like any Allesha, doesn't it? How can I explain why she's different? It's not so much what she is, but how she makes you feel. She uses her abilities to cut through people, to expose their deepest fears or uncertainties, probing until you begin to doubt everything."

"Yes, very Alleshine."

"But with one major difference. She uses her skills as a weapon rather than a tool. Still, that may be my own fears speaking. Perhaps she's merely an Allesha who won't be turned from what she believes in, even when it means disrupting the Peace of our Valley. Isn't that something to be admired?"

"You sound like you're trying to convince yourself. Why can't you describe what you think of her without trying to see it from all sides at once? Tell me honestly, do you hate her?"

Tayar considered the question, gauging the true weight and shape of her emotions. "No," she decided. "I don't hate her."

"A woman capable of murder?"

"That's yet to be proven."

"But that was your first thought when you heard that Caith was dead. Not that some old woman had an accident, but that she'd been killed for the guns."

"That's my failing," Tayar said ruefully.

"Or your insight. If you don't hate her, what *do* you feel?"

"Discomfort with her ideas, her vehemence, because it is so compelling. It would be easy to agree with her. Yet, I abhor what she espouses."

"Which is…?" Dov pressed.

"That all Mwertik should be killed indiscriminately. Even children." Tayar shivered, remembering how Kiv had implied that Tayar was bound to agree.

"But what would you have thought of her ideas before you met me, before you discovered my birth?"

Tayar might have been staring at Dov, but she realized she'd been seeing Kiv, sitting opposite her at this table. However, Dov was here now, watching her so earnestly, using skills she had taught him, helping her probe her own thoughts and feelings. Dov, the Mwertik, who would soon be her first Alleman. Did that change who she was, what she felt and believed? She took a slow breath, seeking the truth within herself. "Your parentage," she decided, "hasn't changed my views, only strengthened my resolve. Somehow, we must find a way to make the Peace work for them, as well as for us."

"That's why I'm here. To get them to listen."

"Yes."

"While that other Allesha is busy trying to kill them. And despite the fact that I'll be just another Alleman, meat for their knives."

Tayar struggled for an answer that might save her Winter Boy.

"Not if we can devise a way for them to find the truth about you, without it appearing to come from us."

"More deceptions."

"No, the unveiling of the truth, finally."

"And manipulations."

"For the sake of your life… for our Peace. Or would you have us relinquish the future to those stolen guns?"

"Tayar, do you still believe in everything you've taught me?"

"Yes, I do."

"Then what has you so off balance?"

"Caith."

"Yes, and the guns." Dov flicked his hand dismissively. "But there's something else. You used to be so sure. Recently, you've been acting like you're walking on hollow ground that might collapse if you put too much weight on it. Then, in the storehouse, I saw you with those other Alleshi."

"What do you think you saw?"

"It wasn't that you weren't respectful, not in your words or actions. But you didn't treat them like Alleshi."

"That's because I'm one of them."

"No. I think it's because you don't quite feel that you are — or, maybe, that you don't want to be. But you can't turn away from them. Can you tell me why?"

"Dov, you are truly becoming an Alleman."

"You're avoiding my question."

"Perhaps."

"And you're not ready to answer."

"Not yet, dear. Mostly because I'm not sure of the answers."

"Can I help?"

"Yes, you do help."

"I mean, with finding your answers."

"So do I. We're both discovering a lot about ourselves. By the end of our Season, I wonder which of us will be the most changed." Tayar picked up her spoon and began to eat the soup. "You know, Dov, you're right. I am hungry."

"Well, that's one thing that will never change about my Allesha," Dov said with a smile that didn't reach his eyes.

Chapter 72

After finishing her morning chores, Tayar/Rishana kissed her Winter Boy and left to join all the other Alleshi slogging through the mud toward the Communal Hall. Few greeted one another, and then only in hushed tones of grief and shock. Word of Caith's death had reached every sister in The Valley, and it appeared all were determined to attend the Council meeting, even those in Season. So many Alleshi converged on the hall entrance that a throng milled around on the outer platform, awaiting entry. Though the sun had finally broken through the low grey clouds, warming The Valley with hints of the coming spring, Rishana gathered her cloak around her, warding off a chill that had nothing to do with the air.

Rishana saw Savah/Peren walk slowly among their sisters, stopping to whisper to a select few. Peren's complexion was blanched, with dark circles under her eyes. Her step faltered, as though she were having difficulty supporting her own body. She must have been searching the library all night. When she approached Veryl, Rishana positioned herself to overhear Peren's muffled question, "Have you seen Elnor?" Rishana couldn't make out Veryl's answer, but Peren moved on, shaking her head.

Why was Peren looking for Elnor? Hadn't they spent the night in the library together, searching for answers? Rishana couldn't remember a time in recent years when Elnor hadn't devoted her off Seasons to assisting Peren. But Elnor was more than Peren's research assistant, she was Peren's second self, her shadow, and would undoubtedly succeed her as lead researcher when the time came.

Slowly, Rishana drifted forward as Alleshi filed into the building. It was so crowded in the large vestibule that it was almost impossible to remove her coat, let alone hang it up on one of the wall hooks. Jostled from all sides, Rishana accidentally stepped on Heinda's foot. She had no sooner apologized than someone jabbed her in the ribs, followed by a muffled, "Sorry" behind her. Taller than most, Rishana scanned the hall. Meika beckoned to her from the doorway of one of the smaller meeting rooms, but the press of bodies made it impossible for Rishana to move in any direction other than forward. Next to the double doors to the

Assembly Room, Michale stood at a podium with a roll call sheet. Rishana found her name and signed next to it, handing the pen to the woman behind her without looking back to see who it was.

The Alleshi funneled into the Assembly Room, breaking off with sighs of relief and dispersing into small circles of friends who comforted and questioned one another in subdued tones. But when Rishana was disgorged from the doorway, she didn't know where to go. She'd usually sit with Peren, Dara, Meika, or sometimes, Caith. Now where, and with whom, did she belong?

As was usual for a Council meeting, chairs and tables were scattered in clusters, angled to face the large fireplace at the front of the room. Rishana proceeded up the tiered floor that afforded an unobstructed view of the front from any seat. She chose an armchair about a third of the way up.

Rishana watched the roomful of women for hints, studying postures, gestures and expressions. How did these interlinking circles of friends relate to various factions? Who were the leaders? Who the followers? Were any Alleshi unaligned and free to think for themselves? Whom could she trust to not want to harm her Winter Boy? And what of the limping woman whose tracks returned to The Valley?

Rishana blurred her vision, as she had been taught, to seek patterns of movement, refocusing only to investigate any disruption which might reveal an uneven gait. A figure toward the rear of the room — Heinda — walked unevenly; Rishana didn't believe their minor collision in the vestibule warranted such an exaggerated limp. Had Heinda been favoring her left foot before Rishana accidently stepped on it? Near the doorway, the flow of Alleshi entering the room deflected around one — Devra — whose left hand rested on her lower back as she hobbled slowly. A back injury or simply age finally catching up with her? No doubt the winter chill had settled into old bones throughout The Valley; several others moved as though the warmth of spring would come none too soon.

Group by group, the Alleshi settled into chairs; murmured conversations subsided. A cough here and there, the sibilance of a few whispers, the scraping of furniture and the clinking of pitchers and glasses. The room was not quiet, but a tense expectancy descended.

Hester stood up from her seat near the fireplace and turned to speak, stilling even the softest whispers. "As all of you now know, Caith is dead. Michale found her yesterday, at the foot of one of the storehouse ladders."

"Was it murder?" Yalaene demanded.

Several voices called out.

"Murder?"

"What is she talking about?"

"Never!"

Hester raised her voice to be heard over the commotion. "Please allow me to give my report." She waited for the company to resettle, then continued. "She had considerable bruising, consistent with a fall, though no bones were broken, which meant it probably couldn't have been from too high. However, the body appeared too well composed to have fallen in place. After removing her to the clinic for further examination, I found contusions almost encircling her upper arms, as though she had been gripped roughly there. In addition, other troubling information has been unearthed. Two hundred of our most advanced guns are missing from the armory, and we have reason to believe they were taken at the same time as Caith's death. We found fresh tracks leading from the storehouse toward the southeast pass, which appear to coincide with the theft and death." Hester paused, glancing around the room. "They seem to indicate that two women left this Valley with the thieves."

"Two of us?"

"Who?"

"Must be outsiders."

Hester nodded to Michale who stood with the roll call sheets in her hands. Seeing and understanding, the company suddenly hushed. Hester returned to her seat.

"Has everyone signed?" Michale asked.

Oriane, Lin and Stepha came forward and, leaning on one of the nearby side tables, signed their names.

As they returned to their seats, Michale asked, "Anyone else?" She looked around the room, her eyes resting on each Allesha in turn. When she came to Rishana, it felt like a gentle probe requiring a response, even if no more than a nod. No one else stepped forward.

Michale slowly studied the sheet and announced, "Five signatures are missing. Ruth."

"She's in Season." Someone said from the back.

"Yes, but has anyone seen her since yesterday afternoon?" Michale asked.

"I did. She was out walking with her boy this morning," Oriane said.

Michale glanced down at the sheet. "Natar."

"I went to see her yesterday evening to tell her about the Council," Heinda said. "But her boy is struggling against a key transition. She told me she wouldn't be coming."

Michale pulled the next name from the roll call. "Lavar."

"She has a terrible cold," Hester said. "I told her to stay home, as much for our sakes as hers."

Michale didn't refer to the sheet before saying, "Kiv."

"Gone," Devra allowed a touch of sadness to flavor the word.

"Gone?" Michale asked.

"Yes, with the guns."

The entire company turned in their seats to stare at Devra.

"I tried to stop them, but they were determined." Devra sighed against the weight of all those eyes. "Kiv… and Elnor… that would be the fifth name on your list."

Peren spun around in her seat to look at Devra, who nodded back. Peren fell back into her chair's cushions, her head bowed, her shoulders curved inward.

"Devra, please tell us what you know," Michale said as she sat down.

Devra stood with difficulty, pushing herself up with her right hand on the arm of the chair, while her left supported her back. Though her torso was bent more than usual, she raised her head high, so all could hear her. "I was on my way to the storehouse when I heard a horse neigh, and saw silhouettes of animals and people headed uphill."

The room crackled with anger, irritation, confusion and questions.

"Who?"

"What time?"

"Where?"

Rishana blurred her vision once again and tuned her hearing, seeking the rhythms and undertones that might reveal the truth behind the words being thrown about, the patterns of affiliation and dissent within the room.

"Ten Allemen, Kiv and Elnor, with nine horses," Devra responded.

"Allemen?" several exclaimed in an ascending scale from gasps to shocked cries.

"Which Allemen?"

"What did they say?"

Rishana felt, rather than saw, a disruption of movement as Hester stood. "Please, Sisters, let Devra tell what she knows. Then we can try to fill in the gaps with our questions." Hester returned to her seat, restoring the physical equilibrium of the room without relieving the tension.

"With this back of mine, I never would have caught up to them if they hadn't stopped in the glade just above the storehouse." Devra rubbed her lower back with her left hand. "That's when I saw the guns, when they were rearranging the bundles on the horses." Her voice caught in her throat. "I tried to talk them into returning with me. But they refused, saying the guns were needed immediately to defend border villages, and they couldn't wait any longer through endless Council debates."

"What did they say about Caith?" a neutral voice that might have been Lin's inquired.

"They didn't."

"You didn't ask?" came from the left, almost directly opposite Rishana's own position.

"I didn't know." Devra shook her head heavily. "How could I?"

Rishana pictured the scene as yesterday's muddy tracks had painted it in her mind. None of the new footprints, certainly not Devra's lopsided ones, had led from The Valley directly to the clearing. Why would Devra set out for the storehouse in the middle of the night, when walking was obviously so painful to her, unless it was to rendezvous with Kiv? Devra was lying. But Rishana wasn't about to confront her. Not until she understood how the answers would change the shape of the room and affect Dov's safety. And not until she could figure out who else was involved.

"So, what did they say?" Meika asked Devra.

"Kiv did most of the talking."

"She would," rasped someone a few rows behind Rishana, but Devra didn't appear to hear it.

"I asked Kiv what they intended to do with the guns. 'Stop the slaughter,' she said. 'Protect our people.'"

"Stop slaughter with slaughter? That makes no sense," complained someone toward the front.

"Does sitting here waiting for the Mwertik to strike again make any more sense?" came from behind.

"We're not sitting and waiting, any more than we have with others. We study, plan, find their weaknesses." Another near the front.

"We can't even find the Mwertik."

The shape of the room was forming in Rishana's mind. Of those Alleshi who spoke out, only a few appeared to have taken sides. Or were they avoiding exposing themselves until they were ready? Through it all, Dara and Peren remained uncharacteristically silent. Sitting beside them, Ayne watched everything, gauging and weighing, perhaps in the same way Rishana was.

"Kiv thinks she knows where the Mwertik are," Devra said.

"Is that why she wanted the guns?"

"Yes."

"What did you do?"

"What could I do?"

"You could have told us right away when we might have had some chance of stopping them."

"How? By the time I returned home, they were long gone. Ever since my fall, I can't move as quickly. I was exhausted by the effort of just getting home." Devra paused, "And I didn't really know what I wanted to do."

Jolted out of her concentration, Rishana found herself calling her own question, "What do you mean, what you wanted to do?"

At the same time, Meika asked, "Are you saying you agree with what Kiv has done?"

Devra adjusted her stance, unable to find a comfortable posture. "It's complicated. I feared what would happen if we went after them... a band of Allemen and Alleshi... twelve of our own. I didn't know what you... we... would do, if we did catch up with them. If I couldn't stop them with my words, what would it take?" She paused. "And perhaps it was all to the better."

"The better?" Meika bristled.

"Maybe, with the decision out of our hands, we can finally move forward. Stop the Mwertik." Devra searched the room, studying the effects of her remark.

Numerous Alleshi raised their voices in a cacophony of agreement or protest.

"She's right."

"How can you even consider such a thing?"

"Why not? Maybe it's time we became more realistic."

"All it will do is cause more trouble, more deaths."

"Mwertik deaths for once."

"Finally." The latter was definitely Beatrice. But was she responding to the previous speaker, or referring to Ayne slowly unfolding her tall, lean frame from her chair?

With Caith dead, Ayne was now the oldest in The Valley, but her age was a thing of effortless grace rather than fragility. Ayne didn't say a word until all saw her and, one by one, quieted. Even then, she rested within the silence of the room, guiding others by example as she breathed slowly and deeply, calming the Council to order. She spoke first to Devra. "Thank you for your report."

Devra began to respond, but instead shook her head and lowered herself into the chair.

"But who were the Allemen?" Meika protested.

Acknowledging Meika's question, Ayne turned to Devra for her answer. When Devra started to get up once more, Ayne waved her down. "No, dear, please don't discomfort yourself any further. I'm sure you can project your voice from where you sit."

"Kiv and Elnor Allemen," Devra said. "Gerard, Tevan, Bran, Frank, Kal, Stave and Nacam."

"That's only seven. You said there were ten," Meika prodded.

Devra shifted her weight in the chair. "I couldn't see the faces of the other three. They were farther uphill, in the shadows behind the horses."

"You didn't ask?" Dara demanded.

Devra stared at Dara for several tense breaths. "You weren't there. You can't know what it was like. No, I didn't think to ask the names of the other three. I was too busy just trying to—"

"Yes, of course," Ayne interrupted Devra. "Again, thank you for your report."

"But she hasn't answered," Dara began to protest, then stopped herself, retreating once more as far into the background as possible.

Neither ignoring nor acknowledging Dara, Ayne asked, "Does anyone have additional information to contribute?" When no one spoke up, Ayne prompted, "Rishana, I believe you made the initial connection between the missing guns and Caith's death. Please tell us what you know."

Standing, Rishana poured a glass of water from the pitcher on a nearby table, as much to give herself time to compose her thoughts as to slake her suddenly dry mouth. "Caith had told me that Kiv wanted to arm her Allemen and others to go against the Mwertik."

"So? That's nothing new. Kiv's been arguing that we should fight back for a long time now," Veryl interrupted. "And she isn't the only one."

"There was something about the way Caith was talking that made me think Kiv was being aggressive about it, demanding Caith release the guns to her immediately."

"But what caused you to link Caith's death with the guns?" Ayne asked. "Why would you make such a leap about one of our sisters?"

"Don't forget who her mentor is," Devra mumbled, though loudly enough for everyone to hear.

Rishana glared at Devra. "Dara may be my mentor, but I am my own woman."

"Then why?" Yalaene asked so softly that it cut through to Rishana as Devra's challenge never would.

"I don't really know how to answer. It wasn't a thing of logic. Now that I think about it, I'm almost ashamed I should come to such a conclusion so quickly. What bothers me most is that I was right — about the guns, that is."

"And the murder?" Veryl asked.

"No! I never accused Kiv."

"Maybe not directly," Beatrice reminded her.

"Not indirectly either," Rishana insisted, her voice trembling with emotion. "It was about the guns, and only the guns."

"Which happened to vanish just when Caith was killed and Kiv fled," Dara interjected, effectively deflecting the focus from Rishana and her motives.

"Kiv and Elnor."

"With their Allemen!"

"That's what we should be discussing. We're wasting time while they're getting farther away," Michale argued. "Ten fully trained Allemen with guns that could make each man more powerful than ten traditionally armed opponents."

"With those guns, not ten. More like fifty… or even a hundred." What had frightened Rishana most, when she'd fired one during her apprenticeship, was that she'd imagined a person — a Mwertik — standing in place of the shredded wooden target. If only she'd been with Jared, in the Red Mountains, with such a gun to defend him.

"We could be talking about a return to the Great Chaos."

"Why? Just because our Allemen have decided to defend us and our ways?"

Ayne asked, "Rishana, do you have anything else to say?"

"Nothing that hasn't been said more fully by others." She sat down.

"Does anyone else have something to add before we deliberate?" Ayne asked.

Meika stood. "The Southeast Battai reported he heard no disturbances in the night, but confirmed finding fresh tracks on one of the auxiliary paths. The Northwest Battai sent word that two other Allemen have just arrived. Our first melt runners from the outside. Hester's Tedrac and my Eli."

"Eli!" The name burst from Rishana's lips and Meika looked up to her, nodding with a smile.

"We thought it best to send Tedrac back out to the others right away, to get information about the guns and what little we knew to the Council of Allemen. Eli awaits our instructions."

"Who is we?" Beatrice asked.

"Those of us who found Caith and discovered the missing guns.

Hester, Dara, Peren and me."

"Yes, of course, it would be," Heinda mumbled.

"Do you object to our quick action?" Meika challenged.

"Anything else you wish to add?" Ayne asked.

Meika shook her head and returned to her seat.

Ayne eased back into her chair, relinquishing the floor to whomever wished to speak next.

No one stood. Initially, all were lost in their own thoughts, absorbing what had been said — and what hadn't. Much had yet to be decided, but first, each Allesha had to consider the facts and implications, and weigh the comparative merits of whatever solutions came to mind.

This phase of a Council meeting never failed to remind Rishana of a stove filled with simmering pots of broth. All she could do was wait and see which ideas came to a boil.

One by one, various Alleshi turned to nearby companions to whisper asides or discuss fine points, some of which were picked up by an adjoining group, bringing them into the same conversation or causing them to veer in other directions. As the noise in the room grew louder, Rishana could hear certain words and phrases repeated over and over from different clusters.

"Caith."

"Kiv."

"Kiv and Elnor."

"Murder."

"Thieves."

"Two hundred guns."

"Massacre."

"Mwertik."

"Kiv's right."

"Without Council."

"Allemen."

"Renegade."

"Chaos."

"Must stop them."

"Must help them."

"We need to act now."

Slowly, the voices coalesced into a handful of distinct conversations, then a single conversation taking the form, once more, of a Council meeting.

"We must find out how Caith died."

"Only Kiv knows for certain."

"Kiv and Elnor."

"How can we now believe anything they say?"

"If they were, indeed, present at the time of death."

"What if Kiv or Elnor did kill Caith? What do we do then?"

Meika stood. Gradually, each Allesha recognized the signal and settled into a partial silence of hushed words and uneasy rustlings, so they could hear what she had to say. "Eli and Tedrac are only the first of our early melt runners. Let's send Eli out with instructions to organize a small group of loyal Allemen to find the renegades and try to convince them to give up the guns and turn back. If Kiv's people won't listen, our Allemen are to follow them and keep us informed."

"Then what?" Heinda asked.

"That's something we can debate and decide today, tomorrow — however long it takes until we agree," Michale suggested.

"While we debate, the Mwertik kill," Heinda argued.

"Then it's even more critical that we get the guns and the Allemen who carry them within our control," Hester said. "Let's send Eli out and prepare our instructions for the next runner. Now that the melt has begun, Allemen will be returning to us with their usual spring eagerness. Others will be here within the day, two days, at most."

"Are we agreed, then… at least on the instructions I should give Eli?" Meika gazed around the room.

While the volume of whispers increased, and various Alleshi fidgeted and frowned, no one objected. Meika waited a few more moments, then turned to leave the Assembly Room. At the door, she glanced over her shoulder to Rishana, who was already out of her seat and following.

Chapter 73

———— ❁ ————

Quickly dismissing any misgivings about intruding on a private meeting between an Allesha and her Alleman, Rishana/Jinet hesitated only briefly before following Meika into the small meeting room where Eli awaited instructions. This was her son, whom she hadn't seen for months. And this was an Alleman, who might have answers she needed.

"Mom!" Eli jumped up, tossing the book he had been reading onto the long table and nearly toppling his chair in his rush to hug her.

The familiar shape, texture and smell of her son was so like his father — taller than Dov, with wide, well-cushioned shoulders at just the right height for her to lean her head. Eli wrapped his thick arms around her, and she remembered what it had once been like to be Jinet, when she'd had a home, husband and children, when she had been safe and protected. An illusion, she now knew, but a comforting one — as long as it had lasted.

"I was hoping I'd get to see you, Mom. You look good. Tired, but good." He held her at arms length, and his broad, sparkling smile dimmed, his grey eyes clouding with concern. "And something else. What is it? How are you?"

"Do you think I wouldn't do anything to see you, once I knew you were here?"

"But I knew you were in Season."

Jinet drank in the sight of her son and realized how much he had changed. His once-fair face was so sun-darkened that his multitude of freckles had all but disappeared. The lines around his eyes and mouth, that had been accents of his frequent grins, were now permanently stamped into his flesh, along with new deep creases on his forehead. While his dark auburn hair was still thick, with those beautiful waves that had embarrassed him as a child, his hairline was beginning to recede. Jinet realized that, for the past few months, whenever she thought of Eli, it wasn't as the 25-year-old man he was now, but as a child learning and growing under her care. Hers and Jared's.

Behind Eli, Meika flicked her hand, reminding Jinet where they were, and why.

Eli recognized the message of his mother's almost imperceptible nod toward his Allesha and squeezed Jinet's hands before letting go. Then, pulling his chair away from the table so his back wouldn't be to either woman, he sat down.

Jinet watched Eli in wonder as he changed from her son to an Alleman. All it took was a squaring of his shoulders, a purposeful positioning of his hands and a slight forward tilt of his body, signaling his relaxed readiness. But in those few moments, she saw Jared in him more fully than ever.

With a glance at her sister Allesha to assert exactly whose meeting this was, Meika turned her focus on her Alleman. "Eli, the Council has decided that you should organize a group of loyal Allemen to follow and, hopefully, stop the renegades."

"That will take too long; I'll follow them right away before we lose their trail."

"No!" The word exploded from Jinet, forcing her to come up with a reasonable explanation for her outburst after the fact. "You must have support; this won't work as a solo mission."

Meika glared her disapproval; Jinet turned away in embarrassment. Picking up the small leather-bound volume Eli had discarded, Jinet recognized the handwriting. Why would Eli have one of Mistral's journals?

"Eli, your mother is correct. We'll need several Allemen on this mission. One to try to talk the renegades back — and that must not be you, because your father was too fully identified with his Allesha and her disagreements with their leaders. Plus you will need several other Allemen to help track them and periodically report back to us."

"In other words, you assume we'll fail when we catch up with them, that they won't listen or be deterred."

While Eli and his Allesha planned a potentially deadly encounter, Jinet tried to distract herself by flipping through random pages of Mistral's journal, hating that she could do nothing to keep her son from harm's way.

"I fear they've gone too far to be stopped by words," Meika replied.

"But we must try," Eli insisted.

The journal was filled with first-hand observations of the Mwertik. How was that possible? How much did Jared and Mistral really know about them? What else hadn't they told her?

"Yes, you must try, but very carefully," Meika warned. "The guns they stole are incredibly powerful."

"They're Allemen! They wouldn't shoot at us," Eli protested.

"We can no longer be sure what they will do. All I know is that they are angry and better armed than anyone, anywhere."

With a shock, Jinet realized that Eli wasn't being fully briefed because Meika knew nothing about the hidden cache of ancient artifacts that Kiv and Elnor had unearthed. Were Dara, Peren and Hester purposely keeping Meika, and therefore Eli, in the dark? Whatever the artifacts were — and she feared the worse — Jinet had to warn Eli.

"We must restore parity," Eli reasoned. "Distribute similar guns to the Allemen who will follow."

"No, Eli. Arming you with similar guns would increase the likelihood that we'd have Allemen fighting Allemen. We must find another way to resolve this."

"It isn't entirely up to us, is it? If they start shooting at us…"

Jinet nearly dropped the journal. Staring at her son, she ached to place her hand on his, to be his mother once more and not simply another nameless Allesha.

"Do we know which Allemen remain loyal and which have turned renegade?" he asked.

"Ten were involved in the theft of the guns. We've identified seven Kiv and Elnor Allemen: Gerard, Tevan, Bran, Frank, Kal, Stave and Nacam. Others are definitely involved. Don't trust any from their circles of influence."

"Then whom can I trust?"

"Your own Triats and your father's. For your spokesman to the renegades, choose from among my Allemen. Dram is the closest. The rest of your cohort should remain unseen. If the renegades refuse to turn back, don't let them know they're being followed."

"Wouldn't they assume they are?"

"What they guess and what they know are different things. That element of uncertainty may help protect you." Meika stood. "Unless you have other questions, you should leave right away. I'll give you one of my ponies."

"I have a horse at the Battai's. You know my legs bunch up on your ponies."

Realizing the meeting was ending, Jinet left the room and closed the door, giving Eli and Meika privacy for a proper farewell.

Chapter 74

Jinet fell into step with Eli as soon as he left the meeting room. Slipping on their coats, they headed for the Northwest Battai's inn. How easy it was to match his pace — a steady, distance-covering rhythm that came naturally to her from years of being his father's companion. Yes, he was Jared's son, but hers, too. She saw her influences in his coloring and his broad, all-encompassing smile. However, the way he carried his strong lean body, gliding through life with no apparent doubts — that was Jared's influence.

Without breaking stride, Eli turned to his mother. "Can you tell me what's bothering you?"

"You mean other than the obvious?" Jinet heard the bitterness in her voice, but did nothing to counter it. "That we're careening out of control toward a war that could destroy everything I've ever believed in?"

"Yes, beyond the obvious. Why are you acting so strangely, like you're not yourself?"

"But I am not myself, Eli. I'm an Allesha."

"Please don't play word games with me, Mom."

Jinet studied her son, seeking to understand the man behind the familiar form and mannerisms. "The Allesha who was killed was my friend." She smothered the words, not wanting to acknowledge the full truth of them.

"But there's more, isn't there?"

Jinet was uncertain how much to tell. "How are Brithine and the children?" she asked, anxious to know about her grandchildren, but also needing to find a path back to being with Eli as family rather than as an Allesha and Alleman.

"They're great." The furrows around Eli's eyes became crinkles of delight. "Little Jared is a handful of mischief, reading everything he can get his hands on, whether it's meant for him or not. His baby sister shows every indication she'll be just as difficult to control, if not more so. Ever since she learned to walk, she's been running. They're good kids, Mom, but they never let us forget that they've got minds of their own."

Jinet had spent so little time with her grandchildren. Even now, as she tried to picture them, she found herself filling in the gaps with memories of her own young family, of Eli and his sister Svana, romping together. "When this Season is over, I'm coming for a visit." *Then home,* she thought. *It's time for me to go home.* "What have you heard from your sister?"

"I got word just before I came here. Svana's had her baby, Mom. A boy, with bright red hair. They've named him Janar, for Kael's grandfather. They're both fine."

"You had bright red hair when you were born. Svana had the finest, whitest blonde." Jinet stared into the distance, back to a time of wonder and certainty when everything rested on the beauty of a newborn, the caress of a beloved.

"Look at us now." Eli raked his gloved hand through his dark auburn hair.

Suddenly, all the joy of her memories drained out of her, and she felt torn between a mother's pride and a woman's doubts. "Tell me, Eli, what do you know of Mistral of the Birani?"

"He's Dad's Triat."

"Yes, but what do you know about him, about his family?"

"He's the son of their headman, what they call their Chancellor, which means he'll likely inherit his father's position. His wife's a quiet sort, but she married outward, from one of our older villages. That could explain a lot."

"And their son?"

"What about the boy?"

Jinet stopped short and, grabbing his arm, spun him around to look at her. "What do you know about him, Eli?"

Before her eyes, he became an Alleman once more, squaring his stance solidly over his firmly planted legs. "Why do you ask?"

"He's my Winter Boy."

"What?" Eli staggered as though he had been hit, but recovered almost immediately.

"I'm your mother and an Allesha! Tell me what you know."

Eli rubbed his upper arm where her fingers had dug through the wool of his coat; it was a small gesture, but one that forced her to consider and control her agitation. Glancing in all directions, he confirmed no one else was near. Then he took her elbow, to guide her off the path to a nearby clearing where they could see anyone approaching. As they had both been trained, they positioned themselves so their combined field of vision assured no eavesdroppers. "Have you noticed anything unusual about him?" Eli moved his right foot almost imperceptibly.

She didn't answer immediately, realizing Eli was testing her. But how much did he know? Was it dangerous to pull him in further than he was meant to be? "Yes," she said under her breath.

"Was it familiar? Have you seen the markings before?" His hand grazed his chest.

She swallowed away the taste of bile in her mouth. "On your father's body, the cuts…"

Eli exhaled a quick raspy undertone, "Mwertik."

"But what kind of people would brand a newborn?" she shivered at the chill horror of it.

"I understand it's a ritual of purchase or ransom, because he's the headman's first son. It may be to permanently mark him so the women can't dupe the men into accepting the wrong child as their leader. But it could also set a standard of fierceness and bravery from his very first breath."

"You know much more than I expected."

"Dad told me, but only after I vowed not to tell another living soul, not even my Allesha." He rubbed his face with both hands the way he used to as a child when baffled by a new idea or problem. A lapse of control? Or a habit he had learned to use to conceal his thoughts and intents from those adept at reading him? "Does anyone else know?" he asked.

"The only ones I'm sure of are the Alleshi of your father's Triad. Mistral's Allesha is my mentor."

"And the Alleshi who stole the guns?"

"I don't know; I pray not." She pulled his hands from his face. "Eli, why were you and Tedrac the first melt runners? It can't be a coincidence."

"It isn't."

"Then why, if you didn't know?"

"I knew the boy was here, but not that you were his Allesha. Now that I think of it, you'd be the natural choice. Damn, I shouldn't have been blindsided like that, just because you're my mother." Eli consciously adjusted his posture to help him sort his thoughts. "So, tell me about him. Will he be able to achieve anything of what Dad had hoped?"

"Your father never shared any of it with me." Jinet hid none of her resentment. Here, now, with Eli, the time for secrecy was past. For, if not Eli, whom could she trust? Why then did her heart feel like a steel hand was squeezing it within in her chest? "Why did he take you into his confidence?"

"Because Dad knew he might not come back."

392

She was almost afraid to ask. "When?"

"That last mission. The one he didn't return from."

"But it was a hunt, a bride's gift of a white antelope for Brithine."

"No."

"He lied to me." A part of her wasn't surprised. Still, to have her doubts confirmed was a new kind of death, trampling her memories, conclusively destroying the dream of what she thought she had shared with Jared.

"Mom, it wasn't like that. There are times an Alleman must hold things close."

"I haven't taught my Winter Boy to lie."

"If someone should ask him about his blood parents? Would you have him tell the truth?"

"Of course not, but…"

"You can't have it both ways, Mom." Eli glanced at the sky; dark storm clouds were forming over the Western mountains. "I've got to keep moving."

"Not yet, Eli. You still don't have the full picture. The renegades found something from the Before Times. We don't know what it is, but it may be even deadlier than the guns they stole."

"I know, Mom. Dad's Allesha told me."

"But your Allesha doesn't…"

"No, she doesn't." The statement hung in the air between them, unexplained. Jinet felt that Eli was about to say something further on the subject. Instead, he resumed walking. "Mom, I really must get going."

She fell into step with him once more. On the path to the Battai's, Eli constantly swept his eyes to and fro, glancing back every few moments, as any Alleman or Allesha would when covering potentially dangerous terrain — an ingrained habit which was now uncomfortably appropriate, even here in The Valley.

"Are you ever sorry you became an Alleman, Eli?"

"Sometimes, when I'm frustrated or confused or forced to choose between two terrible options."

"Or forced to lie."

"Yes. But sometimes, it's what I must do to accomplish what's needed."

"And to survive," Jinet acknowledged. As the path wound uphill, winter trees with their barren limbs gave way to evergreens. Life and death, it was more than the cycle of nature. It was a dance, a collision, a wary balance. Did it make any difference that Jared died on a dangerous mission rather than during a meaningless hunt? No longer a victim of some random, irrational violence, he was still just as dead. "I posed no threat to Jared."

"No, but the knowledge he possessed could have been a threat to you."

"Or is it that secrecy is a habit that isn't easily broken?"

Eli turned toward his mother, altering the rhythm of his constant surveillance of the path and forest to include her. No less vigilant, he softened his gaze so she could see his care and concern. "Don't you understand? Anyone who knows about the boy is in danger from the Mwertik — and maybe from some of our own. How could Dad have functioned as an Alleman if he had to also constantly worry about your safety?"

"So he kept me in ignorance, like a plaything he could return to when he tired of the real world."

"You're hurt right now, Mom. That will pass. Dad loved you."

"Yes, I know. But what about me? Did the man I love ever truly exist?"

"Yes and no. The man who lived by your side, who was Svana's and my father, who worked and laughed with you and sometimes made mistakes. Yes, he was very real. But the legend you built up about him after he died, no."

"You tried to warn me, didn't you? I just didn't understand what you were saying about how becoming an Allesha would change more than who I was."

"Mom, are you sorry you became an Allesha?"

Jinet knew Eli was redirecting their conversation by flipping her question back to her. But, once asked, it couldn't be avoided. "Sometimes." She thought a moment, then added, "Was I better off when I was blissfully ignorant? My whole world has been crumbling, bit by bit, ever since Jared was murdered. But how could it not when it was built on paper-thin myths?"

"You're disappointed that coming to this Valley didn't stop your world from disintegrating, aren't you?"

"You make it sound like a childish tantrum."

"No, Mom. It's just that you were lucky in your birth and marriage and life before coming here. Whatever problem you encountered, you could face it squarely, knowing that with perseverance and intelligence, you would eventually find reasonable solutions. Nothing was insurmountable."

"Except death."

"Except death," Eli agreed. "But the world outside our village isn't like that, Mom. It's messy and doesn't always resolve into sensible solutions."

"Of course not."

"And now you're an Allesha, whether you like it or not. Even if you left this Valley, that's the one thing you could never leave behind you. However hard you try, you'll never unlearn what you now know, never be able to deny who and what you've become."

"If I stay here, I'm part of the lies."

"And of the ultimate truths."

"You still believe we can save our Peace, Eli?"

"It's what I've devoted my life to, Mom."

"Even now?"

"How else can I keep going? Two Alleshi and I don't know how many Allemen are out there, about to start a war. I've got to stop them."

"Do you know the Allemen involved?"

"Some I have called my friends."

"Will you fight them?"

Eli didn't answer; nor did he need to. His mother knew he would fight with all his being to save the Peace. But the choice would be wrenched from him only after he tried everything else he could think of.

"What if they're right? What if the only way to save our Peace is to show the Mwertik that we're willing to kill?"

"Strength isn't found in violence. You know that, Mom."

Something about how he said it, perhaps his deadened tone or the way his shoulders hunched forward, made her ask, "Eli, have you ever killed anyone?"

"Yes." For several steps, his eyes no longer swept back and forth, but looked inward to a place his mother could not follow. "Yes, I have."

Jinet felt an empty space form in her stomach, aching with a mother's mourning. "And you would again."

"Only if all other options failed. If it were absolutely necessary."

"I didn't know."

"I never wanted you to know, Mom. I would have liked to have one person left who still saw me as that red-headed innocent you once adored." His voice was soft and distant. "I guess it's one thing that will never stop haunting me. What else could I have done? Why did I fail so miserably?"

She touched his arm. "Eli…"

He jerked suddenly, as though awakening to a loud report. Resuming his watchful guard, he walked faster and more determined than before. "Does the boy have it in him to be what we need?"

"If you're asking me if I believe in this boy's abilities, yes, I do. Still, I'm not willing to send him out to be sacrificed by schemers who…"

"That will have to be his choice. Not yours. As much as the Alleshi guide us, Allemen must make their own decisions."

"But Eli, he was taken from the Mwertik at such a young age. Stolen by one of ours. Why should they accept him as a leader now?"

"I don't think they will. Still, he could influence them."

"Like the men in *The Northern Border?* I won't send him out like that, with nothing more than a dream of peace to build on. "

"That story comes from long ago, before this Valley existed. Don't use it to gauge what we're capable of now. With your boy's help, plus the generations of knowledge we've accumulated, we might yet find a way."

"But people will die before then. I don't want it to include my First Boy… or my son."

"I wish I could tell you no one will be killed. But I won't lie. It is a possibility; it's always a possibility. However, if we don't try, it will be a certainty. And if we're lucky and others are willing, maybe, just maybe, no one will have to die."

"Then hope is a cancer in more ways than one."

"Mom, please don't be so bitter. It's a wondrous thing that you're doing, preparing a boy who might avert a war and save our Peace."

"And if I fail?"

"You taught me that allowing the possibility of failure to stop you from trying is the worst kind of failure."

"That was before I understood what was at stake."

"And that makes failure even more unacceptable."

The path made one last twist through a well-groomed garden, which gradually spread out around a pebbled clearing in front of the open gate to the Battai's. Turning to face his mother, Eli took both of her hands. "Mom, I must leave. They have such a solid head start."

"Allemen against Allemen. An Allesha killed. What has our world come to, Eli?"

"I don't know Mom. We plan and struggle, but we can never know for certain where our actions will take us."

"Eli, come back to me soon."

"I will try my damnedest, Mom."

"I can't lose you, too." Jinet stroked his cheek, memorizing his face. Then they pulled each other inward, holding tightly for several silent breaths.

Eli was the first to let go. "Tell your Winter Boy that I look forward to meeting him."

He started to turn away into the gate, but Jinet rested her hand in his elbow, stopping him. "We've had so little time."

"You and me, or you and him?"

Jinet saw her own winning smile play on her son's face, and her heart lightened for a moment. "Both."

"I don't know if I've told you before, Mom, but I'm proud of you, and I love you."

"I love you too, Eli. And I know I've told you how proud I am of you."

"Even now, after learning what you have?"

"Especially now."

As they held each other one last time, Jinet inhaled his fragrance — a spicy scent of autumn fields, so similar to Jared's. Before turning to leave, he kissed her on each cheek and then between the eyes, the way she used to kiss her children at night in their beds before extinguishing the lights.

Jinet watched her son walk through the gate to the Battai's inn. Yes, he had Jared's graceful lope and strong straight back. And like Jared, he was now walking away from her to seek danger for the sake of their Peace. It would have been easier to imagine both of them on a hunt for a white antelope. But she hadn't come to this Valley for the sake of her own ease, any more than they had.

Chapter 75

The late afternoon twilight darkened as the storm over the Western mountain rolled in. However, Tayar saw no lights in the windows of her home. Dov didn't rush out to her when she entered the greeting room, nor did he respond when she knocked on his bedroom door. Though the kitchen table was set for supper, the oven and stove were cold and no food had been prepared.

Tayar considered going out to the barn to look for Dov, but something drew her, instead, to the inner room. She found him, sitting cross-legged and fully clothed on an upper platform, relaxed but straight-backed, so still that the only movement in the dark room was the flicker of the single candle burning in front of him. He acknowledged her by focusing on her face when she sat on the other side of the candle. Arranging herself into a comfortable cross-legged pose, Tayar slowed her body and mind to his quiet rhythms before speaking.

"What are you doing here?" she asked.

"Considering my options."

"What decisions have you made?"

"I don't have enough information to make any decisions yet. Tell me about the meeting. What has the Alleshine Council decreed?"

"They don't have enough information, either."

"Yet, if we combined our knowledge… theirs, mine and yours…"

"No!" Tayar's hand shot out almost of its own volition, instinctively trying to block Dov. The candle flame danced at her sudden movement.

"No, of course not," he said. "Not yet."

With measured breathing, Tayar focused on calming her heart and mind.

Only when Dov saw that she was ready did he speak again. "My options are limited, but not as limited as Le'a would have them be. Le'a and that other Allesha, the one we visited."

"Please tell me."

"I could return to the Birani, marry Lilla and live the life I always thought I would."

398

"I don't believe you could sit at home, warming yourself by the hearth fire, while others were in danger. Not when there was any possibility that you could save them."

"If I believed in such a possibility."

In the stillness, Tayar's slight nod felt out of place.

Dov barely moved, only his lips, eyes and slow, even breaths. "When I first came here, I considered leaving, going somewhere neither the Alleshi nor the Mwertik had any influence. I would take Lilla and find another life. Sometimes, that still appeals to me."

"But only sometimes?"

"When I feel tired and confused, when I need to picture myself claiming control over my life. It's a fantasy I play with from time to time." He paused. "Tell me, Tayar, what do Le'a and that other Allesha have planned for me? I know they want me to be their bridge to the Mwertik, but I'm not sure how they expect me to do it."

"They haven't discussed their plans with me. I imagine it would be a gradual contact, as though you were any Alleman approaching a new village. A variation on Mistral's role."

"Yes, that's how I picture it, but even if I chose that option, I could surprise them. I could choose to return to the Mwertik, as a Mwertik, leaving behind all this. But I couldn't take Lilla with me." Dov's tone remained temperate, though his words were harsh. "Besides, why should the Mwertik accept me? If nothing else, they'd have no reason to believe I could change my allegiances after a lifetime with their enemies."

"Could you change your allegiances? Could you fight Mistral, learn to hate Shria... me?"

"Still, I am Mwertik and maybe that's where I belong, if I belong anywhere."

"You belong here, Dov." Even as she said it, she wished she could take it back. Half truths wouldn't help him.

"Only for a few more weeks." Allowing himself a thin smile, Dov gently traced her jawline with his fingertips, then drew his hand back into his lap.

Tayar's throat burned with tears she dared not shed. "You've already decided, haven't you?"

"Only what I will not do. I cannot marry Lilla." He said it as a sigh, fastening his resolve. "Not only because I love her too much to subject her to the danger and uncertainty, but because I must remain marriageable. It's one way I could be a true bridge."

Tayar couldn't deny his logic. "Then you have chosen that path."

"No. I'm just not closing doors. Until I know more about those guns and the men who took them, I can't know how they'll alter the future. Have you learned anything more about them?"

"We know which Alleshi lead them and the names of some of the Allemen."

"Alleshi and Allemen… there's no doubt?" he asked.

"As little as there can be without having seen it myself. One Allesha has confirmed it."

"And they killed that woman, Caith?"

"It appears so."

"What's the Alleshine Council doing about it?"

The balance between them had changed. Tayar realized her role, the one Dov had chosen for her for the moment, was to provide information. "We have sent two loyal Allemen after those who stole the guns."

"How do you know they're loyal?"

"One is my son, Eli. The other is Tedrac, your father's Triat."

Dov nodded. "What are their plans?"

"They will organize a group of Allemen to follow the renegades and try to persuade them into returning to The Valley."

"That will fail."

"Probably, but they must try. It will be Allemen talking with Allemen. That has to make a difference."

"Or maybe that will make it even more difficult. Both sides know the other too well and will have no difficulty reading each other. Besides, what advantage can Eli offer, when the other Allemen already have what they want?"

"Peace."

"The one thing they obviously don't want," Dov countered.

"Peace with their own people — Alleshi and Allemen, and all those who remain loyal to The Valley."

"Do you really think the renegades believe they're doing anything other than being loyal, protecting everything this Valley stands for?"

"Perhaps." Tayar paused, as she pictured Kiv sitting at her kitchen table, so sharp and sure, determined to save the Peace, whatever it would take. "You're right; that is exactly what they believe."

"If so, they'll see Eli and his band as obstacles to be pushed aside. Or worse, enemies who would stop them from doing what's necessary."

Tayar shivered despite the moist warmth of the room. "And they may have an advantage that we can't give Eli. Those rapid-fire guns aren't the only things the renegades took from the storehouse." She paused, realizing how much Dov still didn't know. "They appear to have discovered a hidden cache — some lost secret, perhaps from the civilization destroyed by the Great Chaos."

Dov didn't respond. Tayar recognized the signs; he was waiting for her to fill in the blanks. When she didn't continue, he said, "The more I learn, the more complex the questions become. What are the Alleshi doing to find out what the renegades uncovered?"

"Searching the library and storehouse, sending Eli and others after the renegades, while trying to control who has full information, to avoid further escalation. I believe that only Eli and the Alleshi of your father's Triad know about it, though Mistral and Tedrac will probably be informed."

"The Alleshi have so many secrets; no wonder they can't remember all of them."

For several breaths, both were silent, lost in their own thoughts. When Dov spoke again, it was with a husky rasp, as though the words were forced from his throat. "Tayar, when did the Mwertik start raiding across our borders?"

"They've always been raiders."

"Like they are now?"

"No…" Her voice trailed off.

"What's the difference?"

"The ferocity and how far within the Peace borders they now come."

"When did it change? Was it about eighteen years ago?"

Tayar stared at him. "I don't have an answer for you."

"Skies! What if I'm the cause of everything?" Though his body remained still, it was with a rigidity rather than ease. "Tayar, do you blame Pa?"

"We can control only so much." Tayar's gaze clouded over as she listened to Eli's voice within her.

"I wish I could give you back your dream, Tayar. You believed in it all when I first came here, didn't you?"

"And you think I don't anymore?"

"You want to, Tayar. But it's harder for you now."

"Perhaps that's part of the messiness of life, Dov. Maybe, we'll never find real answers, only more questions."

Chapter 76

As Tayar settled into the sofa, she leafed through a small leather-bound volume to find the entry she wanted. "I'm going to read from another Alleman's journal tonight."

Dov stretched out in his corner of the sofa. "Tayar, we have so little time left, and we haven't finished *The Traveler's Tales*." Dov reached for the book from the side table and opened it. "Look, there's only one story to go, called *In Silence*."

Tayar closed the journal and leaned her head back against the upholstered arm as he began to read.

I wandered from village to village, staying a season here, a few days or weeks there. I no longer allowed any to name me, choosing to belong to no one and nowhere. Instead, I became known as Alleen. Not that I had planned to take my friend's name, but when asked who I was, it was the first to come to my lips.

I was able to trade my healing skills for shelter and food in most places. As I healed, I told my stories of what might be if only we could find the way to peace, but they did not take root. Most dismissed my tales as fantasies suitable only for children. Others rose up against me for suggesting such treasonous ideas.

Eventually, I became known and my arrival at villages anticipated. Not for my tales, but for my skills. Those healers who were not jealous of my knowledge sought me out to learn and to teach. Headmen and councils would sometimes give me messages to carry, and being a messenger often gave me a small amount of safety on the open road ~ as long as the people I met were the ones I sought.

I sometimes became caught up in battles, but as Alleen Healer, not as a nameless victim. More than once, I became bounty for the victors. Over time, I learned to avoid wars whenever I could. Perhaps it was cowardice for a healer, but I'd had enough of the mindless bloodshed ~ and of the cruelty that continued even after the battle had been won or lost. I traveled along the edges of the chaos, visiting villages that would have me, leaving quickly when I was no longer welcomed or needed, and before I could learn to care too deeply for anyone.

The last village I visited was no better or worse than many others that had spanned my years. They welcomed me while the sick needed me, stoned me out of their midst when a child died. What had changed was that I was weary, and my feet began to falter. I wondered if it were time for me to finally stop walking.

In my travels, I had heard of a group of men who had retreated from the world to live in the caves of the White Mountains. It was said that they spent their days in silence. I made my way to them, walking through the spring into early summer, avoiding all villages along the way. The closer I got to the White Mountains, the more often I would encounter other travelers who knew something of the hermits I sought. Then I would share their evening fire, and glean what I could of the men of the caves.

The White Mountains are at the north end of a wide, fertile plain that was gentle on my feet. But the climb to the caves was steep and forbidding. Ofttimes, the path I followed ended at a cliff, requiring that I backtrack and try another approach. I spent the nights on small ledges, sleeping only fitfully, fearful of rolling off into the crags below. After several days, I finally spied the caves above me and set up camp behind an outcrop of stone.

I watched for one day and night, to learn what I could. About thirty men lived in a series of caves, though I couldn't tell whether each had his own private cell, or if all the entrances I saw led to one large cavern. Each man went about his daily chores without imposing on his neighbor. For hours, they sat quietly in the sun and wind, staring into the distance. It reminded me of my days with Alleen, when we would listen and see and become part of the life that surrounded us. Here at last, I thought, I had found people who understood peace.

Set apart from the others, one man perched on a large boulder above the caves, as guard or leader, or both. He was nearly as dark as I, though he was burned by the sun, not his lineage. Compact and scrawny, he had no hair, not even eyebrows; his parched skin stretched over jutting bones. His clothing, like that of the others, was a rough weave wrapped around his torso, arms and legs. As the day warmed, he loosened it to the breeze.

Of all the hermits, only the man on the boulder was nearly motionless, as though he had become part of the rock. Others had varying levels of skill and distinct personalities. An old man, whose white hair and beard reached past his waist, fidgeted with pain in his hips, yet smiled inwardly as he meditated. A small man with improbably bright red hair chewed on a twig all day. Might it be a soporific, I wondered, or his way of keeping his mouth busy so he wouldn't accidentally break the silence?

The one who appeared to be the youngest was probably also the newest of the hermits, judging from his lack of focus. In his late twenties, he had thick dark hair, round cheeks, pale skin and large darting eyes. He had difficulty sitting for long, disrupting his meditations to rearrange his clothing, move an offending stone, or shake out a muscle cramp. He often disappeared into one of the small cave mouths, though not the one directly behind his perch.

In the late afternoon, the young one ascended the cliff to sit below the dark man's boulder. Eventually, the man above acknowledged him, and the young one climbed up onto the boulder. That was the first time I saw any of these recluses speak. Though I couldn't hear what they said, the young one was clearly upset. With a single sharp nod, the dark one dismissed the supplicant. The young one appeared cowed by whatever had transpired; he slowly retreated from the boulder, returning to his own far perch on the lower tier of the caves.

That night, I lit a large fire on my ledge, to be sure my presence wouldn't be a surprise.

The next morning, I waited until all the men had finished their tasks and had settled into their meditations. Each sat in the same place and pose as the past two days. On their tiers of ledges overlooking the plains, they resembled wild birds roosting on the many branches of a tree, though I didn't know if they were scavengers or nesters. When each had attained the level of quiet he was capable of achieving, I left my belongings where I had camped and climbed to sit just below the leader's boulder, as I had seen the young supplicant do. I crossed my legs, arranged my hands on my lap, rounded my shoulders over my straight back and gave myself to meditation. But I kept the leader within the periphery of my sight so I would not miss his summons.

Composing myself as Alleen had taught me, with my body relaxed but centered, I opened my senses. I was not as still as the leader, because my body flowed naturally with the rhythms of all around me. The air stirred with the passing of a flock of birds. A small rodent scurried with a hard-earned berry. Water cascaded out of sight but nearby. Yes, this was a place I would enjoy getting to know.

For two days, I sat below his boulder, leaving it only to eat, sleep and eliminate. He avoided passing near me when he left his perch, taking a higher path to his cave at night. On the second morning, I thought I saw him react to my return, as though he were surprised or pained by it. But it could have been a muscle spasm in his neck.

Only the young supplicant from the other day appeared affected by my presence. He seemed to recognize me, and it disturbed him. I wondered if he had once lived in a village I had visited in my travels. Growing increasingly agitated, by the end of the second day, he didn't even attempt to meditate. On the third morning, I was about to leave my camp to resume my vigil under the leader's boulder, when the young one rushed forward to sit there instead. The leader beckoned to him. When they spoke, the younger one shifted from one foot to the other, and his hands flew with his words, pointing often to me. The leader listened a short while, then dismissed him with a scowl.

When the rhythms of the community calmed as much as they could be with the young one so troubled, I resumed my supplicant pose below the leader. Almost immediately, he nodded to me in such a manner that I knew he meant for me to approach. I climbed up to his boulder and, keeping the distance between us that I had seen the other men maintain whenever they were near one another, I waited. I felt his eyes on me, examining every feature of my face, every aspect of my body. Only after he had completed his survey did he speak. His voice had an incisive edge, with no embellishment of tone. "You are Alleen Healer."

I lifted my eyes to his and said, "Yes."

"Why are you here?"

"I wish to live among you."

"We have no women. You would be a disruption." His upper lip curled in distaste.

"I know how to be silent," I explained. "I need silence."

"Why?" he asked, though his voice was so flat that only the word defined it as a question.

I did not need to ponder my answer; I had lived with it for too long. "Words are the scourge of the world. Only in silence is there peace."

"Then go and be silent elsewhere."

"Some of your brothers are in pain. I can help."

He glanced below us where the young one waited, watching our every move and gesture. "Their pain is given to them to bear."

Something in the way he said it made me wonder at the young one's agitation. This man had spoken to me for a reason. He knew who I was.

"Someone is ill," I said, guessing but stating it as fact. "Allow me to help."

He did not respond, nor did he dismiss me. I quieted my heart and waited, knowing he was trapped between two difficult choices. To allow me to heal his fellow hermit would mean bringing me within his community. A stranger. A woman. To turn me away would be to risk greater sickness. Perhaps even death. And if the illness were contagious, disaster.

Finally, without looking at me, the leader motioned to the young one, who led me to the small cave that had commanded so much of his attention. I had to bow my head to enter. Turning before going in, I saw that the leader had resumed his meditation, but I doubted he was as unaware of me and my actions as he wanted either of us to believe.

Next to a well-tended fire lay a young man who looked so much like the one who had brought me here that I had no doubt they were brothers. While the one who stood by my side was in constant motion, checking the fire, arranging the blankets around his brother, running his fingers through his own hair, the one on the ground was as still as death, burning with fever and wheezing with each laborious breath.

I had never attempted to heal anyone without being able to speak; my voice is part of my healing. Still, I had chosen their life of silence and would not be the one to break it. I gestured to the healthy brother that he should boil some water while I fetched my packs. Hoping I was coming here to stay, I had gathered a large collection of plants, saps and other medicinals. I brewed a bitter tea to soothe his fever, created a hot compress to ease the congestion in his chest, and massaged an unguent into his skin to stimulate his sinews.

My patient whimpered almost constantly with pain. Only once did he cry out, "Tren!" and his brother ran to him, stroked his brow and whispered, "Shush, Ket, shush." His words were so soft I might have mistaken them for an exhaled breath. However, Ket did quiet at the sound of his brother's voice. During the day, Tren did not leave Ket's side. But at night, he had to go to his own cave while I slept by my patient.

The crisis came the next day, with the fever cresting so high Ket's flesh felt like fire. Though I spread unguent under his nose and in his mouth to force my medicines into his lungs, his congestion was so thick that breaths came only sporadically and with great effort. I had to act fast or lose him. Rolling him onto his stomach, I straddled his back, pounding it with my fists, while I had Tren bathe him with cool water. I fought hard for his life, with brews, ointments and vapors, knowing that I could do only so much. This time, I won. He was soon breathing more easily, and his fever subsided.

When Tren realized his brother would live, he smiled for the first time since I had arrived. He sat at my feet and, when I did not respond, reached for my hands, kissed my palms and then pressed them to his head. Ket was still weak, but he pulled himself to a sitting position and repeated his brother's gesture of fealty and thanks. Then the two of them embraced, both convulsing with noiseless tears and laughter.

Pitching my tent over Ket, I created a steam hut to clear his lungs completely. I no longer feared for his life, though I knew it would take weeks for him to mend.

The next morning, Tren silently greeted me and my patient, and then gathered my few belongings. He shouldered my packs and led me to a vacant cave on the edge of the community, far from the leader's boulder. To this day, I don't know if the leader had given him permission or if he had acted on his own, in gratitude.

I cannot say that I ever became part of the community. I was tolerated but ignored, acknowledged only by the two brothers. But I did find peace within the silence. Every morning and evening, I ate alone in my cave. I spent the hours of the day in silent meditation on my sun-baked ledge. The only things I missed were the songs that came to my heart but could not be sung.

The mountains were rich with everything we could want. I would go out from time to time to gather for my medicine pack and my meals. Any extra food or water I had, I would leave outside the caves of the older men. They never thanked me, but they did not refuse my gifts. I believe some of them came to accept my presence. I know I saw a twinkle in the eye of the one with the long white hair and beard when I came near. And the herbs I secretly sprinkled into his food seemed to ease his pain.

The hermits seldom gathered their own food. Nor did they allow themselves to be distracted by the manual labor required to fashion the basic goods even ascetics need. Instead, they accepted gifts from the plains people, who considered the community sacred. Villagers left offerings nearby, always maintaining a respectful distance. Rarely did any approach the leader's boulder, and of those, few men were granted an audience.

One autumn morning, when I greeted the day, I found a young woman sitting outside my cave. Her legs were folded and her head bowed in the same supplicant pose that villagers used when they approached the leader of our community, though no woman had ever dared come within his sight since I had arrived. In her arms was a child of about five years, who barely moved. She held the child out to me; I did not hesitate. It didn't occur to me that perhaps I should have asked permission from the leader first.

I carried the child into my cave, and the mother followed me. After examining my patient, I showed the woman how I prepared and applied my medicines, mimed to her that it should be done three times a day for each treatment, and gave her a portion to take home with her. The child would heal if the mother did as I had instructed. With tears of gratitude, she bowed before me and, like Tren and Ket, kissed my hands and pressed them to her head. Then she took her child in her arms and left.

The following morning, it was a man with a festering cut. On the next, a boy with a limp. Every day, someone new was at the mouth of my cave, seeking my help ~ often several people. They came with severe problems, illnesses beyond the skills of other healers, not disturbing me with ordinary cares and illnesses. And they did so without words. Mothers swathed the mouths of crying children, to avoid offending the silence of our community. I turned none away.

Then, one afternoon, four men brought a boy on a plank, rushing forward with no preliminary supplication. The boy had been wounded severely; the arrowhead was still in his abdomen. I'll never know how they made it up to the caves in time. Perhaps they had been hunting the White Mountains and were already close.

I gestured that they should bring him inside my cave, and I worked with all the skills I could command to save the boy. Soon, the song came, unbidden but necessary, for the child was slipping away from me. I sang his life, fighting the call of death, while I cut the arrowhead out and mended the flesh. Unaware of the passage of time, I worked with him until I knew my ministries had finally taken effect. Then I left the boy and men in my cave, all sleeping soundly, and went outside for air, surprised to find it was dawn.

Tren was sitting outside my cave, waiting for me. He might have been there all night, or he might have just arrived. His lips quivered with words he ached to say. Instead, he turned toward the leader's perch, to show me he had been sent. Then he went into my cave, and sidestepping the various strangers who barely stirred in their sleep, he packed my belongings and handed them to me.

I threw my packs on the ground and stomped off to the leader's boulder. Not waiting to be acknowledged, I climbed up, speaking without permission. "You're sending me away." I wanted to say so much more, but being unaccustomed to words, they failed me.

He had to stand or have me tower over him. "You are a woman and a disturbance. You have strangers coming and going. Now you have broken the silence."

"To save a boy's life," I pleaded.

"You have broken the silence." His face twisted with anger and distaste, but his voice remained toneless.

"Does nothing else matter to you?"

"You have broken the silence," he repeated, with the same exact lack of inflection.

"No, nothing matters," I answered my own question. "You have

nothing more to say because you're empty inside. You've become as solid and untouchable as this boulder. No wonder you can't hear the songs all around you. Your silence isn't peace. It's death."

I leapt from the boulder, almost colliding with Tren and Ket, who must have heard what I had said. For that, I was sorry. They believed in this community, especially in their leader. For their sakes, I would have taken back my words, but my regret didn't fade the sense of truth I felt. The silence of this community separated the men from one another, from life. So much so that they couldn't bear to touch another, even accidentally. I had absorbed myself in their silence, hoping it would bring me peace. But what is peace without words, without songs to give it breath? I would never again allow anything to silence my songs.

Awakening one of the men in my cave, I showed him how to care for the boy, giving him more than enough medicine. The unexpected sound of my voice aroused the others. I told them that regardless of what happened, they were not to move the boy until his wound was set, which would take at least three days. But they were to remain silent and not offend on the community.

Tren and Ket were kneeling outside, waiting for me. Each pressed one of my hands to his lips and brows. Once more I had failed. Perhaps I would always fail when what I sought was to never again care for another. Not even in silence was I able to escape that burden. And now, I had injured these two.

Needing their forgiveness, I sat beside them, in supplication. Soon, the three of us were holding one another, sobbing soundlessly. I was the first to let go, not because my tears were spent, but because it was time to leave. As I stood, they raised their faces to me without moving from where they knelt. And I saw in their eyes not so much pain, though there was that also, but a vitality and joy which hadn't been there before. I did not realize it, but that too was my doing, that life which shone from within them.

I reached into my smaller pack to give them a mixture of herbs, gesturing to White Beard. Unlike the others, who ignored me, I was sure they had seen me stir it into the food I had given the old man. I hoped Tren and Ket would find a way to continue easing his pain.

I then shouldered my packs and left that stony community of silence. Looking back only once, I saw Tren and Ket still kneeling in front of my cave, watching me. I believe that if I had beckoned, they would have followed. Instead, I turned from them, allowing my feet to carry me away once more.

After Dov had been quiet for a few breaths, Tayar stirred from her listening pose, but stopped when he turned another page and said, "That's the end of that story, but there's a bit more to the book. Just a few more pages."

She curled back into her corner of the sofa.

I had no desire to try living in yet another village, but my feet dragged, needing to finally rest. Seeking the peace of solitude I had once shared with Alleen, I made my way to a valley I'd seen on my journey to the White Mountains. It was wide and green, surrounded by gentle mountains that were sure to cut the coldest of the plains winds, even in winter. In the center of the valley, where two streams met and formed a small lake, was a deserted farm. The farmhouse was in disrepair, with its roof open to the sky, but the barn was still solid. Here, I was determined to live the rest of my life, apart from any other person. But springtime hunters from the Attani..."

"Hey, the Attani — that's your people, Tayar, right?"
She nodded without opening her eyes, and Dov continued.

But springtime hunters from the Attani found me. Soon, I was busy healing as before, with people coming from far and wide, seeking my help. Now, however, I was in a position to define how things would be done. I told my stories to everyone I treated, of what might be if only we had peace. What's more, some began to hear and understand.

In the autumn, men from the plains villages came to my valley and rebuilt the house, while the women provisioned my winter stores with the best of their harvests. Tren and Ket were among them, laughing and joking aloud. When the brothers introduced me to their wives, the women thanked me, vowing that whatever I should want or need they would give to me, at that moment or any time in the future.

I found peace in that valley, though not the peace of solitude I had sought. Often, I was truly alone, especially in winter, but I turned no one away who needed my help. Every year, pilgrims came from farther away, until one autumn day, a boy of about eighteen stood at my door. He was large in all dimensions, his hair so fair that it looked almost white. I hadn't seen anyone like him since the Murat and Mukane.

"I seek a woman," he said.
"You have found one."
"You are Alleen Healer?"
"Yes."
"Were you once also called Meysrit?"

Overwhelmed by all the memories that long-ago name held, I grabbed the door jam, holding on tightly. "Who are you?" I demanded.

"I'm told I look like my father. If you are Meysrit, maybe you already know who I am."

"I knew a boy once, so many years ago." I stared at this improbable giant, but saw instead all the others ~ Dawn and Bisrit, Dac and Thim, and ~ "Wen?" I asked.

He nodded. "Wen's my father."

"Please, come in, come in." I led him into my greeting room. "You must be weary; please sit. Are you hungry?" I started for my kitchen, to get him some refreshment, but turned and stared at him once more. "Were you truly seeking me?"

"When my father heard the stories of Alleen Healer, he sent me to find you. He said no one else would heal using stories of hope, of what might be. He wanted you to know that they finally listened; the Mukane and Murat no longer war, though they fight. You should hear my father and mother go at each other."

"Your mother?"

"I was told to tell you she's Darrint's granddaughter."

"Darrint? The old Murat headman? But that's impossible. Wen's..."

"Mukane. I know. Ma never fails to remind him of that when she's angry with him."

I stared at the boy, unable to form all the questions I had.

"All my life, Pa's told me about you. How it was you who first taught him healing, and so much more. About the cancer of hope, that grows even when you try to cut it out of your heart. About how Grandpa loved you and gave his life for your peace. Everything. Even if Pa hadn't sent me to you, I would have had to come."

"Wen..."

"My name is Marrint. They named me for you... For you and for my great grandfather."

"Marrint, I want to hear it all ~ about Wen and his wife, about the Murat and the Mukane, and especially about you. You'll stay with me for a while, I hope."

"That's what Pa wants, too. He told me to ask you to teach me."

"But..."

"I'm strong. I can help you through the winter."

"I live alone, Marrint."

"I'm to stay at your doorstep until you agree."

"Why?"

"Because you were right about the Mukane and Murat, because you are a great teacher, probably the wisest woman alive."

"That's doubtful."

"Because I want to understand."

"What is it you want to understand?"

"Everything." He shrugged with a slight wince of embarrassment.

"You may stay for a few days. However, you will leave before the first snow."

But he didn't leave until the next spring, changed, as I was, by our winter together. He returned often over the years, even after he followed his father as the Mukane Healer, spreading the cancer of hope to anyone who'd listen.

Marrint was the first. Other boys followed, season after season. And women too. But the women didn't leave. Instead, they formed a new community, becoming known as Alleen's women, the Peacemakers. I don't even mind that a village has now taken shape around me, here in my valley. I still can enjoy my solitude and my songs, just as Alleen taught me. But never in silence.

Dov closed the book. "It was this valley?" he asked.

"Yes." Tayar uncurled her legs and rearranged the cushions behind her.

"Alleen, the Traveler, was an Allesha?"

"The first, though the title didn't exist until well after her death."

"It makes sense, I guess." He flipped through the book, to glance at some of the earlier stories. "Someday, I'd like to reread these, now that I know. See how it changes them."

"Oh?"

"I suppose it's like a First Meet. The more you know about a person's heritage and language, the better you'll understand his actions. But with these stories, it isn't her background; it's her future. Ours, too. We're here now because of her. And the things that happened to her in these stories could explain that, too."

"Yes, that's why these stories foreshadow—"

"But she didn't get it right, did she? Any Alleman knows you don't go into a First Meet after only one day and night of observation, much less try to become part of the community with so little information. That was a big mistake. Still, I guess that's why Allemen know it, because she made that mistake, and we can now learn from it."

"Exactly." Though it was taking them in directions she hadn't planned for this evening, Tayar was pleased how quickly Dov parsed the lessons from the story. This was going to be a stimulating discussion. "What should she have found out about them before revealing herself?" she asked.

"No, not right now." Dov stood and put the volume away on a bookshelf. "The story and the book have many more implications than I realized. I need to think about it for a while." He walked briskly toward his bedroom. Turning back, he said, "Will you meet me in the inner room?" Then he left.

Tayar tried to figure out exactly when it was that she had lost control. She reached for the Alleman's journal she had been planning to read and leafed through it. Tedrac's handwriting was even and clear, every word well considered. One of the most respected Allemen for his scholarship and wisdom, Tedrac had once been a boy in Season just as Dov was now. Did Hester have the same kind of difficulties with Tedrac at this stage? Were boys all around The Valley challenging their Alleshi tonight? Or was Tayar's inexperience, coupled with all that had happened, at fault?

Tayar thought about Marrint, the first Winter Boy. Of Tren and Ket and the leader of the hermits sitting so solidly on his boulder that he couldn't learn to bend. Alleen quickly outgrew that community and its leader, as did Tren and Ket. Any student would who had a mind of his or her own. That was the key, Tayar realized. Dov would soon be an Allemen. In only a few days, the Separation Stage would begin, when they would start learning their new roles as Allesha and Alleman, two halves of a partnership who must remain always close but forever apart.

This evening, she'd lost control because she had no right to have control over Dov. Not anymore. From now on, they would have to work things out together, even through disagreements.

Leaving the greeting room to prepare herself, Tayar was determined to initiate the lessons she had planned for the inner room, but knew that she could no longer predict where they might lead.

Chapter 77

—————❖—————

Tayar/Rishana now made a point of going to the Communal Hall daily, usually after lunch. So many Council meetings were being convened, and with such frequency, that no one bothered with a callout any more. At all hours, the Communal Hall was a flurry of activity, with far more Alleshi than usual milling about the rooms and outer courtyards. Everyone seemed in motion, even those who stood in small circles of hushed exchanges. In the Assembly Room, Council deliberations were only slightly more orderly.

Every day brought troubling news or unverified rumors that fed the pervasive sense of escalating disaster.

When a southeast pass guard returned to his post after the long winter, he reported finding the remains of recent camps in the foothills and near the summit, apparently indicating that the renegades weren't just a small band of Allemen acting alone. The guard found the tracks of as many as three score men and several dozen horses.

A runner reported that Eli and Tedrac had recruited a band of loyal Allemen. Eli and the others had set off in search of the renegades, while Tedrac embarked alone on some unspecified mission. They had armed themselves with rapid-fire rifles, almost identical to those the renegades had stolen, though they shouldn't have had access to such weaponry beyond the Alleshine storehouse.

Then, as soon as the passes cleared enough for unobstructed travel, Devra and Beatrice disappeared, apparently accompanied by some of their Allemen.

About a week after Caith's death, Rishana was on her way to the Communal Hall when she found a message waiting under her gatepost candle. She recognized the writing as Savah's, though it was unsigned. "Please come to my home this afternoon. It's important. The outer door will be closed. Come in anyway."

After all the years she had spent loving and trusting Savah, she no longer knew what she thought about Jared's Allesha. Had she ever truly known the woman behind the title? Rishana hesitated with her hand on Savah's doorknob. No, not Savah, she reminded herself — Peren. The knob turned easily, but of course it would. No one ever needed to lock their homes in The Valley. Would that change, too?

In the vestibule, Rishana heard animated voices. Peren, Le'a/Dara, Hester and Ayne were seated in the greeting room. As she entered, they stopped talking. What was Ayne doing here? Now the oldest of The Valley, Ayne had always been somewhat aloof from Rishana. The young Allesha knew the tall, elegant woman mostly from her constant presence in the Council.

"Rishana! You're just in time." Peren appeared glad to see her, as though nothing had changed between them.

Rishana accepted Peren's embrace, then sat in a bentwood chair that had been brought in from the kitchen. "In time for what?" she asked.

"Yes, Rishana, I'm sure you have many questions. Allow us to answer them one at a time, in our own way," Ayne said in that quiet, authoritative tone that she used to bring even the most unruly Council to order. "To answer your first question, this is a meeting to decide how to best respond to these threats to our Peace."

"The four of you, alone, outside of Council?"

"No, the five of us, dear." Peren seemed to think that including Rishana made it acceptable.

Ayne glanced at Peren only briefly, but it was enough for Rishana to realize Ayne considered herself in charge of this meeting. That Peren leaned back into the sofa cushions, almost as a retreat, seemed to indicate she agreed.

"Rishana, the Council is large and often unwieldy," Ayne explained. "They can spend many days deliberating, when immediate action is necessary. More importantly, they don't have key information which we don't dare give them. Isn't that true?"

Rishana wasn't about to answer Ayne until she could be certain how much the old woman knew, and if she could be trusted. Openly studying each Allesha, she tried to form a picture of their relationships and intentions.

Dara seemed almost relaxed, though that may have been a pose for Rishana's sake. Her limbs were too well arranged, her return gaze unexpressive.

Pushing a strand of hair back into her bun, Hester didn't hide her irritation, which seemed directed more at the other women than Rishana. But then, Hester was one who didn't easily tolerate delays in what she perceived as the proper order of things. What had the others done that she considered out of order? Or was it something they were about to do?

Peren was anxious, glancing often at Rishana, trying to restore the connection they once had. In her lap was an open journal, its pages yellow with age.

Ayne was the most difficult to read, but then Rishana hardly knew her. At first, she was a blank slate, sitting rigidly unreadable until she released her pose under Rishana's gaze. What Ayne allowed her to see was someone who was concerned, friendly and open.

The one thing that all four women exhibited was an apparent lack of fear. Despite all that was happening in their Valley, in this place and with this company, they felt safe and confident.

"What key information are you referring to, Ayne?" Rishana kept her tone even and noncommittal.

"For one thing, your boy, of course," Ayne responded.

"What about him, Ayne?"

"That he's Mwertik."

"Why do you say that?"

"Please, Rishana, don't banter with me. It's a waste of time."

"Then tell me what you want from me, and I will try to assist you."

"Rishana, you can be open with Ayne," Dara tried to reassure her. "She's one of us."

But too much about this meeting was unorthodox for Rishana to relax her guard. "Us?" she asked.

Dara gestured at the other women in the room. "We four — now five — who know the truth about your boy and have laid plans to use that truth to save our Peace."

"You mean use the boy." Rishana's words were clipped and sharp.

"Yes, of course," Ayne acknowledged. "As any Alleman is used. As we ourselves have devoted our lives to being useful for the sake of our Peace."

"It's not the same thing. He didn't have the chance to choose."

"And you did, Rishana?" Ayne asked.

"None of us was truly given a choice," Dara said, "Not an informed one."

"Rishana, you have been very naïve, and your naïvety has been useful to us. Now you must assume a new role in our plans," Ayne informed her.

Rishana felt buffeted from all sides by people she had once trusted. "What if I refuse the role you're offering?"

"It isn't an offer." Ayne said.

"Are you claiming I have no alternative but to blindly accept… whatever it is?"

"No," Dara said. "But to refuse would be against your nature."

"A nature we helped formed," Hester added, "which we know as well as our own."

"How dare you!" Rishana jumped up so quickly that she almost lost her balance. "I am not your puppet!"

"Rishana, sit down! Get control of yourself!" Ayne actually raised her voice.

"If you walk out of this room, you'll never know the truth." Peren was the one who spoke softly now. "Never again have this opportunity to learn it all."

Rishana hesitated. "Everything?"

"Everything you will need to know, which is more than almost anyone else." Ayne immediately resumed her cool, quiet way, perhaps as an example to Rishana of proper Alleshine discipline — or perhaps because the slight emotion she had displayed had itself been a mask, used for effect, then discarded.

"Consider Ayne's answer carefully, Rishana," Hester cautioned. "She could have lied or hedged, but she is being honest enough to say some things will still be withheld."

"You think that's good enough?"

"It's all we have to offer for now. Perhaps in the future, when your role again changes…" Ayne said.

"How can you sit there so calmly and inform me you plan to continue manipulating me?"

"Because it's the truth," Ayne responded.

"Just as we were all manipulated." Dara glanced at Ayne. "*Are* manipulated."

Clearly, Dara was referring to something specific, and it related to Ayne. "Tell me, Dara."

"Rishana, this isn't relevant to the reason for our meeting," Ayne insisted.

"Ayne, if you want me to stay and listen, and it appears it's important to you that I do, then it's on condition that Dara tells me what she meant. If I am to trust you, I need to know the truth."

Ayne stared at Rishana for several breaths, but Rishana didn't flinch under the older woman's scrutiny. Finally, Ayne nodded to Dara. Rishana pulled the chair slightly away from the others before sitting down.

"Rishana, you know I selected you as my successor. In a similar way, Ayne selected me. But what you don't know is that it's about more than learning how to handle problem boys. The strength of will and personality that makes us equal to that task is also what allows us to become more than we seem. Of course, I didn't know that when Ayne chose me, just as you were kept in ignorance."

Hester scowled. "But Rishana was kept in the dark much longer."

"For her own protection," Peren responded to Hester, almost too quickly, as though this were an old argument.

"My protection! To keep me ignorant?"

"To allow you to remain innocent for a while longer," Peren explained. "And to keep you from being a target for those who would try to stop us."

"Until you were fully trained, anyone could have read you and known the truth," Dara added.

"And until we could be sure of you, we didn't dare expose ourselves to you," Ayne asserted.

"Sure of me?" Rishana turned to her husband's Allesha, the woman who had been her friend and confidante her entire adult life. "Peren, you weren't sure of me?"

But it was Ayne who responded. "You are Jared's widow. You, more than any of us, have every reason to despise the Mwertik."

"But you know me, Peren, better than almost anyone."

"That is why we couldn't be certain that Peren's judgment of you wasn't tainted," Ayne answered while Peren remained silent.

Rishana refused to allow her anger to divert her from extracting whatever she could from these women. "Dara, please continue. You say you were kept in ignorance, but not as long as I was. What did they withhold from you? Did you also have a boy who wasn't what he appeared?"

"No," Dara replied. "Ayne never told me about the Guardians until she was sure that her training of me had taken effect. Only when she was certain that I'd never betray them, and that I'd be a suitable candidate to join them, did she even hint at their existence."

"Who or what are the Guardians?"

Dara glanced at Ayne as though she were asking permission to answer. Instead, Ayne nodded to Peren, who picked up the journal in her lap and handed it to Rishana. "This will provide you with some answers, dear. Please be careful with it. It's very old, very brittle — and very dangerous."

Rishana took the journal from Peren and gently leafed through it, fearful that the dry, yellow pages would disintegrate at her touch. Though the ink was faded, the handwriting was neat and round. "What is it?"

"Veitas's Dialogues, compiled by Faen," Peren explained. "We are the only ones alive who have read it."

"Veitas? I've never heard of her."

"Few have, and that's one of our responsibilities as Guardians, to assure that she remains unknown. But over four hundred years ago, she was a great teacher and the original framer of our Peace."

"I thought it was Alleen."

"No. Alleen taught people to dream of peace, but it took several generations to take root. And it happened only after some of the bloodiest wars recorded."

"Why all the secrecy? What makes this book so dangerous?"

Peren paused before answering. "Among its many dangerous ideas is the formation of the Guardians, an inner circle of Alleshi who are the true architects of our Peace."

Rishana felt a chill against her back, though her skin was hot.

"The hidden authority," Ayne added. "We oversee the Peace by influencing the actions of others according to the principles laid out by Veitas."

Rishana reminded herself to move slowly, concentrate on the details. Closing the journal, she placed it on her lap and crossed her hands over it "What are these 'principles' that give you the right to subvert the very essence of our Peace?"

"Not subvert it, dear. Protect it and ensure that it continues," Peren countered.

Rishana's jaw ached with the effort of keeping her rage in check. "With no respect for the right of councils and consensus."

"What we do is what allows our Council to be the voice of consensus and authority it must be," Hester insisted.

"I understand how difficult it is for you to accept this right now," Dara said. "I once sat in that seat, just as angry and astounded as you are. We all did."

"You have three choices at present, Rishana." Hester counted them off on her fingers. "You can sit there quietly, seething at us for all that we have done to you. You can bolt out that door and never know the truth. Or you can open that book and read."

"You have in your possession a book that few know exist, and even fewer have ever seen," Peren said. "We could go in circles all day with questions, accusations and justifications. Instead, I suggest you go into my second bedroom and read the Dialogues, which hold so many of your answers."

"And the four of you will wait out here while I read?"

"We have other business that will keep us occupied." Ayne dismissed her with a wave of her hand.

"Perhaps I should stay and hear…"

"After you read the journal." Peren gestured toward the bedroom door, then smiled, and Rishana thought she saw her old familiar friend re-emerge for a brief moment.

Chapter 78

Rishana closed the bedroom door behind her and leaned back against it, taking comfort in the solidity of the barrier between her and the four Alleshi beyond.

Here, in this room, Jared had once spent a Season as a Blessed Boy. He had slept in that narrow bed, his feet probably sticking out from the sheets as they always did. In that armchair, he had read some of the books lining these walls, or gazed out the window, dreaming, thinking, planning. And through that door, he had entered Peren/Savah's inner room, becoming the man, the Alleman, she had loved so completely.

She had come here, herself, as a widow, to mourn with Savah, sleeping in the same bed Jared had once known, though visitors from the outside usually stayed in one of the Battai's inns. At the time, she hadn't thought of it as breaking with tradition so much as two women needing to comfort each other. Rishana now wondered if that had been the beginning. Had it been her own idea, after all, to return to The Valley two years later to become an Allesha, or had Savah influenced her decision even then, that spring they had mourned Jared together?

Rishana curled up in the oversized armchair. The book was leather-bound and small enough to fit into a large pocket. Stained and worn, the cover was mottled, with leather missing in places. The paper was foxed and brittle. The opening page said only *Veitas's Dialogues, told to Faen by Aefna.*

Where should she begin? Reading the entire volume would take the rest of the afternoon and late into the night. But to read only those sections marked with leather strips would be to allow them to dictate what she learned from this book. Still, it would be a good place to start. She turned to the first marked section.

Veitas did not meet with us for several days after receiving news of the battle of Ronefield. She sequestered herself behind her closed door; we thought it was to grieve, and perhaps that was part of it. But when she came out, she appeared neither sad nor defeated.

And Veitas said, "Alleen's dream is collapsing. Her cancer of hope

421

has spread, but what good is it? As long as our world is organized for the purpose of war, war will be inevitable."

Aefna asked, "How is society organized for war?"

And Veitas said, "The prime purpose of every town and city is to support the great armies. With warfare, they acquire land and goods, attempt to secure their borders and consolidate power in preparation for the next war. In exchange, the people contribute the products of their hands and fields to the upkeep of the armies. How could they not, when the army exists to protect them? Are the soldiers not their sons, brothers, husbands and fathers? Should a farmer or smith refuse, the army takes by force what is not given freely."

Aefna asked, "Why does that make war inevitable?"

And Veitas said, "Cities exist to support the armies. But the demands of large armies often outstrip the ability of the cities to support them. So they must forage farther and farther afield. Should a city be prosperous, easily able to meet the needs of their army, what man can sit still and not do the task for which he was trained? Armies exist to fight, and so they fight. Even a city that lacks its own army soon may find itself garrisoning and provisioning one."

Aefna asked, "How should society be organized?"

And Veitas said, "We must abandon the cities and start with the towns and villages, seeding them not only with the dream of peace, but the tools to accomplish it. Help each develop a specialty it can trade with others. Have no single town or village able to stand on its own without raw materials or products from its neighbors. When trade and not war is the basis of prosperity, war becomes a disruption to profit. Armies become inconvenient drains, unnecessary and impractical."

Aefna asked, "And you believe we can change the entire structure of society around us?"

And Veitas said, "I cannot see the whole world... only as far as the horizon. But if you walk a day, can you not see farther? We must start with the three closest towns, then the next three and the next, building an ever-expanding circle of peace around our valley. Each generation that follows us will create a wider horizon."

Aefna asked, "But won't we still need to defend those who live at the borderline between our circle of peace and the world of wars?

And Veitas said, "We must find some way to defend them that doesn't require large armies."

Rishana was surprised that the entry ended so abruptly. But it certainly didn't contain anything she would consider dangerous. She turned to the next marked section.

The converging armies were coming closer every day. Runners reported about 12,000 from the west, another 15,000 from the northeast and a third army of 20,000 from the south.

Rishana stopped and reread that last sentence several times, making sure she hadn't seen the wrong number of zeroes. Never in her life had she heard of such large groups of people, such enormous armies. How could they move, stay supplied, coordinate maneuvers? No wonder Veitas talked about how their world had to be organized to support such vast fighting forces.

Runners reported about 12,000 from the west, another 15,000 from the northeast and a third army of 20,000 from the south. Though they came out of hate for us, what need did they have for so many against a few score women? No, we were merely the rallying cry for massive armies destined to fight and destroy each other. When they finally clashed, we would be among the spoils.

Men who believed in our vision of a world without armies came from nearby cities, towns and villages to protect us, but Veitas sent them away, not wanting to be the cause of their deaths. Then Veitas called us together.

And Veitas said, "The armies will soon overrun us. Those of you who wish to flee to safety should leave tonight, while there is yet time."

Aefna asked, "Will you come with us?"

And Veitas said, "I will stay, because if I run, there will never again be any place where armies don't rule."

Aefna asked, "But how can you still hope to change the world? They will kill you."

And Veitas said, "Perhaps. They certainly hate us enough. Our ideas threaten their very existence. But if I don't resist, if I survive, I may yet find a way."

Aefna asked, "May we stay with you?"

And Veitas said, "If you do, you must realize you cannot fight them. You must allow them to do whatever they wish. You will watch them as they destroy everything we have and are, and you will do nothing. Those of you who are beautiful will survive because of your beauty, and the soldiers will use you until that, too, is destroyed. And still you will do nothing. If you stay, it must be with the understanding that you will obey me in this and in everything I ask."

Of all the women of the valley, only a handful escaped into the night. All the others stayed with Veitas. When the armies clashed, blood ran like streams down our mountains, pooling in our fields. The men who died were among the luckier ones, for they did not linger screaming to the sky, hacked into pieces that no healer would ever be able to build back into living creatures. When it was over, we were given the bodies of our sisters who had run but had failed to escape, and we buried them far from the mass graves of the armies.

Rishana laid the book on the table, unable to continue reading. In her mind, she saw this beautiful valley overrun with armies so massive they would have covered the mountains and spread out onto the fertile plains of her home beyond. Where now there were gardens and paths, there had once been swords clashing, body parts strewn. She imagined the mud she had walked through to get here today, and pictured it made of blood rather than melted snow. The dead and dying everywhere.

Was that what those four out in the greeting room wanted her to see — the ghastly vulnerability of The Valley? No, there must be more to it. She opened the book to the next marked section.

The southern army had defeated both the northern and northeast-ern forces by first standing away from the battle, so the two might exhaust each other. Soon, the generals of the south came to divide the spoils. Aefna and some of the younger women were lucky, taken as they were by officers for their own tents. Veitas and the others were given to the rabble. The oldest women were killed; others died of their shame or wounds. But Veitas survived, her spirit never diminished. Even through the rapes and torture, and the terror of watching her followers dwindle to less than a score of broken women, she lived and watched and learned.

And Veitas said, "If we are to be sex slaves, then sex shall be our tool and our weapon. And we will wield it with all the grace, beauty, sensuality and knowledge we can muster. At no time are your men to know it is a mask you wear. They must believe you are truly enamored of them, would do anything to please them, and while you are with them, you will believe it yourself. For how else are you to abide the ordeal?"

Aefna asked, "How can sex be a weapon?"

And Veitas said, "By ensnaring the men, we will have power and influence over them. Though we will be their slaves, unable to leave or refuse them, they will be ours, unable to resist or hide from us. Enslave the enslavers; find their vulnerabilities and use them. Then we will strike."

The next section was only a few pages further.

The valley couldn't support the entire army of the south through the winter. Once their battle lust was spent and the spoils divided, the bulk of the army left the valley to be quartered closer to the coastline where food and water were plentiful.

Only Gerone, Aric and his brother Armon, the three commanding generals of the south, remained with a few thousand of their personal forces, as much to enjoy the comforts of the valley through the winter as to develop their strategies for the spring campaigns. Being from the south, they didn't realize that the mountains that protect us from the fiercest of the winter winds would also seal them in with us, making communication with their armies impossible. Yet the generals were confident that the harsh discipline of their captains and commanders would keep the troops in line. Winter, after all, would last only a few months.

And Veitas said, "As they did to the armies from the north and northeast, we shall do to them. Allow the three generals to fight our battle by destroying one another. Aefna, Yva and Olane, you three are the favored of Armon, Aric and Gerone, so all depends on you. Each of you must ask your general to tell you of his adventures, then display wonder at his brilliance and bravery. Question aloud why an army needs three commanders when a body requires only one head.

"Yva, prepare to avenge yourself on Armon. But first, we must build the flames of hatred between the brothers and Gerone. Aefna, whisper to Aric of Gerone's glances at you and his envy of all that Aric and Armon possess. Warn Aric out of love for him, so he knows that it is your concern for his well-being and your awe of his might that prompts you. You must be delicate with your words, as you are with your body, seducing him to slowly learn to fear and hate Gerone. When Yva finally strikes Armon, you, Olane, must bear witness to Gerone's treachery. Aric and Gerone will destroy each other, and we shall be free of all of them."

Aefna asked, "But these are only the generals. What of the army, which will return in the spring?"

And Veitas said, "What is the infighting of their leaders to the plain soldier? Once they discover the generals are destroyed, the troops will rebel against all who are above them, while the captains and commanders will vie against one another to take command. Amidst the chaos and broken discipline, they will be unprepared for the springtime battles their enemies are plotting even now."

As Veitas planned, so it happened. We whispered to our generals in the night, until they could barely sit in the same room without screaming and threatening one another. Then, one night, before the mountain pass winter snows melted, Yva struck, stabbing Armon in the back, piercing his heart with Gerone's jeweled knife which Olane had stolen. Yva smeared herself with blood and, running to Aric, cried out for vengeance against Gerone. Aric fell on Gerone, while the soldiers around them rioted, some out of loyalty, others to grab what they could, most because the smell of blood incited them.

We hid in our cellars for three days, while the fighting raged around us. On the fourth day, we came out and found no living man left in the valley. It was a gruesome task burying the many bodies and cleansing our land, but it was ours once more.

Only one more leather strip remained, at the very end of the journal.

For many years, Veitas led and taught us. Slowly, we rebuilt our valley, gathering around us a small circle of communities that chose peace over war, trade over battles. It was a fragile construct, but strengthened a bit more with each new village.

Veitas lived a long life, much longer than most, and she saw many of her teachings come to fruition. Finally, she could fight no longer, and she called only a few of us to her deathbed.

And Veitas said, "Soon I will die, my daughters. But because of you, my dream and that of Alleen will live on. Our valley is safe, our people content and well governed, for they govern themselves through consensus. It is a good life we have created. But I am afraid for you and for those who will come after."

Aefna asked, "What is it that frightens you, Veitas?"

And Veitas said, "The Circle of Peace is so very narrow. Even if it covered the earth, terror abides in humankind. We must insure that no army ever again comes to our valley, or anywhere within our Circle of Peace. Never again can we allow our people to become enslaved or enslavers. You must promise me, you five alone, to protect our Peace and our people. But they must never know."

Aefna asked, "Why must our people never know? Would you have them forget what it was like before our Peace came?"

And Veitas said, "No, they must never forget the times before. But should it come to pass that you must commit distasteful acts for the sake of our Peace, I would not have others share the guilt or the responsibility. You will guard our Peace, and like guards in war, you must move silently, doing whatever is necessary to ensure that our people never again submit to the terror we once knew. Do you understand and agree?"

And Aefna said "We shall guard your Peace, Veitas. Now, and forevermore."

Veitas never spoke again.

As Rishana turned that last page, a small folded piece of paper dropped into her lap, much whiter than the yellowed pages of the book — covered with Jared's handwriting. Almost afraid to find what it contained, she slowly unfolded the paper and read it.

Dear S,

I leave tomorrow on a mission, which may be my last. Jinet sleeps peacefully in our bed, and as I look over at her, I wish I could explain to her why it is so important that I risk my life and our happiness. She thinks I go to hunt a white antelope for our son's betrothal feast. Perhaps, if I am successful, I will be able to bring one back with me, just to please her.

I believe this will be the most important mission of my life, for I might yet be able to avert the coming war. You'll understand when you receive my report, which I sent through our usual secure couriers. But that will take longer than a simple letter. So I send this to apologize for not informing you about this opportunity and awaiting your approval. I cannot delay, nor would I be willing to not go, even if you asked me.

If this meeting goes well, I will come to The Valley immediately after my son's betrothal to give you a full report. If it doesn't, then I ask you to help Jinet understand. My life with her is so very precious, but what is one life when the future of our Peace is at stake? I must make this rendezvous, even if I never come back from it.

Yours, J.

She had thought she'd spent all her tears on Jared's death, that her mourning had been over for years. But when she pictured Jared sitting at his desk writing this letter, while she had slept blissfully unaware, new tears streamed unchecked. One drop fell on the journal, and for that she was sorry, for it was so very old and fragile. She folded the letter, put it back into the book, and went out to confront the Guardians.

Chapter 79

When Rishana returned to the greeting room, she sat in the same bentwood chair. She looked at each Allesha, her eyes finally falling on Savah/Peren. "What was Jared's last mission? Who was he meeting?"

Peren sighed deeply. "We never found out."

"But his report, the one he sent you by courier…"

"Never arrived."

Rishana was about to challenge Peren's denial, then realized that wasn't the point. "Who were the couriers he would have used?"

"Fellow Allemen." Peren's voice was hollow. "It was the beginning. To discover that an Alleman might not be trustworthy…"

"Did no one know Jared's plans? What about Eli?"

"No, Jin… Rishana, no one."

That one slip, almost calling her by the name of her former life, their former relationship, convinced Rishana that Peren was telling her the truth and that the old Allesha was unnerved by it.

"You and your accursed secrecy." With a sweep of her hand, Rishana included all four in her condemnation. "If you hadn't built up so many layers of intrigue, if Jared had told his plans to someone, anyone…"

"Yes." Ayne wielded her agreement like a wedge, creating an opening through which she could force the conversation's direction. "But whom could he trust?"

"The two people he should have trusted above all else, you had taught him to doubt. His wife and son."

"No, Rishana, Jared never doubted you," Peren protested. "He needed to protect you, not involve you."

"Not involve me in his choices and his risks? I was his wife, his partner. You take your secrecy too far, cutting yourself off from the people you need most."

Hester smiled, only a small upturning of her lips, though it seemed sincere. "Perhaps that's why we need you, to remind us."

"No, you need me because my boy is the key."

"That's an important part of it, but who do you think selected you for the boy?" Dara asked.

"I want to be sure I understand clearly what you are asking: you want me to become a Guardian?"

"Yes." Ayne and Peren answered at the same time, but quite differently. Peren with all the warmth she could put into her posture and voice; Ayne a void with all emotion tightly withheld.

"What if I refuse?"

"Then everything will return to the way it was before, with you being kept in ignorance of the futures planned for your boy and son." What was it about Ayne's eyes that bothered Rishana so deeply?

"You would have little influence over that future," Peren added. "And would never know what you could have achieved or helped to avert."

"How do you know that I won't betray you?"

"You'd do nothing that might endanger your First Boy." Ayne's voice held only the slightest tinge of threat. "Any betrayal of us would also be a betrayal of him, exposing him to his enemies before he — and we — are ready."

Rishana opened "Veitas Dialogues" to Jared's letter. "You said we're the only ones alive who have read this book. Did Jared?"

Peren stared at the letter. "No, but he knew some of what it contained."

"And Caith?"

"Yes, she had read it," Peren replied.

"Was she a Guardian?"

"No," Ayne said. "She chose to not join when our predecessors asked her, and I believe she chose wisely. Caith was unique, a great teacher and remarkable observer, but she had her quirks. However, she did report to us from time to time."

"If she had reported more often, she might still be alive." Hester's words were clipped, her tone prickly. Rishana couldn't tell if it were Caith's death that Hester resented or Caith's exclusion of them.

"Yet you would cut me out should I refuse."

"You're not Caith; the role you're destined for is not as a mere observer," Peren said.

"Destined, or designed by you?"

"Some of both," Dara admitted. "But only in the same manner that you and I worked with the boy until his true nature could be revealed and strengthened. Rishana, you were the right Allesha for him, and you are the best candidate for a Guardian we've seen in a long time."

"Are there others?"

"No, only us." Hester answered, thinking Rishana was referring to

Guardians.

While Ayne said, "None we have invited to join us," assuming Rishana was asking about candidates.

"If the Guardians have been able to remain hidden, how do you know The Valley doesn't have other secret circles that influence and manipulate the Council?"

"Alliances will inevitably form from loyalties and friendships, cliques that anyone can see." Ayne dismissed the idea, but with a hard edge that shielded her true thoughts.

"However, we didn't see the connections between Kiv, Elnor, Devra and Beatrice. Perhaps there are others." Was Hester contradicting Ayne, or being more forthcoming?

"That's the kind of information Caith was so adept at uncovering." Dara stared off into her memories. "Which may be why she was killed."

Rishana felt chilled by Dara's accusation and thought back on what she had just read. "Have the Guardians ever used assassination?"

"Not in recent times," Hester answered.

But Peren amended it. "Not that we know."

"Would you?"

"Rishana, you've helped inventory the storehouse armory; you know all that it holds. Just because we have so many weapons doesn't mean we plan to use them. Still, we have them, and we will use them if they are ever needed," Ayne said. "We Guardians have our own tools, which we will implement if our Peace is threatened — including assassination."

"However," Hester said, "we have the benefit of the experience of generations of Guardians who developed other, more effective, less conspicuous methods which create fewer problems."

"Still, to be a Guardian is to accept the fact that someday you might have to order an assassination, reluctantly — and only after trying everything else — but resolutely." Something about the way Ayne's hands curled tightly in her lap made Rishana wonder if the old woman were speaking from personal experience.

"I don't believe I could do that."

"Not even to save your Winter Boy... or your son?" Hester asked. "Or, if one death could avert a war?"

"Do you think that's what Jared was doing?"

"We can only guess, but it doesn't seem likely," Ayne said.

Rishana remembered Eli's eyes when he confessed he had killed. "Was Jared an assassin?" she asked.

Peren paled at the suggestion. "No, never!"

"But he had killed." Saying it, Rishana knew it was true.

"Three times," Peren admitted. "Once when he was ambushed, another when Mistral was about to be attacked."

"And the third time?"

"That's a long story." Again, Ayne was dismissive, blocking the path of conversation.

So she hadn't been shown all of Jared's journals. "In other words, it's another of your secrets."

"One you may eventually know, but not today," Ayne answered.

Rishana chose not to argue the issue; she had more immediate puzzles to unravel. "Dara, you said that being one who trained problem boys made you suitable for the Guardians, but Hester and Peren didn't specialize in problem boys."

"They were needed for other qualities. Hester for her precise, orderly thinking. Peren for her scholarship and deep understanding of our history."

"As far as we know, one of the Guardians has always been a librarian," Ayne added. "It helps us control who has access to the true histories."

"One thing I don't understand. You know I abhor these intrigues, that I don't believe I could order an assassination. Yet you want me to join you as a Guardian. Is it that you believe you can change my mind?"

"Partially, but perhaps you'll also change us."

"Ayne, you really are a master at this, aren't you?" Rishana said bitterly.

"Yes, she is," Hester agreed. "But that doesn't change the fact that you have the strength of will and intellect to influence us. To become a Guardian is to be one who affects others, including other Guardians."

"If I agree, what is the new role you would have me assume?"

"To start, we'll need you to work more closely with us, to coordinate your boy's future," Dara replied.

"Tell me your plans."

"Are you agreeing to join us? Or are you still asking questions?" Ayne asked.

Rishana studied each of the Guardians: Hester, always the Healer, never satisfied with easy answers. Dara, the sculptor of clay and people, who wielded her chisel so delicately that Rishana could only guess at all that Dara had done to her. Peren, the scholar, who had always seemed so nurturing and knowledgeable. And Ayne, who led them with an iron will and unreadable mask. Then she glanced at Jared's letter, its words already seared into her memory. "Both," she answered. "I will join you and honor your secrecy, but I must have answers."

"And we must have your questions," Ayne said, the first hint of a smile teasing at the corners of her mouth, though that, too, was undoubtedly purposeful.

Chapter 80

Tayar was late coming home, so Dov prepared their supper alone. Tomorrow, the End of Season Service Days would begin, and he wanted to make the evening a celebration. Yet, a part of him felt there was nothing to celebrate.

While his Season still had some weeks to go, after tonight, it would no longer be focused only on the two of them. He'd be spending his days with other boys who were about to become his fellow Allemen, under the guidance of other Alleshi and Allemen. And Tayar would be elsewhere, doing whatever Alleshi do when they aren't with their boys —perhaps preparing for her next Season, interviewing boys to choose the one she would Bless.

Dov didn't savor the idea of someone else here in the kitchen cooking with her, in the greeting room reading and talking, or in the inner room touching her. But more disturbing was the idea that this time of wonder and discovery, this Season of love and friendship, would soon be ended. Tayar and Dov would be no more, only private names they'd remember as they moved away from each other, to different lives.

But he liked being Tayar's Dov, the man he had become with her. Seeing himself through her eyes, he was smart, caring, and so very alive. Who would he be without Tayar?

And what of his Allesha? He wanted desperately to support her, care for her, protect her. What did it matter that she wouldn't be Tayar after he left The Valley? She'd still be a woman he loved, who had helped him become the self he had always been, beneath his bluster and fear.

Dov basted the fruited roast, put the potatoes into the oven, and sliced the bread to prepare garlic toast. If Tayar didn't come home soon, he'd have to do something to keep the meal from being ruined. What was keeping her? Was there yet another crisis? So many things seemed to be happening all at once, but they knew little of how events were unfolding beyond The Valley. Could the Peace really collapse?

How thrilling the tales of the Before Times had once seemed to him. But never in any of his childish musings did he really want their world to return to chaos and wars. Whatever came to pass, he was determined to do everything in his power to protect the Peace. Perhaps it was lucky, after all, that Pa had stolen a Mwertik boy. Dov knew he was only one man, but maybe, just maybe, he could do something to help, to save the Peace, to protect Tayar and Ma — and Lilla.

Poor, sweet Lilla. While he still loved her, he had difficulty picturing her. He remembered pieces of the girl, flashes of moments shared. The gesture of her hand when she pushed her long black hair away from her face, the flicker of an eyelid, the shape of her lips. But he couldn't seem to put them together into a solid, real woman. Often, he'd catch himself thinking of her as a child, one who needed guidance and protection. That was unfair of him. No doubt she had grown during their time apart. Even before, she'd had a mind of her own, a spirit not easily bridled. It was one of the things that had attracted him to her in the first place. That, and the sound of her laughter.

Lilla had every reason to believe he was coming back to marry her, to raise children and grow old together. What would she do when she discovered he'd be turning his back on the future they'd planned to share? If not for Lilla, he never would have willingly come to The Valley. Now, because of The Valley, he could never return to Lilla.

Dov heard the outer door close, so he went into the greeting room to welcome Tayar home. As she entered, he wrapped his arms around her, picked her up and twirled her before she had time to put on her slippers. It was something he had planned as a way to start their evening with joy and fun, but the feel of it wasn't what he had expected. Not that she didn't giggle with surprise. Not that the heft and smell of her wasn't a pleasure. But, still… He set his Allesha down onto her feet, smoothed her ruffled hair, and studied her face.

"What's wrong, Dov?"

"I was about to ask you the same thing."

She didn't respond immediately. Maybe she was deciding how to start, or how much she wanted to tell him. "I've had quite an afternoon, and I'm exhausted and feeling a little sorry for myself," she said.

"Me, too. I mean, the feeling sorry for myself. We're so close to the end of this Season. I should be happy, but I'm sad. So I succumbed to self-pity, dressing it up in worry for the people I love."

"That doesn't make the worry less valid." She squeezed his hand. "Whatever you're cooking smells wonderful. Let's wash up for supper, and meet in the kitchen. I'm famished, for more than food." She brushed her lips against his, then pulled away as though she thought better of it. "We've a lot to talk about."

Tayar came into the kitchen just as Dov was placing a basket of hot garlic toast on the table. Wearing the same dress as on their first night, with its cinched waist, multitude of buttons and wide playful skirt, she gave him one of her big, brightening smiles. Dov realized it wasn't really a pose — just Tayar choosing to express that aspect of her feelings. He pulled out a chair. "Dinner's almost ready. Please sit and talk to me."

With a nod, she sat, draping her skirt around her crossed legs. "What a nice surprise, having you take care of dinner."

Dov took the roasting pan out of the oven, then lifted the meat onto the cutting board. "Well, it's our last night, sort of. Tomorrow will be different, and I wanted to give you — give us — something we'd remember."

"I'm glad you understand, Dov, that it is truly our last night."

"Oh?" He stopped carving, to give her his full attention. "I think you're implying something else, aren't you?"

"The inner room has no more lessons for you that you couldn't learn in other ways."

He hid his disappointment by concentrating on slicing the roast. "But it was more than lessons."

"Was it, Dov?"

Dov paused in mid-cut, but only for a few moments. "No, I guess not. At least, it shouldn't be. It would complicate things terribly if it were more, wouldn't it?"

"I knew you'd understand. You will be a fine Alleman."

He filled two plates with generous servings of food and brought them to the table.

"Mmm. It looks as delicious as it smells. Thank you."

For a while, they ate in silence, sharing the sensual delight of each morsel. The crisp, cool salad. The resistance of the potato's salty surface yielding to a steaming, soft core. The crunch and bite of the garlic toast. And the chewy, pungent meat. Only after she had tasted each item on her plate, giving herself fully to the individual textures and flavors, did Tayar break the silence.

"Have you given any thought to the name you will take as an Alleman?"

He nodded while swallowing a bite of toast. "I tried out a bunch of names, but in the end, I decided Ryl is best. It's something of the Birani that I can take with me when I leave everything else behind. Someday, I may have to take a Mwertik name, but I don't know any, and I don't feel that one would fit me right now, even if I did know their language. So, for now, I will be Ryl."

"Would you be surprised to know that most Allemen choose to take the names they had before they came to our Valley? However, between us, I will call you Dov, for as long as we live."

As long as they lived. He considered the phrase, trying it on to see how it felt. It would be a long time, much longer than a single Season — if they were lucky. "It's difficult, thinking about what it will be like after this Season. But what's really hard to understand is how natural it is for me to contemplate life without you. My heart should be fighting it more."

"Your heart is being wise, helping both of us make the transition we must."

Yes, he realized, *the transition has already begun.*

"Tell me about your day. What kept you so long?"

Tayar fully chewed and swallowed the piece of meat in her mouth before replying. "I was with Le'a, Jared's Allesha, and the Healer Allesha you met in the storehouse."

"The Alleshi of my pa's Triad?" He nodded. "Yes, of course. What did you learn from them?"

"We discussed your future and their plans for you. And we were correct; you will have your apprenticeship with Mistral, though Tedrac will be working with you, too. But it won't be a traditional apprenticeship, because the crisis is here, and we don't have two years."

"Will I have a Triad?"

"Yes. The other boys haven't yet been selected, but several candidates are being considered."

"May I know which ones?"

"I think it would be better to let it unfold naturally during the Service Days. If you knew which boys were being considered, you might react differently to them, changing the value of the interaction and observations."

"How will they be chosen?"

"Every Triad is different, but each Alleman must complement the other two in skills, expertise and personality. For instance, in your father's Triad, Mistral is the lone adventurer who can survive by his wits in exotic, dangerous situations. Tedrac is a quiet man, a respected scholar who often gets lost in his books, but his analyses and strategies are brilliant, and his intuitive leaps sometimes groundbreaking. Jared was the diplomat who could get along with just about anyone. He was the anchor that kept his Triad on track."

"With him gone, how are the other two kept anchored?"

"To a small extent, Jared's son, Eli, has assumed that role."

"But your son has his own Triad."

"And that complicates matters, especially for Eli, because the two Triads' loyalties have different priorities."

"So my Triad will be chosen to complement who I am."

"And what you must achieve. In some ways, your skills and personality are similar to Mistral's, but your Triad will need to be structured differently, because the situation you face is unique."

Taking another forkful of salad, Dov pictured the other boys at the Battai's. Who among them would be willing to be bonded to a Mwertik? "If it won't be a traditional apprenticeship, and you say I won't have the full two years, what about our training? I know enough to know how much I don't yet know."

"Mistral and Tedrac will give you whatever you need. You'll be going to a secret camp they've set up on the western border, where the Mwertik raids started. You need to learn the terrain, languages, cultures and environs. It's the best way to give you the training you require within the little time we have."

"Will Tedrac be there, too?"

"Periodically." Tayar used her napkin to blot some gravy from her lips. "Dov, you have to understand about Tedrac. It's true that he seldom leaves the comfort of his library. But don't be misled by his soft voice and appearance. His mind is as sharp as the best knife you could ever wield. What he has to teach you could become your most valuable safeguards."

"So we'll sit on the western border…" Bit by bit, Dov was piecing together what his future would hold, but there were still too many gaps.

"Not quite. You and Mistral will venture often into Mwertik territory, more and more as your training progresses. But Tedrac and your Triats will not follow."

"Then what?"

"Yes, that is the weak part of the plan. Or, maybe, you and I haven't learned enough of the details."

"When you think about it, Tayar, a lot will depend on what Pa and I discover on our scouting forays."

"True, though I've a feeling Mistral knows more than we realize. We can ask him tomorrow."

"Pa? Here? I thought he wasn't coming until after the season ended."

"Surely you knew that some Allemen are always involved in the Service Days."

Pa was here in The Valley, probably at the Battai's inn, while they sat calmly eating, trying to figure out what he already knew. Dov looked inside himself, wondering what he felt about seeing Mistral, the man he'd always thought of as his father. For so many years, they'd been at odds, fighting over the smallest things, silent over the essentials. "I need to talk with him right away."

Dov started to get up, but Tayar reached across the table and put her hand over his, fastening him in place with one gentle touch. "Tonight is ours, Dov. Tomorrow will be soon enough."

Dov stared at Tayar, his beautiful Allesha, but all he could think of were the questions he had for Mistral. "When?"

"Probably after the first assembly, before the work teams disperse."

"Will you be there?"

She withdrew her hand. "For the first assembly, definitely. From time to time, I will attend your meetings or observe your work teams. We'll still have our evening meals together."

"And when I meet with Pa?"

"No. You won't need me there."

Dov leaned forward, his forearms on the table, watching Tayar, trying to decipher what she was avoiding saying. "You'll be meeting him on your own. Will you tell me what you learn from him?"

"Probably, but until I know what it is, how can I say?"

"It's like what you were saying about Eli now being involved in two Triads, isn't it? Conflicting loyalties. You're more than Tayar. You're an Allesha whose other names I may never know, whose loyalty to me I must trust, even when you hide behind your mask."

"I would never withhold information from you that you might need."

"Not intentionally. But I've also learned that the Alleshi make mistakes, as do Allemen."

"Yes."

"So, we'll just have to trust that we'll each do our best, and hopefully, when we work together, we'll offset each other's weaknesses, complement each other's strengths."

"Yes."

"And that's why I'll have a Triad, even though I'll be going off alone much of the time."

"Yes. A fine Alleman, indeed. Dov, I am quite proud of you."

Chapter 81

Tayar's meditations before entering the inner room normally involved opening her heart and mind. Tonight, she needed also to prepare herself for a closing, a walling away of any feelings that didn't further her Winter Boy's needs as an Alleman. And it mustn't be merely a mask. After tonight, she could never again allow herself to ache for his touch, for the intimacy that had indelibly etched him into her thoughts and body.

With Jared, it had been different; death was an undeniable barrier. Dov would continue to live, without her, but connected to her. And she was supposed to move on, to other boys who would burrow into her soul, Season after Season, then leave her.

Caith had tried to caution her. Eli, too, though his warnings were different. Being an Allesha meant being fully a woman, responding with all that she was to everyone and everything she encountered, especially her boys. But being an Allesha also meant never allowing the woman in her to respond so completely that she would ever be less than an Allesha. In the end, she was truly only her title, moving through the lives of others whose naming of her would temporarily lift her out of the role, so she might become a flesh-and-blood woman once more.

This was the life she had chosen. Eli was right. Even if she did decide to leave The Valley, she'd never leave this one truth behind. She was no longer Jinet. After tonight, she would no longer be Tayar. But neither was she only Rishana. She was an Every Woman. Not just the symbol of every woman within the world, but every woman within herself.

For the first and last time this Season, when she entered the inner room, she would discard all those others and simply be herself — a woman with a man. Then she would lock Tayar away, burying her amongst other sweet memories.

She sat in her armchair with her eyes closed, listening to her heartbeat until it became calm and slow once more. Then she removed her clothes, extinguished the lights and went into the inner room.

Tayar stood in the doorway, at the threshold between her airy bedroom and the moist warmth of the inner room. At first, all was pitch dark. Then a spark flared, as Dov lit an oil lamp near his bedroom and carried it forward toward the pool. Patterns and shapes danced about the inner room, molded by the lamp's flickering light and the shadows it cast, so that, with every step, he redefined the contours of the room. He bent to place the lamp on the carpet near the edge of the stone floor, then slipped into the pool, creating small lapping shadows in the water.

This room, the center and heart of her home, was as familiar to Tayar as her own hand. Yet Dov had transformed it simply by walking through it. Tonight, it felt deeper, quieter, a welcoming darkness filled with subtle colors, as Alleen's desert might have been on a new-moon night. Tayar shifted her weight from one foot to the other, which must have changed the nature of reflected shadows, because Dov now looked directly at her.

"Please join me." His voice was a warm invitation, with no prodding or pleading.

As Tayar stepped into the pool, he filled his hands with oil. She glided toward him, aware of the pressure of the water against her flesh as something that linked rather than separated them.

Reaching out to touch her, he held her at arm's length, with his oiled hands on her shoulders, so he could look at her, memorizing every small detail of her body and face. She, too, studied the man before her, knowing that this would be the last time they would see each other like this. Not just naked, but exposed, unguarded.

Initially, she focused on every movement and sensation, using her training to heighten her perceptions and sensual response. His hands on her shoulders gradually began to move, gliding over the slick fragrant oils in small kneading circles, reaching upward along the sides of her neck, down the long muscles of her back to cup her buttocks, pulling her forward against the silky rough textures of his chest. As his palm and fingers alternately brushed and kneaded, she felt an awakening wherever he touched. His pulse in the hollow below his ear tapped against her lips, luring her tongue to taste, her nose to inhale. When his right hand traced the line of her hip forward to her groin, his fingers lightly parting her nether lips with assured but gentle strokes, she felt it as a shock that broke through her concentration, melting the minute details together into an undelineated sensuality.

Only a small corner of her mind vaguely noted the change from monitoring and directing as an Allesha should, to simply giving and responding. It was a fleeting thought drowned out by the smell, taste, touch of him. Wrapping her legs around his waist, she pulled him inside her, and suddenly all was still, as though time itself had focused so tightly onto the two of them that it had sealed itself shut. No doubt they moved, but Tayar experienced only fractional moments, each distinct from the next and the next. All that existed were the almost painfully intense waves of constriction. She heard her own cry, but it felt like laughter, a sacred vow sealing her to Dov for the rest of her life.

She floated within that warm aura. But soon the Allesha awakened once more, with the full understanding of why it was important that this be the last time — before another kind of love could take root, one which would do more harm than good.

They bathed each other tenderly, then walked hand in hand to a high platform, leaving the oil lamp beside the pool. With no other light, she felt as though they were entering a cave, dark, safe and separate.

This time, their lovemaking was slower, less insistent, more thoughtful, but she would not allow herself to become lost in it. The closing had to begin now, before it was too late.

Eventually, they had exhausted each other. Dov pulled her to him, her head on his chest, and soon his breathing slowed to the rhythms of a deep sleep. Slipping out from under his draped arm, Tayar left her inner room and her Winter Boy, looking back at him only once. He had rolled onto his side, as though he were reaching for her in his sleep, but something about the angle of his body and the sound of his breaths made her wonder if he weren't looking right at her, in his own quiet farewell.

Chapter 82

—————❀—————

Wave after wave of body warmth, unfamiliar smells and strange voices pummeled Dov/Ryl as he followed Tayar into the Communal Hall. Over the winter months, his world had become so small, revolving around only Tayar and Le'a. To now have more than one hundred Winter Boys and their Alleshi so close was a sudden, shocking reminder of how removed he had been from everything that defined his life. With a jolt, he realized that, for the time he had spent in The Valley, not even his name had been real.

Tayar was only a breath away; he could have held her hand as they moved through the crowd. But they, like the other Blessed Boys and Alleshi, barely looked at each other as they walked side by side, muscles rigid to remind them that what had been a natural part of their everyday was now and forever taboo. When they entered the Alleshine Assembly Room, Tayar separated from him to sit with other Alleshi in the back, where the tiered floor gave them an elevated view. The boys were instructed to sit toward the front.

Ryl observed everything with a clear, focused mind. But a part of him felt like a gawking child. Here he was in The Alleshine Assembly Room — the center and the source of their Peace — where Alleshi and Allemen made decisions that affected everyone within the Peace borders, and beyond. And it wasn't a mistake; he belonged here, with this company.

Half again as many Alleshi as boys poured into the enormous room, which could have held four, maybe even five times as many people — all the Birani, plus the neighboring Beirjoun — without being crowded. With great formality and uncertainty, the boys greeted one another, some with no more than a nod, others in short, polite salutations.

Ryl acknowledged those he recognized from the Battai's Petitioners dormitory, but with little more than a glance. Even when he saw Sim, whose company he had enjoyed before his Season began, Ryl didn't know what to say or how to behave. So much had changed over the winter.

Ryl sat in a comfortably cushioned armchair about three rows from the front, where twenty empty seats faced the company. Once the boys and Alleshi had settled, a group of men and women came in through another, smaller door and took those facing chairs. Mistral was among them.

Mistral scanned the room, and when his eyes fell on Ryl, his face brightened. What surprised Ryl was that he was happy to see his pa. Not that Ryl wasn't still confused, even angry, but those emotions felt more like an echo of the past, vague rather than visceral.

A tall, wizened old woman stood and leaned on a high reader's table. Tayar had pointed this Allesha out as an important leader among the handful who knew the truth about him. Did that mean she could be trusted?

"Watch her carefully," Tayar had said. "She has skills and secrets you'll want to learn."

Under the old Allesha's commanding look, the shuffling of chairs and murmured conversations quieted. "Welcome and good morning," she said. "This is the day you've been striving toward for months, when you become members of our community, not through ritual or awards, but through hard work and service."

"During these Service Days," she continued, "you will spend your mornings here in our Assembly Room, learning and planning. Lunch will usually be across the hall." She gestured toward the other side of the building. "In the afternoons, you will be assigned various duties around The Valley, under the guidance of Allemen and Alleshi, though not your own Allesha. In the evenings, after you dine privately with your Allesha, you will return to the Communal Hall for informal discussions and to prepare for the next day."

The old woman's eyes glided over the gathering of Winter Boys. "Look around you at the other Blessed Boys assembled here. You may think you know some of them. You don't. No more than they can know you, not after all you have learned. Today is a new start for you. So please take a moment and introduce yourself to everyone within reach." The Allesha sat down.

At first, no one moved or spoke. Ryl glanced around him. When the boy to his right returned his gaze and nodded, Ryl put out his hand and said, "Hello, I'm Ryl."

A head taller than Ryl, he had a ruddy complexion, small grey eyes, sandy hair and a firm handshake. "Garin of the Mukane. What's your village?"

"Sorry, right, I'm Ryl of the Birani. But, hey, Mukane? Like in the Traveler's story *The Northern Border*?"

"Yes." Garin grinned.

"Glad to meet you, Garin."

"Me, too."

Ryl turned to the boy directly behind him, but he was already engaged in conversation. One seat over from him, Ryl recognized the slim boy he had seen crying at the Battai's. A fresh start. Did that mean also forgetting that the reason Ryl had called him a wimp was out of fear and arrogance? Ryl extended his hand, stretching to reach him. "Hello, I'm Ryl of the Birani."

The boy shook Ryl's hand vigorously. "Hi, Ryl. It's great to see you. You kept your name, too? Oh, sorry, I guess we're supposed to do this according to form. I'm Aidan of the Nigan."

"It's good to see you, too, Aidan." Ryl could hear the deep sincerity in his own voice, but felt he wanted to say something else to Aidan, that he owed him some acknowledgment or apology or something.

Aidan leaned over to clap him on his shoulder before turning to greet another boy.

Ryl met five of those surrounding him, amidst a growing hubbub of goodwill. Back at the Battai's, when he was certain no Allesha could ever Bless him, he had dismissed the other Petitioners. How different it was now. He was surrounded by more than one hundred Winter Boys from so many villages that their colors, sizes, shapes and features were almost as diverse as the Peace itself. But each had more in common with Ryl than anyone back home, because they'd all gone through a Season with an Allesha, and were about to become Allemen. He wasn't accustomed to feeling part of something so large, and he welcomed the sense of belonging it gave him. Still, none of them knew what he knew, or carried a similar burden.

The same old Allesha stood once more, and the company quickly quieted, giving her their full attention. "Today, at lunch, you'll sit with at least two of the boys you just met. Until you are told otherwise, we will expect you to sit with new people every day. That way, you'll get to know as many of your fellows as possible. Now I will turn the podium over to one of our Allemen, Mistral of the Birani."

Wyrin, the boy seated in front of Ryl, turned around and mouthed the one word, "Birani?"

Ryl whispered, "My pa," and felt a sense of pride as he said it.

Mistral strode forward, instead of standing behind the tall reader's table. "Well, fellas, you've done it. You've had a Blessed Season and are about to become Allemen." He moved around as he spoke, cutting through the room's formality and turning the moment into something shared among equals and friends. "Today, you feel like you've just awakened from a dream. I know. I've been there… in that chair, to be precise." He pointed at a seat in the fourth row. "I remember how dazed I felt, thrust among so many people, where the rules seemed suddenly skewed. Believe me, that feeling will pass. Until then, your training will carry you through. It's that training we'll now begin to hone, while you spend the rest of your Season helping to open The Valley and prepare it for spring.

"You've already been told what you can expect during your Service Days. Lots of work, camaraderie and discussions. But that's only the framework. What will be important are the undercurrents and relationships that develop during these days. From these we…" Mistral gestured to the men and women sitting behind him, "will gauge how best to form your Triads and assignments."

Mistral strode back to stand behind the reader's table. "You'll be interacting not only with Allemen, Alleshi and other Blessed Boys, but also springtime Petitioners, villagers with their tributes, maybe even representatives from beyond our borders. Watch everyone and everything closely. Use this opportunity to learn and discern." He leaned forward, resting his forearms on the small high table.

"Yes, learn and discern. That's what you've been trained to do. Even among strangers, the smallest gesture can reveal what they wouldn't have you know. How much truer that is with your Allesha, especially now, when the two of you are so sensitized to each other." Mistral didn't exactly frown, but the lines around his mouth and on his brow became more pronounced. "Depending on your Allesha's style, you may already know what has transpired recently. Even if you haven't been told the details, you couldn't have failed to sense that something is very wrong. We don't want you to have to depend on rumors and hearsay to uncover the truth. So we are altering the normal course of your Service Days to share with you what we know. I wish we didn't need to do this. Not on your first day, when you're so raw and open. But it can't be helped."

No one moved or talked. The room was still.

Mistral poured a glass of water and took a sip before proceeding. "We don't have all the facts at present. What we do know is that three disturbing events have occurred in recent days, and they appear to be related. First, a beloved Allesha, the caretaker of The Valley's storehouse, is dead. Second, two hundred of our most advanced guns have been stolen from the storehouse. Third, several Alleshi and an unknown number of Allemen were apparently involved in the theft and have disappeared."

Mistral's stark delivery of the facts put the past week into fine focus for Ryl. Judging by the postures and faces around him, he realized that none of the other boys had known the full story until now. All eyes were fixed on Mistral in varying expressions of shock, disbelief and confusion. All, that is, except Aidan's. In the growing susurrus of nervous fidgeting, coughs and muttered asides, Ryl confronted Aidan in a forced whisper. "Why are you staring at me?"

"Because you're not staring at him," Aidan answered, pointing to Mistral.

Ryl studied Aidan for signs of threat or hints that perhaps he knew more than he should. But all Ryl could see in the slight boy's manner was a friendly curiosity and a sharply aware intelligence. Or had Aidan become more skilled at dissembling than Ryl credited him? Ryl quickly turned away, fearful that Aidan might be better at reading faces than Ryl was at hiding his thoughts.

Mistral stood silently watching the company, giving the boys time to absorb and consider the facts and their implications.

Finally, one boy spoke loudly enough to be heard by everyone. "Was she murdered?"

"The caretaker?" Mistral asked, but didn't wait for a reply. "Possibly, but she was very old. She could have just as easily fallen from the great height of the storehouse shelves."

"What do they plan to do with the guns?" another boy called out.

"I've told you what we know. Everything else is only guesswork," Mistral responded.

"It's obvious, isn't it?" a redhead in the second row said. "They want to defend the Peace. Kill Mwertik. Right?"

"That's one likely scenario," Mistral acknowledged.

"So, what's so bad about that?" the redhead asked. "The Mwertik are killing us."

Ryl heard Aidan's whisper behind him, "We'd become nothing more than murdering raiders ourselves."

Ryl looked over his shoulder at Aidan. "It would be a massacre," Aidan said almost under his breath, his voice a suppressed sob. Then why didn't he speak out?

"It would be a massacre," Ryl said aloud to the company. "That's what's wrong. We'd become just like them, the Mwertik. And that would be their victory over us." He turned in his seat so everyone could hear him clearly. When he faced front again, he saw Mistral nodding approval.

"He's right. I'm sorry I don't know your name," said a dark fellow to the far left.

"Ryl, what's yours?"

"Rominic of the Verrakeem," he replied, then continued, "Ryl's right. We're Allemen. At least we're going to be Allemen in a few weeks. That has to mean something. If we act like Mwertik, what makes us better than them? What Peace would there be left to protect?"

"But it's Allemen who did this. Allemen and Alleshi," someone protested. Ryl couldn't see who it was.

"That doesn't make them any less wrong," Rominic countered.

"Allemen can make mistakes," came from the other side of the room. "And this one is a monster of a mistake."

"And the Alleshi?" asked the redhead.

"They keep telling us they have no magic," Sim said. "That it's just observation, skill and knowledge. They're human, and the Alleshi involved are wrong."

"If it's Allemen and Alleshi who did this, who can we trust?" All Ryl could see of the boy who had spoken was the back of his head, but it was bowed and shaking in disbelief.

"Only ourselves," Aidan was so thin and small, but there was an incisive edge to his quiet, spare words.

Ryl looked over his shoulder at Aidan. Neither of them moved for several breaths while they stared at each other. With a slight movement of his head toward Mistral, Aidan broke the spell.

Ryl stood to speak to the company. "We can trust only those whom we know to be trustworthy. When we aren't sure, we'll have to trust our training and instincts to guide us. But we can be certain of our Triads, when they're formed. Our own Alleshi. Ourselves."

"So the old ways are gone?" the redhead asked.

"Which old ways?" Ryl responded.

"When we could believe in any Alleman or Allesha."

"Blindly, you mean? Without question? Like Sim said, they have no magic." Ryl suddenly felt uncomfortable being at the center of the discussion. With a glance toward Aidan, Ryl sat, wondering why he had stood at all.

"But it was the foundation of our Peace," Garin said.

"You know better than that," another boy responded from his chair. "The foundation is much more complex. It's trade and communications and our hope for the future."

"And the Allemen and Alleshi," Garin insisted. "Without them there is no Peace, no Alliance."

"Yes, Allemen and Alleshi," Sim said. "But it's the people who have earned those titles. Not the titles themselves."

The redhead turned in his seat to confront Sim. "You're wrong when you try to make it sound so ordinary. Everything's changed. An

Allesha has been killed. Guns were stolen. Allemen and Alleshi have turned renegade."

Mistral held his open hands chest high, calling the assembly to attention. "Now you understand why we had to tell you about it today, before we start your Service Days," Mistral said. "These events will complicate our lives for a long time to come. But it's important that you don't allow rumors or conjecture to foment reactive behavior. Deal with the facts, posit scenarios to examine implications and potential solutions as you have been trained, but don't confuse the one with the other. We know three facts at present. That's all." Mistral paused. Then, in a less somber voice, he said, "Now, Konar of the Hauks will speak with you about mediating disputes, something that every Alleman must do, some more often than others. It's Konar's specialty to which he has devoted his life, quite successfully." Mistral sat down and, with a deep sigh, released himself to the comfortable chair.

Tall and sinewy, Konar approached the reader's table with an almost feline gait. He was smooth-voiced, but power emanated from him. So much power that he didn't need to express or show it.

Ryl paid close attention to what Konar said, partly because he knew he needed the skills Konar could impart, but also because the Alleman's voice and words were so compelling. At the same time, Ryl considered what had just transpired — the patterns that were unfolding in this room, and the personalities that had been revealed. Among these boys were two he would learn to depend on more than anyone else: his future Triats. Who would they be? And which of the others would he be able to fully trust? A year from now, how many of them would know what he was? Would any of them respond to the news in a way that could prove dangerous?

Yes, he would need Konar's skills for diplomacy. But Ryl also recognized that he'd have to learn the old wizened Allesha's ability to keep secrets so close that no one could know that anything was hidden.

After Konar finished his tale of how he had solved a dispute between neighboring villages in which both claimed a fertile valley, he answered questions. The discussion was subdued. Everyone was still in shock from Mistral's revelations. Soon they were dismissed for lunch.

While everyone piled out of their seats and headed for the large doors through which they had originally entered, Mistral gestured to Ryl to follow him through a smaller door on the other side of the room.

Chapter 83

Working his way against the surge of so many people moving in the opposite direction, Ryl may have stepped on some toes and pushed a bit too forcefully against shoulders and backs to reach the door through which Mistral had disappeared.

Ryl closed the heavy door, shutting out the din of the Assembly Room. On the far side of the room, Mistral was standing at a large window, as though he had been pacing back and forth and happened to glance out as he turned. They faced each other across the expanse of a large, long table, its dark wood thick with shellac and pitted by generations of scratches and scribblings. How many arguments and crises had this antechamber witnessed? And how many silences?

Mistral took one step forward, then stopped.

"Hello, Pa." The word came easily because it was what Mistral had always been — Pa — but as Ryl said it, something inside him struggled against it.

"Hello, Son." Mistral's tone was colored, too, with his uncertainties.

Ryl strode forward to his father, hesitating only slightly before pulling him into a bear hug. Mistral returned the embrace, not quite comfortable in the moment, but welcoming it. They stepped back at the same time and grinned, mirror images of each other, so that Ryl saw in his father's eyes answers to many of his unasked questions. Answers that had been there all along, even if he hadn't known enough to see them.

They sat on the same side of the table, with their chairs turned so they faced each other.

Mistral leaned forward in his chair. "You're looking good, Son."

Ryl settled back. "You too. How's Ma?"

"She's well. She misses you. We both have."

Ryl crossed one foot over his thigh, then realized his Allesha would have commented that it could look like a barrier. Mistral had the correct posture for an Alleman trying to open a dialog. Ryl put both feet flat on the floor and leaned forward.

Mistral reached for the pitcher from the center of the table and poured some water into a glass. But he put the glass down without drinking. "Ryl, I'm sorry. There was so much I wanted to tell you."

"But you didn't."

"Would you have heard me?"

"Probably not; I'm ready to listen now." Ryl fought the urge to sit back and cross his arms over his chest.

"First, I want to apologize for not telling you the truth, but it wasn't possible at the time. I assume you know it all now, correct?"

"Does anyone ever know it all when it comes to the Alleshi and Allemen? I know about my birth. What I really am, and that you've been making plans to use that — to use me."

"Son," Mistral began to protest, but caught himself.

"Don't worry. I think I understand that part. I mean, if I can help save the Peace, who am I to want to have my own life, to settle down quietly… with Lilla?" Ryl hadn't realized how bitter he still felt deep within himself, until he heard it in his own voice.

"I wish it could have been different for you, and for her." Mistral sighed in such as way that Ryl could almost believe he was seeing the man behind the Alleman. But he shook off the feeling.

"You could have warned me, Pa. She deserves better than this."

"What did you think I was doing? Arguing for the fun of it?"

Ryl considered the question, forcing himself to see the boy he once was. "Sometimes I did… or that you had nothing to say to me but corrections or arguments."

"I should have handled it differently. Before you stopped hearing me."

"How could I hear you when you didn't tell me anything. You and your damned secrecy."

"You were a child, Ryl."

"How much does Ma know?"

"That you'll never marry Lilla."

"And Lilla?"

"That you won't be returning to our village any time soon."

Lilla. In all this, the one true innocent. And the one who would be most hurt. "How is she?"

"Still hopeful, but your ma is trying to help her." Mistral drank some of the water he had poured. "I've encouraged others to court her."

Ryl's stomach twisted. "You had no right!"

"Would you want Lilla to spend the rest of her life waiting for you?"

"But it was my decision. Mine and hers."

"What decision would you make?"

"That's not the point."

"No, I guess it isn't. But I weighed her rights against yours. Would you really want her pain and disappointment to be greater than they need be?"

Ryl had known that he couldn't marry Lilla, that his future would be different from anything they had planned or hoped. But only now, in trying to picture Lilla going on without him, did the concrete truth settle fully within him. "Who did you choose for her?"

"Erl or Noaq."

Ryl nodded. "Both good men. Has she given her consent to either?"

"No, not yet, but we've blazed the paths to make it easier for her once she accepts that you won't return."

"You were that sure of me."

"I knew the Alleshi would help you, in the same way your ma and I have been helping Lilla."

"Manipulate me, you mean." The words came without thought, an ingrained reaction that no longer fully represented how Ryl felt. But he hadn't yet figured out what he felt about what the Alleshi and his father had done to him.

"As we are all manipulated." Mistral countered, then thought better of it. "No, it's more than that. I was sure of you because I knew it wasn't in you to avoid making the right decisions, regardless of how difficult and hurtful it might be."

"What if you'd been wrong?"

"Then you wouldn't be the man I've always believed you to be."

Ryl stared at Mistral, caught off balance by the compliment. "How long have you been planning all this? Did it start when you stole me from my real mother?"

"No, you were just an infant then, squalling and vulnerable.... Ryl, what would you have done? Could you have watched a newborn being tortured, perhaps killed?"

"But you misinterpreted the situation."

"I've gone over the scene in my head so many times since then." Mistral gazed into the empty space between them, as though he were no longer seeing the room around him. But he snapped back, fixing his eyes on Ryl. "I've never stopped asking myself how I could have learned more before stumbling across the birthing ritual. It was a lousy accident that my first encounter with the Mwertik would be laden with such alien, fearsome rites. I was so damned young, unseasoned, but that's no excuse, just a fact that no one has the power to change."

"Would you, if you could? "

"Ryl, you are my son. How could I want to change that? Yet, what are my personal feelings in the face of all that has happened?"

"Pa, tell me, how bad were the Mwertik raids when you first went looking for them?"

Mistral didn't respond, which was its own kind of answer.

Of course, Ryl had begun to suspect the truth days before, but to have his suspicions confirmed left a bitter taste in his mouth. "Damn! You mean it started then? Didn't you even try to talk to them? Return me?"

"It developed so slowly." Mistral's voice was soft and steady, though the muscles in his neck corded with the strain. "We didn't understand until it was too late. By then, the anger and hate were so thoroughly entrenched on both sides, spreading until it no longer mattered what the beginning was. I doubt that most people even know how it started."

"So, what use could the truth about my birth be, if the Mwertik won't listen, if everything has spiraled so out of hand that people don't remember that my being stolen was the beginning?" Taking a deep breath, Ryl altered his approach. "Let's go back to what you do know. All that time you were away from us, what did you learn?"

"I never stopped trying to find an answer. I've spent more time in their territory than watching you grow up… studying them, learning their ways. When they faded into the landscape, I tracked them by the currents of chaos they caused as the violence and frequency of their raids escalated."

"Did you find them?"

"Occasionally. But they're a nomadic people, adept at disappearing, seldom using the same campsite twice."

"What about their home?" Ryl asked. "Certainly, they must have some place they return to, where the women, children and aged are kept safe."

"Yes, they must. But regardless of how far and how long I travel and whom I ask, I haven't found it. Not yet."

"Do they know you've been tracking them?"

"I believe they're aware of someone shadowing them, but they don't appear to realize it's the same person they've sought all these years."

"The abductor of their headman's son, you mean. What makes you think they haven't put the two together?"

"They haven't killed me yet."

"Like they did Jared." Ryl poured his own glass of water, not realizing until he downed it in three gulps how dry his mouth was. "But what is it you think I can do, if no one really cares how it started anymore?"

"One thing I've learned is that they're rooted in their traditions; blood ties are sacred. They might hate what you've become, but I believe, if we handle it properly, we can use the fact of who you were meant to be, to get at least some of them to listen to you. Their traditions should force them to treat you differently than a stranger."

"Or kill me."

Mistral shook his head, though not in denial. "I never wanted it to get this far... All these years... So much time away from you and your ma... Trying to find some answer that wouldn't bring us to this juncture. And it's been for nothing."

Ryl had never seen his father so bared, but even now, he wasn't defeated. Just sad and tired. Or had he been like this all along, behind that mask of Alleman discipline he always seemed to wear?

"Pa..."

Mistral straightened his back and squared his shoulders. "Don't worry, Ryl. I haven't given up, won't ever give up as long as air fills my lungs."

"I know, Pa."

"I'm so very sorry, Son."

"Me, too."

"You? What do you have to be sorry for?"

"I didn't make it easy for you."

"That's for sure." Mistral smiled. "But you were only a boy, struggling with the normal problems of growing up, combined with the uncertainty of our life, of me not being there for you. And, you are, after all, my son. Did my Allesha tell you how difficult I was at your age? My father had nearly given up on me."

"But you never did."

"We're a stubborn family, Ryl. Once we take hold of an idea or a person, we don't let go. It's one of our strengths — and sometimes, a weakness, too."

"And always being away from us, from Ma and me, it was part of that, wasn't it? Part of not giving up on me. It had nothing to do with not wanting to be near me."

"Is that what you thought, that I didn't want to be with you?"

"You never seemed satisfied with anything I did. From the minute you came home, you were planning to leave again, as though the one place you didn't want to be was with me."

"No, Son. It wasn't you. It was me. My guilt and fear. And my stubbornness. I'd always been restless, even before I found you. Your ma understood that when she married me. That's why I was on the frontier in the first place, because the Alleshi took my restlessness and adapted it to a skill for seeking. But after I realized what I had done — taking you from the Mwertik — I became driven. I had to try to mend everything."

"I understand, Pa. But I wish…"

"Me, too, Son."

Mistral reached out with both hands. With no hesitance this time, Ryl grasped them, allowing the warmth and strength of their flesh to say what neither was ready to voice. Only then did Ryl see the toll of the years in the deep furrows around Mistral's mouth and across his brow.

"It's been a long haul for you, Pa. Now it's my turn to try."

"Our turn. We'll do it together, Son."

"Leaving Ma and Lilla behind."

"Because we have no choice. All our choices were taken away that day I thought I was saving your life. Yes, if I could, I would change it, but I can't. And part of my guilt is that I'm glad, because you are my son."

Chapter 84

The banquet room was noisy, with all the Winter Boys seated at large round tables, chatting and laughing. Not that the Alleshi and Allemen were much quieter; if they wanted to be heard above the din, they had to raise their voices, too. As in the Assembly Room, the boys occupied the center, while Alleshi and Allemen sat at tables around the edges. A couple dozen waiters and waitresses from the Battais' inns wove their way among the scores of tables, serving lunch.

When Rishana entered, Dara waved to her. Peren, Ayne, Hester and Dara had saved a seat for her, and it would have been awkward to refuse it. Besides, if she were going to work with these women, she'd need to learn as much as possible about them. The three Allemen seated with them stood as she approached. When Hester introduced them, Rishana couldn't hear their names over the cacophony. She mouthed, "Hello," instead of shouting.

Rishana studied the room, seeking currents that might indicate established alliances among the Alleshi and Allemen, new ones developing among the boys. The way the men at her table interacted with the women, she judged that the two on either side of Hester were her Allemen, while the older one was Ayne's. Did that mean they could be trusted, because their loyalties were to women who were ostensibly loyal to her? On the surface, that felt logical. But wasn't that the basis of their society, the interlocking circles of allegiances which were cascading and collapsing around them? Was it because key links had proven brittle, or was the system itself fatally flawed?

By the time Ryl/Dov and Mistral appeared, most people had started to eat their soup, reducing the noise level to a quieter roar. Seeing them together, no one could doubt they were father and son. Not only in their dark coloring and compact shapes, but their stance and the way they surveyed the room. Both saw Rishana on their first sweep — Dov with a brightening of his face that warmed her heart, Mistral with a piercing stare that riveted her.

"Ryl, over here." A boy stood to shout and wave. "We've saved you a seat." Rishana had noticed him in the Assembly Room. Slight in form but intense, he had sat behind Dov, and something had definitely passed between them. What was the history they shared? Who was his Allesha? Was he one of the Triat candidates being considered for Dov?

Dov turned to Mistral to say something and then went to join the other boy.

Before leaving the room, Mistral glanced at Rishana in an unmistakable summoning. In all the commotion, she doubted anyone noticed when she left to follow him. No one other than the Guardian Alleshi and their three Allemen — and Dov.

Mistral was pulling on his overcoat when Rishana came out of the banquet room. With a quick glance at the only other person in the entry hall, a grey-haired Alleman coming out of the lavatory, Mistral opened his hands to her in full ritual greeting. "Allesha, I wish to thank you for your care and training of my son," he said. "You have honored my family and village."

Filling his hands with hers in the appropriate traditional gesture, she responded, "It is my honor to serve."

The Alleman appeared not to notice them as he pushed through the door to the banquet room. However, Rishana knew to not trust outward appearances.

Before Rishana could take her hands out of Mistral's, he grabbed one and gently tugged. "Come," he whispered. "Walk with me." He helped her on with her coat, though she couldn't tell whether it were out of courtesy or because he wanted her to move more quickly.

Outside, the morning downpour had dissipated to a drizzle. "Shall we go to your home?" He led her toward the house without waiting for her reply.

"I won't melt in the rain."

"We need to be sure we're not overheard." Mistral didn't look at her when he spoke. Instead, he constantly scanned the path ahead.

Why did she feel annoyed with Mistral? she wondered. Certainly, she was as eager as he to talk. That he wanted to do so in private indicated that he planned to be honest with her, or at least discuss sensitive information that neither of them would want others to hear. "What have you heard of Eli?" she asked.

"Nothing you don't already know. Tedrac should have more for us when he returns, before the last of the Service Days." He looked at her briefly, fitting it into his sweeps of the terrain. "Jinet, you've done a great job with Ryl."

Jinet! That was the problem, or part of it. He was still treating her as his Triat's wife. "Mistral, we have known each other for a long time, but you presume a great deal with an Allesha."

Hearing the ice in her voice, Mistral turned toward her without breaking stride. "My sincere apologies, Allesha. I meant no insult."

"Apology accepted." It was the correct response, though devoid of the warmth it should have conveyed.

Placing his hand on her elbow, he forced her to stop and turn toward him. "No, truly, it isn't just words. Please believe me, I'd never wish to insult you, of all people. I've always held you in great respect... not just because you wear a title... but that title does give you the right to expect better of an Alleman."

She looked down at his hand on her, and he quickly removed it.

With a sheepish grin, he shrugged. "We both know this isn't about the respect you require and deserve. My apology is heartfelt, and you know that, too. Now, let's move on. We've too much to discuss to waste any more time."

Rishana considered her reaction. Why did she seethe at his informality? She'd known and liked him for years, and not simply because he was Jared's Triat. True, he had some strange attitudes about her role as an Alleman's wife. And she had often felt uncomfortable with the way he watched everything, as though he thought if he stared intently enough, he could pierce through anyone's private thoughts. She remembered the stories he would tell about his adventures, the laughs they shared, and the many times he and Jared would withdraw from her to discuss private Alleman affairs.

He had posed as a friend, had sat at her table and slept under her roof, had entertained her with his tales of life beyond the borders. But none of it had ever come close to full candor. In fact, both Jared and Mistral had been more honest with each other than either had been with their wives. She resented Mistral and all that he had shared with Jared, down to the truth of his death. A death that Mistral's actions may have caused.

She was angry at Mistral because he was here and Jared wasn't. And because she was terrified of losing Eli — and now Dov.

Recognizing her underlying turmoil, Rishana buried it. Mistral was correct; they didn't have time for that.

When they reached her home, he held the gate for her, waited for her to open the outer door, as was proper, then closed it again, to safeguard against others disturbing them. In silence, they removed their coats and boots in the vestibule. Then, as they entered the greeting room, she turned to him with a suitable smile of welcome. "Please come into the kitchen. We can talk over lunch," she said.

They threw together a cold meal of roast beef sandwiches, salad, applecake and cider. Without asking or being asked, Mistral assisted, as any Alleman would with an Allesha. Not at all the way he used to behave in her kitchen at home where he was always sitting and watching. As Jared's Triat, he'd been treated like family, but he had never crossed over that invisible threshold of familial informality with her. Now she was no longer his Triat's wife, but an Allesha. Yet she could feel Jared's presence as she hadn't in a long time. It should have been a comfort.

When they sat down to eat, she put out an offering saucer and placed pieces of her food into it, knowing Mistral would have the same beliefs as her Winter Boy.

"Thank you for honoring our rites." Mistral added his own offering to the saucer. He bit into his sandwich and swallowed quickly, not taking the time to fully taste it. "No doubt you've many questions. Please ask."

She took a forkful of salad and chewed thoughtfully. All her questions started at the same place.

"Tell me about Jared's last mission."

"I can only guess what it was."

"Then give me your best guess."

"Jared and I didn't always agree, as I'm sure you know."

"Assume I know nothing. In many ways, that's true."

Mistral put down his sandwich and leaned his forearms on the table. He became quite still, allowing no distraction from his words. "Jared and I saw things differently. Jared liked direct paths. If he had a question or problem, he'd go right to the center of it, to the person who had the answer or caused the difficulty. He'd find what they wanted or needed, offer compromises, and when practical measures failed, win them over with his charm and generosity."

"You don't?" His stillness seeped into her, deterring her natural inclination to move in rhythm to her words.

"I can't. Not with the Mwertik; they're a hidden people. I don't just mean that they're difficult to find, but that they hide behind their rituals and traditions. Maybe it has something to do with being a nomadic tribe. What I've learned about them indicates that they're not even direct in their personal relationships. Everything is circuitous. Some would call it devious; I believe it's more about their sense of the sacred."

"Sacred?" She stared at Mistral but couldn't help seeing Dov. It wasn't only their dark coloring or the chiseled angularity of their faces crowned by thick, lustrous hair. How was it that a father and son unrelated by blood could be so similar?

"I'm not sure I can explain it. Sometimes, when I'm tracking them and I find one of their old camps, I'm struck by the way they try to wrap themselves within the land, arranging small stones and twigs in patterns that have no obvious sense or value. And how they place their tents and fires, aligning them to the terrain, with everything pointing west. I'm not describing it well, but whenever I see the remnants, it feels sacred."

"Perhaps your reactions have more to do with who you are than what they believe."

"I don't know." Confusion played on his face for only a few moments and was quickly replaced by more characteristic resolve. "I've spent so much time and energy trying to think like them. I believe I am seeing them clearly."

The tendons in her neck began to ache with such unaccustomed immobility. Shaking off the spell, she stretched her back and willed her body to move naturally as she spoke. "Mistral, how different are the Mwertik from the Birani? Your people are also steeped in the sacred, so much so that they erected a building around a tree rather than cut it down."

"It's an unusual tree."

"When I hear you speak of the Mwertik, I'm constantly reminded of the Birani. Then I look at you, and how much like your son you seem. No wonder others don't question his bloodlines."

Mistral frowned in thought. "What are you trying to say?"

"Do the Mwertik and Birani have common ancestors?"

"I don't know." His gaze became unfocused for a moment, turning inward. "I've never been able to find their roots. But, yes, it would be worth looking into."

"You still haven't told me what you think happened on Jared's last mission."

"I think he made contact with someone, or learned something that he felt would make them listen. What, I don't know; I wish I did." Mistral paused, apparently making a decision. "Did you read his last message?"

"Yes." The memory of Jared's last letter, written while she slept — though not to her — cut through her, a knife slicing off the layers of titles, names and roles that she had built up around her pain.

"Then you know it was a sudden opportunity he felt he couldn't ignore or delay. I believe it was a trap. He wasn't the type to walk blindly into danger. Still, if someone were willing to talk, or if he had discovered some leverage… Perhaps he got caught between two factions."

"Factions? Among the Mwertik?"

"Well, that was Jared's theory. That the Mwertik couldn't be monolithic, that no group of individuals can be always in accord."

"Have you found evidence of factions?" she asked.

"Only the normal rifts over leadership, hunting methods and raiding strategies. But no signs of any Mwertik who disagreed with the idea of being at war with us. Still, I know only of those who lurk near our borders, and wouldn't they be the most warlike? Perhaps if we can finally find their home base…"

Rishana didn't respond immediately. Instead, she drank some cider, while watching Mistral over the rim of her glass. What was he trying to say — or hide? Putting the glass down, she patted the corners of her mouth with her napkin, then asked, "How far into their territory have you gone?"

"Through the border forest into the Antoyn Mountains, almost to the shore of the great western ocean."

"The ocean? Could the Mwertik come from there? From a land off the shore?"

"That's one of Tedrac's theories, which is why I was so far away when Jared was killed. Otherwise…" His hands balled into fists without moving from their rigid position on the table; the muscles in his forearms pulsed with the motion. "If I had been here, maybe I could have stopped him or gone with him. Oh, Jinet!" He slammed his left fist down onto the table. "Excuse me — Allesha. It should have been me, not Jared. He was the best of us. I was gone so long, I didn't even know until months after you buried him. Please forgive me. It should have been me." His voice trailed off, and in the silence, Rishana could clearly hear his anguish.

Rishana knew that deep inside she did hold Mistral responsible. He never should have stolen the baby. Then none of this would have happened, and Jared probably wouldn't have gone off on that fatal mission. But that baby was Dov, her Winter Boy, his son.

She placed her hand on his. "Mistral, we can't change the past, no matter how much we want to. And Jared wouldn't want you to blame yourself." She felt him shiver — a release, or just the shock of her touch?

"Can you forgive me?" he asked.

"For being alive when Jared isn't?"

"For causing all this."

"It isn't my forgiveness you need." She withdrew her hand. "I can't absolve you. That's something you'll have to do for yourself."

"Yes, of course." He leaned back in his chair and grabbed his sandwich with both hands. How quickly Mistral took control over his emotions.

Rishana also ate, working the flavors of the beef, bread and spice sauce over her tongue, while she tried to understand the shape and purpose of this meeting. "What's so important that it couldn't wait? What do you need from me?"

"As I said, Jared and I didn't always agree, but his questions kept me balanced. Without him, our Triad is unhinged. We need your help."

"Mistral, you can't be asking what I think you are," Rishana snapped. "I'm not your Triat. He's dead."

"What I'm asking isn't unprecedented. You are an Allesha."

"Your son's, not yours." She stood, grabbing her plate and his, though they hadn't finished eating. "This meeting is at an end, Mistral. Please close the outer door as you leave."

"No, not until you hear me out," he demanded, but quickly gentled his voice. Standing, he gestured at her empty chair. "I've been clumsy. My apologies once more. Please..."

Putting the plates into the sink, she leaned back against the counter, her arms crossed over her chest. "I'm listening."

"We both carry something of Jared within us. Can't we take solace in that, and at the same time, work together to protect the Peace? All I ask is that you challenge me as Jared would, as it is your nature to do. Keep doubting me, as you always have, but not in silence. Help me see what I might otherwise be blind to. If nothing else, it would be to your advantage as my son's Allesha and Eli's mother and a Guardian to know my thoughts and plans. I would share them with you as though you were my Triat, but, believe me, I know the difference. You are not Jared. You could never be Jared. Still, we could help each other."

"What does your Allesha think of this?"

"I haven't told her about it."

"Do you think it was wise to approach me in this manner without first consulting her?"

"Dara is my Allesha and a Guardian. I honor her and owe her my full allegiance. However, she's become set in her thoughts. Part of it is probably due to age, but there's also her hate and fear. She can't see the many facets of a situation the way she used to. Maybe she's been over the same paths too many times. It's the only reason I can think of that she didn't anticipate the theft of the guns, the Alleshi and Allemen going renegade. But you did. Please don't tell her I said this. I mean no disrespect for her. After all, what Jared gave me — what you could give me — is something different from the way Dara and I are together."

"Why would you keep this hidden from your Allesha if, as you say, it is not untoward?"

"Because it would be a closed subject if you refuse. Only if you say yes will she need to know."

Rishana turned to the sink and ran water over the dishes. Mistral said nothing. When she faced him again, he hadn't changed position. "What I don't understand," she said, "is why you need to approach me in this manner. Don't you already report to the Guardians? We will work together in that capacity."

"That's not the same thing. I'd like your permission to come here to your home when you're not in Season. Or we could meet elsewhere, if you prefer. Just the two of us. To talk, separate from the Council and the Guardians."

Rishana couldn't help wondering what he wasn't telling her. Didn't he trust the Guardians? "And you will be honest with me?" she asked.

"I will tell you everything I can."

"That's not the same thing. I require your complete honesty, with nothing hidden."

"And you will trust my word if I agree?" he asked.

"No, not fully. But then, you say it's my doubts you seek."

"Then you agree?"

His posture, the way he looked at her, with those dark intent eyes so like his son's. She could not bring herself to refuse him.

"You may call on me or send me messages, and I will consider responding. We'll see how it goes. But yes, for now, I agree."

"Thank you, Allesha."

"You may call me Rishana."

Chapter 85

In many ways, the Service Days were everything Ryl had been led to expect: lots of work, discussions and instruction. That first afternoon, workgroups were organized based on the boys' lunch companions, so that Ryl found himself clearing a mountain path with fifteen fellow Winter Boys. Two Allemen supervised, laboring side by side with them, as they broke up and gathered fallen tree limbs. Ryl enjoyed the fresh air and the exertion of the work, a sharp contrast to all the time he'd spent indoors over the winter with women. What surprised him was how easily he fell into working with men he barely knew. Ryl was sure that no one among the Birani who had known him as a rebellious loner would recognize the genial team worker he had become.

During a break, Aidan sat next to Ryl, which made about as much sense as Aidan seeking him out at lunch, given the way Ryl had treated him at the Battai's. Ryl was drinking from his canteen, trying to find the words to apologize, when Aidan spoke first.

"Ryl, I owe you an apology."

"What?" Ryl sputtered, practically dropping the canteen.

"I didn't treat you particularly well at the Battai's." Aidan spoke with the rhythm of a skilled orator, though so softly only Ryl could hear him. "In my arrogance, I thought you were an ignorant oaf and dismissed your ideas. I didn't understand how different people have various ways of using their intelligence. It's something that's been bothering me all Season, and when I heard you speak so eloquently today, it brought home to me how wrong I had been about you."

Ryl stared at Aidan, uncertain how to respond.

Aidan held out his small, thin hand. "Will you accept my apology?"

Ryl looked down at the offered hand and chuckled.

"What's so funny?" Aidan shifted his slight frame on the ground.

Ryl took Aidan's hand and pumped it vigorously. "I was getting ready to ask your forgiveness."

Now, it was Aidan's turn to be astonished. "What? Why?"

Taking a slow breath, Ryl was determined to give as dignified a response as Aidan's. "Because I called you a wimp and treated you badly.

I didn't understand about the different kinds of strength people can have. I hope you'll accept my apology."

One look at Aidan's toothy grin and crinkling slanted eyes, and Ryl's attempts at propriety melted away. They burst into laughter.

"Hey, what's the joke?" Garin called over to them.

"It would take too long to explain," Aidan responded with a wink to Ryl.

Ryl found the physical demands of the daily afternoon work more engaging than the morning lectures. Not that the Allemen who spoke weren't intriguing, providing important information and guidance. But he didn't like sitting in the dark Assembly Room when the world outside was calling. Plants were beginning to unfold, and the paths, fields and forest bustled with people. Life was returning to The Valley, and Ryl wanted to be part of it.

Despite himself, Ryl was often drawn into the animated discussions that followed the morning lectures and continued throughout the days. He hadn't expected the other boys to be so interested in his ideas and opinions. But he often preferred remaining quiet, so he could listen and watch. Soon, he would need to know who among these boys he could depend on. Some might end up his enemies, once his Mwertik bloodlines were revealed. Two would be his Triats.

Mistral and Ryl didn't have any further private time together, though Mistral occasionally supervised Ryl's workgroups, and they were sometimes in the same evening discussion groups. Still, Ryl knew Mistral watched him, as much to protect his back as to gauge what he had learned.

The workgroups were reassigned daily. At first, the boys were assigned to cleaning up winter damage and preparing for spring. Clearing and grooming the paths took several days. Then, in groups of about a dozen each, the boys and Allemen were assigned to work under the Battais' foremen — repairing and painting buildings and equipment, mending or replacing broken gas lines and water pipes, supplying and maintaining the steam plant, sowing The Valley's handful of fields, helping the regular maintaince crews, and assisting with whatever needed to be done in the various workshops that ringed each inn.

Whatever the boys did and wherever they went, it was always under the watchful eyes of Alleshi and Allemen.

On the tenth morning of the Service Days, after the Alleman Jakot of the Waleen explained ocean, river and lake water rights and the various attitudes different villages have about them, Lev of the Saranoi took the podium.

"The spring caravans have begun to arrive." Lev's announcement was greeted with a few yelps of joy. "I understand quite clearly what a caravan's arrival has always meant to you, but it's different here in The Valley, especially for Blessed Boys and Allemen."

"More work, you mean," Donel called out, to the accompaniment of good-humored groans and laughter. "So, what's new about that?"

"What's new is that this will be the first time since you were Blessed that you'll be interacting with so many strangers. It will be an exacting test of your discipline."

Everyone was suddenly very quiet.

Lev leaned on the podium. "The Caravan Convergence is a keystone of the Peace, in many ways as crucial as our Allemen. However, as with any meeting of diverse groups, we're certain to witness disturbances. One of our responsibilities is to cut through any disruption before it can ripen into violence. Keep your senses open, but don't try to take on potential problems without help. Report immediately to the closest Allesha or Alleman, who will work with you to defuse the situation."

Lev stepped out from behind the podium to stand closer to the first row of seats. "As Blessed Boys, you'll be in an awkward position. On one hand, you'll be held in awe by many. Some of the superstitious believe that by being good to you — or by bribing you — they'll be able to partake of your Blessed state."

"They'd think twice if they knew how much work it was," Wyrin quipped.

"Lev's not talking about the kind of people who think twice, are you?" Sim responded.

"No," Lev agreed. "Superstitious folk seldom think their beliefs through. You must be gentle but adamant when you refuse, regardless of whether it's a sincere but misguided offer or an out-and-out attempt at coercion."

"You said, 'on one hand,'" Aidan noted. "What's the other side?"

"Jealousy. For the time being, you're not to walk alone. Be with at least one other boy, preferably more, or with an Allesha or Alleman. Should you encounter antagonism, you're to allow them to believe they've intimidated you, if that's the only way you can get out of the situation without inflaming it."

Ryl cringed at the memory of the Autumn Boy he had tried to bait. Vetram had been his name, son of Vexam, the caravan leader. Someone else he'd have to seek out and apologize to.

Lev looked around the room. "There's one other thing you'll have to deal with for the rest of your lives. Women. Some have their own beliefs or hopes regarding Allemen, especially Blessed Boys."

"Have you heard the superstition about girls who lose their virginity to Blessed Boys fresh from their Alleshi?" one boy in back shouted to everyone's glee.

"It's not a laughing matter to the girls or their families. Each of you has discussed this with your Allesha, and you know our rules regarding intimacy. If you haven't learned that lesson..." Lev paused, then toned his voice to a ominous rasp that couldn't fail to chill, "then you aren't ready to be Allemen."

For long moments, Lev was silent. No one filled the emptiness.

Ryl found himself thinking about Lilla and how far from their shared dreams their separate futures would take them. Work and responsibility. It wasn't only about the Service Days, but the life he had chosen. Or had been chosen for him. As an Alleman, he would always be separate, constantly watched and watching. Nothing would be simple ever again, because there were no easy answers to the challenges he'd have to face.

Ryl glanced around him; all the boys were deep in thought.

With a sigh, Lev broke the stillness. "Now, do you understand?"

No one answered, but heads nodded solemnly.

Over the next two weeks, the patterns of their days gradually broke apart, becoming less predictable. The boys continued to attend the morning lectures in the Assembly Room, after which they dispersed throughout The Valley in increasingly smaller workgroups. With the Caravan Convergence came the many springtime tributes. Every boy participated in receiving and inventorying the wide diversity of goods arriving at the storehouse. Handfuls of boys and Allemen often had lunch at one of the four Caravan tradegrounds or at a Battai's inn. When Ryl saw the spring Petitioners at the inns, he couldn't help but wonder which of them would be Tayar's next Blessed Boy. Sometimes, it wasn't a hot iron in his chest to think about it.

Eventually, the boys were sorted out into different groups of three for every assignment, with test Triads changing as often as a few times a day. When they weren't darting about on errands or tackling assigned tasks, they were given entry to actual councils and conferences, as well as witnessed disbursements, pronouncements and new treaty negotiations.

As they learned and observed, the morning lectures became more demanding — and more stimulating.

Toward the end, Ryl's test Triads tended to be made up of rotations that included Rominic, Aidan, Garin and Sim. Soon, the selection dwindled down to only Aidan and Sim. It happened so gradually that Ryl found himself accepting the arrangement before it became evident. Aidan's shrewd mind and quiet authority and Sim's skillful diplomacy proved natural complements to him. Besides, the more time he spent with them, the more he looked forward to spending time with them.

Every evening, Ryl/Dov dined privately with Rishana/Tayar. The first night had been difficult, punctuated by awkward silences. But with each supper, they gradually became accustomed to their new roles. Only once, that first night, did he wonder how solid the change was.

Tayar had gone to sleep, or at least she wasn't in the greeting room or kitchen when he returned late from the evening meeting at the Communal Hall. Just before getting into his own bed, Ryl stood at the door to the inner room. The knob turned easily, but he went to bed without opening the door which would be closed to him for the rest of his life, even when it wasn't locked.

Chapter 86

The young Allesha was still in Season, but her Winter Boy was nowhere to be seen, gone from her in all the ways that mattered. Even so, they had one evening left that would be theirs alone.

With great care, Tayar planned their final supper, accenting it with sensual reminders of the everyday delights, adventures and mishaps they had shared. She roasted venison from the hunt when he had named her so quickly, simmered a fruit compote with wine the way he had learned to prefer it, baked a fresh loaf of bread in one of the strange-shaped pans they had to use the time he had made too much dough. Each dish had a story, a sense memory: the smells, flavors and textures of their Season together.

Most of all, she wanted to give them reason to smile, perhaps even laugh together one last time as Dov and Tayar, a Blessed Boy with his Allesha.

During supper, Dov gave every indication that he appreciated her efforts, savoring each morsel as she had taught him. It was a pleasure to watch him and know that she had, indeed, trained him well. More than that, they had indelibly marked each other.

I am his creation, as much as he is mine.

They concentrated on ordinary conversation about the people they had met and things they had seen over the past few weeks. If pauses between subjects were longer than normal, or smiles more tender than joyous, neither chose to acknowledge it.

They had just begun their dessert of apple cake and tea when they heard an insistent tap at the back window, even though the front door was closed, signaling that they weren't accepting visitors. When Tayar glanced outside into the cloud-shrouded moonless night, she saw Le'a/Dara and another form in the shadows.

Tayar opened the door but stood blocking the threshold. "This is a surprise, I understood that you had your farewell with Dov this afternoon. And I'm certain I had closed my outer door."

The other figure — Mistral — stepped into the light.

"Rishana," Dara whispered, "Tedrac has arrived. Bring your boy to

Hester's immediately."

"Does he have news of Eli?"

"We'll talk there." Dara and Mistral disappeared into the darkness.

Gesturing to Dov to follow, Tayar cut through the kitchen and greeting room, grabbed her coat in the vestibule and headed outside.

"Rishana?" Dov asked, as he trailed her at the same swift pace. "Is that your true name?"

"It's my Alleshine name. I no longer know what my true name is."

"Rishana. I like that. But you'll always be Tayar to me."

Though Hester's front door was closed, Rishana didn't hesitate, knowing they were expected. All the Guardian Alleshi had already gathered in the greeting room. All but one Guardian — herself.

The furnishings were plainer than Rishana's, with fewer curves and flourishes, but filled with unexpectedly bright colors. On the yellow sofa, Ayne was flanked by Dara and Savah/Peren. Hester and Tedrac sat to the side on matching upholstered armchairs. Mistral was seated on a small hardwood chair he had pulled close to Dara.

Moving with a slow, almost ponderous grace, Tedrac stood and opened his hands to her in full ritual greeting. "It is good to see you again, Allesha."

Instead of filling his hands with hers, Rishana clasped them, "Tedrac, tell me, what news do you have of Eli?" Then, realizing the unintended insult she had just given her husband's Triat, she completed the greeting, resting her hands in his. "It's always a delight to see you, Tedrac. But please do tell me."

"I had a message from Eli four days ago; he is well."

The relief that washed over Rishana made her feel suddenly light-headed. When Tedrac offered her his armchair, she collapsed into it.

While Tedrac greeted Rishana, Mistral stood and brought Dov/Ryl forward to formally introduce him. "Guardian Alleshi, I am pleased to present my son, whom you have watched and protected." In a soft aside, he told Ryl, "Everyone here knows the truth of your birth, and our plans."

Each of the Guardians said, "Welcome," and Ayne gestured to Ryl to take a seat in a blue high-backed chair separated from the rest by the low table that held the tea service.

"I am honored to be invited into your home and meeting," Ryl said with dignity worthy of an Alleman.

"You are here, Ryl, because we have learned that we can trust you.

Precious few know of the existence of the Guardians, and fewer still are invited to join our meetings," Ayne told him.

"The Guardians?" Ryl asked.

"A clandestine group of Alleshi who will use whatever and whomever they must to safeguard our Peace." With a shrug, Rishana added, "They are also the Alleshi who have protected you and the secret of your birth."

Ayne stiffened, but it was Peren who spoke. "Ryl, you should know that your Allesha has recently joined us as a Guardian, and her description, in its brevity, leaves out much of which you would approve. For as long as the Peace has existed, a small, hand-picked group of secret Guardian Alleshi has worked to protect all that you cherish."

"And you trust me not to reveal the fact of your existence?" Ryl asked.

"We trust you with much more than that," Hester said.

"Why?"

"Because we have been watching you ever since you were a baby," Dara explained.

"You mean a stolen baby, don't you?"

With a sharp look of impatience, Ayne silenced any response Dara might have given. "The point is, we know your nature," Ayne said. "And we chose you long ago to be one of our Allemen."

"Your Alleman? No, I'm Rishana's."

"And she is ours," Ayne stated flatly.

Ryl looked to his Allesha, who nodded. "So you think you know me. What do you want from me?"

"First, we want your oath that you won't disclose anything you learn here tonight, including the existence of the Guardian Alleshi," Tedrac said. "Then sit back and listen. You will hear things you need to know and understand; as of this moment, you have become one of us."

"A Guardian?"

"No," Dara said. "But one of the few Allemen who are our confidants and agents."

"So, do we have your oath?" Ayne asked.

"I will not disclose anything that is said to me tonight, unless you tell me otherwise."

"Done!" Peren clapped her hand on the side table. "Now we can begin. As I'm sure you are aware, we sometimes give Allemen who work with us our true names."

"As true as any name is." Ryl softened his retort with a wry smile.

Peren glanced at Rishana, as if to say it was obvious who this boy's

Allesha was.

"As that may be, we will give you our Alleshine names, which we share only with our sisters and those Allemen who have reason to know them. I am Ayne."

"Dara."

"Peren."

"Hester."

The others looked at the young Allesha, so she added, "Rishana."

"I am honored," Ryl said with a slight bow of his head.

Ayne turned to Tedrac, who had settled into another cushioned chair and was finishing the last bites of a sweetcake. "We have your written report." Ayne pointed toward a thin leather packet beside the tea service. "Please give us your analysis of the key issues."

Tedrac carefully placed his plate and fork on the table next to his chair, uncrossed his legs and leaned forward. "The question of loyalty. That was the first puzzle we had to unravel. You already know the roster of Allemen who went after the renegades with Eli. But when I left The Valley to spread the word, I had to make choices about whom I should contact." He enumerated the facts in an even, unemotional tone, as though they were nothing more than an inventory of ideas, rather than information crucial to the survival of the Peace. "But how do you prove disloyalty before any is committed? We can never accurately predict what another man will do, especially under duress. We can only make guesses rooted in prior knowledge and intelligent reasoning, then hope our guesses won't prove wildly off the mark."

"But you can know if he would have reason to be disloyal or to especially hate the Mwertik," Dara said.

"Then Eli would be the first to be eliminated," Tedrac replied. "Who among us has more reason to hate the Mwertik? And we all know how freely Rishana voices her doubts and questions. Would you disqualify her? On the other hand, Beatrice had seldom been anything other than nurturing and accepting, and yet she left to follow Kiv."

"So, how did you choose which Allemen should be called upon to go after them?" Ryl asked.

"Instinct and history, with a bit of serendipity thrown in."

Dara shook her head in disapproval. "Not exactly a formula for security. Serendipity, indeed!"

Tedrac arched one eyebrow, but didn't respond. Instead, he proceeded as before, detailing his analyses. "We had no way of knowing who is or isn't part of the conspiracy, so we decided to treat every Alleman who rallied to us as a friend, and watch him as an enemy. What other choice did we have? We had to move quickly, ready to adjust our plans as we gain new knowledge and insights."

"Your logic is all well and good, Tedrac." Rishana concentrated on speaking deliberately, though her stomach churned. "But you're not playing strategy games in your study. If you're wrong, people may die."

"What would you have us do? Nothing? The real world has no guarantees, only likelihoods. I can't promise you Eli will be safe, that we'll be able to restore our Peace, or even that you and I will live to see the end of tomorrow."

"But some things are too precious to risk so easily," Rishana insisted.

"Other things are too precious to not take the chance that you can save them," Peren reminded her.

"How many men went with Eli?" Ryl asked, deflecting attention away from his Allesha.

"Twelve," Tedrac replied.

Ryl considered the odds. "Against nearly four score!?"

"Even if we could have assembled more in the time available, I don't believe it would have been the correct response," Tedrac explained. "When two armies meet, war is all but inevitable. When a scouting party follows a horde, they have to find other ways."

"I'm surprised you know the number of Kiv's followers." Ayne addressed Ryl but stared at Rishana. "What else have you been told?"

Rishana refused to be cowered by the older woman's disapproval. "Whatever I felt he needed to survive all this."

"Did they secure the village of the..." Ryl paused, pulling the name out of his memory. "Forreze?"

The four older Alleshi and two Allemen stared at him, but Ayne was the first to respond. "Did your Allesha tell you where Eli and the others were headed?"

"No, just that they were going after the renegades."

"Then how did you know?"

"It's obvious, isn't it?" Ryl said with a shrug. "The renegades would need ammunition for those guns they stole, and they couldn't have carried enough when they left here. The horses were too loaded down as they were." Ryl turned to Tedrac. "The Forreze make those bullets, right?"

Tedrac pointed to the thin leather packet on the low table between them. "I have Eli's report. Shall I read or summarize?"

"Read it, please," Rishana answered.

Tedrac pulled several papers from the packet, then rearranged his bulk, settling more fully into the cushions. When he read, it was with the finesse of a master storyteller.

Dear Gs,

Our journey to the Forreze held no real surprises. We moved as quickly as we could, bypassing other villages for the sake of security and haste.

We timed our arrival at the Forreze village for nightfall. After hobbling our horses where they wouldn't be heard by the renegades, we hid in the surrounding forest, which is separated from the munitions workshops and the village by a series of firebreaks. Much of the forest consists of fir and spruce, which gave us good cover.

The renegades had camped in the firebreak between the workshops and the munitions blockhouse. At the door to the blockhouse were a dozen carts, partially loaded with crates which we presumed contained the bullets and magazines the renegades needed for the stolen guns. One cart was full and had been pulled out of the way.

We waited until the moon set and most of the camp and village were asleep. While Ralf went to warn the Forreze headman, the rest of us set to work. Approximately ten renegade Allemen stood guard around the camp perimeter, but only four watched the carts and blockhouse. We surprised and restrained the four before they could raise alarm. After setting our fuses, we fled the area, dragging the unconscious guards with us until they were out of danger. We were safely back in the forest by the time the sky lit up with a series of explosions that rocked the earth.

The blockhouse went up first. Within moments, the carts exploded, one by one, starting with those closest to the blockhouse. That's when I saw our mistake. We had cut the fuses the same length, but ignited them at different times, beginning with the blockhouse. That gave quick-thinking renegade Allemen time to save the one fully loaded cart, pulling out the burning fuses and dragging it away from the sparks and exploding bullets.

I confess that a part of me was proud of how well they worked together amidst the chaos, though I knew how deadly the repercussions of our mistake and their discipline may be. All of them were burnt by the embers, Marten, Ben and Nacam were struck by bullets.

Though the renegades and villagers quickly organized a bucket brigade, no one could approach the fires, where bullets were flying every which way. All they could do was watch the fireworks from a distance and attend to the injured among the Allemen who had rescued the cart. At least the workshops and village were safe, isolated from the blockhouse by firebreaks, and none of the villagers was hurt.

Kiv seemed to be everywhere, shouting at those tending the injured, then at the idle bucket brigade, prodding them to do something, anything. Back and forth she ran to no real purpose, because there was nothing she could do. Suddenly, she darted from the camp to a clearing near the forest where we hid, and screamed, "Show yourselves!"

Dram started to step forward, but I stopped him. Yes, I know Meika had instructed me to appoint another to speak for us, but I couldn't send him out into that melee, with Kiv screeching, fires burning, bullets flying wild and everyone's nerves frayed to the breaking point. Instead, I went out into the clearing alone, my hands held wide and open in the universal sign that I was unarmed.

As I came within the penumbra of the fire, Kiv saw and recognized me. "You! Why am I not surprised that it's you?" With an almost gleeful sneer, she added, "A son who would side with his father's murderers against an Allesha."

By now, Beatrice and Devra had joined Kiv, as had some of their Allemen. Elnor hovered nearby, within earshot, surrounded by a protective guard of her own Allemen. Kiv's Tevan had his gun raised and pointed at me, but I couldn't believe he'd actually pull the trigger. He had danced at my wedding.

"I'm amazed that you dare come out in the open," Kiv cried. "Aren't you afraid of being shot?"

I tried not to look at Tevan, to avoid any challenge to him. I stared only at Kiv. "You mean the way you killed Caith?"

"That was an accident," Beatrice said.

"Not according to Hester's autopsy. Someone pushed her, and I have a strong feeling I know who."

Beatrice turned toward Kiv. "You told us it was an accident! That she was already dead when you found her. That she probably fell when she heard unexpected noises in the night."

I was close enough to them to see the fires reflected in their eyes, but in Kiv's was a rage that burned from within. Kiv snapped at Beatrice, "You can be such a fool."

I'll never forget the look on Beatrice's face, the raw horror quickly turning to rancor as the truth sunk in. Without a word, Beatrice stomped away. Devra retreated more slowly.

Tevan lowered his gun and gradually backed away from Kiv. He briefly locked eyes with me, and I understood. She was his Allesha. He owed her everything, would have done anything for her. Now he walked away from her, accompanied by most of the other Allemen who had come forward to confront me ~ including other Kiv Allemen.

I should have felt triumphant. Instead, I was filled with pity for Allemen who had been forced by their Allesha's actions to break their covenant with her. That, more than anything else I have seen or heard, brought home to me just how damaged the foundations of our Peace have become.

Kiv was left standing alone, with only Gerard and Bran at her side. For perhaps the first time in her life, she was wordless, not from shame but fury. She grabbed Bran's gun and pointed it at me. Even faster than I could respond, a hand shot out from behind her, pushing the barrel toward the ground. Another pulled me out of the way. Fanor, the Forreze headman, now stood in my place, facing Kiv. Two dozen armed villagers surrounded her and her Allemen.

Fanor is a small Alleman, but he didn't flinch when Bran and Gerard leapt into a protective position in front of their Allesha. "I've had enough of your treachery, woman. Get out of my sight," Fanor commanded. Speaking to me, he said, "You and I have some reparations to discuss."

I followed him away from Kiv, certain that the armed villagers would be able to contain her. That was my second mistake, turning my back on that woman. The greatest insult anyone could give Kiv would be to ignore her. The next thing I knew, what felt like a hot poker tore through my upper arm, twisting my body with such force that I lost my balance and fell to the ground.

"No!" Rishana cried, jumping up from her chair.

Startled, Tedrac dropped the papers as he struggled to rise, but Ryl reached her much more quickly, putting his arm around her shoulders while guiding her back to her seat.

Tedrac reassured her in the only way he knew, through logic. "Eli is fine. Otherwise, I wouldn't be reading a letter from him."

"Please continue," Ayne commanded.

Tedrac settled back into the cushions, picked up the papers, found his spot, and resumed reading.

I lost my balance and fell to the ground.

Suddenly, I was surrounded by a swarm of people. I tried to reassure them that it was only a flesh wound, but they wouldn't listen. Later on, I was told that Kiv had moved so fast grabbing Gerard's rifle that none of the villagers had time to act. It was Bran who jarred the gun barrel just as she shot. She was his Allesha, but he wasn't about to watch her shoot a fellow Alleman in the back.

I heard rather than saw Fanor clomp away from me and slap Kiv in the face. "Bitch!" he yelled. "I should have you hanged from the nearest tree for everything you've done."

The Forreze Healer cleaned and bandaged my wound and gave me a draught, which he said would speed the healing. I didn't realize it would also make me sleep through the night and well into the day. If he hadn't, perhaps I could have prevented what happened next.

Somehow, Kiv and nineteen renegade Allemen managed to sneak away in the middle of the night with the one loaded cart. Fanor estimates that it held about 20,000 bullets and 400 magazines, enough to kill every Mwertik many times over."

Marten succumbed to his bullet wounds almost immediately, while Ben lingered until dawn. You can't imagine what it felt like to bury two Allemen who were killed because of me. Marten had such an open laugh; Ben and I had been friends since we were kids. I never wanted them to be hurt. I never wanted any of this.

I tried to leave right after their burial, but Fanor and his council insisted we draft an agreement regarding reparations for their cata-strophic loss. What's more, we had to contend with scores of renegade Allemen who claimed to be loyal once more. We sent Peter and Dram as scouts to follow Kiv while her trail was fresh. Unfortunately, an afternoon downpour obscured the tracks.

The Forreze were tough negotiators, but they had right on their side. The signed agreement and a formal report to the Alleshine Council are enclosed in this packet.

Elnor, Devra and Beatrice took charge of those of their Allemen who remained, organizing them into teams to help rebuild the Forreze blockhouse. Can we trust them not to hand over new ammunition to Kiv as it is manufactured? Fanor assured me that his villagers were capable of keeping them in line, now that he knew the truth about them being rene-gades. But I insisted that the three Alleshi send some of their Allemen away so they wouldn't have the force to overpower the Forreze.

As for the many Allemen who no longer belonged to Kiv but could never again belong to us, that was much more difficult. Some slunk away in the night, perhaps to rejoin Kiv or return to their homes. A few asked to accompany us in our hunt for their former comrades. I weighed their request carefully. They might have information that could be of value. But how could I trust them? It's a question with too many ramifications to solve in a day. So I'm leaving it to Ralf and Fanor to figure out what to do with them.

We'll eventually have to deal with the former Kiv Allemen who didn't stay with the Forreze. No longer loyal to The Valley or to their Allesha, what laws and responsibilities will they recognize? What further disruptions will they cause as individuals or bands who owe allegiance to no one? You'll find in this packet two rosters of the Allemen involved. While both list who went with Kiv, who disappeared, and who remained, the one meant for your eyes alone includes my comments about many of those named.

Tomorrow, we will finally be free to leave here, to follow Kiv and recover the guns and bullets.

Please send my love to my mother, but don't tell her about the wound. It is, after all, minor, and I wouldn't want to give her further cause for concern.

Respectfully, Eli.

Tedrac looked at Rishana sheepishly. "Eli didn't know you had joined the Guardians."

Rishana nodded, not trusting herself to respond.

Tedrac opened another page. "He penned one more report before he left the Forreze."

Dear G's,

This morning, as I prepared to leave, Elnor came to me. I'll not take the time to write about the regrets she voiced, for which I had little patience. Instead, I've enclosed her letter to the Alleshine Council. But I doubt you will want to deliver it, because we dare not share what she has divulged.

To get to the core of the matter, the Before Times weapons that Kiv unearthed are far more dangerous than anything we could have imagined. Elnor called them "Windspeakers." According to the one reference to them that Elnor found in the hidden archives, these palm-sized devices allow people who are some distance away to talk to each other.

I fear these Windspeakers and the chaos they might unleash. The strategic advantage they could give Kiv is terrifying ~ allowing her to instantaneously communicate and coordinate far-reaching movements. Beyond that, should their existence and how they were uncovered become generally known, the Alleshine Library and storehouse would be torn apart by those who would seek more and more advanced weapons, bringing on an unstoppable escalation of war.

According to Elnor, of the approximately one hundred Windspeakers that they found in the storehouse wall, about eleven appeared intact. Elnor claims that Kiv hasn't yet figured out how they work, beyond the fact that exposing them to sunlight causes them to emit a blue light. I now have one in my possession, which Elnor says she stole from the renegades' cache.

I managed to extract a promise from Elnor that she wouldn't disclose any of this information until she hears from you or me. But I don't trust that she's as contrite as she claims, and wonder what advantage Kiv might gain by inserting Elnor back into The Valley and its library. So I've arranged for Fanor to keep her at Forreze and not let her out of his sight."

Respectfully, Eli.

For several moments, the only sounds were the rustling of paper as Tedrac folded and put away Eli's reports. Peren reached for the leather satchel, removed Elnor's letter and quickly scanned it. Then, with a sigh, she folded it and put it into her skirt pocket, carefully buttoning the flap.

"We must destroy that," Hester insisted.

"You don't yet know what it says," Dara countered, holding her hand out to Peren for the letter.

Peren passed it to Dara, who shook her head as she read it.

"But we can't trust anything Elnor says," Mistral reminded them. "Are these Windspeakers what she claims? If so, are they truly non-functional, or is the one that Elnor gave Eli a trap in some way?"

Tedrac cleared his throat, making sure he had everyone's attention. Then he reached into his pocket and pulled out a rectangular device, about the size of the sweetcakes still on the tea tray.

"Is that it?" Ryl asked, as he stood to look at it more closely.

Silver-colored, with brownish dents, scratches and wear-spots, about half its front was covered with a circle pattern of slots. On the top was a sloping mosaic of tiny mirrors. It had a hook on the back and three black knobs on the side.

"Have you figured it out yet?" Rishana knew that Tedrac would never let go of a puzzle until he solved it.

"Not yet. But Elnor was right about one thing. When I exposed it to the sun, this area lit up." Tedrac pointed to the circular pattern. "It was faint at first. By this afternoon, it was quite bright — but emitted no heat. I haven't the foggiest idea how. It's unlike gas, candlelight or any other natural luminant I've seen."

"What do those knobs do?" Mistral asked.

"Logically, I can surmise that one turns it on and off. Perhaps one controls the strength of it. And the third... I've no idea. This is beyond anything I've ever encountered or read about."

"Well, let's see what they do." Mistral snatched the device from Tedrac.

Dara jumped up to stop Mistral, shouting, "No, don't! We can't know—" just as Mistral turned one of the knobs. But she didn't get to finish the thought.

Suddenly, the device emitted a strange sound, like hot oil sizzling, followed immediately by Kiv's voice. "What the hell! Dara? How'd you get…" The buzzing faded in and out, revealing Kiv's voice in an uneven staccato. "…too late… think you know… you'll never beat… not only Windspea…"

Tedrac grabbed the device and turned the knob in the other direction, silencing it. No one spoke, terrified that Kiv might still be able to hear them. Nor did anyone move until Tedrac stood, turned to Hester to silently mouth "inner room," then gingerly carried the Windspeaker into Hester's second bedroom. The others were still frozen in place when he returned.

Hester tentatively whispered, "Is it safe?"

Tedrac answered in his normal voice. "It's deep in your inner room; no sound escapes those walls. Even so, I piled some cushions over it."

Rishana's mind whirled with questions. All she knew for certain was that, as bad as she thought things had become, they were now much worse.

"What did she mean, 'not only Windspeakers?'" Ryl asked. "Does she have other Before Times weapons? What do we do now?"

"We deal with the facts, and not let these mysteries distract us from what must be done," Tedrac responded. "For now, you should return to your Allesha's home, to prepare for tomorrow."

"No," Ryl decided. "We've too much to discuss."

"Boy," Mistral interrupted, then stopped, realizing his mistake.

"No, Pa, not a boy ever again."

"Yes, I know. My apologies."

Ryl sat down, crossed his arms over his chest and stared at Ayne. "You planned for years to bring me to this point, to make me one of yours. Tomorrow, you'll be sending me out into a world tumbling toward war, to seek my real parents who will probably want to kill me on sight. We're racing against a rogue Allesha who has unimaginable weapons, and we can't know who she'll use them against first — the Mwertik or Allemen. If you believe you can continue to keep me ignorant, denying me information that I might need to survive, then you don't know me as well as you think you do."

Ayne studied Ryl, and for the first time all evening, smiled. Then, without acknowledging Ryl's demands, she directed, "Tedrac, please give us your initial analyses."

Tedrac began to enumerate. "These Windspeakers may bring about the greatest changes to our world since Alleen's Circle of Peace. But we mustn't allow ourselves to become overwhelmed by cataclysmic potentials. Let's break it down into areas of investigation and action.

"First, we must figure out how these Windspeakers work. How does Kiv's possession of them change the nature of our dispute with her? Second, should we consider any alteration to our plans for Ryl? Third, what are the dangers to The Valley, beyond the possibility of being attacked? Eli's fear is valid. I see no way to keep knowledge about the Windspeakers — and possibly other weapons hidden in the storehouse — from becoming widespread. The keg that has been bonged open can never be resealed, and I doubt we'll have much control over the rate of flow of information. But is there any way we might minimize the chaos that could be unleashed? And, fourth, if The Valley is attacked, what do we do? Do we use whatever weapons we have or are able to unearth to save it? If so, would saving it be its destruction?"

Through the night, they debated the ramifications of the Windspeakers, Kiv's threats, and the rogue Allemen. While none expected to find viable solutions in a few hours, they did distill the questions, and each now had defined areas to pursue.

Rishana was proud to see Ryl hold his own, facing down the men and women who had planned to control them both. Tedrac had been right, and so had Eli. Being an Allesha wasn't anything like Rishana had imagined it would be. It had shattered the beautiful illusions she had once allowed to be built up around her, and had set her adrift from everything she had held true. But watching Ryl, she realized she would rather have truth than comfort, as messy, unresolvable and horrifyingly dangerous as facts can be. That was the one thing Jared hadn't understood about her; that perhaps she hadn't understood about herself.

Chapter 87

The final morning arrived. Tayar found Dov in the barn, playing with the goats one last time. Standing in the doorway, she watched him silently, though she had no doubt he was aware of her presence. The boy he had once been would have done anything to avoid being seen frolicking in such an undignified manner. Darting this way and that, he made himself an easy target for the goats, who alternated between nudging his pockets for the treats that were always there, and butting at his hands to be scratched and rubbed. Tayar wasn't sure who was enjoying the game more, the goats or Dov.

Kneeling, he reached out to the animals to ruffle their heads one last time. "Goodbye, girls. Take good care of my Allesha." Then he looked up at her and patted the ground. "Come, sit with me a few moments."

Tayar stepped more fully into the barn, but remained standing. "It's time for you to go to the Communal Hall for the ceremony. Are you packed?"

"You know I am. I sent my things to the Battai's early this morning."

"Good." She held out her hand to help him up, then, realizing what she was doing, withdrew it.

Dov stood, but instead of moving toward the doorway, went to the back of the barn. Reaching behind an old cupboard, he retrieved a package covered in blue linen, about the size of a large loaf of bread. "I made this for you."

When he placed it in her arms, it was heavier than she had expected. He removed the cloth, and Tayar was astonished to see that it was a sculpture of hands, his hands, held open in the traditional greeting due an Allesha.

"I never did master that pottery wheel of Le'a's, but the clay was fun to cast and mold."

"It's beautiful." The words snagged in her throat. "I'll treasure it always."

Dov caressed the palms of his sculpted hands. "You know, at first, I wanted to put your hands in there, filling mine. But I couldn't get them right. Every time I thought I understood how to model them, it didn't work. Then something remarkable happened. The more I worked on this, the more I understood about the greeting gesture." Taking one step back, he opened his hands in the pose represented in the clay. "I used to think it symbolized me being willing to open up to you, to let you fill me with whatever you were willing to give. And it's that, too. But the other part is my responsibility, to hold your hands, to support you whenever you need it. And I will, Tayar, whenever you need me. Just send me word, and I'll come. Not because of the Agreement, but because it will be you summoning me." Tenderly, Dov cupped his hands around her face. "I want you to know one thing: if we lived in a better world, I would never leave you."

"Dov..."

"I know. But let me say it this one time and never again. I love you, Tayar. Not because you're my Allesha, but because I have come to know the woman you are. But this is the only world we have, and the only way to try to keep it from destroying itself is for me to leave. I understand that now, because loving you has made me understand so very much." Leaning forward, he gently kissed her right cheek. "Thank you." Then her left cheek. "Dear, sweet Tayar." And then her lips, brushing them softly with his own.

Not trusting herself to speak, Tayar turned and left the barn without looking back. She retreated into her bedroom, and placed the sculpture on a table where the early morning sun always shone, rearranging everything around it to make it the centerpiece. Then she placed her hands into Dov's clay palms, closing her eyes to more fully feel the contours and comfort.

The sculpture was devoid of the warmth and flexibility of his flesh, stripping the greeting gesture to its essentials — not only a symbol of her relationship with her Winter Boy, but also the space where she fit, as a woman who was also an Allesha. She washed her face, brushed her hair and composed herself, determined to not mar Dov's last day in The Valley with inappropriate emotions.

He awaited her in the greeting room. They embraced, hands on shoulders, bodies barely touching. Then he left. Watching from the front window seat, as he fell in step with other new Allemen headed toward the gathering, she didn't allow herself to cry. She'd had enough of her self-pity. When he was no longer in view, she began to prepare for the ceremony.

The Alleshi gathered in the Assembly Room to don their voluminous green ceremonial robes.

The first time Jinet had seen so many Alleshi in their robes was at Eli's End of Season ceremony, seated beside Jared, in an honored position as a parent and an Alleman wife, in the chairs aligned on the gravel in front of the Communal Hall. Her heart had fluttered when the Alleshi had flowed out onto the platform, accompanied by their new Allemen. There, before her eyes, was the embodiment of what she had fully believed was The Valley's unity of purpose and the enduring sanctity of the Peace.

At her own initiation, the procession had been reversed; all the Alleshi had enveloped Rishana as she had stepped up to the platform, pulling her with them into the Communal Hall. She had thought it had been a choice based on faith that had brought her to that moment. But she'd been wrong. The people she had trusted most had lied and manipulated her to bring her to the Alleshi, to her Winter Boy, to this uncertain future.

Rishana had participated in various Alleshine ceremonies since her initiation, though always in the background, as a green-robed body helping fill the ranks. Today would be the first time she'd be a full active participant, and the first time her eyes would be completely open.

Looking around the Assembly Room, she saw the individuals within the ceremonial anonymity of their robes. She also saw the gaps in the company where others should be. Caith. Beatrice. Devra. Elnor. Even Kiv. Fissures had formed. No, she corrected herself, they had always been there. The circles of loyalty didn't always overlap, and rifts were now shaking apart the Alleshine Peace.

Meika pushed through the crowd to make her way to Rishana. "I've had word from Eli."

Rishana caught herself before saying, "I know." Instead, she clasped Meika's hands and pleaded, "Tell me, please, is he safe?" How easily the pose settled on her.

"He's safe and well, and they've even stopped Kiv, at least for now."

Rishana embraced her son's Allesha. "Thank you."

"Good news?" Dara asked.

Rishana hadn't realized that Dara and Peren had also made their way toward her.

"Yes, news from Eli," Meika replied.

Peren's forehead crinkled with her worry for her Alleman's son. "Is he well?"

"Yes, he's well. I've a letter from him for the Council."

"What of Kiv?" Dara asked, allowing a trickle of her usual venom for the renegade Allesha to escape. Rishana had to admire the performance.

"She escaped, but most of her Allemen have deserted her," Meika said.

"And the guns?" Peren asked.

"Nearly useless. Our Allemen destroyed most of the ammunition she had stolen."

"Wonderful news, indeed." It wasn't the volume of Peren's voice as much as her energy that caught the attention of other nearby Alleshi.

"News?"

"Meika, have you heard from Eli?"

Soon Meika was surrounded, and Peren and Dara had navigated Rishana away from the throng. But before they could say anything to her, the signal came for them to begin the procession. Dara and Peren took their places behind Rishana, so close that she could feel their breath against her ears when they leaned forward to speak to her.

"The North Battai has a worthy candidate for your Spring Boy," Peren whispered.

Rishana stared forward. "Not now."

Slowly, the front of the line began moving, while others formed up toward the back.

"But this one is different," Dara said. "A gentle, quiet boy who needs—"

"I said no!"

"Rishana, dear, you don't understand," Dara insisted. "Sometimes, we give ourselves tender Seasons."

Whipping around to face them, Rishana stated firmly, unequivocally, "I doubt I'll be giving any Seasons to anyone, ever again. Now, leave me alone." Saying it released something inside her, like a storm-flooded stream breaking out of a dam. But as Rishana moved forward, following the snaking line of green-robed Alleshi, knowing that to anyone looking on, she would appear the same as the others, Rishana couldn't shake the picture in her mind of the two who walked behind her — how very old Dara and Peren suddenly seemed — and the look of hurt on their faces.

In the large entry hall, the new Allemen created their own processional to walk beside their Alleshi — though apart. Rishana could hear the excitement erupt from the outside courtyard as the first Alleshi and Allemen appeared. On the large platform in front of the hall, the two lines diverged again. The Alleshi arranged themselves in eight rows of chairs to the right, with those who had just given a Season seated in front; their young Allemen sitting on the opposite side of the platform. A podium had been placed at the front edge to the far right.

Hundreds were standing, cheering and applauding in the gravel courtyard where chairs had been placed, as well as from the surrounding lawns where numerous blankets were spread. In front were the Allemen who would be taking apprentices. The rest of the seats had been reserved for the Battais, other Allemen and their wives, some of whom were also parents, then other parents, and, in the back, caravan and village leaders. Somewhere in the crowd were a handful of representatives from beyond the Peace borders who had come to negotiate and trade.

Every once in a while, Rishana distinguished a name being called out from the audience. Two of the new Alleman waved back from their seats on the platform. But most barely moved, keeping their hands in their laps. Everyone quickly quieted and settled down when Ayne came forward to stand at the podium.

Ayne waited several moments, testing the uncertain silence of the large crowd, giving them a chance to focus on her and the solemnity of the ceremony. Though Rishana couldn't see Ayne's face, she knew from experience what a powerful presence the older woman projected, even when all she was doing was allowing her gaze to drift over her audience.

"Welcome to our Valley and our Winter's End ceremony. Before you are the newest of our Allemen, sworn to uphold our Peace and protect your well-being."

Rishana found herself unable to concentrate on Ayne's words. But then, she wasn't trying very hard. She knew whatever the old woman said would include nothing of the truths, hardships and intrigues of the past Season — or the looming catastrophes. This was a time to reaffirm the bonds of the Peace and reassure their people that everything was as it should be.

Directly across from her, Ryl was far from the largest of the young Allemen, but he sat tall, with squared shoulders, fully aware of everything around him. Watching him observe the assembled representatives from both sides of their borders, Rishana realized he was already making plans and testing out new scenarios, considering the mission ahead of him. Soon, he would be on the western border, seeking the Mwertik, his people. Perhaps nothing he tried would divert the coming chaos. Perhaps he would be killed. All she could do now was sit in this Valley and await his reports, hoping against hope for his safe return.

Or, maybe, it was time for her to leave, too. She ached to go home, to the warm, happy farmhouse she had shared with Jared, Svana and Eli, filled once more with children, her grandchildren. It could be a good life. Couldn't it?

Thankfully, Ayne kept her remarks brief. With more than a hundred new Allemen to acknowledge, the ceremony would be long enough. Ayne arranged the papers on the podium, put on her spectacles and announced the first Triad. "Garin of the Mukane, Lewen of the Verterrali and Kerix of the Grevatine."

Certainly, the young Allemen had already guessed who their Triats would be, but this was the first time it would be confirmed publicly. The three shook hands as they walked across the platform to stand before their Alleshi. Whispering final words of gratitude, encouragement and farewell, the couples faced each other while each Allesha draped a chain and medallion around her Alleman's neck.

Rishana fingered Ryl's gold medallion in her pocket, the familiar ridges of the hands and flower. She remembered returning Jared's to Peren — no, she corrected herself, to Savah — on her widow's pilgrimage to tell her husband's Allesha of his murder. No Allesha should outlive her Alleman. It wasn't natural. Please, she fervently prayed, don't let it happen to me, to Dov.

The three Alleshi walked side by side with their young Allemen to the front of the platform where a Triad waited to take charge of their new apprentices. Returning to their places among their sisters, the three Alleshi watched, one with tears in her eyes, as the six Allemen walked away from the Communal Hall through the cheering crowd, headed for a Battai inn before they left The Valley.

So it continued, Triad by Triad. Rishana found her mind wandering from the repetitive ceremony, thinking instead of Dov, Eli and Jared, the Allemen of her life. Each a lie of one sort or another. Each a joy. And, in the end, each a heart-rending loss. But the only way she could have avoided the pain of losing them was never to have loved them. How like Alleen's desert, with its shadows and light, the one giving shape and form to the other. Sadness wasn't the opposite of laughter; silence was — the emptiness where human conversation and touch should be, as in Alleen's caves.

"Aidan of the Nigan, Ryl of the Birani and Sim of the Emet," Ayne announced, jolting Rishana back to the here and now. But as Ryl shook hands with his new Triats and began to walk toward her, Rishana realized that her thoughts had been leading to this point all along.

Ryl stood before Rishana as her Alleman, and she was devoid of words, because she had too much to say, because it had all been said. They faced each other, trying to capture one last moment of connection, knowing it was already gone. Ryl bent his head and Rishana placed the chain around his neck. Taking the medallion in his hand, he looked at it with wonder and a bit of surprise that it was, indeed, his. He smiled and silently mouthed, "Thank you."

Rishana walked by Ryl's side, joined by Aidan, Sim and their Alleshi, to bring them to Mistral and Tedrac, her husband's broken Triad — to the space where Jared should have been. Then she returned to her seat, no longer noticed by the crowd that cheered her new Alleman and his Triats.

Craning her neck, she tried to glimpse Ryl, but the standing, cheering audience blocked her view. She could judge their progress only by the movement of those who turned to watch them. Soon, however, everyone was seated once more, their attention focused on Ayne, who was announcing the next new Triad.

Rishana felt a light touch on her shoulder and Peren's breath on her ear. "Rishana…"

She shook her head, not wanting to respond, to be aware of anyone or anything else. Not yet.

Ryl and his companions turned onto the gravel path toward the West Battai's inn. As they were about to disappear around a bend, he looked back briefly. Knowing she would be watching, he waved. Then he was gone.

Rishana felt her breath leave her body. She was weightless, unrooted.

"Rishana," Peren said once more, her voice soft with worry and regret.

Dara's hand rested on her other shoulder, but the older woman said nothing. What surprised Rishana was that it wasn't so much a pressure as a presence, a connection.

With her eyes still on the bend in the path, Rishana whispered, "Tell the North Battai I will meet the boy."

"Good." Dara squeezed her shoulder before letting go and settling back.

"You won't be sorry," Peren said.

Rishana continued to focus on the path leading away from The Valley, on the empty space where Ryl had been. "Yes, I will," she said. Shadows and light might shape her life, but the only certainties she would be able to depend on would be the pain and the joy ahead.

THE END

Addenda

*Please support this author by reviewing **The Winter Boy** on your favorite book website(s), and by telling your friends about the book. Thank you.*

THE WINTER BOY STUDY GUIDE

A free *The Winter Boy* study guide is available for book clubs, teachers, librarians and other discussion group leaders from the Pixel Hall Press website (pixelhallpress.com/study+guides.html).

ABOUT SALLY WIENER GROTTA

Sally Wiener Grotta is the consummate storyteller, reflecting her deep humanism and sense of the poignancy of life. As an award-winning journalist, she has authored many hundreds of articles, columns and reviews for scores of glossy magazines, newspapers, journals and online publications, plus numerous non-fiction books. Her fiction includes the novel *Jo Joe* which was published by Pixel Hall Press in 2013 to critical acclaim.

She is currently working on *Sex Witch*, the next Alleshine novel, about the Mwertik, Jinet/Rishana, Dov/Ryl, Lilla and Kiv.

Sally Wiener Grotta is a frequent speaker at conferences, schools and other organizations on storytelling, creativity, photography, and the publishing industry. She welcomes invitations to participate in discussions with book clubs and other reading groups (via Skype, Google Hangout, online chat, phone or occasionally in person). She is sometimes available to do readings. You can also connect with her on Twitter (@SallyWGrotta), Facebook (Facebook.com/SallyWienerGrotta), and her website (Grotta.net).

ACKNOWLEDGEMENTS

My heartfelt gratitude goes to the many people who helped me over the years as I created the world of the Alleshi, Allemen, Mwertik, et al. Most notably, thanks once again to Cynthia Dadson of Pixel Hall Press.

Also, I send my appreciation to Molly Glick of Foundry Literary Agency for her excellent editing and faith in *The Winter Boy*. Chelsea Lowe was a thorough and creatively challenging copyeditor. The Nameless Workshop was a great sounding board, even when (especially when) we disagreed. Barbara Krasnoff gave me invaluable feedback and comments on the next-to-final manuscript. Pixel Hall Press's ever-vigilant Beta Readers — Sandra Ulbrich Almazan, Robin Baum, Gail Gabrielson, Chip Hitchcock — were great at finding typos and other details that I and my editors might have otherwise overlooked. Hugs to Norma Krasne-Levine for her friendship and invaluable precision. As always, Daniel Grotta and Noel J. Wiener helped me with much-needed brainstorming, suggestions, morale boosting and unstinting edits. Of course, any errors in judgment or otherwise are mine alone.

Sally Wiener Grotta

ABOUT PIXEL HALL PRESS

Pixel Hall Press (www.PixelHallPress.com) is a relatively new, old-fashioned small publishing house that focuses on discovering literary gems and great stories that might have otherwise been overlooked. Our mission is to publish books that energize the imagination and intrigue the mind, and to be a conduit between readers and provocative, stimulating, talented authors.

Please go to the For Readers & Book Clubs section of the Pixel Hall Press website, to find out about various programs we offer readers. These include free Study Guides for book discussion leaders, our Beta Reader program which offers access to free pre-publication eBooks, and the Author Connect Program which helps to set up book discussions with our authors for reading groups. We also have volume discounts on books for discussion groups, organizations and classrooms.

Join in on the discussion about books, reading, writing and the publishing industry on Pixel Hall Press's Facebook page and on Twitter: @PixelHallPress.

Made in the USA
Lexington, KY
14 April 2015